Signs of Passing

Connected Stories by Owen Thomas

Text copyright © 2015 Owen Thomas

Author Website: http://owenthomasfiction.com

Cover Design by Endeavor Creative (http://endeavorcreative.com)

ISBN-13: 9780692494318

ISBN-10: 0692494316

Library of Congress Control Number: 2015913711

OTF Literary, Anchorage, AK

For my brother

Part one

Chapter 1

Chapter 2

Chapter 3

Chapter 4

Chapter 5

Part two

Chapter 6

Chapter 7

Chapter 8

Chapter 9

Chapter 10

PART ONE

"Anticipation of the unknown is the midwife of a contentment always promised but never born and that's what it means to love the world."

— *Jack McMannis, Private Eye*

Chapter 1

WINCHESTER COUNTY

Winchester County was the best show ever. That's what Tyler thought anyway. It didn't much matter what anyone else thought about it. Least of all his father who sat in the kitchen chewing fried meat off of the chicken bones that he pulled out of a greasy red and white paper bucket. Tyler's father, Kevin was his name, liked to read the newspaper or a magazine about cars when he ate his dinner.

Tyler liked to watch *Winchester County.*

The show was a Western, what his friend, Pillsbury, liked to call a *classic shoot-em-up.* Pillsbury's real name was Warren Lemiski, but Tyler called him Pillsbury because Warren Lemiski was a white, doughy sort of a boy that tended to spill out beneath the hem of his shirt. Tyler knew *Pillsbury* was not an especially nice name, but he called him that anyway, mostly because Warren said he liked it and because whenever Tyler referred to Pillsbury by his real name Tyler's father liked to make a wise crack about *ol' Jew boy,* which, the way his father said it, sounded a whole lot worse than *Pillsbury.*

Tyler guessed that he and Pillsbury were friends, even though they only saw each other at Dolly Madison Elementary, and even then Pillsbury was shy and didn't talk much unless Tyler really worked on him. But Pillsbury would talk to Tyler more than he talked to the others, and *Winchester County* was Pillsbury's favorite show too, so Tyler guessed that made them friends. Maybe even *best* friends. Tyler really did not have any other friends to speak of. He was about as popular as Pillsbury, so maybe that was another reason they were friends. On the other hand, Pillsbury had just turned nine and even though Tyler was only a year older, there was a great big pile of difference between nine and ten.

Winchester County was a show about a sheriff named Henry Winchester, only everyone either called him *Hank* or *Sheriff Winchester* or lots of times just plain *Sheriff.* No one ever called him Henry. Hank's family owned the town, which only had four long dirt streets that came together into one busy intersection, where there was a bank and a general store and the jail, which is where Hank worked, and a saloon. The Winchesters owned the whole town because they had lots of money from punching cows, which was another way – a really dumb way, in Tyler's view – of saying *ranching.* In all his years of watching *Winchester County,* Tyler had never seen anyone, let alone Evangeline Winchester or Miss Kitty or Papa John or Hank Winchester, or anyone else in the family actually *punch* a cow. Not even Sam the deputy, who wasn't real smart sometimes and couldn't shoot much more than one guy off a roof in any one show. Not even Sam ever punched a cow.

The show started the same way each time, with a real close up view of a wagon wheel, spinning, spinning, spinning fast and tight like a top, only you knew the wagon wheel was upright and rolling, not sideways and spinning, and then there was a gunshot and music would start that sounded kind of like galloping, and if Tyler stared at the spinning wagon wheel hard enough sometimes it made him a just a little dizzy. Sometimes he laid on his side, placing his head directly on the cushion of the green couch that was almost worn through from so much sitting – the couch his father liked to strut about; *I got the couch, be goddamned, I got the couch! She didn't get that! They wont be doin' it on the couch!* And with the worn green couch cushion on one side of his head and one of the ratty blue pillows on the other side of his head, Tyler could block out everything in the room except that spinning wagon wheel and he would enjoy feeling a little dizzy with it all.

Then there was the gunshot and you could tell it was Hank Winchester's rifle because it had a special sound. Pillsbury says it's because Hank Winchester had the truest shot. He never missed.

4

Pillsbury was right about that. Hank Winchester never missed. Unlike Deputy Sam.

After the gunshot, the music started and the wagon wheel slowly got smaller and you could see that it was really the front wheel of a stage coach and that the stage coach was being pulled by four horses running full out – or *huckledy-buck* as Pillsbury liked to say – and clouds of dust spitting out from behind, and Hank Winchester standing up on the coachman's seat with the reins twisted tight in one hand and his rifle in the other, shooting off into the distance as ponderosa pines as big as mountains flew past in the background.

Channel 12 had taken to showing four, half-hour episodes back-to-back for two hours every night starting at six o'clock. At five fifty-five every afternoon – and earlier if he could manage it – Tyler was either sideways on the green couch at his father's place or squeezed into the wing of the red loveseat in the home of Mark Wilton, the man his mother had taken to living with, and would wait with great anticipation of that spinning wheel and that dizzy feeling and the gun shot and the galloping music. Tyler looked forward to Hank Winchester shooting that rifle with deadly aim and gripping those reins and gritting his teeth, determined to protect his town and his family and all the good people of Winchester County.

No, Tyler more than looked forward to it. It is fair to say that he *lived* for it every day of the week.

The only part of the opening sequence of the show that Tyler did not love concerned the horses. He liked horses, especially horses running full out, huckledy-buck. But he had never really cared for the spotted kind, what Pillsbury called *Palamentos.* Tyler thought horses, real wild-western horses, should either be all black or all brown. Horses certainly should not look like Dalmatians, which was a kind of dog that his grandmother in Wichita used to have before she died of smoking – grandma, not the Dalmatian – and they sent her to a shelter – the Dalmatian, not grandma – because no one wanted to take care of her. In any case, there was just something wrong about big Dalmatians pulling a stagecoach and when the opening of *Winchester County* showed those horses, Tyler winced just a little inside his tiny chest and wished that all four of those horses pulling that stage coach were either all brown or all black. Sometimes he squinted so that he could barely see them, just to make it so.

On this evening, as his father sat in the kitchen stripping fried meat with his teeth from chicken bones and reading a magazine, and as Mrs. Davis the upstairs neighbor ran her vacuum like she was trying to destroy the place, and as the late summer air pressed with both hands and with some desperation against the small window on the far side of the room that, for want of a crank, did not open, Tyler lay in the failing light, on the couch, sandwiched between the worn green cushion and the ratty blue pillow, *stunned.*

He sat up, still a little woozy from the spinning wagon wheel, and looked around the room for some other person; *any* other person, even his father, who was really the only other person there could have been. But his father was still turning magazine pages in the kitchen and excavating the greasy paper bucket.

So Tyler looked back at the television, the dizziness completely gone now.

One of the horses was brown. All brown.

The show started and Tyler lay back down on the couch wondering why they – the Winchester County television people, *whoever* – had changed one of the horses in the opening scene, which was the same every time. Except *this* time.

The episode, the last of the evening, was the one where Hank's younger brother, Benjamin, is visiting from San Francisco where he works in some kind of business. Every so often Benjamin – they all call him *Ben* or *Baby Ben* when they want to tease him – will show up in *Winchester County* wearing a suit and tie and bringing presents for everyone and usually with someone in tow, like a fiancée – for whom it never quite works out because she usually dies – or a business partner, or a lady friend that falls in love with a storekeeper and decides to stay. One episode Ben brought along a big parrot on his shoulder and gave it to his sister, Miss Kitty. But tonight's show was the one where he brings the fiancée and she dies at the end or *bites the dust big time* as Pillsbury says. Sometimes

6

Ben goes along on the cattle drive and brings his guitar and they all sit around the fire singing under the stars about not being fenced in.

"Turn it down!" His father shouted from the kitchen.

"I can't hear 'cause of the vacuum!" said Tyler, with only the muscles of his mouth moving.

"It's too loud, Tyler. God damn it! Turn it down!"

Tyler got up off of the sofa and walked over to the television and turned down the volume a little. It seemed like Mrs. Davis found a way to turn her vacuum up whenever he did this and Tyler sat down, Indian-style, on the burnt-orange carpet so that he could hear over the ruckus upstairs.

Baby Ben and his fiancée, Madelyn – Ben called her *Maddy* – were climbing off a buckboard out front the Winchester General Store. Maddy wore a fancy hat. Evangeline Winchester was gonna *love* her!

"Tyler, turn it off and come in here," said his father.

"I turned it down, dad!"

"Turn it off, boy! And bring your scrawny butt into this kitchen."

"Dad, it's *Winchester County*!"

"Tyler!"

It was the one-word sentence. Tyler knew he had no choice in the matter when the one-word sentences started. He turned off the television just as Hank Winchester and Sam the deputy were coming up the street to greet Baby Ben and Maddy. Tyler moped into the kitchen and sat down at the table opposite his father and the greasy bucket of chicken and bones.

"How was school today?" His father asked, not looking up from his magazine, which had bits of whitish gristle speckled all over the slick pages.

"Dad, it's *Winchester County*," said Tyler like a leaky bicycle tire.

"Tyler. How was school today?"

"Okay I guess," he said. "Pillsbury got in trouble for not coming when the teacher told him to."

"You mean Warren Leminski? Good ol' eat-the-entire-box-of-donuts Warren? You still hangin' out with ol' Jewboy?"

"I call him Pillsbury."

"Whatid your mom have to say today?"

"What do you mean?"

His father looked down at him for the first time as he turned the page. He was still wearing his uniform and it needed a washing. The dirty green baseball cap was on the counter by the sink. Even if the grease would not come out, it would still look better washed every now and then. His hands holding the drumstick were red from scrubbing but still black beneath the nails.

"Well she picked you up, didn't she?"

"Yes."

"And she dropped you off, didn't she?"

"Yes."

"So what did she have to say?"

"About what?"

"About anything. About me. Here, want some more chicken?"

"I had some."

"Have some more," said his father, tipping the paper bucket his direction, "just don't take a leg. I love the legs. I'm a leg man. You know what a leg man is, Tyler?"

"No."

"You will," he said with a laughing sort of a snort. "You're my boy and you will one day know what it means to be a leg man. And then God help you."

Tyler fished out a piece of chicken and held it in his fingers, examining it in the used up yellow light of the kitchen with its doorless cupboards and its cracked floor and its dripping sink full of last night and the night before.

"What's this one, dad?" Tyler asked, holding the piece out for inspection.

"Huh? That's a breast," he said flatly.

"I'm a breast man, then," said Tyler and this made his father roar for reasons Tyler did not really comprehend, and when his father's mouth came open with laughter Tyler could see bits of chewed up meat and gristle on his teeth.

But Tyler liked to see his father laugh and so he laughed too, giggling over the piece of chicken between his fingers. He brought it to his mouth for an enthusiastic bite that was too big for him.

"Hey, dad?" Tyler asked after he swallowed, and with just a little electricity in his voice.

"Yeah," said his father, washing down the laughter with the last of his beer.

"Tonight on *Winchester County* one of the horses pulling the stagecoach was a different color. See, it was brown and usually…"

"So what did your mother have to say?"

"Huh?"

"Was she bad-mouthing me at all?"

"No."

"Was *he* with her?"

"Who? Mr. Wilton? He's at work. He never picks me up."

"You don't have to call him Mr. Wilton. Does she make you call him that?"

"No. I just do."

"Did she come inside? Because you know the judge said she can't come inside."

"She just dropped me off like she always does, down at the corner so she doesn't have to turn and go around the block. She never comes in."

"Be glad next year when you ride the bus."

"Yeah," said Tyler. "I guess so."

"If she ever comes in you'll tell me about it won't you?"

"Yeah," said Tyler, his head slumping a little, no longer feeling like a breast man. "I'll tell you."

"And if they ever try to take you away, like on a trip or something, I don't care where, you won't go with them, will you?"

"No."

9

"Mark… Mr. Wilton has people out east. They ever talk to you about going out east?"

"No, dad."

Tyler's father looked at him hard, as though squeezing him for a drop of truth that wasn't there to be squeezed.

"Okay then," he said at last, "go watch your show. But keep it down."

Of course, there *was* a drop of truth to be squeezed. Tyler did not like lying to his father, but he knew things would not go well between his parents if he told the truth. For there *had*, in fact, been talk of going east to see Mr. Wilton's people.

Only there had never been any talk of taking Tyler.

———

The next day at Dolly Madison Elementary, on the playground where Tyler and Pillsbury mostly walked the fenced perimeter of the school grounds like a couple of cons serving out their time, Tyler asked Pillsbury if he had seen the brown horse.

Pillsbury had not seen the brown horse and Tyler found this very disappointing. But Pillsbury had seen something; or at least he said so. Pillsbury said he had seen a dog, a brown dog, through the spinning wagon wheel, running huckledy-buck on the other side of the stage-coach, keeping up with Hank Winchester as he twisted the reins and gritted his teeth and fired his rifle, a brown dog running all out between the stagecoach and the pine trees as big as mountains flying past in the background.

Tyler did not really believe Pillsbury, mostly because Pillsbury copied Tyler a lot. He walked with one hand in his pocket with the thumb sticking out like Tyler did and he tried to snap his fingers whenever he had an idea. Since Tyler had not seen any brown dogs, it seemed pretty clear that Pillsbury was just making it up so as not to be left out of the mystery. Besides, Pillsbury wanted a dog of his own something awful and it was not unusual for Pillsbury to work the *word* dog into every other sentence. But Pillsbury's mother was not having a dog in *her house.* She paid good money to keep a clean house and she called dogs and strange men *mongrels.* Pillsbury liked to say that his father would have let him have a dog if he had not killed himself.

Pillsbury liked to say that his father never came home from Korea, which is really what his mother liked to say about it, even though his father had come home from Korea and had even started selling ice cream out of a bicycle cart he had built himself. The way Tyler figured it, only part of Mr. Lemiski had come back. The part of him that liked ice cream and bicycles.

But Tyler chose not to blow the whistle on his friend for making up stories about seeing a brown dog because he did not really see the point of blowing the whistle. And also, Tyler supposed, because it was more fun to imagine that there *was* a dog on the other side of the stagecoach. So they both agreed to pay close attention to *Winchester County* and to look for brown horses and dogs.

After his mother dropped him off at the corner and he had walked the half a block to his building and had let himself in with the key around his neck, and after he had kicked off his shoes and fed the fish in its murky bowl and pulled some baloney and cellophaned cheese slices from the refrigerator, Tyler fell upon the worn green couch and stared disinterestedly at the *Looney Toons* gang, eating his snack and waiting for six o'clock to finally arrive.

The phone rang during *Road Runner.* Tyler got up and answered it by the third ring. It was his father calling to say he was working late that evening, although Tyler suspected he was just *up to no good with those low-life friends of his,* as his mother liked to call them. Tyler said *okay* anyway, just like he hadn't blown the whistle on Pillsbury about the brown dog. He hung up a little too quickly and the phone rang again before he had grabbed some more cheese and made it back to the couch.

"Is your mother there, Tyler?" His father asked suspiciously. "Is she?"

The red and white paper bucket, with stains of grease on the outside that looked like the shadows of passing dark clouds, sat on the floor next to a can of garbage too full to take any more. Inside, a mess of wadded-up napkins tossed over a pile of bones still slick with gristle and scraps of skin was beginning to smell sour.

"No," said Tyler. "Just me."

"You'd tell me wouldn't you?"

"Yes."

"You'd tell me if she was over there packing up your things." It was not a question.

"Yes. She's not here, dad. It's only me. She dropped me off at the corner."

"Okay then. I'll be home when my work is all done."

"Dad?"

"Yeah, Tyler, what is it?"

"If it's okay with Pillsbury's mom will you take us to a ranch on Saturday to ride horses?"

"Tyler, I'm not gonna tell you this again. Listen up real good. That's nothin' but a waste of good money. Okay? I'm not made of money. Besides, Mike and Dale are comin' over on Saturday and we're gonna work on my own car for a change."

"What about on Sunday? Can we go on Sunday?"

"No Tyler. I need to get back to work, now."

"Can I ask Mom and Mr. Winston?"

"*Hell* no. Did she tell you she would?"

"No."

"Have you asked her?"

"No."

"Good. She'll send me half the damn bill, Tyler. The answer is no. Repeat after me."

"The answer is no," repeated Tyler flatly.

"Then that's enough talk about horses. You sure she isn't over there?"

"I'm sure."

"You'd tell me if she was packin' up your things, wouldn't you? If she was talkin' to you about goin' out east?"

"Yes."

"Okay then. Stay out of trouble Tyler. I'll be home in a little while."

His father hung up and the noise in the background of his words – like lots of people talking and the tinkling of glass and someone shouting *your turn, your turn* – all fell into abrupt silence.

Tyler did not like lying to his father. He did not like lying at all. But there would be big trouble between his parents if his father knew what his mother had said to him on the corner where she dropped him off so that she would not need to drive around the block. She had said that she would not be picking him up and dropping him off tomorrow, or for a while after. That she had paid her neighbor, Mrs. Filbert, to wait for him after school and to bring him home for a while. That Mr. Wilton had an opportunity out east and that they were going on a little trip. That she would bring him something when she came back. That she wasn't going to tell his dad because he would go all crazy again, but that it was okay if Tyler wanted to tell him.

But Tyler knew better, and knew he would not be telling his dad anything of the sort. So he had smiled and waved goodbye to his mom as her car had disappeared up the street, and he had walked the rest of the way home by himself just like he always did. And when he had stood in the yellowing kitchen next to the souring paper bucket of gristle and bones talking to his father over the sounds of tinkling and shouting, Tyler had not said a thing.

The first two episodes of *Winchester County* were exciting – lots of people falling like rain from the rooftops into the dust – but completely uneventful on all matters relating to horses and dogs. The Palamentos were pulling the coach *huckledy-buck* and there was no dog at all in any of the episodes.

In the second episode Baby Ben came to town and gave everyone gifts from San Francisco – everyone always called it just *Frisco* –, a hat for his mother, Evangeline, and a saddle for his father, Papa John, and an engraved rifle for his older brother, Sheriff Hank, and they all slapped him on the back, except Evangeline who kissed him on the forehead and left a mark, and told him how glad they were he had come to visit.

13

Baby Ben also brought a lady friend, Lilly, a very smart, delicate woman who knew how to sing like a bird and hang sheets out to dry in the hot sun. Lilly fell in love with the horseshoe maker that, just out of the goodness of his heart, had hired the Black man who used to be a slave, and then she – Lilly – almost got picked off by an angry rustler. Hank Winchester put an end to that mischief, with his *new* rifle. Knocked the rustler off the roof of the General Store with one shot, and the rustler staggered and staggered and staggered until he fell off the roof and straight down into a long wooden box where the horses drink their water. *Splash!* And then just a few bubbles and he was *deader'n-a-doorknob* as Pillsbury said sometimes.

By the time the third episode was ready to cue up, Tyler had stopped caring so much about horses and dogs, even though he had promised Pillsbury that he would pay close attention. He went to the bathroom and then washed his hands and then went to the kitchen where he slipped another slice of baloney and another slice of cellophaned cheese out of the refrigerator. He suspected his father would bring home part of a pizza or some fried chicken when he was through with his work. But Tyler thought that maybe if he filled up on baloney and cheese, then he wouldn't have to eat any of what his father had brought home for him.

Tyler returned to his position on the couch just in time to see the wagon wheel spinning and spinning and spinning; spinning so big that it filled the screen and made him feel a little woozy like normal. For a moment in the dizziness, Tyler thought he could smell summer dust laced with a hint of pine and the soft pungency that the sun will bring out in large animals. The smells stirred in his head with the spinning wheel and the dizziness that was stronger this time than ever before. The wagon wheel got smaller and Tyler could see again that it was really the front wheel of a stagecoach that was under attack and going *huckledy-buck*. And then he saw something to take his breath away: two of the horses were black and one of them was brown, leaving only one Palamento horse.

Tyler sat up and gasped. He could not believe his eyes. Not one horse, but three horses! And still one Palamento, but three *real* horses.

He looked hard for a brown dog, like Pillsbury had described, through the spinning wagon wheel, keeping pace with Hank Winchester on the other side of the stagecoach. He squinted. There was no dog.

But there was something.

A person. A *boy*. In little boots and a straw hat that hung down his back from a strap around his neck. Faintly through the wheeling spokes – there and gone, there and gone, there and gone – like a scratchy old time movie like they showed sometimes at Dolly Madison Elementary when a teacher is sick, up there on the big wall of the *gulag*, which is what Pillsbury likes to call the cafeteria, because that is where they serve *goulash* and even though neither Tyler nor Pillsbury knew what goulash was, it didn't sound very good and that's what they both thought about the Dolly Madison cafeteria. The old movies that they showed up on the big wall of the gulag were so beat up and cut and scratched to ribbons that a boy or a dog – Tom Sawyer or Old Yeller or whoever – might be up there on the wall one second larger than life, and then there would be a popping sound over the speakers and he would disappear and then reappear on the other side of the wall like magic. That's kind of what it was like watching the running boy through the spinning spokes of the wagon wheel. There and gone, there and gone, there and gone.

And could this kid ever run! *Man alive* – as Pillsbury liked to say sometimes when he was excited – he was keeping up with that stagecoach. He was keeping up! And Tyler imagined that this boy between the spokes would be there when Hank Winchester shot his rifle and picked off the rustlers and said *Whoa there, horses,* which he never actually said in the opening but Tyler knew Hank Winchester had to say it eventually. *Whoa there horses!* And the horses, only one of which now was a Palamento, would whinny and stop and stomp their big hooves, and Hank Winchester would drop his big arm down over the side and swing this fast little kid up onto the coach and give him a ride back into town before his supper got cold.

Tyler was so amazed and befuddled about the start of the episode that he almost couldn't concentrate on the actual show, which was the one where Miss Kitty gets taken hostage by some counterfeiters and shows everybody in Winchester County that she can shoot her way out of a mess as good as any man. It was a good episode, a two-parter, but Tyler had trouble focusing on the story. He heard people talking, but he wasn't paying any real attention to what they were saying. It helped that he had seen this episode at least eight or nine times before.

What he *wanted* to do was call Pillsbury. He wanted desperately to know if his friend had seen the running boy and the three non-Palamento horses. But Tyler had never called Pillsbury on the phone before and it seemed strange to do so now. He tried his best to put the horses and the running boy out of his mind and focus on the show.

Miss Kitty was in the barn up at the ranch brushing down a little foal which Tyler already knows is where she will get nabbed by the counterfeiters, or, at least, by the bad men who work for the counterfeiters, who is really just one wiry little man wearing a green visor and carrying a magnifying glass and making pretend money.

Oh, she'll put up a struggle. She'll holler and scream. That Kitty Winchester is as pretty and sweet as a whippoorwill, but she's tough too; and she's *really got a set of lungs on her* is what Pillsbury likes to say about her. She won't go down without a fight.

But Tyler knows that Hank Winchester is in town taking Evangeline to see the preacher and that Papa John and the others are out tending the herd and Baby Ben is back in Frisco and that Miss Kitty will fight and make a lot of noise but that there is no one home to hear her calling out and the bad men will take her. They will tie her up and fold her over the rump of a black horse and trot her off to a hideout up in the hills where the wiry man in the green visor will show his manners and pretend to be polite and ask her questions and pretend to protect her from his men, like he really cares about her; but he doesn't really care and Miss Kitty knows he is not her friend. And up there in the hills above Winchester County they will put her to work, making her haul buckets of water and making her cook for them – for just about all these men will ever do is stand guard over the hideout and eat food, bowls and bowls of stew – or *goulash* is probably what it is, like what they serve at the Dolly Madison Gulag – and Miss Kitty will spoon it out to them from a big black pot which she heats over a fire. And when she hauls the firewood, Miss Kitty will stumble and fall and over the course of many days with the counterfeiters, black marks will begin appear across her face and arms like streaks of coal and her shirt will be torn above the shoulder and the bad men will laugh at her and treat her poorly. But all the while Miss Kitty will know that her brother Hank and Papa John and Evangeline and Sam the deputy will be worried sick about her and will be out calling her name and searching for her day and night. And what Miss Kitty won't know is that even Baby Ben will come home when he gets the telegraph from Evangeline, and that Hank Winchester will get so worried for her that every time he talks to Papa John about it you almost think that this great big fearless man who can make a stagecoach fly and pick off rustlers like he was swatting flies, you almost think he is going to open up and cry broken-hearted tears of lost love for his only sister.

That was just how much they loved her.

But it will be a long, hard wait for Kitty Winchester and when no one comes and no one comes and no one comes, she will realize that it is all up to her and she will walk outta that snake pit of a hideout up in the hills. She will slip a revolver into the pot of goulash when no one is looking and then she clean it off in the stream when the men are asleep and she will steal a horse and she will simply decide to go on home where everybody is waiting for her. And she does. Oh, they will try to stop her, and they will get the horse back and when the shooting starts, there will be heck to pay for it all, but Miss Kitty will go home. She will near stumble out of a grouping of tall pine right near the Winchester Ranch on the edge of town, and then fall smack into the arms of her brother, Hank Winchester. And he will hug her and she will cry on his shoulder and she will tell him everything.

And then Sheriff Hank will leave Miss Kitty to Evangeline and then *oh-brother-take-cover* as Pillsbury often said.

Tyler looked at Miss Kitty brushing the little brown foal in the hay of the barn and knew all of that was coming. *A real shoot-em-up.* He tried to let the show unfold and to enjoy it as though he did not know what was going to happen. But he could not really see the show at all. He could

17

not see anything but the picture in his head of the spinning wheel and the three non-Palamentos and the smell of dust and pine and the dog that was really a boy, running and running and running. And as the late summer air pressed up against the crankless window and the sour fumes rose from the bones and the gristle in the paper bucket and as the Miss Kitty episode played on in the background of his mind, as though from very far away, and as the pistol disappeared beneath the goulash and as bad men fell from the rooftops and the treetops and out of the sky like rain, Tyler slowly began to understand what needed to be done about it all.

When the show was over, Tyler removed the ratty blue pillow from the side of his head, sat up, left the worn green couch, went directly into his bedroom and packed as many of his clothes into his backpack that he could manage.

———

The next morning, Tyler climbed into his father's truck early, rather than waiting to be called to hurry up like normal. His father was bleary-eyed and didn't say more than six words to him the entire way to school except to say that he had a wicked headache. He was wearing his greasy green uniform and matching baseball cap, both of which still needed to be washed and which Tyler thought were beginning to smell a little sour like the bones and gristle and soiled napkins at the bottom of the paper bucket in the kitchen. He had the green cap pulled so low over his face that Tyler wondered how his father could see the road.

But he could see the road just fine. Tyler's father knew everything about cars and was a very good driver.

When they reached the school, Tyler's father pulled the truck over to the curb. He laid his head back on the seat and closed his eyes, pulling the cap down even further like he was planning on going to sleep. Tyler pulled his pack from its place beneath the seat and climbed out.

"Tyler, you'll tell me if your mother says anything, won't you? You'll tell me everything."

"Yes sir."

"Atsa boy. A father protects his kid. Nothin' bad is gonna happen to you as long as I'm around Tyler. You remember that."

"Okay, dad," said Tyler.

His father did not lift his head or open his eyes, but snapped the bill of his greasy green cap with his finger. "Go on now."

And Tyler did go on.

He went on to find his friend Pillsbury, who was really Warren Lemiski and who his father liked to call *ol' Jewboy*, but who Tyler called Pillsbury because Pillsbury was his best friend and that's what Pillsbury liked to be called and that's all it meant and all it ever would mean.

When they were alone at recess, walking the fenced perimeter of the yard like a couple of cons looking the break out of the joint, Tyler asked Pillsbury and Pillsbury asked Tyler the questions they had been holding inside of them for hours upon hours. Tyler had not seen a dog, but he had seen a boy. Pillsbury had not seen a boy, but had seen a dog, running all out, *huckledy-buck* with the stagecoach, not on the far-side, between the coach and the pine trees as big as mountains, but on the *near side* this time, in between the spinning wagon wheel and Pillsbury.

"Tyler, it was the same dog!" exclaimed Pillsbury. "Man-o-man! It was the same dog only closer this time! And the horses! Same as you saw, Tyler ol' pal!" Because that was the kind of thing Pillsbury called Tyler sometimes. "Same as you. Two black, one brown and one Palamento."

Pillsbury could have just been copying, but Tyler knew that he was *not* just copying and that he and Pillsbury really did see things the same, even if a little differently.

"Man alive, Tyler! What do you think all of this means?"

Tyler told his friend what he thought all of it meant. And before they had finished walking the yard, they had resolved a great many things about the world and what to do about it.

When Dolly Madison Elementary sounded its final bell, and the children spilled from the big double doors and down across the weary lawn and into the cars and arms of those who were waiting for them, Tyler and his friend Pillsbury went out another way, through the single

19

metal door in the back of the gulag, avoiding Mrs. Filbert who, Tyler suspected, would be waiting in her blue station wagon to earn the money Tyler's mother had given her.

"Make sure you just take what you need," said Tyler as they turned their backs on the fenced playground, heading away from the school. "Don't load yourself down."

"Okay," said Pillsbury

"Will your mom be home?"

Pillsbury pulled a key on a chain from his front pocket and smiled.

They walked up the block to the lock in the doorknob that fit Pillsbury's key. Inside, Tyler sat hunched on a gold-tasseled, red velvet-cushioned stool in the entry hallway of the Lemiski home. He held his backpack in his lap, and waited as Pillsbury plodded up the stairs to his room.

Across the hall was a kind of parlor. He could see a high-backed chair with arms that scrolled into little wooden fists and part of a brown couch with a black pillow that had white stuffing coming out of the seam. The window shades were drawn and the air hung heavy and low and old along the floor. In the corner was a television console that stood on three wooden legs and a can of tomato soup. Tyler guessed that was where *Winchester County* came into Pillsbury's world.

The Lemiski house had a smell. Emptiness has an odor. Nothingness has an odor. Stillness has an odor. The clingy, sickly sour of rot and decay. The stench of gristle and bone in the bottom of a forgotten bucket. It made Tyler want to cry and shriek and break things and tear the curtains off the windows in the parlor. It smelled like something no longer living, like dander and scurf. It smelled like death.

The late Mr. Lemiski stared down at him from a gilded oval portrait on the wall. Eyes like glossy black marbles, abandoned on the shelf of his face, looking out over the razor-ridge of a nose and thin, pink lips. It seemed to Tyler that Mr. Lemiski had wanted to speak but could not comprehend the chaos of sound in his own heart. His forehead was almost imperceptibly worried, like a deep lake had swallowed the scream of a rock and was resealing itself into glass. Somewhere a clock ticked out a thin memory of heartbeat.

Tyler stood up and went outside. He sat down on the stoop and watched the sun set fire to the trees.

In a few minutes, Pillsbury was closing the door behind him. He had a lumpy blue laundry bag slung over his shoulder and a straw cowboy hat on his head.

"I'm set to mosey," said Pillsbury.

"Me too," said Tyler.

And so they walked on through the late summer air, gold with dust that billowed out in soft, dreamy shapes from between the trees that lined their path. The sun was still out, but on its way down, marking their progress like a reflection in the cloud-mottled sky that would meet their young and hopeful souls precisely at the horizon, way, way out there where the sidewalk beneath them stopped and the world ended. They walked beneath the dreamy sunlit shapes in the air and beneath the trees that seemed to get taller and taller into the distance rather than the other way around. And as they walked, their bodies got smaller and brighter and smaller and brighter and they kept walking and kept shrinking even as the trees got taller until they were but tiny specks, lit like motes in the afternoon sun or two bits of electric static.

And then, just like that, they disappeared.

———

When Kevin Freeman returned home from work that evening, he was surprised at first to learn that his son, Tyler, was not at home. Tyler was always at home when Kevin returned from work in the early evening, or in the mid-evening if Kevin went out for a drink or two after work to blow off some steam. Tyler was always waiting for him. That was the arrangement with his ex-wife. That, by God, was the arrangement.

But tonight, early evening, Tyler was not home.

Kevin placed the box of pizza on the table in the kitchen and fanned his face on account of the smell of the garbage he had expected Tyler to take out to the dumpster. He left the kitchen and toured the whole apartment looking for answers to the whereabouts of his son. Finding nothing, Kevin returned to the kitchen angry and pounded the counter with his fist.

"That, by God, was the arrangement," he said to no one, throwing his greasy green cap onto the table and picking up the phone, "and I, by God, will *enforce* the arrangement."

When he dialed the number of Mr. Mark Wilton, the man with whom Kevin's ex-wife had recently taken up, and about whom his ex-wife was increasingly fond of bragging, Kevin heard the message that the number had been disconnected.

First he heard it. Then it sunk in and he felt it.

And Kevin began to feel a fear and an anger that was like the sour smell from a pile of bones and gristle that have been sitting around too long. He pounded the counter again and cursed the emptiness around him and charged off again to Tyler's room, this time opening drawers and the closet and seeing that some of his clothes were gone. His toothbrush was gone. And his ball glove. And his cowboy boots. And his cap gun from the windowsill by the bed.

"You've stolen my boy!" he screamed and stormed back to the kitchen to call Mr. Mark Wilton again only to be told, again, that the number he had dialed was no longer in service.

For the next hour Kevin Freeman stomped and kicked and shouted himself around his empty home until the garbage in the kitchen had been more or less evenly distributed across the floor and he had one fewer lamps to his name. He collapsed still angry but exhausted on his couch and turned on the television, because he could think of nothing else to do with himself.

It was *Winchester County.* A two-parter. And, not that Kevin would know it, an episode not even his long lost son had ever seen before.

It was the one where Baby Ben comes home from Frisco, dressed in a spiffy suit with a bunch of presents for his family – some dresses and a saddle and another rifle – and also with an orphan boy and his dog that he had saved from certain doom along the way. Sheriff Hank smiled and tousled the boy's hair and the dog barked happily and spun in quick circles and smiled up at everyone, and Miss Kitty kept hugging on them and telling them they were *finally home, finally home, finally home,* because Miss Kitty said things like that.

They were, of course, welcomed by all of Winchester County with open arms.

And *man alive,* how they could run.

Chapter 2

THE OFFICE

Lydia grabbed three more bottles by the necks like they were so many dead chickens. She put them on her tray next to wadded up napkins and the salted nuts and the six dollars and took them to the bar.

She was careful to chart a course around the men swinging their sticks by the pool table. They were regulars, most of them anyway, and they all called her by her first name when they needed another drink or if they wanted a bet settled. They wore greasy green uniforms and green baseball hats that advertised a local garage. Several of the men liked to turn their hats backwards on their heads so they could see the cue ball better in the dim yellow light that the smoke liked to hold close up to the ceiling.

"It's your turn! Kevin! It's your turn!"

Two of them were shouting over at another who was in the corner talking on the pay phone in the short hallway to the bathrooms. The man was hunched over and covering one ear so he could hear.

"Come on, Kevin. We're not getting any younger over here! Tell her you *looooooove* her and hang up."

The man on the telephone straightened and turned and made an obscene gesture and they all laughed raucously like it was the funniest thing they had ever seen.

"He's talkin' to his kid," said one of the men who sauntered away from the pool table and lowered his face into the red glow coming out of the jukebox. Howlin' Wolf was singing about how the wolf is at the door. "Leave him alone," said the man into the red glow.

There were bottles and glasses around the pool table that were empty and needed to be collected. Lydia knew that there would soon be an accident and bits of glass would be all over the floor again.

But she was in no hurry to do the prudent thing. The pool game had stalled as the men all waited for the man on the phone to finish his call. She knew that with nothing else to focus their attention, the men would be all too delighted to start up a conversation with the female help. They would ogle her legs and ask her about her personal life and she would smile and act like she didn't quite understand what they were getting at. If push came to shove she might ask them a question about their wives and that would just make them mad and all the more determined.

All of that was coming eventually. There was no escaping it. But she could delay it until she had absolutely no choice in the matter. That was the way Lydia handled things at *The Office*.

She left the tray of bottles and napkins and nuts and the six dollars on the bar for Ryan to take care of and picked up the three whiskey sours he had left for her to take to the women sitting in the corner booth.

They were secretaries, or maybe bank tellers, thought Lydia; young women – thirties maybe – who were not professionals but who were close enough to think of themselves in that way. They wore silk tops and pearls and rings on their fingers that they had not purchased. They had not been to *The Office* before and Lydia knew they would not be back again. They had realized by now – their second round – that this was not the place to troll for men in suits rebounding from misguided love and courting fresh heartbreak. It was not the first time people had been misled by the name over the door.

When Lydia approached with the drinks the women stopped talking and took a renewed interest in the cigarettes they were smoking. They all blew up into a bluish cloud above the table like they were trying to create their own weather.

"Here you are," said Lydia with a smile, placing the glasses on the table. "Three whiskey sours. Anything else I can get for you?"

"I ordered a glass of ice," said the one with the bracelets and the lips that were uneven and fleshy in the middle. She certainly had not ordered a glass of ice. Lydia would have remembered.

"I'm very sorry," she said. "I'll bring that right over. Anything else?"

"Just the bill," said the blonde one with a long exhale up in Lydia's direction, and then she leaned into the table and continued the discussion with the others, something about a man named Peter and a woman named Laura.

Lydia asked Ryan for a glass of ice and a ticket for table seven.

"Yep," he said. "Your gonna be pickin' up glass again you know." Ryan jerked his head in the general direction of the pool table as his hands took care of business beneath the bar. A lick of thick brown hair flopped against his forehead. He was a big man and handsome, she supposed, in an over-stuffed bear sort of way. Ryan ran the bar whenever Milo was out of town. Sophie still handled the diner, but Ryan was in charge of *The Office*.

Ryan's style was to get things done by making observations that implied some action was required. Like, *table nine looks a little cluttered*. Or, *sounds like the ladies' commode is plugged again*. Or, like tonight, *you're gonna be pickin' up glass again, you know*. Lydia supposed that there were worse ways to govern. Better than Milo, anyway, who liked to snap his fingers and point.

"Yeah," she said heavily, "I know. You're right. Is Conni coming in at all?"

"Sounded pretty bad to me," said Ryan shaking his head. "Wouldn't count on it."

"Okay. I'll be right back for the ice."

Lydia grabbed an empty tray and headed for the pool table, wiping down table number three and pocketing her tip along the way. She started cleaning things up, moving quickly and hoping she could pass through without incident. But she could feel their eyes on her and she knew she should try to set the tone before they did.

"You gentlemen mind if I collect some of these things?" she asked everyone and no one. Howlin' Wolf growled his way out through the smoke that held the light against its will up against the ceiling.

"Sweetheart," said one of the men, "you can do anything you want to do as far as I'm concerned. Just don't call us gentlemen."

The men laughed and those with pool sticks jabbed them at the floor so that the rubber stoppers made thick thumping sounds like someone beating his fists against the door of a locked room. Lydia smiled and laughed a little and continued pulling glasses and bottles off the rim of the table.

"You got a man in your life yet, Lydia?" asked the one whose stubble was closest to an actual beard.

"Oh, I have lots of men in my life," she said, reaching for a bottle and thinking darkly that she meant all of them and their kind.

"I'll bet you do, sugar. Legs like those, I'll bet you do."

"Bet your wife has some pretty legs," said Lydia casually, as though just making conversation.

"You listen here, sugar…"

"Leave her alone, Ross."

It was the same man in the long hair and the bandana around his arm who had sauntered over to the jukebox and told them to leave the man on the telephone alone.

"Oh, I'm not doin' nothin'," objected Ross. "I'm just complimentin' Lydia on those creamy white gams of hers. You know, like a gentleman."

There was another round of laughter as Lydia brushed splintered shells and peanut husks into her hands. She reached for a shell on the corner of the table and as she did so, she felt a thin polished reed of wood slowly slip its way from inner calf, up around the protrusion of knee, to inner thigh.

There was more laughter, husky and low this time. The man with the long hair and the bandana who liked for people to be left alone was busy in the red glow of the jukebox. Lydia moved out of reach to the other side of the table. She filled her tray and returned to the bar without asking if there was something else that she could bring them.

27

She passed the tray of bottles and glasses and broken shells to Ryan, along with the rag with which she had wiped down table three, and she picked up the glass of ice and the ticket for table seven. They were all looking at her as she made the delivery.

"How hard is it to get a stupid glass of ice?" said the uneven lips. "I almost finished my entire drink while you were over there flirting with the grease monkeys. What is your name? What does that say? *Lydia?* Is that your name? What am I going to do with a glass of ice now, Lydia?"

"I'm sorry, ma'am. I'm the only one waiting tables tonight. I... I needed to get..."

"Save it. I don't really care what you needed to *get*. I needed to *get* a glass of ice and I hope that you didn't really need to *get* a tip."

"Now, Ruth," said the curly one in the blazer with the broach that looked like a silver insect, "it's no big deal. Let's just go."

"I'm sorry, Gayle, but it *is* a big deal. No one cares about service any more."

"Have a nice evening," said Lydia and left them with the ticket.

She returned to the bar where Ryan was drying glasses and putting them back on the shelf.

"I need five minutes," she told him.

Ryan surveyed the room with his eyes, still drying glasses.

"Those boys okay for beer?" he asked, flipping his lick of hair toward the pool table.

"They're okay," said Lydia.

"Dunno. Been awhile."

"They're okay."

"What about table seven. Ladies look like their clearin' out. Probably gonna need cleaning."

"Five minutes, Ryan."

"Okay, okay. Bad night already? We're just gettin' started, Lydia. You're not gettin' sick too."

"Just need a break. I'll be in the diner."

Lydia crossed the bar, walked through the curtain of plastic beads hanging in the doorframe and headed down the hallway of stained and split linoleum where the light got all slick and yellow and seemed to pool on the floor like it didn't have enough energy to get itself up into the air.

She pushed her way through the swinging, slatted saloon-style half-doors that led into the diner and found an empty booth along the wall of windows. The diner smelled like cheese and grease and chili and as she sat down the vinyl cushion stuck to the back of her legs.

She sat quietly, with her hands folded neatly on the table, staring out into the nothingness of the parking lot and at the sign that flickered Milo's name on top of the tall, white metal pole. The sign used to turn in slow circles, but that had stopped years ago.

"Heeey! Eesa Leedia. My Leedia," said Sophie from behind the counter. She was older looking and ethnic and small with craggy skin and sharp, dark eyes that peered out from beneath a mop of black curls. Lydia liked Sophie and Sophie liked just about everybody. Sophie *was* the very heart of *Milo's Diner* and everybody who had ever eaten there knew it.

"Hey, Sophie. How ya' doin'?"

"I no complain, Leedia. Sophie happy. Leedia happy, yes?"

"Conni's sick. It's all me in there tonight."

"Like Kreesta. Kreesta sick, sick, sick. All Sophie in *here*. See?" Sophie extended her arms to the half-full diner and laughed. "See? Sophie too. Only Sophie."

"When's Milo coming back?"

Sophie made a sound with her lips and a comic role of her little dark eyes to show the ridiculousness of the question. "He say Wednesday, but... we see."

"When's the funeral?"

"Yesterday. He trying to help his seester. Oh, Leedia. So sad. Poor Bianca."

"Poor thing," said Lydia shaking her head out at the parking lot. The wind was picking up and she had the feeling that it might be raining soon. "How long were they married?"

"Feefteen, I think. Years. Feefteen years. Oh, but he so sick for many years." Sophie chopped at the air with her hands and shook her head. "Many years."

29

"Poor thing."

"Yes. He do same thing every ten years."

"He does what every ten years?"

"Bury husband of seester. Twenty years past, his seester Eva husband die two weeks after we open diner and he leave me alone to run business." She put one hand on each side of her face and shook her head. "Oh, Leedia, what a mess. I know nothing then but cooking. We have kitchen fire when I help customer with too much money making change. Oh dear. Then ten years pass he go again for other seester. Rosaria. Her husband dead too. Kaput. Dead. So Milo go over and help Rosaria bury and hold her hand and stay with her. He stay whole week. She was baby; Rosaria. No like Eva. Eva was tough that one. She tell Milo go home, go home, go see Sophie, leave me alone. Eva have money. Rich and tough. No like poor Rosaria, who cry and cry and cry. And no like this one. Bianca. She poor and sweet, like a little bird, no rich and tough like Eva. These seesters, Leedia, Milo's seesters pick men to die early."

"So sad."

"Yes. I bring you something?"

"No."

"Chili?"

"No."

"Tea?"

"No. Thank you, Sophie. I just need five quiet minutes."

"Oh, Leedia. Sophie know. You need rest. You rest. You relax."

Lydia sat, and she looked out at the parking lot and at the wind playing with the trash and dust and at the flickering sign that had stopped turning long ago.

But she did not relax.

She was afraid that if she relaxed, if she slackened her grip even just a little, she might just slip beneath the surface of her life and drown, never to be heard from again and never to be missed by a soul. She did not relax because she could not let go of the thing that kept her afloat, which was simply the hope that life would get better; that one day the world would spin out of the shadows and into a new orbit where all the rules changed and everything worked differently. Where people were kind and appreciative and where children did not die in the womb and where men did not cat around and beat you and leave when they got bored, and where parents lived forever and they would take you back so you could start all over from the beginning. Lydia could not afford to loosen her grip on the hope that a new day would be coming around on the big wheel, maybe tomorrow, or if not tomorrow, then maybe the day after tomorrow, and that the new day would hold something entirely different for her than all of her other days that stretched end-to-end, back, back, back, back into the cracked and peeling sepia horizon of her own memory.

The new day did not have to hold something brilliant or magical or miraculous. That would be marvelous. It would. But that was not the particular hope to which Lydia Watson clung. She was long past that. The hope was only this: that a new day would come and offer within its widespread arms something different. That was all. Something different. Because as long as the new day came and offered something different, that would get her by; that would be proof enough, at least for the time being, that the world was still spinning and that time had not stopped and that change was possible. *Possible.* That was not so much to ask. *Possible.* That at least would get her to the next day. Something different. Something. Anything.

Lydia sat for several minutes watching the wind and listening to Sophie sling endearments with the pie and coffee. Then Sophie came by and slipped into the seat across from her and patted her on the hand.

"You still go to... eh... island? What you call... island?

"Fiji Islands."

"Ah, Fiji islands. Yes."

"No. I was just talkin', Sophie. Someone left a magazine in the bar. All about the Fiji Islands. I said I wanted to go. Not that I was actually *going.*"

"Ah... lots money, yes?"

"Yes. A lot of money."

31

"Bah! Fiji a waste. Waste of money, Leedia. You stay here. With Sophie."

Lydia turned away from the window and looked at Sophie who flashed that irrepressibly good-natured smile at her and Lydia laughed in spite of her mood. She liked Sophie. Everyone liked Sophie.

Ryan appeared in the doorway with his hands on his hips and the lick of brown hair nearly touching his eyebrow. He looked at Lydia and Sophie sitting around the diner and laughing about money.

"Excuse me there, Sophie," he said, never taking his eyes off of Lydia, who instantly began scooting herself out of the booth, trying to hold her skirt to her legs.

"Ah! Meester Bigga Boy Ryan. How you do, meester Bigga Boy?"

"Well, we're fillin' up in here, that's for sure Sophie. These people are so thirsty, I was just beginning to wonder when the riots are gonna start."

Lydia walked past him through the swinging doors and headed back down the hallway towards the bar.

"You be nice, meester Bigga Boy," said Sophie, chopping the air with her hand and then getting back to work.

"I'm bein' plenty nice, Sophie. Milo would'a just snapped his fingers. You know that. It's no time to be sittin' around."

For the rest of the night, Lydia did the work of two people, hustling out the fulls and rounding up the empties. She took orders and suffered abuse. She brought cracked wooden bowls of roasted nuts out to women who made it very clear that, pretty or not, Lydia was not in their league, and to men who, married or not, wanted to take her to bed or touch her legs or at least ogle at the way she filled out her uniform. She did not ask for another break.

The best parts of the evening were when she had to clean up a newly empty table. When she seated customers, she was all performance, smiling and happy to see them and ready to take their orders and their disrespect. Same as when she brought them their drinks and their roasted nuts and salted pretzels. And when they settled up the bill, she had to smile and wish them well and bid them a nice evening and thank them for nothing.

But when she grabbed the wet rag and the tray and went out to clean up a table, that was her favorite. Because when she cleaned up, she was just Lydia again – she didn't need to smile and pretend things she wasn't feeling. As she wiped up the nut dust and the lemon pulp and the ice puddles, she could scour downward through all the smoke and the music and the noise and find herself again, quiet and desperate and wanting some evidence that the world was still turning and that a different life was at least possible. It was about the only time that she was free to feel the sickness of not knowing how much longer she could last.

The Office closed at two o'clock in the morning, long after the diner at the other end of the hallway was dark and quiet and Sophie had gone home to her husband, Frank, who was in a wheelchair for serving in the war, and her daughter, Rose, who taught school over at Dolly Madison Elementary. Rose was not pretty and couldn't find a man who would love her, so she lived at home even though she was almost forty. But Rose was sweet and always seemed happy whenever she came over to *Milo's* to visit, and when she did she was usually wheeling Frank around so that he could tell his jokes to the regulars and eat pie and drink coffee. The two of them would laugh and laugh at Frank, who was a real card, and then Frank would start laughing, at nothing really, just laughing, and soon the customers would be laughing as they ate their food.

When it was two o'clock in the morning and *The Office* was closing Lydia often thought of Sophie and Frank and Rose – who was all the happier, in Lydia's opinion, for never having found a man – all sleeping under one roof and happy to have each other.

Lydia lived in a two-room apartment just large enough for a person and a medium sized dog. The owners did not allow pets, so Lydia did not have a dog and had finally given up wanting one. The apartment did have a nice view of a copse of tall pines that swayed in the wind and that caught the sun in the mornings when it was clear and that continued to drip water into deep puddles long after it stopped raining. She kept the place clean because it was small and there was not much else she had to do with her time when she was not working. She did not have a television, but she liked to listen to the radio and to read books about *other* people and the things *other* people did and what *other* people felt about those things.

The apartment was eleven blocks away from *The Office,* which made it a convenient walk to work in the early evening and a dangerous walk back in the very early morning. On her walks in the early evening, on her way to work, people were just coming home from their jobs; returning from the office – *real* offices – out there in the world where things happened and where people had to struggle just to keep up with all the new developments. And when they came home at the end of the day they pulled sharply into their driveways in their big cars with the windows down and the stereos on with the sound of Sam Cooke and Elvis Presley and Nat King Cole sloshing out into the street like a glass so full of wine that it's too much for one person to drink. And almost before they can step out onto the driveways, children spill out of the doors and from the bushes and from the back yards with their basket-balls and their squirt guns and their questions about what was going to happen next, maybe supper or maybe a movie or a double-header down at Diggers Field.

Lydia tended to walk to work with her hands in the pockets of her jacket, eyes forward, looking at the gray squares of concrete passing beneath her feet, all as though she was counting her steps and failing to notice the commotion of the people coming home from their offices. But she noticed, all right. She always noticed. She could hear them just fine, and out of the corners of her eyes, she could see what it must be like to come home from the wide world at the end of the day.

That was all on the walk to work in the early evenings, before the sun had plowed itself fully into the earth, pushing the night up out of the soil, growing everywhere like a black moss that covers the trees and the buildings and clinging to the air with its scent of desolation. On the walk home, in the very early mornings, the streets were quiet and dark and full of menace, as though something hungry and heartless came out of the shadows once everybody was safely inside their houses and tucked into their beds.

Years ago, Lydia had been fearful of the walk home, and she had covered the blocks quickly, looking over her shoulder most of the way, sometimes running that last stretch past Murphy's and the Neighborhood Pharmacy and Diggers Field and the empty drive-in, so that by the time she had climbed the stairs and opened the door and closed it behind her and turned the bolt, she was panting hard and sweat dampened the hair near the skin of her nape.

But that was a long time ago. Now, even the fear was gone. The fear was gone and she missed it. She missed it along with everything and everyone else that no longer touched her. Not that there was no reason to be afraid. There certainly was and the newspapers could prove it just about every day. But Lydia had simply stopped feeling fear.

And sometimes that concerned her. Sometimes it gave her an uncomfortable buzzing in the pit of her stomach. Because when you stopped feeling fear walking home in the dark mornings, when menace was on the prowl and the moon hung in the night like a slender blade of sharpened white bone, what else was there left to feel? If not fear, what is left?

After the last of customers had slipped into the night, Ryan shut and locked the door and balanced the till and did the closing up paperwork. Lydia grabbed the broom and started sweeping peanut shells over by the jukebox, which was mercifully quiet for the first time all night. Ryan zipped two stacks of soft green bills into a black deposit bag and pulled on his leather jacket.

"Why don't you leave that for tomorrow, Lydia," he said, pulling his licks of hair back through his fingers. "Go on home."

"Oh, I will," she said. "I won't be but a few more minutes. It'll be nice to have it all swept."

"You're a good worker, Lydia. You did good tonight. Conni owes you one."

"Thanks Ryan."

"I'm going to make the deposit and go on home then. You'll lock up?"

"I'll lock up."

"Good night then."

"Good night."

Ryan left the bar, stepping out into the dim glow of the parking lot, and Lydia closed and locked the door behind him. She swept for a minute and then sat down at table number three and looked around the now perfectly empty bar and down the dark hallway that led off to *Milo's Diner.*

She sat quietly, listening to the stillness, which was at first like a deep cold lake sitting in a cup of granite that kept it from moving. But after a few minutes the stillness began to move and flow, finding its way in, seeping into her ears in tiny streams, then crashing in around her in ever greater waves of unbearable loneliness until she ached so much inside that her narrow shoulders started to shake. She put her head on the top of table number three and cried.

A knock on the door, three sharp raps, snapped her to attention. She sniffled and wiped her nose and blinked rapidly to clear her eyes and grabbed the broom.

"Ryan?" she called.

"Yep," said Ryan.

She unlocked the door, looking over at the bar for the keys he must have forgotten. The door flew open suddenly, with such force that it caught her in the shin and the face and she cried out in pain, falling against the opposite wall.

The man had a short scraggly, beard and he wore a knit green skull-cap. From the beneath the cap, greasy gray strands of hair escaped like tendrils of dirty snow slipping off the back of a tire.

It was not Ryan.

Lydia placed her hand carefully where the door had caught her in the face and checked for blood. There was no blood, but it hurt and she winced. The man slammed and locked the door behind him and then turned to face her.

He was considerably taller, but not much older than she was. He was hard and lean looking and wearing an army jacket that was dirty and ripped, showing a white, threadbare shirt beneath. A pallid ridge of skin cut across one of his eyebrows, leaving a thin trail where the hair wouldn't grow. He was breathing hard, like he had been running, and he held his mouth open to let in the air. Lydia saw that his teeth were crooked and yellow and that the thatch of beard growing from his chin was matted with the blood that glistened from over the surface of his lips.

Wrapped around the fingers of his left hand was the end of a half-full duffle bag. Gripped in the other hand – the one with the knuckles stripped raw that he had used to turn the deadbolt back into place – was a large, toothy hunting knife.

"We're closed," she said sharply, looking at the knife. "You need to go. Please leave, sir!"

"Naw, y'aint closed," he said, out of breath but otherwise calm. "Not for me y'aint. I'm gon' stay a spell. Go on and sit down. What's your name?" He looked at her nametag and squinted. "Lydia? G'on and sit down, Lydia, if you know what's good for you." He flicked the tip of the knife away from the door, towards the middle of the room.

Lydia did as she was told, stepping backwards so that she could keep him in sight. She realized that she was still holding the broom and thought in a sudden rush that maybe it had potential as a weapon.

"Why don't you just drop the broom there, Lydia," said the man reading her mind. "I reckon the place is already clean enough. You ain't got to be sweepin' no more."

She let the broom drop and it fell between them. The man stepped on it and stood for a moment apprising himself of his surroundings, craning his neck slowly this way and that.

"Anyone else here, Lydia?"

She shook her head before it occurred to her to lie. She backed into table three and started to sit down.

"Naw," he said. "That won't do, Lydia. You go sit in that booth over there where I can keep an eye on ya." He pointed to table seven where, earlier in the evening she had set down the whiskey sours and the woman in the pearls and the fleshy uneven lips had flicked her cigarette and claimed to have ordered a glass of ice. "I'll be sittin' here," he said, nodding at table three.

Lydia sidled her way over to table seven and slipped into the back of the booth, trying to hold her skirt to her legs, which seemed suddenly cold and covered in goose flesh.

The man pulled out the chair on which Lydia had been crying only moments before and straddled it. He released his grip on the duffle bag and set the knife on the table. His breathing slowed but his eyes were still quick, darting around the room, and they caught Lydia looking at the sharpened, serrated steel he no longer held.

"I can reach it right quick," he said, looking sideways at the knife. "You'll never even make it out from around that booth. So you just sit and relax there, Miss Lydia. Just relax your bones a spell."

Lydia sat quietly and thought to herself that there was nothing she could do. He sat at a table that was between her and the door through which he had entered on the left, and that was also between her and the hallway that led to Milo's Diner on the right. There was no way to leave the room.

Aside from the one in the diner, there were only two telephones. One on a shelf behind the bar and the payphone in the back, towards the restrooms, where the man named Kevin had been hunched over covering one ear and trying to talk to his boy as his greasy pool-playing buddies had teased him about being in *loooove* before the long-haired man in the glow of the juke box had told them to leave him alone. There was no way she could reach either phone, let alone dial a number and ask for help.

Lydia knew that Milo kept a gun behind the bar, a snub-nosed pistol that she had only seen once, but she had no idea where exactly it was kept because even in all of her years working for Milo, she had never taken an interest in such things.

So Lydia sat quietly and watched the man catch his breath and look around the room. He came to a slow but focused attention as the sound of sirens, long and searching with their high-pitched tendrils, rose up out of the silence from different directions and mingled in the night, exchanging information like wolves. The man stiffened slightly as he listened. The sirens grew louder and more complicated and the man looked hard at Lydia as he listened and his hand again lay over the handle of the knife.

After several tense minutes, the sirens seeped back into the earth and all was quiet once more. The man let the knife alone on the table and scratched his head through the green skullcap.

"We don't have any money," said Lydia at last.

"Got me plenty of money," said the man grinning his crooked yellow teeth. He reached down and moved the duffle bag from beside his chair to beneath the table.

"What…" But she didn't ask it.

"Ain't none of your business what I did, Miss Lydia. You just mine your own."

He picked up a pack of matches from the table as he listened some more to the night sitting over the quiet earth. One by one he struck the matches and watched them burn down to his fingers. When they were all gone he tore the matchbook in half and scooted the pieces around the table with a finger. Then he picked one of the pieces up and examined it more closely.

"Why they call this place *The Office*, anyway?"

Lydia looked at him, but did not answer. The man smiled to himself and slowly picked up the knife. He turned it in his hand until he was holding it like a flag, point up, over the table. He brought the butt of the knife down violently against the wood of table number three and the noise was so loud and jarring against the silence that Lydia's entire body jumped.

"I said…"

"It's kind of a joke," said Lydia nervously.

"What kinda joke?"

"The joke is that people can come here and drink and stay late and then go home and when their husbands and wives and children ask them where they have been, they can truthfully say they were at *The Office*."

"Ha! I like that," said the man, smiling full out, teeth pointing everywhere. "At *The Office*. Helps 'em out with the lie."

"Yeah, I guess."

"The lie about what they been doin' with all their time."

"Yeah."

"At *The Office*. That's right clever."

The man nodded to himself and the smile slowly shrank into the faintest of grins like the last rim of sunlight before the earth turned another click and the hills inched up on the horizon and darkness started to come.

"I used to work in an office," he said. "You ever work in an office?"

"No," said Lydia, looking at the table.

"I used to. Working in the mail room."

"Here?"

"Naw. 'Nother state. Hated that job. Same thing every day. Sort the mail, deliver the mail. Collect the mail, package the mail, stamp the mail. I weren't much good for nothin' else and they'd never let me forget that. And it was just mail, mail, mail until I thought I'd plum bust into flames."

"Mmm," said Lydia, feeling wrong about having anything like a civilized conversation with this man. So they sat in silence for a moment until she could not help herself. "What did you do?"

"Huh?"

The man jerked his head up with a sudden snap, his features hard and mean.

"About your job, I mean. About the job in the mailroom. Did you quit?"

"Oh, that you mean." He slumped back into the chair. "Naw. Got fired."

"Why?"

"Got tired of waitin' for somethin' to change I spose. Ain't nothin' was gonna' change in that place and I got that itch that kept comin' on and comin' on and there was just no scratchin' it. I reckon I just got sick of it."

"Mmm."

"Yeah. So I started stealing stuff. Little things, you know, do-dads and whatnots from peoples' desks when I'd drop off mail and they weren't there. And then I started breakin' some things like cuttin' the telephone cords and unscrewin' the hinges on the doors. Boy, somma that were *real* funny too. One time a whole door came off in a fella's hand. People thought he was Superman. I laughed 'til I bust a gut."

The man smiled again at the memory, but briefly, and slapped his knee.

"Then I started pickin' fights and I hit a guy in the face. Broked his nose all up. And I 'spose someone just said *well that's enough of that mess* and sent down the word from on high to just kick me out. Can't say as I blame 'em much."

He sat back in his chair and, coming out of his reverie, looked around the bar. Lydia watched him warily, as though she were sitting in the middle of a zoo with no cages. He held her firmly in his gaze for a few long seconds and then inclined his grizzled chin.

"Lydia, ol gal, I want you to get me a drink. This is a bar, even though it's called *The Office*, this is a bar, and even if you say you don't got no money, I bet you got whiskey. And that's what I want, a whiskey in a clean glass. I don't want no funny business and if you give me any – and I mean *any* – funny business, you can bet your pretty face that I will gut you like a fish in the mud. Do you understand what I'm tellin' you, Lydia?"

Lydia froze at the words, but eventually found the strength to nod.

"Good, now scoot on out of there, go to the bar and pour me a whiskey in a glass. You leave the bottle on the counter and you bring me the glass and then you put it on the table just like I was a reg'lar ol' customer."

Lydia did as she was told and slid out of the booth, trying to keep her skirt up against her legs, which had lost their goose flesh but now felt heavy and slow. She made her way to the bar like a crab, stepping sideways, and as she stepped, she could not help but think about the telephone and about the snub-nosed pistol hiding in its unknown place behind the bar. She thought about how she had never fired a pistol before and she thought that if she shot and missed it would be the end of everything that she knew forever.

The idea of the end of everything forever did not frighten her as much as getting from here to there. It wasn't death that scared her so much as the last part of life, just on this side of death. She looked at the man at table three with his knife and his crooked yellow teeth and his bloody beard and she knew that he would be the one to take her from here to there if she shot at him and missed. He would be the one to show her the way. And that scared her.

The whiskey bottles were perched on a glass shelf up on the wall next to a big square mirror set into an elaborate gold frame that Milo had brought back from New York. It had fluted gold scrolls on each corner, one of which had suffered a triangular wound when Milo and Ryan had dropped it trying to hang it on the wall.

Lydia did not look at the bottles up on the shelf.

"I don't know where he keeps the whiskey," she said. "I'm not a bartender."

As she said these words she began looking beneath the bar as though that was as good a place as any to start the search for a bottle of whiskey.

She did not see the gun. She did see the telephone. She resolved to take the receiver off the cradle and dial the emergency number and just leave the phone off the hook and hope somebody would come by to see if there was a problem.

"Oh, I think this might be it," she said as hopefully as she could, reaching for a bottle of crème de' menthe with one hand and the telephone with the other.

"Naw," said the man. "That there's a telephone, Miss Lydia. Whiskey's up there on the wall, next to the big ol' mirror that lets me see behind the bar."

"No, no," said Lydia, "oh, no I meant this," she stood up clutching a green bottle the shape of a genie's lamp.

"Whiiiiisssskeyyyyyy! Now!"

The man pounded the table with the hard butt of his knife screaming the words like they came from a fire raging in his throat. Lydia
dropped the bottle of crème de menthe on the floor and it broke open,
the neck snapping off with a dull popping sound and sticky green fluid
gurgling out onto the floor. She spun to the shelf, forgetting the phone,
forgetting the gun she could not find, and grabbed a bottle of whiskey.
She found a glass, one of the tall clear ones by the register, and filled it
to the top.

"At a girl, Lydia," he said. "I knew you'd figure it out. Now you leave
the bottle on the bar and bring that to me."

Lydia did as she was told, though her heart shook in her chest. The
shaking radiated out through her arms and hands and fingers so that for
a moment she was afraid she would drop the glass before she reached
him, like she had the crème de menthe, and although she knew there
was lots more whiskey, she also knew that it wouldn't matter because, if
she dropped it, that would be the end of Lydia Watson.

But she did make it to the table. One slow step at a time, she made
it. She stretched forward to set the glass carefully between the man and
the unattended hunting knife with all of its gleaming silver teeth and
she knew in that slow second that this was her only chance. Slim as it
was – he could easily overpower her – but still: her only chance. As the
table took the weight of the glass, Lydia loosened her grip.

"Don't you touch that knife," he said calmly, reaching out and
grabbing the whiskey so that his hand, large and rangy and raw at the
knuckles, held her own hand to the glass like they were about to drink
it together.

"Knife don't belong to you, Lydia. That'd be stealin'."

"I wasn't," she said, trying to pull away. "I wasn't. I just…"

He released his grip, holding onto the top of his glass with two of
his fingers. Lydia took several steps back and stood before him, nervous
and shaking.

"You sure are a pretty thing, Miss Lydia. Bet you hear that a lot in
here."

Lydia shrugged and looked around uncertainly, flattening her skirt with her hands.

"Go on sit down," he said, looking at the amber liquid in the light, holding the glass up as though he was toasting a whole room of fellows at a bachelor party.

He waited until Lydia was back in the booth to take his first sip. A cloud of blood from his split lip billowed down into the gold drink and he winced and kissed the back of his hand.

"Damn," he said under his breath.

"What, uh… what happened to your mouth?" Lydia asked, hoping now for the polite conversation she could not even contemplate initially.

"Aw," he said smiling and shaking his head like he was embarrassed, "I got all tangled on top of a fence and I fell on my face. Thas all."

"Must hurt," she said.

"I 'spose. Didn't much hurt before I started to drink this."

"Did you get another job after the mailroom?"

He smiled a little at that. "Tryin' to make small talk, are ya? That make you feel better bein' 'round a man like me? Small talk 'bout the places I worked?"

"Just what do you plan to do with me?" she snapped, flattening her hands on the table and pressing her ribs against the wood, leaning out towards the man at table three. But she regretted the harshness of her tone even before she was done speaking the words, not knowing what effect it would have on him, and she slowly leaned back against the cushion of the tall booth like she was inching her way back into the womb.

The man set the glass back on the table and picked up the knife and pulled the tip lightly across his palm like he was tracing his veins.

"Well, I tell ya Lydia. I been thinkin' 'bout that very thing. That very thing."

He continued to pull the tip across his palm for a moment as though finishing up his thoughts. The he looked at her and all motion and all thinking stopped.

"I'm gonna do one of two things. I'm either gon' kill you with this knife of mine, or I'm gonna sex you on that pool table back there. And I tell you what." He pointed the knife at her casually, like it was just a steak knife and they were talking politics over a steak dinner. "I tell you what, Miss Lydia. I'll even let you choose. If I sex you, at least you'll live. If I kill you, then least you won't live the rest of your days with dreams of my ugly mug to wake you up at night. Understand? If you choose that I should kill you, then I promise I won't sex you first and I don't never sex dead women so you don't need to worry about me doin' nothin' after you dearly depart. And if, on t'other hand," he rolled the handle of the knife from one hand into the other, "if you choose I should sex you, then I won't kill you when it's over. You can go about your life and come back here tomorrow to serve your drinks and collect your tips and finish out your life, but you prob'ly gon' see me every time you close your eyes. You understand what I'm saying?"

Lydia stared at him, hearing the answer to her impertinent question again and again in her ears, but said nothing.

"Lydia? Cat got your tongue there?"

She swallowed and shook her head but still could not bring herself to speak.

"Well, tell you what there Lydia." He traded the knife for the glass, which he admired again in the light. "You don't have to decide right away. I'm gon' sit here and drink my drink and rest my legs. You tell me what you want me to do whenever you're ready. In the meantime, we can talk about whatever you want to talk about, 'ceptin maybe what I been up to tonight. But here's the deal, long-legged Lydia. Here's the catch as they say, 'cause there's always a catch. If you don't decide by the time the drink runs out, I'm gon' decide for you. See there? That's how life works. Either you decide how it's gon' go down, or that question gets decided for you."

Lydia felt herself go numb. A low voltage buzzing coursed through her bloodstream and traveled to every inch of her body simultaneously. She blinked slowly and swallowed but there were no words and no thoughts. She simply stared at him. He gave her a toast in the air and took a gulp of whiskey, wincing again as it passed his lips.

"Ooo!" he said. "That does burn somethin' wicked. *Ooo-Wee.* Well, anyway, you asked so I 'spose I'll tell you. After I was fired from the mailroom, I tried to find me another place to work. I reckon I looked pretty much everywhere but no one would have me. That's 'bout the time I met my wife."

The man took another sip of whiskey and winced again, closing his eyes as it went down. The clear golden color had deepened into a cloudy, reddish brown.

"Lilly's her name. Like the flower. I met her at wunna them Market Fresh stores. Y'all don't have them stores round here but they was all over back home. She was buyin' apples. An I don't recollect why I was there, beer or soda prob'ly, but I don't really remember 'cause meetin' her pretty much blocks out everything else. Understand?"

He waited a beat for Lydia to respond. Her mouth was too dry to speak.

"Anyway, we got to talkin' 'bout diff'rent kinda' apples an, oh, we jus talked about all kinda' things that day, an it was like talkin' to a little bluebird on a branch. She didn't talk as much as sing to me right there in the Market Fresh next to all them apples. Great big ol' pile of apples, all shiny and new. I'll never forget that, Lydia. Never in my whole entire life. They shine in my mem'ry even today.

"We met the next day and the next an so on and so forth until we admitted we was sweet on each other. We got married in three weeks time and I moved out of my rat trap and into her apartment which was all neat and clean and just so and that became my home. Lilly an' me'd go out lookin' to find me some work bein' as I hadn't found any to replace the mailroom. And it took a lot of lookin' and I got plenty discouraged with it all. I even asked around at the U.S. Post Office bein' as I was already experienced with the mail. But thems good jobs at the Post Office and they was all fulled up so I come up empty.

"But Lilly stuck by me and stuck by me and stuck by me. You know, encouragin' me to keep at it. *Keep tryin' baby,* she'd tell me when I'd come home from lookin' and askin' and all long in the face. *It's gonna get better, baby*, she'd say to me. And even when I was about to give up she'd tell me it was only a matter of time 'fore things got better. *The big ol' worl' keeps a turnin' baby*, she'd say, *an its gonna bring us somethin' good. Just you wait an see.* Sometimes when Lilly'd go with me to apply for jobs and I come up empty like at the U.S. Post Office, she'd tell me that I can do better than that anyhow. I knowed she was lyin', but it was a good sorta lie that a woman can tell her man to keep his spirits up."

He stopped talking abruptly at the sound of a siren in the distance, cocking his head toward the back wall behind him, listening intently to how the wailing and howling moved and shifted around the room like a ghost. When it faded away and all was quite again, he took a drink of whiskey and continued.

"Ventually, I got me job at a Winkie Burgers; cleanin' things and moppin' and handlin' all the trash and what-not. You don't have them Winkie Burgers up here neither, but they serve some pretty good burgers. An' big ol' milkshakes. I got my food for free. One meal a day 'cause I worked there. You get free drinks here at *The Office?*"

"N-no," Lydia said softly, shaking her head.

"Winkie Burgers weren't no office, kinda like this place ain't really no office even though that's what you call it. Anyhow, I stayed there for near three years. Best job I ever had. It was the same every day, but it didn't feel the same. I felt happy there, even though I knowed they wouldn't put me in front of a customer to save their lives or let me 'round the register. But I knowed all that and I didn't care none. And I never, ever, not once felt the itch whilst I was workin' at Winkie Burgers like I did in the mailroom. An I figured this, Lydia. I figured it was 'cause I had somethin' to come home to. See. That was the whole difference and nothin' else. Lilly an Samuel. That's our baby boy. Not Sam. Samuel."

He sat for a moment, lost in the past, holding a half-glass of whiskey in his lap and staring off into space. He came to slowly; present consciousness filling his eyes like water. He took another drink and looked around the room as if apprising himself of the present all over again.

Lydia let her mind feel the contours of the choice he had laid before her and which was now only half a glass away. The choice between death on the one hand and defilement on the other. Between leaving the world and suffering the world. But her mind could not feel the contours of the choice and she closed her eyes and avoided it entirely.

"What happened next?" she heard herself ask in a shaky half-whisper.

"Huh?"

"At Winkie's. What happened?"

"Aw, yeah, well," he said resting his elbows on his knees and turning the glass in his hands. "Winkie Burgers got gobbled up by Tasty Stop and the Tasty Stop people, well, they didn't want a bunch of us around no more so *that* was pretty much *that,* as they say. I started lookin' for another job right away 'cause I had to, see, 'cause Samuel was almost three by then and Lilly stayed home to bring him up 'cause we didn't have enough money to buy us any help. Her people lived up north and they didn't like me much, I 'spose, but they gave us money to keep us and Samuel floatin' okay. But aside from that it was up to me to make the money. So I looked and looked and Lilly kept tellin' me to not get discouraged. *The big ol' worl keeps a turnin' baby,* she'd say, *an its gonna bring us somethin' good. Just you wait an see.*

"It was in her bones, even then. We didn't know it, but she had the cancer in her bones even then."

Another drink, a big healthy gulp this time, and he rubbed his face with his bloodied hand.

"So after a time of searchin' I found a job with a custodial business. You know what that is? Custodial?"

Lydia nodded.

"Means like a janitor. We cleaned people's offices after they'd gone home for the day. I was back in an office again. An office-office. You know. And that was okay I 'spose. For a few months anyway. I did my job good. That's where I met Cecil who was a friend I 'spose in a no account kinda way. Cecil stole things all the time and he's got him a brother that's got friends that robs rich people's houses and what-not, and I just tried to keep my nose out of it and do my work and go home to my family. And that was easy and I was happy.

"But when I was workin' as a custodian was when the cancer came on and we went to the doctor one day cause of the pains and he did some tests and called us back a week later and he took us back into his office, which wasn't really nothin' but a little tiny room, but he called it his office just the same. And he sat on his little stool and he told my wife she had six to eight months. Six months left of livin' and he said that the last three months prob'ly wouldn't be worth livin' on account of the pain."

Lydia watched the man's head sink a little towards the floor under the weight of the past. He took in a breath that was a little ragged at its edges and swished the whiskey around in the glass a few turns. He let the air out through his nose in a long, slow leak before continuing.

"Lilly, she took the news pretty good. She took that news better than I did, that's for sure. She was a strong-hearted woman. She took the news and tried to make it right with me and Samuel. Yeah. She had a strong heart all right, but her body didn't even last three months. See. She didn't even make it half way to the six months, and I 'spose that if you could choose, dyin' before your life ain't worth livin' is pretty much the way to go. That's what Samuel and me told ourselves. Yeah. Sure enough, that's what we told ourselves. But that ain't no kinda fair choice. Sure ain't no kinda fair choice."

He fell silent and sipped the whiskey. Lydia could see his mind was trying to climb the slippery hill back up to the present. But the hill was too steep and too wet.

"Her momma come down and she knowed some fancy lawyers and they took Samuel with them to live. They took him. All the way up to Boston, they just took him. They never liked me much anyhow. But the judge said I could visit my boy any time I wanted, long as I behaved and minded the law. And I tried, Lydia, sure as I'm sittin' here I tried. I wanted to save all my money and move to Boston so I could be near Samuel. But that's a whole lot of money just to get to Boston. That's a lot of offices to clean. That's a lot of days and nights and days and nights of comin' home to nothin' and sittin' in the dark and listenin' to the weather in the trees. And after awhile I could feel the itch comin' back to me. Small at first but then bigger and bigger. Sometimes when I was alone pushin' a vacuum around a hallway or on my knees cleanin' out a toilet bowl I could hear my wife tellin' me that the big ol' worl was gonna' turn an bring me somethin' good one day, to just hang on an wait. *Wait for it,* I told myself. *Just hang on and wait for it.* And so I tried to wait, Lydia, I surely tried my best. But the itch kept comin' on and comin' on and Cecil was at me and at me and at me and I knowed that life was just too short to wait any more for somethin' good to come along. Life is just too short, Lydia. I couldn't wait no more for the good that weren't never comin'. See. I'd already had the good. An' it weren't comin' again. Not ever.

"So one day I stopped waitin' for things to get better. I was pushin' a vacuum through a man's office and I saw that drawin' on the wall, like a little kid draws with a crayon, with a stick house and a stick dog and a stick tree and all these little stick people and without even thinkin' I just tore it off the wall and wadded it up into a tight little paper ball put it in my trash bag and kept pushin' the vacuum. An' the itch felt just a little better. Cecil thought that was about the funniest thing he ever seen in his life doing somethin' like that to a little ol' piture. Yeah. Well, I stopped hearin' Lilly's voice after that. It's been a lotta years now. Lotta years."

It was the better part of two minutes before his mind made it back up the slippery hill. He blinked slowly at Lydia and then seemed to come to, clearing his throat and looking at the whiskey left in the glass. He scratched his bloody half-beard and stood. Lydia's heart went slack and all she could think was that she had forgotten how large he was when he was not slumped down in a chair.

The man passed the glass to the other hand, grabbed the knife and walked up to table seven where he towered over Lydia like a dark, condemned building casting a shadow that goes on forever. He sighed and scratched the white ridge of flesh through his eyebrow where the hair no longer grew.

"Well, Miss Lydia, I'm plum talked out," he said. "You got somethin' you wanna tell me before I finish this drink?"

Lydia swallowed and looked at him and she felt the tears come to her eyes and roll like drops of rain from the branches of the tall pines outside of her apartment window into the deep puddles on the earth. Her lips were dry and seemed glued together, but she managed to speak the only words that came to mind.

"What ..." she faltered, "what color were the apples?"

The man's eyes widened at this and Lydia could see a mixture of surprise and alarm and anger, giving way to soft reverie like rock will eventually give way to water. She could see his mind slip a little ways back down that wet hill that leads to the past. Then he smiled a crooked smile and looked at her and his yellowed teeth poked out as he brought the glass to his lips and poured the rest of the whiskey into his mouth. It must have hurt him less this time, because he did not wince and he took it in smooth like a drink of warm chocolate.

He turned the glass upside-down over the table to demonstrate the obvious. He and Lydia locked eyes for a very long second that stretched out to the horizon.

Then he righted it again, and spit the last of the whiskey back into the glass.

"I ain't got no small bills for a tip," he said. "So I figure I'm gonna give you some more time to think about things." He swished the remaining whiskey around in the bottom of the glass and he set it on the table. "It ain't no kinda fair choice anyhow."

He turned, walked back to table three and collected the duffel bag. He tossed the knife into the bag, walked to the bar to grab the bottle of whiskey and then to the door, which he unbolted with a sharp sound of metal.

"They was green," he said without turning. "All of 'em was pure green like a big ol' field of grass in the summer, exceptin' two bright red ones, big and juicy, right there in the middle of the field."

Then, as suddenly as he had come, he was gone.

It was a long time before Lydia found the presence of mind to re-bolt the door. She moved slowly and broke into uncontrollable fits of emotion far too complex to label or fully understand. She walked over to *Milo's* and wrote Sophie a note that she set on top of the cash register and then she came back down the dark hall, through the beads hanging in the doorway and to the restroom where she changed into her street clothes and left her uniform folded neatly on the bar.

She mopped up the mess behind the bar with a rag and threw the body and the neck of the broken bottle into the trash. From her purse, she extracted enough money to pay for a bottle of crème de menthe and a bottle of Jim Beam whiskey and she slipped the money along the polished bar so that it was just poking out from beneath the frills of her folded uniform skirt.

And then, with a final twist of the bolt, Lydia Watson left *The Office* for the last time.

———

When Sophie opened up *Milo's Diner* the next morning, after she had lifted the blinds over the five big windows to let the sun pour in over the tables and along the floor and flood up the posts of the stools around the counter where it burst into brilliant shards of spark that flew off the hammered aluminum skirting, she found a folded piece of paper on the register which she opened and read.

Dearest Sophie,

I met a man tonight who told me that sometimes life is just too short to wait around for something good to happen. What I think he meant is not that life is too short, but that it's too long. It's so long, Sophie, that the something good we're all waiting for might just be too far off to bear if you have to wait for it all by yourself. So long that if you're waiting for it all by yourself, your life becomes nothing but waiting. And if that happens, Sophie, your only choice is to either die waiting or to spend your life wishing you would die, and as this man told me tonight, that's not any kind of a fair choice. So I'm moving on, Sophie. I need to feel the earth turning under my feet. I don't know quite where yet; maybe just down the road or maybe the Fiji Islands. Wouldn't that be something?! Give a kiss to Frank and Rose and tell Milo that I will miss him. Your friend, Lydia.

Chapter 3

JIMMY D'S THRIVE-N-DINE

She was new at this, he imagined.

She had never been a widow before. Maybe new to death entirely.

Mid-fifties. Well-connected in society, judging by the turn-out. Money, yes. Money enough, that was certain, judging by the fine cars lining the drive at the bottom of the hill like stones of polished onyx, and by the fine black dress that hung from her bones like wet grief in the still heat. She was put together. Even now, she was put together. She was comfortable in her life.

And, yet, perhaps, here was something she had never experienced.

Garrett watched the small, brittle woman, and realized that she must have felt all of the eyes upon her, weighing her actions against the moment, and she must have felt self-conscious.

She plunged the silver shovel deep into the pile of soft, coffee-colored loam and he thought that it was all wrong. She moved with far too much resolve; with vigor too easily interpreted as eagerness or even excitement at the task.

Maybe, Garrett thought, *maybe she was glad to see him go. Maybe she had hated him. Maybe she had killed him – poison,* he surmised, *it would have to have been poison – and maybe this burial was but the denouement to a long and twisted plot to free her from a marriage rotted by violence and deceit.*

He panned the mourners discretely. *Her lover was certainly among them. Her husband's brother. His business partner. The priest. No, not the priest. Maybe the alderman.*

She withdrew from the middle of the mound what would be her third heaping load of soil. Straining under its weight, her knees buckling slightly and pushing out against the fine limp grief of her dress, the new widow swung the shovel over and down into the earthen rectangle that held her former husband. There was a small grunt from her effort and the dirt made its soft, muffled contact with the cleanly polished cherry wood down in the hole.

There, Garrett thought, his compassion returning, *that will do, now. That will do.*

But the new widow rotated her tiny shoulders back to the mound, driving the shovel in hard and deep for another load, and another straining expression, and another little grunt, as though this was the way it was done. As though grieving required some solitary feat of strength in the midday sun as others watched on in silence, judging the sincerity of her loss by her willingness to suffer physical injury.

The man they called Milo – her brother, Garrett guessed – stepped in to take the shovel and pat her on the shoulder. He was a big man, depositing a load of dirt into the grave like he was spooning cream into his coffee. He handed the shovel to the bald man in the sunglasses who looked like he worked for the government.

A meadowlark alighted on the branch of the young sycamore that would one day split the polished planks of cherry wood with its roots. The bird cocked its head and chirped a lackluster condolence before moving on.

Garrett stayed until the shovel had been propped against the tree and the mourners were filing somberly, hands pocketed, across the cemetery to the bottom of the hill where the small asphalt road was lined with waiting cars. The human confluence along a narrow path of earth eventually pulled Garrett in behind Milo and a white-haired man who was still holding his program from the service. The program was rolled into a tight paper stick that he flicked around like a wand or a tiny scepter.

"How's business?" asked the man.

"Good. Business good." Italian, Garrett guessed. Milo clapped the man on the back. "Everyone need food."

"Food? I thought ..."

"No. I sell flower shop. No everyone need flowers. Everyone need food. So I sell flower shop and open diner."

"A diner?"

"Yes. *Milo's Diner.* Soon I build bar onto diner. Everyone need to drink."

"A bar too. Well, very good, Milo. Very good. How's it doing?"

"Only open two week. I leave Sophie all alone. Oh, Robert, she scare to death."

"Sophie," the man with the paper scepter laughed a little laugh. "I haven't seen Sophie since all of us went to the fair. She doin' okay, Milo?"

"Sophie still Sophie," Milo laughed.

The man bobbed his head forward in the direction of the new widow, now almost at the bottom of the hill. "Eva seems to be handling things okay."

"Oh, yes, Eva strong. She want me to leave already. You know little Bianca?

"Yes, we spoke at the church."

"She getting married."

"No, really?"

"She so excited. Today she try hard no to smile. For Eva."

"It was a nice service," said Robert.

"Yes," Milo agreed after a moment of listening to the line of hard-soled shoes touch against the sloping trail, nodding his head, "it was nice service."

And it *was* a nice service, Garrett had to agree. The nicest so far. He twitched his fingers around a coin in one pocket and a pair of keys in the other.

Garrett did not know the man in the cherry wood box, or Eva the widow, or Milo the brother, or the man with the paper scepter, or Bianca the betrothed, or any of the others. He should have felt awkward for having been there; for having witnessed the marriage of flesh and earth among intimates not his own.

But he did not feel awkward.

He felt frustrated. He was still stuck. Another man buried. And yet nothing had come to him. He was no closer to anything except his own untimely demise.

At the bottom of the hill he walked along the narrow road to his car. The air was too sweet and too heavy and he wanted to sleep. He wanted to drink and he wanted to sleep, which was always what he wanted in the grip of hopelessness. He climbed behind the steering wheel that was too hot to touch, and sealed himself inside thinking of the man in the cherry wood box.

He looked in the rear view mirror and saw that her car was still there – sky blue with white wall tires and an improbable slash of red over a corner of the hood. It sat, quietly, three fine black cars behind his own, which was neither fine nor black. She was still behind the wheel, whoever she was. Waiting for him, he imagined. He started his car, and she started hers.

He drove along the narrow asphalt road, unspooling like a small black thread down and between the lush undulations dotted with gravestones and shade trees, down to where the landscape flattened out and the small thread grew fat and gray, like an old sun-faded ribbon. He drove in a straight line with the top down and the wind and the sun having their way, keeping his hat on the front seat, on top of the notebook and the paper program from the funeral service, which chattered in the wind. *Flap-gatta-gatta-flap-flap-gatta-gatta-gatta.* He imagined that this is what the man in the cherry wood box was now saying – in fear, in grief, in anger – shouting up to the old wife and the new widow who had left him alone and could no longer hear. *Flap-gatta-gatta-flap-flap-gatta-gatta-gatta,* as the soft dirt fell in swift, heaping loads at the hands of a black man and his two sons whose job it was to silence the dead.

Garrett realized he was hungry and pulled off into Wilsonville to find something to eat. He knew he should have pushed aside the hunger and kept driving. He should be at home working. He should be hard at it, looking for the words that would not come on their own. But futility hung in the air with the heat and together they weighed on him like sopping blankets. He had no energy now to resist elemental needs.

Anyway, Imajean was home with the boys today. *That* was not an environment ideal for coaxing timid words out of the dark and onto the white page.

He found a parking place across from a small white diner that called itself *Jimmy D's Thrive-n-Dine* in looping red letters across a pane of half-shuttered window. Garrett sat quietly in the parked car for a moment, waiting for the slowest, wettest part of the heat that had trailed him from the cemetery to catch up.

He looked through the windshield out at the looping red letters and thought about the diner owned by the man named Milo. He wondered what city the diner was in and what it was called and if it looked anything like *Jimmy D's Thrive-n-Dine*. A woman named Sophie, he imagined, was working in the diner even now, wiping her hands on an apron and pulling a clean cup from beneath the counter. He wondered if Sophie was Milo's wife or his daughter or his mother or his mistress, or if she was just some woman who was always the same and who may as well own the diner, but who did not want anything to do with the adjoining bar because that was just who Sophie was in the world, and you could take that to the bank seven days a week and twice on Sundays. Garrett wondered if Sophie was the type of woman who exuded the truth about things, even when she walked or pointed or picked up the telephone. Maybe, he imagined, looking out and up at the looping red letters, maybe Sophie was the type of woman who knew how to put a man back on the path of the life he expected.

He grabbed his notebook and his hat, stretched his arms beneath the hot blue sky and went inside, creaking the door on its hinges as bells tinkled unnecessarily above his head.

He hesitated and turned back, standing on the bright sidewalk a moment, considering the top of his car and looking up and down the street.

Two men in hats and nice slacks with suit jackets slung over their shoulders waited for somnolent traffic to pass and then crossed the street to the bank. In the distance, five or six children rode bicycles along a dirt trail that disappeared into a stand of larch. In the other direction an attendant at the service station bent beneath the hood of a dark green Buick as a woman behind the wheel pursed her lips into the mirror. A squall of laughter came from a small, colorful mob of women who were clustered like chiffon flags on the lawn of a Presbyterian church. Down the block he could see the corner of a marquee casting a shadow over enough cars to suggest a matinee was in progress. Across the street, a collie turned in slow circles looking for the right position in the shade of the blue awning that sloped over a doorway to the *Fix-It Factory / Help Yourself Hardware.*

Garrett reentered the diner deciding to leave the top down after all. Lunch at a diner was not a funeral and it was not unseemly to arrive or to leave in a car with no top. It was all right for people to think he was enjoying himself – that he was free to lose himself in the winds of high velocity living – even if he wasn't.

He took a seat by a window facing the street and pulled a paper menu from a stand on the table. It was late for lunch and early for dinner, so he had the place to himself. The diner was clean and quiet and he was grateful to be alone. The floor was a pattern of large black and white squares, like a checkerboard that was so clean it seemed lit from below.

When the waitress came with a pad and a pen he ordered a soda and a cheeseburger and a basket of fries, but only because this diner, inexplicably, did not offer corned beef on rye with a pickle, which is what Garrett always ordered in diners. He did not have the energy to be upset at this, and even appreciated the general congruity of the disappointment with his overall mood. He agreed with the waitress that it was a lovely day, even though he did not really think so, seeing nothing particularly lovely about the heat, which was pressing its swollen, sweaty palms against the window to get in.

Three wicker-bladed fans quietly stirred reassurance into the air from above. The waitress – her nametag read *Glorious* – turned with a bright swishing sound and disappeared through a swinging door behind the arc of a white Formica counter to place his order.

Garrett tossed his hat in the seat next to him, fished a book of matches and his last cigarette out of his pocket, and opened his note-book. He fanned through a dozen pages until he found the three para-graphs he had read every day for the past three months. He lit his ciga-rette and read them again:

He lay on his back, in the grave he himself had dug in the dark woods, and she above him, her legs straddling the opening, pointing the long barrel down at his face, her finger caress-ing the trigger. The autumn night enveloped all but what the orange glow of the lantern could find. Her features, still beautiful, flick-ered and shifted in the air above him and her dress wafted in the light breeze. Every so often he could smell the perfume that had been his undoing, even through the layers of soil and decay that now surrounded him. Church bells rang in the distance. Life was proceeding with-out him, oblivious of the irony that after a life of criminal detection, after three decades of staying one step ahead of hardened, schem-ing, treacherous villainy, the likes of which his beloved city had never before encountered, Jack McMannis had lost his edge to a woman. And not to the flesh of a woman, for Jack was bet-ter than that and no slave to lust. With his wife gone six years now from a stray bullet, Jack was as true as they came and would sooner die than betray the memory of the woman he still loved. No, Jack McMannis had lost his edge not to a woman, but to the very essence of a woman, or perhaps to love itself, floating within a cloud of perfume past the innate cunning and suspicion that had always kept him alive. He stared up into the long lamp-lit barrel in her hands; up into that tunnel of black steel that held within its charred hollow the sum of his experience in the world; a life of violent justice and righteous vengeance brought to an untimely end by mere sweetness in the air. It was fitting, he supposed, that he should smell it now, again, in the instant before it all ended.

He had done a poor job of the digging. The grave was too narrow and his arms were pinned to his sides, his powerful shoulders suddenly a hindrance. He could feel the butt of his Colt Pocket Hammer - the Hammer, he called it - pressed between his leg and the wall of dirt. She should have bothered to frisk him. That was the sort of oversight that could get you killed. Just the same, Jack realized as he stretched his fingers towards his pocket that he could not reach his gun without either sitting up or swinging his legs skyward. The slightest twitch either way would earn him a quick bullet in the head; a hole in the skull to match the one in his shoulder that was still burning like a white fire. One smooth movement would do it; one quick sit-up like the billion or so he had done in the army and he would be able to reach his gun.

But not while she was pointing that canon at his face. He would have to distract her. He would have to get her talking; get her focused on something else just long enough to make a move for the Hammer. But what did one say to a face like hers? To whom should he address this last effort at distraction: to his memory of love or to his assassin? For she was both of these to him, and only one would be willing to let him live long enough to speak the words that would save him. If, indeed, he was to be saved at all. Jack McMannis swallowed hard and spoke out from beneath the ground:

Garrett sighed to himself, folding the notebook over his hands. He leaned back in the booth and closed his eyes and tried again to put himself in the grave – in Jack McMannis' very body.

But the words did not come. The words never seemed to come any more. Jack McMannis had, by the narrowest of margins, escaped certain death dozens of times – on the cliffs above Niagra, in the trunk of a car sinking to the bottom of the East River, strapped to a bomb in the torch of the Statue of Liberty – over narrative landscapes and labyrinthine plots that spanned six novels. And now, Garrett had quite literally written his hero into a corner – *a grave!* – from which he could not escape. There were no words to come to his rescue.

Garrett opened his eyes in time to see the woman in the sky blue car with the white walls and the red slash trolling down the street, moving across the window, through the looping red letters, written backwards now, through which he peered. She looked casually this way and that as she rolled slowly past the diner, eyeing every automobile until she found his.

She slowed momentarily and squinted in the sun at the window of the diner, but then continued for another block, parking across from the bank. Garrett saw the tail lights go out and imagined that she would wait for him to leave.

Glorious delivered his food with a wholesome smile, turning the plate just so in front of him and uncapping the catsup before placing it on the table next to his soda. He thanked her and with an assuring nod and a crisp swishing of her skirt she was gone again. Garrett ate his cheeseburger, thinking in spite of his mood that it was perhaps the best thing he had ever tasted in his life.

The thought that Imajean would not be happy crept in somewhere between the crisp French-fried potatoes and the cold, caramel bubbles of soda. She would not be happy that he had been gone for so long today. She would say it was worry, but it was not worry. No matter what she said. He knew it was not worry. It was displeasure. It was the displeasure of incomprehension. She did not like him to be gone where she could not see or understand. She needed to understand his time. She had understood the time in school. She could have understood time working at her father's firm had he been sensible enough to accept the offer. She probably could have understood time working for *anybody* doing just about *anything*. For Imajean was a smart and understanding woman.

The wicker blades stirred the air calmly above Garrett's head and he tried to think of the words to save the life of Jack McMannis. But the words would not come. He found in his thoughts the image of the man in the cherry wood box, riven by roots and rot, calling out through the dark earth: *Flap-gatta-gatta-flap-flap-gatta-gatta-gatta.* And still, the words did not come.

His thoughts fell back to his wife. Yes, Imajean could have understood him spending time doing just about anything for just about anybody, but she could not understand the time of a writer. He may as well conjure spirits or count clouds or trace leaves for a living. He may as well spend hours off in the weeds out behind the Clarkson County Raceway assigning foreign sounding names in alphabetical order – Jacques, Jean-Paul, Jules – to all of the gnats that roiled in dark pillows of air beneath the cooling shade of the water towers. To his wife, writing was that incomprehensible.

His success as a writer was no more comprehensible to her than the endeavor itself. In her eyes, his success – still modest and mostly local – certainly did nothing to validate what he did with his life. She seemed utterly immune to the indisputable fact that other people *liked* what Garrett wrote down on paper. Other people – important people – liked his *make believe world,* as she liked to call it. They liked Jack McMannis. They cared about him like he was a real person. Cared if he lived or died. Even Imajean liked what he wrote most of the time and she frequently told him so. But she liked his stories in the way she liked small hard candies that dissolved into nothing on the tongue. It was not a serious appreciation.

Then again, Garrett had never been the object of Imajean Wilbanks' serious appreciation except insofar as she had seriously appreciated just how much marrying an aspiring writer who lacked social connection as much as he lacked family or fortune, would anger her father, a man who had spent his life getting his way in whatever he set his mind to, including controlling every golden hair on his daughter's head. In professing her love for Garrett Webb, let alone marrying him, Imajean had broken all of her father's rules. Marshal K. Wilbanks' had been dealt the comeuppance that could only come from his daughter.

Garrett had believed it had all been about him. He had, after all, loved her. He had actually believed that love had inspired his flaxen-haired beauty queen to rebel. To thumb her perfect nose at her inheritance and to follow her heart which, he had been led to understand, yearned for the company of a man who was not established, not a part of the work-a-day machinery; a man who carried the world around in his head and wrote it all down into tattered notebooks and then typed up what he had written. She had swooned when he read to her. It had all been very romantic.

And yet, in the end, Marshal Wilbanks had paid for the wedding and invited all of his well-to-do friends. In pretending to concede the war against his daughter, he had regained her loyalty in a way as to utterly erase all signs of conflict. Marshal had even offered Garret a job as an assistant clerk pushing paper for the promise of a future managerial role as a junior account executive. Garrett had respectfully declined, just as Marshal Wilbanks knew he would. Imajean, for her part, had never forgiven him for rejecting the kindness of her father and for so stubbornly shirking his responsibility to maintain her in a lifestyle consistent with her upbringing.

The marriage had launched itself inauspiciously from the underwhelming honeymoon at her father's sprawling estate and proceeded to lurch from one recrimination and declaration of disappointment to another, some of them meritorious and others simply piling on, meticulously measuring the distance between Garrett and Marshal and cataloguing his succession of his shortcomings as a husband as if she were reporting on a sad, rainy parade.

He loved his sons, of course, and they him. If anything continued to bind Garrett and Imajean to the sacrament of marriage, it was Evan and Marshal Jr. But even in their eyes, Garrett was no match for Grampa Marshal.

The door to the diner creaked and the bell tinkled as it opened and closed again. A woman walked in and looked up at the fan and then took a seat at a table near the wall. She did not look his direction, keeping her gaze at the shiny, checkered floor so that her dark hair fell in a sheet across her features. Her dress was simple and sleeveless and the color of a June watermelon.

Garrett had to look twice before he realized that it was her.

He had never seen her upright, moving her arms and legs, and it was odd now for him to think of her as a whole person, as something more than a bare shoulder and a profile framed in sky-blue metal.

He watched as Glorious brought her some water and took her order, which he could overhear was a chicken salad sandwich and a lemonade with extra ice. He realized then that his imagination had gotten the better of him and that she had not been following him after all. He could see that she was a normal person, and lovely at that, with an appetite and a thirst and other motivations that were not the least bit unsavory. Like getting out of the heat.

Garrett returned his attention to his notebook and tried to re-conjure the mental image of the grave in the woods and a wounded man inside of it with a gun and one last chance to talk his way out of death.

But then Glorious came to collect his sandwich plate. She set a wedge of cherry pie in front of him, redness bubbling from beneath the crust into a growing stream of white vanilla. She smiled and told him it was on the house. Garrett looked at the piece of pie and then back at Glorious, surprised and a little bewildered.

"Why?" he asked her, and she laughed delightedly. She patted the tips of her fingers together and told him that the last piece in the pan is always free at *Jimmy D's Thrive-n-Dine.*

"Jimmy," she explained, "liked to keep people wondering about the vicissitudes of fortune."

Garrett thought this a highly improbable phrase from someone like Glorious, but he thanked her anyway and ate his pie in heaping fork-fuls that meandered through the ice cream before ascending from the plate. He looked out the window at the afternoon. The heat floated off the hood of his car in waves, bending the light. Over the top of the car, he could see the sun reflected in the windows of the two-room boarding house that sat above the *Fix-It Factory / Help Yourself Hardware.*

He listened to the fan stirring the air and thought that maybe he should bring Imajean and the boys out here one day. It was a long way and they would complain at first, but they would settle into the trip soon enough. They could get a room for the night and eat a meal or two at *Jimmy D's Thrive-n-Dine,* which Garrett decided he liked very much, and they could see a new town. It would be a good change for them all, just for a day or two. And, he thought nodding his head, that might just do the trick.

He looked back up at windows of the rooms perched above the hardware store and tapped the brim of his hat against the table with a finger. They could rent *both* rooms. They could make the drive to Wilsonville – *good old Wilsonville* – on a Thursday or a Friday and he could take one of the rooms and Imajean and the boys could take the other. They could explore together during the days, maybe horseback riding at the *Dixie Dell Ranch* only twenty miles or so up the road, and then after a day about the town, and after cheeseburgers and pie all around, Imajean and the boys could set off to find a good picture show and he could retire to his room and write his book into the early hours.

Garrett pulled another piece of pie off the fork and held it on his tongue as he thought about things.

Yes – it was just the thing they needed. And then on Sunday morning before heading home they could go to service just up the street at the Presbyterian Church. Imajean always felt at peace after a good service and liked to sing in the car on the way home. They rarely went to church any more because the boys were so restless. But they would surely like the newness of a service in Wilsonville. They would sit still for that. And Imajean would sing for hours in the car all the way home. Now how would *that* be? He thought about this for a moment and smiled a little smile. It would be *fine*.

With the makings of a new outlook rising in his eyes, he finished his pie and soda. Glorious was suddenly right there with the ticket, which he paid with a smile and a dollar bill and told her to keep all the change and promised he would be back one day very soon. She blushed a little for no apparent reason, thanked him with a dainty kind of salute that twirled her skirt and then set about cleaning up his mess.

Garrett could tell that the woman in the watermelon dress was listening to them as she ate her chicken salad sandwich. Suddenly and strangely optimistic about his future, he now felt a directness and an energy for curiosity that he would not have previously thought possible. He strode up next to the woman's table and tipped his hat.

"My name is Garrett Webb," he said.

She looked up at him with a slight widening of the eyes and then dabbed her mouth with a napkin and looked back down at her plate. Garrett took this as a rather endearing timidity that he found both sweet and sad. She swallowed and looked back at him.

"I'm Delia May," she said, reaching up to shake his hand. And then, with a quizzically astonished expression, "Garrett Webb, the writer?"

It was Garrett's turn to blush a little, for he did not expect this at all.

"Yes. I'm a writer," he said, thrusting his hands into his pockets and adding stupidly, "I write books."

"I'll say you write books! And boy do you ever," said Delia May. "I've read them all."

"Have you? Have I bored you to tears, Ms. May?"

"Heavens. That Jack McMannis is never dull, is he? Is he still up to his old tricks?"

"Always."

They both laughed at this and after a moment her face settled into a more bashful expression as though to compensate for having temporarily forgotten her timidity.

"Can I help you in some way, Mr. Webb?" she asked.

"No," said Garret, "oh, no. I just… Well, I saw you yesterday."

"Did you?"

"At the funeral. In Kempton."

"Really? Were you there too?"

"Yes. And then I saw you this afternoon up in Harsgrove."

"Oh. Yes, I saw you there, but I did not know your face. I guess writers aren't movie stars."

"No. I suppose not."

"Were you a close friend of Wilfred? Did you know him well?"

"No," said Garrett feeling a twinge of discomfort, "no, not well."

"And what about Helen?"

"No," he said, and then added, "Poor woman. At least she has friends to help her through."

Delia looked up at him perplexed. Garrett saw in her eyes that were a simple, implacable green, that he had made a mistake. She spoke slowly at him. "No. *Helen.* In Kempton? Yesterday?"

"Oh, Helen. I thought you meant… the widow of… silly me. No, no, I was not especially close to Helen either. Quite a loss though. Quite a loss. And quite a coincidence," he said, mightily changing the subject, "wouldn't you say, seeing each other at two different funerals so far apart."

"Yes. We must know the same people," she replied, seemingly unimpressed with the odds of it all. Garrett laughed and shook his head a little, fidgeting with his hat.

"What is it?" Delia asked him, scrutinizing his face and suddenly not seeming so timid. "What's so funny?"

"I thought you might be following me," he said.

"Following you? Why would I be following you?"

Garrett kicked at a seam in the floor between them. "Just... I don't know. It was just such a... you know, a coincidence."

She stared up at him for a moment, expressionless, her face too busy making sense of his words. Fearing he had offended her, Garrett concluded that it was time to leave and began to reach for the hat on his head and to make the slight bowing gesture one makes as a prelude to departure.

But an almost imperceptible convulsion, from somewhere beneath the surface of the table, caught his attention and stopped him. Delia May's lips tightened and her eyes closed, attempting to imprison the swelling laughter in thin walls of tissue. But it would not be contained and when it came, it escaped her lips in sharp but melodious bursts, which she vainly tried to coax back into her mouth with her fingertips.

Glorious appeared suddenly, as if on wheels or wings, with a scalloped, silver dish of light green ice cream. She reached between them to place the dish on the table, excusing herself.

"It's on the house," she said smiling. "Here at *Jimmy D's Thrive-n-Dine*, pistachio ice cream is free on the second Tuesday of even-numbered months." They looked at her dumbly. "Because *anticipation is the midwife of contentment*; that's what Jimmy says."

The bright bird of laughter finally broke free and Delia raised her face and let it fly around the diner and up to the ceiling fan. Perhaps misunderstanding, Glorious squinted her eyes and smiled in satisfied delight and glided back through the kitchen door. When she had composed herself, Delia looked back at Garrett.

"I think you've been reading too many of your own books, Mr. Webb," Delia said, wiping a tear from the corner of her eye. "You've begun to think like Jack McMannis."

"What do you mean?" asked Garrett, no longer knowing what to think of this woman.

"Oh, consider it just for a moment, Mr. Webb. Detective McMannis is followed in every story. Without fail. In every story he *believes* he is being followed. Every shop owner and cabbie and bellhop seems to have secret designs. He has a keen eye for these things and without fail what he suspects is true." She sliced a spoon through the ice cream and slipped it into her mouth from where the bird had escaped. "You've started to think like Jack McMannis. Don't you see, Mr. Webb? You've become your own character."

Garrett did not know quite what to think about this and could only stare down at her in silence. As he did, the smile on Delia May's face gradually faded, and her eyes dimmed a little, and it was as though a cloud had passed between the earth and the sun.

"I did not mean to offend you, sir," she said softly, holding her empty spoon.

"Oh, no. No offense taken, Ms. May. I assure you." But because he did not know his own mind, he was unconvincing. "I should be on my way and leave you to eat your free ice cream in peace. Very nice to have met you."

Garrett left the diner and stepped out into the merciless afternoon, the heat falling on him like scalding water. He left Wilsonville directly and when he rejoined the main road that stretched like a flat, straight, grey, sun-faded ribbon off the end of the earth, he drove faster than the law allowed, trying to outstrip the heat and the words and laughter of Delia May. But no matter how fast Garrett drove, and no matter how ferociously the wind whipped the funeral program in the front seat into a frenzy – *flap-gatta-gatta-flap-flap-gatta-gatta-gatta* – these things followed him relentlessly and he could not shake the tail.

———

By the time he got home, the moon was up over the house and the kingdom of insects sang and chirped from the tall, cool grasses growing in the vacant lot on the other side of the back fence. Across the street, Mrs. Bloodstone, who was a known night owl, had taken out the light in her living room and was now a shadow passing back and forth like a ghost in the upstairs window.

Imajean was at the sewing machine, which she had set up at the dining table, working on a patch for the tablecloth. He supposed she had picked that project quite deliberately. Imajean could be that way.

Her back was to him and, as it was so late and as the odds that Imajean was indifferent to the lateness of the hour were slim to non-existent, Garrett considered continuing on his way to the staircase and straight up to bed. But he knew this to be a bad idea as soon as it occurred to him. Besides, there was no time like the present to share his idea.

"What'cha working on there, Sugar?" asked Garrett, not kissing her hello and sitting on a chair in the corner of the dining room.

"Trying to fix the hole your cigarette burned into my tablecloth," she said matter-of-factly. "Where you been, Garrett?"

He could tell from her tone that she was angry, but he did not acknowledge the mood in the hopes that it might go away without an invitation. "Oh, you know, working on this book," he said. "Research."

"Mmm-hmm." Imajean put a piece of thread in her mouth and wet the end, pulling it through the end of a needle. Her hair was washed and stacked on her head like a nest pulled from a river. "Boys were home all day today, you know."

"Yes. I know. District ought to bring in teachers from another county. Punch a hole right through that picket line. Fire every last one of them. The kids are the ones who pay the price. The teachers don't think about the kids for a damn minute. Not a damn minute."

It was a stronger opinion than Garrett normally expressed on such topics. He harbored some hope of coaxing the conversation off of its course. But there is no besting gravity.

"They both wanted to know where their father was, but I didn't know what to tell them, because I didn't know myself. I told them you were working and Lord in Heaven knows I do not like lying to my own children."

"But I *was* working, Imajean. I..."

"No, Garrett, you were doin' whatever you were doin' but it sure wasn't work. Drivin' around God knows where, burnin' up gasoline, making up your stories for your books," she thrust the needle at him from across the table, her face pointed and sharp, "but in *my* book Garrett, in *my* book, in my daddy's book, in *your* daddy's book, that ain't work."

"Jeannie..."

"It's not a living, Garrett. Daddy turned eighty-one years yesterday. *Eighty-one!* He still pays for most of what we need to live."

"No he doesn't."

"He does so, Garrett. He pays for this house. He pays for our food."

"Some of it."

"Most of it, Garrett. Most of it."

Garrett braced his elbows against his knees and bowed his face to the floor, weathering the storm.

"We had a party for him down by the river yesterday. Whole family was there except you. You couldn't bother to be there because you were off – what did you call it again? Working? Let me ask you something. Any of this hard work of yours brought any money into this house in the past year? Anything since that last book that paid for, what, seven house payments?"

"Nine," he said stupidly.

"Well 'scuse me for my error. *Nine* house payments."

"Bernard says they'll consider another printing."

"Well that's just fine. We'll keep milking the *old* book. Maybe somebody in this town will want to buy it *again*. Maybe people will want to buy one book for each eye."

"Imajean..."

"How about the new book? You anywhere close to being done with that?"

"No."

"Did you write anything today?"

"No."

"Yesterday?"

"No."

"It's been weeks and weeks, Garrett."

"I'm stuck, Imajean. I told you a hundred times. Sometimes the words are just stubborn. Sometimes I need to just…"

"Just what? Oh, just *what?*"

He looked at his wife, pleading in his eyes.

"Just sort of… to be out in the world, watching and listening for the words I need."

"Garrett, you don't need to be looking for new words. All of your stories are the same. Detective Jack McMannis caught in a web of corruption and villainy. Jack McMannis wounded in a shoulder. Jack McMannis shot in the leg. Jack McMannis, ever-true to the memory of his dead wife, looking for her killer, looking for the man with the money, is almost seduced by a murderous *femme fatale* who gets her just desserts in the end. New York City is saved again. You don't need any new words for old stories, Garrett."

She was angry and trying to hurt him. And it did hurt him to hear her opinion, even if he told himself that this was not her real opinion but only words that she chose to carry her anger. But he did not show the pain and he did not let the pain blossom into anger of his own. He sat still and quiet hoping to wait out the storm.

"Where do you go to find the words, Garrett? Where exactly do you go all day long as I am here with your children and your typewriter and your mortgage?"

"I've…" he hesitated, not sure whether he wanted to tell her; knowing she would not understand. He could lie. But he didn't want to lie. "Funerals," he said to the floor. "I go to funerals lately."

"Whose funerals?"

"Various people. I don't know them."

"Garrett, why on earth…"

"I don't know. I just feel like it might help somehow. It's like the words I need will be close to death. You know? In the grave. That they will come from desperation and hopelessness. You're not a writer. I don't expect you to understand it, Imajean."

"Well that's a great big relief, Garrett, because I don't understand it one bit. Not one bit. If that's how you are spending your time, going to the funerals of strangers, rather than tending to your own family, then... well, it's just a little sick if you want to know the truth."

Garrett sighed and stood up and walked to the oaken sideboard at the end of the room, a wedding present from Imajean's father. Thin curtains over the window soaked up the moon, burning coldly as a dog barked out its nightly warning. The grandfather clock in the corner ticked its wooden drops somewhere it the hollow of its heart, but its hands, as ever, did not move.

He righted a tumbler and poured himself a bourbon. Taking a small drink, he closed his eyes, feeling the warm amber spread through is body. He pulled out another chair and sat down at the table. He began fishing for a cigarette, but then decided that now would not be a good time.

The bourbon made his stomach growl and that made him think about the free pie he had enjoyed hours ago at the diner, and the cheeseburger and French-fried potatoes before that. For a moment, he was not sitting at his dining room table, but at the window table at *Jimmy D's Thrive-n-Dine* looking out across the street at the windows above *Fix-It Factory/Help Yourself Hardware*. For a moment, just for a moment, he expected Glorious to appear out of nowhere with a plate of something good that surprised him and then share something of her boss' philosophy of living.

"Garrett," said Imajean, her tone now just a little different somehow, giving him hope that she was softening and that the storm was passing. But she did not continue. She pulled the tablecloth closer to her face and squinted at it, as if trying to find an invisible stitch in the fabric he had ruined. Garrett took another sip of his drink before she spoke again.

"Are you steppin' out on me? Is that where you are all these days? Are you courtin' on some gal?" Her voice was level and hard, and

Garrett understood that the change in her tone had not been a hopeful sign after all.

"Jeannie." His voice was soft and weary. "Where would you get such an idea? I told you where I've been. I've been out working on my writing."

Imajean was quiet and focused on the tablecloth. Garrett felt like a ghost; a spirit of a man long dead that no one could hear, shouting up through the damp earth after all the mourners had left. *Flap-gatta-gatta-flap-flap-gatta-gatta-gatta.*

"I'm not a cheater, Imajean. You should know that just isn't possible. I'm as true as they come. You are my life Imajean Webb, and I would sooner die than be with another woman. I am a good man. With good and honorable intentions. And I love you like the day we were married."

If the words moved her closer to a sympathetic thought, it did not show. She sat like a machine, a human sewing appliance, moving the needle precisely around the scorched hole in the fabric. Garrett felt a surge in his chest, a swelling of optimism born of desperation.

"Lets go away Jeannie. You and me and the boys while the teachers are striking. I was way up in Harsgrove today, for a funeral, and on the way back I passed through this real quaint little town, Wilsonville, I believe that's where Charlie Digger is from, and it was just a lovely little place; clean and well kept, and they have a nice diner and the Dixie Dell Ranch is nearby, and they have a theater and fishing creeks and places to walk. We could make the drive on Thursday or Friday and stay until Sunday. Just to change things up a little. They have a Presbyterian church there that looks like new, Imajean, and we could take the boys to a nice service and then come on home and maybe sing songs in the car. And this diner, Imajean, has the best cheeseburgers you ever tasted in your life and free pie if you're lucky enough to get the last piece in the pan. There's a couple of rooms above the hardware store for rent. If we wanted to stay longer, I could use one for writing and you and the boys would be right next door so I could work while you were sleeping. What do you say, Imajean. A change. For a few days. Jeannie?"

Imajean sighed and set down the tablecloth, taking care to position the needle at an angle so that it would not get lost in the folds of fabric. She looked at her husband in the eyes for the first time that night and he back at her, his face hopeful and encouraging.

"What I think, Garrett, is that it's very late and I'm going to bed," she said standing, her features coldly beautiful and expressionless. She turned off the light as she left the dining room. Garrett sat in the dark, his spirit slowly deflating, and listened to the stairs creak, one by one, as she ascended to the place where they made their bed.

Over the next four days, Garrett stayed close to home. He worked at odd jobs around the house; the gutters needed a good cleaning and the back fence he had repaired last summer still needed painting. He and the boys played their three-person version of touch football, but it was too hot and they grew tired of the game within twenty minutes. He read more of the paper than normal and helped to keep the house present-able and even went with Imajean to shop for groceries at the *Country Cupboard,* which he hated. He tried not to lean all over the shopping cart like an invalid while she traded gossip with one friend after another.

"That's Ruth," she would say walking up the aisle away from him, ready to resume the hunt for food. "Her husband owns a construc-tion company" or "That's Marilyn. Her husband was a very successful accountant before he died, but his sons have taken over the practice. I think that's wonderful."

He rose early on these mornings, dressed, and slipped quietly down-stairs to sit at the dining room table in front of his typewriter and his note-pad and a stack of pages that, one by one, had led Jack McMannis into an open grave. But the words would not come. Garrett stared at the blank page until the dining room was full of activity and the smell of Imajean's breakfast bacon grease was so thick in the air that he could not concen-trate, at which point he would put his things away and start the day.

He tried writing again in the evenings, sitting across the table from his wife who busied herself with her sewing projects and as the boys played card games in the living room. They did not talk to each other, he and his wife, but attended exclusively to their respective tasks. This was fine with Garrett since he could not concentrate on his book and hold a conversation at the same time, although he did feel self-conscious about the fact that Imajean could hear that he was not typing anything as she sewed. He imagined that every moment of silence from his end of the room was an aggravation to Imajean's nerves.

Every so often Garrett typed gibberish onto the page – a list of food he liked, every word he could remember from the Declaration of Independence, the alphabet forwards and backwards – just to send some reassurance of progress across the table. He typed with great authority and enthusiasm in the rhythm of his finger movements, almost punching the keys, and wished like he had never wished for anything in his life that the words he typed had been the words he needed.

Imajean's mood did soften somewhat as the days passed. She spoke to him, if not kindly, then at least courteously about the practicalities of their existence, articulating her half of the marital bargain as it asserted itself into every passing moment. She did not apologize for the things she had said to him about his writing and when she smiled, which was rarely, it was a complicated smile that bespoke something other than pleasure or contentment.

On Sunday, when he could no longer bear the agony of staring at an empty page as Imajean clattered around in the kitchen, talking to her father on the telephone about needing help again with the mortgage, he retreated into the living room to read the newspaper. He forced himself to read about government and business and international relations and all manner of things for which he cared nothing.

He was not looking for the obituaries, but found them soon enough. A man named Elmer Wentz had died in Broughford County. Services at *Our Lady of Everlasting Devotion*, and burial at the *Broughford Lawns* cemetery, were scheduled for next Thursday. Elmer, who died of lymphoma at 83, left a wife, three children and five grandchildren.

Garrett stopped reading. There was no point any more of scanning the obituaries. He folded the paper neatly in thirds and took it into the kitchen and stuffed it firmly into the garbage, crushing eggshells as he pushed.

He carried the bag of garbage from the kitchen out to the side of the house where he stuffed the bag into one of the silver metal pales. He pulled the pales, first the one and then back for the other, out to the curb for the garbage men who would be making their rounds in the morning. The sky was trading its periwinkle for still deeper shades of evening and the stars were slowly spilling over the earth.

Mr. Walatke's car, an import the color of a rutabaga, trundled towards him. Garrett held up his hand in perfunctory acknowledgement of his existence, without caring to look up from the trash pales long enough to attempt any personal recognition. The obituary page was still face up on the top of the bag of trash. Beneath a smear of yoke he read the words: *James Diamond, dead of natural causes at age 90. Memorial service and burial, Monday the 13th of August, 11:00 a.m., at the First Presbyterian Church, Wilsonville.* Garrett stared down at the paper, rereading the words just to be sure he had understood them correctly.

Wilsonville.

He looked up, half expecting to see Mr. Walatke's rolling rutabaga stopped in the street with its owner watching concernedly as he read the newspaper out of the garbage can on the curb. It was odd, therefore, and even the cause of a slight adrenal rush, when he saw the taillights glowing smaller and smaller towards the stop sign at the end of the street. He realized then that not one, but *two* cars had passed him. The second set of tail lights were like beacons, burning through a cloudless sky of light blue metal, traversing the darkening earth on a quiet set of white wall tires.

That night Garrett ate his dinner, kissed his children and went up to bed early. He undressed and lay quietly beneath the single cool sheet in the dark, arms to his sides. He stared up at the ceiling for a long time imagining that it was a sky of still gray clouds with the forest moon tucked out of sight in a downy pocket. When, after a long time, Imajean finally came up to bed, he did not move. She did not steal into the room, but walked upright, bringing her full weight with each step, stopping like a declaration at the foot of the bed. Garrett could hear her breathing, slightly labored from climbing the stairs. He could sense her standing over him, watching his chest rise and fall in a peaceful unbroken rhythm, like a boat on slow water. She was listening to him in the dark; for once, listening. Garrett kept his eyes closed. And for a long time she stood there at the foot of the bed watching him breath; listening intently as he listened to her.

But the words would not come.

———

The next morning, after a night of fitful sleep, Garrett was up just before dawn and was rolling backwards down the driveway as the tips of the tallest trees behind the house had started to burst into bright baby green flames in the early sun.

The street on which he lived and where his family still slept, sloped gradually past the houses on the left and on the right, lined up for inspection like uniformed soldiers of unquestioning allegiance, down toward the stop sign that grew up through the cement like a steel flower. The street sloped down to where he had last seen the light blue car idling behind Mr. Walatke's rolling rutabaga – where his street met the road that carried travelers out of the neighborhood.

Garrett let the car roll soundlessly down to the intersection without starting the engine. He pushed his hat down on his head, lit a cigarette, and put the top back on the car. When he reached the stop sign where he had last seen the taillights that had burned through his dreams, he started the car and steered in the direction of Wilsonville, where he planned to bear witness to the burial of James Diamond.

He arrived late. It was a long drive to begin with, even longer than he remembered. He had needed to stop at a service station for gasoline, which had entailed a series of detours around some road construction that seemed to have cropped up over night. The inconvenience had frustrated him and he wondered openly why he had bothered to get up so early if he was only to drive in sloppy circuitous loops around the suburbs.

But once he had made it to the open road, he felt an inexplicable sense of freedom coursing through the ventricles of his heart. He swung

79

his arm over the back of the seat and lay his head back, the sun and wind splashing off the brim of his hat, trying not to think too specifically about Imajean's reaction when she came downstairs for her cup of coffee and read the note:

Jeannie – Ran out to look for better pipe wrench to fix furnace. Fix-It Factory in Wilsonville probably best bet. Back late. G.

He told himself that she would not have believed or accepted the truth. He was right, of course. She wouldn't. But the truth would have been a much safer bet than the note. The note would only compound her suspicions. Nobody travels two hundred miles for a pipe wrench. Somewhere in the dark, deep down in the fecund cavity of his being, down where the light of the moon did not reach and where life and death traded their fortunes, Garrett understood that he had chosen his words poorly. And that he had chosen them on purpose.

When at last he pulled onto the main street of Wilsonville, he noted a stillness to the surroundings, as though time itself had stopped. There were no people to be seen. No traffic. No children on their bicycles. The service station looked closed. He drove past the *Fix It Factory / Help Yourself Hardware* where the same collie was still curled up in the shade of the awning, a sight that gave strange comfort.

He drove past the Presbyterian Church, sitting alone on a large open green lot with a fountain of smooth white marble that seemed to rise up out of the earth into the hot air like ice glistening wet in the sun. The parking lot in front of the church and both sides of the street down to each corner were choked with parked cars.

Garrett drove back to the hardware store and parked across from the diner in exactly the same place he had parked on his first visit, which made him laugh a little to himself. He dusted off his shoes, straightened his tie in the mirror, and walked to the church with his hat in his hand and a slow deliberation in his step. It was just as hot as it had been on his last visit. Hotter maybe. But somehow he minded it less.

The church was so full of people that it was all Garrett could do to get inside the large mahogany doors. People turned as he entered, rotating halfway around from their torsos, giving him melancholic smiles that he returned in kind with a nod of his head. They politely shuffled their feet sideways a few inches, parting shoulders just enough for him to be able to see up the aisle to the front of the church.

A roundish woman in spectacles, with an unfortunate lack of curl to her hair, but who had an earnest and good-hearted expression, was on the dais looking out at the assembled mourners.

"I guess that's all I can offer you," she said with a sigh and a shrug. "Jimmy Diamond was the best man I've ever known. I will miss him almost as much as anyone in this room." She drew in a small breath and held it, looking out at all of the dewy eyes looking back at hers, as though thinking about whether to let the words out of her body.

"But he would not want this sadness," she said. "He would not want it. He would not. And those of you who knew him, know this to be true."

And at this Garrett could see dozens of heads nodding in slow, quiet assent.

"He was grateful for the life he had and he was too humble a man to expect more than what he was given. When I was fourteen my parents imposed a nine o'clock curfew upon me and my younger sister. As pertained to young Lilly, it was a sensible decree, but as to me, an unpardonable travesty against all that is decent and just. Never before or since has the world seen a more pitiable human specimen. You'd have thought I had been sentenced to a life of exile with the spiders and the stinkbugs in the cellar of our home.

"Jimmy was on one of his walks through Wilsonville – you all know that whole long route he used to do every evening as the sun was coming back down, up to the dairy to read to the cows from that book of quotations by which he seemed to live, and all the way back around the library and through the cemetery, through the woods and around this very church over to Melville and then up Brookline to tease Martin Dell about his yard and, well, you know the path he traveled – and when he got to our house he saw me crying and pouting on the tire swing out in our front yard. Well, he asked why I was carrying on, and when I told him my troubles, he gave me that sideways look of his – you know the one."

There was a ripple of soft breathy laughter that moved through the church like a breeze.

"And Jimmy told me something I have never forgotten and that I know he would want me to remember today of all days. He said, *Miss Molly, in this life you make the most of what you're given, that's all there is to it. And you don't come a cryin' when it's all done. You don't come a cryin'. It ain't never worth a tear over the shortness of the day, 'cause no matter how long the day is, it always gonna be too short. It's how you spend the day that really matters, and if you're disappointed when it's all done, you've got no one to blame but yourself.*

"And then he swatted me on the arm and continued on his walk. But after he had walked a few yards he turned back and pointed out there in the direction of the town square – this was back before we put up the cinema – and he said: *You go see how much trouble you can cause your momma 'fore that clock on the tower over yonder strikes nine."*

The mourners thought this was funny and chuckled to themselves, but out loud and together at the same time, and the mood lightened a little.

"Jimmy was not afraid to cause trouble in the world. Lord knows he knew how to mix it up and break all of the rules that tie us down and that obligate us to one another. Been in jail twice that I know of, both for disturbing the peace, which was an ethic we all know Jimmy held dear. Peace and security and comfort and acceptance by his fellows were all over-rated in Jimmy's book. All of that made him feel restless and made him want to, well... made him want to disturb the peace a little. It wasn't enough that he believed the things he believed, Jimmy needed to shout the things he believed – and I mean standing on a sidewalk, arms out, head up, shouting – like his very life depended on you believing his anger, believing his joy, believing his sorrow. It's just that at three o'clock in the morning, not everybody cared to be a believer.

"And money. Any of you who have had occasion to talk to Jimmy about aspirations of wealth, know that he was no friend of money.

Which maybe explains why Jimmy had so many friends. He hated the stuff. You've all been to the diner. Where else in this world is the pie free? *Free!* Anyone here ever *not* been served the last piece in the pan?"

The mourners laughed openly now and a couple of them clapped.

"That's right. You know what I'm saying. He gave money away like it was cherry pie with ice cream on the side. Jimmy's always been able to make it and never cared to keep it. He was always poor and always the wealthiest poor man I have ever known. His kind of wealth just never ran out and we're all the richer for it."

"Amen, Molly" said somebody near the front and somebody else gave a little laugh.

"He married six times, and except for Mary Willis who went on ahead last year – we do miss you Mary and we know you are looking down this afternoon – except for Mary, all of Jimmy's great loves are here in this church today. And they would tell you that Jimmy lived to break those rules, even the sacred ones, and that they could not help but love him for it. They would tell you that they envied his freedom from rules, from those formulas of living. Because for Jimmy it was not the rules of living but living itself that was sacred. *There are no formulas for happiness. There are only formulas for unhappiness.* He put it right there on the back of the menu for everybody to think about. Jimmy Diamond loved every minute of his time among us and I can promise you," she said ferociously, summoning everything to hold back the tears, "I promise you, that he did not come a cryin' when it was all done. There is such a thing as a life well-lived and there is no grief in that."

The woman took a deep and shaky breath and wiped her face with her fingers as she stepped down off the stage. The minister, in his white robe and gold rope around his waist patted her on the back as she went.

"Thank you Molly," he said. "Thank you, Mayor Jenkins."

When she was finally off the stage, the Mayor of Wilsonville was crying hard. She came to a stop before the front pews that were always reserved for immediate family on such occasions, and she stood with her arms outstretched. Several people stood and took turns embracing her and patting her on the back and swaying in the hot church as the mourners looked on. Garret watched the grieving faces and realized then, for the very first time, that Jimmy Diamond had been a black man. The man who would have wanted no grief; the man breaking rules and disturbing the peace by shouting the things he believed; the man living a full life and walking the sun into the ground every day, had been a black man.

The minister assumed the pulpit and read from the Bible about the last days of Jesus Christ in a deep voice that sounded like dark chocolate held on the tongue in winter. He lead the mourners in prayer and then everybody stood and sang *Amazing Grace* and cried through the part about the ten thousand years and through the part about how *we have no less days to sing God's praise*, and as an organist from somewhere Garrett could not see laid into the final notes there was more crying than singing.

When the service was done, a group of mourners, all men, rose from their seats and filed up onto the stage and assumed positions around the casket that had been too low for Garret to see from his station near the front doors. They carried the casket – simple pine this time, no polished cherry wood for Jimmy Diamond – out through the back of the church, which emptied behind them like an hourglass of black sand out onto the green summer lawn. The pallbearers hoisted the body of Jimmy Diamond onto a flatbed wagon that had been hitched behind two large black horses standing patiently and twitching their tails in the heat.

The coachman, accompanied by two middle-aged black men who Garrett took to be children of the deceased, sent a quick ripple through the reins and the wagon began to roll across the field towards a wide green belt of oak forest. Garrett imagined that Jimmy Diamond had walked that very path every day as the sun grew swollen and mottled and red, burrowing its way into the darkening earth.

The mourners watched quietly for a moment as the creaking of the wagon and the sound of the turning wheels grew faint, and then in twos and threes, hand in hand, arm over shoulder, saying very little, they began to saunter off to their cars and their trucks, which waited to carry them over narrow, unevenly paved roads, around the belt of hardwoods to the small cemetery on the face of a gentle southern slope. There they would wait one last time to see Jimmy Diamond coming around the bend.

Garrett stood on the steps of the church, put his hat on his head and lit a cigarette. He watched the automotive procession slowly disappearing around the corner. The heat was brutal, but he didn't mind, for the sun too, in all of its might, had come to pay its respects.

He thought about the burial to come, about the moment when the heat-swollen hands of the pallbearers would grip the handles of wide leather belts and lower the box into a hole in the ground. He thought about the sound of soft soil falling on the lid of a hollow pine box. Garrett knew there would be no calling out from that grave. Jimmy Diamond had already spoken his mind and when it was all done, it was all done, and he would not be one to come a cryin' or to call out when the mourners finally shuffled away into the afternoon. There would be no more words. There would be no more sound at all. There would be only the simple swelling silence that is the only song all of us will ever sing together.

A butterfly alighted upon a bush of roses, beating its wings against the heat.

"You going to the funeral?" asked Delia.

Garrett looked around at her calmly, saying nothing. He considered his cigarette before stubbing it out on the heel of his shoe. He dropped the butt into an ash can and walked over to where she was standing. Her dress was like it was made of the ocean.

"No, Ms. May," he said. "I'm not. That's a private affair."

"I lied to you, Mr. Webb. I'm sorry."

"Can you call me Garrett and still be sorry?"

She smiled, but without a trace of sheepishness.

"Why are you following me?"

"I do that sometimes."

"Do what? Follow people?"

"Yes."

"Can I ask why, Ms. May?"

"You can if you call me Delia."

"Alright. Why do you follow people, Delia?"

"You ever felt trapped in your own life, Garrett?"

He did not answer her, taking his hat off and slicking his hair back with his fingers.

"Ever try to make yourself laugh?" she asked. "I don't mean remembering something funny that you were not expecting. I mean actually *trying* to make yourself laugh."

Garrett put his hat back on and narrowed his eyes, trying to understand. "You mean like telling yourself a joke?"

"Yes. Like telling yourself a joke that you've heard a hundred times before. Like a joke you've been telling yourself every day and every night for years."

"Okay."

"Well one night I woke up in a cold sweat knowing that I might never laugh again. I packed a bag and I wrote a note for my man to read whenever he decided to come home and dry out. I pawned my ring and I went to the bus station where I got in line to buy a ticket to I didn't know where. The woman in line ahead of me was headed to Scranton and so I went there too. Scranton. I've been following people ever since."

"Hmm." Garrett fished another cigarette out of his shirt pocket and rolled it between his thumb and forefinger, but then thought better of it and put it back.

"I don't like knowing what's going to happen next," she said. "I like not knowing whether I'm turning right or turning left or whether I'm going to a funeral or a diner or the seashore."

"A little odd, don't you think?"

"I suppose it is," she said, shrugging.

"I mean just a little unnatural."

"No. Not unnatural. It may be odd; I'll give you that. But it's as natural as the birds and the bees, Garrett. Unnatural is telling yourself the same joke over and over and telling yourself that you're happy. Predictability is unnatural. Security is unnatural."

"You think?"

"It is in this world."

Delia looked away at the last of the cars rounding the corner for the cemetery on the far side of the woods. Then she looked back at him, tucking an errant wisp of dark satin hair behind her ear. Her mouth was simple and red and moved effortlessly by some mysterious force.

"For the living, anyway."

With all of the mourners gone, the town felt suddenly empty of people and the air was sweet and quiet in the swelling heat. Garrett extended an elbow.

"Walk you to your car?"

She slipped her hand in the crook of his arm and they began walking toward the now deserted street.

"Where are you parked?"

Delia smiled. "Across the street and down the block from you," she said. "Where else?"

Garrett laughed at this and she joined him. Neither of them really knew why this was so funny, only that it was and that it did not matter why.

When they reached Garrett's car, he could see that she had parked down the street by the service station and started off in that direction. Delia stopped him and pulled him up onto the sidewalk. They stood staring at the sign on the door of the diner. It read: "*Open for Funeral. Free Pie. Please Help Yourself.*"

They sat together in the empty diner for an hour, eating pie and listening to the fan stir the air. They laughed and spoke in full stories and toasted the late Jimmy Diamond with spoons full of cold vanilla ice cream.

When the people of Wilsonville began to filter back through the streets, and when Glorious returned to the diner, quiet and sad and yet still somehow beaming her enthusiasm for the world, disappearing to change into her work clothes and then wiping down the lunch counter to prepare for the dinner crowd, Garrett and Delia strolled across the street to pet the collie curled up beneath the awning. Together, they stepped inside to ask the man at the *Fix It Factory/Help Yourself Hardware* about the signs in the windows looking out over *Jimmy D's Thrive-n-Dine*.

But not while she was pointing that canon at his face. He would have to distract her. He would have to get her talking; get her focused on something else just long enough to make a move for the Hammer. But what did one say to a face like hers? To whom should he address this last effort at distraction: to his memory of love or to his assassin? For she was both of these to him, and only one would be willing to let him live long enough to speak the words that would save him. If, indeed, he was to be saved at all. Jack McMannis swallowed hard and spoke out from beneath the ground:

"The case is yours, doll," he said.

She pulled back the hammer and aimed the barrel down at his head. "Whatever do you mean, Jack?"

"I mean that the keys to my office are under the flower pot, and the keys to the safe are under the coffee pot, and in the safe is a ledger and on the ledger you will find the name of the man who will lead you to the money. If you are good enough to find me, then you are good enough to find him, and if he has hurt you like he has hurt me, then he deserves what he has coming to him and you are just the right dame to deliver the pain. But I want you to do one thing when you find him."

"What's that Jack?"

"I want you to tell him that I sent you. I sent you because you are not what he's expecting. You with your hair and your face and your perfume. Just like you were not what I was expecting. Tell him that expectations are for suckers and saps. They're nothing but a longing for sameness and that way lies rot and regret and so many words left unsaid that you cannot stop jabbering as they lower you down into the cold earth. Tell him that what you expect to happen is never worthy of your life. Tell him that life happens in the anticipation of what you do not expect. Tell him that anticipation of the unknown is the midwife of a contentment always promised but never born and that's what it means to love the world."

She cocked an eyebrow and gave him a wry smile, lowering the gun.

"Anything else?"

"Tell him I've moved on. And tell him to take heart; because there's always one last piece of pie in the pan. Always. And it's always free."

Chapter 4

STILL LIFE

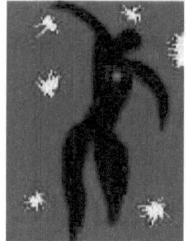

Mrs. Foves quite resented the look.

Even when he was not in her sight, she felt him from the corner of the gallery. Felt his unapologetic appraisal. Felt his wariness.

Such suspicion in those eyes, she thought. As if she were a saboteur of the order. As if, at any moment, she might act upon some grandly irrational impulse.

She stole a glance at him as she turned from *Mona Lisa* to consider *Whistler's Mother.* His eyes were dark and soft in the center, like something primal and molten, rimmed with a pure, bloodless white. It occurred to her that the eyes were a reflection of the man himself, black as midnight and wrapped in the starched white uniform of the museum.

That he thought her capable was incomprehensible. That she might desecrate some masterpiece as this one or that one, or mark upon the marbled walls or take a hunting knife to the glossy floors, or that she might suddenly regress into the shape of some beast given to howling and clawing at the peace and grandeur, struck her as preposterous.

But the eyes did not see it that way.

Mrs. Foves tried to remember the name of this place, but could not. She had seen it chiseled above the entrance, but that must have been a very long time ago, or, at least, she *supposed* it had been a very long time since she now had no recollection of ever crossing the threshold.

She knew that the name of the museum had been stenciled in a thin, slanted looping script into a small rectangular plaque and pinned to the uniform of the security guard who still looked at her from the only shadow of the gallery. Another hard look at him and she might remember.

But she quickly thought better of it. She did not wish to deliberately encounter the appalling suggestion in those eyes.

It seemed to her that they were the only souls in the place and it unnerved her to be alone. She walked along the polished floor, which seemed to flow from gallery to gallery like a river of wood, and her heels made sounds like the knocking of stones beneath the water. She adjusted her handbag and smoothed her dress against the tops of her legs in a way that would have betrayed her discomfort had there been anyone else to see it. She stepped calmly out of the room, and across the hall.

Here was an entirely different gallery. Mrs. Foves was surprised to find the walls were bare and, by what must have been a trick of poor lighting, they seemed to pucker and bow in random splotches of darkness. She turned and looked intently, knowing that she had surely missed something.

When she had come nearly full around, she saw that the black man in his white uniform and his invasive, uncompromising eyes was in the corner. The sight of him surprised her, since she had not heard a sound of his moving so quickly. She continued to turn in a casual manner, as if his presence was of no particular consequence. She did not want him to have the power of knowing her discomfort.

Never let them see you stirring, is what Robert had always told her. And she would follow his advice, as always, even now.

But she *was* stirring. In spite of herself, she was... stirring. She could feel it. Deep in the bottom of a place she could not name, something was turning over.

It was certainly time to be leaving. Time to be moving on.

She gripped the strap of her handbag on her shoulder as though clutching the railing of a ship in heavy seas. But as she turned, Mrs. Foves realized that she did not know her way. She could not recall the direction from which she had entered this dismally empty gallery and, now that she looked with a sharper focus, she could not discern any doors at all.

But that cannot be, she thought, fighting a rising tide of concern and trying her best not to look into the darkened corner. *Surely there is a door. Surely. Come now!*

And, indeed, there was a door. She realized that she had missed it quite foolishly in her state of needless worry about the security guard who was, after all, merely doing his job.

She made her way with a brisk step and, as she approached the adjoining gallery, found further consolation when her eyes caught a glimpse of her dining room table. And not just the table, after all, but the entire room, with the grandfather clock that Robert liked to wind with such precision and the lavender draperies that had been too bold for his taste but which he had endured for her sake. And there, too, behind the table, was the heavy oak buffet that held the good china and, on the table, the arrangement of dried lilies in the vase painted the color of a field.

And wasn't it all now ever so much better?

She quickened her step towards the gallery that contained her dining room, which, it turned out, was much farther away than she had first believed. She walked and walked and walked and suddenly she was there, one hand resting upon the smooth mahogany scroll of a chair and the other reaching over the table to fuss with the dried lilies in the way that Robert liked to roll his eyes about.

At first she thought him her father. He had the same posture. The same presence. But then she realized that she did not actually know the man sitting at the head of the table. Nevertheless, it seemed natural that he should be there and Mrs. Foves was unconcerned. Perhaps it was the expensive dark suit that put her at ease, or the shine on his shoes. The tie was like a crisp blue stream through a bright green valley. She thought it was only proper to ask if she might bring him some tea or a light lunch, but she could not find her kitchen. A red fruit sat on the table before him, an apple she thought, and he rolled it slowly from one hand to the next.

A large black dog entered the gallery, his eyes flashing white and his nails clicking on the glossy floor. This gave Mrs. Foves some pause, for she had never seen a dog in a museum gallery, or in her dining room, and she did not know what to think. His mouth hung open and the flesh inside was brightly sanguine in its prison of bleached bone. The dog, which was very large indeed now that she looked at him, paid her no mind and he curled up at the feet of the man like a pool of cooling lava.

Something pulled her at attention. The pulling came from the wall behind the buffet. From the wall itself it seemed, which was not the yellowing white she expected, but blue. And not just any blue, she saw, but the coming of night while the day is everywhere still melting from memory into dream.

She saw that the wall stretched upward from behind the buffet for a very long way, up into blackness. In the blue ink of dusk was the sprawling silhouette of a man, as though cut from the blackness above, tumbling down, down, down through a constellation of exploding yellow light, like solar munitions, and a burning red in the center of his chest, like a flaming seed, where the stars had finally found their mark.

Mrs. Foves could feel the burning hole in her own chest now. The tears came and she let them fall. She reached up to the sprawling tumbling man, her entire hand the size of his flaming heart, and she knew that this was Icarus. At least, that was the name in her head. She looked at the man sitting at her table and he moved his head in a slow nod, continuing the roll the fruit from one hand to the other.

Then he spoke her name.

But Mrs. Foves did not recognize the sound of it. She could see now that the man sported a trim gray beard over a weathering face much older than her own. His pink lips moved with a smile.

Qu'avez-vous dit? she asked, surprised to hear a language she did not speak.

Vous êtes si jeune pour mourir, the man replied, patting the large dog on his head. *Vous brûlez à l'intérieur.*

He looked at her directly now, for the first time, and with such intensity that a lily stem snapped between her fingers. She looked down at the broken stem in horror, and then back at him. His eyes glowed a deep red and he held up the fruit by the tips of his fingers. It burst into flame and he smiled.

Brûlure, Amelie. Brûlure!

———

Mrs. Foves woke with a start in the middle of her bed. The dawn was seeping into the room from beneath her curtains, slipping to the floor in cold, gray sheets. She sat up and quickly took stock of the familiar – the fluted bedposts, the bureau, the oval mirror with the chip, the night stand with its glass of water and its vase of dried wildflowers, the portrait of Robert she had painted from an old photograph and the memory of the grim determination of his features.

All was as all had ever been.

The images in her head blurred at the edges and soon became unrecognizable, like sea foam disappearing into the sand. In another moment, she had no memory of what had been so upsetting and her heart settled back into its familiar rhythm.

She rose and dressed for work. Because she was up earlier than normal, she took extra time to arrange and pin her hair and to iron her clothing. She made the bed and then went into the kitchen for a soft-boiled egg and a piece of toast. She poured herself a glass of juice and sat down at the dining table to eat.

After a brief moment she began to feel a sharp uneasiness, which she decided must have something to do with the dried lilies that were always giving her grief. The flowers were arranged in a vase of black ceramic sitting on a doily at the center of the table. Mrs. Foves had long concluded that her house had a draft that caught and turned the wide petals when she was asleep or away at work or in the kitchen with her back turned.

Today the flowers would simply not consent to a lifelike arrangement and Mrs. Foves gave up, suddenly rising from the table in exasperation.

In truth, the flowers were only part of the problem, for the dining room in general, quite inexplicably, had set her ill at ease this morning. As she sat and fussed with the arrangement, she could not avoid the disconcerting feeling of a bather paddling into an overgrown lake, toes losing contact with the earth, naked legs beneath the murky surface a flurry of blind, fearful reconnaissance, knowing that something is there, biding its time. Not that she believed anything was beneath her dining table, and not that she even looked.

But still.

The pill bottle was before her, with a solitary white pill on the table next to it. It was her practice to take her evening pill and to place her morning pill on the table on the right side of the bottle so as to be sure not to miss it, and, similarly, upon taking her morning pill, to replace it with an evening pill on the left side of the bottle for when she came home. In this way, her nerves remained steady and her doctor well pleased. Mrs. Foves popped the chalky, bloodless ovule beneath her tongue, washed it down with a swallow of juice and tumbled an evening pill out onto the table.

She gathered her food and repaired to the sitting room, where she settled into the embroidered wingback chair that she and Robert had found in a boutique in Chicago visiting his mother after their honeymoon. It was the only chair she ever used in the sitting room, though there were others. She could not bring herself to sit in Robert's chair, which was large and leather and still smelled of tobacco, or so she thought. There was no sense in changing chairs now.

The morning outside had taken on some color and was pushing its way through the translucence of the draperies over the front windows that faced out onto the small lawn and the street beyond. Mrs. Foves appreciated her privacy in the mornings and typically did not, therefore, open her draperies until it was lunchtime. She sat quietly, with a long silver spoon, eating her egg in its cup and watching the curtains brighten. It was not yet 7:30 and she could already smell the dust in the air. That meant it was going to be another warm day. It was the heat of the sun that aerated the dust. That's what Robert had told her. The earlier you smelled the dust, the hotter it was going to be.

The street outside was starting to come alive. She could hear the Wilsons' spaniel take issue with something fast and temporary; a squirrel or a bird, she imagined. Michael Clancy emerged into the soundscape saying something to Eunice about bacon. A car door closed and an engine started and then rumbled off down the street taking Michael Clancy to his day at the Home Appliance Center where, his wife was fond of reporting over the hedge, he had just been promoted to the Executive Sales Team.

Before Michael Clancy's engine faded away, another engine grew louder and then stopped with a sputter and a clank. There was a sliding metal sound and the clinking of bottles.

Bo was here to deliver the milk.

Tom Douglas was his real name, but for reasons unknown to Mrs. Foves, his customers called him Bo. The name seemed to sit just fine with Tom, always whistling to himself, with his heavy step and the bottles clinking. The dairy dressed him in white from head to toe like he had been dipped in a vat of milk to fill his bottles before making the rounds. With his cap on he almost looked military, although without any of the silver insignia, the ribbon bars and the gold buttons or the white polished shoes instead of the dark boots that Bo tended to wear.

There was a knock next door and then a singsong *G'monin' Miz Clancy!* It was Bo's way to knock on the door and to sing out a greeting and to leave the milk in the porch shadows and then to move on before the door could open. That was just fine with Mrs. Foves, who valued her privacy and was not much for small talk with the milkman, even some-one as likeable as Bo.

The whistling picked up again and footsteps approached, growing louder and heavier, and the clinking bottles sounded like wind chimes in a gale. There was a sharp knock, three quick blows against the wood that made her heart quicken even though she knew it was coming.

G'monin' Miz Foves!

She listened quietly, invisibly, her spoon suspended between cup and mouth, as Bo's sound, like an aroma, became fainter and fainter and finally disappeared into the morning hidden beyond the curtains.

Mrs. Foves finished her breakfast, gathered the bottles of milk and put them in the refrigerator, cleaned up the dishes and, after collecting her shawl from the hall closet, made the walk to the corner of Macomb Street and Nellis Way, near the school yard where the Number 6 bus stopped. It was not a long walk, nor the least bit unpleasant, stretching only five blocks through a quiet neighborhood of modest and aging homes.

The bus was mostly full by the time she climbed aboard. She navigated the elbows, nodding hello to familiar, nameless faces and they all nodded their good-mornings back to her. A man in a seersucker suit and a smart gray hat gave up his window seat for her. She thanked him in a way that was sincere but not overly encouraging and swayed and bounced and looked out the window at the farmers in the fields as she listened to people talk about their lives.

She opened her handbag and retrieved Celia's letter, reading it again for reasons entirely lost to her. She liked the slant and the fluid artistic loops of Celia's pen and perhaps that was enough. Or maybe it was the entertainment inherent in the invitation which was so prepos-terous as to be instantly dismissed, but which brought Celia and her impulsive folly to life and kept one's attention even on second reading while leaning up against the cool window of a morning bus.

... The other thing about Miami, my dear married recluse, is the men. Everywhere men. There are enough on my little street to have a new one every

night of the week and three on Sunday. Gentlemen
in the evenings and rogues in the afternoon. They
are not all Cubans as you might expect, though they
too are in good supply and deliciously scented like
tightly rolled cigars. And the women... my, but I am
a long ways from home. No need to commit any of
that to writing I suppose.

Oh, I do so miss my art school conspirator. Are
you still painting? I fear true love has broken all of
your brushes. Were it not for your dear Robert off
fighting the good fight for God and country I would
abduct you to this paradise and we would share a
studio and live to render our daily scandals in slick
tropical oils. Oh! Have I told you? I saw my first
Matisse! Three of them, a month ago. I have to say
they were exquisite. The colors! Now I cannot stop
imitating. I have to stop; I am becoming a butcher.
They will arrest me soon.

So, I must say that I am happy. I have made
so many friends and we drink and dance in night
clubs like you have never seen – Tyrone Power was
having drinks at one of them only last week – and
while I can easily forget that my mother no longer speaks to me, I do miss you and wish you were
here. When Robert returns, if he has not already,
give him a hug for me and remind him that his gain
has been my loss. Remind him that if he does not
treat you like the Queen that you are, you will be
on the next plane south. Are you still working for
Mr. Wilbanks? Such a serious life you have. Goose
him for me and see if that doesn't liven things up a
bit. And if you see my mother, tell her you heard
from me and that she should not believe everything
she hears from Mrs. Davidson, whose sister – as luck

would have it – works down here in a local library. Write me. Much love, Celia.

Mrs. Foves folded the pages back into the envelope and returned the envelope to her handbag, which she closed with a snap. The Number 6 route had added eight new stops in the past year and the ride was now up to forty-three minutes before reaching her stop at the end of Nightingale Boulevard. She leaned her temple against the window and watched the ground on the surface of the world spin away beneath her, its colors blurring into a single streak of movement, as she sat motionless above.

Having disembarked, Mrs. Foves stood in a pool of sunlight on the street corner watching the bus labor to push itself up along the sloping arc of road that circled around the library and then up behind the museum and then, moving downhill now, roar past her back up Nightingale from whence it had come. The man who had given up his seat was back in the window tipping his hat.

She started to cross the street and begin the next and final four blocks of her commute to work. She stopped suddenly, one foot on and one foot off the curb, and looked up the hill at the museum. She found something strangely compelling about the site of the edifice – two stories of dark brown, window-speckled stone, with fluted flourishes along the roofline and down the corner columns, perched on a hilly lawn – that she could not explain.

She stood and looked at it, blazing in the morning sun, feeling the heat of the day slowly rising out of the earth, building its strength in the air. She had been to the museum only a handful of times, and not once within the past many years. Her last visit had been for *Stars Among Us*. Billed as a celebration of local artistic talent, the exhibition had really been more of a low-budget filler between far grander, professional displays. But the community enthusiasm for a showing of local color had been surprising, and there was some talk of making the show an annual event. If the idea ever took hold, Mrs. Foves was not aware of it, for she had never been back.

And while she stepped down from the Number 6 Bus onto this street corner almost every day, today was the first time Mrs. Foves could recall having taken particular notice of the museum up on its hill. It was as if someone had quietly carried up the stone blocks and built the museum overnight as she slept and she was now seeing it for the very first time.

No. That was not right. Not the first time. The second time. Like she was seeing the museum for the second time. For it seemed oddly familiar to her. Like an echo.

But she could not understand the feeling so she shook her head, removed the shawl from her shoulders, adjusted her purse, and continued on her way to *Wilbanks, Marshall & Haynes*.

———

When she crossed the threshold, she was not surprised to see Mr. Wilbanks already behind his desk bent over his papers and shuffling through them in a manner that might suggest to the uninformed that he had become confused or had lost something. But the papers were all arrayed in a line of neat stacks on the desk and though he had recently turned eighty-one and was given to fits of muttering to himself, she knew Mr. Wilbanks was still very much in control of his faculties and that he knew precisely where to find whatever he needed.

He looked up sharply when she set her purse down beside her desk, which sat directly outside Mr. Wilbanks' door.

"Ah, Mrs. Foves. Good morning to you."

"Good morning, Mr. Wilbanks."

"Lovely day for a walk to work, wouldn't you agree?"

"Oh, I would certainly agree, sir. Very nice. It will be warm though."

"Yes. Unseasonably. But the mornings are nice."

"Very."

"Grocery was robbed last night. Did you hear?"

"No. Last night?"

"Yes. Two men I'm told. Sylvia's all a-gab."

"Goodness."

"I would like you to take a letter when you are settled."

"Yes sir. I'll be right in."

Mrs. Foves draped her shawl over the back of her chair, grabbed her notepad and one of those new ballpoint pens from her drawer, and presented herself at the doorway, knocking lightly.

"Come in, come in," he said, suddenly irritated. "Goodness, Mrs. Foves. You needn't knock after I've already asked you in. Sit down. Sit, sit."

"Sorry, sir."

She quickly took a seat across from him as he busied himself with a stack of paper, extracting sheaves here and there. His head was an unruly white mop, finally beginning to thin from the center and his eyebrows knitted and unknitted like great gray wings drying in the sun.

Mrs. Foves rested the pad and pen in her lap and waited. The desk before her was heavy and dark with thick muscled claws for feet and a trio of tawny leather rectangles inlaid across its surface. A large pane of glass behind the desk looked out over the street three stories below from which rose the sounds of morning traffic and the newspaper boys. Not too far in the distance were the poplars that shaded the banks along the western bend of the Cleatchee River. The world beyond the river, if it existed at all, was behind a curtain of bright blue sky.

"I want you to take this letter. Are you ready?"

"Yes sir."

"Mr. Harold Carlton. Carlton Engraving Incorporated. Forty-one, fifty-one, Wisteria Way. Dear Mr. Carlton... this letter is to advise you... of the unsatisfactory status of your account with this firm. Our records indicate that... notwithstanding the professional services... duly provided by myself and Mr. Haynes for the benefit of your company... you have seen fit to disregard our invoices. Our recent encounter... at the fairgrounds... has left me, quite frankly, disappointed in your character. No, strike that, Mrs. Foves. I think *appalled* would be better than merely disappointed, don't you?"

"Yes sir."

"Good. Continuing then... If you do not have the courtesy to..."

Mr. Wilbanks stopped and when Mrs. Foves looked up from her pad she saw that he was staring off into the distance behind her. She was suddenly aware of swift movement at the door, moving in from the back of the office.

"This is highly irregular," said Mr. Wilbanks sternly. "You must make an appointment, if you wish..."

"I don't need an appointment to tell you to go jump in the river, Wilbanks. You going to introduce me?"

A woman with dark satin hair was standing next to her now with one hand on her hips and a cigarette glowing between her fingers. She wore gabardine slacks and a white blouse that billowed at the sleeves. She smelled of flowery perfume.

"I most certainly will not," said Mr. Wilbanks. "This is highly irregular."

"Sorry to intrude," said the woman, turning to Mrs. Foves and extending a hand. "My name is Delia May."

"How do you do, Ms. May," said Mrs. Foves with a tentative shake. "I'm Mr. Wilbanks' secretary."

"Really. Well I'm Mr. Wilbanks' private detective. Former private detective, I guess I should say."

She took a drag from her cigarette and looked sideways at Mr. Wilbanks who was turning red in the face with anger. Mrs. Foves thought that she had never seen a more self-assured woman in her entire life.

"Ms. May! That is quite enough!" shouted Mr. Wilbanks.

"I do not appreciate being yelled at, sir," said Delia May calmly. "Nor lied to."

"I have not lied to you. I certainly have not."

"You told me your son-in-law was a man of low moral character. You told me he was a philanderer and a cheat."

"And you say that he is not these things?"

"I know now for certain that he is not."

"Do you now?"

"Garrett Webb is a novelist. He creates characters of low morals, Mr. Wilbanks, but he himself has high character to spare. Perhaps you were confused."

"You followed him?"

"I did."

"And you say that he is not stepping out on my Imajean." Having forgotten his circumstances, he turned sharply to his secretary. "I am sorry for you to hear this, Mrs. Foves, will you please step out so that I may conclude this business?"

Mrs. Foves rose, but Delia May lowered her back into her chair with a finger on her shoulder.

"Don't bother, sweetheart. The *business,* as he has so delicately put it, is concluded." She stepped forward extracting a stack of bills from her pocket and dropped them on the desk. She flicked the stack over with a slender, red-tipped finger. "Here's your money back. Your son-in-law is a good man... missing only what your daughter will not give."

"And how can you know such a thing?"

"You made it my business to know." Delia May turned and looked down at Mrs. Foves and gave a wry wink. "And now I do." She patted Mrs. Foves on the shoulder with her money hand and then strode off behind her towards the door.

"Are *you* now sleeping with Garrett, Ms. May?" said Mr. Wilbanks loudly after her. "Are you? *Ms. May!*"

But Delia May did not stop and all that was left to answer the question that hung in the air was the smoke from her cigarette and the lingering smell of her skin.

After an uncomfortable minute, Mr. Wilbanks sat down heavily in his chair and looked across the desk at Mrs. Foves. She imagined that he was scrutinizing her face for any signs of wavering in her loyalty. She forced herself, for the moment, to dislike everything about the woman who had just left them and then she allowed her face to repeat the lie.

"That will be all, Mrs. Foves," he said. But when she had reached the door, he stopped her.

103

"May I ask you a question that should not be too personal for an old man like me to ask a young woman like you?"

Mrs. Foves paused in the doorframe, but did not answer him, knowing her answer to be irrelevant.

"Were you and Robert happily married? Before the war, I mean?" His voice was soft and riddled with uncertainty.

"We were very happily married," she said. "As happy as any couple I know."

"Yes," he said, nodding. "I suspected as much. My daughter is your age. She is very unhappily married to a man who fancies himself a writer of bad crime novels."

"I'm sorry."

"I knew he was corruptible when they married. I knew there was not enough decency in that man to restrain his lusts." He knocked his old fist against the edge of the desk. "And I'll bet my next dollar that there was nothing in these modern times that could have corrupted your Robert. Am I right, Mrs. Foves?"

She looked at him and smiled bitter-sweetly. "You are right, sir. Robert was always decent."

"Yes, well, that's the Army for you, isn't it?"

"Yes sir. Army Air Corps."

"Air Corps. Yes, of course. One and the same though, really."

"No sir. Not to Robert. To be a paratrooper in the Army Air Corps was... well, it was something special, Mr. Wilbanks. For special men."

"I see. A paratrooper. Well, I suppose leaping from airplanes for the free world is something special at that Mrs. Foves. Special indeed. I'm sure he was quite a man and that he always wanted the best for you, didn't he?"

"I believe so, yes."

"Even now, I'm sure a man of such good Christian character has God's ear for your satisfaction in life. Don't you suppose?"

"I don't know," she said. "I suppose he wants me to be happy even from Heaven, yes."

"As he should. My son-in-law will not go to church without a gun to his head. He will not be seen at his own father-in-law's birthday picnic on the banks of the Cleatchee. Not that I would have him, mind you, but just the same. He would rather drive around in his silly convertible and daydream about crimes of passion and ruining my daughter's happiness." He closed his eyes and rubbed his temples and was suddenly very far away. "That is all for now, Mrs. Foves."

Mrs. Foves returned to her desk, closing the door to Mr. Wilbanks' office behind her, and set to work typing up as much of the letter to Mr. Harold Carlton as she knew so far and when she was done with that, she resumed the various projects that she had left off the day before.

As she worked, she tried to keep Robert foremost in her thoughts, as she always did. It should have been easy enough today given her unusual conversation with Mr. Wilbanks and the way that, together, they had invoked Robert's heroism and strength of character. Standing in the entry of her employer's office she had gripped the door frame and forced herself to imagine Robert gripping the open door of the plane, the hot breath of the valley overwhelming his senses, in that single moment before he stepped out over the darkening Rhone.

But the more she conjured the memory of her husband, the more he seemed to slip away from her, like a wisp of something in the breeze. When she was not absolutely vigilant in keeping her mind from wandering, she found that she was not thinking of Robert at all and that instead, it was the very idea of the woman named Delia May that occupied her attention. It was the way she dressed and smoked and spoke and occupied space; hard as nails and smelling like flowers. Delicate but unafraid. She imagined the man that loved someone like Delia May. The man that would let go of everything in him that was decent, falling from grace just for the pleasure of her kind of love. For those eyes and those lips and that unapologetic ferocity. A damnable, lowly man to be sure, and irresponsible to boot. And yet, she could not help but wonder whether any man was immune. Whether even her Robert might have fallen.

The very idea was preposterous and she forced it out of her mind, mistaking feelings of regret for the pain and self-pity to which she was so accustomed.

At precisely noon, she took her regular lunch at *The Corner Counter* on Smithdale with Sylvia Blake. Sylvia was secretary to Mr. Haynes and was no friend of the spiritually weak. As they shuffled sideways, sliding their trays along the cafeteria counter, they leaned into each other's ears, speaking in hushed but animated disdain for Delia May and her kind. Sylvia thought Delia May a harlot of the worst kind and was not at all reluctant to say so. Sylvia's husband Milton was a Deacon down at the First Methodist and they were both known to speak with some conviction about the temptations along the wayward path, almost all of which seemed to concern *harlots of the worst kind.* Mrs. Foves nodded her head in emphatic accord, and their lunch continued in this enthusiastic manner until it was time to return to work.

But even as their words cut to ribbons this woman they had not known for more than the minute or so that she had been in the office, Mrs. Foves felt a longing in her heart that she could not explain. It was only with some effort that she was able to put Delia May out of her thoughts enough to attend to her responsibilities and the incessant need of Mr. Wilbanks.

At the end of the day Mrs. Foves walked back to the bus stop and waited for the Number 6 to take her home. The air was now so warm that the tips of her hair around her temples, and the thin fabric of her blouse beneath her arms, and the petticoat beneath her dress, had begun to soak in the perspiration spreading over her body.

Two men in ties and suit coats slung over their shoulders were also waiting. One of them was leaning against the bus stop sign; the other rocked back and forth on his heels. They eyed her appraisingly but did not speak, nor she to them.

She looked down the street, but found no sign of the Number 6. In the other direction, up on its green hill with the loop of Nightingale Boulevard draped like a gray ribbon necklace from behind, sat the museum. It too seemed to eye her appraisingly, its windows glinting. For reasons she could not begin to fathom, Mrs. Foves felt the pull of the familiar, of a conversation to be continued, and she turned to stare up at the building directly.

"Excuse me, sir. Do you know when the Number 3 is due?"

The men looked at her with contained surprise and then at each other and then at their watches.

"Not for another ninety minutes," said the younger one with the dark eyes and large hands. He took a step closer. "Can I be of some assistance to you?"

"No, thank you," said Mrs. Foves, smiling up at him and, without a further word, she turned and crossed the street.

———

The museum was cool and quiet and nearly empty. A kindly woman with glasses hanging from a beaded string extended a leaflet with a wrinkled hand and inquired perfunctorily.

"Oh, just looking as I wait for my bus," said Ms. Foves, nodding and walking into the main gallery.

It was a large, two story room finished in a dark, glossy wood that seemed to soak up the light and let it back out in a soft glow. The upper story was rimmed by a circular balcony behind a wooden railing. Behind the balcony, Mrs. Foves could see the entrances to smaller galleries, and she remembered now that the *Stars Among Us* exhibition had been upstairs in those rooms.

In the main gallery hung twelve large, ornately framed oils of sailing ships tossed upon the watery lips of dark and angry seas. The spume was like snow in the air and seemed likely to come off on her finger had she ventured a touch. She consulted her leaflet instead. The artist, a Mr. Carlyle, was a native of Boston and it seemed that in forty years of painting he had garnered an impressive list of distinctions. They were listed in the leaflet in a bold, scripted print, which Mrs. Foves generally noted without reading.

Turning the leaflet over, she read that one of the upstairs galleries – referred to as *The Stansfield Gallery* after some devoted bene-factor – featured the works of Staff Sergeant Arthur Griggs, a local from up near West Quincy, which was only about thirty miles beyond the river as the crow flies. His oils, it said, were a tribute to the common soldier and to the brotherhood born of sacrifice. The leaflet included a small self-portrait of the artist in a little box above the text. His face was clouded with some unknown emotion and his eyes, deep-set beneath a shelf of brow, were dark and disproportionately large, as though it took something extra for them to stare out of the leaflet and into the world.

Resolved to see the exhibit before she left, Mrs. Foves finished her tour of the main gallery and then left the main room for a staircase ascending from a point near where she had first entered.

A man and woman, nicely dressed, married most likely, parted for her on the staircase, the man, smelling of musk, opening his shoulders to her, unnecessarily rotating his body sideways along the rail, allowing her passage but holding his courtesy for so long after she passed that his companion continued her descent without him, calling up after him from the bottom. He skittered down the stairs in a controlled, obedient tumble.

Walking along the upper balcony she paused to look over the railing at the gilded works of Mr. Carlyle. It was a god's perspective to be sure, there, from up in the lights, looking down upon the dark and roiling, foam-flecked seas. Ms. Foves imagined a body in the water, limbs flailing, features frozen in horror at such a long fall from the masthead. How easy for a god to save the fallen, she thought, to reach out and pluck a drowning sailor from the pitch and to leave him gasping and grateful on the deck.

In the Stansfield Gallery, the featured works of Sgt. Griggs was not the same grand affair on display below. The paintings were small. They were hand-framed in a dark wood and hung in two even rows on each of three walls. The room itself was insufficiently lit and between the shadows and the size of the paintings, Mrs. Foves found that she needed to stand very close to the wall in order to appreciate the display.

The paintings were of men; of soldiers and comrades in uniform, posed indulgently as if for a photograph, arms draped over shoulders, leaning on shovels, smoking in the doorframes of scarred and battered Quonset huts, reclined upon the hood of a jeep, caps askew, hands on hips, standing as totemic fixtures in the mud of foreign soil. Mrs. Foves moved quietly and slowly from one to another, taking them in, scouring the faces. In each portrait, the artistic perspective was unreservedly reverential, as though the act of painting had taken place from deep within some hole at the feet of the subject. Heads and shoulders were carefully framed between clouds against a blue sky. Except for the occasional building or vehicle, the soldiers may well have been suspended in mid-air.

"Emily?"

She turned to see a man at the entrance of the gallery looking at her. He wore khakis and short sleeves and held a hat in his hand.

"Emily Foves, isn't it?"

"Yes," she replied, looking around uncertainly. "I'm Emily Foves."

The man stepped towards her quickly, but with a decided limp, extending his large, sculpted arm. He had a solid posture. He took up space, pushing the air between them aside with his chest. As he approached she was suddenly and almost fearfully preoccupied with his physicality. She felt a quickening in her body and knew that if this man did not have honorable intentions, there would be nothing in this empty room to stop him. But suddenly he was before her, shaking her hand, and the rising feeling of alarm began to quietly seep away.

"I'm Artie Griggs. I know your brother, Bobby. We were in basic training together at Fort Benning."

He paused, waiting for her to respond. But she continued to stare at him uncomprehendingly, grasping his hand, lips parted and eyes fixed.

"I recognize you from your camera picture," he continued. "Boy, oh boy, you look exactly like that picture. I mean your hair is up and all and the clothes are different, but, boy oh man, if you don't look exactly like that picture. I see a picture and I never forget it. It just burns itself right into the ol' noggin." Letting go of her hand, he pointed to the walls around them in an over-enthusiastic swooping gesture. "All of these I did from camera pictures and memories of camera pictures." Artie Griggs tapped his temple with a finger. "I never forget a picture."

Mrs. Foves stared at him, not knowing what to say. For all of his muscle and frame, she saw that he had a boyish face and a couple of wayward teeth and watery green eyes.

"You mean... *Robert?*" She said at last.

"Oh, yeah, well, we all call him Bobby. Sisters are too formal I guess. My sister calls me Arthur, but everybody else calls me Artie. Where is the old rascal, anyway? He still living around here?"

"No. Robert's ..."

"Don't tell me he finally got hitched, that dog. Eddy Rivers bet me that I'd get a divorce before Bobby Foves ever got hitched. I been divorced a year now, come October." He arranged his face into a mockingly dramatic expression. "So you've got to tell me, Emily: is Bobby Foves livin' the married life?"

When at first she did not answer, his face broke into a mischievous grin, but she could see that he was not acting out of malice.

"No." Mrs. Foves cleared her throat with a small sound. "No, uh no, Bobby's not living... he's not living the married life."

"That dog!" Artie Griggs slapped his hat against his leg with a popping sound. "I knew it. Now I got to send Eddy Rivers some money. Dad-gummit! Well, it was a dumb bet, anyway. Bobby's not the marrying type. Good thing, too. He's a looker, that one. Boy, Bobby could sure tell some stories. And did we ever have some passes into Atlanta on a couple of those weekends..."

Artie Griggs stopped abruptly and the cheeks of his baby-skinned face began to flush. "Well... listen to me ramble on. I guess Bobby wouldn't appreciate me talkin' like that to you of all people. I need to learn my manners again, I guess."

"Quite alright, Mr. Griggs."

"Please. Call me Artie. He's a good man, your brother. I was always sorry we didn't ship out together. You gotta be made out of something special to be in the Air Corps. Jumpin' outta those planes. Bobby was made of the right stuff and I wasn't. I was strictly infantry and even then all I wanted to do was take pictures and paint. I saw plenty of action, but it was always on the ground. I'll bet Bobby could cut down Krauts like they were standin' still. I'll bet they were all dead before he even hit the ground."

"You… you painted all of these, then?" Said Mrs. Foves from the only part of her that was not suffocating beneath the weight of an inexplicable comprehension. Artie Griggs looked around at his own work and then back again.

"Yeah. My leg got all tore up and they sent me back and I started painting. I got my divorce and moved to San Francisco for a bit and had an exhibition there and then I moved to Houston and had an exhibition there and now I'm living back here and, well," he looked around again at the paintings on the wall matter-of-factly, "now I'm having an exhibition here."

"They're all very nice."

"Yeah, I guess. My wife never liked 'em much."

"I'm sorry. They are very nice, though. Very realistic. Maybe she likes more abstract paintings."

"No. What she likes are the still life paintings. You know, fruit and flowers and that kind of thing. I'm strictly portraits."

"Isn't a portrait just another still life? A human still life?"

He laughed and shook his head appreciatively. "Well, I guess you have something there, Emily. I never thought of it like that. I wish I'da thought of that. I could have settled an argument or two with that."

"Too bad."

"Aw… It's clever all right, but it wouldn't have made a difference. She said my portraits reminded her of me being away, thinkin' I wasn't ever coming home. I came home, sure enough, but it wasn't the same between us. It wasn't the same, because I wasn't the same. See, war changes a person, Emily. I've been to Paris. Madrid. I've seen good men die for no good reason and for the best of reasons. I'm not the same. I'm sure Bobby's not the same either."

"No."

"Yeah, I came back a different man and Lucy was exactly the same. *Exactly.* It was like," he paused to consider his hat and picked at the band for a moment. Voices – women and at least one man – echoed up from the main gallery. It was laughter, she knew, but just shrill enough for Mrs. Foves to imagine the sounds as screaming, as pleas for help as the ocean flooded into the gallery from the massive Carlyles on all sides and as the waves crashed in over their heads.

"It was like she kept herself on ice the whole time I was in Europe, see, like in one of those big chest freezers, and the world just passed her by for almost two years. And when I came back, well, like I said, I was a different man than the one she was waiting for. Fact is, I guess I don't ever recall being the man she was waiting for. I don't ever recall being that person. She had a lot of time to herself. You think that changes how you remember someone?"

"I, I don't..."

"Anyway," Artie Griggs shrugged, "on top of it all, she didn't like my paintings, so that was that. Say," he reached out and touched her elbow with his fingertips, "would you like to have some coffee someplace?"

"What? No. Thank you, no, Mr. Griggs."

"Are you okay? I mean, you look like you're burning up. Are you feverish, or...?"

"No. It's very warm; that's all. I have a bus to catch. It was nice meeting you."

"I have a car, Emily. It's not much to look at, but I promise it runs smooth as silk. Can I take you someplace?"

"Oh, that's not necessary, Mr. Griggs. Really. The bus is quite convenient for me. Thank you for the offer." She smiled as best she could and moved past him toward the doorway and the railing beyond, the blood boiling beneath her skin and her breath coming in sharp, short gasps.

"Tell Bobby I said hello then will you?"

Mrs. Foves waved back at him in a way she believed would be taken as agreement, as if to say that she would give "Bobby" the message the very next time she saw him. But she was running hard now and by the time she extended a backwards-flailing arm to Artie Griggs, she was already half way down the stairs, sinking into Carlyle's ocean and well out of sight.

———

The tears came in torrents, but only once she was home again, with the door safely closed and locked. Hysteria rose in her throat like an acid bile and she felt as though she was choking and that her home was becoming smaller and smaller. She felt exactly as she had, three years before, upon opening her door to a bright blue sky glimmering at the backs of two sober young men, there, suddenly, in their perfect uniforms, to anoint the new widow.

She paced the rooms, mostly, like a beast in a cage, covering her face with her hands as she walked, sitting every so often on the bed, or at the dining room table and once in the sitting room, in Robert's chair, trying to get a sense of him for comfort, for continuity. She groped blindly for him, for even the smallest, inconsequential memory. His voice. His scent. Even his scolding.

But he was truly gone from her and she no longer felt him anywhere beneath her existence. She felt every bit the desperate flailing form she had imagined drowning in the violent seas of a Carlyle painting, the ship suddenly gone and all the world a watery grave. How easy for a god to save the fallen, she thought again. To reach out and pluck the lost and drowning from the pitch. But if we have imagined our gods, if we have merely deified our wishes like so many golden coins in a lonely hilltop well, do the gods not drown along with us?

Mrs. Foves could not bring herself to eat or to drink, and when she was exhausted from pacing, she collapsed in a heap at the dining table, sobbing into her arms. When she looked up, she was staring at the bottle of pills she had set out for herself that morning. Next to the bottle sat the single pill that was to be her evening medication; the pill that was promised to hold at bay the very despair and anxiety that now engulfed her like an ocean engulfs a granule of sand. Behind the pills loomed her arrangement of dried lilies, still and composed in its perfection.

An hour passed before she rose from the table. Unscrewing cap from bottle, she held the collection pills aloft, level with her lips, and without any ceremony or hesitation, she poured them all into the heart of the thatch of dried flowers, then smashing the bottle against the wall.

That night, sleep did not come easily and did not stay long. When sleep did come, it came like a wild beast from the woods moving cautiously and only as the campfire dwindled into darkness.

She found herself back in the museum, moving along the polished floor, which seemed to flow from gallery to gallery like a river of wood, as her heels made sounds like the knocking of stones beneath the water. The security guard, his blackness wrapped in whiteness, walked behind her, and then with her, his hand in her hand.

At the table sat the impeccably dressed man in the white beard and the brilliant blue tie flowing from his neck down his chest like a river through a valley of green silk. Delia May sat next to him, sleeves rolled up, smoking a cigarette rolled from a dollar bill, one arm draped over a chair, naked beneath the table. On the table was a blue ceramic bowl filled with large red fruit.

The security guard let go of her hand, sank to his knees, and crawled under the table where he curled up into black ball at the feet of the man, who reached down and patted the head of what had suddenly become a large black wolf.

Bonsoir, père, said Mrs. Foves upon entering, not because he was her father, but because he felt like her father.

Good evening, said the man. Delia blew her a smoke ring with a kiss in the center. They both looked at her expectantly. She turned to study the wall above the buffet, discovering it to be a soft pink.

Où est Icarus? she asked.

Icarus is gone, said the man. *Drowned in the sea.*

Et n'y a-t-il ne plus rien?

Is there nothing left? asked the man incredulously. Delia May shook her head and laughed to herself. *She does not know her Bruegel,* she said with a blue funnel of smoke, and the man nodded.

My dear, he said to her. *This is your spring. You are too young. You are burning inside.*

She looked again at the wall that towered above the little buffet. The soft blush had become a backdrop for an undulation of blue ink, folding like a silk ribbon into the shape of a nude woman, her legs a tangle of flesh beneath a firm feminine form, rising up along the wall, the breast flowing forward to graze the rising thigh, one arm extended and folded back upon itself, elbow out, so that fingers might submerge themselves into the blue river of hair.

Icarus was gone. And everything was left. *Everything.*

Delia was laughing now. The man lifted Delia's hand from the back of the chair and brought it to his lips, kissing it with appreciation, and she stroked his beard. The bowl of fruit began to overflow; a stream of crimson juice traversing the table, then spilling over the edge, down to the floor into a pool of flame. The wolf lapped at the puddle contentedly.

The man turned his blazing eyes upon Mrs. Foves, and they danced and flickered, reflecting some unseen fire that must have been raging within her the whole time.

"Burn, Amelie," he said softly, patting his black beast on the head. "Burn!"

———

When she woke it was still dark and the world beyond her bedroom window was suspended in its slow, dewy gloom. She propped herself up against the headboard and stared at the clock on the wall until the darkness parted enough for her to be able to make out the time. It was just after three-thirty in the morning.

If she had been dreaming, she did not know it. She knew only that she did not feel like she had been sleeping and that the act of waking was one born of distraction: an act of shifting attention from one thing to another. While it was still very early in the morning she did not feel tired, nor did she have any compulsion to go back to sleep.

Not that she felt at all good or refreshed. He eyes were swollen and raw and her head throbbed from the hours of hysterics that preceded her collapse into bed. She sat in the dark and listened to her own breath and felt the weight of being alone. She remembered the museum on the hill and the portraits of soldiers and Artie Griggs and then, in quick succession, his Bobby, and her Robert, and she felt another flood of anxiety, seeping in through the cracks of her understanding, filling her up like dark water in the leaky hull of a Carlyle ship. Her impulse was to take one of Dr. Gleason's chalky-white pills. It would soon be a full twenty-four hours since she had "eased her nerves" as he was fond of saying to her over his glasses as he scribbled out a prescription.

She could not remember ever having gone a full twenty-four hours.

But as quickly as the impulse arrived, it dissipated, and to her own surprise she thought that if the hysteria came to take her, then it could have her. It could carry her away over its shoulder as she screamed and shrieked and wailed into the night. She would not be fishing pills out of an arrangement of dead lilies.

Robert Foves, the consummate soldier and husband, looked at her soberly through the dark from his oval frame on the nightstand. Her own sketch of him from a photograph. Her own sketch of him from a memory. She thought of him falling; drifting limply through the hot dark air, his heart bleeding freely into the night, until he dipped into the silky black Rhone. She wondered, again, whether he had still been alive when the water touched his face – whether the gods could have plucked him from the river and laid him on the bank. She picked him up in her hand, holding the frame between her fingers, and brought him to her, pressing him against her chest and weeping for the last time.

Eventually she rose and showered, scrubbing her body clean of the previous day. She toweled off and, rather than warming the iron and considering what she should wear to the office, she brushed out her hair to its full length, pulled her night gown back on, and set immediately to work.

When the sun first began to show itself, she took a break to have some juice and a soft-boiled egg and a piece of toast. She settled in the sitting room, watching the morning light slowly blaze its way up the draperies. The spaniel up the street loosed a long series of singular barks out over the neighborhood, announcing rather matter-of-factly that he had again survived the night and had resumed his post in the yard. The sounds of Michael Clancy emerging into the morning were the same as always; a snippet of conversation with Eunice, severed by a car door and followed by an engine coming to life and becoming smaller and smaller until it disappeared entirely.

She finished her glass of juice and laid the long silver spoon down on the plate next to the eggcup. She started to rise but then remembered. She smiled a little and resettled herself and waited.

It came soon enough.

"G'monin' Miz Clancy!"

The milk bottles clanked against each other on the stoop next door as Tom Douglas gave three light sharp knocks. She could hear his whistling now as he crossed the yard. She could hear him pause to readjust his load, and then picked up the tune again. He set down a single bottle of milk at her door and knocked three times.

"G'monin' Miz Foves!"

She opened the door almost before her name had left his lips.

"Oh!" said Tom Douglas, looking surprised. "Well, good monin' there Miz Foves. I don't mean to disturb. I just…"

"Good morning, Mr. Douglas. You're not disturbing me."

"Aw, now, you can call me Bo, Miz Foves; you know that."

"And you can call me Emily, Bo."

"Emily?"

"That's my name, Bo. Emily. Why don't you come inside?"

"Inside? Well… I just making my rounds Miz… Emily. I don't mean to disturb or get you up with your night clothes still on and all. I …" He shifted uncomfortably on his feet and readjusted his grip on the two gray wooden crates, hanging by wide leather straps under each arm that were full of bottles. Half of each crate contained bottles of milk, the other half empties. The bottles, full and empty, were evenly distributed within each crate so as to keep the load even.

"Come inside, Bo. Set those things down a moment. I have something for you. Close the door."

Emily turned on her heels and headed off towards the hallway she had paced so many times the previous night. Tom Douglas came in behind her and closed the door, standing awkwardly in the entry with his empty arms and wide, unburdened shoulders and his large black boots.

"Have a seat, Bo, I'll be right out." Emily opened the door to the storage closet and began to rummage, first near the opening and then back among the shelves where the dust was old and long settled.

"You plannin' on takin' you a trip, Miz Emily?" he called out to her from the sitting room.

"Yes, Bo, I am. That's very observant."

"Ma'am, thas about the biggest suitcase I ever seen in my live long days. Ain't nothing special 'bout noticin' a thing like that. Where you off to Miz Foves?"

"Emily," she called out from the bowels of the closet.

"Sorry. Where you off to Miz Emily? That is, if you don't mind me askin'."

"I have friend in Florida. I'm going off to see her for a little while."

"Flo'da. I been there a time. Yes, Ma'am. Thas a fine place, Flo'da. It sho is, Emily. You gon' have a *grand* time. I won't bring you no eggs and no milk then 'til you come back." After a minute of nervous silence, he added, "Gon' be another hot one today. Can already smell the dust in the air. Gon' be real hot."

Emily reappeared from the hallway to find Tom Douglas, all five foot eleven inches of him, midnight skin wrapped in his starched white delivery uniform, sitting carefully on the edge of what she had always thought of as Robert's chair. Her heart skipped one beat; and then resumed.

"My husband used to say that," she said. "About the dust, I mean."

He stood quickly at attention when he saw her and then bashfully averted his eyes. She was barefoot and still wearing her nightgown, which, while not especially revealing or immodest, it was quite obviously the only thing she was wearing.

"My daddy telled me that," he said to the floor, "'bout the dust. When I was a boy he told me that all the time."

"I'm going away for awhile, Bo. I may not be back for a long time. I may never be back. And when I think of this place, I will think of you. I will think of you coming to my home every morning and singing out my name like you do; and no matter what happens to me, you bring me a song in your heart and a bottle of milk and a new day. What a beautiful thing to bring someone, Bo – a new day."

Tom Douglas was blushing mightily now; not that she could see it in his face, but she could feel it in the room.

"Now... I just doin' my job, Miz Emily. You know that."

She walked over to him and gave to him what she had excavated from the closet. He took it carefully in his hands, almost as if she had handed him an infant.

"I want you to have this. I painted it a long time ago. Won an award too. It's called *Still Life of a Pomegranate.*"

Tom Douglas took a moment before he could find words to speak. "My, Miz Emily, this sho is a pretty pichure. My, but it sho is pretty. You done this yo-sef?"

"I did, Bo. I'm an artist. That's what I do. Do you know what a still life is?"

"No, ma'am. I don't know what that is?"

"Do you know what a pomegranate is?"

"No, ma'am." He looked at her worriedly and confused, and then, with a wincing and hopeful look, he pointed to the canvas. "*That* a pomegranate, huh?"

Emily laughed and nodded and Tom Douglas laughed too. His eyes widened in relief and delight and his expression seemed to break open into shafts of daylight. Looking at him, she felt a welling up inside of her. A welling of something ancient and forbidden and lost that hurt her chest so much she thought she was having a heart attack, as though her ribcage was an old wooden boat, finally crushed by the beautiful sea, splintering into a thousand pieces that were determined to float, spreading out across the surface of the water rather than sinking to its bottom in that old, familiar shape.

It occurred to her that not taking those pills might just kill her.

She erupted in another swell of laughter and Tom Douglas laughed back at her even harder and she back at him and so it went until she remembered. She remembered the feeling of joy. She remembered the gratitude of the living.

The laughter gradually began to subside, but before it was gone entirely, Emily stepped in and stood on her toes and brought her lips to his, pulling Tom Douglas down to her gently with the palms of her hands. The buttons of his uniform pulled at the thin cloth of her night-gown. She closed her eyes and let him soak into her like spring rain into the desert riverbeds. The feel of his skin. The pungent smell of the farm. The sound of his heavy breath escaping. The solidity of his presence. All of it, soaking into her in an instant. In the space of a memory.

She withdrew from him, slowly, releasing him to his full height, but leaving the tips of her fingers on his mouth as the curtains behind him now blazed in the glory of full sun. His eyes were wide and he clutched the painting between their bodies with such force that the frame might have broken had the moment lasted any longer.

"Thank you, Bo. Thank you for this new day. I will not forget this feeling ever again."

———

That night, Tom Douglas sat in his home, a two room cottage his father had left him that sat only three miles from the northwest corner of the Yulecrest Dairy Farm. It had been a hot day again, just as his father and the husband of Emily Foves might have predicted. In the late afternoon a slight breeze had picked up from the east, closing the sensory gap between his home and his employer so effectively that he might as well have been living out in the pasture among the cows.

The radio was on and he was listening to *Chicago Big Band Swing*, which he usually liked to hear while he worked on his carving at the dining table after he had eaten his food and before bed. There was also *Captain Midnight* and *The Green Hornet*, when he couldn't sleep. He could read some things, but not very well. And since he did not have a family, the radio kept him from talking to himself and, in that sense, it was a valuable check on the creeping threat of insanity.

That and the carving. There was lots of good carving wood he picked up on the walk to and from work each day, and which he put into an old blue and white cloth laundry sack that he stored in the back of the delivery truck while he was working. He owned three or four different knives he used for carving. He liked to sit out on his porch and sharpen them on a long, gray slab of pumice when the sky darkened and the earth around him seemed to green itself up just knowing that the rain was coming.

He carved farm animals, mostly; lots of cows, and the smaller ones became sheep and goats, and there were hogs and even several chickens that looked more like small pointy lumps than anything that might produce eggs. He had amassed a collection of these animals, numbering some thirty or forty, which he arranged on a long wooden shelf he had installed over the fireplace. The wooden carvings had been conspicuously arranged by species. The cows with the cows, and the chickens with the chickens, and the sheep with the sheep. This, it had originally struck Tom Douglas, was as God intended things. There was no sense in mixing the cows with the chickens or the goats with the hogs.

But Tom Douglas was not working on his carvings tonight, and, although he certainly heard the music just fine, he paid little attention to the radio. Tonight, he sat in his chair and stared at the painting given to him that morning by Ms. Foves – by Ms. *Emily* Foves – who had laughed with him and stood on her perfect pink toes in her very thin nightclothes and kissed him on the lips with her eyes closed and with her hands on his face, and with her long damp hair and her skin smelling like soap.

He had not stopped thinking of those moments, every detail of them, since they had unfolded around him in her sitting room. They had left him restless and agitated.

Not unhappy. No. Not that.

But wanting more.

Of her? Yes, of her.

Yes, of everything. Yes of everyone. Yes of himself. Yes of Life.

Still Life of a Pomegranate, it was called. He had hung it above the shelf of carved farm animals, frozen in their wooden clusters according to divine expectation. A wide, cerulean dinner plate sat in a field of sunlit lilies. On the plate was a large round fruit with a husk the color of mottled fire. A wedge of the fruit had been cut out and removed and was laying on the edge of the plate, revealing an interior that was molten with red juice. No longer contained, the fruit was spilling itself upon the plate. Plump sanguine seeds, translucent in the sunlight, flowed in sticky rivers across and over the lip of the plate and into the field, staining lilies as they went and changing all that they touched. The fruit burned like an enormous liquid sun over the cows and the sheep and the quiet assemblage of still life below.

Tom Douglas sat in his chair and stared in awestruck wonder at the wall above his homemade mantle, not hearing Glen Miller or the Green Hornet, not hearing the crickets in the field, or the owl on the wing, or knowing that the moon had come up over the pasture like a ball of ice, coaxing the earth to give up its heat to the dark air. He stared in restless memory, wanting so much more than he had, feeling only the wild beasts prowling his soul and knowing that he was changed forever.[1]

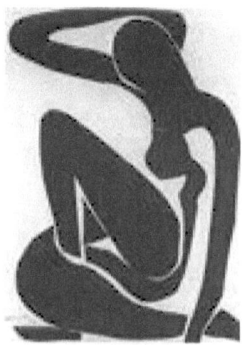

---

[1] An interpretive note to *Still Life* is included at the end of this collection.

Chapter 5

THE NUMBER 6

The kestrel was soft and muscled. It pulled an elastic, membranous string of something visceral from one of its talons, glistening in the new light as it shortened. It made Harlan think of the wet, over-sauced spaghetti Winifred served on Sundays at *The Gravy Boat Inn*, just across the line into Clement County. *The Gravy Boat Inn* was a good ten minutes past the end of Route No. 6.

When the string was gone, the kestrel gave its halting, chirping cry and hopped off the metal roof of the bus barn and floated down onto one of the seven stacks of tires sitting in the dust near the corner of the fence. The kestrel knew, just as Harlan knew, that the rabbit – a little pink eared, brown and white ball of baby fluff – had made for the tires the moment the dark feathered shadow had crossed the yard.

The kestrel would lose this one, Harlan thought, yawning. As long as the rabbit was content to live in those stacks of tires. He stretched and sat up in his seat and scratched his head all over with his fingers.

'Course, the kestrel stood a good chance if the rabbit ever wanted any kind of a life. That was the dilemma for all of God's critters, and it wasn't up to God, it was up to the critter – it was up to the bunny rabbit quivering under the tires what kind of life he wanted. The way Harlan figured, it was only those kind of choices that kept God interested in the first place.

Harlan looked carefully through the open window and around the bus yard, turning his head this way and that to see if the coast was clear. All was quiet except for the kestrel going on and on about the rabbit. Mr. Janicek was certainly not out and about this early, although he would be there soon enough to make sure all of the drivers showed up to work on time. Mr. Janicek was a stickler for his people being on time.

Mr. Janicek liked to show up at the front gate with all of his drivers standing there in a neat line and waiting for him to unlock the padlock and remove the chains and to swing open the iron gate that kept his busses where they belonged over night. Then Mr. Janicek handed out the bus keys, each one wired to a small slab of pine with words "Summit County Bussing" burned into one side and the bus route number burned into the other side. He handed out the keys like he was hand-ing out bibles or gold bars or loaded weapons or the keys to his own house or the keys to city – anything more important or valuable than the ignition keys to the rusted silver tubes that daily rattled the people of Summit County to and from their various affairs. Mr. Janicek drove a clean white car with tail fins and red leather seats.

It might have been a smart system Mr. Janicek had devised. If one of his drivers ever lost a key, the finder would know where to return it, but would not know which particular bus it started, only the route number of the bus to which the key belonged. To steal a bus, a felonious opportunist would have to know that, for instance, the key for "Route 3" started Bus Number Seventeen. The fact that Summit County Bussing Company only owned six operable busses could have only added to the confusion and helped to snuff out criminal impulse before it sparked itself into an action that could not be taken back.

Of course, if the same opportunist was fortunate enough to ride Bus Number Seventeen along Route 3 every day of his life, then there really would be no mystery in matching key to bus, and even less mystery after Mr. Janicek made blue laminated route number signs to hang from the rear view mirrors.

None of this, in any event, applied to Harlan, who, for the entire period of his employment by the Summit County Bussing Company

– had been assigned to drive *Bus* Number Six to and fro, day in and day out, along *Route* Number Six. Should the felonious opportunist of Mr. Janicek's darkest dreams stumble upon the key that he ceremoniously handed to Harlan every morning outside the iron gate, then there would be no stopping him.

This all assumed that anyone would want to steal a bus in the first place, something that Harlan could never quite fathom.

He slid the window closed until he felt the latch click. Then he bent himself in half at the waist and leaned sideways, reaching under the seat for the sack that contained his personals. He pulled the sack up next to him on the seat and fished out the beech wood frame with a mirror in it that used to belong to his mother. The frame, into which had been carved a tangle of vines and flowers and even a small wren on one corner, had a twine attached to it that Harlan looped around the window latch so that the mirror hung where he could see his face.

He could have used the rear-view mirror up at the front of the bus, but that was too risky. The busses were always parked facing the front gate and anyone, like Mr. Janicek, who happened to be around would see him and he would lose his job for sure. So he tended to stay near the back of the bus whenever possible.

He gave himself a good look in the mirror. Because of a twist in the twine, the mirror wanted to turn around into the window and reflect the bus yard outside. Harlan's eyes were red and shot with veins. A pinkish line cut a diagonal path across his cheek where he had pressed up against a hard seam in the seat cushion. He looked tired. But he did not look old. *Older*, and certainly not a young kid any more; but still, not yet *old*. There was still time.

He reached into the sack for his comb and straightened up his hair, smoothing it back in places with fingers that he moistened on his tongue. Fortunately, Harlan's hair was fine and light colored – like baby's hair people told him – and he could go a good two or three days without having to shave. He found some tooth powder and brushed his teeth with his forefinger and then opened the window again and spit out into the yard. He put on his Wednesday shirt, which he saw needed a good washing, and then he took it off again and stuffed it back in the bag and swapped it for his Thursday shirt, which was torn at the bottom but which Harlan thought looked much better.

And smelled better.

He stood and stretched and looked cautiously out the windows on all sides. In a quick sequence of movements that he could have performed with his eyes closed, Harlan removed the plank of wood that he used to connect the back two seats of the bus into a makeshift bed that accommodated his entire length. He slid the plank beneath the seats and up against the back wall of the bus where it was difficult to see. He fastened up his britches, belted them, pulled a reasonably fresh pair of socks out of the bag, put them on and then laced up his shoes.

Kneeling in the aisle, Harlan lifted up a flap of vinyl in the edge of the seat where it had come loose from the seam. He stuck his hand into the slit all the way up to his shoulder and fished around for a moment until he pulled out a small bottle of whiskey.

But whiskey was not what he had been looking for and he shoved it back into the shredded foam padding. He fished a bit more until he found the paper bag of dollar bills. Looking over his shoulder, Harlan carefully extracted the bag and dumped the bills into a pile on the seat. He scooped the pile of paper into a neat stack and then counted the bills out in a slow whisper.

One hundred and twenty-three dollars. Same amount as yesterday morning, which he knew would be the case. But still. One hundred twenty-three. And that amount would go up to one hundred and twenty *eight* dollars by the end of the week when he got paid. Harlan wanted to be able to remember back to the days when he only had one hundred and twenty three dollars, just like how he now liked to remember back to the days when he only had one hundred and eighteen dollars, and so on.

Harlan knew he would need a lot more than the tidy sum stacked on the seat like a column of dried leaves. Good farmland was not cheap and three and a half acres was more than he had any right to think was even possible. But it was already one hundred and twenty-three dollars more possible than it had been this time five years ago.

Of course, Harlan had made some foolish bargains between then and now, like the guitar with a glued-on neck, and the wrist watch that lasted almost three weeks before he traded it plus fifteen dollars for a bicycle with a weak front rim and brakes that ceased to function only after the seller had vanished into thin air. He had also played many a game of five-card stud down in the back room at Murphy's where the regulars were always generous with their drinks and friendly in lightening his load.

But, in spite of these and other misadventures, Harlan had forced himself to save his earnings. Week after week. Month after month. Year after year. To that greater end and with a nightly ritual of counting in the dark, he had sacrificed many an indulgence. At least the way Harlan kept score, his saving streak had now almost lasted longer than his losing streak and he was determined to own a piece of the earth that would sustain him. A piece of earth that no one could ever take away.

There was a fluffing of air outside. Harlan looked and saw the kestrel repositioning himself atop the tires, hopping about and twisting his head.

Three and a half acres was certainly more than his father had ever owned. Though, to be fair, there was no telling what his father might have been able to buy if he could have kept working and saving. They might have owned a great deal more than that tiny plot of land – two acres and a quarter of good farming soil that Harlan knew by the square inch in his memory – had it not been for the fever. His father had said that if the fever was the devil setting the righteous and god-fearing afire in their own skin, then it was the bank paying the devil's wages.

Taking up residence in the same bus he drove for a working wage had helped Harlan's savings plan immensely. It was not the only place he lived, of course. He could always stay at Henry Skolpot's place for maybe a week, or at least until Henry's wife got fed up and told Henry to tell Harlan to leave.

But he had not been back to Henry Skolpot's for a long time. Not since the oldest daughter and one of her friends had made fun of his walk. Harlan had stepped outside one morning to bring in the newspaper and the milk as the two girls were leaving for school. He was wearing his short pants that morning and so his leg was fully visible. They had gawked and giggled inside their hands and then scampered off whispering and giggling some more.

His bones just didn't fit quite right at the knee. They never had fit right, like one of them had belonged to someone else. Someone taller. Actually seeing the bones moving disjointedly like that beneath his skin just made his limp all the more dramatic.

Harlan often told himself that his leg had probably saved his life because it had kept him out of the war. The Army was just not interested. Sometimes knowing that he owed his life to his twisted leg made him feel better. But not always. Had he known the Skolpot girl and her friend were around, he would have worn his long pants. He should have worn long pants. Or he should have just not walked around like no one else would be outside to see him.

That was one benefit of driving a bus for a living; no one was the wiser when he was sitting behind the wheel of the Number Six.

Sometimes Lucy Walton's Boarding House let him have one of the back rooms when he cleaned things up for her in the fall and spring, but that was never for more than a night and Lucy Walton was getting more demanding and less and less appreciative in her old age. Whatever benefit there had once been to Lucy's schoolgirl friendship with Harlan's mother had long since been tapped dry. Sometimes he even paid to stay at the boarding house as a guest, and even though on such occasions he made it clear to Lucy Walton that he expected to be treated as a paying customer, she still treated him like an employee who owed her a favor. And, despite himself, he acted like one.

Bus Number Six was by far his favorite shelter, at least when it was not winter and so cold out that he needed a fire to stay warm. Aside from the fact that sleeping in the bus was an illegal trespass and that every moment of his occupancy threatened his very livelihood and reputation, it did not require Harlan to accommodate the interests, demands, needs or considerations of any other person in the world. The bus yard was only an hour's walk from town and Harlan came and went as he pleased after nightfall, although as carefully and quietly as he could. He could, and often did, sleep naked on the bus without any concern of offending someone like Elizabeth Skolpot or Lucy Walton or Lucy Walton's boarders when he got up to relieve his bladder in the middle of the night. Furthermore, possession and consumption of strong drink or tobacco was never a problem in the bus and, for that matter, Harlan was free to be his own man in every respect.

When it rained hard in the summer, Harlan liked to lay on the seat in the back of the Number Six and imagine that he was still a young boy back home only two counties to the south lying in his bed beneath the tin roof that made drops of water sound like arrows of stone that had arched earthward through the heavens from the great bow of Sagittarius, while his father did his carving and smoked in his chair and his mother quilted as she sang her hymns. He also liked to read when it rained at night, or when he had trouble sleeping. He made it a point to keep a flashlight in his bag and a book or two that he had not read in a while, usually a Garrett Webb mystery novel starring Jack McMannis, private eye.

When the night sky was clear, Harlan liked to prop his head up against the side of the bus and drink a little whiskey and sing songs to himself and stare out at the stars through the bank of open windows across from him. He made up his own star shapes, his favorites being the dog with the cigar and the upside-down boat and the giant haystack with feet. There were many others and Harlan tried to remember them and to find them the next night. But he mostly just made up new shapes since the daylight seemed to wash in like a wave over the dark sky and mix everything up while he was busy scattering people around Summit County, as though the stars were little shiny trinkets that the day had scattered across a black beach.

He had never actually seen the seashore, a place where a great ocean washed up over the earth. Neither had his parents, for that matter. But that was still how he liked to think of his days: enormous bright waves that scattered new glittery things on the beach of creation for him to look at and admire and to turn over and over in his mind until his lids grew heavy like pockets too full from beach combing. And only when Harlan was so tired from the day, or so mellowed by the whiskey that he felt himself drifting into dream, did he put the bottle away, roll over, and fall asleep to the sound of crickets.

So it was mostly the roof of the Number Six over his head at night. Harlan did not, at any rate, have to pay room and board to his Uncle Del. In light of his parent's untimely demise, Harlan's aunt and uncle had felt obliged to offer him a room under their own roof. But – as Uncle Del was always quick to note – ain't nothin' in this world for free.

Uncle Del's *pay-to-stay* rule had come down hard on Harlan's seventeenth birthday. The *pay-to-stay* rule marked a dramatic change from the unwritten *play-to-stay* rule that had characterized Harlan's previous six years with Uncle Del. Del's wife, Aunt Frieda, was a frail stick of a woman put on this earth to do what Del damn-well told her to do, which certainly included staying out of his way when he took a drink, which was often, and to go work in the field or the barn when Del wanted to *educate* his nephew about things she wouldn't understand.

It was a *man thing*, Del often told her. And it certainly was a man thing, although Harlan was nowhere close to being a man at the time.

By the time Harlan had reached age seventeen, Uncle Del had lost the coercive influence he had once enjoyed over his nephew. The cost of Harlan's room and board was thereafter three dollars a week. For the ensuing thirteen years, Harlan had lived with his aunt and uncle only sporadically, when there were no other alternatives. On those few occasions, Harlan had been polite and appreciative to his Aunt Frieda and avoided all but the most trivial of interactions with his Uncle Del, unless one counts as more than trivial the three occasions in those thirteen years that Harlan found to beat his drunken uncle senseless with his fists, making it abundantly clear that *play-to-stay* was no longer a rule Harlan cared to observe.

Del and Frieda allowed Harlan to store his clothes and some keepsakes from his parents without charge or complaint. Harlan was, after all, family.

Harlan put the money back in the bag and then folded the bag tightly around the stack of bills like a skin. He stuffed the bag into the seat with the whiskey where, he had decided, it was much safer than in the burlap bag with his tooth cleaning powder and clothing. A bag can be stolen or misplaced, but not a bus and not a piece of land, except maybe by a bank and the devil, but Harlan would just have to take his chances there.

He untied the mirror and returned it to the sack and then tied the top of the sack into a loose knot. He walked carefully to the front of the bus and looked out of the windshield. Nearly a quarter of the sun was above the eastern horizon where the corn looked like a million tongues of green flame in the distance, and the wheat like wisps of feathered bullion. The smell of the dust was already in the air. It would be another hot one today, he thought, tucking his bag down in the corner between the driver's seat and the side of the bus. He took a last look around to make sure he had not forgotten anything. Satisfied that all was in order, he pulled the silver handle next to the gearshift, opening the doors just enough to allow him to slip through and hobble out into the morning.

Once he was outside, Harlan did not waste his time. Any place outside the shelter of the bus, and inside the locked bus yard was dangerous for there would be no acceptable explanation he could offer. He walked quickly, with long purposeful if uneven strides, through the back of the tin-roofed bus barn to the far north end of the property. There, where the fencing had come free of its post, Harlan slipped through the opening and walked through the adjoining field, wading though the milo until he reached the split rail fence and the dirt road on the other side. The dirt road eventually met up with the two-lane paved road. Setting foot on the paved road meant that he had made it to safety again and that he could relax.

So he did. Harlan slipped his hands into his pockets and whistled *Go Tell It On The Mountain* as he limped his way up the road up to the locked front gate of the Summit County Bussing Company storage yard. He leaned up against the front post beneath the *No Trespassing* sign and looked out at the sun climbing up over fields of green flame and the hardwood clusters that seemed to spray out of the ground here and there off in the distance. He pulled a lighter and a pack of cigarettes out of his pocket and had a good long smoke as he waited for the other drivers and, ultimately, for Mr. Janicek to hand him the key to the Number Six.

———

Built in 1940, the Number Six was the only TD-5401 model ever made by the Yellow Coach Company, which tended to limit its bus lengths to the twenty-five to thirty-five foot range, at least until General Motors gobbled up Yellow Coach in 1943 and changed the designs. Of all the busses servicing the whole of Summit County, the Number Six was the largest at forty-one and a half feet long and ninety-six inches wide. It was a two-toned beauty, silver with a wide blue band beneath the windows that swooped up in the back like the wings of a jay. The Number Six had a low, powerful growl that came from a Detroit Diesel 6-71 inline six-cylinder engine. Fully loaded, at a speed of between twenty and thirty miles per hour, particularly on an incline like on the Nightingale Boulevard loop around the museum, you could hear the Number Six coming two and a half blocks away. All of Summit County knew the voice of the Number Six. Harlan knew it had served Detroit and then Chicago before coming all the way over to Summit County, although he had no idea of just how anyone, including Mr. Janicek in particular, comes to acquire something like a bus.

It was entirely appropriate for the Number Six, as the longest bus in the fleet, to serve Route No. 6, which was the longest route serviced by the Summit County Bussing Company, stretching from the borders of Deer County to the West, Fulton County to the North, and within six miles of the Clement County line to the South. Harlan had come to think of the route as kind of like a long-legged spider with stretches of empty road threading between the unending miles of dusty, sunbaked, silo-dotted crop land toward the center of the county, gathering people along the way, one and two at a time; then in past the slaughterhouse and the grazing fields and the dairy farms where the air was thick and musty with livestock and where he picked up the fares three and four at a time; and then across the Cleatchee River and in through the outer neighborhoods and the school grounds where the cars were clean and the people waited on neatly sidewalked street corners in groups of five or six and where ladies wore dresses and the men wore their hats and ties; and, finally, looping into the city itself – the small body of the spider – where, over the course of four stops, the Number Six Bus disgorged most of its load and headed back out along another spindly leg toward a different neighboring county.

He stopped at the corner of *Macomb* and *Nellis* and four people climbed on and paid the fare and found their way to their seats. He knew all of them and none of them. That is, Harlan saw each of them almost every day, and he greeted them like friends with a hearty *good morning* or a genial nod of his head, and they each in their own way returned the greeting, but he knew none of their names, nor anything about them. To pass the time as he drove, Harlan liked to single out people in his rear view mirror and imagine things about their lives, like why they were going into the city and how they earned their money and what they liked to do in the evenings and what they wanted most that they didn't have.

The third person of the four at *Macomb* and *Nellis* was a young and lovely woman who was usually dressed, in Harlan's opinion, too old for her age. Her hair was up and she wore a dress with a knitted shawl about her shoulders that was surely too warm for the day that was coming. She smiled and said good morning as she paid the fare and Harlan smiled back and said good day and told her that she looked lovely. She smiled with her sweet kind of sadness and moved past him to her seat halfway back near the window. Harlan could see the men on the bus watching her, tipping their hats and nodding their heads as they always did as she passed them.

Harlan had long since decided that this woman was a nurse who worked out at the hospital and who changed into a bright white uniform with white stockings and a white hat when she got to work and that her job was looking after people who were so sick they often never got better and died. That accounted for the sadness, he thought. She wore a ring on her wedding finger, but she did not seem to Harlan to be a happily married woman. He could not decide whether she was married to someone who did not love her – which Harlan found difficult to imagine given her attractiveness and sweetness of disposition – or whether she was widowed. He decided that she was widowed and that her husband had been killed in the war and he felt sorry for her. Sometimes Harlan worried that she might mistake his friendly greeting or his compliments as an invitation of the same kind offered by the other men on the bus with their looks and their hat tipping. It was certainly not an invitation of any sort and he had never thought of her in that way.

The woman – his widowed nurse – always disembarked, appropriately enough, at the end of *Nightingale Boulevard*. She did so again today with a soft smile and a timid wave as she stepped down onto the sunlit pavement and looked up the hill towards the museum.

Harlan waited before closing the doors after her. He stood up and craned his neck around the bus, looking for Christopher out of the windows on all sides. When he spotted him on the run towards the corner, Harlan sat down again. He eyed the back of the bus in the rearview mirror and was pleased to see that no one was sitting in the last row in the seat that held his whiskey and his one hundred and twenty three dollar bills. People rarely sat that far back, and even when they did no one ever seemed to sense that there was anything other than yellow foam stuffed into the seat. But it was always a relief just the same.

Christopher Dupree lived with his cousin in a house one and a half blocks from the *Nightingale Boulevard* stop and each morning he waited to come running until he saw the bus pass his front porch. Harlan always stood up to see if he was coming and within seconds of standing, he could pick out Christopher rounding the giant pin oak a block behind the bus, his arms and legs moving with such a fluid, graceful rhythm that some days Harlan remained standing and pretended to still be searching for him as he watched him gliding up the street towards the bus.

Christopher Dupree leapt in through the doors with his usual broad smile and pale, sky blue eyes breathing heavily through even rows of the whitest teeth Harlan had ever seen. Harlan pretended to be concentrating on the widowed nurse who was still on the corner looking up the hill at the museum.

"Good mornin' Harlan, ol' boy!" said Christopher, clapping a hand around the back of Harlan's neck. "How you doin' this glorious mornin'?"

"Mornin' Christopher," said Harlan rather flatly.

Christopher paid his fare and took his usual seat directly behind the driver. Harlan glanced in his mirror in time to see some of the men he had picked up at Granger Meadows looking at Christopher and then looking at each other sideways and shaking their heads.

They all knew about Christopher Dupree and so did Harlan, although Harlan pretended he didn't know anything except where he was going next.

"Almost missed it this time," said Harlan, closing the door and heading up the hill.

"I always make it, Harlan," said Christopher in a playful way. "You know I do."

"Only because I wait for you."

"You're a good soul, Harlan Buck," said Christopher. "You truly are. Thank you for your kindness. I am much obliged."

"Aww, now stop it," said Harlan in a voice meant to suggest annoyance. "You just try to be on time. One of these days I'm just going to pull off without you and you're just gonna have to hoof it to the prison."

Christopher Dupree always smelled clean, like he'd spent his morning soaking in a tub of alfalfa soapsuds. He had high apple cheeks and fine, shiny hair like Harlan's, only it was darker and long enough that it took the wind when he ran.

"That's too far, Harlan. I'd die and the hawks'd swoop in and pick me clean on the road in a quick minute. You know that."

"Damn right it's too far. So be on time."

"You'd never leave without me, Harlan. You're too good a soul."

"You just be on time."

"You can't be cross with me today, Harlan Buck. Not today."

Harlan looked at him in the mirror. "Oh yeah? Why's that exactly?"

"'Cause today is my birthday, that's why."

"Everyday is somebody's birthday and everyday somebody walks to work."

"You're too good a soul. You don't fool me one little bit."

Harlan drove up the hill that looped around the museum and headed back up *Nightingale* the way he had come. He turned west on *Montgomery* from which he would pick up a different leg of the spidery Route No. 6 and head back out of town for the sparseness of the country roads that led toward Fulton County where they still worked the quarry that his grandfather had worked when he was a boy.

Next, Harlan stopped on the corner of *Clyde* and *Winslow* across from the barber shop and right in front of *Bubba Z's Shoe Shine Stand* with Bubba, who was so black he was darker than his best work and who looked all of one hundred and fifty years old, still hanging out his rags and doing his little shuffle and bidding people good morning. Harlan opened the doors and emptied most of the Number Six onto the sidewalk. Keeping their seats were Christopher Dupree and an older couple off on their weekly visit to kin living somewhere up near Black Hills.

The men in hats, who had looked at each other sideways when Christopher Dupree boarded, took another long look at him as they passed, tipped their hats to Harlan and stepped off the bus directly into the charms of Bubba Z who slipped as easily into his sing-song sales pitch as if it was a pair of loafers.

"Well, good mawnin! Good mawnin, Mista Sir! And to you too, Mista Sir! Lookin' right fine this mawnin'. I gots you a shine an a smoke to start the day so's you start it off with a shiny step. It's a spanky shine, Mista Sir!"

The men paused in the doorway as if considering the offer.

"Have a nice day there, gents," said Christopher Dupree at their backs in a loud, sweet voice. The men did not respond and continued on their way up the street.

Harlan thought to himself that it would be wise for Christopher to know his place and to not pop off to such men lest they take it personally and get the notion to show him what's what. But Christopher never seemed to care about restraining himself, even though Harlan knew he had already paid the price for such an outgoing nature.

Six men and a woman climbed onto the bus and paid their fares and found their seats; the woman two rows behind Christopher, four of the men about mid-bus across from each other, and the other two, to Harlan's consternation, all the way in the back, on the seat where he stored his liquor and his bag of dollar bills. Harlan eyed them in the mirror and wondered whether it would be better to keep his savings with him up front in his sack after all.

They were youngish men, temporary field workers he guessed on account of their clothes and the old dirt on their hands, and they each carried lunch pales, one gray and one black. The men sat down roughly with their pales on their laps and talked amongst themselves in low tones and pointed at things outside the window. They did not seem to think there was any reason to be concerned about the seat, so Harlan forced himself to put them out of his mind.

Harlan closed the doors, and pushed the Number Six slowly up *Donner Street*, rolling past the six huge maples that were like an iron fence protecting the county courthouse, which had its own tall white columns right in front of the doors. The maples and the white columns, like a double protective fence, coming as they did when Harlan was thinking about Christopher and the price he paid for his out-going nature, made Harlan think about the prison.

"You like working at that prison?" Harlan asked over his shoulder.

"I like it alright," he said. "You like driving the Number Six?"

"It's a living, I guess," said Harlan with a shrug. "Rather drive the Number Six than any of the others. What sort of work they give you out there?"

"Bit of everything. I clean. Help in the kitchen. Help in the laundry. Mostly I do what Warden Mopes needs done."

"Thought the prisoners do all that."

"Some of it. But Warden Mopes don't trust convicts. I help him in his office, see. Convicts ain't allowed back there. Warden Mopes calls them the filthy animals."

"Are they?"

"Just plain folks to me, I guess. Like anyone else." Christopher Dupree smiled and shrugged his shoulders and his eyes were like pieces of cloudless sky. "But Warden Mopes is a man of God. He likes things *extra* clean, see."

"Does he look after you? The warden?"

"I 'spose he does."

"'Cause I remember a time not too far back, you come on this bus and you look like…"

"Convicts don't hurt me none," he said, cutting Harlan off. "Not any more anyway. Not for a while. On account of me working for Warden Mopes."

Christopher Dupree turned and looked out the window and for awhile he and Harlan rode in silence as they re-crossed the Cleatchee and as the tidy, well-kept neighborhoods surrounding the town gave way again to open fields and the sweet and the pungent smells of the country. The rest of the bus was also quiet except for the two lunch pale men in the back – Mr. Black and Mr. Gray – who laughed in rough whispers and slapped each other on the leg and pointed at things out the same windows through which Harlan liked to look at the stars.

"I ain't workin' there forever, you know," said Christopher.

"The prison?"

"Yeah, the prison. I ain't working there forever."

"Where you working next, then?"

"Don't know. Some day I'm goin' to California."

"California?" Harlan laughed. "What do you know about California?"

"I know its better'n here. You ever been there?"

"California? No."

"You ever been anyplace other than Summit County?"

Harlan looked at Christopher in the mirror to see if he was talking down to him, but Christopher's face was an open question, as bright as day.

"I've been to lots of counties," Harlan said. He heard Christopher laughing and he looked up in the mirror at him again and then Harlan laughed too.

"Oh yeah," said Christopher, "I been to all kinda counties. I am one well-traveled cuss, Harlan Buck, so you just look out." They both laughed and shook their heads and then, after another minute or so of road, Harlan looked back up into the mirror.

"So tell me about California, then."

Christopher looked at Harlan's reflection and smiled like his whole face might come apart.

"Aw Harlan! It's like a heaven! Just like a heaven! They got beaches that are made of gold powder and…"

Harlan laughed and shook his head.

"No, I know it's *sand*, Harlan. I ain't no turnip off the back of a truck. But what I'm sayin' is that that sand looks and feels like gold powder the way the sun catches it and the way the sweet smellin' breeze stirs it all around at your feet. And the ocean is so blue with its little tufts of white spray as far as the eye can see that it almost makes you want to cry. And it ain't so flat there as it is here, Harlan. It ain't a square and a square and a square like all this out there. In California they got these great green hills that cover the land like the earth is playin' a mimic to the sea. And the people are all real nice and dressed just so and they got culture up the wahzoo 'cause everyone in California is a writer or paints or sings or acts in the pictures. Shoot, Harlan, just about every person living in California is a movie star or personally *knows* a movie star. And they got a picture show on every corner each one showing somethin' different, not just one old dirty barn three counties away where they show the same dumb picture for six solid months."

"Ain't a barn," said Harlan.

"Smells like a barn."

"Yeah, smells like a barn. That's true."

"And just about everybody in California drives their own automobile and those that don't have their own automobile ride in electric open air trolleys where they hang on to the poles with the sun on their faces or they sit in the shade under the roof. You'd probably be a great trolley driver, Harlan. *Hey!*"

Harlan suddenly felt Christopher's hand slap him on the shoulder. Startled, he looked up in the mirror and saw that the woman behind Christopher and the four men behind her had also looked up. Mr. Black and Mr. Gray didn't seem to notice. He looked at Christopher, who was beaming back at him with an expression made for Christmas morning.

"You should come with me, Harlan."

"Ain't goin' to California," said Harlan.

"Why the hell not? You having too good a time here, Mr. Buck?"

This time Christopher *was* talking down to him, though in a playful sort of way, and Harlan gave him a half-hearted glower in the mirror. But before he was done glowering, a question slipped out.

"What kind farming they got in California?"

"Oh, they got all kinds, Harlan. Everything we got here and more, cause the soil is so darn good."

"What's so good about the soil?"

"Rich dark brown soil, the color of coffee. Not this dusty mess. It just moister and sweeter for growin'. You can grow everything in California and twice as much of it."

"How much for a plot of land?"

"Don't know really, but my cousin up in Fulton, my momma's brother's kid, says they practically give it away out there 'cause there's so much of it and they don't got enough farmers to work it. Crops just comin' outta the ground all over and layin' around waitin' to be worked."

"You're cousin been there?"

"No. But he has a best friend who has a daddy that grew up in California and he knows all about it. We should go together, Harlan. You and me. *Come on, now!* You and me!"

"Ain't goin' to California," said Harlan, swatting at the very idea like a fly on a plate.

"Suit yourself," said Christopher, his eyes showing that he understood a lost cause when he saw one. "I'll miss you out there, Harlan. Every time I ride on one of them trolleys I'll grab on to a red pole and swing out into the sun and I will think of my friend back here driving the Number Six."

Harlan swatted at the invisible fly again. "Trolley won't wait for you like I do. You can just bet on that."

When they reached the southwest corner of Swanson's Field, Harlan pulled the bus over and opened the doors. The prison was still a mile to the east, but it was as close as Route 6 reached.

"Guess I'll see you when you get off work then," said Harlan, not looking up. Christopher stood up next to him and Harlan caught another scent of alfalfa.

"Don't know. Warden Mopes just might let me go early on account of it bein' my birthday. He don't know it yet, but I'll find a time to tell him."

"What'ch you gonna do if he does let you go early? Too far to walk and I won't be back this way for another...."

"Warden's got a nice car," said Christopher. He drives me around sometimes. Or I can hitch. Don't you worry 'bout me, Harlan Buck."

Christopher clapped his hand against the back of Harlan's neck and squeezed and shook it a little and then he laughed when Harlan uncomfortably tried to shrug it off. Christopher trailed his fingers off Harlan's shoulder into a wave as he bounded off the Number Six and began running the southern edge of Swanson's Field toward the prison, dust kicking up from his heels and his body like a sapling in the wind.

Harlan watched Christopher Dupree run as he closed the doors and began to push the Number Six on towards the next stop a long ways now up the spider's leg. As the engine growled higher and higher, Harlan watched Christopher disappear behind the corn and, inexplicably, he *did* worry.

———

By the time the Number Six had reached the Fulton County line, it was empty except for Harlan, Mr. Gray and Mr. Black. The two men with the lunch pales did not show any inkling of wanting to leave.

"This here is the end of the line," said Harlan authoritatively, talking up into his mirror. "I'm headed back into town from here. Where can I drop you?"

Mr. Black, who was on the aisle, looked at his fellow traveler and then arranged a polite look on his face.

"We goin' into town, too."

"You just came from there," said Harlan confusedly.

"And now we goin' back," said Mr. Gray, his tone like an iron pipe and his face like a slab of something hauled out of a quarry.

"You givin' us a nice tour of the county this mornin'," said Mr. Black with an amiability almost convincing and that earned him a swift elbow in the ribs.

"You'll have to pay another fare if you stay on past town," said Harlan. "I got rules to follow."

"We ain't got no problems payin' the fare," said Mr. Gray, which made Mr. Black sputter out a laugh. "You just go on and drive your bus."

Harlan thought for a moment about that back seat beneath the two men and then said as friendly as he could, "why don't you boys move on up closer to the front. The ride is much more comfortable up this way. You sittin' right on the back axle."

Mr. Black started to stand, but Mr. Gray pulled him back down.

"We fine right here. Now, you just drive the bus and let us be."

By the time the Number Six crossed the Cleatchee River, it was nearly full again, mostly with a class of school children and their teacher and a chaperone all coming in to learn about the Constitution at the county courthouse. The girls on the bus sang *You Are My Sunshine* and the *Peter Cottontail* song and the boys tried to disrupt them by making animal sounds and making noises with their hands in their armpits which was always good for some laughs and the girls would have to start over. The other passengers on the bus had to raise their voices to be heard over all the singing and the noise-making and by the time the bus rolled by Mrs. Winter's boarding house on *Blackberry Street,* Harlan could barely hear himself think.

Not hearing himself think was not entirely a bad thing, since Harlan was thinking a lot about Christopher Dupree and about the prison and Warden Mopes and about California, and all of that for reasons Harlan did not understand or did not want to understand, made him feel uncomfortable. Just about the time Harlan grew impatient with all the singing and noise for its interference with his thoughts, he was relieved for the interference and so he did nothing to calm everyone down.

When the bus pulled up along side the salon, which was kitty-corner from the courthouse, Harlan pulled the lever and opened the doors and most of the passengers stood up and began to file down the aisle. The children were excited and unruly and the teacher and the chaperone had to call them down and tell them to stop jumping on the seats. The teacher told them in a loud voice to thank the nice bus driver and each of them did so as they passed. Harlan smiled and told each of them that they were very welcome, throwing in a *be good now* and a *have a nice day* every so often.

After the children and the teacher and the chaperone and a few of the other passengers had left, and as new passengers were climbing on and paying their fares, Harlan started to think about how he was going to go about collecting a new fare from Mr. Gray and Mr. Black. He supposed that he would just shout back at them over the commotion and he looked up to do so.

When he did look up, Harlan noticed that they were both different than before, although he could not quite tell just what about them had changed. They were quiet and still, stiff even, like they were made of wax. They did not talk to each other or look out the window. They faced forward, unblinking, watching the new passengers make their way back, but not really *seeing* at them. The last of the new passengers boarded and Harlan pushed the silver handle, closing the doors. He cleared his throat up into the mirror.

"You two gentlemen in the back, I need a new fare. Like I said, rules is rules."

Mr. Gray and Mr. Black looked at each other through the corners of their eyes, but they did not answer. Harlan cleared his throat again.

"I can't let you ride for another..."

A knock on the doors turned Harlan's attention. A man in a mustache and a brown uniform who Harlan knew to be Stacey Lumm, the county sheriff, stood on the other side of the glass, knocking it with the butt of his gun. Over Sheriff Lumm's right shoulder was a large bulldog of a man that Harlan did not know but who was wearing the same uniform as Sheriff Lumm and who also had a gun in his hand and who, therefore, Harlan figured was a deputy. Harlan opened the doors.

"What's your name, son?" asked Sheriff Lumm in a voice so low that Harlan almost could not hear.

"My name?" said Harlan just as low. "My name is Harlan Buck, sir."

"Mr. Buck, my name is Sheriff Lumm and this here is Deputy Cobb. We have a witness who says that two men who may have robbed the grocery last night boarded your bus this morning."

"My bus?"

"The Number Six," said Sheriff Lumm. "You seen anything odd this morning?"

"Odd? No sir. I don't think so."

"Did everyone on this bus just get on?"

"Yes," said Harlan. "Everyone except the two in the very back. They got on my first trip into town. They say they just touring the county. Guess that's a little odd, ain't it?"

Sheriff Lumm stood on the first step of the bus and craned his neck around the inside, then stepped back out onto the street.

"More than just a little odd, Mr. Buck," he said. He put his hand on Deputy Cobb's bulldog shoulder and said something Harlan did not hear. When he was done, he turned back to Harlan.

"Okay, Mr. Buck, we are going to unload this bus, starting with you. Stand up slowly and step down onto street next to Deputy Cobb and then go on over there by the post office. Don't look around, just come on down here with me."

"But I got a schedule…"

"We'll have you on your way soon, Mr. Buck, but this is police business. Come on down here."

Harlan did as he was told and stood next to the bulldog who directed him with a stubby finger up the street a ways to the post office. As he limped forward in his ungainly way, Harlan looked back over his shoulder and could hear Sheriff Lumm asking the passengers to please disembark and something about a mechanical problem and telling them to follow the bus driver to the post office. When he got to the post office, he leaned against the flagpole with his hands behind him and watched.

A line of confused passengers filed off the Number Six and walked up the street towards him. Mr. Black was at end of the line, stepping out into the sun, but Mr. Gray did not emerge.

Deputy Cobb spun Mr. Black around by the shoulders and pushed him against the bus as Sheriff Lumm stepped up inside. Faster than Harlan would have expected was possible, Sheriff Lumm jumped back down onto the street and ran out of view behind the Number Six. Harlan knew right away that Mr. Gray had used the emergency exit or was trying to that very second. There was a call from behind the bus and Deputy Cobb pulled Mr. Black roughly around to the back.

The passengers were all congregated at the flag pole, clucking like upset chickens, and a small crowd, including women in smocks and pink rollers, was knotting up outside the salon directly across from the bus. The sun was high and big and the heat boiled off the street into the air as the starlings and the grackles and the robins hopped around in the elm shade. It was a day like any other day and yet, at the same time, it was a day unlike any other day that any one of them had ever experienced and Harlan wondered if the stars would look different tonight.

Within moments, Sheriff Lumm emerged from behind the bus pulling Mr. Gray by his arm, which had been handcuffed behind his back. Deputy Cobb followed with Mr. Black, who was also handcuffed. Mr. Gray squirmed and Sheriff Lumm gave him a good yank on the handcuffs and he stopped squirming. They marched the men around the corner to the sheriff's office, which was in a two-story brick building directly across the street from the county courthouse.

The passengers asked each other and then asked Harlan what they were supposed to do and whether the Number Six was still in business. Harlan said he didn't know and that all he could do, as their driver, was to wait for the sheriff because he didn't want to upset the law. At that, two of the passengers walked off in a huff.

After a few minutes, Sheriff Lumm reappeared and climbed up into the Number Six. In another minute he was out again, walking up the street towards the post office. In his left hand he held Harlan's sack from beside the driver's seat. He may as well have been holding Harlan's heart because it started beating around in his chest like a frightened rabbit looking for a place to hide. The sheriff stopped some distance from the flagpole, out of earshot of the passengers, and motioned for Harlan to join him.

"This belong to you, Mr. Buck?" he asked Harlan.

Harlan swallowed hard before answering. "Yessir. Those are some clothes and things. Case I need them."

"You know anything about these boys we just took in?"

"No sir."

"This sack doesn't belong to them?"

"No sir."

"You weren't keeping a change of clothes for fugitives?"

"No sir."

"What else is in this sack then?"

"Mirror in a wood frame that was my mother's; and some personals for my teeth and hair and some clothes. Book. Flashlight. Picture of my dad. Picture of my mom. They been dead a long while now."

The sheriff looked at Harlan and then seemed satisfied and handed him the bag.

"Mmm, hmm. Well, I'm sorry to hear that. Where do you live Mr. Buck?"

"Here and there I suppose," said Harlan. Got an uncle and aunt live out past Briar Flats."

"What are their names?"

"Del and Frieda Marks."

"You know anything about stolen money?"

"No sir."

"Any stolen money on that bus?"

"No sir. Least, not as I know of."

"Okay, son. You can be on your way then. Thank you for your cooperation."

Sheriff Lumm slapped Harlan on the shoulder and then pushed past him to tell the passengers that they were free to re-board.

———

Harlan finished up his day as he always did, in an empty bus bumping and rattling along the poorly maintained roads that lay across the invisible line separating Clement County from Summit County. The sun was a mottled blood orange rolling out of a western sky that had long since begun brooding out of its periwinkle youth. The fields were still so hot from the day that they seemed to be glowing behind a palpable translucence that was made of more than just air and vapor, but of some living substance, some diurnal plague, from deep within the molten core of the earth itself.

Ordinarily he turned around several miles before that invisible line passed beneath the wheels of the Number Six. But today was Tuesday, and it was well worth a short detour into Clement County before returning to the bus yard in the dark, even given the distinct possibility that Mr. Janicek would be waiting on him to collect the key.

But Harlan knew it was just as likely that Mr. Janicek would spend any such waiting time relishing time away from Mrs. Janicek, who would not let him drink a single drop of liquor once he returned home. Mrs. Janicek was Born Again – a concept Harlan did not pretend to fully understand, and was very strict about such things.

In any event, on Tuesdays Mr. Janicek often attended a Knights of Columbus meeting out at the Miller farm up on the ridge on the other side of the Cleatchee. That meant Mrs. Janicek expected her husband to arrive home late on Tuesdays, which meant that Mr. Janicek, whether or not there was actually a Knight of Columbus meeting, got to wet his whistle and didn't care so much whether Harlan was a little late returning the Number Six. All of which meant that, on Tuesdays, Harlan got to stop by *The Gravy Boat Inn* six miles into Clement County, the very day of the week that Mrs. Winifred served up her meat loaf and potatoes and biscuits. It was a weekly indulgence that Harlan always found impossible to resist and that the universe had strangely accommodated.

Harlan looked out at the horizon and could see the day withdrawing its wave of light into the great sea of history, slipping away from the black, glittering shores of night. He was good and hungry and he looked forward to his dinner and to his time tonight looking out at the stars with the crickets out in the fields and the invisible owls on the wing in the dark air; for the day had washed up something new and interesting for him to pick up and to hold between his fingers before he went to sleep.

The unwitting transport and subsequent arrest of two bonafide robbers, while initially disconcerting, had become like a small but sharp electric charge in Harlan's veins, giving him a little burst of excitement whenever he thought about it, which had been all day long. Once the passengers who had witnessed the arrests had all disembarked, Harlan had no one with whom to recount the excitement. His efforts to work the event into a conversation with other, unknowing passengers were less than satisfying, forcing him to exaggerate some of the details. At the last telling of the story, both Mr. Black and Mr. Gray had pistols in their belts and Sheriff Lumm – whom Harlan had taken to calling *Ol' Stacey Lumm* – had expressed genuine concern to Harlan that the robbers would try to shoot their way out of the bus or take one or more of the passengers hostage. That version, at least, had really raised some eyebrows.

But then those passengers, inevitably, had also disembarked and he found himself alone again with a bunch of familiar strangers who did not know the story and Harlan would have to think all over again about how to strike up the right conversation while he drove. During one long stretch of the afternoon, when the closest passenger was five seats behind him, he felt like he might just pull over and stand up and turn around and make an announcement to everybody on the Number Six all at once, and to tell them just how it felt to be in the middle of it all.

But Harlan had never been very comfortable talking to more than one person at a time and, fortunately, he now concluded, he had never screwed up the courage to hold court on the side of the road. After all, people had places to be and others were out there waiting in the heat to see the silver mantle of the Number Six rising out of the dust with its blue laminated sign swinging in the window.

Harlan had been disappointed to drive by Swanson's Field late in the afternoon and to see that Christopher Dupree was not waiting for him. He knew this meant that Warden Mopes had most likely let him off work early for his birthday and had probably even given Christopher a ride home in his car. Just the same, it would have been good to share the story of Mr. Black and Mr. Gray with someone who could really appreciate it.

Harlan pulled the Number Six to the side of the dirt road that ran behind *The Gravy Boat Inn.* He stood and stretched and was about to open the doors when he saw what he thought was a bit of litter in the aisle about three quarters of the way towards the back. He let go of the door handle and walked back through the quiet, darkening bus and picked up a rectangular piece of paper the size of a playing card that felt kind of heavy and glossy in his hand. He held it out in the failing light and examined it.

On one side, the paper showed a watercolor of a little rabbit on a green hill that rose up in the foreground over an ocean. A round yellow sun dominated the upper left corner. The bunny, which looked to be nosing his way into a tuft of clover, was a soft earthen brown. In yellow script lettering written over the water it said: "*God Is Watching Out...*" The "G" in "God" was written fancy and was much bigger than the other letters on the card and at first Harlan didn't recognize the word at all because the "G" looked like the number "6" to him and that was how he read it.

Harlan turned the paper over. The back was all white with the word "*FOR:*" printed in the upper left corner, followed by a bold line on which was written, in a careful young hand, the name "*Emily Potter,*" which was followed by an address on South Mill Road. The paper card had been punched with a hole in the corner through which there was still a short piece of brown kite twine.

Harlan thought back to which of the children on their way to the courthouse might have been Emily Potter, but they were all a blur and he could not single any of them out in his head. He remembered them more by sound that by sight.

Harlan put the card into his pocket and then suddenly froze in his own skin. Under the seat next to the place where he had found the card, sat a gray metal lunchbox.

He looked over his shoulder and slid it out into the aisle and looked at it for a moment. He crouched down and opened it. Inside the lunchbox was a yellowing apple and what looked like a thin sandwich wrapped in a sheet of wax paper. Harlan used two fingers to open the wax paper. He found two pieces of white bread and a light brown slice of meat.

Harlan frowned and leaned back against a seat. He closed and latched the lunchbox and set it up on the seat next to him. He got down on all fours and looked under the seats. On the other side of the bus, more towards the back, he saw the black lunch box. He crawled over on his hands and knees and fished it out into the aisle, his heart rattling the bars of its prison now that the initial stupefaction had passed.

Not so gingerly this time, he opened the black lunchbox. He could tell instantly that it contained the same apple and the same thin sandwich wrapped in a sheet of wax paper. But while he knew the food was there, he paid it no notice and it played no role in the silent explosion that lit up Harlan Buck's eyes like tiny light bulbs. Harlan blinked, and then fell back into stupefaction all over again. Lying on top of the sandwich and the apple was Harlan's own bottle of whiskey.

He could tell it was *his* bottle of whiskey because he had torn off the corners and edges of the gold label to make it round, and he had scratched out the words *distillery* and *proof* and *volume* with a fingernail for no reason other than to pass the time alone laying in the back of the Number Six drinking and listening to the arrows of Sagittarius pocking the metal roof.

Harlan cursed and stood up sharply and stepped over the lunch box, making his way for the seat in the back.

His seat. *His bed. His safe.*

He lifted the flap and jammed his hand inside. The bottle was certainly gone. His fingers crept along the foamy trench along the back of the cushion and for a terrifying moment felt only foam. He cursed again, only this time it was more fearful than angry.

Then he felt paper between his fingers and he began breathing again. He extracted the familiar worn paper bag wrapped tightly around a small stack of bills. He closed his eyes and placed his forehead against the seat. He raised himself and then sat heavily on the seat with his life savings in his lap and he marveled at the razors edge on which the future always seemed to balance itself.

And then he realized that things did not feel quite right.

Harlan stood and got back down on his knees and lifted the flap and felt around again in the place he had been sitting. His fingers found paper. He pulled out a brown bag the shape and size of a brick and dropped it on the seat in front of him like it was a snake.

It took Harlan a full two minutes of looking at the bag to summon the resolve to open it and to count out in neat piles the five hundred and forty-three dollars inside. He re-counted it and then re-combined the small stacks into one big stack and put the big stack back into the paper bag. He set the big bag next to the small bag on the seat and then began to pace up the aisle of the bus, tripping over the black lunchbox he had left sitting in the aisle and scattering the food and the whiskey across the floor. He cursed under his breath and crawled around collecting the contents and packing them back into the lunchbox, which he then closed and latched and set next to its gray companion. Then he continued pacing; up and back, up and back, unsure what to do next. He sat in the driver's seat and after a few minutes of that he paced some more.

Eventually, Harlan decided there was only one thing to be done. He fetched his sack from beside the driver's seat and went to the back of the bus. No longer trusting the security of the back-seat cushion, he put the small bag and the bigger bag of money into the sack, where they sank into the cushion of his clothing. Then he lowered the black lunchbox and the gray lunchbox into the sack, which was now as full as it had ever been, but Harlan could still tie a loose knot at the top. He looked around the bus and then headed up to the driver's seat. The sack was now too big to fit next to him, so he laid it in the seat directly behind and started the engine. Having lost any appetite for food, Harlan pulled the Number Six away from *The Gravy Boat Inn* and left the smell of meatloaf and sweet onions hanging in the heat.

Harlan drove non-stop into the darkness with only one thought in his head except the money glowing in the sack behind him. The shapes rising up and falling away in the gloom just beyond the reach of the headlights seemed alien and haunting. Silos rose out of the earth like huge nightmarish mushrooms. Rolls of wheat lay like great knuckles of flesh in the fields, fallen from the sky. Grain elevators loomed like dark towers on which to perch dragons. The Number Six sailed through the dark, splitting the air like a forty-one and a half foot long silver bullet unable to stop or slow down or change direction. Harlan had made his decision and as he crouched in the front of the bullet, he ground his teeth, determined to hold firm. And all the way he heard the voice of Christopher Dupree: *you're a good soul Harlan Buck... you're a good soul Harlan Buck... you're a good soul Harlan Buck.*

The long silver bullet finally came to a rest on Winslow Street next to the rose bushes that framed the gardens outside of St. Mary's Methodist Church. Candles burned beneath a statue of polished white stone in the courtyard, dwarfed by enormous pin oaks on all sides. The candles flickered their tiny lights, heaving monstrous shadows in all directions and coaxing the smooth stone into a ghostly dance.

Harlan cut the engine and sat for a moment in the dark, steeling himself against any last minute change of mind. When the thoughts came, as he knew they would, he blocked them out by mindless action. He yanked the key out of the ignition, grabbed the sack off the seat and hopped down and out of the Number Six, walking clumsily up the block and around the corner to the Sheriff's Office.

In a back corner of the room, beyond a chest-high counter that separated the inquiring public from the inner-workings of the Summit County Sheriff's Office, Deputy Cobb sat behind a desk with his shit-kickers up, still in his brown uniform but now without a hat which was crowning a coat tree in the corner next to a glass water cooler. He had a smooth, bald head and a flat nose and a large white neck that could have been made of stone from the same quarry as the statue in the church courtyard only not as polished and with two thick bluish veins running the length of each side. Deputy Cobb, who was cleaning his fingernails with a small knife, looked up when the door opened.

"Mister bus driver," he said matter of factly, going back to his work.

"Harlan Buck," said Harlan, looking around uncomfortably.

"What can I do, Mr. Buckeroo?"

"Lookin' for Sheriff Lumm."

"Sheriff's gone havin' supper. Won't be back 'til mornin'."

Harlan stood in silence with the sack hanging at his side. After a moment, Deputy Cobb looked up and let his knife hand fall against his leg.

"Well... so come back tomorrow or state your business."

Harlan seriously thought about turning and walking out and coming back in the morning, but his feet were rooted into the floor like tree trunks into the soil. It had been hard enough tonight. Hard enough to even get here. He did not know if his resolve would last the night.

Except that he did know. He'd be busy driving the Number Six tomorrow and something in him knew that he would use every stop as an excuse to postpone visiting with Sheriff Lumm until another day had passed, and by then it would feel like he couldn't live without it. Like it was water. Like he was a man dying alone in a desert holding on to the one thing he needed that the laws of God and man forbade him to drink.

"It's… it's about them two robbers… them fellas you arrested today," said Harlan.

"What about 'em?" Deputy Cobb put down the knife, leaned back in his chair and crossed his arms, suddenly willing to give up his full attention.

"Well…" Harlan stepped forward with his bad leg and heaved the sack up onto the counter. He untied the knot and pulled out the two lunch boxes, setting them next to each other. "These are theirs. I mean, they came on the bus with them, but they left 'em on the bus."

Deputy Cobb sighed. "Yeah. Sheriff said he searched two lunch-boxes. You sure they belonged to those two, huh?"

"I'm sure."

"Okay then." Deputy Cobb scratched his head and dropped his shit-kickers on the floor with a heavy slap. He started opening drawers in the desk. "Guess I should log them in. Where are those damn… Why didn't you tell us this earlier, Buckaroo?"

"And there was also this," said Harlan, pulling out the big paper sack wrapped tightly around a five hundred and forty-three dollar brick and placing it on the counter.

"And what is that?" Deputy Cobb narrowed his eyes and looked suspiciously from the bag to Harlan and back again.

"That's money," said Harlan. "Five hundred forty-three dollars."

Deputy Cobb strode over to the counter in five loud, authoritative steps. He unwrapped the brick, opened up the paper bag and looked inside. Then he looked up at Harlan sharply.

"Where'd you find this money, Buckaroo?"

"On the bus. On the Number Six."

"We searched that bus. You told us there was no money on that bus."

"It… It was in a place… I didn't know. It was in a place in a seat…"

Deputy Cobb was busy opening the lunch boxes.

"That's mine," said Harlan when Deputy Cobb pulled out the bot-tle of whiskey. Deputy Cobb looked at him and Harlan could see little flecks of red around the part of the eye that didn't have any color at all.

"No, no, no, Buckaroo. You said these lunchboxes belonged to Carney and Wallace."

"To...to... the robbers. But the whiskey is mine. It was in the seat."

"Maybe you just want a drink, Buckaroo. This is not sounding right to me, fella. Not right at all. What else we got in here?"

Deputy Cobb dumped the sack out onto the counter and rummaged around in the clothing, tossing aside the flashlight and the two tattered Jack McMannis mysteries, until he found the smaller brown paper brick.

"And just what is this?" he asked, holding it under Harlan's nose.

"My money," said Harlan.

"Oh, this here is *your* money. Wrapped all nice in a brown paper bag just like this money over here, but this is *your* money."

"Yessir. One hundred twenty-three dollars and no cents."

Why don't you come around here and sit down in this chair, Buckaroo, so you don't run out on me. I'm not in a chasin' mood. You understand?"

"Yessir," said Harlan, who pushed through the swinging gate between the counter and the wall and sat down in a wooden chair across from Deputy Cobb's desk.

"Been in the war?"

"No sir."

"Born with that leg?"

"Yes sir."

"Guess you don't play a lot of baseball."

"No."

"Pity. Well... one hundred twenty three, you say."

"Yessir."

"Ever heard of a bank, Buckaroo?"

"I don't trust banks no more."

"Trust 'em or don't. A bank is where people keep their money. Not brown paper bags."

"Not all people."

Deputy Cobb finished sorting through the contents of Harlan's sack and left it strewn on the counter. He collected the lunchboxes and the two paper bricks and brought them back to his desk and sat down.

"No, not all people. You are right about that, Buckaroo. Some people, like those who rob the local grocery, use brown paper bags."

"I didn't rob no grocery."

"Maybe you helped."

"I didn't help."

"Maybe they paid you to drive 'em around all day and to keep quiet about it. Keeping them off the streets while Sheriff Lumm and I were out lookin'."

"No, sir."

"Or maybe you just found a brown sack of money and decided you wanted some all for yourself and were just stupid enough to bring it into the Sheriff's office."

"That's my money," said Harlan, feeling the nervousness starting to give itself over to anger. "One hundred twenty-three dollars. I saved it. That's my money, sir."

Cobb pointed at him from across the desk with a muscular finger that seemed big enough to knock a man out.

"You might think about lowering your voice there, Buckaroo. I got a right mind to put you in a cell on charges of…"

"I didn't do anything, sir!" shouted Harlan, starting to stand. Cobb pounded his fist on the desk.

"Sit your ass in that chair, boy."

Harlan did as he was told.

"On charges of robbery, conspiracy to commit, accessory after the fact, obstructing justice. I got a whole list of reasons to lock you up. Okay?"

Harlan nodded and looked around the room to keep the tears from coming out of his eyes.

"You're two cross words from a world of hurt, Buckaroo. You understand what I'm telling you?"

"Yessir."

"Good. Now why don't you tell me everything you know about this whole mess, including the two men we got locked up downstairs and all of this money. I'm gonna listen and you gonna keep your voice down and your tone respectful."

Harlan told Deputy Cobb everything he knew from the first moment he had laid eyes on Mr. Gray and Mr. Black, to the arrest, to his discovery of the lunchboxes, to the concern for his own money, to the discovery of the stolen money, to his appearance in the doorway of the Summit County Sheriff's Office. As he spoke, Deputy Cobb nodded his head as he made notes on an evidence form with a dull pencil. When Harlan got to the part about the arrest, Deputy Cobb held up a finger and told him to *hold that thought, Buckaroo.*

Harlan stopped talking and Deputy Cobb gathered up the evidence form and the two lunchboxes and the large brick of money and walked through the door in the back of the room. The words *Stacey Lumm, Sheriff* had been burned into a rectangular plaque made of oak. The words had been painted a goldenrod yellow and the entire plaque had been shellacked so that it gleamed a little in the office lights.

Through the open door, Harlan could see a polished wooden desk and a flag and part of a large safe off to the side. Deputy Cobb placed everything in his arms on the desk and stood in front of the safe. The safe door opened and Deputy Cobb loaded in the two lunchboxes and the brown paper sack. Then he closed the safe and picked up the evidence form, which he placed in a basket on the corner of the desk. Deputy Cobb closed the office door behind him and sat down.

"Now," he said, "you were telling me about the arrest."

Harlan told him about the arrest and about everything else he knew, including how he had taken to sneaking into the bus barn and sleeping in the Number Six and storing some of his belongings, like liquor and money, in one of the back seats. When he had finished, Deputy Cobb stood to his full height, opened his desk drawer, dropped in the smaller brown brick and closed it.

"You drive the Number Six here tonight?" he asked Harlan, who was still looking at the place where the desk drawer had been open.

"Yessir."

"Good. I think you need to show me this secret compartment in the seat."

"What about…"

"Don't you push your luck, Buckaroo. Get movin'." Harlan stood up and headed for the front counter. "And put all that mess back in the sack. May as well bring it with you."

By the time they had reached the bus, Deputy Cobb had taken to using a friendlier tone and once even using Harlan's real name. He asked Harlan to sit in the driver's seat as he inspected the back. He hunched over the back seat and stuck his huge arm into the opening of the cushion. He felt around, stretching one way and then the other. When he was done, Deputy Cobb stood up empty handed and then proceeded to inspect all of the other seats in the bus for similar hiding places. Finding none, he walked up to the front of the bus and slapped Harlan on the shoulder.

"I'm gonna let you go, Mr. Buck, and I thank you for being a good citizen. I'm gonna give Sheriff Lumm a full report in the morning."

Harlan opened his mouth to speak, but Deputy Cobb kept on.

"The good news for you, sir, is that I do not see the point in including in my report the suspicious circumstances surrounding your reporting of stolen money. And however odd all of this may look to others, a jury for instance, I'm just gonna trust your good character and let it go. Least for now, anyway. I'm gonna choose to believe your outlandish story, Mr. Buck."

"If you believe my . . ."

"And I think for now it would just complicate things for me to get your boss . . . what's his name . . . Mr. Janicek involved. I just don't think he would understand a lot of this mess. Do you?"

Harlan stared up into Deputy Cobb's face and, in the silence of everything he did not say, he could feel his heart shrink back from the bars of its boney cage and shrivel in desolation like the dying of a dream and his chest was suddenly the hole into which they had lowered his father. Someone had extinguished the candles it the courtyard and the Virgin Mary had returned to stone locked in a circle of oak.

"You have a good night there, Buckaroo," said Deputy Cobb. And then he was gone.

———

Harlan sat in the bus a long time before starting the engine. He slowly trundled his way through the quieting streets to Parson Road, which would take him west of town, running parallel to the five mile stretch of the Cleatchee that flowed almost perfectly straight until it finally banked away from the great green swell of earth that lifted the cemetery in which his parents were buried, just a little closer to the sun. Another three miles past the cemetery was the bus barn where Mr. Janicek would certainly be waiting to fire him for being so late.

The moon was just now rising in the east, showing itself in the dark water like the lip of a silver ladle, dipping and emerging between the sycamore stanchions that lined the river. Harlan, utterly disconsolate in his loss, and betrayed as only the righteous can feel betrayed, saw the moon and yet did not care to see it. His conversation with Deputy Cobb circled endlessly in his head, the things he might have said but failed to say wounding him from the inside like an angry, savage bird trying to peck its way out of the prison that was Harlan's natural timidity.

Between the second and third mile up Parson Road, Harlan entertained the notion of talking to Sheriff Lumm; of explaining himself all over again and of noting for the record that *two* bags of money had been confiscated by his trusted deputy and that only one of those bags had been put into the safe. Harlan envisioned an embarrassing confrontation between Sheriff Lumm and Deputy Cobb in which Cobb slumped and stooped and confessed everything, and tearfully apologized to Harlan for abusing his trust and taking his money, and then wailed as Sheriff Lumm put on the handcuffs and took him downstairs to a cell next to Mr. Black and Mr. Gray.

But it took less than a mile for Harlan to admit to himself that, as gratifying as such a fantasy might have been, it was only a fantasy. Deputy Cobb held all the cards. Harlan would likely go to jail for a crime he never committed. At best, he would lose his job and go to jail for a crime he had, in fact, committed every single night and that he was about to commit again. His anger blunted up against his unforgiving sense of stupidity, bending it inwards, fueling the old loathing for himself and his loneliness in the world. The Number Six groaned and creaked on all sides as it rolled over the uneven road and Harlan felt as if he had been imprisoned in the shadows of the happiness and opportunity that belonged only and always to others.

A deer crossed the road in front of him not two hundred feet away and while some part of Harlan knew the deer was there – had seen the fleeting flash of starlight on the road – the rest of him was oblivious and uncaring, lost in his own piteous night.

Three or four minutes later he nearly hit a man walking along the road. The man was headed in the opposite direction, back to town. He was a just another shape of darkness on the side of the road that would have been hard enough to see even if Harlan had been looking. But Harlan was not looking and the Number Six passed within two feet of the man. Harlan almost didn't even blink at the realization of how close he had come to killing him, but after a couple hundred feet he glanced at the receding shape of darkness in the side mirror.

Whether it was the delayed realization of what he had seen for half a second in the headlights, or the shape he saw now in the faint red wash of the taillights, Harlan snapped into the present moment with a jolt and slammed on the brakes so hard that the Number Six seemed to shorten a little and pitch its entire weight down and forward. The Number Six came to a noisy, swaying stop and Harlan squinted into the mirror.

Christopher Dupree never stopped walking.

Harlan watched him, moving through the blackness in slow, somnolent steps like a man possessed of the dead. Harlan put the Number Six in reverse and pushed back until Christopher was a full hundred feet in front of him, walking into the white spray of the headlights. Harlan opened the doors and waited. Christopher was shirtless and his face was a pale, living stone. He walked into and out of the light and passed the open doors of the bus without the slightest acknowledgment. Harlan got up and jumped down into the road.

"Christopher?" he said, uncertainly, to no effect. Then he shouted. "Christopher Dupree!"

Christopher stopped with a jolt and turned to face the sound like he was waking from a dream.

"That you Harlan? That Harlan Buck?"

"Yeah, it's me. 'Course it's me. Christopher... what's got into you?"

Christopher blinked and stared at him for a couple of beats. Then he shuffled back past Harlan and without a word, climbed up into the bus.

Harlan followed. "Where's your shirt? What'r you doin' out in the middle of the night... Christopher, what's wrong?"

Christopher curled his body up into a tight ball in the seat directly behind the driver's seat.

He breathed in and out, chest rising and falling like something small falling down a hill over and over. In and out. In and out.

Harlan looked down on him in silence and felt something old and fragile and precious break open inside of him and he wanted to cry. But he didn't cry or make a sound. He stood and he looked down, transfixed. *In and out. In and out.* Here was Christopher. The skin of his arms and chest was smooth and strangely luminous and his fine, sleek hair, which seemed to strain and filter the darkness for tiny filaments of light, lay across his cheek over a streak of color that Harlan knew in the sickening of his belly was a smear of blood. He knelt carefully and placed a hand on Christopher's bare shoulder.

"Christopher..."

"I want to go home, Harlan."

Harlan stood up slowly and let him be. He drove the Number Six a good mile up the road until he could find a place to turn around and then headed back into town. He asked no questions. But the questions filled his mind anyway and he thought about what the answers were likely to be and each of them left him with a chill wrapped around his spine and a hot pit burning in his stomach. He looked in the mirror at Christopher and then at the darkness behind the Number Six out of which Christopher had walked for God knew how many miles and he tried not to think of what horror lay in that darkness for the sun to discover. His own troubles had not been forgotten, but they were now a distant memory hardly worth the thought. Earlier in the day the urge to go on about Mr. Gray and Mr. Black had been irresistible. And minutes ago he would have given just about anything to lay waste to Deputy Cobb for anyone who would listen and offer some tiny commiseration. But all of that was now so distant. Harlan's self-pity gave way in a near instant to a consuming dread.

Christopher Dupree never spoke or even looked up during the drive. He must have been conscious of their progress because when Harlan pulled the Number Six around onto Nightingale Boulevard, Christopher sat up a little and waited for him to stop outside his house. Harlan opened the doors.

"You okay, Christopher? You want me to come inside with you?"

Christopher unfurled his half-naked body from the seat and stood up. Without looking at Harlan, he stepped down and out of the bus.

"You're a good soul, Harlan Buck."

He walked in slow steps up the walkway of the little house, opened the door and disappeared inside.

———

Harlan watched the door close and sat idling in the street wondering what to do next. A wave of fatigue washed over him and he remembered that he had never had any dinner. He was too tired and upset to eat. All he wanted was to lie down and be still and to let the world grow quiet. The front door to Christopher Dupree's house stayed shut and the window shades betrayed no light. Not knowing what else he could do, Harlan turned the Number Six around and headed back for Parsons Road and the Summit County Bussing Company bus lot. Home.

When he drove into the lot, the gate was still open. His headlights washed across and Mr. Janicek's clean, white car along the side of the iron gate. A figure came to life and stirred inside. He drove into the open gate, circled around and then backed the Number Six into its designated spot. He turned off the engine and the lights and grabbed his sack from beside his seat. Mr. Janicek was waiting for him when he opened the doors.

"This better be real good, Buck," said Mr. Janicek who smelled strongly of liquor. Mr. Janicek liked to call him Buck when he was drunk.

Harlan gave him a sanitized version of the story about Mr. Black and Mr. Gray, explaining that he had been out at the Sheriff's office providing a statement. His own story sounded so unconvincing to Harlan given the lateness of the hour that he thought he had made a mistake and that he should have gone with the flat tire or the empty gas tank excuse.

Fortunately, owing largely to his condition, Mr. Janicek seemed satisfied and took possession of the key to the Number Six without further interrogation. He did not, however, miss the opportunity to pass blame as they walked back to the gate.

"You always late, Buck. You know that. You always goddamned late. My wife 'bout skin me alive every Tuesday night 'cause I'm waitin' on the goddamned Number Six to show up."

"Sorry sir. But with the money and the robbers an' all . . ."

"What money?"

"The robbers. I'll try to be on time tomorrow."

"Best see that you are, Buck."

Mr. Janicek chained and locked the gate and pulled hard twice on the chain to make sure it was secure. Then he headed in the general direction of the waiting car although it was only through a series of over-corrections, swerving him one way and then the other that kept him on track.

"If you had you a girl I'd be right inclined to think you was out get-ting' some. Know what I mean, Bucky Boy? Getting' some in my bus parked out in the fields."

"No sir."

"You know I don't tolerate such as that."

"Yes sir."

"I'm a good Christian and this here is a good Christian company and you driving a good Christian bus there, Buck."

"Yes sir."

"Christ an' I don't put up with such mess."

"No sir."

"You hearin' me?"

"Yes sir."

"Christ might forgive you one day, but I'll fire you on the goddamned spot if I so much as smell hanky-panky on my bus. You understand me?"

"Yes sir."

Mr. Janicek stopped as he looked through his pockets for his car keys.

"In your hand, sir."

"What?"

"Your keys."

"Oh. Goddamned keys. You ain't got no girl, do you Buck?"

"No sir."

"Fact... I don't recollect you ever havin' a girl."

"Guess not."

"Why is that? You got looks enough. 'Cept for that leg of yours, I guess."

Harlan shrugged as Mr. Janicek opened the door to his red leather, white finned automobile and climbed in like he was positioning himself inside the flesh-lined, scooped out carcass of a great white shark.

"You ain't no fuckin' dandy, are you Buck?"

Harlan looked down at him fumbling with his keys, polluting the air with his breath, his paper-thin lips contorting over his teeth with the effort of simple tasks. The skin on his scalp was sallow and scratched and pocked with little sores. Mr. Janicek tossed the key to the Number Six onto the passenger seat where it landed on top of two brown paper bags. One of the bags Harlan knew contained a bottle of something potent and the other contained the four other bus keys collected hours ago. They made Harlan think about the paper sack of his life's savings down at the Sheriff's office and he wondered how long the money would stay in the bag.

Mr. Janicek leaned out of the window and hocked and spit a blob of yellow phlegm into the dirt. Not all of it separated from his mouth and he wiped himself with a sleeve. He looked up at Harlan sharply.

"Well? Are you boy? That the way you like it?"

Harlan's sense of being alone with this man surrounded by darkness and miles of open, empty fields was powerful. He felt his muscles tense and his teeth come together and the fingers of his free hand open at his side to a circumference the size of Mr. Janicek's throat.

And in that moment Harlan marveled at the order of things, and just how arbitrary it all was in the end.

"No sir," said Harlan.

Mr. Janicek laughed until he lapsed into a fierce coughing spell, which must have provided the focus he needed to finally start up the white shark car.

"Give you a ride?"

"No sir. I'll walk up to my friend's place. My uncle can pick me up there."

"Suit yourself, Buck. Now, you be on time in the mornin'."

Harlan watched Mr. Janicek back up and speed off, narrowly missing the right and then the left shoulder of the road on the way to the corner. When he could no longer see the taillights, Harlan turned and followed the fence along to the back of the bus lot where he slipped in through the same hole through which he had emerged at the start of his day, now so very long ago.

He squeezed in through the doors of the Number Six – which was now so quiet that it felt like a windowed tomb – dropped his bag on the floor and fell back into a seat in the middle of the bus. His stomach growled and he felt the hunger knotting up his insides. But he was too tired and pre-occupied to concern himself with food, which would require an hour's walk unless he cut across Cougar Connelly's farm and that just wasn't smart after dark. Not that it mattered, because even if he had the energy to go out and buy something to eat, which he didn't, he now had not one single red cent to his name.

The fact of his sudden impoverishment was new all over again, as though Harlan was realizing it and feeling the shock of it for the very first time. His chest tightened and he closed his eyes and saw in his mind the back of Deputy Cobb's shiny bald head, moving away from him in the dark, daring to be severed from its pillar. Harlan slammed his hand hard against the frame of the seat next to him, accidentally knocking his wrist bone against metal. He cursed in a whispered anguish and squeezed his hand between his legs.

Once the pain had subsided he found himself thinking about Christopher Dupree and the almost ghostly visage that had appeared out of the darkness along the side of Parson Road. Like he wasn't even human. Like he was an empty body.

Harlan remembered and shivered and looked out through the windows across from him at the dark, open fields disappearing seamlessly into blackness. He wondered what horror was there that he could not see but that he had felt in touching Christopher Dupree's naked shoulder. He wondered why, when the prison was south, Christopher had been coming from the north, where there was nothing but open fields for fifty miles. He wondered if Warden Mopes had given Christopher a ride home for his birthday. He wondered whose blood was drying on Christopher's skin. Harlan felt a sickness come over him, coating his gut like rancid oil, and he had to stop wondering.

He turned and sat proper in the seat like he was waiting for the bus driver and looked up at the sky through the open window. It was a clear night and the stars were out, strewn over the black sand beach of creation. He looked for familiar patterns. Orion's belt. The dippers. The dog with the cigar. The upside-down boat. He found none of them. Nothing was familiar in the lights.

True, it was quite a bit earlier than his normal viewing hour, and he was looking north out of the right side of the bus rather than south out of the left side like he normally did.

But still.

Nothing was the same up there. Nothing. All was foreign and strange, like he had spent the day walking a great distance and on the crest of night had come upon the lights of a foreign city. He found the absence of this small continuity, when perhaps he needed it the most, very unsettling.

As the minutes passed, the night got darker and the lights grew brighter and the more he stared at the stars the more he felt like they were all staring back at him, watching to see what he would do next. Harlan's discomfort grew into a presence within him that he could not contain and he stood up sharply and paced the aisle a couple of times, not thinking that it was still early enough that someone could be out there on the road, which was close enough to see him hobbling around inside the bus.

He sat down in the driver's seat and put his head down on the steering wheel. He took in a deep breath and tried to clear his mind. But Harlan could not clear his mind. Now when he closed his eyes all he could see were unfamiliar stars and all he could feel was Christopher Dupree curled up on the Number Six clutching his knees and telling Harlan he wanted to go home and the feeling of not knowing what to do next.

He stood up and walked back to where he had dumped his bag. He rummaged around until he felt the flashlight and the book. He tried his best to focus his thoughts on the life and death worries of detective Jack McMannis, whose best friend was his snub nose revolver and who all of the beautiful dames wanted to kill for some reason or another. But Harlan had read the book so many times that he was not worried in the least for Jack McMannis and his attention kept skating off the page into a pile of the wholly unfamiliar worries that were suddenly all his own.

He turned off the flashlight and put the book away and after a minute or two of staring at the floor, Harlan decided he would try to sleep. He knew that if he couldn't even read his book then sleep would likely be impossible. He longed for the whiskey in the black lunchbox.

He took off his shirt and stuffed it into his sack and then fished out the mirror and the comb and the tin of tooth powder and the pictures of his parents and put them all in the seat with the flashlight and the book. He wadded up the bag of clothing into a makeshift pillow and stuffed it into the corner of the back seat where he normally slept; the seat which had seen so much unfortunate activity this day. He kicked off his shoes and then knelt and reached under the opposite seat to remove the wide plank of wood that he used to lay across the seats and bridge the aisle.

The plank was not flush against the back of the bus as he had expected. It came free from its hiding place easily and when he pulled it towards him there was a soft thud of a sound against the floor of the bus. The sound of a small weight falling to rest. The sound of fate and of inevitability and of consequence all wrapped in the life we surely deserve, but the why's and how's of which we will never understand in a million years, because we were not made to understand the *why* or the *how*, only the *what* and the *what next*.

Now sleep really was impossible. Harlan never even lied down. The owls took to the dark air and the crickets sang up into the night. The unfamiliar stars – glittering in their fascination and suspense so far above the Number Six as it sat in its wire pen amid the endless fields that blanketed the crust of earth still seething with the day – never stopped watching.

———

When Mr. Janicek drove up to the gate in the morning, Harlan was smoking and leaning up against the fence. Three of the other drivers were sitting in the dirt, their backs to the fence posts. Another driver was off in the milo taking care of business.

Mr. Janicek was surly and he looked terrible, like all night long large birds had been swooping down and pecking at his head. He didn't say much other than to curse at the lock that would not open without an extra couple of yanks and to tell Harlan the he would fire him on the spot the next time he was as late returning the Number Six as he had been the night before and that he didn't care about any goddamned business at the Sheriff's office. Harlan took this to mean that Mrs. Janicek had really let him have it when he got home.

Before his first stop, Harlan drove out to the filling station where the Summit County Bussing Company had an open account. Company policy was to fill up at the end of the day, not the beginning, so that the busses could run on time without having to make detours for gas. Harlan had been too pre-occupied to think about diesel fuel and the tank was almost bone dry. Fortunately, Mr. Janicek had been too drunk the previous night to investigate.

Harlan filled up the tank and topped off the oil and changed the window wipers. When he finally made it out to the main road headed for the first stop into town, he was a good five minutes late. He made up some time on the way, but even so, he could see that some of the passengers were looking at their watches and wondered what had kept him.

When he reached the corner of *Macomb* and *Nellis* he was disappointed and a little surprised to see that the pretty woman who always dressed too old for her age was not waiting for the Number Six. Today of all days she was not there. Even with five other people waiting, the corner seemed empty without her. He wondered if she was sick or if she had taken a trip. If she was a widowed nurse as he had always imagined, maybe she had been fired by the hospital. Maybe she had fallen in love with a patient and they had run away together. Harlan wondered if the sadness that she always seemed to hold like tiny seeds in her eyes had finally bloomed. He could tell that the men on the bus were also wondering where she was. They looked out of their windows up and down the street, pressing their faces so close to the glass as Harlan pulled away from the curb that their hat brims bent.

169

By the time he turned onto Nightingale Boulevard, the Number Six was near full. Something about Wednesdays brought everyone out to the corners. The sun was out too, already pressing up against the bus and prying at the widows. The passengers were agitated and restless. Maybe it was the sun. Maybe. Or the heat it promised before noon. Or maybe the new stars they could not see were upsetting them. Whatever it was, the Number Six was full of it.

Harlan pulled up to the stop at the end of Nightingale and opened the doors and let out seven people. He stood up and pivoted on his bad leg and looked out the back windows.

There was no sign of Christopher Dupree.

This scared Harlan a little and he felt his heart skip and flutter at the image of Christopher on the road in the dark. At the same time, it was what he expected. He knew Christopher would not come running today.

He sat back down and closed the doors and pushed the Number Six up the hill and looped around the museum and back up Nightingale Boulevard, eventually turning west on Montgomery to Clyde and then over to Winslow in front of the shoe shine stand where Bubba Z was already set up and ready to go. Harlan stopped and opened the doors.

"G'mawnin' Mista Sir! How's about a spanky shine to go this mawnin?"

The passengers filed off, one by one, contending with Bubba as they left. No one boarded. Harlan looked in the mirror. There were four passengers still on the Number Six and they all looked like short-timers. He closed the doors and drove up the block to Donner Street where he turned and rolled between the colonnaded courthouse and the Sheriff's office across the street. He took a hard look as he passed the building in which so much in his life had inexplicably changed. The door to the office was closed and Harlan saw no sign of either Sheriff Lumm or Deputy Cobb. He stopped at the corner and popped open the doors to the Number Six before the wheels had fully stopped turning.

Three of the passengers stood up and filed off the bus and went their separate ways. When they were gone, Harlan looked in the mirror at the hatless man seven rows back reading some papers he had taken out of a satchel. The man looked up at the front of the bus and then back down at his papers, showing no intention of leaving.

"End of the line, sir," said Harlan. The man looked up at him, confused.

"What? This is the Number Six, isn't it?"

"Yes sir."

"Then it goes out to Wesley and Tull. By the dairy. I mean, doesn't it?"

"Not today it doesn't, sir."

A look of astonishment came upon him and he looked around as if for confirmation of what he had just heard.

"Why? Why *not* today?"

"Schedules have changed all up on account of one of our drivers quittin' on us. More work for everyone now. Number three goes to the dairy. Pick it up in front of the shoeshine man in about an hour."

"An *hour?*" The man's heart pumped a mottled red into his face.

"Sure am sorry," said Harlan, looking out the window.

The man huffed and stood up, stuffing his papers into a satchel he pulled up from the seat as he rose. He marched up the aisle and off the bus with a hard look but with no words. Harlan closed the doors behind him and took the blue laminated square down from the mirror and stuffed it into his sack by his side.

He accelerated the Number Six up another block before looping all the way back around to Nightingale Boulevard. He pulled up alongside the curb directly across from the home of Christopher Dupree. He cut the engine and stared at the little house. The shutters were closed and there was no sign of life. Even the air over the windows seemed old and still.

Harlan disembarked, limped up the walkway and stood nervously on the porch. He knocked purely out of courtesy, not expecting an answer, fearing the worst and wondering if he was prepared for what the worst would look like. He had imagined the worst; he had seen it in his dreams. But he had never actually seen it up close. He was not a little boy any more and there was no sweet nurse around to take him for a soda and a few carefully chosen words.

No one answered. Harlan twisted the knob and stepped inside.

Christopher Dupree was dead to the world.

But he was not dead.

He was sitting in a chair at a small table off the kitchen. He was alone, and for the moment just before he realized he was no longer alone, he had his head on his arms, which were folded on top of the table. His spine bowed beneath his skin like a young tree beneath a heavy snow. He wore his short britches and nothing else. His skin glowed with the day pouring in through the front door, his hair like spun starlight. The spatters and smears of blood though – on his side stretching like claws around to the top of his chest, and over his neck and coating the tips of his hair – were more extensive than Harlan had been able to observe the night before in the darkness.

Christopher sat up slowly and looked at Harlan in the doorway, but said nothing. His eyes and nose were red and moist and his face was twisted in an arrested anguish that hit Harlan hard from the inside somewhere in the center of his chest.

"Is your cousin home?" asked Harlan. Christopher stared at him as if waiting for the words to reach him as they traveled through a tunnel of hot oil. Then he slowly shook his head.

"Get dressed. Get your things. We're goin'. Sun's well up. We don't have much time now."

Harlan shut the door and hobbled across the room, swinging his bad leg a little off to the side like he did whenever he was in a hurry. He moved past the kitchen to the tiny bedroom beyond where he found an unmade bed of tangled white sheets, a long oval mirror and a wooden bureau. A shade of stiff blue cloth had been pulled down over the only window. He went to the bureau and began pulling open drawers and tossing what clothes he found onto the bed. Then he stopped suddenly and went back to the doorway.

"This your room?"

Christopher looked at him from across the table and wiped his nose with his bare arm. He nodded once and sniffed. Harlan turned and went back to work. He found a suitcase under the bed and stuffed the clothes in the suitcase and then strapped it shut. When he turned around, Christopher Dupree was standing in the doorway with a face of grief and stupefaction.

"Harlan Buck..." he said, the tears like a torrent across the hot, reddened plains of his face. But he did not seem to know how to finish.

———

They made good time, stopping only once by the Cleatchee where Harlan grabbed Christopher by the wrist, pulled him off the bus and led him down the bank to the river. He soaked his Thursday shirt in the cold, clear water and sponged the blood from Christopher's body and hair and then dried him off as thoroughly as he could with his Friday shirt. Christopher took it without complaint, like a child who knew better than to resist his Sunday bath.

Every now and then when Harlan tried to find a dry part of the shirt to use, he caught Christopher looking at him as if up from the bottom of a dark well. Harlan said nothing and focused on soaking up the water. When he had finished, Harlan pulled is Monday shirt out of his sack and held it out to Christopher who put it on without a word and buttoned it most of the way up the front. Harlan climbed back up the bank and walked across the road to the Number Six with Christopher following slowly a few paces behind.

Harlan kept to the small roads, little ant-trail seams between walls of corn, careful to stay away from any bus routes, until they got far enough North that they could pick up Warren Flats Road which was a straight shot to the highway. Once they picked up the highway he turned east, making a beeline for anyplace between the fields of his childhood and the Atlantic Ocean.

The Number Six did not ordinarily travel such wide flat roads for such uninterrupted distance. Harlan felt a strange, almost vicarious exhilaration in opening it up and working that six cylinder Detroit Diesel engine for all it was worth, letting it roar over the road like it was some pent up stallion set loose upon the prairie.

They did not speak for a long time.

"Where we goin', Harlan?" said Christopher eventually, his first complete sentence since he had boarded. Christopher sat in his normal seat, right behind the driver, with his hands in his lap, looking out the window. Harlan looked in the mirror and smiled at him with a little wince.

"I figure we need to get maybe as far as Kentucky. Tennessee maybe. Across the Mother Road and then some."

"You mean I gotta find work in Tennessee?"

"No."

"What we gonna do for money?"

"I got plenty of money. Don't you worry about money."

"You got work in Kentucky?"

"Only thing I'm doin' in Kentucky is turnin' around and headin' the other way."

"Turn around? I don't... why we turnin' around?"

"'Cause when they find the Number Six I want 'em to keep lookin' east, that's why. We'll hitch ourselves halfways back across the country by then. Maybe more."

"We're gon' hitch?"

Harlan was relieved to hear just a little of the old attitude back in Christopher Dupree's tone. "Yeah. We're gonna hitch. You got a problem hitchin?"

"Harlan Buck... We got us a damned bus!"

"By tomorrow this time they'll know enough to be looking for *you* in this damned bus as you call it. You *and* me. Coupl'a scrawny hares between a hard plowed field and a clear blue sky."

Christopher fell silent, looking out the window at the world flying sideways. After a minute or so he looked up again, his face twisted in shame.

"He... Harlan... He tried... He had that gun a'his. I didn't..."

"I know," said Harlan, focused forward on the hot road flattening beneath the tires. But then he looked up and caught Christopher in the mirror. "It's done. The world don't ever roll backwards. Not ever."

They rode in silence a long time, each thinking about the unbroken fields up north where the wheat grew so tall that a person could hide a car, or even hide the Number Six bus, for a solid month before some unsuspecting farmer came along and took off his hat and scratched his head and then decided to have a look inside.

Christopher was the first to speak.

"So we're gon' turn around."

"Yep," Harlan nodded. "We gonna double back, pick up the Mother Road and ride her two thousand miles all the way."

"And go where, exactly?"

Harlan snapped his fingers to an imaginary orchestra. "Flagstaff, Arizona, don't forget Winona, Kingsman, Barstow, San Bernardino."

"Harlan Buck. . ."

"I seem to recall someone tellin' me they got beaches they're made of powder."

"Like gold," Christopher whispered.

"And the water is so blue it makes you want to cry."

And Christopher Dupree did start to cry, not in wretched anguish, but in a single clear stream, as his features broke open ever so slightly, just enough to show a memory of daylight in his expression.

"And trolly cars," he said with the beginnings of a smile.

"And trolly cars."

"And movie stars everywhere you look." Christopher wiped his eyes with his wrist. "Right, Harlan?"

The road ahead was flat and clear and Harlan could see for miles. The sun was full on now and the heat and the dust from the road and the country boiled into the open windows. The Number Six roared forward in a mad dash for the horizon directly beneath a trio of hawks circling in the updrafts over the baking fields. Harlan smiled a little to himself and gave the Number Six a pat on the wheel. He pushed his bad leg down and put on some more speed.

"Yep," he said. "Stars everywhere you look."

———

Dear Emily Potter:

You do not know me and I do not know you except I saw you once with all of your school friends, even though I do not really know which one of them was you. I am returning to you something I found a long time ago when I was living in Summit County. I hope you are still living at the address on this nametag but I guess if you are not still living there then you will never know about this letter. Anyways, I am sorry that I did not send this to you sooner than today. I did not steal it. I found it. I cannot say I am not a thief. I am a thief or I was once a thief anyway. Back when I found your nametag I was a thief. But even though I did not steal it, I should have sent it back sooner and I am very sorry. I kept it for such a long time because I guess when I look at it makes me think about things. My friend says it has been so long that you are a big girl now and do not care about a nametag. But it is yours and you should have it back anyway.

Emily, if I knew you, which I don't really, but if I did, I would want to ask you what you think when you read on the nametag that GOD IS WATCHING OUT. When I was living where you live I knowed people who would say God is watching out for the righteous good Christians to protect them and see them out of the Devil's way. Me and my friend though think it means that God is watching out to see what we will do next in the world. Me and my friend are not the righteous and God does not care too much what it is we do so long as we do something that is worthy of the air in our lungs and the love in our hearts. That is what we think anyway. Because even if we are not loved like the good Christian, we ache with love just the same and even if we are not the righteous, we ache for life just the same as the righteous. Sometimes I think you have to do bad things just to show God you are worthy of another day.

I have never read the Bible but I have read a lot of mystery stories and in one of my favorite stories, which is about a private eye named Jack McMannis, a woman kills her husband so she can run away with the man she loves. Jack McMannis catches her and as he is handing her over to the law he asks her how such a beautiful dame could do such an evil thing and she says to him that what is done for love always takes place beyond good and evil. And it seems to me that is how God must see things too because I am still alive to write you this letter and my friend is still alive to stand over my shoulder to correct my spelling.

I do not pretend to have God's favor, but I do believe that me and my friend have God's attention. Our lives will most likely catch up with us one day and the God of the righteous will swoop down and pick us off like a hawk on a hare. But

we will not hunker down in the dark, Emily, cornered like rodents afraid of our own shadows.
Such a person is not worthy of another day. We
will run and we will breathe deep and we will
love until we feel those talons in our shoulders
and our feet rising up above the earth.

Even though you should be careful taking advice
from strangers, Emily, I will give you some advice
to think about as you grow up and every now
and then look at this nametag that you used to
own and then lost and then was returned to you.

One Day you may realize that you have been
living upside down and backwards because the
only time you really look at the world is when it
shows up behind you in the mirror as you gaze at
yourself. And one day you will realize that your
whole life you thought left was right and right
was left and up was down and so on and so forth.
And if that day comes, Emily, you must be ready.
You must be ready because on that day you will
be lost. You will realize that the people who you
believed are good are not good, and the people
you believed are evil are not evil. You will be confused between the letters and the numbers. You
will realize all of a sudden, like a thunderclap
in July, that your home is also your prison. You
will realize that you have hated your own love
and that your dreams are too small for you. You
will realize that God is a hawk, Emily, and that
he IS WATCHING OUT and that you must finally
meet Him in the open field running for your life
because you were born to run under the open sky

and because you do not ever, <u>ever</u> want to give your life back by hiding from the day.

Anyways, I am sure you are a fine young lady now who could probably teach me a thing or two about living in the modern world. I hope this letter finds you in good health.

Sincerely,

Your Friend (and his friend)

PART TWO

"Tomorrow. Always a tomorrow. What a curse that can be to hopeful people."

— Sheriff Hank Winchester

Chapter 6

NEXT
("THE CAGES")

"Three times," said Maribel. She held up her fingers like a pitchfork. "Once because someone was a little careless. Two other times because Anna was just a little smarter than everyone else."

She took another step backwards, but none of them were budging. The sky, seething in its darkening gray, began to spit.

"What about Sam?" The same girl with the same bottomless curiosity.

"Sam knows he's got it good. Sam and Jake, both. They're not going anywhere. Even Anna. She always comes back."

"How old is she?"

"Twenty-eight next month."

"Twenty-eight? That's older than my sister. And she'll keep getting bigger?"

"No, no. She's done all the growing she's going to do."

"How much does she weigh?"

"Almost 175 pounds. That's about full size for a female."

"How come she's not with Sam and Jake?"

"Wants to be alone, I guess." Maribel shrugged. "Chimps live in male-bonded societies. The males control all of the resources and tend to be more social than females. They do more grooming like Sam and Jake over there. And they almost never leave their natal family, whereas ..."

"What's a natal family?"

The mother put her hand on the girl's shoulder and squeezed. Maribel caught the mother's eye with a reassuring smile. *Part of the job* she said in a glance.

The same glance found the back of the man across the trail, now standing in front of the dingo pen. He looked around as if he had actually felt something hit him between the shoulder blades. He was still alone. Maribel saw his eyes take in Sam working his way through Jake's hide. Then they slid sideways to find Anna slouching in her characteristically unfeminine pose against the boulder at the far end of the habitat like she was watching a television somewhere beyond the fence. He turned around, his back to Maribel, watching the small pack of dingoes obsessively patrol the perimeter of their confinement.

Maribel considered him.

Maybe, she thought to herself. She looked at her watch before answering.

"The natal family just means the family that the chimpanzee was born into. Same thing with bonobos and orangutans and gorillas. But the females aren't programmed with that same family bond. The females will tend to wander from community to community as adolescents until their first pregnancy and then they pretty much stay put after that."

Maribel looked from one profiled face to another, eight of them comprising three families as far as she could discern. They each leaned against the iron rail and stared across the gray water in the concrete mote, utterly rapt at the mundanity unfolding on the other side. Before them was the zoological equivalent of watching Maribel painting her nails or brushing her hair or blinking hypnotically into the electric blue glow of a television. *The lobotomy box,* as he father called it.

Anna rolled languorously onto one haunch to reach the half-eaten orange that had so occupied her attention during the ten o'clock tour. She pulled it through the worn grass and smelled it and looked around and let it drop. She picked it up again and let it drop. Again. Drop.

Sam had left Jake for the tallest and centermost stand of rangy beechnuts. Each tree had been topped where six steel beams brought all sides of the habitat together like a wire mesh bag of monkeys tied off at the apex, fifty feet above the middle of the moted island habitat. Sam, the smaller of the two males, sat and watched the watchers. Jake, the larger, made his way slowly past the tire swing, pausing at the old termite hill on his way to wait at the brown metal door in the back of the island. If you lived on *Monkey Island* at the Summerfield Zoo, then the brown metal door was the place where life changed first.

A cell phone began bleating something tinny but vaguely familiar. Sam arched his eyebrows and looked around, peeling back his lips. His muscles came to attention beneath his skin and, for a moment, he was focused and listening to the jungle with ancestral ears. The older girl with the mouthful of gum fished a hand into her pocket. The sound stopped and Sam's attention slackened. He pulled himself effortlessly into the canopy.

"I'm at the zoo," she said. "Yeah, really. Monkeys. Nothing. Just sitting there. Soon. Maybe an hour. No. Okay. Okay. Later." She snapped the phone closed and stuffed it back into her pants. Her father looked at her but seemed to know better than to ask.

Maribel felt rain on her cheeks and a breeze carried bison and llama and elephant through the zoo like a circus train. She saw the Dingo Man pull up the collar of his jacket and thrust his hands into the pockets of his jeans. They were pressed and creased and stopped crisply at a pair of hard mahogany loafers.

A gust came and the mote started to pock and pucker. Maribel looked at her watch then pulled her hair behind her ears, remembering as she did Evan's quip that these were unconscious mannerisms that may as well have been turn signals. *I always know when you're ready to change directions, Maribel; when you've had enough and it's goddamned time to go.*

"Any more questions?" she asked. The father of the twins took another picture of Sam who scratched himself and looked away. Maribel walked backwards. "No? Okay, then lets move on this way and finish up the tour over in the Reptile House where we can get out of the rain."

At the far end of *Monkey Island* she stopped at the smiling park ranger sign, flipping over the wooden plaque so that the message changed from *Tour in Progress!* to *Returning Soon!*

———

The Dingo Man drove a foreign car, sleek and silver like a bullet. It gleamed around corners dripping rain. Its taillights smeared like red paint across her windshield.

Maribel had not planned to follow him. Of course, such was never her plan. It was always a last minute conspiracy of coincidence that convinced her to do this sort of thing. A compulsion aping an impulse.

He passed the on-ramp and slowed, then stopped at the intersection, a single amber glowing pulse now joining the flaring red smear across the wet glass. *Pulse. Pulse. Pulse.* He waited for the on-coming cars, one after the other, like a parade of miserable wet cats, each hesitating at the shore of the lake-sized puddle in the southbound lane.

Pulse. Pulse. Pulse. The Dingo Man was not interested it seemed, in the efficiencies of freeways.

She had thought him long gone. The rattlesnake had been relocating himself to another shelf of rock, uncoiling and recoiling, and the questions in the Reptile House had been relentless. By the time she had emerged, the sky had fully opened its soft slate coffers and was pouring the sea back to earth. The Summerfield Zoo had been almost deserted: those who were free to go were gone or going. Those not so free had taken refuge.

Maribel had made a dash for the Safari Canteen, which connected by way of the gift shop and then a series of wide thatch-sheltered walkways to the administration building in which the Veterinary Services Office was located. Once inside, she had unclipped her radio, placed it in the charger and then busied herself straightening up the desk and finishing the inventory she had started several hours earlier, before her first tour. She reviewed the new blood test reports on Dolly and Ben and wrote a note for Dr. Klatch about the loose stools at Cat Mountain and the limp that had reappeared in Billy's gate. *Always after he jumps*, she had noted. *May need to reset the left-hind.*

She had clipped the note to the blood test reports and placed them in a neat stack on the center of the desk where he would see it when he arrived that afternoon. On her short days, when she and Dr. Klatch only infrequently crossed paths, Maribel wanted there to be some evidence that she was tending to her responsibilities. She often left notes just to show Dr. Klatch what she thought, in her paraprofessional opinion, needed tending.

After writing the note, Maribel had gone to the employee break room, changed her shirt, returned her patch-emblazoned Summerfield Zoo ranger-wear to her locker, and left, sprinting through the deluge for the parking lot. She reached her car just as the Dingo Man was closing his door. It was, she thought, with the rest of the day to kill, an irresistible coincidence.

Maribel turned on the radio. The potboiler summary of current events in the Middle East was ceding the frequency to Elgar. Cellos scooped up the rain like great sonic ladles. The Dingo Man turned and headed towards the business district.

He seemed to be in no particular hurry. The traffic was slow, because the traffic on South Topeka was always slow and because the rain seemed to push and pull against forward progress with every drop. But even when the lumbering furniture truck had pulled off the road at the filling station, leaving a hundred yards of open lane ahead, the Dingo Man maintained his speed as though nothing had changed.

It meant nothing to Maribel. If he was in no hurry, then she was in no hurry.

He left South Topeka Road for Lincoln Street, which was less congested by half, unrolling west for miles out over the croplands. Microtels and minimarts gave way to auto supplies and farm equipment and dingy white warehouses with big bay doors streaked with grime. None of them had paved lots or signs or claims to ownership or boasted purpose. Each seemed to have a man waiting outside in an idling pickup truck, blowing cigarette smoke out into the rain. Silos stood quietly in the distance like iron sentinels, standing guard in the weather. A flicker. Then another. There. And there. Bone lightening licking rain from the rim of the world.

Maribel bet herself that the Dingo Man was headed for the old post office to mail a package. Everyone knew that *The Mail Slot* on South Topeka Road was always crowded this time of day and that it would not accept packages over ten pounds.

The Dingo Man, she thought, was mailing a box of old letters to a woman who no longer loved him. Years of ardent declaration returned to the source. Keepsakes to be kept no longer. What was once eternal suddenly reduced to historical fact. She – the woman to whom the box had been addressed with a firm hand – would not see this coming. She would hand the postal clerk a pink slip and he would retrieve an eleven pound box and she would see that the box was from him, the Dingo Man, and when she got back to her car and opened the box she would hear the echo of her own declaration of independence and it would wound her to the core and she would dissolve into tears in the post office parking lot. And then, on the way back home, she would wish she could go back to the way things were in spite of it all.

But the Dingo Man passed the old Post Office without even slowing. At the stop sign he made a left on Jefferson and then another left on Springfield, heading back the direction from which they had come.

He's lost, she thought. *I'm following a tourist.*

No, she corrected herself. *He's not sightseeing. He's looking for someone. For her house. For her work. He's making amends. He has things to say that can only be said in person. He won't leave until he's said them.*

A police cruiser hissed past her, headed west, and she remembered.

All state cruisers reminded her of her father. Her family was full of cops going back to her great grandfather, Stacey Lumm, who served thirty-five years as Sheriff of Summit County, back when the name Stacey could still connote a sense of virility. The story was that Sheriff Lumm lived to one hundred and one and still had his wits about him. His grandson, her father, would soon be only seventy-six and the wits were long gone.

The siren wailed behind her. Watery red and blue smears out the back window. Smaller and smaller.

Well, it wasn't *his* fault, she reminded herself. She should call him. He won't remember her, she knew. But she should call anyway. He's used to not knowing the people who seem to know him. The people on the refrigerator. The people on the mantle and on the wall in the study. He has people to sing to him. To help blow out the candles. To remind him of his name and the day he was born.

Maribel bet herself that Claire would be right there with him. Like a wife. Like a goddamned soul mate.

But still. She should call for his birthday. And that would be enough. She didn't need to fly out to see him this year. It's not like he remembered the visit last year and was expecting another. It's not like he knew she even existed; let alone her name. If he could not remember his own daughter, then he also could not remember that she had kept her mother's secret. Or that the first time he had wandered off into the night was more than Maribel could stomach and that she had abandoned him to his fate.

She did not have her sister's penchant for familial sacrifice. Why remind him? This year she would just call.

The red smears were like wet, seeping wounds that would not be cleaned or staunched. The Dingo Man turned off the road onto a slab of asphalt that belonged to *Shocks & Struts*, a low, gray, windowless cinderblock of a building surrounded by flooded potholes. Red neon beer signs adorned the exterior. A poster promising *Ladies Night* incentives had been tacked to the door at three of its corners, the fourth curling in the wet air up towards the center.

Maribel drove past the building, turned around and parked on the opposite side of the street. The Dingo Man slipped his silver bullet into a parking space near the back of a building. He turned off his lights and cut the engine. Maribel did the same.

It was not what she had expected of him, this place. Not that she was disappointed exactly. She was not supposed to have expectations anyway. That was not the point. Understanding, yes. Curiosity, yes. But not the fulfillment of expectation. Expectation imprisoned the mind. We will see what we expect to see. Experience what we expect to experience. We expect and then we repeat. We repeat and we are not free. We are not free and we are not happy. Which is what history teaches us to expect out of life in the first place, but we follow expectation anyway.

So she told herself to remain open, uncommitted to outcome.

The Dingo Man climbed out of his car and closed and locked the door. He wore a black baseball hat now. He kept his head bent down and his arms up against the rain, moving quickly for the door. It opened and swallowed him whole like a gray concrete toad eating a bug.

Maribel put the seat back and stared out at the relentless sky through the moon roof. Thunder, suddenly, from somewhere beneath her, under the street. China exploding. She turned off the radio and closed her eyes and tried to feel the sound deep within her chest, radiating out in waves that moved through her bones.

Evan would be home in another three hours. There would be more angst. She should go buy some fish and make a salad. Buy some wine. What vintage went with angst? What if the angst was only the shallow superstitious kind; an offering to the disturbingly whimsical God of Forgone Conclusions? Evan should know better; the job was his for the taking. Like everything. He just wasn't one for tempting fate. Angst was part of the process, a distraction as he secretly counted his chickens.

She wondered what he would say to her if he knew. If he knew what? What was there to know? If he knew that she had two short days a week at the zoo? If he knew how she had fallen to filling those days before he came home? He would understand. He would understand that he did not understand. *That*, sometimes, was an acceptable state of affairs when it came to relationships. But then that was Evan. He always understood more than she did.

There was a sharp sensation, stabbing through the flesh of her lids, of the world blowing to pieces and vanishing in a silent, brilliant pulse. She opened her eyes as the light vanished and sound from everywhere split the moment like an atom. It was just enough to trigger the impulse, pushing her to act against her better inclinations. She climbed out into the rain, slammed the door and made for the building that had swallowed the Dingo Man.

———

When her eyes adjusted, she saw that there were three of them going at it simultaneously, one per pole and barely a stitch between them. Two wore boots. The third wore silver cuffs that caught the blue spot beams through the smoke. The one in the cuffs climbed a pole and hung upside down, locking her bare feet at the ankles, her hair suddenly like a black horsetail swishing at the dust. She rattled metal against metal in mock protest as the other two paced the stage with mock authority wearing police hats and palming their batons in menacing and suggestive ways. Three expressions of over-affected savagery, utterly failing to convey any sense of lustful abandon, betraying boredom so intense as to invite violence as a welcome improvement. They bared their teeth at a dozen men that lined the platform, popping their eyes down at them with every other step. The men looked on, darkly impassive, silent amid the pounding drumbeats, motionless except to lift a glass or fling a dollar, as if merely bearing witness and afraid to be counted.

The Dingo Man was not among them.

"Looking for your man?"

Red hair like Christmas tinsel and a kimono, loosely sashed, carrying a blue drink in a cloud of perfume. Serious heels. The music pounded between them. The woman had perfected the soft shout required for such places.

"No," said Maribel, pushing her voice above the music.

"Looking for your... *woman?*" The woman bent her knees, lowering herself so that she could look directly into Maribel's eyes as she touched her on the arm. Maribel smiled and forced herself not to look away.

"No."

"You lookin' for work?"

"No, just curious."

"Ah. Sure?"

Maribel nodded. "Sure."

"It's good work. You know? Itch is always lookin'." She looked appraisingly at Maribel. "He'd like *you* alright. Money's good. Work's steady. Keep most of your tips. King Itch takes care of just about anything you need."

"King Itch?"

"*Mmm hmm.* He owns this place. And he can hook you up. Substances. Business opportunities. You know. He can keep you happy. Even has a housing plan if you need a roof."

"A roof?"

"Hey, it beats the street. Beats the fucking jungle. Lots of girls leave and when they see what's out there waiting for them, they always come back. Always."

Maribel smiled and nodded. She looked around the room for an out of the way table. There were none. She scanned faces and the backs of heads. This was a mistake.

"What's your name?"

"Anna," said Maribel.

"Crystal." They shook. "Drink?"

"No. Thanks. Just looking around."

"If he's not out here, then he's in one of the private party rooms." Crystal jerked her head in the direction of a hallway that disappeared out of the back of the main room.

"I'm not looking for anyone," Maribel repeated.

"Right," said Crystal, disbelieving. "And I'm Lady Godiva." She smirked and sucked some blue up through a straw. "Look, Anna." She swallowed. "It's not the end of the world. Okay? So now you know. This shit happens. Sometimes they're just lookin' for something a little different. A little nastier. A little raunchier. Not better, just different. You know? Sometimes the same ol' same ol' just don't make 'em happy any more."

They looked at each other for a long few seconds through the smoke and the music. Maribel nodded.

"Good. Now, my guess is he'll only be back there about ten minutes. He'll buy a beer and take in a dance or two just so as not to look like a punk getting' his rocks off and then he'll leave. Okay?"

Maribel nodded.

"I suggest that you just take off. Don't let him see you. Now you know where he comes. Gettin' in his face ... well domestic situations are bad for business here anyway, know what I mean? Go home. Say nothing. And then either find a way to spice it up or, if you can't do that, just let him get his jollies. It's harmless. But, hey, if you stay, then it's my job to make sure you either buy a drink or show the ladies out there some appreciation. So..."

Crystal let the question hang. On stage, one of the women was writhing on the back of another, pulling black fingernails slowly through her hair like a comb. The woman cuffed to the pole strained to reach them. One of the men extracted a cell phone, looked at it and returned it to his pocket.

Maribel walked back out into the rain.

She put the seat back and waited. Her clothes were wet and the windows began to fog. She sketched her initials with a fingertip and then cracked the window. Thunder came like a celestial rockslide, crashing and breaking in jagged chunks all around her, settling into a cloud of sound.

He is trying to convince her, she thought at last. The Dingo Man is shouting at her that she is better than this, pounding his fist against the wall.

You're better than this and I'm not leaving unless you come with me!

She surely had not expected to see him barge into the small dark room where there was only a filthy couch and a chair. He was lucky she was not... in the middle of something. She's crying. Sobbing. And the Dingo Man is still yelling. Pounding his fist against the wall. No one can hear him because of the music. But she can hear him.

This is no way to live! Free yourself, damnit! Why do you keep coming back to this? Why? Do you think this will make you happy? Do you? Why do you keep coming back to me only to keep coming back to this? Is this what you want? The Dingo Man is crying now, she imagined. *Come back! Stop this. Please come back! I can make you happy!*

He is determined and she will relent. She knows that the other life, his life, will make her happy. She will wipe her eyes and smile.

The air ignited and, in an instant, was transparent again. Then thunder, an aural apocalypse, from within the hollow of her bones. The door to *Shocks & Struts* opened and three men came out holding their hands up against the rain. The last of the three held the door for a fourth, not with them. He was alone.

Maribel sat up and started her car. The Dingo Man pulled his cap down low and walked quickly. He climbed into his sleek silver machine and brought it quietly to life. The lights flared and he was in motion.

He seemed to know where he was going now. Or, if he had always known where he was going, he was far less circumspect now about getting there. No more meandering. He continued east on Springfield, back toward South Topeka Road, tailgating and rolling through stop signs. He pulled into the parking lot of the *Mini-Quikmart* and darted next door to the *Summerfield Cork Stop*, leaping awkwardly over one puddle and the next.

Maribel hit her hazards and double-parked the car, letting it idle. She needed to tend to her own life, she thought. Evan would be home soon. She needed groceries.

In three minutes he was back out in the rain, gripping a bottle of wine by the throat like a dead pheasant, holding his other hand to the sky. He pulled back out onto the road, speeding past her.

Together they worked the traffic and the rain, weaving to avoid potholes and slow moving trucks. There were always two or three cars between them, but the Dingo Man was not difficult to follow, particularly once they had left the business district and mounted the freeway, heading north where the sky showed some signs of clearing.

In twenty minutes they had skirted the city and were off the interstate, gaining altitude in the long climb out of the valley up Ridgeline Drive. The road eventually began to turn, coiling through hardwoods that had been left to grow old. They punched through light pillows of fog along the road, the vapor curling in great misty fingers behind each of them, first him, then her, as prelude to complete reconstitution, like an ocean smothering and assimilating the wake of tiny boats.

As they leveled off, the miles were marked by single-lane side-roads, private driveways snaking off through the trees to large houses that Maribel could not see but knew were there. Some of the driveways were gated and posted with legal admonitions. Most featured mailboxes that identified the owners. *The Baxters,* said one. *Sam and Joyce Davenport,* said another.

Ridgeline Drive forked and they veered to the west. The woods thinned and then dropped away altogether. Maribel could see down into the valley now, still getting hammered with rain but the western wall of the cloudbank was taking on color and contrast, the dark grayness now shot through with great tines of peach and the underside beginning to boil with blood orange marbling.

The Dingo Man turned onto a parkway that dead-ended at a divided driveway separated by a roof-sheltered kiosk. On the far side of the kiosk, bisecting the entire driveway, was a black iron gate. The wet silver bullet stopped at the gate and Maribel pulled over to the side of the road.

Across the face of the gate, in great copper script, were letters that read: *Welcome to Springhill Family Estates.* Beneath the soaring letters was a square white sign with black capital letters that Maribel could not read but which were no doubt a stern qualification to the foregoing welcome.

The Dingo Man's arm extended from the side of the car. His hand communicated briefly with the kiosk. The iron gate slid open as a shaft of sunlight slipped past the clouds at the top of hill and lit the silver car like a Christmas ornament. Maribel could see the Dingo Man, silhouetted in the new light, take off his cap and toss it in the back seat. He messed with his hair. The gate waited. The car finally slid forward, the gate closing behind.

She watched him as long as she could, pushing slowly up the hill to a stop sign where the car was little more than a silver glinting splinter in the sun. It remained idle at the stop sign for a long time – a full two minutes – before rolling off to the left and out of sight.

Maribel sat at the side of the parkway looking at the gate, hands still on the wheel, watching the clouds over the hill try to recapture the sinking sun. But there was no catching it now. It had escaped and was dropping like a stone to water, plummeting to the opposite side of the world where it could be free and new in the sky, as though entirely unknown.

But it would surely be back.

In her rearview mirror, Maribel watched a deep blue minivan approach and pass her. It pulled up to the kiosk. A woman's arm emerged. The gate began to slide open and the minivan inched forward into the x-rays streaming down the hill through the windshield. Maribel counted two children. The gate closed and the minivan rolled up the hill to the stop sign.

Her perspective changed with the light. There were not two children, but one child and one dog. The dog, lean with sharp ears, bounded back and forth, window to window, circling the confines of his world, desperate to get out.

———

"Mmm. Smells like feeding time." Evan dropped his keys into the bowl and leaned his umbrella in the corner of the hall by the door.

"Fish," said Maribel. "Twenty minutes maybe. Wine?"

"You're joking, right?" He knelt to untie his shoes.

"Tough day?"

"Tough day."

"Any word?"

"No." He placed his shoes on the mat beneath the coat rack and padded into the kitchen. "I'm beginning to worry."

"Beginning?"

He kissed her, pulling her waist into him. She tried to keep the spatula over the stove.

"Hello, Yes," he said, smiling, so close he was almost out of focus.

"Hello, Next," she replied, always charmed to hear the old endearments.

"I think they may actually give the damned contract to C.M.I.," he said, moment gone, letting her go.

"Why?"

"Don't know." He rummaged around in a drawer. "Just ... I don't know. I've got a bad feeling. Corkscrew?"

"By the sink. You said they can't offer the same networking capabilities that..."

"They can't, they can't, but I haven't heard anything from Greer or Davis in three days." He opened the bottle, pulled a glass from the cupboard and filled it with Riesling. "*Davis*. I was talking to him every day. It's been *three* days now. That's more than enough time. Something's not right."

"Evan, it's a hospital," she said with help from the spatula. "It's going to be complicated and bureaucratic. And you said yourself that doctors don't know anything about I.T. security. It's going to take time. But you know that in the end they'll give it to you, because you..."

"No I don't know they'll give it to me."

"You do. Do I get some?"

"Sorry. I thought you had some." He poured a glass of wine and held it out to her. She opened the oven and poked at the fish with the spatula and then closed the door and took the glass from him and drank. She pushed the potato slices around the pan.

"Have you ever failed to get a contract you really went after? Ever? You just worry too much. Your problem is that there is no problem. You need to relax. Let go of the fear."

"What fear?"

"*Losing*. Losing what you have or might have. I honestly don't know what you'd do without something in your life in danger of slipping away. Just relax and let whatever is going to happen, happen."

"I'll relax when the ink is dry."

"No you won't. When the ink dries, you'll start worrying about the contract renewal three years from now. You'll start worrying about... whatever it is you geeks always worry about. Firewall decay and Buster viruses or..."

"Bunker busters."

"Whatever. As soon as you get what you want, you'll start worrying about losing it. You're the most stable person I know and the person least likely to appreciate stability."

Evan laughed. "Don't even talk to me about stability, little miss I want to be an anthropologist; no, I want to work in the Forest Service; no, I want to become a caribou migration expert; no, I want to be zoologist; no, I want to be a veterinarian; no, I want..."

"Hey, just because I don't always know what I want doesn't mean I look for reasons to feel upset."

"I'm not upset." He spread his arms as if to exaggerate his innocence. He put his glass on the counter and loosened his tie and then took off his suit coat and draped it over the stool. He stood behind Maribel at the stove, pulling her back into him as though her heels were hinges screwed to the floor. Maribel let her body fall backwards.

For a self-described digi-geek, Evan was strong and remarkably fit. He was devoted to his daily cardio-exhaustion. He made his body a priority lest he end up conceding anything unnecessarily to nature's decompositional agenda. Like his work, Evan was never quite satisfied with the results of his own effort. He was a man in a boat, head down, watching for leaks.

"I'm not worried about losing *you*," he said in that playful way of his.

"You're petrified of losing me," she said. "As well you should be, mister. You should never pour the wife's glass last."

"Yes. For shame. I don't deserve you. Please forgive me. Please don't leave. I don't want to have to cook for myself."

Maribel turned and played up the offense, a frozen gasp on her face. She threatened to hit him with the spatula. He caught her wrist and kissed her again.

"I do love you," he said.

"I forgive you." Maribel smiled up at him. "But only because you have sense enough to know that you're helpless without me."

Over dinner they discussed the information technology problems inherent in the delivery of medical services. Privacy, Evan insisted, had become almost as important as medical malpractice on the worry radar.

"All of this stuff is digital," he said. "The security issues are huge."

He ate carefully. Precisely. Sizing his bites. Segregating his potatoes. Separating the pink flesh of the fish from the dried skin. Maribel thought of Anna and how, years ago, she had liked to painstakingly peel away the rind of an orange, stacking the pieces in a neat pile on the ground at her haunch and then biting each piece of rind in half and rebuilding the pile before taking a single bite of fruit. It was an act of savoring, she thought, not so much for the food as for the experience of certainty – an intricate subdivision of time by needless replication of function all to hold at bay an uncertain future. Each moment a lifetime of its own, as when the moment is the only thing you can count on.

"Medicare fraud has really become an information security issue."

Maribel listened and nodded and contributed enough to the conversation for him to know that she was impressed with the complexity of his professional concerns, but not enough to convey genuine interest.

"Sorry," he said. "I'll shut up."

"No, it's interesting."

"No it isn't."

"Evan..."

"No, I'm sorry. How was work?"

She tried to feel bad that he had understood; that she had made him feel like a self-preoccupied ass. But she didn't feel bad. However much she tried, she *couldn't* bring herself to feel bad and *that* made her feel like shit.

"It was okay. Pretty slow."

"Crappy weather for a day at the zoo."

"First half of the day was okay. One tour after another, though, so I didn't really get any work done."

"Well, the deluge the second half of the day must've fixed that."

She laughed a little and nodded, not wanting to lie. Not to him. As if allowing someone to believe in a reality that does not actually exist is somehow different than lying. Above her, the roof creaks in the wind under the weight of evening.

"You must have spent the rest of the day building an ark."

Maribel laughed again and Evan divided the rest of the wine.

"Doc Doolittle still on track to retire?" he asked.

"Please. Bruce Klatch has been retiring for fifteen years. He leaves and they throw him a party and then he's back with his arm up Kimba's ass like nothing has changed."

"God, I hope Kimba's an elephant," said Evan.

"Funny. The point is he keeps coming back.

"Loves his work, I guess."

"Mmm, not really. Doc is the most out-of-sorts S-O-B you've ever seen. You'd think he hated it out there. Good thing he's a vet. Human patients would never put up with him. Good teacher. He knows what the hell he's doing. I'm learning a lot. But, no, I think he can't really get used to all of the free time. He's used to being needed. So he keeps coming back. He'll still be there when I'm finally licensed."

"And then?"

"And then it will be time for him to go. *Again.* Summerfield doesn't need two fulltime vets and I'm not working for apprentice pay. Bruce will just have to move on."

"And if he doesn't?"

"If he doesn't, then I'll go to Wakefield. They're expanding. Or Lakeland. They're even bigger than Summerfield. Or there's still that offer up in Braden."

"The bison guy?"

"That's a fragile herd and a good study he's running. He needs the help."

"He needs money is what he needs. The help will follow. You don't need to be working for free."

"We'll see."

"And a hell of a commute. Way up there."

"We'll see."

"You know I'll support whatever you want to do."

"Yeah," she said, smiling. "I know."

"I mean we could move north and I could commute this way."

"We'll see what happens."

"Could start your own practice. You know... dogs, cats, parakeets."

"Parakeets?"

"Hamsters."

"Too confining. Too domestic. God, I'd go crazy. I've got to be outside. I can't do the whole nine-to-five wall-to-wall pain-and-suffering thing."

"Tell me about it. If we get this bid I'll have to do a lot of initial on-site work." He swallowed and made a face. "I hate hospitals. God, I'm going to be pissed if we don't get this job."

He slipped back into his bubble of sound.

It was funny, she thought, that Evan, of all people, should worry about losing her. Funny that he should be so solicitous of her affection; as though she will one day declare that she has had enough of him and walk out in the middle of the half-sautéed mushrooms. Or that she might just decide one day to not come home from work.

Had five years really changed him so much? Or was it her?

Five years ago she would have done almost anything to have him. He should have been preposterous for her to contemplate. Entirely out of her league. More attractive by orders of magnitude than any man she had ever dated. Smarter. More successful. More sensitive. More attentive. A nuptial virgin.

In a word, *perfect.*

Not just in some culturally generic sense – although her girl friends had been agog and disbelieving at even that basic level. He was perfect for *her.* For Maribel Lumm. His arid humor. His shyness, like an underground stream, pooling beneath his daunting confidence. His love of nature. His progressive instinct. The sacred stacks of *Blue Note* vinyl. The way he dipped into his late father's collection of biographies when the air turned cool and the leaves started to flutter and fall with the first breath of autumn. All of this quintessentially, magnetically, Evan, a walking contradistinction to the soullessness of the digital age to which he had sworn his professional allegiance.

He might have had any woman, for any woman would have had him. And yet, he had allowed himself to be chosen by her. By *her* – *Maribel Lumm.* He had seen fit to reward her improbable persistence. One date. Then another. Then another. A dinner. A lunch. An afternoon of kites in the park. The hot air balloon. Always her request; always his acquiescence. Saying *yes.* Looking past everything in her that was *not* perfect. Allowing for substance. Allowing himself an open mind and inviting her inside. Inside of him, inside of them, where she had stayed, curled up like a cold stray by the warm fire. *Cold* because the world was what it was to a stray, scavenging for scraps of happiness. *Warm* because she would never again want for that which would make her content.

And yet, he acted as though he could not keep her; as though she was a wounded bird in a punctured shoebox healing her way to inevitable release. Did he think her affections, her loyalty, so impermanent that she might one day leave him for no reason?

No. She knew him better than that. He was as confident as ever. He knew damn well she would never leave him. It was all just Evan's way. She was another inestimable treasure in his life of charms; another rare value that he had secured and made his own. Inside he was determined to keep her. To not lose her. His manner with her was all process, masking the arrogance of certainty in an uncertain world, ever careful not to offend the gods by any lack of ceremonial humility. Was it such a price to pay – his gratitude, his solicitude, his deference – if it meant she would never leave him? If it meant the impossible *stayed* impossible?

It should have been an ideal state of affairs.

"It's not that they're incompetent," he was saying. "They do decent work. Their techs are all trained. But those guys don't have the service range to handle a large hospital."

Evan was not Vincent. That much was certain. Although she could not forget that she had picked Vincent, too. Vincent, whose name was really *Vince* and who, in the cruel light of retrospection, was all too much like a first husband. Vincent, who had been too willing to accept that she tended to confuse obeisance with love. Too willing to believe that it was a work of great magnanimity – a credit to his moral decency – for him to tolerate her educational pursuits while he earned a living. Vincent, who had been too willing to step in for her father in a pageant of substitution; two cops meeting in a church to negotiate a transfer of custody; her father handing her over, quietly ready to be rid of the daily memory of her betrayal. Vincent, whose betrayal was yet to come, receiving her, knowing nothing of forbearance or compromise, except to waive speeding tickets for the right woman. Vincent, for whom marriage was less a sacred vow to be honored than a sacred contract to be enforced.

Of course, Maribel knew she had not been a perfect wife. And she knew that Vincent had not been completely unforgiving. She had been too critical of him. Finding fault in shortcomings of which she had been all too aware from the very beginning. And she he had deliberately asserted herself in ways that Vincent, in all sincerity, had found unbecoming in a woman. He had, most often, seen fit to let her go with a warning. He had a cop's idea of forgiveness.

"Wonderful dinner as always, Maribel," said Evan. "I'll bet you cook like your mother cooked."

"Oh, if only," she said. "Mom was a culinary sorceress. Whenever we had guests over, dad would eat the last thing on his plate and lean over to whoever was sitting next to him and say something corny like *Anna could cook her way into Heaven;* you know, just loud enough for her to hear. She'd protest. He adored her."

Evan smiled and reached across the table and patted her on the hand. "Well, then it does run in the family. Let me get the dishes."

She finished her wine, watching him stand and collect the plates, marveling that she could have been married to such different men.

Maribel knew that she had not been a perfect wife to Vincent. Indeed, she had been caught – trapped and caught – in the very state of her imperfection. Hers had been a flagrant violation of marital law for which there could be no pardon. Not from Vince. There was no getting around that ugly fact.

That she was justified in her behavior – just once with an old friend – had seemed so clear at the time, especially in light of the evidence that Vince had, from the very beginning, indulged in a far more regular pattern of sexual indiscretion. The old friend had produced a handkerchief, had dried her eyes, and had been outraged on her behalf. They had finished both bottles. They both had felt so much better afterwards. It was all so clear. She was free because she wanted to be free and had found a way. Happy, because she wanted to be happy and had found a way. No telling how long that clarity might have held.

But she had never considered the possibility of surveillance. Cops.

She admitted everything. Vince admitted nothing. The good friend ultimately found a better friend. And suddenly *nothing* was clear. Suddenly she was alone and nothing was clear. All was lost in a black storm of recrimination and longing.

She had moved back home then, mostly for the comfort of memories. But then she had seen first hand what Claire had been telling her and had somehow dismissed or discounted. Memories, she abruptly realized, no longer lived at home. Her father had left the gate open and the memories had all scattered off into the night. And her father, the new and disagreeable stranger, had taken to wandering off alone in search of them.

Too much. Too much.

So Maribel herself had wandered off in the middle of the night, leaving him to Claire who had gracefully, selflessly, ennobled herself from sister to surrogate wife and mother, wielding tone and judgment and authority over the house like a chef clearing a kitchen.

So, yes, Maribel had wandered off too.

She had wandered off across the Great Plains beneath cold, indifferent stars, moving ever North, like a lone calf looking for the herd, deep into the coniferous void, from boreal to taiga and back again. Tracking ancient migrations. Tracing the rock-worn veins of instinct and reading the palm of the world.

Later, much later, she would say that she had been looking to find herself, and that she had done so, out there in the woods, on the plains, on the cliffs. It was the story she told on the way to explaining her vocational direction. It was the story she told on the way to explaining her disappearance from the places where her own history was recorded.

But while she had found the Canada Park Service, and while she had found the North American Wildlife Research Foundation, and while she had found the Conservation Society, she could not say that she had found herself, Maribel Lumm, who was forever cresting some far ahead crag or submerging into a sea of velvet pine, disappearing into the distant foreground.

The animals in that foreground were always so much easier to follow. Animals never considered the possibility of surveillance. Even after the dart. Even after the collar. They woke up and shook it off; without question or confusion or nagging doubt, they simply resumed the only life for which they were made.

So Maribel had lived among the lesser kingdoms and those who studied them. She became an acolyte of men without walls; a fledgling member of an order of peripatetic worshippers who believed that God was in the elements and that shelter was a sacrilege. She believed as they believed, that happiness came with freedom, that freedom came with distance, and that distance came only with scientific objectivity and a good pair of field glasses.

She convinced herself, looking back down along the course of her own migration, that she had found the opposite of where she had once lived, drowning in domesticity, pacing the length of her relational identity, living on table scraps of esteem. And she had breathed deeply and smelled something like freedom, something like happiness off in the distance. Just over the ridge.

It was the orphaned and injured they found along the way that had made her an emissary to civilization. Three or four a year. A stray cub. A pup curled up against a cold, milkless corpse. An owl with a broken wing. Animals suddenly, tragically incompatible with their own environment. Her betters preached the gospel of non-interference, out of respect for the will of nature over any individual. But Maribel simply could not abide. Tempers swelled and receded. Eventually they found her weakness endearing and impossible not to encourage. *Maribel's Mercy Missions*, always with rolling eyes.

There were lighthouses. Outposts in the liminal corridor between worlds. The animal parks. Neither purely here nor there and yet a bit of both. Places to go when one needed to come in from out of the cold. Off the plains. Out of the forests. Down from the cliffs. Places from which the unforgiving laws of nature were held in kind suspension.

And yet, it was always a Faustian trade to be sure: living for life.

A rapport of merciful intentions developed in Vancouver, where they named the rescued black bear cub Maribel. A job offer materialized out of the ether. God is all in the timing.

For it was in a cheap Vancouver hotel, excursion gear packed for the morning, the newest member of the team in post-coital slumber on old yellowing sheets, that Maribel realized she was not happy. From the bathroom, she had watched the rising and falling of his chest, young and hairy, as if he were a living clock with a bellows instead of gears. As if he contained his own ocean that ebbed and flowed in tides that would expand and contract his body forever.

And everything had been suddenly and perfectly clear. She toweled off and dressed quietly with an entirely new head about things. She left him a note to share with the others and was gone with the click of the latch.

The next time she saw any of them she was busy planting trees; busy making an environment. A habitat. They called down to her and waved from the lip of a concrete barrier posted with information about the hibernation and eating habits of *Ursus Americanus*. They all looked filthy and tired and hungry. And as happy as ever. Maribel smiled and mopped her brow with the back of a glove and waved up at them, fighting back a sickening sense, like black foaming water rising up in a basement, that she had been wrong; that she should have stayed with them. They disappeared beyond the barrier and she resisted the urge to scale the concrete wall and give chase.

It was only ten weeks of putting the zoo into zoologist that she had met Evan. By chance, they sat together in a darkened auditorium listening to passages from a new biography of Jane Goodall. He was alone and quiet and relaxed. He smelled of soap.

The biographer was a stooped, tufted man with spectacles that flashed in the lights whenever he looked up from the text, which he read emphatically and with unexpected humor. When he had finished reading, he took questions. Maribel had her hands up around her head, adjusting a wayward barrette. God is all in the timing.

Yes! said the biographer, pointing at her.

Maribel froze and then pointed at herself.

Yes, yes, said the biographer, the finger now vibrating in command. *Yes, yes!* as though it were her name. *You.*

Oh, no... I was just... Maribel shook her head. The biographer retracted his hand.

My apologies, young lady. I thought I saw a movement of commitment back there. I am like the bird looking for the worm up here. I am all about the movement. If you are not next, then who is next?

Evan rose from his seat.

Ah! Very good. There's commitment for you! You are next then?

I am next.

And not only next, but next door!

A wave of laughter all but knocked them together, Maribel smiling up at him in full blush and he looking down at her with a wink and a pat on the shoulder. *Gotcha' covered*, he had said.

Speak man! And make it a good one.

Do you find it difficult, as a biographer, to maintain any sort of rigorous objectivity about someone for whom you clearly have such admiration and affection?

The biographer nodded his head and wandered away from the podium and back again scratching the top of his head.

Good question. Except that rigorous objectivity is a fiction anyway, isn't it? Rigorous objectivity, as you put it, is generally unobtainable about anything, let alone about the people or things that we love and admire; let alone still further those that we commit to writing about. I do not claim to be perfectly objective.

He scanned the room and seemed about to choose another hand but stopped himself and pointed back at Evan who had taken his seat.

No, I am not perfectly objective, but there is less lost there than you might think. Dr. Goodall faced a lot of criticism early on for her practice of naming the Gombe chimps. I mean this is a woman who had no real scientific training to speak of. She couldn't even claim a bachelor's degree to her credit when she began her research of nonhuman primates. And when she began her historic research in Gombe, she did not know that conventional scientific practice would have counseled against using feeding stations to attract the chimps out of concern that their normal foraging and socialization patterns might be altered. Similarly, she did not know that conventional scientific practice would have counseled that she identify her subjects by numbers. Cold and impersonal symbols. But she didn't know that. She gave them names. Like people. Like friends of hers. 'Flo.' 'Flint.' 'Freud.' 'David Greybeard.' Primatologists have been saying ever since that the very act of naming a subject invites a sympathetic relationship that necessarily clouds objective analysis. And they are certainly right. Dr. Goodall herself acknowledged that the names were a mistake. But again, there is less lost in that mistake than you might think. Because the act of naming is also an act of claiming. It's an act of possession. It's a declaration of ownership. Not possession or ownership of another being so much as an ownership of one's own personal relationship with that other being. You can never truly understand any being in this world, and certainly no sentient being, unless you enter into a personal relationship with that being. You must declare that relationship. You must take responsibility for understanding who or what is on the other end of that personal connection. That, whether she knew it or not, is what Dr. Goodall did with the Gombe chimps. We now have a far more meaningful understanding of chimpanzees than we would otherwise have precisely because of her less than perfectly objective, pristinely scientific approach. Because she had named them, she knew them. Because she knew them, Dr. Goodall was compelled to understand these chimps – these hairy, rubber-faced children of the forest with names and personalities – at a level far deeper than traditional science could have reached.

He had paused, staring out at them, gears still turning. Hands and arms began to grow like weeds out of the audience. He ignored them, taking off his glasses and blowing at a lens.

Dr. Goodall was an activist long before she ever knew that about herself. She was an activist doing magnificent, groundbreaking methodologically flawed work as a scientist; but she always had the heart and soul of an activist. How do I know this? 'Flo.' 'Flint.' 'Freud.' 'David Greybeard.' Names. Relationships. That's how I know. You see, as a biographer, if I wish to truly understand another person, I pay close attention to their relationships. I pay close attention to who and what they have reached out and given a name. Who have they claimed? What connections do they care enough about to own? We own with names. In those names I find love and longing and identity. I find passion and grief. I find great reflections of the self that elude conscious understanding. I find deep identity that cannot be forced up into the light by simply jabbing a lot of impertinent questions down into the dark in hopes of spearing the great fish of the soul.

Evan had shifted in his seat and Maribel had stolen a sideways glance to find a pensive face with clean, precise features focused to a point of understanding. He must have felt the attention. He had turned and might have been about to whisper something, but Maribel had turned away and made a point of re-crossing her legs.

So, to get back to that most excellent question, I suppose it is a fair comment that in this book I have made Dr. Goodall – Jane – my own David Greybeard. I confess to being less than perfectly objective. I have not pretended to treat her as a number. She is a friend and in some ways a colleague. And you should read this biography through that lens. But much like Jane's chimpanzees, I think you will come away with a better, not a lesser understanding. And if you want to learn something about yourself, I commend to you the following exercise.

The biographer pushed his glasses up his nose and stared intently at his listeners, seeming to take independent measure of them.

To each one of you, the vast majority of the people in this room are complete strangers about whom you know nothing. Common human primates with good taste in non-fiction literature and a kindly patience for doddering old writers. Pick out one of these strangers – wait until you are out in the lobby, milling around – pick someone and shake his hand. Shake her hand. Give that person a name. Say it out loud. It's not their name, of course. It's your name for them. Say it out loud anyway. Go write it down someplace. Commit to it. Stand by it. Be able to repeat it. Then tonight, when you are home brushing your teeth, ask yourself why, out of all of these people, did you pick that particular person to name? And why did you choose that particular name in the first place? The answers will be slow in coming. But if you are honest and diligent, you will learn something about yourself. And if we all continue to do this throughout our lives, we may just save our own species. It is so much harder to destroy that which we ourselves have named. For suddenly, they are us.

In the wave of applause, Evan had turned to her.

You must be 'Yes', he had said, extending his hand. Maribel took it and squeezed.

That always depends on who's asking, she had said. *And you must be 'Next'.*

He had smiled through a slow beat of silence. Then, finally, *We'll see.*

And they had seen. She had been unable to keep him out of her head, despite the obstacles of which there had been plenty. Like his erstwhile but admirably undaunted girlfriend whose well-turned ankles alone had put the whole rest of Maribel to shame. Or like his almost single-minded devotion to climbing the ladder of his incomprehensible profession, which even in those first days had been incubating a decision to strike out on his own. And then there was the earth-splitting news that he was leaving Vancouver, that he and an old friend were starting a business in Summerfield, of all places. And, perhaps above all other obstacles, there was the absence of any obvious and compelling reason that he should have wanted her in the first place.

But Maribel, perhaps by the force of her own powers of denial, had been undeterred. They became light and shadow. Sound and echo. She learned his schedule. Studied his habits. Watched from across the street as he and his office mates, in their loosened ties and rolled up sleeves, ate their lunches and drank their beer and threw darts to settle the tab. And every so often she would screw up the courage to wander in, as if by coincidence, and he would invite her to join them. *Are you sure?* She would ask. *Yes, yes,* he would respond. *Please.* And he would pull up a chair next to him and give it a pat.

Yes. It was always Evan's response. Whatever she asked, his response was always an unqualified *Yes.* He never took the initiative. He never asked her. He trained *her* to ask *him.* He tamed her to come closer in, like some small woodland creature to a handful of bread. And every time she did come closer in, every time she dared to ask – the dinners, the park, the balloon rides, the symphony, the movies, the walks – he said *Yes. Yes. Yes.* Like he was calling her by the name he had given her from the very beginning.

And then, like a dream, floating in a bubble of color above the city and the ocean of pine beyond, he had asked her the one question she had once vowed, and then feared, never to hear again. She had said her own name back to him – *Yes, Yes* – and in that moment, her shining immortal Evan had become *Next.*

———

It is the insidious agenda of snow to bury the world, but to do so with such delicacy that we can only marvel at the beauty of the effort. We are complacent in the certainty of seasonal rescue. We push it into piles and roll it into balls and fashion it into comically rotund likenesses. But ice ages are as much an accumulation of snowflakes as any life is an accumulation of seconds. We are a species prone to seduction, slowly immobilized by infinitesimal pieces of time and the happenings that they carry on their tiny crystalline backs. It is never that we are taken by surprise. We simply succumb to an advantage of patience far greater than we can conceive.

Lady Ocelot stood, head down, watching her boots slowly disappear. The weather built its momentum. A lick of wind snaked out of the north, cold and dry. She pulled up the collar of her long tawny coat, tugged at her scarf, and returned her hands to her pockets.

Maribel stood quietly back from the road, on the far side of three young, underdressed bucks smoking cigarettes and reveling in their truancy. Together, they formed an ineffective windbreak but decent camouflage. If Lady Ocelot had been inclined to turn and look behind her, back towards the Summerfield Zoo, the boys' incessant hocking and spitting and bawdy commiseration against the cold was ample deterrence.

Maribel stamped her feet and looked up the road intently, focusing on the single spot in the world from where she knew change would come next; the point on the horizon at which she would be able to catch that first glint of the *S.B.L. Number 60* coming over the top of the hill.

Maribel had not particularly relished the idea of a bus ride. It was cold and her gloves were in her car and, in any event, she had been telling herself all day that it would be good to use her free time to make soup for Evan. Something hearty and full of vegetables. Something to thaw them out. But, one step at a time, Maribel had been pulled in a different direction.

Dr. Klatch had been in a particularly disagreeable mood, even in the context of the last three months, which had proven to be no picnic. He had blamed himself for Kimba's death and there was nothing anyone could say to bring him around. The local criticism had certainly not helped. But he was not an unintelligent or inexperienced doctor. He knew that it was not really the infection or an overly passive veterinary response that had killed Kimba any more than simple advanced age. Dr. Klatch knew that Kimba had done right by the statistics, outliving her wild African cousins by a good and relatively carefree fifteen years. There was no one to blame. But there was a penance to be paid nonetheless.

He was often surly and morose and vacillated between vehemently forswearing another single day of veterinary practice and vowing that he would never leave the Summerfield Zoo for fear of the living nightmare of learning that it was only his personal attentiveness that was keeping the animals alive and that he had abandoned them all to some cruel fate. So he had stayed on against his own will, a hostage to the brutality of circumstance and a morbid fear of his own happiness.

All of which had made Dr. Klatch exceedingly difficult to be around. For Maribel, it meant that she could do nothing right. Her diagnoses were always lacking, either because she was jumping to conclusions and thereby offending science, or because she was so prosaic as to unquestioningly accept lab results rather than trusting her gut instincts and professional intuition. She could not win. Dr. Klatch insisted that he did not need her assistance, when he clearly did, and he insisted that she remain close and available when it was clear that she was more of an irritant to him than anything else. The visitor tours had, therefore, become the bright spots of her days rather than the obligatory distraction from the real work to be done.

Today, at Dr. Klatch's insistence, she had left him alone with a pregnant llama and made herself available for tour duty. When it was one o'clock and she was signing out for the day, Dr. Klatch had shaken his head in disappointment, saying nothing and saying everything. Her half-day schedule, his sigh intoned, was not a creature born of budgetary concern, but a manifestation of laziness and lack of caring emblematic of all that was wrong in the world. So Maribel had taken off her coat and followed him back to the infirmary. She stayed for an extra hour until Dr. Klatch was so irritated that he all but asked her to leave. It had been an effort for her to smile and to pat him on the back and to bid him a pleasant day, but she was not without compassion.

Lady Ocelot had been standing at the front turnstiles pulling on her gloves and meticulously arranging her thick rosette-spotted scarf beneath her coat. She had pulled a tan knit cap out of her pocket and put it on as five children were racing through the parking lot for the entrance. They stopped in a skid at the ticket booth and waited impatiently for a threesome of adults who were busy locking something in the trunk of a blue Chevy. Lady Ocelot watched the children, blinking slowly, registering nothing.

At several minutes past two o'clock, Maribel had assumed her long gone. But their paths had converged, or re-converged, after all.

During her last tour of the day, Lady Ocelot had repeatedly joined and abandoned and rejoined the group. She asked no questions and seemed to pay no attention. She stood impassively at the back of the gaggle of fifteen, the only one without a companion or a child. When the tour meandered away from one habitat and made its way along the winding path to the next habitat, sometimes she would follow. More frequently she would not follow, letting Maribel pull the people from her like an engineer carrying a trainload of humanity away from the platform. Walking and looking backwards, Maribel almost found herself looking for a wistful wave or a stricken expression of longing. *Don't forget to write! I'm sorry! I love you!* But Lady Ocelot was always in her own world, never looking. Never caring. The first flakes of snow lightening her reddish curls.

She was in exile, Maribel had thought, watching her discretely in the House of Cats. She had been banished from a heartless place. She had dared to love the wrong person. Or she had refused to love the right person. She was a child of the old regime, daughter to the deposed king. The people loved her. They dared not jail her, nor kill her, so they sent her away. And here she was, in another place entirely; free, yes, but bound by chains to those forbidden feelings in that forbidden place.

Maribel had guided the group out of the House of Cats and on toward Monkey Island, leaving Lady Ocelot behind, alone, to look up into the foliage of amputated trees and to speak telepathically with the twins, Oscar and Ophelia, who looked back at her in luxuriant disinterest, registering nothing.

The *Number 60* bus pulled away with a half load, Maribel in the back and Lady Ocelot at the window behind the driver. The truants carried on obnoxiously in between, sprawling across the seats and kicking at each other. There was a red, handwritten message on a flap of cardboard affixed with silver tape to the metal overhang above the driver: *Sorry, Heater Broken*. Columnar plumes rose from the passengers like the smoke of distant signal fires, each seat another hill, another ridge toward the horizon.

Lady Ocelot did not acknowledge the green-coated man next to her, even if his body language suggested that he was more than just a little open to that possibility. She sat motionless but for the rocking of the bus and the occasional pothole. Her gaze through the frosted window and the snow remained fixed on freshly bleached fields that she did not see, but that served as invisible backdrop to the secret images in her head.

Four stops into town, on St. Louis Boulevard across from *Levitt's Shoes*, Lady Ocelot rose, stepped past her disappointed bus-mate and disembarked. Maribel stepped down onto the sidewalk after her. The wind was stronger than it had been at the zoo. Maribel tried to hunch herself further into her coat. She plunged her hands into her pockets and wished she had her gloves. In fact, she wished that she had just gone on home. She wished she were warm and listening to music and making soup like she had planned. But then, such wishes had become predictable and they, as much as anything, were what kept her warm.

The *Number 60* pulled away from the curb.

Lady Ocelot stood at the window of *Levitt's Shoes*. A young icy-white mannequin kicked at a soccer ball suspended from invisible fishing twine, artificial turf eternally green beneath his red leather soles. Behind him, faceless parents – in hiking boots and heels – cheered him on. There was a sudden lash of wind and she turned her back, heading slowly south up St. Louis Boulevard. Maribel watched, letting the wind take Lady Ocelot for half a block. Then she followed.

It was sixteen slow cold blocks to the City Plaza and Nellis Park. Every window held some empty interest to be perfunctorily examined and left behind. *Chocolate Scoops. Summerfield Drug and Sundry. Carl's Stationers. The One-Stop-All-Shop. Video Barn. Braverman Books.* The snow was falling harder now, muffling the sounds of the city. The world was softer and out of focus. The wind, too, had picked up, but was mercifully at their backs. Maribel's ears were numb and the blood burned at the tips of her toes. She tried her best to ignore the sensation of life freezing in her veins.

At the ice rink, Lady Ocelot took a seat on the top tier of the wooden bleachers. The three bronze horses rose up in semi-circular rage behind her with Nellis Field stretching out to the west like an empty white carpet. The horses were wild, frozen forever in time, ears back, teeth bared, their massive necks as if from dragons, twisting and pulling mightily in three different directions, muscles and veins straining against their smooth bronze hide like the rigging of a ship heading into a hurricane.

On the ice below, a half a dozen skaters were trying, with very little success, to coexist. Maribel seized the opportunity to cross the street and duck into an empty coffee shop to warm up. She sat in the window watching through the curtains of snow, hoping she would have at least a couple of minutes. She ordered a hot chocolate to go from a girl too young to drive. She watched Lady Ocelot watching the skaters. The milk steamer began its congested lament.

Two of the youngest skaters – or at least the smallest – collided. A taller figure with a hockey stick swooped in, pulled them up by the arms, adjusted their clothing and then took after another skater who was slapping his stick on the ice. They zigged and zagged and stopped and started until they too were sprawled across the ice and loose sticks were imperiling the other skaters. The scene repeated itself as it were a loop of film.

The hot chocolate arrived and Maribel paid. She wrapped her fingers around the paper cup and sighed. It was too hot to drink, but the relief was instant. Feeling in her ears and toes began to return in anguish. She took a cautious sip, scalding her tongue, and held the cup to her cheek. She watched through the sideways static for signs of life.

Lady Ocelot remained still, as if she herself had been bronzed, as if frozen – a daughter of Pompeii beneath the falling ash.

The long walk, Maribel surmised, had done Lady Ocelot little good. She remained hopelessly transfixed by a past frozen into the skating rink, just as it had been frozen into the shop windows and into the eyes of the people who passed her on the street, and into everything and everyone else she encountered. She decided that Lady Ocelot and her illicit lover, the man she could never have, the man from whom she had been banished, had used to steal away and skate upon the country marshes and ponds on winter afternoons, hidden among the wide bands of forest so far away from the prying eyes of the government and the spies of the city that they were free to drop their guard entirely and to be unapologetically happy and in love.

He had had convenient connections, this lover of hers, perhaps a loyal servant or a fellow officer who had a friend who owned property in the same woods. Property with a modest, leaky home and a bedroom fireplace and a great fur rug. Property that was seldom occupied in the winter since the friend of the loyal servant or officer had grown old and sick and had taken to staying close to the city once the ground froze. That, Maribel knew, must have been true happiness.

But those days must now seem like ice ages past. Maribel wondered if there was not yet some tiny spark in that frozen form across the street that glinted with the hope, however remote, of seeing him again. He would be looking for her. He would stop at nothing. She had to believe that much. She had to believe that change was a fundamental property of existence. Ice thaws and water softens the ground and the world turns green. Those once lost, return. Or could return, and that is enough. Change and happiness are improbable lovers, with no future save an eternity of shallow, impermanent consummations. Improbable, yes. But no more improbable than gliding across water on blades of steel. There is always hope, she thought.

Lady Ocelot rose and descended the bleachers. She walked to the statue of the rearing horses and looked out over Nellis Field. Her hair whipped in the wind like an auburn flag on a long forgotten field of battle. After a minute or two she turned and headed back for the ice rink and the sidewalk beyond. Maribel stood and moved for the door.

They covered almost two blocks, back in the direction from which they had come. Maribel stayed on the opposite side of the street, one hand in her pocket, the other clutching her cup like it was a lantern cutting through the dark.

Lady Ocelot stopped outside *The One-Stop-All-Shop*. She stood at the window looking at a family of Styrofoam snow people clustered around a sign advertising extra low prices on everything from donuts to shaving supplies.

Then, quite unexpectedly, she went inside.

Maribel started to cross the street, but a stream of traffic set her back on her heels. By the time she was free to cross, she had thought better of it and changed her mind. She loitered outside *The Little Depot*, looking in at the toy train speeding past herds of unconcerned plastic cows and children gathered at the water wells and farmers waving from tiny yellow tractors. The train disappeared into a hole in goat-dotted cliffs. Maribel watched the *One-Stop-All-Shop* across the street in the reflection.

When Lady Ocelot emerged she turned south again, back towards the ice rink, now carrying a gray plastic bag at her side. At the rink, she cut in sharply towards Nellis Field, moving past the bleachers to the horses. There, at the base of the sculpture, amid the flurry of hooves, she lowered herself into the snow.

Maribel crossed the street, pausing at the rink out of caution, but then pressed forward to the bleachers. She ascended to the third and highest tier and sat down on the planks of frozen wood scarred with the hieroglyphs of love and slander. She wished that she too had a full-length coat for insulation. The underside of her legs began to lose feeling, as though portals to her body had been thrown open and the cold was flooding in like icy seawater into a shattered hull. She stood up again and turned, looking for her, the cold having overcome caution.

There was no sign of her at first. All was white, windswept static. The snow was falling as heavily as Maribel could ever recall. The wind drove needles of ice into her eyes and even when she hazarded her hands for assistance she had to keep her lids all but closed. She turned her back to the wind for temporary relief. The skaters had had enough and were changing into boots. The smallest of them was crying from the cold. Maribel turned back into the wind.

A movement caught her attention. Lady Ocelot was directly behind the horses, still sitting in the snow, hunched and motionless except for the occasional and inexplicable thrust of an arm. Another. And another. Sharp and jerking. Maribel sensed distress; a pulse of alarm in her blood. She felt that some vicious pain had suddenly broken free. It was howling with the wind like a wounded animal, gnashing at its own limbs, devouring itself down there in the snow. Consumed with inexplicable urgency, she wanted to break from her hiding. She wanted to fling herself over the back of the bleachers down into the snow and to fight her way to the frozen horses. She wanted to provide solace. *Change is coming,* she would shout over the wind. *There is always change and change is coming!* She would have done anything in that moment to save her. Even lie.

But, true to her training, Maribel remained quiet and did not move.

In a few bitter moments, she saw Lady Ocelot stand, fighting against the force that pushed at her entire body. The bottom of her long coat was caked with snow. She removed her cap and stuffed it into her pocket and began to push forward. She had walked a dozen halting steps out into the white emptiness of Nellis Field before Maribel understood what was happening. Then she felt a gasp opening her throat to the cold.

A bright red, gaping wound sliced open. Left then right then left again, a scarring scarlet pain ripped and fluttered up and up and up across the bloodless sky with a long trickling tail that whipped and lashed at the cold air in abject torment. The wind took it higher. Higher. Higher. Higher. It fought her with every step, careening violently one way and then the other, trying to snap its invisible leash.

Lady Ocelot walked with slow resolve to the center of the field, unspooling twine as she went, until the brilliant red diamond was nothing but an airborne flame; and then a lone spark in the white wind. Every so often its luminance seemed to flutter and flash in the air like a distant beacon in salt spray, both hope and warning in a single pulse.

Lady Ocelot turned her back to the fury of the horses, to Maribel and to all of humanity. She dropped to her knees, inclined her face to that jeweled, flaming drop of blood, and screamed in full-throated rage and anguish up into the storm. Again and again and again she howled herself raw, her fists clenched and her head back and her long hair like ropes of fire in the violent white air.

The snow took her voice like the sound of a leaf leaving the branch and the wind carried it away for no one to hear.

With a violent pull, Lady Ocelot snapped the leash of twine from the spool and dropped her hands to her sides. She stood, watching that curse, watching that burning prayer, as it soared upwards for a moment, hanging for an instant of indecision, and then cart wheeling suddenly south and then down, end over end, falling like a drop of blood from the finger of God. It lodged in the top of a tall pin oak at the south end of Nellis Field. The tree burned like a candle.

The minutes passed slowly in the cold, fighting the wind, and it seemed like a long time before Lady Ocelot pulled herself to her feet and walked back out of Nellis Field. Maribel had lost all feeling in her hands and feet and her face, but had dared not leave. The light was beginning to fail and the temperature promised to drop even further. She waited until Lady Ocelot was past the now empty ice rink and back onto the sidewalk before descending the bleachers.

They walked further south until they reached Beamish Road and the Police Station and then walked east six blocks to the train depot. The station was crowded and Maribel had to search for her once she was inside the terminal, forcing herself to focus through the pain of feeling that came with thawing. She ricocheted from one knot of travelers to another, looking for the coat, looking for the hair, and finding only people.

Just as she had decided to give up and to catch a cab back to the zoo and her car, she spotted Lady Ocelot in the line for Lottsberg.

Lottsberg, She thought to herself. *Why Lottsberg? What was in Lottsberg?*

Maribel looked at her watch. Lottsberg was only a thirty-five minute ride. Soup was out of the question now anyway. She could bring food home. Evan had mentioned he might be working late.

The train car was not crowded, but still full enough for Maribel to easily obscure her presence when she needed to by leaning forward behind the woman in the blue coat with the shopping bags, or rocking back behind the large-gutted man with the football shoulders. As it turned out, neither maneuver was necessary. Lady Ocelot sat as she had on the *Number 60*: in the front of the car, head to the window. Never looking up. Never turning around. Registering nothing.

Maribel leaned back in her seat and suddenly felt exhausted. She wanted to be home. She wanted to be home with Evan. Why was she here? What sickness was this? Was this a curse of genetics? A precursor to her father's wandering darkness? She wondered if he had ever suddenly come to his senses in a strange place and known the feeling of wanting to be home; wanting to be surrounded by the familiar; longing sharply for the life he had unwittingly abandoned.

She should have gone out to see him, she thought. It was his birthday. She should have done more than just call. Maybe if he had seen her face; putting it together with a voice and a smell; a presence. Maybe he would have remembered.

A girl, maybe thirteen, with healthy black hair escaping a white wool cap sat across the aisle with a pink plastic cage on her lap. Two green eyes blinked from inside.

"Pretty little cat," said Maribel.

"Thank you," said the girl.

"Boy or girl?"

"Girl."

"What's her name?"

"Miss Loulabell."

"That's a pretty name."

"My dad just calls her Lucky."

"Oh. Is Miss Loulabell lucky?"

"We rescued her from the shelter. They were going to kill her."

"Well that is lucky then, isn't it? She sure seems calm and quiet in there."

The girl lifted the cage into the air up to eye level. She twirled it clockwise so that the front was facing across the aisle. The calico feline tensed and locked eyes with Maribel in the shifting light.

"She's real scared," said the girl. "Miss Loulabell doesn't like cars or trains or planes."

"Oh, poor Miss Loulabell." Maribel brushed the back of a finger against the outside of the cage and cooed. "Are you scared, baby? You don't need to be scared."

"I think she just doesn't know where she's going or what's going to happen when she gets there."

"But you're so loved, Loulabell. You're so loved."

"She thinks we're never going to let her out again."

When the train stopped in Lottsberg, Maribel let Lady Ocelot disembark first, not entirely confident that she wouldn't just opt on a whim to ride on to Kimbelston Platte or all the way out to East Wilson. But she did disembark and made her way almost somnolently through the Lottsberg Terminal, threading clusters of people and luggage and lines.

After a brief stop at the restroom, she walked to the main entrance and looked outside. It was snowing lightly and there was a breeze that kept the flags animated but at less than full attention. It was impossible to tell whether the storm had just left Lottsberg or was just arriving.

Lady Ocelot pulled a cell pone from her pocket and made a brief call. She walked outside and sat on a bench and waited as the sun began to roll off a shelf somewhere behind the white curtains.

Maribel stood directly behind her, inside the terminal at the big window next to the automatic doors. Lady Ocelot bent forward, elbows on her knees, as if contemplating the frozen ground. Maribel wondered if she was thinking about the seventy-foot candle burning in Nellis Park. She wondered if she could feel it burning in her mind. There was no way to tell.

Lady Ocelot sat up again and began grooming, pulling her fingers through her wind-knotted hair, first the left side, then the right, both hands tending simultaneously to the same snarls and then alternating in long, smooth rakes from scalp to tip. She was, Maribel realized, in mid-transformation. She gathered the strands together as one auburn rope, which she then flipped effortlessly into a single, simple knot behind her shoulders. Her posture became more erect and her head tracked every movement as though she was taking stock of her environment in minute detail. There was a deep intake of air and a billow of steam that she released as she shook her head and hands in a small, frenetic, coordinated spasm. Something like calm returned almost before the steam was gone.

In ten minutes the shuttle was there to pick her up. It was a cheerful pink color with darkly tinted square widows with the string of a painted balloon tied in a bow and looped around the blue-sky *C* in *Children's.*

Lady Ocelot rose from the bench. The doors folded open and a grave-looking man with a baldhead and glasses stepped out pulling a small rolling bag. He winced as the frigid air met his face. He pulled a gray overcoat closed over his thin, light blue scrubs, smiled perfunctorily as he passed Lady Ocelot and darted into the terminal. She stepped up into the shuttle and disappeared inside. The doors closed.

Maribel strained to see her, but to no avail. The windows were dark and impenetrable. She surmised that privacy was the whole point of a shuttle like that.

But she knew where Lady Ocelot was sitting anyway. And she knew what she looked like in there. And now she knew why.

As the shuttle pulled away from the curb, Maribel decided that the pink paint job and the balloon and the fanciful sky-blue lettering were unnecessary, however well intentioned. It took either a love for what was inside or a fear of what was outside. The color of the cage never mattered.

———

"Sorry I'm late. Are you starving?"

Evan was reading by the fire with his feet up. Sarah Vaughn was like a blanket of smoke wafting around the lamp and casting shadows. He closed his book over his finger and lolled his head backwards toward the sound of her voice.

"Well, if it isn't the lovely *Yes*."

"Hello handsome *Next*."

"Give us a kiss then."

She kissed him upside down, his nose along the underside of her chin. She unzipped her coat.

"You shoveled the driveway," she said.

"You smell like pizza."

"There's a good reason for that on the kitchen counter," she said. "I'll bring you a piece if you forgive me."

"You need to be forgiven?"

"Yes."

"Okay. You're forgiven."

"Don't you want to know why you're forgiving me?"

"Um, for letting the pizza get cold with a lot of kissing and silly questions. Is there something else?" He stood up and followed her into the kitchen.

"I told you I'd make you soup tonight."

"Hey... that's right. Soup. That just might be unforgivable."

"Really?"

"Well let's see how the pizza is." He opened the box and stuffed half a slice into his mouth, chewing contemplatively. "Mmm. Close. You always seem to squeak by. One of these days you'll beg to be forgiven and you're going to come up short and then won't you be sorry?"

"Oh, I will. I'll be very sorry. I'm sorry tonight."

"Stop groveling. You're forgiven already. Let's have it."

"Lucy went into labor, or so we thought."

"Which one's Lucy? Here," Evan pushed the box across the counter and pretended to be his mother. "Eat, eat, you're like a rail over there. You're like a stick. I can barely see you you're so thin."

She folded a piece in half and devoured it. She was starving. She felt like she had been wandering around in the wilderness for days.

"Easy there, cupcake," said Evan, now imitating his father wagging his finger. "I told your mother it was enough already with the extra helpings when you were a baby. She spoiled you, your mother. Now look at you... going after the pizza there. You're enormous."

"Evan."

"Sorry. Who's Lucy?"

"Llama."

"Everything okay?"

"Yeah, I think so. False alarm. Doc's worried, but Doc is always worried. I would have called, but my cell is dead and I kept thinking it would only be another ten minutes and so now it's eight o'clock and there's no soup. Obviously. Sorry."

"Okay, here's the deal. Three Hail Marys and another slice of pepperoni and we're good. Forget about the soup."

Maribel chewed. She felt a seismic settling in the hollow of her chest, like the shifting of walls that define an empty space, threatening to collapse. It was always too easy, his forgiveness. Evan's acceptance came like tap water. She could have told him anything and he would have accepted it. He may not have actually *believed* it. He probably *didn't* believe it. She would never know. He had too much self-control. But he would have accepted anything she told him. As if believing or disbelieving was irrelevant. As if it was wholly unnecessary for her to earn whatever indefinable thing she needed from him. Whatever she needed was hers. She wanted for nothing. She had been given the secret handshake and the keys. No questions asked. Nothing to prove. She was always on the inside. It was not possible for her to be outside of Evan.

The truth was almost always innocent. Strange perhaps, but innocent. Like tonight. But it bothered her to imagine a contrary truth. An ugly truth. And if she could imagine it, why couldn't he? Did he really not care? Was a little skepticism so beyond the pale? An unsettled quality to his voice suggesting the possibility of consequence? A look from which she might imagine his fear? His pain? Betrayal? Simple disappointment?

No. He gave her nothing to overcome. The door to Evan was always wide open.

But the truth tonight really was innocent. Or so Maribel supposed since, when she really stopped to think about it, she did not actually know what the truth meant. Had she known, had she been able to explain it to herself, she might simply have told him. She might have let it loose. She might have set it free.

"Well I heard a strange one today," she said when they were in bed, after an evening of eating and cleaning up and television. The last of the fire still popped and hissed its way to extinction out in the living room.

Evan folded Abe Lincoln's life over his finger and looked at her. "Yeah?"

"This gal I work with has a friend who is married to a guy who follows people."

"Follows people."

"Compulsively. Just follows them around. Not every day. Just every so often."

"It's called stalking. There's a lot of that these days."

"No. It's not stalking. He doesn't know any of these people. He just watches them."

"It's a sex thing," he said, opening his book again. "It's a perversion of some sort. Voyeurism."

"Not just women. I mean anybody."

"So. Maybe he's attracted…"

"No, no. I don't think – she doesn't think it's a sex thing. He's supposedly a perfectly decent guy with no indication that there is something loose or out of balance. I mean he's perfectly normal."

"How do you know he's normal?"

"I don't. But his wife does. I assume."

Evan closed the book and placed it on the nightstand. He rolled over and propped himself up on an elbow.

"So he got himself arrested?"

"No. It's nothing illegal."

"Well he obviously got busted somehow."

"Yeah, I guess his wife found out about it. I don't know the details except that she confronted him and he confessed."

"Confessed to what exactly?"

"He sees someone that interests him, you know, that piques his curiosity in some way, just someone out of a crowd, and he just shadows the person as long as he can."

"You mean like in a car?"

"In a car, on foot, bus, train, whatever it takes."

"Doesn't make contact?"

"No. I mean, not as far as anyone knows."

"What's his explanation?"

"Doesn't really have one. He says he just likes to, I don't know, follow people. Watch what they do."

"Hmm."

"What?"

"Something's wrong there."

"Why?"

"I don't know. There just is."

"Why can't it be just..."

"What?"

"I don't know. Curiosity. An innocent... an intellectual interest in other humans. You know. What they do. How they act."

"You're reaching."

"Why?"

"What's he do for a living?"

"I don't know what he does for a living. Why does it matter?"

"Is he a behavioral psychologist?"

"No. Not as far as I know. I doubt it. But what does it matter? What if he's a truck driver? What if he's a hot dog vendor? Can't he still have a legitimate interest in understanding people? Learning from them?"

"No. Not to the extent of following them around."

"Why? I mean why can't..."

"Because, Maribel, there are only so many hours in the day."

"What do you mean?"

"I mean that you can hypothesize all you want about knowledge for the sake of knowledge, but in the end all of this is time taken away from this guy's own life. His family. Why do you think that is? Don't answer, I'll tell you. He is either looking for something he doesn't have or he's escaping something or someone he doesn't like, or both. If you can rule out a professional interest – gumshoe, spook, process server – then something's wrong. This is extreme dissatisfaction. Something's missing."

"Like?"

"Like sex. He's not getting enough. He's not getting the right kind. Maybe his wife is a real bitch and he can't bring himself to go home. Maybe he's bored out of his skull. I don't know what it is but something is out of balance. And the odds are overwhelming that he's up to no good. It's something addictive. It's drugs. It's gambling. It's sex. I'll bet it's sex. It's always sex."

"Maybe its not always sex or something bad. Not for a good man."

"FDR was a good man. You know how he treated Eleanor? JFK was a good man."

"When did you become so cynical and suspicious?"

"Read any newspapers lately?"

"I think you're excluding other possibilities."

"Like?"

"I don't know. Just to learn."

"Learn what?"

"I don't know."

"What'd his wife do about it?"

"I have no idea. She's not even my friend. I don't even know her."

"Well, if one of your friends provides you with convincing evidence that I spend my spare time following strangers around the city for no discernable reason, then I suggest you kick me out and change the locks until you get some straight answers."

"What? Is that what you'd do? If you found out something like that about me?"

"No."

"If someone told you that I'd been sneaking around behind your back following people? Following men?"

"Of course not."

"Why? Would you believe it?"

"No."

"Why?"

"Because you're incapable of guile."

"I am not."

"Yes you are. See? You can't even lie about guile."

"What if you were wrong? What if you found out it was true?"

"I'd know it was because you had a professional interest in primate behavior. I'd realize that you were subconsciously leaping from veterinary science back to zoology back to cultural anthropology."

"It would never occur to you that I was out looking for sex?"

"No."

"Why?"

"Because you'll never find a better lay than me and you're smart enough not to waste your time. Come on... it's *me* we're talking about. Look at this body. I'm all about the sex, baby. Pizza and sex."

Classic Evan. Humor that was indistinguishably dismissive and deflective. She wondered whether he was genuinely unconcerned or protecting himself. Or was she once again over-reading an open book?

He fell back and grabbed Lincoln by the spine. "Anyway, that's not who you are," he said, trying to find his place.

"My mother had an affair once," said Maribel, surprising herself, the lock on the old secret shame having crumbled with rust.

"Really?"

"With the public defender."

"Ouch." He closed the book again and looked at her. "Bet that went over swell with Officer Lumm."

"Yep. Dad locked 'em up and David J. Fossey, Esquire, set 'em free."

"He found out?"

Maribel nodded.

"At the very end. It was all over the squad room."

"But you about it knew first, didn't you. You're trying to prove your guile."

She nodded again.

"How?"

She did not answer.

"Maribel?"

"She started going for walks on Tuesdays and Fridays. Like clockwork. I got curious."

"Mmm."

"I followed her. I saw what I saw. It was something."

Evan was silent, watching her intently.

"I never told him," she said. "It was six months after she went into remission. I was afraid of, you know, upsetting things. Cancer came back anyway though. I should have told him."

"Maribel... that's ridiculous."

"No."

"So... I'm guessing he found out about it and then he found out that you had known all along."

She could only look at him and nod.

"Guess it doesn't really matter now, does it?"

"Guess not. Maybe there's some mercy in that disease of his after all."

It was Evan's turn to nod.

"I should have gone down to see him," she said.

"You called him."

"I know. I always call. I should have gone down again. I'm going. I'm definitely going. Maybe this month."

"Maribel. Maribel?"

She looked at him.

"You've got to stop this. You've got to stop trying to go back."

"Claire went back."

"Claire never left. Claire has no life of her own. She walked in your mom's shoes her whole life and she's still wearing them, that's all. It's different."

"He's *my* father too. His condition doesn't change that."

"Right. But you're the only one who doesn't accept his condition."

"Yes I do."

"No. You don't. You want to go back to someone who doesn't exist any more. Remember the last time? Remember how you felt? He's happier without any memory at all than with a ghost of a memory. You're just haunting him."

"Evan..."

"I'm sorry. But you just want to see some glint of recognition in his eyes. Some knowing smile."

"Yes. I do."

"Why?"

"Because he's my father."

"No. Because you feel guilty and you're ready to take any hint of recognition as forgiveness."

"So."

"So? So that's the thing you can't have, Maribel. You want it and he can't give it to you. That's that. You need to let it go. You're trapped right now. It's like you've built yourself this cage out of your guilt and his lost memory. You can't go back. And you can't go forward until you accept. He can't forgive what he can't remember. He's just not there anymore."

"That's not true," she whispered. The room began to flood around her. Evan let go of the book and pulled her head down onto his chest. He stroked her hair. His voice softened.

"Recognition is the last thing he wants, Sweetie. The flicker of a ghost is all he'll ever get. You're willing to tempt him with the very thing he cannot have. And, in exchange, he will tempt you with the one thing that you cannot have. It's cruel in both directions. How is that in anybody's best interest?"

"He's my father."

"Look. I'm not saying don't ever see him. I'm not saying you don't owe Claire some help, if she'll take it. I'm not saying don't go buy a ticket tomorrow."

"Then what are you saying?"

"I'm saying all pain comes from resistance and all happiness comes from acceptance. I'm saying he can't free you from these feelings. I'm saying he can't save you from yourself. No one can. You're the only one that can let yourself out."

"I know."

"No. You don't, Maribel. You don't accept that there is nothing left to be forgiven. You don't accept that he loved you. Knowing everything, he loved you. You don't accept that I love you. Knowing everything, I love you."

"There's nothing to know."

"If you say so," he said.

"There isn't."

"You want proof, but love is not provable. It simply is or it is not. You either feel it in the room or you don't. And if you feel it, Maribel, then you are forgiven."

"I accept that you love me," she said. "I do. I'd die without you. This has nothing to do with you."

"You're right," said Evan. "This has absolutely nothing to do with me."

———

"Will she come back?" asked the boy.

Six, she guessed. Maybe seven. He held his sister's hand like he was swinging on a rope. The short, spiky red hair made him look like a lit match.

"Oh, I think she'll be back. Anna's gotten loose a couple times before."

"Why does she come back?"

"This is her home. This is where she gets all of that yummy food you see in there. And this is where people take care of her when she's sick."

Mr. Bird was like a statue in a park, a couple of bronze shoulders and a hat, maybe an outstretched hand, on which the pigeons roosted between sorties to exploit human carelessness and generosity. He was still except for his hand, which was incessant, like a sparrow in a bath. From his vantage point on the wet stone bench, it was easy to imagine that he was staring at her.

"This is where Anna's friends are," she continued, tailoring her words and pointing up into different trees. "Sam… there, and Jake… there. Anna was rescued when she was just a little baby. She comes from a forest in a country called Gambia. That's in Western Africa, a very long way from here. When she was found she had been abandoned and was very sick and would certainly have died."

"Why was she abandoned?" asked the sister.

"Well, her mother probably died. Baby chimpanzees learn almost everything about living in the jungle from their mothers. If the mother dies, young chimps don't stand a very good chance of surviving. But, fortunately for Anna, there was a boy just a little older than you are…"

"Me?"

"Yes, you, handsome little man."

The match-boy burned brighter, looking up at his sister. Behind them, Maribel could see Mr. Bird recross his legs and adjust the pad in his lap. His hand paused and he inclined his chin to the thatched eves of the pump house across the trail behind her as the adult barn swallows brought in another load of immobilized insects to the nest. Maribel tested his focus with a smile. There was no return. The hand began again.

"And that little boy found her and took her home to his father, who was a minister in Gambia. They nursed Anna back to health and they raised her as one of the family for several years. They tried a few times to release her back into the forest, but Anna had become too accustomed to people and to being fed rather than searching for her own food. To make matters worse, none of the troops of chimps in the area would accept her and it actually became dangerous for her not to live with people. And so every time they released her, or escaped, she would always find her way back."

"How come she came here to that, that, um, how come, how come she came to that place in there?" The boy pointed over the railing into the habitat on the other side of the mesh.

"My goodness, Ryan," said the grandmother. "So many questions for this poor girl." The sister laughed. The hand-holders in matching windbreakers stayed in the back whispering.

"No, no. That's why I'm here," said Maribel with a dismissive wave. "Ryan, that's a real good question although I'm afraid it's not a very nice story. You see, the minister died of a disease and his family moved back to London. They couldn't take Anna with them, so they gave her to some friends who did not take very good care of her. They sold her to a circus …"

"A circus!" He bounced and swung.

"Yes, a circus, where fortunately she did not stay for very long because they did not take very good care of her either. The circus was shut down and Anna ended up in the hands of a humane society in Tunisia. The humane society ultimately placed her with a zoo in Morocco, which sold her to a research facility in London …"

"Did she see her people family there?"

"No, London is a very big place for a little monkey. Her people did not even know she was there. After a while Anna was sold to a zoo in Kentucky and then she came here to Summerfield. And we've had her about sixteen years now."

"Had," said the sister.

Mr. Bird's hand stopped and he inclined his head again, this time closing his eyes to the sun burning a bright blue-rimmed hole through the brooding anvils hanging low over the Summerfield Zoo. The rain was done now. Maribel could feel the warmth on his face; could feel the muscles around his eyes relax; could feel the years melting in his veins. Winter had gone.

"Excuse me?"

"You *had* her," the sister repeated. "Now she's gone."

"Right. She's close by someplace. She's probably still on zoo property, up in one of these trees. It's only been less than a full day so I think she'll be back. She has everything she needs right here."

"Then why'd she leave?"

"Because she could, I guess. See that big wire door back there? By those two big bushes? Yesterday we brought a big tractor in here to help us make room for a special termite mound and after they took the tractor back out someone didn't close all of the latches on that door and our little Anna was the first to discover the mistake."

"What's a termite mound?" Ryan yanked down. His sister yanked back up, separating his shoes from the earth.

"Well, when it's done it will look like a big pile of hard dirt, but it's actually specially constructed out of concrete and wire and rebar and there's a secret little door built into the back of it. And when you open the little door there are a lot of these little plastic tubes inside the mound that we can push tasty food into. Then Anna, Jake and Sam can pick around the outside of the mound and find their own food to eat. When it's ready, the termite mound will go right over there in that hole."

"Did those people with the tractor get in trouble?"

"Ryan, now that's enough. Stop hanging on Pam. Stand on your own two feet. You're acting like a damned monkey. Goodness."

"Okay. Are we ready to move on?"

———

Mr. Bird drove a station wagon that was old and brown, with a scar of silver blood across the entire length of its passenger side. The right tail-light had been shattered. The aluminum luggage rack had been sharply reconfigured from a rectangle into something no longer fairly within the rhombus family. A long crack, like the leading edge of a crescent moon or the glinting chine of a scythe, laid claim to most of the rear window. The car, whatever its mileage, was remarkably clean.

Mr. Bird was in no hurry, just as he had been in no hurry back at the zoo. He had still been sitting on the stone bench across from Monkey Island for a good hour after Maribel had signed out and was heading for the parking lot.

Dr. Klatch had twice encountered her loitering on the trail behind the pump house, near collisions that seemed to double his irritation at a schedule that took her off the clock after only a half-day of work. *I thought you went home,* he had declared curtly without slowing down. *You must be here first thing in the morning, Maribel. There is much to do.* She could see by the deep creases between his eyebrows that he wanted to ask why, if it was so damned important for her to leave half way through the day, did she insist on hanging about doing nothing. She obviously could not explain about Mr. Bird.

But she also knew that Dr. Klatch had come to anticipate these short days. He no longer feigned surprise when she announced she was leaving. He no longer indulged in temperamental machinations to keep her engaged into the afternoon. An afternoon without an assistant was an afternoon that Dr. Klatch could begin drinking early, a secret practice that had crept into his routine sometime during the winter. The only real secret was that most of the grounds staff, if not the front office, knew all about the flask he carried. A few of them, including Maribel, also knew that Dr. Klatch had been in the primate habitat after the contractors had gone away with their tractor.

Mr. Bird rolled slowly along St. Louis Boulevard, steering around rain-filled potholes left by a hard winter. If history repeated itself, it would take another two months and a dozen broken axels before the city lifted a finger.

The street was still damp, catching the spring sun in a clean sheet of light that coated the ice-bitten road like a salve. At the City Plaza, clusters of t-shirted men darted chaotically at opposite ends of the skating rink. Basketballs arched like tiny orbiting planets.

He merged onto Van Buren, which was Summerfield's fast food alley, and turned into the drive-thru lane of the *Burger Barn*. Maribel turned in behind him. At the haystack, Mr. Bird stuck his head out and opened and closed his mouth in a way that made Maribel think of the baby barn swallows waiting for their next bug. When she reached the haystack, Maribel rolled down her window and thrust her head out towards the metal bale and said that she wanted the same thing that the car in front of her had ordered. The haystack sounded confused and Maribel repeated the order. She pulled around the *Burger Barn* to the pay window without waiting for a further response, afraid that that he might drive off without her seeing his direction.

Mr. Bird had not driven off. He was parked at the far end of the lot facing Van Buren Road and *The Dunkin' Chicken* across the street. Maribel paid the girl in the barn window and drove to the opposite end of the parking lot beneath the revolving sign of the red barn with the haystacks out front. She turned off the engine and leaned in, wrapping her arms around the steering wheel so that she could see through the broken back window of his car. She could see the shape of his shoulders and head above the front seat, perfectly motionless, almost as though he was the seat itself.

She opened the bag and pulled out a Big Barn with wagon wheels, which meant tomatoes, and extra cheese and an order of hay sticks, which were extra-thin French fries. She tasted the soda, which was a root beer. She ate, watching his silhouette in the brown car by the road, wondering what he was thinking. She wondered if identical food tastes identical, no matter who eats it, or if flavors were part of unique experience, chemical data requiring an idiosyncratically cognitive translation. She dragged a bundle of hay sticks through a puddle of ketchup. There was no way to really know another person.

Just the same, she concluded that Mr. Bird was a lonely sort. His wife had left him some years ago. She was an artist and he was not. She thought like an artist and he did not and that was a problem for them. She created things and he went to work every day and earned money. Mr. Bird was a man of science, a man of vectors and square corners and coefficients. They came at life from such different perspectives. Being together and doing the same things was a wholly separate experience for each of them. Eventually, she had had enough such companionable isolation and she had left him, suddenly and without any explanation, like a shoe on the side of the highway. The divorce had been quick. She had asked for nothing. He kept the house and the car, both of which he had purchased because he had the paying job. She hadn't wanted any of the things that defined them. She did not want her old paintings in the closet or the one over the bed. She just wanted out.

Maribel sipped her root beer.

That was their old car he was in. He had the money to trade it in, or to at least fix it up. A new paint job. Get rid of the luggage rack. But he could not bring himself to change anything about the world in which they had lived. He still lived in the same home, every room, every last bit of furniture, still in tact, as though she had simply stepped out to the grocery store and would be right back. He knew she had moved to another country, France or Italy or Spain or Greece, or maybe New York or Los Angeles, which may as well have been other countries as far as Mr. Bird was concerned; places where she could fully indulge her artistic sensibilities.

He knew he would probably never see her again. And yet he could not help but anticipate her. He made trips to their various favorite places throughout the town, expecting in a quiet, forbidden part of his heart that someday, when he was sitting very still, sketching something that she might have sketched, he will sense her arrival, like a flutter of wings just outside some corner of his vision. Nothing will come of such a sighting, of course. She will never know he is there, watching. Sketching. It will be enough for him, Maribel imagined, just to see her.

Mr. Bird sat watching cars and trucks and busses pass between the *Burger Barn* and *The Dunkin Chicken* for a long time after Maribel had finished eating. She opened her window to let the heat out. The sun was rolling freely now in a sky that had cleared and hardened into a glossy dome of beryl shot with veins of melancholic granite that were like great gray rivers retreating into space. She melted cubes of ice on her tongue, waiting.

When he finally started his car and exited the parking lot, Mr. Bird pointed himself East. They left the business of Summerfield quickly, tracing Bright Leaf Road, passing over corridors of greening cropland and into the heart of a loose network of subdivisions which, from the air, looked like the petals of a strange flower carved into the alfalfa and the nascent corn. Every mile, side roads veered to the right and to the left, each an entrance to a different plume of habitat. None of the roads had gates. None of the subdivisions came with signs declaring a name. Eventually, Mr. Bird left Bright Leaf Road through an arc of filtered light from a stand of old Maple that was like a natural gateway all its own.

Within another ten minutes, Maribel could see homes rising up on the near horizon. They were modest and mostly white, arranged in a circular array of interconnected cul-de-sacs, as though she and Mr. Bird were a couple of ants climbing the stem of a giant daisy. She slowed as he slowed, trying to maintain her distance. The road bent and they began to trace the inner circle, passing on the right a new cul-de-sac petal every thousand yards. Mr. Bird turned into the fifth cul-de-sac. Maribel slowed and waited at the corner. Like all of the others she had passed, the cul-de-sac was rimmed with nine homes.

Mr. Bird pulled into the driveway of the fifth house, a simple, two-story, white-clapboard cliché at the very tip of the petal. The driver's door opened and he stepped out, turned and bent back into the car to retrieve his sketchpad and whatever might have been left of his *Burger Barn* lunch. He closed the car door and arched his back, stretching up into the sunlight. He stood in his driveway looking out towards the entrance of the cul-de-sac, from where Maribel was looking back, idling. She knew he did not see her. Just as at the zoo, she was in his field of vision, but was not his focus. One last time, before enclosing himself for the remainder of the day, he was scanning the horizon for any sign of happiness.

Mr. Bird turned and proceeded up a short walk to the front door, and disappeared inside.

Maribel waited a minute or two longer before rolling slowly into the cul-de-sac. Her plan, such as it was, was to complete the small loop of road, never stopping, but slowing enough as she passed his house to take in whatever there might be to take in – a skateboard on the stoop, a cat on the sill, the window coverings, a mantle crowded with old framed photos that she could not see but that she would not have to see – and to then head back down the daisy stem to Bright Leaf Road, and then home, where she intended to make good on a promise involving salad and lasagna. Evan was bidding the school district again. He would be tired and stressed and hungry. It was her mother's lasagna. Her father, always good for seconds, called it sinful.

As soon as she reached the driveway, the plan fell apart and Maribel came to a full stop.

She had not considered the car. It sat unguarded in the driveway. She looked at it, the crescent crack bisecting emptiness. She imagined that this was the car that had carried them – Mr. Bird and the woman who was once his wife – from the church to this very house the day they were married. This is the car into which they had loaded all of her best canvases and taken them to the Summerfield Craft Fair and even to the galleries as far south as Santa Fe, where she always seemed to sell one or two. This was the car they had taken into the heart of a field of high summer corn and folded all the seats down and made love and listened to the radio playing as the stars came out to the sound of crickets and the night wings spread themselves out above them slicing into the hot, dark air. The car was more artifact than transportation; a fossil of old love.

Maribel turned off the engine and listened. The neighborhood was still, like everything about this man. She stepped out into the new spring sun and a breeze of birdsong that was so thick it seemed to push the air.

She closed the door and took several careful steps onto the driveway, peering inside the back window. The back was clean; empty except for a large nylon bag the color of mustard and labeled *sunflower/red millet/ oat groats/safflower/peanut hearts.* Maribel moved slowly up the driveway, tracing the deep silver scar as she went. The back seat was also empty.

"It's a package deal," said Mr. Bird.

He was on the other side of the car, leaning against the house. Maribel jolted and took a step back, looking furtively at her own car at the end of the driveway.

"Oh! I…"

"See," he said, not looking at her, reaching two fingers into his shirt pocket, extracting a sunflower seed and popping it into his mouth. He chewed it and looked up. "If you buy the car, you also have to buy some swampland and a bridge I'm trying to unload."

He was older than she was, but younger than she had expected; younger than he had looked ordering his food, or at the zoo. He had a clean, efficiently built face, with pale blue eyes that looked out at her from deep, unfortunate hollows made by a prominent brow and the vertical planes of his nose, as though he peered at her from the bottom of a deep well at high noon.

For a moment, Maribel feigned a re-examination of the car, thinking that he was genuinely confused and had unwittingly handed her an excuse for being in his driveway. But the words and the tone and the circumstances finally coalesced into meaning and she knew that an explanation was still owing.

"Oh, no, I'm not looking to buy," she said. "I used to own a car just like this and I was just driving by and I, well, I couldn't help making sure. I'm sorry. I know this looks awfully…"

"Not at all. Not at all," he said kindly. He smiled and ate another sunflower seed. "Take all the time you like. I've had it a long time though. I'd be surprised." He pushed himself upright. "My name is Parker Grey."

Maribel gave a meek wave from the other side of the car. "I'm Anna."

"Nice to meet you, Anna." Mr. Bird, now, suddenly, Parker Grey, smiled broadly and his sad, blue eyes seemed to brighten from deep within the well. "Why don't you come on inside and tell me why you've been following me all afternoon."

Without waiting for an answer, he turned and headed back inside.

The urge to get back into her car and drive away was powerful, but short lived. The longer Maribel stood on the sun-bleached driveway the more the urge to flee transformed into an urge to follow him. The sound of songbirds was like an invisible cloud in the air, everywhere and nowhere. She walked around the front of the car and up the shoestring path to the front door. He was there, holding it open.

He led her through a front parlor appointed with polished wood furniture and bright cushions and large peace lilies in the corners, all loosely arranged with attention to a white brick fireplace. The fabrics were all from the same summery family of colors, weight and texture. The patterns were floral. The wall behind the loveseat, opposite the windows, was light blush.

A man had not conceived this room.

A broad stone mantle overhung the fireplace. There were photographs, framed in bamboo, in which Parker Grey and an attractive woman were prominently featured.

As she followed him out of the room, Maribel's blood thickened. Her heart began to labor with the thought that she had been so wrong; that Mr. Bird was really Parker Grey, a real person who lived happily in a lovely home with a beautiful wife who would, no doubt, be home any minute, just in time to make her humiliation complete.

"I'm boiling water," he said from just ahead of her as they stepped into the kitchen. "Can I interest you in some tea?" He turned to look at her. She smiled and nodded. "Good," he said.

It was the brilliance of the room that struck her first. Sunlight snapped and splintered into pointed shards, shattering off of the chrome appliances; off the knives hanging in their rack; off the stemware on the shelf. The far wall of the kitchen was entirely glass. She counted five, ten-foot panes, each three feet across. Each window was joined to its neighbor with a single, floor-to-ceiling beam made of a dark lacquered wood, each only inches wide. The glass wall protruded out in a broad semicircle onto a bright green lawn bordered by a thatch of sprawling larch and raspberry bushes. The glass was so clean that there was a danger of thinking one was free to walk between the dark wooden seams joining the windows together and right out onto the lawn. The illusion of such freedom, apparently, was the whole point.

After the light, it was the movement that caught her eye. Movement everywhere. Darting, swooping, soaring. Appearing, disappearing, reappearing. Color and sound and shape were close behind.

"My God," she said under her breath. "Look at them."

"Hmm? Oh, yes," said Parker, turning. "It's like tornado of feathers, isn't it?"

"It's amazing. Look at them. There must be… God, there must be hundreds."

"Tough to count," he said, pouring steaming water into cups. "But I probably go through a hundred pounds of seed in a week. There's almost forty feeders out there. Peppermint okay?"

Maribel nodded without looking at him.

"Please, Anna, have a seat." He indicated a chair at the round wooden table in front of the arcing wall of glass that she had not yet consciously noticed. "If you sit there you can watch the chaos."

She sat. He handed her a cup.

"So," he said, sipping, "how long have you been a private detective?"

Maribel blushed and stifled a smile. "I'm not a private detective."

"Hmm. How long have you worked for Central Intelligence?"

"I don't."

"The mob."

"No."

"The Summerfield Zoo."

She looked up at him suddenly. He pulled out a chair and sat. Her eyes began to fill with shame and she had to fight back tears she could not begin to understand.

"I'm sorry," she said, almost pleading. "I'm sorry." She put down the cup and lowered her face into her hands. "I don't know what I was doing. I... I just... I saw you and you seemed interesting and... I don't know... I'm so sorry."

Parker Grey reached out and touched her wrist. His fingers were soft and nimble. He pulled her hand from the side of her face. She looked at him, cringing.

"There's certainly no reason to be sorry, Anna," he said. "You've done no harm. And even if you had, there's nothing that can't be forgiven."

"Oh, this is humiliating. I'm sorry."

"Stop."

"I should go."

"Anna, stop. What do you want to know?"

"Oh, God," she said. "Nothing. Please, no. I'll die if you tell me anything now. After all of this. Don't tell me anything. Seriously."

"Okay, then tell me about yourself."

She took in a deep breath and looked out at the storm of birds. There was nothing about the question she could answer. She did not believe that she knew anything about herself any more.

"We've got to talk about something," he said. "Can't drink tea and not talk. That's the whole point of tea."

She looked at him directly, as if surrendering herself to punishment.

"What would you like to know?"

"How long have you been ordering extra cheese and no onions on your Big Barn Burgers?"

She laughed in spite of her humiliation and the tears finally came. He handed her a napkin and she wiped her eyes and blew her nose and looked at him feeling awful but lighter somehow.

"How did you know?" she asked, shaking her head. "God, how humiliating."

"My daughter works at the drive through of the Burger Barn."

There, she thought, gouging herself with a vengeful satisfaction, *you were wrong about him. Stupid fool. He has a daughter and wife. Mr. Bird is not who you thought he was, not who you needed him to be for your stupid little avocation.* When the noise in her head had cleared, he came back into focus, watching her intently.

"Your daughter."

"Yes."

"Works at the drive-thru."

"Yes."

"She was… she was the one at the window."

"Yes."

"And so when I…"

He nodded. "She was almost as curious as I was."

Maribel shook her head in disbelief. "Christ. What are the odds?"

"About a hundred percent if you're following me around."

"Well, I must say, it was a very good lunch."

"The best. Glad you enjoyed it."

"How old is your daughter?"

"Amy is twenty-five."

"Oh."

He smiled a little.

"Not really tearing up the track, is she? Her mother would have accepted it better than I do."

"Mothers aren't as hung up on achievement… wait, *would* have?"

"Yes."

Maribel nodded and sipped, as though she was prepared to let it go.

"Suzanne died when Amy was eleven."

Gears slipped in her mind as the words found their place.

"Oh… I'm so sorry. I didn't… I…"

"It was a long time ago, Anna."

"But not really," she said carefully. "Right?"

"That's right," said Parker Grey. "Not really."

"It could have been yesterday."

"Yes. That pain never really goes away. It has its own immunity to time."

Maribel looked back in the direction of the parlor and the mantle and the photos in the bamboo frames that she could not see. Like blood draining from her head, the realization found its way down into her chest, which began to tighten in a vice of inexplicable emotion.

"This house, then…"

"Yes."

"The car."

"Yes."

"The car. An accident."

"Yes."

"Oh, God." She did not feel the tears. "All of these years." She found his hand on the table.

"Yes." He blotted her cheeks.

"You haven't changed anything."

"No. No. Why would I change anything?"

"How could you not? How could you not just… isn't this unbearable? The car?"

He did not answer. He sipped his tea and they watched the birds out the windows.

"I'm sorry," said Maribel. "It's not my place."

"No, no. Amy feels the same. She doesn't come here any more."

"You can't… leave?"

"Everything I want is here. I could leave. I wouldn't be happy."

"Eventually?"

"No."

"I know it hurts, but…"

"You've lost someone too then?" It was a graceful course correction. Related, but not so painful. Her, not him. Still, it took her by surprise, leaving silence where there should have been an answer. "I don't mean to pry…"

"Oh, no," she said quickly. "Please. Yes. I lost both parents. My mom when I was a teenager. My dad just this winter."

"I'm sorry."

"Thanks. I am too. I went out to visit him for Christmas. You know, just before."

"I'm sure he appreciated that."

"I missed him by years."

"I don't understand."

"He was sick for a long time. He found a way to erase me from his memory."

Parker Grey's eyes smiled.

"He would have been proud of you. You seem like a nice person to me."

Maribel sipped, acknowledging the compliment in silence.

"At least, you're not working at the Big Barn Drive-Thru. You've got that going for you."

"Hey, now, give her a break. I work at the zoo."

"So I deduced. What exactly do you do there?"

"Assistant veterinarian."

"A vet? That's great work."

"Not licensed yet."

"But you will?"

"Yes. Before the year is out."

"That's great."

"I like it. It's good, I guess. Always liked animals." Maribel took another sip of tea and the conversation threatened to become normal. "You obviously like birds." She toasted the backyard.

"Ornithologist," he said. "I work in the Biodiversity Department at the Natural History Museum."

"Really? In Wellstone?"

"Yes."

"I've been there. Last year."

"And now you're here in my kitchen. Small world."

He saw from her face that the humor had missed its mark and tried again.

"Oh, don't look that way. It just as easily could have been the other way around, you know. I could have been following you."

"I don't think so."

"What makes you say that? You think I didn't notice you at the zoo? You think you didn't catch my eye? Spark my interest? Were you following me or was I leading you? Probably never stopped to think about that."

She hadn't. The question played heavily in her head until he smirked and she managed to shake free.

"No, I don't think so. Do all ornithologists spend their spare time sketching common barn swallows?"

"You think there is something common about barn swallows?"

"Isn't there?"

"Hey, you're talking about the national bird of Estonia. You try living in chimneys and bathing as you skim over the surface of a lake."

"Really?"

He nodded.

"Well, see? Tells you what I know. What else?"

"Okay. Barn swallows frequently build nests right beneath the nests of birds of prey that do not eat other birds, like ospreys, which mostly eat fish. So the swallow gets protection from other air-born predators and the osprey gets a built in alarm system."

"Clever." Maribel smiled, squaring her shoulders to him, suddenly at ease and wanting more. "What else?"

"What else? You're a tough audience. Okay. Here's what else. Barn swallows are socially monogamous but genetically polygamous. That means they pair and mate for life, but..."

"But they're free."

Parker sat back in his chair and smiled and looked at her, fishing around in his pocket for another seed. "Yes," he said finally, finding one and putting it in his mouth. "They're free."

By the time the tea was gone, the sun had fallen deep into the tangled boughs of larch and was setting fire to the raspberries, silhouetting birds into quick shadow and sketches in coal. Parker offered a tour of the house. Maribel obligatorily declined, citing fear of imposition and undefined obligation.

"Someone waiting for you?" he asked.

"No," she replied, falsely answering his real question. He left it up to her, knowing better than to pull. She followed.

There was no room in the house that was not a three-dimensional scrapbook, a museum to a memory. *Suzanne. Suzanne. Suzanne.* As they walked, he spoke the name less as a word than a sound of greater meaning. Like he was repeating something ineffable he had heard in the woods. A birdsong. A prayer in the wind. This home, this eddy in time, was her place. Even Amy's old bedroom, which was like the top of a birthday cake with tiny pink meringue bedding and sugar lace curtains, was a monument of sorts to her mother. Photographs. Crayon drawings. The musical jewelry box. All perfectly preserved like a time capsule sealed in her sixth grade year.

"She began sleeping in the guest room after it happened," he said. "She became a guest in her own life, or at least in mine. She never came back. I lost her. I let her move out at seventeen."

"She blames you?"

"Somewhere inside. Yes."

"Is that fair?"

"I don't know. I was driving. I never saw him coming. Amy's moved on in her own way. I do what I can to help."

A triptych of graphite sketches framed in pewter caught her eye from the dresser. The three faces of Amy.

"She was a cute child," she said. "She's got your..." And then she stopped and looked up. The realization hit her that she had been right after all. Parker noticed.

"What's wrong?"

"She did this. She was an artist."

"What?"

"Your wife. Suzanne. She was an artist."

"Yes. She was. How did you know?"

"I don't know. I just... I just knew. You don't sketch birds for your work. You sketch birds because *she* sketched birds. You used to take her places. You used to take her to the zoo and she would sketch and you would show Amy the animals and when you had seen them all you and Amy would come back and she would still be right there where you left her; on one of those benches. She tried to sell her paintings and you helped her. You drove her around. You drove her around in that car."

Parker looked at her without expression, as though there was a satellite delay between them or as though he was waiting for a translation. Silence. Stillness. And then, as nothing came and nothing came and nothing came it seemed to Maribel that she had frozen him solid, turned him to stone, with her own revelation. He blinked slowly. Then extended a hand to her and she took it.

"I want to show you something," he said.

The room upstairs, the one stacked directly upon the glass room off the kitchen, was in every sense a vertical continuation of that lower room. It was as though a glossy maple floor evenly bisected a beveled glass chamber twenty feet high. Parker hung back in the doorway as Maribel entered. The sun was gone now and the spring sky was bruising its way dramatically into black. It was like walking inside a jeweled amethyst. The thin beams separating one window from the next had darkened in the failing light from the color of oak to the black of iron. Parker turned up the lights.

"This is where she did most of her best work," he said.

Many of the paintings were on an array of easels that paralleled the arc of windows. Stretched canvas, no frames. Others were in half-boxes lined up along the interior walls.

They were studies in oil. Slices of the natural world. A yellow-green glade at dawn. A garden of burdened larkspur after a rain. A lakeside fawn against the explosion of autumn. Clouds, like whitewater in a blue river. A dog in snowdrifts. Rolls of hay. Crows in the corn. A meadow-lark. A bathing wren.

"She painted all of these?"

"Well I certainly didn't."

Maribel walked from one to the next, admiring, wanting to brush the ridges and dimples and depressions of paint with her fingertips, tracing the scars of color across topographies of a world interpreted and now gone forever save one man and his collection. But she resisted and did not touch. Parker moved to one of the boxes and began flipping through the framed canvases as though he had opened the drawer of a filing cabinet and was pulling his way through utility invoices with his fingers.

"Ah," he said, more to himself than to her, and lifted a canvas out of the box. He removed the meadowlark from its perch upon the nearest easel and replaced it with the smaller canvas in his hand. He took a step backwards, saying nothing. Explanation pointless.

It was Anna. Looking back at her from a long time ago, before they had ever met. She was no more than ten, maybe twelve. No question that it was her. The asymmetry of her eyes. The triangular notch missing from the top of her left ear. Mostly it was her expression, always a question in the brow. Always a look of pleading. A telltale hope, both savage and relentless, about the next moment to come. The next moment to bring something new. Something different. Anything. *When? What next, Maribel? Next. Next. Next.*

She was in her old habitat, sitting at the base of the large mahogany that had taken on a rotting fungus and was cut down the year Maribel first arrived. In the background, through the fork in the trunk, were familiar smears of gray and black that had to be the elephants. Probably Buster and Peanut, that long ago. Or Tiny Tim. In any event, it was long before Monkey Island had even been built, which was now about as far away from Elephant Kingdom as one could get and still be on zoo property.

"This... is..." she whispered. Parker did not respond. "Amazing. I feel like she's looking right at me."

"Did you know that one?"

"Yes," she said, not expounding, afraid of the name she had appropriated.

Anna's long arms, hands and fingers had unfurled down into her lap, palms up. Her feet stretched out away from her, soles angled towards each other, knees akimbo, like she was a child in a sandbox, claiming the space in the circle formed by her own legs. A half-eaten apple sat in the grass before her. On the far side of the tree a tire hung from a yellow rope. Anna's deep brown eyes bored out of the paint. *Next, Maribel. Next. Next. Tell me what's next.*

"I've… that's her. I mean. I mean she looks at me like this every day."

"Looks?"

"Looked."

As she reacted, something snagged and pulled at her attention, like a lure catching on the bottom of a rocky stream. Something was wrong. A color. A detail. Something. She was so much younger, that was it. And yet, no, that wasn't it. The location. No. The apple. She didn't like apples now. No. Elephants where they shouldn't be. No.

"The mesh," she said at last. "She left off the wire mesh. And the bars. My mind was supplying all of that on its own. I never even noticed."

Parker stuffed his hands in his pockets and nodded. "Suzanne liked to say that there was something in art, or at least in the act of painting, that was universally freeing. There's no point in painting a cage."

"Yes," she said, looking at him. The control of the well-lit kitchen was gone from his features. His face had softened. His eyes, still blue coins, no longer sunken, but floating, begging to be taken. The sun had taken his quiet confidence to ground. He seemed to have forsaken his calm authority, and all that had ever protected him, for something unnamable. For a new star in the dark sky above the well. "Can I see more?"

"Of course," he said.

They moved together in a counterclockwise arc, starting on the right side of the glass studio and working their way, canvas by canvas, from one half-box to the next, speaking in near whispers. Suzanne and Amy and Evan were everywhere now, in every breath, in every pulse, in every accidental touch of fingers. In her mind, Maribel could feel Anna watching; could feel her question like a hammer. *Next; what next?* At the fifth box, eyes closing, tears spilling, Maribel answered her, stepping forward, stretching up to find Parker's mouth, kissing him, hesitant at first, but he offered no resistance. His long, deliberate fingers navigated her hair, cradling her head, his lashes on her cheek, she allowed herself to tumble freely from where she was to where she was not, and in that glorious freefall, for the first time in a very long time, she was truly happy.

———

In the morning the sun streamed into the windows and they found all of themselves that they had shed. The sound of birds rose up around them like a swelling of warm dough and the fecund aromas of spring cleared the mind, promising self-correction. Promising continuation. Promising that the world would now pick up where it had left off so long ago, before the incomprehensible dreaming.

Parker brought her coffee and two warmed muffins and a cup of sliced pineapple and a proper kiss on the cheek, all of which he had arranged on a wicker kitchen tray while she was in the bathroom tending to her hair and breath and reflections of conscience.

When she emerged she saw that he was fully dressed and pulling a sport coat out of the closet. He turned and smiled and laid the sport coat over the back of the chair in the corner. He picked up the tray off the dresser and delivered the food and the kiss. She thanked him sweetly and sat on the edge of the bed and ate bits of pineapple with her fingers, one bare foot still on the floor, eyeing the pile of clothing by the nightstand.

"I borrowed a shirt," she said.

"I see that." His voice had found its old reserve. "You're welcome to it. It looks good on you."

"I don't even like football."

"Neither do I. And, yet, it still looks good."

She laughed, breaking open the muffin. She handed him half and he down sat next to her. They ate in silence until it became uncomfortable.

"Tell me something about birds," she said at last.

He took another bite of muffin and looked at her. "They can see in ultraviolet."

"What else?"

"They can detect star movement."

"What's your favorite?"

"I don't have a favorite."

"Tell me about one of those." She nodded toward the open window where the air was almost alive with color and sound.

He swallowed a bite. "What kind?"

"Any kind. Robins."

"The common robin. Okay."

"Hey, now," she swatted him on the knee. "There's nothing common about robins."

"You're right. Okay, here's something about the robin." He popped the last bit of muffin in his mouth and brushed his hands together. Watching him, she noticed his tie was slightly askew and decided his cologne was a little too sharp. "You've watched a robin hunting worms in a yard?"

"Yes."

"She hops, hops, hops and turns her head this way and that way and then she kind of freezes there for a second? Perfectly motionless? And then she strikes her beak down for the worm?"

"Yes. So?"

"So, why the pause? Why not just hop, hop, strike?"

"She's looking?"

"Yes. But why not look and move at the same time?"

"Tell me."

"Well, a robin's eyes have photoreceptors that gather information for each of millions of ganglion cells in the retina. The ganglion cells process the visual information and send it along to the brain for further analysis. In a billionth of a second her little robin brain has a perfect picture of what is in her field of vision. Every blade of grass. Every drop of dew. Every granule of dirt. When she freezes, when her head stops moving, her brain essentially grays-out that picture. Like turning it into an old black and white photograph. She hops and hops and cocks her head and another photograph is frozen in her mind. Her whole life is a series of frozen mental photographs."

"Because…"

"Because all the robin cares about is movement. All she lives for is change in the latest picture she carries around in her brain. There is nothing about the status quo that can hold any interest for her. Her own physiology considers the details of sameness a distracting waste of time. Change is the only thing that matters and the only thing she is looking for. So when the tiniest tip of an earthworm pops into view, it registers in very sharp relief, neurologically speaking, like a red flare across that black and white photograph."

Parker smiled and leaned forward and kissed her on the forehead.

"So, there you have it. The uncommon robin. And now, dear Anna, I must go to work. Lock the door as you leave."

"Parker," she looked up at him. He waited. "My name's not…"

"I know," he said, stopping her. "It's okay."

"Forgive me."

"There's nothing to forgive."

"Yes. Yes there is." She looked down at her fingers, mashing a bit of muffin into dust. "I'm married."

Parker smiled kindly, his eyes in deep water now, well beyond reaching. "I was awake when you made the call."

"I'm sorry."

"Don't be."

"God… what you must think. I'm broken. I'm lost."

"We're all broken and lost. It's a lot easier if you just accept that. Take it from me."

He smiled self-evidently. Birdsong crashed in sonic waves against the side of the house, sloshing into the open window.

"So what's next, Anna? You're welcome to…"

254

"No," she said too quickly and felt him absorb the point of it. "Thank you. I have to tell him. That's what's next."

"It must be love."

"It is. I just hope he lets me back in."

"Nothing is unforgivable."

She looked up, finding the hand at his side. "Really? Have you forgiven?"

"No. But I'm working on it. Last night helped a little."

"Thank you for that," she said, squeezing. "Good luck, Parker."

"Good luck, Anna."

And Mr. Bird flew away.

———

Maribel was very late for work. Dr. Klatch, who was there to watch her pull into the parking lot, abandoned all semblance of restraint in dressing her down. He had not believed her excuse about car trouble – generic mechanical difficulties she never bothered to specify – a story festooned with purely decorative, half-baked explanations involving an undependable alarm clock and a misplaced set of keys. It was as though she wanted to be caught in the lie.

"I told you to be here first thing in the morning! Didn't I?"

"I'm here."

"I see that. I'm delighted. Elsa is already sedated and prepped and I've already made all the rounds myself."

"What can I do?"

"Nothing. You can do nothing."

He stomped off past the ticket booth, past the wide eyes of the counter help and the people in line. Maribel followed at a distance. In the break room she changed into her uniform and put her things in her locker, still feeling the sting of Dr. Klatch's disappointment and knowing that it was nothing. She knew that Evan had not believed her any more that Dr. Klatch had believed her. The whispered explanation about the old girlfriend and the impromptu dinner and the alcohol was now, in the harsh light of day, an invitation to disbelief. The end of her day promised an ugly, hurtful, exhausting ordeal and she felt her heart flatten at the thought of it.

She had convinced herself on the slow drive in to work that she was as good as divorced. That she would be unloved and tossed back into the wilderness. She had tortured herself with the prospect of causing Evan pain. Had she intended this end? Would he see malice? Cruel indifference? How could he not? Of all the things in the universe that were possible, forgiveness was at the bottom of the list.

Maribel closed the locker door and spun the dial. She walked over to the sign-in board and found her card and stuck it in the clock and returned it to the slot beneath her name. She grabbed a pair of gloves from the box on the table and a radio out of the charger and pushed the front door open with one foot as she snapped the radio into the holster on her belt.

The door to the break room swatting closed behind her, Maribel stepped outside into the sun and into the smell of new soil and fresh hay and morning pachyderm. Invisible birds chattered from trees lit with fresh color. Spring was unlocking the gates of winter and the earth was freeing its prisoners. The fields for miles around were thick with young swarms of redemption and smelled of hope.

One of the new grounds keepers, Maribel did not know his name, passed by with coiled hoses around his shoulders and pushing a wheel-barrow. She watched him and he nodded genially and she waved back. Groups of visitors pushed in colorful knots of excitement along the path, reading signs and unfolding maps and squabbling about which way to go, their children like unleashed pets.

Forgiveness was at the bottom of the list. And yet, she thought, it *was* on the list. Evan, after all, was alive. He would remember who she was. He would not simply forget the unspeakable thing she had done and he could not simply wave it away. If the thing forgotten could not be forgiven, then the thing not forgotten – the thing so painful it could never be erased – *could* be forgiven. And if forgiveness was still possible, then the life she had taken for granted was still possible. It would be a long way through the woods, she knew. But she could make her way back. That singular hope was suddenly the only thing that mattered. It was the only thing moving in a landscape of frozen gray irrelevance.

Since Dr. Klatch was not speaking to her, Maribel walked in the direction of the ticket office to put her name on the list for zoo tours. She stopped at Monkey Island. Sam and Jake were busy grooming. They sat on the far side of the crater where the new termite mound was to be installed. Jake looked up at her, pausing, and then resumed.

There was still no sign of Anna. Maribel turned in all directions, looking around at the treetops brushing the cloudless blue sky with new baby green leaves, as if she might find her in one of them looking down at the world that had once held her and asking: *What next, Maribel? Next. Next. What next?*

But there was no sign of her. It did not appear that Dr. Klatch would be blamed after all. She would have heard something by now. She was glad. For as difficult as he was to work with, Maribel did like him and respect him. And how could anyone not have compassion for a man trapped by such love and loneliness. Anna would be back. She always came back. She supposed that leaving and then coming back was the whole appeal. There was no point in blaming Dr. Klatch.

Besides, getting anyone blamed had never been Maribel's intent in leaving the gate open.

She looked at her watch and pulled her hair behind her ears. Then she walked on, her thoughts again reaching out to Evan. She paused at the smiling park ranger sign: *Tour In Progress!* Maribel flipped over the wooden plaque so that the message for all who passed by the giant metal enclosure read, simply, inevitably: *Returning Soon.*

Chapter 7

SHORELINE DRIVE

"This *is* happiness. Why can't you… just…"

He was a boy again, suddenly, the paroxysmal tone, the urgency in his expression, the sharply emergent moue, all working to pull him back out of his new, ill-fitting adulthood.

"Because, Fen, I think you misunderstand…"

"Who are *you* to tell me it's not happiness? Look at me. Can you even see me?"

He pointed hyper-extended forefingers to either side of a marble smile.

"Yes. Fen. I can see you."

"I'm… I'm *happy*. I practically *floated* through that door. Do you think I'm… what, that I'm just faking… that I'm…"

"No. I don't think you're faking."

"What, then?"

Peter placed the book on the coffee table, trading it for the tea. He leaned back and crossed his legs and drank, wincing because it was still too hot. The boy, for he *was* just a boy, reached out and snatched the book from the table, nearly upsetting his own water. For a moment, Peter saw that he did not exist; that Fen and the book were alone in the room with the tall clock in the corner by the window, slicing off the seconds like dollops of molten wax that splatted onto the hard floor and disappeared.

A car hissed through the rain on the street below and was gone. Peter listened, wrapping his hands around the bottom of the mug like a warming stone.

Fen gazed at the cover of the book, brushing away imaginary dust, and then thrust it face down into his lap as if to protect it from falling debris. He looked up suddenly, self-consciously, as if remembering that he had asked a question.

"What's the big deal?"

"I just don't think what you're feeling right now... with this new thing," Peter gestured vaguely at the boy's covered lap, "this new idea of yours, this interest of yours, is genuine... happiness."

Fen made a sound of exasperation and collapsed backwards into the couch. Peter gave a subtle smile at the display.

"I'm not trying to be difficult. I just don't think this is happiness. And I'm a little concerned that you *do*."

"But *why?* Why is this not..."

Peter furrowed and considered the black porcelain mug in the cup of his hands. The seconds dripped onto the floor behind him.

"Well... I think it's because the largest component of what we experience as happiness is contentment. We are happy, we experience a feeling of happiness, when we accept our... when we accept ourselves... when we accept our lives... and we are content with the way things are. There is no happiness without some seed of contentment in the middle. You see what I am saying? Happiness is not distraction."

"You think ... you think she's a *distraction?*" Peter could see the blood coiling its way through the upper rim of the boy's ears and his face flushing with emotion.

"Yes. Look, try to stay calm." He held up a palm as if to a piece of glass. "There's nothing wrong with distraction, Fen. I'm not saying that. We all love our distractions. I have my own that I love dearly. But a distraction serves the purpose of keeping us from thinking about the things that we don't wish to consider. The things that we don't accept. You see? That's the whole point."

259

The boy rolled his eyes, looking away, scanning the walls of the office that aspired to be a living room.

"Sometimes our distractions *feel* a lot like happiness because... because we are relieved not to be dwelling on our troubles. There is a certain pleasurable relief that comes just from being able focus on something else... anything other than what we don't like about our lives. And so these distractions can be wonderful. And often they can be necessary. But distractions are a poor substitute for happiness. These are not the same thing."

There was no discernable response from across the table. No glimmer of understanding. He knew summarizing was pointless. It wasn't that the boy couldn't understand. He didn't want to understand. That was the problem. The barriers were up. Peter summarized anyway.

"True happiness comes from contentment. And contentment comes from acceptance."

They stared at each other over the hiss of another passing set of radials. Peter took another sip and squinted as if into sunlight.

"Is any of this making sense?"

"She's not a distraction."

"You don't know her. You don't know anything about her. She's not real to you, Fen. She's not... She's not a real person."

"She *is* real. And I am... okay, I know it sounds corny and all, but I am totally in love here. Okay? This *is* going to happen. This *is* the real thing. Happiness. Have you ever seen me like this?"

Peter nodded. "Yes. As a matter of fact."

"Oh, right. Here we go. When?"

"You remember last fall? When you purchased the lottery ticket?"

"No, no. That was different."

"And you happened to come across each one of those numbers at some point in your day. One on a license plate. Others in the newspaper. Others at the bookstore, on a receipt if I recall. All in the right sequence. And you convinced yourself that you had actually won the lottery. You remember how you felt?"

"That was different."

"You felt like an instant millionaire."

"That was excitement, not happiness."

"You're not excited right now?"

"I am. Of course I am. Jeez. I mean," he grabbed the spine of the book and held it face out over the glass table, "just look at her. Look at her."

"Yes. I see. She's very... she's very attractive."

"Of course I'm excited. But even though I'm excited, I'm also happy. I mean *really* happy, because I can see our future and I know that future actually exists."

"As a certainty, you mean?"

"No. No. Nothing is certain. I'm not stupid you know." He retracted the book back into his lap.

"I don't think you're stupid, Fen."

"It's... *possible*. You know? It exists as a real possibility. And that makes me happy. That makes me ecstatic. Lighter than air."

Peter puzzled and sipped his tea. The boy was glowing, radiant with some force that outshone the anger and frustration. He *believed*.

Peter re-crossed his legs and the leather groaned in protest. The boy stared at his own hands tracing the perimeter of the book, up and back, left and right in smooth, regular strokes, moving like sentries posted around Fort Knox. They were lean and pale and scrubbed-looking like the rest of him. They were strangers to the sun, those hands. And they had never known the earth either. The tips of his fingers were incarnadine pads; fleshy crescent bonnets that rose up around his raggedly bitten nails. Fingertips, Peter guessed, that had never touched another person in the way that they now touched this book.

"Okay then," he said. "Tell me how."

"How what?" The boy straightened. The hands stopped.

"How you plan to make this... to make *her*..." he nodded at the boy's lap, "a real possibility. A real person in your life."

The boy smiled lopsidedly and shook his head.

"What. Do you find that a dumb question?"

"Duh."

"Well then let's hear it. How do you find her?"

"Hello? I work in a book store?"

"So."

"So I have publisher contacts." He held up the book, less reverently this time, as if it were just an assemblage of paper sheets. "This is a Vintage Pulp reprinting of a classic Jack McMannis mystery. *The Open Grave?*"

Peter shrugged his shoulders, missing some obvious significance.

"You've never even heard of Garrett Webb, have you?"

Peter smiled.

"He's only one of the best crime writers, like... *ever. The Open Grave* is the last in the series to be republished. It just came out. You know, not the book, the reprint. We just got it last week."

"Okay... so..."

"So I call my friend John Daly over at Vintage in the shipping department and he connects me with..." the boy flipped open the cover of the book and then the first five or six pages and then pulled his finger down to the bottom and tapped it twice sharply, "... Mr. Edward F. Winsom, Jr."

"And who's that?"

"He's written the forward in every Jack McMannis mystery reprint. I've checked. Every last one of them, from *My Darling Dead* to *The Open Grave*. He's the editor in charge of the whole series. And she's on, like three different covers. If there's anyone who knows who she is and where to find her, it's Edward F. Winsom, Jr."

Peter waited respectfully, in case there was any more to it; in case there was actually more substance to the great plan than he suspected. But the boy sat in silent expectancy. He too was waiting. Waiting, Peter supposed, for some concession that his skepticism had been inappropriate; that he had been wrong to doubt him. Waiting for some acknowledgement that it just might work after all.

Peter nodded, because the boy needed something, even an acknowledgement that he had been heard and understood. He took in a long breath through his nose and let it out and took another sip of tea. Beyond the door he heard Henry thundering slowly down the hallway towards the bathroom.

"... of this rain makes me want to pee...," Henry was telling someone, probably Margo, who liked to sit in the common waiting room when the phones in Phil Wagg's office were slow and Phil was in court defending a client from the greedy over-reaching of some soon-to-be ex-spouse.

"And when I got to pee, Margo, it's like a day at the racing stables."

The boy turned around and looked at the door and then turned back and snickered.

"Sorry," said Peter. "Try to ignore that. These walls are a bit too thin."

"Hey... if you gotta go, you gotta go."

Peter smiled and then just as quickly pushed his eyebrows into the shape of professional concern.

"Have you considered, Fen, that it's just a stock photograph? Just a picture of a pretty model holding a gun that someone in the marketing department over at Vintage Pulp had in a drawer or pulled off the Internet?"

"No. No way."

"Why?"

"Look at her." He held the book up again.

"Yes?"

"Look at the gun."

"Okay. So?"

"So if you read Jack McMannis mysteries, you'd know that's exactly *his* Colt Model 1903 Pocket Hammer. The grip is inlaid bone. And that chip out of the corner was from *Hot Night, Cold Comfort* when Jack McMannis almost got chewed up in a threshing machine. And right there," he pointed again, "on her wrist, is a bracelet? See?"

"Yes."

"See the initials?"

"EM?"

"That stands for Ella McMannis, which is Jack McMannis' dead wife."

"Okay."

"Okay so then this is no stock photo, doc. This picture was specifically taken for this cover."

"Okay then. Let's say your right. Let's say you get her name. You get her phone number. Let's say you find out where she lives. What then?"

"What do you mean?"

"Well, I suppose you call her up on the phone, right? You go out to find her."

"Yeah. I guess."

"What do you tell her?"

Henry thudded his way back down the hall. The boy listened and grinned. Peter waited. The boy looked back down at his lap, his entire presence beginning to slip into itself like the barbican of a sand castle beginning to lose its integrity in grainy rivulets.

"I don't know. One step at a time. Those are just... like... I don't know. Details."

"I suppose she doesn't live anywhere around here."

"Probably not."

"How much time off do you have coming?"

"I dunno. Maybe ten days."

"Mmm. Not much time is it? Do you just give notice and quit your job at the bookstore?"

"I don't know that yet."

"Have you told your mother about this plan?"

"No."

"What if you find this woman and she's already in a relationship."

The boy gave a look of alarm that quickly narrowed into a basilisk glare, looking up and out from between the hunch of his narrow shoulders as if from a dark notch.

"Then I'll just have to change her mind. Why are you... why is it so important for you to piss all over her."

"I'm not pissing on anybody or anything, Fen. I'm..."

"Yes you are. Yes you sure as hell are."

"No. But you're annoyance with my questions about details is really quite instructive. The details are all about reality. This fixation you have is not about reality. You get upset and uncomfortable whenever it starts to get too real. Can you see that?"

"No. No I can't. And you're jealous is what I think. You know I'm right but you don't want me to be right. Because if I'm right, then your whole life is... is... a god... damned... fraud!"

Peter leaned back, temporarily ceding the room to the hiss of the rain and the seconds splatting beneath the clock, giving the new hostility a chance to dissipate.

The boy seemed to receive the silence uncertainly. He swallowed hard and looked cagily about the room. Peter puzzled. The boy had asserted himself and sharply so, throwing Peter's life back in his face. Not that the boy knew a single thing about Peter or his life, other than what might be garnered through the loose friend-of-a-spouse affiliation that Peter had with the boy's mother. It was the bluff of implied knowledge that made the aggression and the certitude in the boy's manner all the more remarkable. He was not, ordinarily, given to such displays. In eighteen months that sort of outburst had been wholly unprecedented.

He was interested, of course, in what the boy had meant about his life being a fraud. Or whatever the boy *thought* he had meant by that remark. But Peter knew an invitation to change the focus when he heard it. The session was not about Peter.

He traced the rim of his mug of tea with his thumb, letting the silence do its work. Eventually, the glare lost its edge and the eyes softened. The boy slowly deflated back into the couch, the intensity of the moment hissing away into the rain.

"What would you say, Fen, if I told you that I thought this... this very lovely young woman, is simply a distraction that you have chosen for yourself? What if I told you I thought she's like that old winning lottery ticket of yours; something that you can focus on instead of a reality that you choose not to accept?"

"If you told me that… then I'd think *you* were the crazy one."

"And what if I told you that I think you have a tendency to set yourself up for crushing disappointments? That your idea of happiness is like a thin candle flame on a dark and windy night? That you deliberately pick things to be happy about that – deep down – you know are ephemeral and unrealistic. You know what I mean by ephemeral? I mean something that lasts only…"

"I know what ephemeral means."

"Okay. So what do you think about the idea that you're setting yourself up to actually be *un*-happy?"

"I think it's totally stupid."

"Hmm. Why do you think it's stupid?"

"Why would I do that?"

"Well, one reason might be because the only thing in the world that you really except, Fen, is pain and loneliness and *un*happiness. Probably ever since your father and your brother died. You're convinced it's all so hopeless. And you try to confirm that in everything you do. Even in deciding what it is that makes you happy."

The boy crossed his arms and scowled, now less in anger or defiance than in self-reflection. Peter knew to be silent, to let the boy chase whatever he was chasing up to the surface.

"You don't understand," the boy said at last. "I'm like… I'm an optimist, see? I believe everything will work out. I believe it's all good. Okay? All of it. Even the bad stuff. Because I believe I've seen the last of the bad stuff and it's done and over, like my dad and brother, or at least it's temporary."

"Like what? What's temporary?"

"You. This. These sessions. Some downer customer at the bookstore or when mom gets all… freaked out about me."

"Do you really feel that way, Fen? About our sessions together?"

The boy paused, looking away briefly. "Maybe. Sometimes, like today. But what I'm saying is it's the bad stuff that's ephemeral, see? Not the good stuff; not happiness. I *believe* everything will work out. Okay? So my starting point is that... like... it's all good until proven otherwise."

"You think everything works out?"

"I'm talking about what I *believe*. Everything doesn't always work out, sure, I know that, I'm not delusional. But I *believe* it will work out, okay? For awhile I *believe* it will. And that's happiness. That's *real* happiness. That's where I like to live. Just knowing it's out there, okay? Knowing it's possible."

"Knowing what's out there? What's possible?"

"Whatever. Happiness." He put his palms on the book, framing the woman's face with his fingers. "Her. That's what it means to be an optimist."

"Fen." The boy looked away, unwilling to hear. "Fen."

"What."

"Look at me."

He looked. "What."

"Optimists tend not to want to kill themselves."

———

Last night, while he had slept, clouds had taken away the sky, mummifying the heavens. Mothballing creation. They were low and white and absolutely featureless. They even disavowed the rain, which came from everywhere and from nowhere, seething from unseen cracks and fissures in the air itself. *They,* as if there was a multiplicity at issue above him. No, it was one thing, one cloud. One feeling. No, not even that. Not one thing; one *nothing.* An utter absence of expression. This was the face of meteorological catatonia.

"You know, Peter, if you don't stop staring out of that window I'm gonna have to conclude that you don't really wanna be here."

He heard Henry sit heavily on the couch behind him and pick up a magazine. Henry spent almost as much time in the waiting room reading magazines as he did in his own office.

"Just waiting for Lucy," said Peter. "Late as usual."

"Kids," said Henry flipping a page.

"Not her fault. The guy has never been on time for anything. Not once, Henry. The shrink in me says it's deliberate. It's his way of making sure I remember."

"Remember?"

Peter turned from the window and leaned back against the sill, crossing his arms. He held an expression of self-evident irritation until Henry looked up.

"Ah, right," Henry said. "Second-class step-parent syndrome. How could I forget?" Henry flipped another page, twisting the magazine to ogle a celebrity and shaking his head in admiration, "Mmm, Mmm, Mmm," then flipped again looking up at Peter in the brief second it took that page to settle. "Well the shrink in you may be suspicious of hidden agendas, but the family therapist in *me* says you've got nothing to complain about."

"Oh, really. How's that?"

"Please, Doctor Pete." Henry dropped the magazine in his lap and spread his massive arms like great oaken limbs over the back of the couch. "You should sit in on one of my sessions. You can set your skinny ass on the floor back there behind my credenza and just listen to what *I* listen to every day. I mean these families go to war over what flavor of juice to buy, and who forgot to put gas in the tank or pay the electric bill, and who plays the music too loud. Hell, Peter, I do entire sessions on not abusing bathroom time."

Peter smirked in spite of himself.

"Sure, you go ahead and laugh my friend, but that's the jungle that's out there. Shitting under the tyranny of a stopwatch. I kid you not. But you and Diane have found a way to share custody of Lucy with whatshis-name, the ex, the *real father* as you are inclined to think of him, and you have him over for dinner, and you work him into the whole Christmas routine, and you have birthday parties and nary an argument or harsh word. Am I right?"

"Henry…"

"Nah, don't Henry me, doc. Am I right?"

Peter smiled at Henry's theatrical directness. "Yes."

"I mean I have never seen such a well-behaved cooperative group in all my years. He's dropping off *his* flesh-and-blood loin-fruit at *your* office."

"Loin fruit?"

But Henry widened his eyes in a mock threat, as though the six-foot colossus might just raise himself up off the couch like Poseidon out of the briny deep and smite him with a scepter made of glossy paper and cheap gossip about cellulose and infidelity.

"Yes, yes," Peter said. "Okay. Christ."

"He's dropping her off so that *you* don't have to leave work to pick her up from school."

"He's had her all weekend."

"And yet, you're not picking her up, are you?"

"Because we have an arrangement. Three o'clock. Here. And now its quarter after."

Henry picked up the magazine again and flipped the page. He shook his head in mock defeat.

"Sorry Peter. You're right, man. I don't know how you put up with that no-account bastard. He's clearly fucking with you."

"Okay, okay. Point taken."

"No, seriously. When he does show up, he damn well better stay down in the parking lot. He comes in here," Henry tipped the magazine down and raised his prodigious eyebrows. "I will fuck… him… up. I will counsel his ass right into next week. I will cut his bathroom time in half."

Peter turned back to the window and its cotton sky listening to Henry turn pages. A white truck with a load of rusted iron piping and machine parts in the bed pulled into the lot below and turned around. He saw that something heavy – a meteor, or a hailstone the size of a microwave oven – must have landed on the cab of the pickup where there was a sizeable crater just to the right of the driver's head. The irregular depression in the metal roof of the cab was now filled with rainwater that sloshed and flashed in the diffuse and cloying light as the truck stopped at the street. A greenish van hissed past in a fan of old rain.

"I saw young Fenton earlier," said Henry.

The truck sped off to the right towards the First National Bank, disappearing around the side of *The Yeast We Can Do Bakery.*

"Yeah," said Peter after a moment.

"Getting a little old for you, isn't he?"

"He's grandfathered in. We started before he could vote."

"Mmm. How's he doing?"

"It's complicated."

"Thinks he's in love, doesn't he? I could tell by the dreamy look in his eyes."

"You know I can't talk about it, Henry. It's complicated."

"Isn't it always with you guys? When will shrinks just accept the unfathomable? For me, you know, the lowly counselor without the power of the scrip, love is like a fucking color. It's like the color blue. I don't care what wavelength it is. It's blue. People wear it around. They paint it on things. Then, suddenly they hate the color blue and their life is all about the reds and yellows. Unless he's, you know, in love with his dog or something. Then its time for the pretty pills and the rubber room. Don't tell me Fenton's humping his dog."

Peter ignored the question and poked at one of the raindrops through the window.

"Henry, what if I told you that I loved one of the women in that magazine you're looking at?"

"Get in line, pal."

"No, Henry, not lust after. Not even like or admire. *Love.* Destined-to-be-together love. Key-to-my-happiness love. Don't know her name or anything about her, just the shape of part of her face. Not the whole face, mind you. All I know is part of the face."

"And that does it for you, huh?"

"Over the moon. Like, 24-7, isn't life a grand and wonderful thing."

"Hmm. And how old are... you?"

"Let's say eighteen. A *young* eighteen. I can buy booze and go to war but I live with my mom. Emotionally, think sixteen."

"Is he..."

But Peter held up a cautionary finger, stopping Henry in mid-sentence.

"Christ." Henry rolled his eyes. "Okay. *You.* I meant *you.* Are *you* big into weed?"

"Pot? Nah. I'm a good kid. No access to that kind of thing in my circles anyway."

"It'll pass," said Henry with his casual authority. "It's a... it's just a fantasy."

"Not to me. I'm a believer. I don't know anything about her except that she's the key to my happiness for ever and ever."

"Hmm. Happiness."

"Happiness."

"Not knob-polishing happiness."

"No. We're not talking about you, Henry. Happiness with a capital H."

"It'll pass."

"No doubt. And when it does?"

"You'll move on to another color. Green. Red."

"Black."

"Black. Whatever."

Peter nodded. Behind him, Henry swatted past another page.

A sleek silver coupe slid into the parking lot on a sheet of water; a bullet cutting through the rain. The passenger door swung open to reveal a pitch-black interior. Lucy stepped out. She slung a backpack over her shoulder, stooped, waved, closed the door, re-encasing the blackness in its silver sheath, and then disappeared under the eave directly beneath him. The car, gleaming a brightness greater than the day, glided off out of view into the heart of catatonia.

"Black is not another color, Henry'" he said. "It's the absence of color. Black absorbs all other colors. And then there are no colors left."

———

"But I got her a book *last* year."

Lucy crossed her arms and slid herself towards the front of the seat, bowing her back into a perfect crescent and jabbing her shoes into the darkness beneath the dash. Her head bent grotesquely forward along the seatback, her chin pressed into the hollow of her clavicle.

"No..."

"Yes. *Pee-ter.*" Her tone was plaintive and desperate, casting him again in the familiar role of heartless martinet.

"No."

"You would if you loved her."

"I do love her; you know that."

"I mean *reaaaallly* loved her."

Nine years-old, he thought to himself, and already mastering her mother's genius for emotional manipulation. It was like watching baby Mozart tickle the ivories.

"Lucy, don't be silly. You know what I think?"

She turned her head away from him and looked out the passenger window at the empty sidewalk. It began to rain harder. Water pocked the roof of the car in tiny detonations. His words competed for attention.

"I don't think you want me to buy a dog for Mom's birthday."

"Yes I do. You're not even listening."

"I think that you want me to buy a dog for *you*, Lucy. I don't think this has anything to do with your mom's birthday."

"Does so. Her birthday is Saturday."

"Yes. Her birthday is Saturday. A dog's a lot of work, Honey. Your mom's busy at the hospital. And you're at school and then you spend time with Spencer every other weekend and you two are off doing things."

"He can come with me!"

"To school?"

"No. To *Daddy's*."

"And the other twenty-six days a month?"

"He'll be with me."

"Nope. Sorry, Luce."

"I'm asking *Daddy*. He'll buy me one. He *loves* puppies. He loves *me*."

"I love you too, Sweetie," he said.

He might have simply stopped there. There needn't always be a 'but' to follow such sentiments. The purpose of an endearment needn't always be to soften a blow, or to introduce a correction, or to limit the ambitions of another. There was no need to go further, to change direction, to tack inward.

Except that there was.

For the psychiatrist in him ascribed an overriding importance to truth. To *reality*, above all else. Particularly as to children, who needed to learn early on how to stay balanced upon the thin but certain rims of that which was real in the world. Tilting one's expectations recklessly beyond the pale of reason led to a life careening out of control. So too the indulgence in the childish delusion that motivations are not real unless openly acknowledged. Those 'but' clauses – *yes, but...; I know you're excited, but...; It would be wonderful if that sort of thing were likely, but...* – were like training wheels, enforcing the balance as the speed increased down life's big hill.

"I love you too, Sweetie, but I thought this was all about *Mom's* birthday. I thought this wasn't really about you."

As he spoke the words, he felt the guilt. It pushed against the membrane that separated his conscience from his professional instincts, testing its strength like a prisoner with nothing better to do. It pushed and poked at the very idea that forcing a child to examine her motivations – like pressing the nose of a puppy into a spot of urine-soaked carpeting – was an acceptable thing for a father to do.

Step-father.

He was no alien to the species. He knew what it was to want something just out of reach, wanting it like your entire life hung in the balance. Lucy swung her leg in frustration, saying nothing.

"Don't kick the car, Honey. It's not the car's fault."

"He loves *her* is what I meant. He loves her more than you do."

The rain came now in a steady gush. The windshield and windows had begun to cloud around the edges. The space inside the car – the space between them – seemed to grow smaller. Peter pulled the keys out of the ignition and weighed them in his hand.

"I think you know that's not true, Lucy."

"Yes it is. He married her first and then they made me."

"That's true."

"You didn't make me, Peter."

"That's true."

"And Mom still loves Daddy, she told me she does."

"Of course she does. But she loves me too. And I love you. Just as much as if I made you myself, but..."

"I'm still asking him," she mumbled.

"Sweetie, I suspect you already asked him and if you're asking me now, then he probably already said no to the puppy. Besides, I can't really see Spencer with a puppy."

"It wouldn't be for him! It would be for me!"

"You?"

"No! I mean Mommy!" She pounded the seat with her fist. "Stop psychoanalyzing me, Peter!"

He closed his eyes and took a breath.

"Baby doll, I know you've heard that big word before, but I really don't think you know what it means."

"It means you're a poop."

"So you think calling me names is going to change my mind?"

Something in this must have resonated. Lucy turned, in desperation, her eyes little soft, green pools of heartbreak. "Please? I'll take care of him? I'm sorry I called you a poop."

A bearded man in a dripping leather hat and a black slicker scuffed along the grey wet slab. He stooped as he passed, looking into the window but then looked away when Peter caught his eye.

"No puppies," said Peter with an edge of authority.

"But I apologized. I didn't mean to call you..."

"Let's talk about *actual* birthday presents. I don't have all day so let's get to it. We're already here so why don't we just go take a look and see what they have? If you can't find anything then we can go someplace else."

She sighed heavily, eyes suddenly dry and hard, recalibrating her options.

"What do you have against books anyway?" he asked.

"Nothing," she said flatly. "I gave her a book last year."

"No."

"Yes. The one about the lady and the parrots."

"No. You got her the earrings last year. The book about the lady and the parrots was for Christmas."

"Oh yeah. But it was still a present."

"And a good one. You know she loves to read good books."

"It won't be a surprise," she said, as if he would be sorry to see just how right she was about this.

"Sure it will. Would *you* expect *another* book if you were her?" He knew it was the wrong thing to say. But he said it anyway.

"*See?* Peter!" She swatted him and he laughed.

"I'm joking. Your mom loves good books. It can't lose."

"Heeyyy..." Her voice swelled until it spilled over with new enthusiasm. "I know! I know!"

As if to counter the new diameter of her eyes, he narrowed his own in suspicion. "Yes?"

"We could buy her a parrot! Red and yellow and blue! And he could fly around and sleep in my room and bring in the paper... please? Oh, Peter, pretty please? Wouldn't we all be so happy with a parrot?"

———

Peter toweled off and pulled on the boxers hanging from the doorknob, pausing to listen for Diane's response. But there was none.

"Can you hear me?"

"Yes," she said absently and from a long ways away, although he could tell that physically she was still in bed.

He pushed his face up against the mirror, inspecting his nose for the hair that had been driving him to distraction all day.

"I'm not knocking Spencer," he said, digging a blind hand into the vanity drawer in search of the tiny specialty scissors. "I'm just saying it's about time for a change of approach."

"This is really... *awful*," said Diane.

"What? No. I'm really not trying to be a jerk about it." He snipped out the hair and replaced the scissors. "I mean, no one needs to get their feelings hurt. I'll talk to him and just... explain things. I think he'll understand. For Lucy's sake."

Peter tossed the wet towel over the shower door and then flicked off the light and padded out into the bedroom.

It was a room to behold. Fortress of Solitude meets House of Mirrors meets 1001 Arabian Nights meets Mutiny on the Bounty. The color white and its extended family were well represented, including eggshell, oyster, putty, tusk, parchment, buttermilk and dander.

Two great, plastered ornamental beams skewered the room at diagonals from floor to ceiling, coming from nowhere in particular and going to nowhere in particular but making an architectural declaration along the way.

Two banks of clean windows, jutted out into the airspace over Ridgeline Drive and met along an invisible seem, like the tip of a glass arrow. The windows overlooked what was, when the day was lit, the wet grey serpentine of the Cleatchee River, cutting its way along the base of Marlow Ridge and then meandering southward, across the valley and around the giant thumb of Grant's Butte, flowing towards town. Diane had fashionably encumbered this panorama with billowing swags of heavy white cotton that hung like mainsails over the edges of the windows, as though the view were from the prow of a fully trimmed clipper ship.

Each of the walls that had been deprived of a window to the outside, featured large, divergent reflections of the inside. Mirrored panels, framed in elaborate gold brocade, had been mounted on hinges that allowed an articulation of up to fifteen degrees for each panel. Even the smallest of swivels, as Diane was fond of observing, entirely changed the room.

The bed, which was large and canopied, had been one of Diane's touches, from the over-stuffed jewel-toned pillows, to the silk mosquito netting tied in loose folds, to the back bedposts with thick hemp cords.

The wood flooring and the Egyptian area rugs had also been Diane's touches. The bedroom itself, however, like the house in which it was situated and, for that matter, much of the surrounding neighborhood, had been designed by Spencer Patton, Diane's ex-husband, the man who only two hours previous had called to suggest ideas for celebrating Diane's forty-fifth birthday.

The pillows dominated the bed. So much so, in fact, that it was necessary that they be unloaded every night into the enormous Persian reed baskets that stood like sentries on either side of the arched doorway to the bathroom. As each marriage has its rules and assignments, in this marriage, the rule was that each person was responsible for unloading the pillows from his or her half of the bed. Peter attended to the ritual with an efficiency born of practice, scooping all of the pillows off the bed, pressing them between his hands like an accordion player.

Prior to their removal, the pillows had served as a kind of fluffy silken hedge that defined his wife's side of the bed. There was something vaguely feline about the way she backed into them whenever she was first to bed, lining up the length of her spine with the tasseled demarcation, claiming her bed space in the same way a cat might lay claim to a rectangle of sun painted over a sofa cushion. As he removed the pillow hedge and turned his back on the bed, he got a sense of her, stretched out beneath the surface of white cotton, head propped up, arms holding a book over her face, the sheen of her hair a dark river over new snow.

"I mean, Spencer's got to see the potential for confusion," he said, stuffing the pillows down into the basket like he was feeding some hungry wicker beast that guarded his bedroom. Diane did not answer. "Don't you think?"

"Hmm?" Diane looked up at him, her subconscious hearing the question mark in his voice. "Oh, yeah, well Spencer's Spencer."

"What does *that* mean?"

"It means he's not going to change." She held up the book and gave him a worried expression that had nothing to do with unceremoniously changing the subject. "Are you really reading this thing?"

Peter squinted, actually seeing it in her hands for the first time.

"No," he said, slipping under the sheet. "Yes. Kind of. It's for a patient."

"A patient? Who?"

He pinched his expression reflexively, marking the familiar boundary. "Doesn't matter *who*, Diane."

"Right. Sorry."

"He's developed a kind of obsession."

"With what? Cliché's? Bad dialogue?"

"Lucy and I went to the bookstore today. I saw it. I bought it. I thought it might help."

"It really stinks."

"Doesn't matter. I'm not interested in its literary value. I'm interested in the cover, mostly."

Diane flipped the book closed and scrutinized the woman holding the Colt Model 1903 Pocket Hammer with a grip of inlaid bone.

"The cover? Really?"

"Long story. Long and privileged."

"Oh, come on…"

"No. Can we get back to Spencer?"

She rolled her eyes. "What's to get back to? He wants to get together for my birthday. What's wrong with that?"

"I think Lucy needs a greater separation between…"

"This isn't about Lucy, Peter."

"What? Yes it is."

"No. This is about protecting your familial territory."

"Only in the sense that clarity is important for children who… "

"No, only in the sense that you think Spencer is horning in on what's rightfully yours."

"I'm just saying that the psychological dynamics…"

"No, no, I didn't suffer med school and a hellish residency just to get pushed around by shrink-speak-psychobabble. On top of my pediatrics practice, my dear, I'm a mother. I have a pretty good sense for what is and is not important for children. So you can stop hiding your motivations behind Lucy."

She sat and pivoted, swinging her legs from beneath the sheets like a mermaid slipping her tail from beneath the sea.

Except in the dead of winter, when the wind came howling out of the North over the frozen valley and found its way up along the ridge and into the house, Diane usually slept in the buff. It was a predilection Peter had initially found brazen and tantalizingly exotic given the Lutheran restraint in his DNA. His father's oft-repeated motto had been, simply, *when in doubt, don't.* This from the man who, as a retired mill worker and widower, was arrested at age 72 and fined $5,000 for "operating or materially aiding a gambling enterprise." DNA aside, if Peter had learned anything from his father's life, it was, *when in doubt do it quietly and don't invite the neighbors.*

So Peter had conducted a very discrete and passionate affair with Diane, a married woman. When Peter and Diane were first married he had followed her lead and taken to sleeping in the nude. And he had felt every bit the secret rebel lothario psychiatrist for having so easily and casually thrown his caution and his nightshirt to the wind whenever he climbed into the bed of this lean, long-legged pediatrician that he had stolen and made his own.

All of the extra nudity, over time, had only served to keep him awake at nights. Try as he may, Peter could not sufficiently tame the feelings of proximity and sexual opportunity, which were wholly anathema to all notions of sleep. Eventually, after nodding off one afternoon in the middle of a session, Peter had reverted back to sensible sleeping attire more in keeping with his upbringing. If the world was to continue to function properly, some urges simply needed to be contained.

Diane double-pumped lotion from the jar on the nightstand and began the nightly moisturizing. This, it seemed to Peter, was a ritual that always happened *after* Diane had gone to bed, as though this singularly critical process slipped her mind, night after night, requiring that she extract herself from the covers, turn on the bedside lamp if necessary, and lubricate her legs and her buttocks and her breasts. Somehow, no matter how late Peter came to bed, he always seemed to catch the last show.

"I wasn't trying to insult your child-rearing credentials."

"Spencer is harmless, Peter. He's just... *Spencer.* You know? He's just Spencer. I've been there, done that, got the ring, gave it back, and don't want it again. All of which you already know. Right? I mean, haven't we been through this a couple of times now? I chose you. End of story."

"Well, yeah, except that a little earlier in that same story..." He broke off, recognizing the dead end.

"Yes?"

She started on the other leg, pushing against the mattress with the ball of her right foot for balance. Diane had a swimmer's body – lean and toned. Sinewy. Not entirely at the expense of womanliness. But partly. She had developed angles. Corners that had not always existed. Her physique betrayed a growing rigidity. After-work lap time at the Cleatchee River Health Club had, over the years, crept from a bi-weekly to an almost daily occurrence. The prospect of having to *miss* after-work lap time – for a patient or a husband or a child – increasingly came with a dark cloud of brooding and poorly concealed resentment. Peter could not help but wonder whether these moods were merely an unconscious cover for the unease – the nascent panic – that accompanied frustrated compulsives. He had seen more than a few of those in his day.

"Nothing," he said, knowing that she would persist no matter what he said.

"A little earlier in that same story, what?"

"A little earlier in that same story you were really upset that Spencer chose to leave you and I just..."

"I can't believe we're going through this again."

"I'm just…"

"Yes, Peter. You're right."

Diane splooched out another two squirts of mango coconut crème and went to work on her breasts, her hands making tiny slapping and squishing sounds from moving so quickly and efficiently and independently, as though she were throwing pots, wetting down domes of spinning white clay and working feverishly to shape them into salad bowls.

"Spencer chose to leave me because I was having an affair with a certain child psychiatrist with delusions of inadequacy. That would be you, in case you've forgotten. The marriage was wrong. Broken. Spencer knew it and I knew it. Two years past the fireworks and we're a total mismatch. We were both miserable. It had to end."

"I'm not trying to rehash any…"

"And of course I was *upset*. We had – *have* – a child together. It was not the way it should have ended. I mean I never *hated* him. I never wanted to hurt him. But it was destined to end. It just was. And we're all the better for it. I mean, aren't we? I'm happy. Spencer's happy."

"Says you. I think he wishes he could go back and…"

"He's part of the family and he's happy. You're the only one that doesn't seem happy, Peter, and I can't for the life of me understand why."

"I'm fine."

"Fine?"

"Yes."

"Is that the same as happy?"

"He wants you back, Diane."

"Oh, Peter… honestly. I think it's sweet that he wants to stay involved, but that's all it is. He wants a connection. To Lucy."

"To you."

"To *family*. We're all he's got."

"Bullshit, Diane. Spencer gets whatever Spencer wants. He zips around in his little silver bullet car and he thinks he owns the city.

"He does not."

"One wink and its all his."

"*Man,*" Diane shook her head in that kind of teasing disgust that he hated. She returned the lotion to its station behind the phone and then, all for the good of the sheets, she conducted the once-over check with the flats of her palms to make sure that there were no stray splotches or streaks needing attention. Then she slipped her moistened body back into bed.

"What," he asked.

"That's just a little bitter and jealous to be coming from the one who got the girl."

"I'm not…"

"And anyway, Peter, it was *your* idea to make sure he felt welcome as a part of the family. Remember that? Making sure Spencer was part of the family was as much your idea as anybody's. If I was a psychiatrist – I know I'm not, believe me, but if I was – I might conclude that you had some guilt feelings about getting caught poaching another man's wife. Caught red-handed, mind you."

"You said he was gone for the weekend."

"But I'm not a psychiatrist. As we both know. So, I'll just have to take you at your word that it was critical – *critical* – to Lucy's well-being that her father be included as a regular part of the family unit."

"Diane, that was six…"

"No, no, I was skeptical, but you sold me. And it's worked out great. Except that now, suddenly, you seem to have changed your mind about the whole thing."

"Not the whole thing. And conditions have changed. Lucy's older. And Spencer wants back in."

"Oh, give me a break."

"It's so obvious. It's obvious to me anyway. Maybe not to you, but its obvious to me. And he's buttering up Lucy."

"She's his daughter."

"Yeah, well … she's also his excuse to stay close to you."

"He's bringing someone."

"Who?"

"Spencer. To dinner. For my birthday."

"Who?"

"I don't know. A date."

"So. You think that means he's not still carrying a torch?"

"I'm just saying… he's interested in someone else."

"She's a beard, Diane. He wants you to drop your guard."

"Jesus, Peter."

"She'll be like all the others."

A look of sharp annoyance seized her face and she arched her back, thrusting her hips toward the ceiling. She extracted, as if from a place that knew no mango coconut moisturizer, *The Open Grave* by Garrett Webb.

"Here, darling," she tossed the book onto his chest, "read your pulp."

———

Peter watched Spencer turn on the gas and push the starter. The grill popped softly to life. Spencer unhooked the wire brush from its peg on the railing and began brushing the grill with the kind of casual authority that belongs to a man in the comfort of his own home. As he brushed, he rested the tip of his boot on the lid of the big red cooler and looked out over the valley. He began to whistle a tune that sounded vaguely like *I've Been Workin' on the Railroad.*

Of course, Spencer wasn't actually in his own home. He was in Peter's home. He was in the home of his ex-wife. He was in the home that he had designed and built and then abandoned along with everything else he had relinquished to Diane in the divorce. But the paper facts of legal title did not change anything about the way that Spencer moved through the house, which, to Peter, now was like a shark moving through a familiar reef of coral: through the front door without a knock, up the stairs, through the living room with its photos of the current occupants, into the kitchen, sliding open the door to the deck with the side of his boot and out to the railing over-looking the ridge and the sunlit Cleatchee River snaking along below. Never a hesitation. Never a deferential pause. *Swim, swim, swim.*

Once he had set down the large cooler, Spencer the shark had swum back into the kitchen toward the refrigerator with all of its intimate reminders – *Lucy piano, mustard, garlic, pay Jill, landscapers Thurs.* – and there encountered Peter who had come downstairs in time to see Spencer carry the red cooler through his kitchen and open the back door with his foot.

Now, out on the deck with the grill hissing and the summer dusk gathering her dark hems just out of sight beneath the ridge, Peter handed Spencer a glass of wine. Spencer sipped and promptly set the glass down on the side-table.

"Hope you like salmon," said Spencer.

"Love salmon," said Peter. "Don't eat near enough of it."

He handed a glass of Chablis to Nicollet, the olive-skinned, barely-legal, Mediterranean-born plaything that hung on Spencer's every move. Spencer called her *Nik* and *Nikki* and sometimes *Nico.* She called him *Spender* and sometimes, *Big Spender.*

She called Peter, *Pete,* because that was how Spencer had introduced him back inside by the refrigerator. *Nikki, Pete; Pete, Nicollet,* Spencer had said, followed quickly by *where's the birthday girl?*

Pete. His name was not *Pete.* Spencer knew this, of course. It was the game they played. Peter would not give him the satisfaction of showing that it bothered him. And Spencer knew that too. In any event, Peter had not corrected the introduction. He had been surprised to turn and to find her there behind him, tiny and silent and brown.

"Is good, yes? This fish?" she asked timorously, gesturing towards the cooler with her wine as if offering a toast. "This is good food? Eating food?"

"Salmon? Yes, yes," said Peter a little loud and a little slow. "Salmon is a very good fish. I like salmon very much."

"That's good, my friend," said Spencer. "That's good." He began making a series of short rapid, triple brush strokes on some charred detritus that was resisting the inevitable. "Because you're gonna eat some *serious* birthday salmon tonight. Not that farmed shit, either. These bad boys," he tapped to lid of the cooler beneath his boot, "are straight from the Copper River. My dentist goes up every summer."

"Who? What's his name? Ken Gleason?"

"Yeah. I designed his summer home. Pays me in fish."

Nicollet laughed, covering her lips with her fingertips. Her hair was black and sleek and short, curling in at the clavicle and leaving her neck and shoulders exposed. She wore a tee-length sundress, yellow, with leather sandals adorned with a plastic daisy on each thong.

"I do not shit you doll-baby," said Spencer. "One good Copper River salmon is better than five-hundred U.S. dollars. Maybe a thousand. Maybe you should start asking for salmon tips, honey."

"Spender!" she said in a soft scold, pretending to look cross. The patch of skin between her dark eyebrows wrinkled slightly. *Bad boy*, said the wrinkle. *Mama spank*.

"And just wait 'til you try my marinade," said Spencer.

He stopped scrubbing long enough to look over his shoulder and wink at Nicollet. Or perhaps the wink was for Peter, who could not actually discern the intended target of this over-used affectation. But he was struck by an awareness – and not for the first time – that what might be irritatingly transparent affectations coming from others, tended to translate as entirely genuine expressions when coming from Spencer. Perhaps it was the three-day beard or the unruly coal-black curls boiling out from beneath his nearly threadbare mango-colored cap. Or the ruggedness of his frame wrapped in his perpetually tan hide. Unlike his fellow architects, Spencer had a disarming physical presence; like he was a star ball-player for the Caribbean Castaways. Or maybe it was just the flawless teeth – shark's teeth, Peter thought suddenly – that hypnotized people into believing the sincerity of something as corny as a wink. But whatever the trick of misdirection or sleight of hand that produced Spencer's immunity from harsh judgment, Peter knew better than to think that anyone else could pull it off in quite the same way. Peter was quite sure that if *he* ever winked at another human – even *once*– he would be instantly gored by a bolt of lightning.

Nicollet laughed again, putting a little throat into it this time. Whatever Spencer had meant by *salmon tips* and *marinade,* she had understood.

Peter did *not* understand. He did not care to understand.

Lucy bolted through the kitchen door and onto the deck.

"*There* she is," said Spencer, putting down the wire brush on top of the cooler. He clapped his hands and squatted like a catcher waiting for the pitch. "C'mere fireball."

Lucy bounded past Peter who, even as these words were spoken was stepping back to allow clear passage. Spencer received her and rose in one fluid motion as she clasped her hands around his neck. His fingers found her ribcage and she giggled and squirmed and then shrieked as he spun her in circles over his head.

It was an unnerving thing to watch; this child, this little sparkle of a human that Peter had known and loved since she was only two, now being twirled above a flaming hot grill, over a deck railing that jutted some twenty-five feet above the ground. Peter understood that Lucy was not his daughter. Not genetically. Not legally. But he thought of her as a daughter. He worried for her as a father worries for a daughter. He liked to believe that in Lucy's mind he occupied the same thoughts that are reserved for a father.

He thought of Henry, a font of unsolicited wisdom even in absentia. His irascible embonpoint officemate – a family therapist with two ex-wives, four kids and two failed custody fights to his name – would have slapped him much too hard on the back in false assurance. *Kids are resilient,* Henry would say in that stop-worrying tone of his. *They're pliable. Broken arm maybe. If she misses the grill and clears the corner of the railing and happens to land right. Maybe a concussion. Minor burns and scarring. She'll be fine. Nothing that can't be repaired. You know, nothing psychological, God forbid. And as for the father thing, you're every bit the father to Lucy as Ol' Bio-Dad over there with his boots and his stubble and his millions. So if you want to grow a pair and step in and assert yourself there buddy, you should feel free. After all, it is your fucking house.* And then Henry would go back to reading his magazine, or drinking his soda, or doing whatever it was he was doing before it occurred to him to opine, like some coin-operated fortune-teller giving it away for free.

Peter inhaled, preparing to advocate restraint and caution; preparing to lecture Lucy's father on how not to handle his own flesh and blood.

"Spencer. Let's just –, " he started, but Diane interrupted him from a third-story window looking directly over the deck.

"How's a girl to take a shower with no hot water?"

Peter turned with the rest of them to look up in the direction of her voice. She was cantilevered out the window at the waist, holding a white towel over her torso with one hand and her dark towel-wrapped hair wrapped with the other.

"Hey!" shouted Spencer, putting Lucy down. "There's the birthday girl! And in her birthday suit, no less."

Lucy giggled at this and Spencer gave her another tweak in the ribs.

"I'm wearing a towel. And you're early."

Spencer looked at his watch. "Only thirty minutes."

"Hey Nik," Diane lilted, waving two of the fingers holding the towel that was wrapping her hair. Nicollet smiled, returning the greeting with a schoolgirl wave that was simple and exuberantly wholesome.

Peter was taken aback at the familiarity, as though these two women had been pleasantly acquainted for years. Not *Nicollet*; not even on the first meeting. Not even *Nico* or *Nikki*. It was *Nik;* one syllable was enough.

There was an intimacy in sharing shortcuts, he thought. Diane and Spencer shared a lot of shortcuts. Like when Spencer would say, shaking his head to himself, *that reminds me of the asparagus joke,* and Diane would start laughing because she knew the punch line. Or when Diane would look up from her plate and glance confusedly around the table and Spencer would instantly be up and pushing back his chair and moving away from the table for the kitchen because he knows what she needs; the salt, or the wine or the bread.

Nik. Intimacy lived in the nooks and crannies of normal discourse; spaces only large enough for a glance, a snicker, a thing not said. Intimacy, so often, was found in the act of trimming words; breaking language itself into little pieces that will fit into those secret irregular alcoves where people meet, down there, beneath the roaring traffic of conversation. *Nik*, Peter knew, was Spencer's intimate name for Nicollet, just as he knew that Diane was now making a casual bid to share in that intimacy. The rest of her name was to be uttered only by those on the outside looking in, wanting what was not theirs.

"This is so lovely house," Nicollet said, gesturing broadly. She had a wide smile that turned up the corners of her eyes.

"Oh, thank you, Nik. We're so glad you could join us. We have Spencer to thank for the house *and* the lemon of a boiler he installed."

"Mommy, come open presents!" Lucy hopped in place like a bunny on a leash. Nicollet clapped and laughed delightedly. "Nico and me want…"

"Nico and I," Peter said reflexively.

"Nico and I want you to open presents."

"Hold on now girls," said Spencer conspiratorially but loud enough for all to hear. "The woman has just disparaged my choice of boiler and has so brought my good name and character into question. You see, there is a proper order to things. First, I shall re-ignite the pilot light so that your mother has unlimited gallons of hot water with which to wash her sizeable posterior," Nicollet clamped her hand over her mouth, trying to keep the laughter from escaping, "and so that she may then apologize for her rash and scathing criticism, a condition causing unfair treatment of others brought on by advanced age and, therefore, a condition for which she is not responsible. Pitiable, really, when you think about it."

"Hey!" laughed Diane.

"Second," Spencer continued, "we eat some scrumptious salmon. Third, we sing happy birthday. Fourth, we serve cake and blow out candles. Then, and only then, Little Miss Lucy and Miss Nikki, do we open presents. Are we agreed?"

Lucy and Nicollet laughed and nodded and then laughed toward each other at the fun Spencer was able to bring to any occasion. It was a laughing look they had obviously had previous occasion to share.

Lucy's delighted expression collapsed into something more earnest. "I can play happy birthday on the piano," she whispered up towards her father, standing on her toes. "I learned it from Mrs. Soulak."

Spencer winked at this and a smile bloomed over her face once again.

Raising his chin to the damsel at the window, Spencer called aloud, "Good Lady, we are in agreement that Sir Pete shall tend to the mighty slain river beast as I re-enslave the evil boiler to do your ceaseless and unreasonable bidding."

"Spence," Diane beamed. "Just shut up and fix the damn water heater."

Several years ago, it would never have occurred to Peter that as Spencer opened the cooler and handed him the grill brush and then clomped his cowboy boots across the deck for the kitchen, he was not actually going down to the basement to tend to the boiler, but up to the master suite to tend to his freshly showered ex-wife. But now, as the kitchen door closed and as Spencer's heavy footfalls receded into the heart of the house, this was precisely the thought that came for Peter, swimming silently out of the gloom. And circling.

It was ridiculous, he knew. More often than not it had been Peter defending Spencer from Diane's harsh judgment, encouraging the benefit of the doubt when it came to Spencer's motives and intentions. She liked him, as a person and a father. There remained affection between them, even if it took the form of a thousand barbed exchanges that might leave the uninitiated to imagine a genuine and abiding enmity lurking in the depths of their banter. She even felt sorry for him on occasion, which was an appropriate thing to feel for a cuckold. But, to Peter's recollection, she had never betrayed an interest in rekindling any sort of... *intimacy*.

Nevertheless, the thought persisted, and it persisted with such force that Peter quickly busied himself with the two large blood-orange strips of fish flesh laying in the cooler on a bed of ice – lifting them and poking at them unnecessarily with a spatula – just so that he might quell the urge building in his chest to bolt inside and run upstairs. He attempted to provoke an enthusiasm in young Lucy for salmon, dead or alive, with an animated narrative that included totems, Grizzly Bears, and the migratory wonder of spawning.

"Mom and me say Peter's a know-it-all," said Lucy to Nicollet. Lucy's eyes rolled and her tiny body went dramatically limp on the glossy stained-plank floor of the deck.

"Mom and *I* say Peter's a know-it-all," corrected Peter, looking down at her.

"Really?" said Lucy, "So do me and Mom." She rolled around on the wood until she came to the railing and then she changed directions, making her way back towards the grill.

"Lucy, get up please. You're starting to look like a salmon. What will Nicollet think of a girl who rolls around like a fish?"

"Fish don't roll," she said authoritatively. "Fish swim. Everybody knows that. And Nico knows I am *not* a fish because Nico knows me and *I... am not... a fish.* Am I Nico?"

"No, Lucy," said Nicollet. "But you are a silly girl, yes?"

"I would rather be a silly girl than a fish. Any day I would. Nico's a ballerina. She's not a fish either."

Peter scrubbed the grill like he was trying to get blood out of a carpet, glancing up at the window at which he had last seen Diane, and then sideways at his guest as he feigned interest. "A ballerina. We don't see many of those around here."

Nicollet smiled, demurely.

"This is what we say. *Ballerina.* Me and Spender. Yes?" She raised her eyebrows above a rye smile. "*Ballerina?* For Lucy. You see?"

Peter stopped scrubbing and looked at her. "No."

She smiled, as if to a child. She demonstrated.

"Ballerina holds bar like this." She reached out her free hand and touched the railing, lightly with just the tips of her fingers. She extended one leg – slowly, robotically – so that the toe of her shoe pointed to the kitchen door. Sunlight shown through yellow fabric.

Lucy clapped. Peter gave a smile that he had intended to be perfunctory, but that was not quite so by the time his lips had finished the job. He started to return his attention to the grill, for that was what he wanted; that, and to worry about the happenings inside his home. But he found that he could not tear his eyes from hers.

Nicollet slowly lowered herself on one leg, bending her knee with such ease and silence that it was almost imperceptible, as if she were not bending her knee at all, but rather sinking smoothly into quicksand, bringing her rigidly extended leg – toe still pointing at the door through which Spencer had disappeared – within inches of the floor of the deck.

Inside, behind his professionally implacable expression, Peter gaped. She looked up at him with eyes of purpose. Lucy clapped from somewhere in the distance. With both hands Nicollet clutched one of the vertical stiles near her shoulder running from railing to floorboard. Her left hand spiraled up the stile in a kind of serpentine caress.

"I am *this* kind ballerina, yes?"

Peter did not understand. And then he did. He swallowed and returned to the grill.

"Yes, yes. I think I do. That's great. Very…" He didn't finish. He glanced up at the window, now a rectangle reflecting empty sky. "Lucy, why don't you go in and find your mother. I mean, call out to her from the stairs. Ask her if she wants you to set the table."

"Table's already set, Peter," said Lucy pulling something small out of the flesh above her knee. She did not look up. "Mom did it already. Hey, I have a splinter."

"That's what happens when you roll around on the deck. Go ask Mom for a bandage."

"I don't need a bandage. It's not bleeding."

"Go ask her for some anti-bacterial crème."

"Peter…" she agonized."

"Lucy, no whining. Just go inside and holler up to Mom. Tell her…" he glanced over at Nicollet, who was leaning against the rail, arms crossed, listening with a smile. Listening and understanding everything. "Tell her she needs to take a look at your knee."

Lucy groaned and heaved herself upright, then trudged off the deck into the kitchen. "Mom!" The door closed behind her and the house that Spencer built swallowed her whole, claiming her tiny voice.

"Sweet girl, that one," said Nicollet, gesturing toward the house with her chin.

"She's a handful," said Peter, not looking up. He opened the cooler and extracted the first filet. He held it out in the open air, rotating it in and out of the sun like a signal mirror. The orange translucent flesh glowed and flashed.

"That *is* a nice piece of fish," he said. Nicollet smiled, committing to nothing, and sipped her wine. Peter placed the fish on the grill and reached in for the second filet. "So... where exactly do you... dance? I mean, if I can ask?"

Nicollet smiled as if considering the question. Then she pointed up to the window. "She is pretty. You wife. Good muscle. Yes?"

The non sequitur was enough to stop the spatula. He looked up.

"Oh. Thanks. Yes. Thank you. Yes. She is. Pretty. She keeps in good shape. She works out a lot. "

Nicollet walked in slow, casual circles, as if to trace a figure eight drawn onto the deck, placing the heel of one sandal carefully in front of the daisied-thong of the other.

"No thank *me*," she said, her back to him. "I say *she* is pretty. No *you*." He laughed cautiously, looking for signs of humor. But he could see only the lines of her back. Delicate yellow straps disappeared over the tops of shoulders that were like smooth hillocks of coffee and cinnamon. When she passed closest to the grill she looked up at him. Her eyes were pools of milk floating large dollops of chocolate.

"You worry she is with Spender." It was not a question. She turned and continued on her course.

"Who? Diane? No... you mean..." he pointed up stairs with the spatula. "No." He laughed.

"Yes you do."

"No, no. They're friends but..."

"Then why do you worry?"

"I don't."

"Yes you do."

"No. I'm afraid you misunderstand." Peter needlessly repositioned the fish and closed the grill. "They were married, but they divorced. And for good reason. Do you worry?" Diane would have made a point of his choice to deflect a question with a question. *So like you, Peter,* she would have said; had she been here, and not upstairs. "About that, I mean? Do you worry about them?"

Nicollet looked up and made a face, pushing air dismissively from between her lips. She sipped her wine.

"In Barcelona, my father is marry six times. He is happy and looking very young and handsome and the women love him. Each wife is beautiful woman. Each wife becomes old hag because she know about my father and she worry. You see? They worry. Worry, worry, worry. They wish to keep him, but he is no that way. He is happy always with the one he does not have. He go to Marseille and meet my mother. *Mi Madre* is number seven. She is most beautiful woman he has ever seen. They move to Madrid. She is good wife for two year, but then she sleep with many men. This one and that one and this one, and the butcher, and the florist, *y el banquero, y el jardinero.* Many men. Including my father. You see? She is no satisfied with only him. And my father never catch her because she is clever, my mother. But he know enough to worry, you see? He is suspicious. And he start to shrivel up. *Que un pomelo.* You see?" She squinted at him horribly, scrunching up her face. "Like rotting grapefruit. He start to grow old. He becomes mean and unhappy. This way he dies."

"I'm sorry."

"Si. He was fifty-eight. My mother say keeping her was the only thing my father want. You see? *Keeping?*" She looked at him again, this time balling up one of her tiny fists and pulling it into her chest. "But keeping is no wanting." She opened the fist, fingers wide and straining, as her hand flew away from her breasts like a bird.

Peter nodded just as Lucy pushed open the door.

"I called," she said.

"And?"

"She doesn't hear me."

"Did you go upstairs?"

"No. You said to call. I called. I'm going to watch T.V."

She retreated without waiting for an answer. The door closed. He stared expressionless at the place she had been. Nicollet cleared her throat.

"Sorry. What were you saying?"

"*Wanting.*"

"Oh yes, wanting."

"My father forget it is the *wanting* that keep him young and happy. *Mi madre*, she is *sesenta y siete*. Sixty-seven. She is beautiful woman. She is courted by many men. She is wanting, wanting. So, you say this about Spender?" She gave another dismissive puff of air, brushing the backs of her fingers towards the house. "This is no to worry me. Wanting, wanting. No keeping. You see?"

Peter opened the grill and absently poked again at the salmon. He opened the lid to the cooler and pulled out the large baggie of marinade. It was dark and pulpy in his hand, like he was holding a freshly harvested organ. He placed the baggie on the side tray, opened it, and stirred the marinade with the basting brush that he kept hanging beneath he grill. He drizzled it onto the fish in a thin, continuous serpentine stream of purpled sauce the consistency of honey. He looked up at the window and then back down at the hissing fish and then nodded his head.

She was behind him suddenly, reaching for the basting brush with her free hand. A delicate silver bracelet swung loosely around the base of her wrist. She sunk the brush into marinade and removed it from the baggie. Thick, glopping strands dripped into the grill. Fire rushed up at them in fat, redolent tongues. He stepped back. She did not. She painted the filets in full, luxurious strokes.

"Thanks, Nico," he said. "I mean, not for the basting, but..."

"Do no call me Nico."

"I'm sorry, I thought... I just..."

"*Nicollet,*" she said, reaching past him to slather the last fish. "Nee-co-let. *Me gusta la forma en que mi nombre suena en su boca.*"

The words darted out of her, like a spray of tiny arrows, sticking into pillows of hot, sugary aroma as the fire rushed up to ignite them. All he could do was to look confused. He felt the length of her leg against his own.

"I like this way my name sound in your mouth," she repeated. "Like it is home."

———

The evening was something gauzy and dreamlike. Sickening and wonderful. Passing around and through him like a circus-laden wind. Coming to him in a kind of detached staccato consciousness. Spencer and Diane emerging separately, ten minutes apart, Spencer descending upon the table just as everyone was seated. Diane greeting Spencer in a manner too contemptuous even for their relationship, insulting his mechanical skills and complaining about the temperature of the bath water. Spencer taking no offense and responding with his typically grandiose flair, suggesting that she had become a cosseted, captious princess plagued by a pea at the bottom of a stack of mattresses. Lucy and Nicollet giggling at the show that they rightly presumed to be for their, and his, benefit. Spencer whispering into the fluted hollow of Nicollet's ear. Nicollet laughing and stroking Spencer's shoulder and tousling his hair. Spencer slathering him with a thick marinade of praise for mastery of the common gas grill. Diane joining in, lifting her glass, toasting the chef. Diane and Spencer and Nicollet strenuously dismissing his embarrassed protests that the fish and the marinade had come from Spencer and that the person who merely applied the heat deserved little credit. Spencer pivoting, standing, lifting his glass to Diane, using her middle name, bellowing the name *Stella!* like he was Stanley Kowalski, acknowledging the day of her birth, reciting *Stella's Birthday* by Jonathan Swift, and lingering over the lines – ...*However, Stella, be not troubled, Although thy size and years are doubled* – to hearty applause and laughter and swatting. Diane asking if he knew any birthday poetry by Nicholas Gordon, and Spencer laughing uproariously, both of them brushing away the confused and eager inquiries for illumination, keeping it to themselves. Declaiming, *Nothing! It's nothing!* and shaking their heads and laughing and wiping their eyes. Nicollet tasting the fish, pressing the palm of her hand against the sloping brown plane of her chest, between the yellow shoulder straps of her nothing sundress, just beneath the clavicle, thumb and forefinger framing the supple notch at the base of her throat, the sliver links of her bracelet clinging against gravity to the slightest protuberance of wrist, closing her eyes, losing herself to a silent ecstasy of the tongue as they all watched her swallow, and smile, and then, pivoting her face, and opening her eyes… to him.

After dinner, they all left the dishes and retired to the living room for gifts and dessert. Lucy proudly emerged from the kitchen with a lemon-frosted cake that she and Diane had made that afternoon. Diane's aesthetic contribution could scarcely be avoided. The cake was adorned with thin crescents of lemon, small white flower petals, a healthy dusting of zest and a single tall yellow candle in the middle. Lucy's contribution had been to stir the batter, to rigorously time the cooking, to help apply the frosting, and to wage a heroic and yet losing battle for an accurate number of candles.

Lucy had taken her defeat on the candle issue in stride. Perhaps this was because the battle over candles had come in the context of an even more pointless contest over the cake itself. Diane was not a person who ate desserts. Ever. Sugar and fat were sworn enemies of the body. Birthday cakes were Trojan horses. It did not matter to Diane that it was her birthday, or that her daughter had labored over the cake or that there had likely been more sugar in one spoonful of Spencer's secret marinade than in the entire cake. Diane had attempted to persuade Lucy that fresh fruit with a splash of liqueur might be festive. Or perhaps something creative with watermelon. But Lucy had held her ground. It did not matter that her mother would blow out the candles but abstain from even the smallest sample. There would be cake.

She placed the cake on top of the piano where Spencer was seated and playing a blues-up version of *Celebrate Me Home.* She disappeared and returned repeatedly, skipping and skidding on the glossy floor, transporting brightly wrapped packages from their hiding place into the living room. Nicollet sat on one of the couches opposite the piano patting the side of her leg and swaying in time to the music.

"Spender!" she exclaimed, delighted. "You no tell me you play this!"

"This is the only place I can play any more," he said without any discernable impact on the song, fat round notes falling like rain.

Peter remained standing, crossing his arms. "You should have taken that thing with you," he said, numb with anger and yet nearly drunk on a feeling he could not name, almost saying *that damned thing*, but checking himself in time. "No one in this house plays much."

"Nah," Spencer smiled wryly, shaking his head and not looking at the man who had appropriated his wife and home. "She comes with the house. Looks great in here. Won't work in my place." He broke off to roll his head back and forth at something moving or pathetic in the phrasing. "Besides, Lucy plays."

"Yeah, Pee-*ter*!" said Lucy plopping a small green package on a larger yellow one. "I play! Mrs. Soulak says I'm her best student."

"Sorry, Sweetie," said Peter. "Your right. You *do* play. You play beautifully."

Nicollet, still reeling, reached out and pulled Lucy down onto the couch. "My God! Is like that Elton John, your dad!"

"Who?"

Spencer slipped seamlessly into a rousing *Crocodile Rock*. Nicollet squealed delightedly and stood up, pulling Lucy to her feet. They danced in place, turning and dipping and shimmying to one another, faces radiant.

Peter watched her move, as if from the other end of a tunnel, mesmerized at the fluidity of form and the perfect control of every part of her body, not responding to external stimuli, but moving now like the notes were inside of her struggling to get out. Her face – eyes, lips, the delicate divot beneath the nose, ears like perfect shells – was moving too fast for her black, silk hair, in the same way that her hips and her breasts were too quick for the thin yellow fabric of her dress. The silver bracelet hung on, slamming recklessly from wrist bone to forearm.

They chased her, these things, changing directions every half-second, desperate to catch up, desperate to keep her from getting away. It was an innocent dance. Gleeful. There was no bump and grind here. No erotic pantomime.

And yet.

Nicollet turned, catching his glance, pulling his eyes up to hers. She held out a hand, perfectly still as the rest of her body moved wildly, hovering in the air at the end of a naked arm that waited for him. Peter smiled and waved her off, turning with a sudden giddy sickness in his stomach to retrieve the cognac and glasses from the bar near the rapidly darkening windows.

Diane, having taken a seat on one arm of the sofa, clapped in time to the music, jutting her head forward on every fourth beat – quickly out and slowly back in, quickly out and slowly back in – like an immobilized chicken. Lucy tugged wildly on her mother's arm. After a brief and insincere resistance, the rest of Diane's body happily joined in.

It took *Honky Cat* and *Saturday Night's Alright for Fighting* before the dancing impulse gave way to exhaustion or, perhaps, an interest in the cake that sat waiting on the piano. When they were done and panting, Peter stood from his perch by the windows and delivered a cognac to Spencer.

"Now *this* is what I call a party!" Spencer shouted, Nicollet descending on him like a crazed fan. Lucy and Diane cheered.

"Drink?" Peter asked Nicollet, holding up his glass.

"*Agua,*" she said seizing his arm in mock desperation. "*Fría! Inmediatamente!*"

He offered the same to Diane.

"Me too," she said, nodding towards Nicollet.

"Me three," said Lucy.

He went to the bar and scooped ice from a faux leather bucket. The room chattered and gasped behind him. He filled three glasses with water and delivered them. Nicollet held her glass to her face and neck, one side, then the other, before drinking. She smiled up at him in the way a guest shows polite appreciation for a host. As though they were acquaintances. As though they had not already been together, meeting in the tiny silent spaces between words, as the flames had licked at the lacquered copper flesh.

"Ah, *gracias*," she said.

Lucy bounded from the couch and made a production of evicting Spencer and Nicollet from behind the piano. After a false start, she played the birthday song, in a rapid, broken, halting cadence, probably not in the way taught to her by Ellen Soulak. She bounced and jerked her shoulders from side to side, imitating her father's performance. When she was done, she waited briefly to receive her applause.

"You're supposed to sing!" she scolded.

She played it again. They all sang in a jumbled pile of words like a marching band following a drunken drum major. Then a third time, slower, measured, Spencer's hands on her hands, Spencer's voice like a trumpet into battle. Then a fourth time, perfect and all Lucy. *Mastery by repetition*, as Mrs. Soulak liked to say.

Cake followed. And then presents. Shredded paper and mangled ribbon fell to Diane's feet as she tore into the wrapping with a production of eagerness that left no room for sentiment. From Peter, a watch with a gold band and face of pearl, followed by the latest in mobile telephone technology. From Lucy, chamois slippers and an oversized book on designer gardens. From Spencer, a silk camisole and a French perfume in a fluted, tear-shaped bottle.

"It's from both of us," said Spencer winking at his date. "Nico helped me pick it out."

"Lovely," said Diane, dabbing her wrist and holding it to her nose. "Mmm, Peter, smell this." She stood and reached across the coffee table. Peter bent down to her wrist as if genuflecting to royalty. "Nice," he said.

"Better than nice," she scolded. "Exquisite." She smelled again, splaying her wrist to the room and waving her arm around in the air. "Oh. Divine. Intoxicating is more like it."

Lucy seized the wrist sharply and sniffed. She closed her eyes in the way of her mother. "Is this what you wear, Nico?"

Nicollet smiled demurely and shook her head.

"What do you wear?"

She shrugged and then looked up at Peter, eyes calm and dark. He felt blinded. Lost. "*Nada,*" she said. "*Jabón. Aceite de oliva.*"

"That's French isn't it?" Lucy said authoritatively.

Nicollet laughed, teeth gleaming, breaking contact, looking back at the child who was still holding her mother's wrist. "No is French. This means, eh, soap. And olive oil. You see?"

The words came with unbidden images of Nicollet applying emoluments and the room seemed to Peter to fall into an odd and reverent hush for elongating seconds.

"In Mrs. Soulak's bathroom," said Lucy, "she has these soaps in the shape of apples. And they're even red and everything. Only the soap isn't red when it's on your hands. Isn't that cool? You could trick somebody. She says that's how she gets people to wash their hands 'cause they always want to grab the apple."

Spencer stood up. "I almost forgot. Wait here."

He left the room and returned with a large box wrapped in electric blue shimmery paper with a pink bow on top. He set it carefully on the table in front of Diane.

"Daddy," breathed Lucy, "what is it?"

"It's a gift, silly. For your mom."

Diane squinted, eyeing him suspiciously. His expression was mocking. She reached out to pick up the box. He stopped her.

"The lid comes off," he said. "See?" He plucked a corner of the box.

Diane lifted the lid. She gasped and closed the lid then lifted it again and extracted the tiny bundle of squirming gold fur. Lucy shrieked.

———

Ellen Soulak was Diane's widowed sorority sister. In the years after a boating accident had taken the lives of her husband and oldest son, Ellen had managed to keep herself afloat by helping neighborhood children butcher Chopin for money. Her youngest son, Fenton Soulak, was all she had left. Ellen and Diane had never been particularly close in college, which was rigorously cliquish and stratified for such a small school where even minor variations in eye color and hair length counted as diversity. Ellen and Diane had become reacquainted as adults when the Soulak family moved up into one of the adjoining neighborhoods along the upper ridgeline. Since then, mutual impressions had warmed.

The accident had happened on the afternoon of the Fifth of July at the apex of a blind corner of the Cleatchee River, roughly five miles North of Horsefly Lake. The other boat had carried a retired judge, who had also met his end. It had been a hot, cloudless day with the sun perched in its blue nest at an angle that made it difficult to look much above the ridgeline, and that sprayed light off the water with such force that it was also difficult to look at the first hundred feet of the river in front of the boat. Alcohol had been a factor for both adults. While the newspapers had been delicate, the lawyers and the claims adjusters had not, leaving an emotional carnage that surrounded the event in ever expanding concentric circles like ripples around a stone that has disappeared beneath the surface. The Judge left behind a wife of thirty-four years, seven children and nine grandchildren. Carl Soulak left behind Ellen and Fenton.

The funeral was a quiet, sparsely attended ceremony at the First Summerfield Episcopal Church. For several months thereafter, Diane had made regular visits to check in on Ellen and Fenton, bringing them food to eat and movies to watch and stories from the happier corners of society, or at least those corners that were not rending their clothing in blind grief. Peter, who had known Carl from the Riverside Rotary and had generally enjoyed his company, had accompanied Diane on these mercy trips on many occasions. Aside from a hot summer barbeque and once sitting with them in the bleachers for six innings of a playoff game between the Summerfield Falcons and the Clement County Badgers, he did not really know Ellen or her son. But Diane had wanted him to go with her. She had never been very comfortable in intensely intimate circumstances. The grief was too much for her to handle by herself. She needed him, she had beseeched uncharacteristically. She needed his expertise.

Ellen had been withdrawn, empty, sitting apart in her chair by the quietly humming fish tank. She sat like an abandoned building sits, hollowed out, broken, scarred and littered with glass, on the outskirts of a city, in a place people used to live. Peter brought her tea and sometimes sat down on the edge of the hard, black piano bench, avoiding the empty recliner, and talked to her, with his elbows on his knees, about the psychological importance of grief and about the importance of anger and about the importance of wanting things from life. She had frequently nodded, and had even given an occasional dutiful smile whenever he had attempted to buoy her with humor. Peter sometimes fed the fish as he talked, dusting the top of the water with translucent green flakes, as though he was a natural part of her environment, performing functions unrelated to her state of mind. A link to something normal.

But he knew she did not see him; not really. And he could tell that his words were like windblown trash, coming from a place she could not remember, passing through her empty rooms, and tumbling on towards a place she could not follow.

As time passed, Ellen had cultivated the appearance of someone who was slowly reacquainting with the process of living. Their visits were received with appetizers and fresh flowers on the table and even something orchestral on the stereo. She had begun giving piano lessons – an old vocation dusted off and brought current with new sheet music and exercise workbooks from *Tatterhoch's Music Supply*. Peter's approval, with Diane only an echo away, had been effusive and unsparing.

Ellen had thanked him for his encouragement and his counsel, as had Diane thanked him on her friend's behalf. But while Peter had allowed himself to feel useful, he had known better than to think Ellen had actually survived anything. Caring enough about life to feel something, to feel anything, was a critical step off a very high cliff.

On the good days, she made it through dinner in one piece, the four of them around the table working hard at light conversation. Every so often, Ellen would remark at what Carl or Ben might have thought; how they would have hated or loved something. *Isn't that right, Fen?* She would look at her son with an unconvincing smile, her eyes out of focus, as though her question were a tongue probing for the confirming pain of an excised tooth.

Young Fenton never answered such questions. He was aloof and difficult to engage, usually declining to even look at Peter, who had rattled on about sports and astronomy as Diane tended to the dishes and Ellen sobbed in the bedroom.

A year and a half after Ellen had buried half of her family, Peter stopped going to her home. Or rather, since the frequency of Diane's visits had nearly stopped by that time anyway, it is more accurate to say that Peter made a conscious decision to not go to Ellen's home any more. The decision was precipitated by an unexpected visit that Ellen made to his office one afternoon as he was locking up for the day.

Fenton, Ellen had explained, had discovered her sleeping pills. Stomach pumped, he had been recently discharged from Saint Collette's. The doctor had recommended therapy from a psychiatrist – specifically a male psychiatrist – to work on the loss of Carl and Ben. Fenton, she explained, needed a professional; although that was not exactly the way Ellen had put it. She had said that her son *needed a man* and Peter had pretended that this was the same thing as needing a professional. But he knew that when Ellen had hugged him in the doorway and said that Fenton needed a man, she was actually talking neither about psychiatry nor about her son. Peter had agreed to see Fenton as a patient, but knew better than to tempt fate by making any further house calls.

Acting more on personal instinct than professional ethics, Peter had never relayed anything of these events to Diane who, at least as far as Peter was concerned, tended to take an overly proprietary view of her friends and their lives. She would never have tolerated a professional vow of discretion that trumped her personal interest in knowing whatever there was to know about her sorority sister. She would not care to be excluded by his independent allegiance. Ellen would surely tell her anyway, he thought. Better that it come from Ellen.

Or, at least, that is what Peter had told himself, assiduously avoiding the truth. Ellen, suddenly, in his doorway, was an attractive, forty-six year old widow who appeared to have conquered the demons that had occupied her for the past year and a half. Her eyes, once hollow black sockets, ringed and ragged with deprivation, had become soft and hazel and responsive to his every word. Her hair, still honey blonde but now gathered loosely behind her head, no longer a bird's nest. Her expressions, once bleak and twisted were, suddenly, relaxed and genuine, allowing a return of femininity to her features and her manner. She smelled of perfume and cosmetics. She smiled with sincerity. Had they not been discussing Fenton's overdose, she might even have laughed easily. She had looked as though, one layer beneath her concern, she was radiant with wanting reason to laugh.

And yet he found her suddenly, inexplicably, abhorrent. Loathsome. Loathsome in the way of law-breakers and cheats and spoiled children. He had resisted the urge to push the widow Soulak firmly out into the hallway and to close the door in her face.

Her face. He had wanted to slap it, to physically shock it back into its rightful countenance. But he had successfully resisted such thoughts, in fact denying them almost instantly so that it was nearly as though they had never existed in the first place.

Henry had passed heavily down the hall behind her, sizing her up with his eyes in an obvious way, grinning so that Peter would notice his approval. Ellen had turned slightly to watch him pass. When she turned back, Peter was again a psychiatrist and he had invited her in.

Although their discussion had been devoted exclusively to Fenton, Peter could not help evaluating Ellen, as though she were his patient; taking her measure and comparing her to the grief-stricken husk he and Diane had so often visited. She had, he concluded, come to terms with her grief by owning it, celebrating it, wearing it around her neck like some dark butterfly she had trapped in resin, letting it nestle in the cleft of her breasts on a gold metal rope. She had turned death itself into a keepsake reminder of the feelings she believed she could never have. Ellen, he had surmised, was now to devote herself to a kind of suffering, patiently endured; she would hunt for experience that would fall short, partners who would disappoint, enthusiasms to crumble at her touch like dry sand, all to cause the very pain that would prove to her that she was still alive. The act of living now resided for Ellen entirely in the longing for something else. Something other.

Peter indeed suspected that *he* was something other; an entry somewhere near the top of Ellen's list of wrenching mistakes-to-be. Reason enough to decline her request to counsel young Fen. Too much potential for conflict. Too many cross-fertilizing relationships, each set against the others; Fen-Peter; Fen-Ellen; Ellen-Peter; Ellen-Diane; Diane-Peter; Ellen-Lucy. It should have been an easy request to decline.

But, with no discernible hesitation, Peter had obliged her request, and for reasons that he could not or would not acknowledge, he had then tucked everything about the widow Soulak in with the things he chose not to discuss with his wife, nor even to consider in the privacy of his own thoughts. She did not exist for him but to pay the bill for her son's treatment and to animate the musings of his patient.

———

In the week following Diane's birthday, Peter found it nearly impossible to stop thinking about Nicollet Flores. At work, his mind wandered. Patients repeated themselves through awkward, echoing chasms of silence that Peter, after coming to his senses, pretended had played some critical role in the therapeutic process. He kept his door closed between sessions specifically to keep Henry from lumbering in and dumping himself in a chair, propping one of his scuffed Hush Puppies on the edge of the table, and wasting his time with idle conversation.

And yet, so ensconced, Peter tended to spend that carefully guarded time at his desk with his heels propped up on an open drawer listening to the clock and staring out the window at the cars hissing through the rain and at the people scurrying from awning to awning, leaving *The Yeast We Can Do Bakery* clutching their protuberant white paper bags and crossing the street in the direction of *McClatchy's Seed Company* where they disappeared out of sight beneath corner of his window sill.

He found himself imagining – idly and without any particular effort to do so – that Nicollet might one day decide she wanted a pie. Or a scone. He found himself imagining that he might look down and see her there, exiting the bakery or preparing to cross the street, and that she might look up and find him silently watching her. Looking down at her. She was not the kind to avoid his staring or to care about the rain. She would stop right there in the street and stare back up at him, water running over her face and down her bare brown arms and down her bare brown legs to the tips of the petals of the daisies that adorned her sandals.

That was how it would happen, he caught himself thinking. He shook his head and forced himself to think about something else. But it didn't take and there she was again, looking up at him. As if for help. As if to be pulled up out of a river. And him staring down at her in the river, water raging, rising higher and higher between her legs, as if the simple act of looking at her was extending a branch for her to grab. As if his longing was not the river and she was not the branch. That was how it would start.

At home, when he and Diane and Lucy congregated for dinner after their separate days, he found Diane to be uncharacteristically happy. Not aggressively cheerful in the way she often was when she was overcompensating for a foul mood or surreptitiously spoiling for a fight; but happy in a deeper, more genuine way as though she were actually optimistic about every next minute of her life.

On Monday, her clinic signed two new partners, both top pediatricians from a competing practice, and both of whom Diane had personally recruited. On Wednesday, she topped her own best time for the fifty-meter backstroke. On Thursday she attended a parent-teacher conference at which she was informed by Lucy's summer school teacher that Lucy was among the smartest and well adjusted of her peers. Lucy would start the new school year two years ahead.

Diane had been quick to credit her genetic contribution, jokingly of course. She had not meant to exclude him. She laughed like a large, pale egret.

On Friday, Diane had followed up her nightly lubrication ritual with such a flurry of unsolicited, uninhibited, tropically scented sexual attention that Peter almost convinced himself that nothing was actually wrong between them. Even as she had mounted him in nearly a single leap; and even as, in his surprise, he had gripped her around her waist and buttocks and ribcage, trying to find reliable purchase like he was wrestling with greased livestock at the Summerfield Fair, he had begun to entertain the notion that his concerns about Spencer were, as Diane had always insisted, the product of an overactive imagination, a possessive heart and a guilty conscience. For a moment, the skies in his mind had begun to lighten.

But well before Diane's private symphony had reached its scripted, cymbal-crashing crescendo, Peter felt himself drifting away from the moment, floating above the bed and watching his wife slide up and down a body that was not his own. His attention waned. Hydraulics began to fail. He began to spiral down into the ocean.

It was Nicollet who saved him; stepping out from the shadows in his head; extending one leg into the room; lowering herself slowly to the floor as she had to the decking on Diane's birthday; substituting herself for the screeching, slippery pale siren; taking him into her; bringing him back into the moment in a surge of wanting that which he did not have.

Lucy, too, had found new resilience against the tides that normally pulled her towards the shallow fits of discontentment for which she was known. She had inexplicably taken to sitting in his lap, voluntarily, giggling and squirming like the happy little girl he liked to imagine she was. She generally did as he requested without complaint. She asked for his permission and sought his counsel in ways that seemed almost too alien to be satisfying. He was inclined to interpret this new disposition as evidence of a genuine father-daughter bond that he never should have doubted.

It was likely that he owed most of Lucy's refreshing familial interest to Spency, or *Little Spence*, the inexhaustibly bounding, barking, excreting, shoe-devouring mutt, part Retriever, part Border Collie, part Tasmanian Devil, that Lucy insisted naming after the man who – in direct contradiction of Peter's wishes – had made it all possible. As *Little*

Spence had instantly become the center of Lucy's orbit, the petty power struggles in which she had typically indulged with Peter had become, in the greater scheme of things, far less important to her burgeoning self-concept. Suddenly, it seemed, Lucy felt that she could afford to show some consideration.

And yet, neither Diane's affections, nor Spency's magnetism, nor Lucy's sudden role of adoring daughter in the family play, had been enough to keep Peter's attention grounded in the daily rhythms of his home life. In the back of his mind, always, there was now another rhythm, a deeper and altogether darker pulse to his existence that showed no signs of weakening.

Quite the opposite.

On Saturday, Spencer dropped by unannounced. He was in jeans and a ripped brown Henley and unshaven in his usual way. He and Lucy and his quadrupedal namesake tussled savagely on the floor in the foyer. Peter watched from the stairs like a policeman deciding whether to intervene.

"I need to bum a ride to the airport," Spencer said, pretending to bite off Little Spence's front left paw.

"You do? When?"

"Now."

"Why?"

"Business. Chicago," he said answering a question Peter had not really intended. "Just a few days."

Peter was prepared to ask why he could not simply take a cab to the airport, but Diane was suddenly on the landing behind him.

"Take your own sorry butt to the airport," she said. "Mooch, mooch, mooch. You think I'm your personal assistant?"

"I can take him," said Peter.

"Thanks, man," said Spencer. "I don't want to put you out or anything."

"No. I may as well do it," Diane said. "It's coming up on three. Lucy's got a piano lesson. I'll just drop her off on the way."

Little Spence was on his back, wriggling, mouth open, tongue flopping wildly trying to free his hind legs from Spencer's grip. Lucy pounced on Spencer's back and began biting his shoulder. Spencer groaned and began bucking to throw her off.

"But they're in opposite directions," said Peter. "That doesn't make any sense."

"Well *someone's* got to take her."

"So take her. I'll take Spencer to the airport."

"Why don't you take Lucy and I'll take Spencer?" asked Diane, in a way that seemed to Peter like she was trying too hard to sound casual.

"Why?"

"Oh, that's right. You don't like Ellen Soulak anymore."

"I never said that."

"Seems like it."

"No."

"You don't like to go over there though. To her house."

"She's you're friend, Diane. I certainly don't have a problem dropping Lucy off."

"Fine. You take...."

Spencer roared in mock outrage as he rose from the floor, hanging Lucy upside down from one hand and beating his chest with the other. Lucy shrieked and Little Spence stood on his hind paws barking excitedly and trying to scale Spencer's leg.

"I need you to keep my car for me too," said Spencer to whoever was listening, disconcertingly human and calm. He set Lucy down and picked up Little Spence. The dog squirmed and licked frantically at Spencer's stubbled chin. Spencer scratched behind the dog's ears as the foyer slowly decarbonated.

"What? Your car?" asked Diane.

"I've got contractors working on the garage."

"Still?"

"It's a big project. I can't park on the street while I'm gone."

"Who on earth wants a smaller garage?"

"I do. I only need enough for two cars. I'll get a second office out of it. That's really the point. A drafting studio."

"Where are we going to put your car?" she asked.

"Living room? Linen closet? Hey, I know..." he looked in revelatory wonder from Diane to Lucy and back again. "How about the driveway?"

Diane rolled her eyes.

"It's only for like three days. Four days. Drive the thing all you like. Here."

He reached into his pocket and tossed up a key on a teardrop-shaped leather fob. Peter caught it awkwardly.

"My driveway is full of pickup trucks all day and my garage is a disaster zone."

Lucy bounced on her toes in front of Peter, looking up at him beseechingly. Little Spence, who had in the space of a single week fully attuned himself to Lucy's brain waves, whipped his head around and leaned forward out of Spencer's arms like a furry noodle panting and ready for action.

"Can I take Spency to show Mrs. Soulak?"

"No." said Peter.

"How come?"

"Because you can't just take your dog over to somebody else's house. Besides, there's nothing for Spency to do at a piano lesson."

"He can listen."

"No."

Lucy looked past him, as one might look past any other obstruction, to Diane.

"Peter's right," she said.

"Can we take Daddy's car then? I like Daddy's car."

Diane looked at Spencer, who winked and nodded.

"Hey, it's fine by me," said Spencer. "Can you drive a stick?"

"Nope. Not me," said Diane, waving away the suggestion. "I guess Peter will have to take you, Luce. Looks like I'll be taking your dad to the airport after all. Spency and I will pick you up after your lesson and we'll go to the park. How's that?"

"Really?!"

"Yep. I think Spency wants to play. He's got that look in his eyes."

———

Peter watched his wife roll the deep blue minivan backwards down the driveway. Diane craned her neck back over her shoulder, tendons extruding, her hand braced against the headrest of the passenger seat where Spencer sat waving at Lucy on the front steps. Still inside the foyer, looking through the open door, Peter imagined the tips of Diane's fingers burrowing into Spencer's hair. Spencer held up Spency and waved his paw. Lucy laughed and waved back.

"Bye Spency! Bye Spency!"

The minivan backed out into the street. Diane turned and said something to Spencer. Spencer nodded. Little Spence leapt between the front seats into the back, racing from one window to the next, barking for Lucy.

When the minivan had disappeared around the corner, Peter went upstairs and changed his clothes and began herding Lucy towards the door at the back of the kitchen that lead into the garage. He held the door open with his fingertips, waiting.

"No, Peter," she said, hand on her little hip.

"No? We have to go, Lucy. You'll be late."

"We're taking Daddy's car. Remember?" She dangled Spencer's keys from her finger.

He let the door to the garage close and followed Lucy down the stairs through the front of the house and out across the wet grass to the curb where the familiar silver coupe waited like some sort of glossy watercraft – a speedboat or a submarine – tied up at a dock in a James Bond movie. Lucy was already inside and strapped in before he had even opened his door.

The car smelled like cologne and new leather. It felt small and snug around him, like he had slipped his body into the finger of a velvet glove. He closed the door and the pressure in his ears popped. The air was suddenly close and quiet and it seemed as though he could hear the ends of Lucy's hair move against her collar. Peter put on his seat belt and poked the key along the length of the steering column. Lucy giggled.

"No. It's here," she said, pointing to a glowing amber slot beneath the stereo. He inserted the key and turned it. The engine purred to life. Silver lights glowed. A crystal chimed.

Ellen Soulak's home was a short, twenty-minute drive further up Ridgeline Drive and then due West over once fertile cropland that had long since been submerged beneath the concrete wave of suburban sprawl with its flotsam and jetsam of mailboxes and trampolines and skateboards and basketball hoops and plastic swimming pools and pre-fab kitchen-nook-sun-room-library additions. The gated neighborhoods and riding mowers were considerably fewer out this way. They passed the old Methodist church with the lightbox sign in the parking lot that never seemed to have enough letters to complete it's single-word edicts, like "_OVE" and "PR_Y" and "FORGI_E" and "_RUST." Today the sign read "RE_ENT."

They passed the new middle school. The yellow bulldozer that had been used to clear the ground for the combination hockey rink and basketball court was still parked over in the back of the un-mown field where an end zone would be if the field had been made for a high school rather than a middle school. It seemed that every few miles there was either a video store or a trailer made up with a fake bamboo roof or clapboard shutters framing a large drive up window beneath bright awnings and signs that read *Java Joint* and *The Jumping Bean* and *Shot in the Dark*.

When they reached the Windward Mall, Peter turned north again, pulling the wheel so that the car cut the corner to the bone. He accelerated as he shifted gears. The car growled and sucked him back into its black, velvety center of gravity. Lucy grabbed the edge of her seat and gave him a look but said nothing.

He pulled up alongside the curb in front of the Soulak residence so that the bullet car stopped just past the front door. He was not interested – in fact, he was particularly disinterested – in the prospect of happening into an exchange of small talk with Ellen Soulak.

The door to the house opened as Lucy climbed up out of the car. Ellen smiled and waved and stepped outside, her hand clasping the edge of the door to hold it open. She wore a bright blue dress and her hair was pulled back in a black ribbon. Lucy returned the wave and shut the door as her piano teacher bent at the waist and waved to the driver she had no reason to expect was Peter and who was already accelerating down the street.

———

The car would not let him go. He had every intention of returning home but then, without a flinch or hesitation, he succumbed to automotive momentum allowing himself to whisper past the last turn that would have taken him to Springhill Family Estates and then kept going, rolling like a silver marble down Ridgeline Drive all the way to the bottom. The sky had traded its uniform gray for an unsettled, mottled look, with great pockets of blackening clouds off to the East that moved like granite boulders rolling in slow motion down slopes of dusty shale. As the ground leveled, he banked sharply with the road and headed out across the plains.

He had nowhere in particular in mind to go, so he wandered, letting the car serpentine the streets almost at random, waiting for the rain and trying to understand the beating in his chest, which was heavy and urgent and restless.

He thought of Ellen Soulak in her bright blue dress the color of an unseen sky, and her healthy blonde hair, and her cheery wave, and the more he thought of her, the more he felt inexplicably angry. He wanted to choke her. Scream at her. Humiliate her. He hated her. She made him hate others whom he was otherwise disposed to tolerate. He hated Spencer. And Diane and Lucy. Mostly, she made him hate himself. He wanted to push down on the accelerator with a slow, steady pressure until the engine was whining and the speedometer needle was shaking and the car was a rocket flying over the road. He wanted to scream into the blue of her dress.

But he hadn't the slightest idea why.

He was a psychiatrist and he knew what it was to perceive a thing as a representation of something else. He knew what it meant to lash out at the wife because, somehow, she represents the mother who is conveniently out of reach. He understood pining for lost youth by grounding the child. We are inkblots to one another. We are dots and dashes in a code. We are walking ciphers. We are shards of ancient clay and bone in the dirt waiting to be discovered so that others might understand something greater, more profound, about themselves. We use one another in this way, in this unspoken service, of which we are largely oblivious. But knowing this is so, as all psychiatrists do, was not the same as knowing the answer to the savage beating in his chest. He *wanted*, desperately, he wanted, but he knew not what.

Nicollet was suddenly in his head. "*Wanting, wanting. No keeping. You see?*" It was as though she was seated next to him. The smell of her. Her hand on his thigh as he pushed in the clutch. The links of silver swaying from her wrist. Her hand on his hand as he shifted gears. Her dark eyes watching him watch the road.

The thought of her was like liquid blue fire in his veins. *She* was what he wanted, by God. Right now. He wanted to pull over and ravage her right here in the back seat of Spencer's car. When they were done, he wanted to drive back to the house and lay her out on the top of the piano and to then resume with abandon in the hopes that his wife and step-daughter might return home and find them copulating like wild animals on the very instrument Spencer had so calculatingly left in the living room before pretending to take his leave.

Spencer would then clomp into the room, having missed his flight to Chicago and expecting to stay for dinner, and would stand agape with the others, wanting to speak, wanting to quip and swagger and to be in control, wanting to dominate the room with the sound of his boots, wanting to play his old piano, wanting to disappear with Diane somewhere secret in the house he designed, but then – seeing them and hearing them and smelling them – suddenly reduced to stupefaction, having lost all sense of the world and his place in it.

Black was white. Up was down. *Nic? Nikki? Nico?* Spencer would sputter. *Peter? Just what exactly do you think...* Diane would start to ask in that way of hers. But he and Nicollet wouldn't stop, drowning their audience out, slamming into each other until the baby grand was just a pile of sweaty black kindling.

Peter felt his anger lighten as his lust intensified. He gripped the wheel and shifted into fourth gear as scenes of wanton carnality played in a delicious loop in his head.

Perhaps Ellen Soulak would choose that inopportune time to pay a visit and, having knocked for too long at the door that no one had answered, she would wander into the house looking for signs of life until she too had stumbled upon the spectacle.

Ellen, for her own reasons, would certainly disapprove. He was, after all, married to her close friend and sorority sister. She would be indignant on Diane's behalf. Perhaps even worse, Ellen Soulak had been cruelly deprived of her own spouse. She knew, as well as anyone, that we should never take for granted what can be taken away in a single stroke of fate. After all, hadn't he once rattled on at her in her living room, as she looked at him like a wraith, bleary-eyed from the other side of the empty recliner between them, that happiness lay in knowing what one has, not in recalling what one has lost? Hadn't he told her to find solace in the fact that Fenton – who might have accompanied his brother and his father on their river outing – had not been taken? Hadn't he told her that there were parts of her life still in tact, and that not even the crush of grief would excuse turning her back on those blessings?

No indeed. The widow Soulak, who had somehow managed to find peace in her bright blue dress and her simple existence in her empty house, would certainly not approve of such exercises on the piano, the instrument she taught to children. She would judge him harshly for turning his back on his blessings.

He knew he had lost control of the fantasy when Henry shuffled into the scene, from stage left, drinking a soda and grinning from ear to ear. He plodded past the others to the sofa where he deposited his full girth with a grunt and settled in for the show, putting his Hush Puppies up on the coffee table.

Get the hell out of here! Peter would shout, trying not to lose his rhythm. *This isn't for you!*

Who's it for then?

Them, you moron.

Why?

Get out!

Why?

Because they... because they live like I'm not here! Okay? But I am here, goddamnit! I am here!

You should quit your whining. You want to see real problems? You should come sit in on one of my sessions. Now those are some bad family problems. This? This is nothing. You're on easy street here. Except you're losing your thing there... He points with his soda hand. *You've got to keep moving.*

Shut up, Henry. I'm sick of you. You don't know how they are. You don't know what it's like living here.

Hate to tell you this Pete, but this was all your idea.

What was?

Everything, man. Everything.

The fantasy disintegrated as he was forced to stop behind *S.B.L. Bus Number 60.* His mood, which had been expanding with the force of anger and lust now collapsed around him like the husk of something dead.

The bus hissed and lowered as two people in the back stood and made their way toward the exit. One of them came back and bent toward the back window to retrieve something from beneath the seat, taking her time, oblivious to the fact that he was waiting and that other cars were now lining up behind him. He wanted to honk but now lacked the energy.

The sign on the back of the bus featured a smiling brown chimpanzee beneath the taunt "Monkey See, Monkey Do..." The chimp was dangling from a bowing tree trunk. In his free hand the monkey held a large red letter "F", which he had taken from word "Follow" which was making its way up a green hill just ahead of the words "me to the Summerfield Zoo."

The passengers finally alighted and the bus raised and hissed and lurched forward, slowly gaining speed. Peter followed.

———

He could not remember the last time he had been to the zoo. Years ago. College. High school maybe. He remembered now that he had not liked the zoo. He still did not like the zoo. It was an unusual way to kill time. The novelty and the animals had been enough, then and now, to get him past the front gates. But thereafter, every step along the captivity tour was strangely unsettling. Too many eyes. Too many snouts and trunks and beaks at the bars. Too many straining necks. Was he passing through? Was he just another to be so casually enthralled at thralldom? Did it all make him feel lucky? Or was he the new next-door neighbor?

He wandered the trails with his hands in his pockets, moving slowly so that others would pass and not adopt him as part of their touring experience. The sky had grown progressively darker as the rain moved closer. It sprinkled lightly on his face whenever the trail turned out from beneath the canopy of foliage that was like a leafy green umbrella over the cages. Every so often a cool pungent gust blew through, rattling the boughs. He stopped at each exhibit, but generally without interest and sometimes without even bothering to find the poor animal he was supposed to see.

Nicollet, though, was with him every step. Not just beside him, but in every cage, or rather, on the other side of the bars looking at him as he strained every sense to detect her.

He stopped at the dingo pen and watched what just as easily could have been two domesticated dogs fighting over a length of old rope. He thought of Spency and wondered how long he would last with a pack of dingoes. Three others, reddish-brown, drawn and lean looking, darted out of their den and approached him. They advanced at a trot, picking his scent out of the air, detecting nothing that resembled food, and moving on along the perimeter of the enclosure, stopping, doubling back, and then doubling back again, as though hoping to discover some break in the fence, some exoneration, some pardon from their circumstances, that they had missed a million times over.

He was out in the open. The rain was light, but no longer intermittent. He turned. Across the clearing was a tall fenced enclosure for the monkeys. *Monkey Island* according to the sign. A zoo guide was pointing to a chimp up on a branch for a small group of visitors. They were asking questions and the zoo guide was answering, pretending that she did not mind the rain. She turned and looked his direction, pausing her explanation, as if she were about to ask him why he was standing so far away from the group. As if to ask how he had gotten loose.

And he was loose, he thought, looking back at her. *Wasn't he? He was loose.* He knew then where he needed to go.

———

Shocks & Struts was not the only strip club in the greater valley. There were three others and Nicollet might have been in any one of them. Peter had never been inside these establishments, but like all human males over the age of twelve, he knew exactly where they were and what they looked like on the outside. If he closed his eyes, he could see the parking lots and the signage just as if he had grown up across the street.

He started with *Shocks & Struts* because it was the closest, and because he had once heard Spencer tease Diane that the new shoes about which she had been raving and which she had modeled for them after dinner one evening – dark, clunky and ridiculously expensive things – were too sensible and boring. *You really should go take a look at what they're wearing over at Shocks*, Spencer had said. It had been just another opportunity for them to laugh at Spencer's pride in his own low character. But now the comment had taken on additional meaning. Abbreviation suggested familiarity. *Shocks.*

It had taken a lot of aimless driving in the pouring rain to screw up his courage and to plan out what he wanted to say, but eventually, as though Spencer's silver bullet had driven itself, he awakened from his own thoughts to find himself pulling into the parking lot of the familiar low gray building. The lot was strewn with potholes now filled with rainwater and the smear of neon like a reddening oil slick.

He turned off the engine before he could change his mind and sat for a moment, listening to the rain hit the roof like acorns. Lightening flashed around him followed by a splitting and a crash that seemed to come from inside his chest.

He opened the glove compartment looking for breath mints. Instead, he found an empty flask and a flashlight and a rolled up baseball hat. He took out the hat. It was black and beaten and frayed along the bill. On the front above the bill was a simple line of gold thread in the shape of a bird in flight, a single bolt of lightening clutched in it talons. He put it on and looked at himself in the mirror. Then he stepped out into the torrent.

Inside was dark and loud. It appeared a low square cavern with a raised stage in the middle. The place was mostly empty of patrons except for ten or twelve men scattered among the tables around the stage. Three women in minimalist costumes worked the poles. They grimaced and growled and clawed at each other. One wore handcuffs. Another brandished a policeman's bully club. None of them was Nicollet.

Peter was relieved. As much as he wanted to find her, he did not want to find her here. Not like that. Or, at least, that was how he explained his relief. For as much as he *wanted* to find her, *needed* to find her, he did *not* want to find her. Not here. Not anywhere. Searching was one thing. Even searching with intent. But finding was something else entirely.

He surveyed the room more carefully. None of the faces were familiar.

A chesty redhead at the bar caught his eye and began making her way through the percussive gloom. She wore an open cream kimono and high heels.

Peter shook his head and waved her off, thumbing towards the front door to show that he was headed back out into the weather. She stopped and shrugged and headed over towards the tables, percussion exploding around her. The strobe over the stage went into a rapid frenzy rendering the room in a kind of dream language, allowing her to float above the floor. The dancers clung to their flashing silver poles, reaching for each other to keep from drifting away in the storm.

Nicollet's hand came from behind, slipping into his own like a small, hairless animal looking for shelter. It was soft and smooth and vulnerable to the touch.

He started, the composure of his expression falling away like rain. She smiled and pulled. He followed. They cut through the room, she floating and he stumbling, traversing the length of the bar and skirting the far edge of the stage to a shadow that became a hallway. The hallway turned once, twice and it was suddenly too dark to see. He gripped her hand, blindly following the pull. She stopped. Knocked. She opened a door into a dim red glow.

The room around him was barely large enough to accommodate a plaid sofa along the wall, a wooden chair across from the sofa, and a round table in the corner. On the table were several empty beer bottles, a box of tissues and white ceramic lamp with a red acrylic scarf draped over the shade. On the floor in front of the table was a black portable stereo, glowing with thin green lights that blinked *12:00 A.M.* like the iridescent eyes of some timid underground forest dweller. She closed the door.

"Nicollet..."

She placed her fingertips on his lips and maneuvered him to the couch, sitting him down into the sagging springs so that this tiny sprig of a woman was now towering over him. She wore black stilettos and a lacey blouse that dropped to just below the swell of her hips. Her hair hung loosely at her shoulders. Her wrists and fingers were bare. The deep brown of her eyes was relentlessly black in this room. The pounding music from the bar was like a muffled heartbeat in his ears. Her kneecaps were at eye level. He reached out for the flawless skin of her legs.

She stepped back, once, twice, around the chair, as if she had eyes in the back of her head. She stooped and pressed a button on the stereo coaxing new sound into the room. A slow, syncopated synthesizer slithered out of the walls and when she stood again, rising from the floor, she was like a cobra rising from a basket: head and shoulders and hips and knees all following each other just a beat behind the rhythm. She removed her blouse and draped it over the back of the chair.

Peter struggled off of the couch to his feet.

"No. Nicollet. Stop. I don't want this. Not this. Not here."

She smiled, pressed her fingers into his chest, pushing back against the couch, her breasts like perfect raindrops swelling from her shoulders. He kept his balance.

"No, Nicollet. I don't want this. I want... I want you. Let's go somewhere."

She dropped her arm and the smile faded. She shook her head.

"No," she said softly.

"Yes." He reached out and took her hands. "Yes. You and me. Spencer is still after Diane. You could see that, I know you could. When you came for dinner. You have no future with him. Not with that guy. He's a lout. He's a wolf. A shark. He'll never love you. All he does is chase. That's no kind of life, Nicollet. You have no future with Spencer. I'm sorry, but you don't. I think you know that. Let's do to them what they have done to us."

He couldn't tell whether he was actually speaking these words or if it all came from his eyes. It was not exactly as he had rehearsed. There had been more and he had intended more calm, more reason. The counselor in him had counted on inexorable logic and not so much passion. But the gist of it was in tact.

He realized that he was squeezing her hands as she wrenched them free. She walked over to the small black box on the floor and tapped it several times with her foot until the music stopped and the dull thudding from the bar returned.

"Nicollet?" Desperate. Wavering.

She retrieved her blouse from the chair and put it on, shaking her head.

"You're better than this," he said. "I'm not leaving you here. Come with me. I want you, Nicollete."

She looked at him coldly, part pity, part disgust.

"No. To have what Spender has," she said. "Always, with you it is to take and keep. Not to want. You take and keep like wet fingers around match. You put match in pocket and carry around like dead slobbery stick." Nicollet balled up her right fist and placed it inside her open blouse. "You want only keep. You see? Dianne take and keep. Lucy take and keep. Nico take and keep. *Pero custodia no es lo mismo que querer.* I am for wanting. Life is for wanting." She opened the fist, fingers wide and straining, as her hand flew away from her breasts like a bird. "I wish you to want, Peter. Just want." She opened the door, gave him one last look, and was gone.

———

Autumn came early. The sun slunk away in the wind and rain and the hardwoods worked to purge all memory of summer in extravagant tantrums of red and gold.

As the world changed its clothes, life adjusted its routine. Little Spence, for instance, abandoned his oral fixation on shoes, broadening his interests dramatically to include boots and slippers, as well as table legs, houseplants and everything else that was in reach.

Lucy started middle school ahead of schedule and with an attitude made of equal parts superiority and trepidation. Her interest in clothing, jewelry and candied perfume increased almost as dramatically as her interest in Little Spence decreased.

Spencer developed a yen for Sunday brunches with his ex-wife and daughter, appearing on the doorstep with enough waffle batter, strawberries and syrup to feed an army. He also volunteered to share custodial responsibility for Little Spence if Diane would teach him – Spencer, not Little Spence – to swim, claiming to suffer from negative buoyancy and a mild phobia dating back to childhood; weaknesses which he had somehow made to sound endearing and to confirm his virility.

Not coincidentally, Diane added an extra night of swimming to her weekly exercise regimen. She spent untold hours picking up and dropping off both Spencer and Little Spence at Spencer's home. Swim-lesson nights became less regular, increasingly sporadic and so difficult to predict that if Diane was ever not at home in the evenings, the standing assumption was that she was either off teaching Spencer to swim or, if Little Spence could not be heard gnawing on the furniture, picking up the dog. Upon her return to the house, Diane invariably confirmed one or both of these explanations.

Peter, meanwhile, threw himself into his work. He stayed late. He worked many Saturdays and almost always found a reason to be out of the house during the hours that corresponded to Sunday brunch. He exceeded his usual client load by a significant margin in large part by expanding his practice to include clients of all ages and by riding the wave of anticipatory seasonal depression that began to build as October arrived with promises that winter was, once again, highly likely.

It was common for him to stay at the office in the evenings even well past the end of his last session. Since Henry usually liked to leave his own office at the stroke of five, the hours between five and eight provided Peter with a stretch of quiet opportunity to work on his notes without any worry of being interrupted.

When he was done with his work, he tended to stay for a while longer, leaning back in his brushed leather chair and listening to the quiet of the building. Whenever he was particularly disinclined to go back home he propped his heels up on an open drawer of his desk and stared out the darkening window. He watched the last of the sun glugging from the bottle, staining the tablecloth where it dropped over the side of the horizon past the western croplands. He listened to the rolling rubber river beneath him; the internal combustion of people leaving work, leaving their lives of relative competence and professional restraint, and racing both directions past *The Yeast We Can Do Bakery* for home, where, he assumed, they were all more or less content but most vulnerable to losing the illusions that kept them so.

It was on a Thursday, in the middle of one of these contemplative vigils, that he was startled back into the moment by a knock at the door. He dropped his feet, stood up, closed the desk drawer and crossed the office. He opened the door, wishing he had steadied himself first.

"You *are* still here," she said.

She looked different that when he had seen her last, the image of her looking at him with her hand on the open door was still etched in his brain. She wore a long black open raincoat over a slash of rumpled white, faded black denim, and heeled boots that made her taller than she really was. Her face was composed and, he could not help thinking, lovely and womanly, with soft wrinkles at the corners of her eyes and those cheekbones that pulled everything up into the semblance of a smile.

And yet, somewhere just beneath the surface of her appearance, he sensed an aching sadness, a certain crestfallen despair that was impossible to avoid. Her eyes seemed slow and slightly unfocused, like she was listening rather than seeing. She seemed to him in that moment like a perfect little house overlooking the sea from the edge of a grassy bluff, except that she was preoccupied with the feeling that the bluff was steadily eroding beneath her, one relentless gray wave at a time, into the shape of a thin overburdened crescent.

"Ellen..." he said, not covering his surprise.

She pushed past him into the office, walking slowly over to the couch. Peter watched her, his hand still clutching the doorknob. She rotated one way and the next, taking in her surroundings with an interest that was alternately general and particular, as if looking for something she could not identify.

"Ellen, what's ..."

"Where is he?"

"Who?"

"My son. Fenton. Where is he?"

"I don't..." He closed the door and walked over to her, looking at her directly. "Ellen, I don't know where Fen is. Is he..."

"He's gone."

"Gone? How do you know he's gone? Here, for goodness sakes, take off your coat, please sit down."

He raised his hands to her shoulders and she turned her back to him, reluctant but obliging, so that he could help her with her coat. She sat heavily on the sofa as he hung the coat on the rack in the corner.

"Would you like some tea, or..."

"No. I would not like some tea. I would like to know where my son has gone."

Peter sat in his chair across from the sofa and leaned forward, elbows to knees.

"Ellen, I haven't seen Fen for months. You know that. You have to know that. He stopped coming. I haven't sent you a bill since..."

She looked away sharply.

"What's going on, Ellen?"

She was quiet for long moments. The clock behind the desk ticked away and the cars passed on the street below with enough regularity that Peter heard them as little gray waves eating away at the bluff.

"I was gone," she said finally. "For a week. With a friend. He has a cabin. At a lake." She spoke to her hands. Her fingers made elaborate lattice patterns on the curve of her black denim knees. "It was just for some fun. There's no phone up there."

She realized she was fidgeting and stopped abruptly and looked at him. A beat passed and she started the finger-weaving again. "Fen was staying at the house, I mean he still lives there, with me, well I guess you know that..." she shook her head violently in frustration. "Christ!"

"Ellen," he said calmly. "It's okay. Take a breath. Just tell me what happened."

She gave a forceful exhale, reaching behind her head to unfasten the barrette into which she had gathered her hair. She pulled her fingers absently through the honey-blonde tresses, arranging them over her shoulders. Her fingers obsessed over the barrette like a lost child.

"When I came home, he wasn't there. I figured he was off at a friend's house or something. After three days I began to really worry. He's slipped off before, but only for a night or two. I can count the number of actual friends he has on one hand."

She opened one of her hands as if to make sure. She showed him. He nodded.

"I called them all. They had no idea. So then I started to panic. You know me; he tries to kill himself one time and so if he's not exactly where I expect him…"

"You assume the worst. I know, Ellen. It's normal. Any parent would."

"Finally, I found the note."

"He left a note?" Now it was Peter who could not help but assume the worst. "What kind of note?"

"That idiot kid left a note, for me, in his own room, on his own desk, under a half empty soda can." She looked up at him with a look of twisted incredulity on her face. "Why not the refrigerator? Why not my goddamned pillow?"

"Ellen, what note?"

She returned her attention to the barrette.

"He said he's gone to California. He said he didn't want to tell me because he knew I would have a cow. That's something Fenton says. *Have a cow.* It means …"

Peter nodded. "I know what it means. Lucy keeps me current."

"He said that he's finally found his wife. *His wife.* That's what it said. *His wife.* The woman of his dreams. He said that after they are married they will buy me a new house somewhere near where they live. On a hill. Over looking the ocean."

She leaned back on the sofa and stared at the ceiling. A thin stream streaked down her face. She blinked and wiped her cheek with the back of her hand.

"Where is he Peter?"

"I don't know, Ellen."

"If you knew, would you tell me?"

"No," he said. Ellen shook her head in silent futility and disgust along the back of the sofa. "But I really don't know," he added.

"Has he talked to you about this woman; this wife of his?"

"You know I can't talk about anything that your son and I have discussed."

"Does she even exist? I mean this is Fen we're talking about. Is she even fucking real?"

"How did he seem the last time you saw him?" he asked, deflecting.

She nodded bitterly, an acknowledgement that he would not answer her questions.

"I wish I smoked," she said. "This is when I would really love to need a cigarette, I mean really crave one of those things, you know? And to reach into my coat pocket and light one up and to feel that nicotine in my blood and to feel just a moment of satisfaction, just for a second, like at least that one little act accomplished something. Just a little bit of control at my fingertips."

"I used to smoke," he said, leaning back. "I miss it sometimes."

"It's a vile habit for insecure people."

"Ellen…"

She sighed and combed her fingers through her hair. "He seemed okay. He seemed better than okay. He seemed… really good. He seemed happy."

"He's an adult. He's free. At some point he's got to figure things out on his own. We all have to do that. We all have to leave. To go away. To search. It's not for us to control him. We have to let go."

"You mean *I* have to let go."

Peter didn't answer.

"He's not ready," she said. "You know that. You're not saying it, but you know that. He's not ready for the shit that's out there."

"He's got a lot of learning to do. He's not as equipped as others. Emotionally. I'm not hiding from that, Ellen. I'd prefer he was still here. I'd prefer to have him in therapy. He's got a lot of tough lessons ahead of him. But I think he's far more resilient than you're giving him credit for being. He's come a long way. There's a good chance that this... journey, this walkabout will be good for him."

"Oh, is that what it is? A journey? A Walkabout? I thought he was getting married."

"I think he'll be fine and I think that if he needs you, he'll reach out. He'll call you."

She looked up crying. Her eyes shone hope for the first time.

"You really think so?"

"I do," he said, smiling. "I really do."

"God, Peter, I hope you're right," she said. It was the first time that evening she had said his name kindly, as though he was someone she trusted.

He leaned forward in his chair, closing the distance between them. "Ellen, I'm far more worried about you than Fen."

"Me?"

Peter nodded.

"Why are you worried about me?"

He leaned back again and crossed his legs. He brushed away imaginary lint, shaping the silence as he slipped back into his professional skin. "Because you are blaming yourself."

"No."

"Yes. I think you are. I think that is what you do when the men in your life leave you. I think you blamed yourself when Carl and Ben went off to the river and never came back. And I think now Fenton has left for the ocean and you are terrified that he will meet some tragic end and that he will never come back. I think that you are preparing to blame yourself. I think you have already started in earnest. I think you are telling yourself that it is all your fault."

"Isn't it?" she asked, barely above a whisper, staring at her hands and shaking her head.

"No, Ellen. It absolutely isn't."

"You don't know everything."

"Would you like to tell me?"

"No."

"I know what I'm saying here. I'm not guessing at this."

"You don't know everything," she repeated.

"I know more than you think."

She looked up at him, green eyes rimmed in red. Alert. Suspicious. "Like what?"

"I'd rather hear it from you."

"And I'd rather you tell me what in the fuck you're talking about."

He looked at her for nearly half a minute, re-enlisting the silence, his old ally, trying to draw her out into the void, luring her confession into the open with a handful of quiet seconds. But her burning stare was unwavering. Eventually he smiled in surrender. He would have to put the cards on the table.

"I know that you stayed home that Fifth of July because you had other plans."

"Yes?"

"With... with someone else, Ellen."

She looked at him as someone made of wax, with no apparent pulse or respiration. Her mouth opened in a kind of slow, silent horror. She did not speak.

"I'm not judging, Ellen. I'm not. I promise you that. But I am saying that I know you have been torturing yourself with guilt. And I know it must have made your grief that much deeper and that much harder to bear."

He paused, giving her a chance to express herself, but she said nothing, staring through him to the clock on the wall.

"I saw you a couple of times this summer. Dropping off Lucy for her lessons. You waved from the house. You seemed to be doing so much better. I thought maybe you had found some perspective. I thought maybe you realized none of it was your fault and that you had forgiven yourself and moved on. I was really happy for you, Ellen. You looked beautiful. You looked happy. But now... Now Fenton has left. And he has left while you were up at a cabin with... with a friend. I don't know if it's the same friend or a different friend. Doesn't matter. Because that's fine… that's wonderful. Except that *you* don't think it's fine. *You* don't think it's wonderful. You think that makes you a bad person. You think it makes you guilty. And I think all of this stuff with Fen is now collapsing back to the Fifth of July over two years ago. You're life stopped then. On that terrible day. That's why when I say…"

"How could you know that?" She interrupted in a plaintive wail, coming to life as if by some electric shock. Her nose was running. She tried to wipe it with the back of her hand but that only made it worse. Peter stood and retrieved a box of tissue from his desk. He handed it to her and sat back down.

"How I know is not import…"

"Bullshit! Don't tell me that. There is only *one* way you could know that. *One!* I knew I should never have told her. That bitch. That bitch! How could she?"

"Ellen, look, there's no point in being angry about it. Husbands and wives talk. They confide. We were both concerned about you. You know that. Diane was not trying to hurt you. She thought it was important that I know. She has not told anyone else and I certainly haven't told anyone. But look, this is a part of your life that you must come to terms with. Do you understand?"

She did not answer him, twisting a soggy tissue around her finger like a tourniquet, squeezing the blood up past the first knuckle until the nail took on a purplish cast. She showed no sign of responding, so he plunged back in.

"Ellen? Do you understand? Do you?"

Not understanding that it was he, Peter, who did not understand. Not understanding what he was saying. Not understanding what he was feeling.

"This will keep tearing you apart until you deal with it. You need to talk about it, Ellen. Openly." A moment. Pressure building in his throat. Words he knows better than to say. Words wanting out. Words fleeing captivity to be with her. "I will do that with you. I will be your therapist. I won't charge you a dime. And if you don't want to call it therapy, then we will call it friendship. We'll call it whatever you want. I will help you work through this. Let me help you."

She released the tissue allowing the blood in her finger to flow back into the rest of her hand. Two minutes passed. He let the silence steep. Then she looked up at him coldly.

"Husbands and wives are not the only ones who talk, Peter. You know who else talks?" He waits, not answering, still reeling at his own offer. Like he has been sick and knowing in the pit of his stomach that there is so much more to come. "Sorority sisters talk. They talk about *everything.* You think I don't know? You think I don't know how you two lovebirds started up? You think I don't know what your blushing bride is up to now?"

She let the question hang in the silence that was suddenly *her* ally. He felt blood rush into his cheeks, as though someone had released a tourniquet. He wanted to protest that she did not understand. He wanted to lecture her about the sort of patience that every good marriage requires. He wanted to insist that he had never judged her and that she was showing her immaturity in lashing out at him in this way. He wanted to suffocate her with a smile and professional detachment.

But more than that, he wanted to slap her and lash at her. He wanted to lie. He wanted to tell her the truth.

The clock ticked and the gray sound of traffic kept digging from beneath the window.

"How's it feel, Peter?" She asked finally, pulling her hair furiously back into a barrette. "How does it fucking feel? You're every bit as pathetic as I am. How dare you judge me from your big marital mansion on the hill. How dare you." She stood, stuffing the tissue in her pocket, and made her way to the coat rack.

"Ellen..."

"To think I ever, even in the fog of grief, took any solace in your words. To think that I ever waited for you to visit me. To think that I ever wanted you or envied Diane."

Her words were like a freak rockslide in a field of corn, burying him where he sat. He watched helplessly as she put on her coat.

"You mean…" He didn't know what else to say. He was stuporous.

"Like you didn't know. Like you didn't lord yourself over me like the living over the dead. Sitting in my living room, perfectly out of reach. Perfectly untouchable."

"I didn't. I… I'm a psychiatrist. You were grieving. There are rules. I'm married. Ellen."

"Fuck you, Peter. You deserve her. She deserves you."

She moved for the door, leaving him in stages. First her eyes. Her shoulders. The small of her back. Moving away. Away. Moving away. Like some celestial object spinning out of its solar spray and into a new, unlit orbit. In his imagination she was already through the door and down the hall and then out of the building entirely, in her car, down the road, away, leaving him alone in his little boxy office made to resemble a living room, now with the scent of her in the air. Alone with all of the things he might have said. Alone with all of the old regrets he had so deftly denied and rationalized away. Alone with his once untouchable self that was now, suddenly, like a body engulfed in a kind of flame.

"I don't know what I'm doing any more," he said, swallowing. "Not for a long time."

Ellen Soulak paused, rotating back to him. She waited, anger disintegrating to irritation and then into a grudging patience. Her silence took on a professional air. Finally, when he said nothing else, "What do you want, Peter? Start there."

He leaned back and rubbed his face in his hands, a gesture intended to disguise the flailing that shone in his eyes. The cliff from which he had stepped rose above him. The bird in the cage of his chest beat its wings furiously and with such force as to break his bones. There was no going back.

"I don't know what I want. Not any more. I thought I knew. I had to have Carol. Then I desperately needed to be out of my marriage to Carol. I found Diane. I had to have Diane. I had to have that fucking house. I had to have Diane's daughter as my own. Don't ask me why. I don't know why. I don't know. I just did."

Silence. The clock. Traffic. Rain.

"A few months ago I practically proposed to a stripper. She thought that was an odd thing for me to do. And it was, of course. It was odd. But I was angry with Diane. And Spencer. And Lucy. I was ready to trade them all in for something…"

"Something what."

"Different. Something that would shock them. Shock me."

"But…"

"I know. Don't ask me why. The point is I don't trust what I want any more."

"What do you…"

"You, Ellen. I want you."

Silence. The hissing of water on the street. The beating heart of the clock.

"Me?"

He nodded, just once, not looking at her. He is as surprised as she is.

"Since the beginning. Since the very first day. When Carl was still alive. At the barbeque. You probably don't even remember. You wore that blue dress, no shoes. I've never admitted that to anyone. I've never admitted that to myself. It has always been true and yet it has never been true until just now. I shouldn't have denied it. Shouldn't have locked it away. I'm so good at compartmentalizing my own feelings sometimes, they become like forgotten prisoners. Just… locked away. You're right about that. About me. I have been untouchable. I should have been honest with myself. Maybe I would have, eventually. Maybe one of those barbeques… ballgames… But then Carl and Ben died. It was so terrible. I wanted to help. I treated you like a patient. It was a safe way to be with you. When that became too difficult I stopped coming to see you altogether. A psychiatrist is not supposed…" He abandoned the recitation of the canons of his profession. He looked up at her. "We can go slow and easy, Ellen. As slowly as you need. We could make each other happy."

"We make ourselves happy, Peter. You told me that. When Carl and Ben died. You told me that. So you should know better than to think I can make you happy. I can't."

She walked slowly across the office and put her hand on the knob. Peter tensed, gripping the arms of his chair. Nicollet's voice came to him from her dark little room. *Life is for wanting. I wish you to want, Peter. Just want.*

"What would make *you* happy, Ellen? Tell me. What do you want from me? Anything?"

She opened the door and stopped, her black coat seeming to melt into the dark hallway behind her so that the white of her face nearly glowed. She thrust her hands into her coat pockets and stared quietly at the floor, thinking. Then she looked up.

"I want you to be my therapist, Peter. I want to talk to you about my missing son. About my dead husband and my dead child. I want to talk to you about my lovers and my terrible, terrible dreams. We will meet on Sundays. Noon." She pulled a folded sheet of paper from her coat pocket and tossed it on the floor in front of her. "This Sunday we're going to talk about Fenton and this damn note. I will pay your fee and I will expect your absolute discretion without any exception for Diane, my dear, dear sorority sister, who must never know about our sessions."

"I will," he said. "I will do that, Ellen..."

She held up a finger. "On this condition, Peter."

"What condition? I said I would do anything."

"If you ever leave your wife, you will never see me again."

He could only stare at her, uncomprehending.

"Do you understand that I am absolutely serious about that?"

Peter nodded slowly.

"Not a divorce. Not a separation."

He nodded. She moved out into the hall, the darkness threatening to swallow her whole and his heart contracted.

"Ellen," he nearly shouted from his chair. She stopped. Turned. "Can I see you ... in a... in a *non-professional* capacity?"

"A non-professional capacity?" Came the voice from the hall, moving away from him in the dark. "You're a psychiatrist, Peter. And a married man. There are rules, aren't there?"

He sat listening to her boots on the stairs and then on the tile in the foyer. The front door to the building opened and closed again. Minutes passed as he stared across his office through the open door.

Eventually, he stood slowly, as if his muscles were sore from some recent over-exertion. He walked over to the door and closed it. He picked up the square of paper at his feet and unfolded it.

Mom:

I am leaving you this note because I knew that if I told you what I have to tell you in person you would probably only have a cow and try to stop me. I have left for California. I am in love. I have finally found my wife. It has taken a lot of time and a lot of looking but I have found her. I always told you I would make a good detective!

She is the woman of my dreams, Mom. It may take me some time, but after we are married we will buy you a new house nearby so that we can see each other and so that you won't worry like I know you are worrying right now. It will be a beautiful house on a hill over-looking the Pacific. The water will be as blue as a cloudless sky and you won't have any worries ever again. Not about Dad. Or Ben.

If I told you how all of this got started, you would not believe me and then you would start up again about therapy. I don't need therapy. I need hope. There is no hope without desire. You have to desperately want something before a hopeful life is even possible. Even if everyone including your psychiatrist tells you that the thing you want is just plain pie-in-the-sky crazy. Doesn't matter if it's crazy. Doesn't matter if it's wrong. I know what I want. That's enough to give me hope. The hope is enough to keep me happy. The happiness is enough to keep me alive.

You always tell me that you would do anything to make me happy. But we make ourselves happy, Mom. And it starts by believing. We can't just say the words. We have to actually believe that happiness is possible. Right now you are up at that lake, believing. And I am off to California, believing. And I'm happy and I hope that you are too.

I won't call you for a while. Maybe not for a long time. Because I know you will try to tell me I am crazy about all of this. You will go see Peter and the two of you will try to come up with the words for you to use to bring me back. I'm not coming back. It's a big world, mom. There is so much to want from it that sometimes I can't sleep at night. That's what living should be. I never want to lose that feeling. So don't have a cow. And don't worry. I love you. Fen.

———

Peter waited another hour before making his way home. The driving people of Summit County had, for the most part, reached their evening destinations and the roads were clear. The five-mile stretch of two-lane pavement between Nightingale Road and Ridgeline Drive did not have the benefit of any streetlights. People liked to complain about this in the letters to the editor of the Summerfield Times. There had been a few bad accidents in that stretch of road because deer and sometimes people crossing the road had been difficult to see until it was too late. Peter had always agreed that the city needed to budget the funds and light the road. He had once even written a letter to the editor.

But tonight he could not complain.

Right across the Cleatchee River Bridge, after the turn up Ridgeline Drive, where the valley starts to drop away beneath the tires, almost as though the car was taking flight, the lack of streetlights made it possible to appreciate the night sky, sprawling above him like an infinite black sea. A razor-thin icy sliver of moon floated just above the trees. Tonight, Ridgeline Drive might as well have been Shoreline Drive. When he bent forward directly over the steering wheel and looked straight up out of the front windshield, he could see brilliant blue flecks of starlight float-ing in the firmament like phosphorescent algae. As he climbed above the valley floor, the scattered lights of the houses and the farms and the cars grew smaller and fainter until they too appeared as starlight. From the right perspective, he could imagine himself floating in the cosmos, in his little boat of a car, completely surrounded by stars.

Which, ironically enough, was actually true.

The trick, he realized, was never looking at any of the lights directly. Never like he owned them. Never like he intended to hold them ever accountable for their location. But rather, always keeping the lights off in the corner of his peripheral vision, just visible enough to have a sense of them. Just visible enough to believe they were there, out in the interstellar dust of our own consciousness where what we hope for is indistinguishable from what we know.

He reached into the white paper bag in the passenger seat and extracted the last of the raspberry scone he had picked up at *The Yeast We Can Do Bakery*. He popped it into his mouth and chewed.

He thought of Ellen. It was Thursday night. Sunday noon loomed in his mind. Distant. Imminent. He imagined and dared to hope. That was how it would begin. Sundays at noon, while the rest of the world ate brunch. That tiny fleck of light was his new home. That was where he lived, out on the blue, blue sea gazing at the silver-lit shoreline and wanting. Only wanting.

He leaned his head back against the seat, sighing up into the stars. The sensation blooming in the center of his chest, the beautiful ache, welling in its tidal surges, again, after so many years, was excruciating.

Chapter 8

PHOTOPHOBIA

"You're not what I expected," he said. His accent was soft and blended. A faint flavoring of language. A hickory finish. "Not by a country mile."

His eyes slid sideways, away from her, as if to deferentially excuse his attention over the wrought iron railing of the café and across the street to the window of the ice cream shop. She should be left to consider his approving statement, alone and unobserved.

But, of course, his attention was not waiting across the street. He was as present as ever, his interest in her keen and palpable. His mouth was wrinkled at the corners. But he smelled young, his cologne sharp and acidic.

"Really?" She leaned back in the chair and sipped her coffee, tucking a thin blonde wisp behind her ear. "What were you expecting?"

Conrad gave an apologetic smile. He was trying to see through her sunglasses.

"Most of the women in your line of work – at least that I've encountered – tend to be…"

She watched him pretend to be delicate. He pushed a glistening, freshly expelled strand of sausage gristle around his plate with a tine of his fork, through the carnage of egg, around the sopped, rejected corner of toast, as he pondered his words. His fingers were red and chapped, the nails bitten short in irregular planes. She imagined that most people never really noticed the actual fingers. It was difficult to get past the ring, which was remarkable for its plump yellow diamond set between two waves of elaborately stenciled gold. Not a ring the living tended to purchase.

"Mmm…" He wrinkled his lip. "How to say this… they tend to be… *plain*. Rather tomboyish, I suppose."

"Lesbian, you mean."

He looked up suddenly from his plate, mocking surprise.

"Am I wrong?" he asked, covering his question with a smirk.

"Wrong about women photographers or wrong about me?"

Conrad laid down his fork and held up his hands, palms out.

"No offense. I find you exceedingly attractive. That's all I meant."

She forced herself to soften.

"There is no offense taken, Mr. Kurtz. I am flattered."

"Please, call me Conrad."

She smiled into her cup of coffee.

"Alright. Conrad."

"What kind of name is Jack for such a lovely creature as yourself anyway?"

"Jacqueline." She twirled a pinky in the air.

"Much more suitable, if you ask me."

"A bit regal for my taste," she said. "My aunt had a certain yearning for Camelot I think. I didn't really have a vote."

"Even so, you can see why I might be surprised. To see you, I mean. I expected *Jack* to be a man."

"We spoke on the phone."

"I meant after the letter. Yes, after we finally spoke on the phone I expected…"

"A butch photog."

"I'm sorry."

"Don't be. I'm used to it."

"You like it, I think." Teasing now. As if he were her brother.

"How's that?"

"You like the way it keeps men off balance."

Jac smiled implacably. "Some men."

"I'll bet you have to beat them back with a stick. Or your boyfriend does."

Subtlety was not his strong suit, she thought.

"I'm in-between boyfriends," she said, regretting the phrasing more than the candor. She braced herself for the inevitable segue into troilism. A joke, a quip, a raised eyebrow. Or, God help her, a personal anecdote. She saw it – whatever it was – pass over his face. He let it go.

Conrad looked at her directly, smiling, lingering on his reflection in the dark glass lenses. First the left, then the right. He wanted to see her eyes. He wanted her to take the damn things off. There was no need for them here, beneath the awning. The sky was leaden. It was going to pour later.

But he resisted. He returned to business.

"So, is there a publication date that you have in mind?"

"Too soon to tell," she said. "A year. Eighteen months. I'm not suggesting anything comprehensive. It's not like an encyclopedia of small wineries. Just a picturesque sampling."

"How many?"

"Up to the publisher. Maybe a dozen vineyards."

"So none of this has been discussed?"

"In general terms. They wouldn't pay me without *some* idea. I'm taking some pictures, scouting some wineries. I'll mock something up, make the pitch. They'll tell me if they're interested."

"So, this is kind of a... a..." he searched for the idea up in the taut ochre awning above him, "kind of a coffee-table thing you have in mind."

She sipped. Nodded. "Oversized. Glossy. You know. Foldout overleafs for the panoramas. Lots of close-ups. Last light, first light. The grapes. The process."

"No text?"

"Some text. Mostly pictures."

"Who's writing the text?"

Jac shrugged. "Not me. I'm just a girl with a camera."

"Why SRV? We're a pretty minor player."

"I'm not looking for successful business models. I'm looking for photogenic vineyards. Sol Ridge is up high. I can get the valley. Mt. Chardonnay as a backdrop. Saratoga below. And Cupertino. Dramatic sun. There's a lot to like about it." She pointed at him, extending her finger through the handle of her cup. "You're thinking about the wine business. I'm not. I'm thinking about the photos."

"But Jeez-Louise, Jackie-O, there's wineries all over those hills. Why Sol Ridge?"

"Mr.," she stopped, corrected herself, "*Conrad.* I gotta start somewhere. It doesn't have to be SRV, but..."

"No, no. Don't get me wrong. I'm not turning away free publicity." He paused to look at her, drinking her in. "It's just... its all enough to make a man look over his shoulder. You realize the berries on those vines are like little peas right now? Not much to photograph."

Jac nodded. "I know. But beginnings are important. They put the end product in context."

The server collected their plates and stood a black leather folder in the middle of the table between the salt and pepper. Conrad reached.

"I've got this," Jac said, snapping it up. "I was the one who asked you."

"Only because I wouldn't let you up."

"Right. And why is that anyway?" She slipped a credit card into the folder.

"SRV is not set up for tours or public tastings. We're almost twenty-five hundred feet up a crappy dirt road. I don't need a bunch of tipsy looky-loos rolling their cars sideways down into the valley. Visits are strictly by appointment."

"Believe me," she said, "I tried to make an appointment. I even wrote you a letter you never answered. And when I called, your staff told me it was invitation only. I didn't have an invitation."

"My staff." Conrad laughed and shook his head.

"The woman..."

"That was Iris. She's not much for people. She'd have said the same thing to the Pope. She can be a little jealous for my attention."

"So she's…"

"My step daughter," he said, tossing his eyes.

Jac crumpled up the empty packet of sugar and dropped it in the cup. "You're married," she said, fully intending the tonal disappointment. She knew it would please him. "Does your wife work for the business?"

"Until she passed away." He held up the back of his hand, thumb hidden. "Four years ago." The yellow diamond on his finger was like an old third eye, secretly taking her measure.

The server came and went, snatching the folder.

"Sorry," said Jac.

Conrad remained still, as if counting to himself until it was safe. He retracted his hand to someplace beneath the table.

"Life goes on," he said. "Grapes keep a'growin'. Lots of picking to do in this life."

———

It was almost two hours up to the winery. Conrad, wrist draped over the top of the wheel, elbow out the window, body swaying and bouncing with the buckled and puckered dirt road beneath them, was in no hurry. Conversation had dropped off after the first hour and he had taken to humming something vaguely reminiscent of Home on the Range. Jac popped the pressure in her ears and watched the brown cloud of wheel-spun dust kick up behind them in the rearview mirror. It curled into the pale fog like chum into a frothy wake, losing its identity completely twenty yards or so behind. The lengthening hillside unrolled steeply beneath her into the valley like a spongy, mottled green and brown carpet. The air was wet and white and gauzy, hanging low, filling the valley like a bandage staunching a greenish wound.

"Is this common?" she asked.

"What's that?"

"Driving into cloud."

Conrad shrugged. "Foggy mornings are pretty common, but it burns off. This isn't fog. This is weather. Whenever the Santa Cruz range gets any serious weather we're pokin' our nose right up into it. That's for sure. We're at about thirteen hundred feet right here."

He looked at her, waiting to see if there was more. He turned forward just in time to steer up onto the lip of a deep rut, then looked back over at her. This time he was looking at her glasses. A soft black leather, fan-shaped blind connected the left lens with the left stem, blocking his access to her eyes even in profile. His brow pinched in irritation. He went back to humming and driving.

Jac was convinced that she could have made the trip in half the time. Conrad, though, had insisted on driving, telling her that the road was bad enough when the weather was hot and dry. He had pointed to the slabs of broken slate up in the sky out behind the café and arched his eyebrows. He had leaned in until she could smell the eggs on his breath and told her that it would get messy up in the hills before the day was over.

At that point he might still have been persuaded to let her drive herself. But when he saw her little white Yugoslavian tuna can of a car he was adamant.

"No way, girly. You're riding in the truck with me. You're just asking for trouble in this thing." He kicked the tire with the toe of his boot.

"I'll be fine."

"I insist," he had said, bowing toward her, bending over his forearm. She supposed that thirty years ago his hair would have been an irresistibly thick tangle of chestnut. What he presented to her now was a thinning oily mat flecked with dandruff. "Why, it would be my honor, Miss Jacqueline," he had said, laying on the drawl.

Jac had considered balking at the counterfeit chivalry. She might have proposed that she wait; that she come back and call him when his vineyard could offer a clear sky. But she had already told him that she was looking for some weather. *Rain paints with a soft light that you can't get any other way,* she had told him. She liked dusk. She liked dawn. She liked clouds. She liked rain. Garishness was not an artistic sensibility.

Full, brutish illumination was simply painful; an ice pick in the eye of the beholder. The sun needs a filter.

No. The sun needs nothing. We need the filter.

She might also have said something about her suspicion that his true intention was to keep her stranded up at the winery over night with no way to get back to town. *It's getting dark*, he would say. *The road is a mess with all of this rain. I'll take you back to town in the morning. Have another glass of wine. I'll make you a bed.*

Jac was no stranger to predation. She had that look to which certain men are drawn from a long ways off. Without a father, the look had developed at an early age. It was in her eyes, mostly, but also in the way her mouth slipped out of a smile, and the way she moved through a crowded room, and the way she coaxed the last drop of anything from a glass. A longing, barely contained. Loneliness wrapped in a tough but threadbare self-sufficiency. That was the look.

But nature provides. With the look had come the vision. Jac could sense dark billows roiling just beneath the horizon of seemingly good intentions. The years of trying and failing had been good for something at least. She had learned to ignore hope and to heed instinct. The *hope* was always that here was a man who was different. The *instinct* was that here was a man who was just the same as all of the others. There may as well only be one man in the world. One man with a lot of different clothes and a lot of different smiles and smells and a lot of different ways to say he wanted her. Needed her. Loved her. A lot of different ways to say he was sorry. But, said the instinct, still the same man.

Jac had opened up her car and fished out the three backpacks – one for clothes and personals, and two for camera gear – as Conrad had gone to fetch his oversized diesel pick-up, a *Limited Edition Erebus V.8 Charger* according to the chrome scrawl beneath the side mirror. The truck gleamed a dark, midnight black, snorting and hissing behind her like a bull pawing at the ground. The Sol Ridge Vineyards logo sprawled in purple and silver along the length of the bed. Full, pregnant grapes tumbled off the top of the letter 'S' into a barrel. Conrad had hopped down and come around the back of the truck to help with the backpacks.

"Not this one," she had said at the last second, tightening her grip on the shoulder strap of the pack full of clothing. "This one stays." She had unlocked her little Yugoslavian housecat and returned the pack to the floor of the back seat.

She had felt him watching her from behind as she bent into the car. When she extracted herself and closed the door, locked it and turned, Conrad had extended a hand to help her up into the truck. She had lightly gripped the red raw-looking fingers and Conrad had cupped his other hand against the lower small of her back. As is almost always true when two bodies make first contact, the sensation was electrical in nature, a low-voltage thrumming in the central nervous system acknowledging the significance of the first contact and, simultaneously, anticipating the next.

The truck jolted sideways. Jac's head knocked against the window. The higher they climbed, the farther they traveled from the last main turn off, the more the road seemed to degrade into a pair of hard, not-so-parallel ruts in the dirt that were either too narrow or too wide for the wheel base of the truck.

Conrad was waxing philosophical about extended maceration. Skins and seeds and stems mixed in with the juice, softening tannins and allowing extraction of color and flavor. He spoke in pseudo-paternalistic terms of *maintaining character*, as if the juice was some *essence-of-child* to be refortified with the memory of its upbringing; only not so much the memory as the actual detritus of the transformational carnage – the torn skin and crushed seeds and broken limbs.

"You'd think they could fix this road," she said, cutting him off and shifting her weight away from the window and toward his side of the cab. She knew it looked like she was trying to get closer. She didn't care.

"Who's *they*, exactly?" he asked.

"The county. The state. I don't know."

Conrad just laughed.

"You ever take those things off?" he asked, not looking at her.

"What things?"

"Your sunglasses."

"Why?"

"No reason. Just never seen your eyes, that's all." The hand over the steering wheel came suddenly to life and swept back and forth at the windshield. "Nothing but clouds in every direction. Seems odd that someone as gorgeous as you would keep your eyes so under wraps."

The hand drooped limply again. He looked over at her and smiled, intending to confirm for her, in case she had missed it, that he thought she was gorgeous; reminding her, in case she had forgotten, the extremity of his earlier expressed attraction.

His lips were beginning to thin. And his complexion was yellowing a little with age. But she could tell just from looking at him that in his day he must have been a handsome, silver-tongued devil. She bet that he could have had any woman he wanted, and probably did.

He wanted to see her eyes. She was not inclined to deny him. He was a widower, after all.

Jac returned the smile – acknowledging the compliment, giving him the hope he needed; the hope she wanted him to have – and removed her sunglasses.

Conrad saw that her eyes were, in fact, every bit as beautiful as he had suspected. Perfect almonds of a deep sea glass green with flecks of gold. Like she had plucked them from the sockets some Amazonian panther.

The truck jolted. Conrad focused forward for an instant to correct his steering then looked back. Jac's expression was a strangely intense study of discomfort. Her brow was deeply furrowed, like she was trying mightily to read his mind or to reshape her frontal lobe into a point.

"What's wrong?" he asked.

"Nothing." She smiled unconvincingly.

Conrad looked forward at the road and then back at her, squinting. She closed her lids. She kept them closed allowing him a full view. Her forehead relaxed, smoothing itself as if from an abatement of wind.

At first he thought it was a bruise or a cut; a purplish-red streak running from the side of her nose, up across her left eyelid, disappearing into the soft black tangle of her eyebrow, and just barely emerging on the other side.

He had seen such stains before, of course. His grandmother had had one on her chin that wrapped down like colored cellophane over her upper neck. And he had known a boy in high school – Jarrid or Jason or Jasper – who had a splotch over the right hinge of his jawbone that stretched onto the lobe of his right ear. And then there was the red geography quiz on Michael Gorbachev's forehead.

But this one seemed somehow different. Its color was not uniform. Not purplish-red, but increasingly purple in one direction and increasingly red in the other direction. It was deeper and wider towards the nose and thinner and lighter towards the eyebrow. And its shape seemed to follow the natural topography the terrain, bending around the curvature of the eyeball and pooling up against the bridge of her nose. It was less a stain and more of a subcutaneous flow, as though gravity more than genetics was at play. Conrad could not help but imagine Jac lying on her right side, dead or unconscious, head drooped over her shoulder, so that a cut just above her left eyebrow would produce a stream that followed the same path.

"Well my gracious sakes," he said. "Is that little thing what those glasses are all about?"

Jac opened her eyes a slit and looked sideways at him.

"Jackie-O, if I may be so bold, you are a beautiful woman and nothing but nothing about that cute little birth mark of yours changes that. You've got no need to be hiding behind a pair of shades."

Jac gave him a crooked smile and put her glasses back on, not caring to correct him. "You were telling me about extended maceration."

———

"Okay, my little shutterbug," said Conrad, patting her thigh. "Where do you want to start?"

The truck hissed and popped and rattled itself down into a hot silence in front of a large Spanish mission-style home that looked out over the deepest cut in the valley. Ridges on the far side of the dale stretched out in the distance like granite waves coming in to beach through the low-hanging clouds.

"So, you live here then?"

"Yeah. This is the barn. We call it that, anyway. I'm not sure why. Doesn't really look much like a barn, does it? Iris and I live here with Buddy, Elmo and Gator. Those are the dogs. Two labs and a mutt. They pretty much have the run of the whole area. And then if you follow this road," he pointed out the window, past the picturesque monstrosity he called a barn, "it goes up over that little ridge and up there is a big flat plateau. That's where we keep the warehouse, and the equipment – the juice box we call it –, and the tractor barn, the stables, got four horses up there, Oreo, Nellie, Maggie Mae, and Diablo, and then the bunk-house is up there too where *Señor* and his bunch live."

"*Señor?*"

"My chief picker, Ernesto de la Cruz. He calls me *Hefe*, I call him *Señor*. He's got two sons and three nephews that all live up there in the bunkhouse. Sometimes more. Some cousins. All men up there except Celia. That's *Señor's* daughter. I don't let them bring their girlfriends up. Nothin' would ever get done. They all come and go. I lose track sometimes, to tell you the truth. I can't tell 'em all apart."

Conrad gave a self-deprecating half-laugh at this. He was unnerved not to be able to see Jac's eyes.

"Iris can tell though. She knows 'em all. She and Celia are thick as thieves. Celia's sixteen and sweet as blueberry pie. She stays here at the house with me and Iris a lot. To get away from all the yahoos in the bunkhouse. You can hear those boys at night sometimes, drinkin' and cuttin' up. Before the harvest wears 'em out, anyway. Then they're work-ing so hard all they want to do is sleep. They roll their own tobacco, the real kind *and* the wacky kind, and they waste a lot of time on the horses. It's a good day when I can get a smile out of any one of 'em. But they sure know how to bring in a crop."

"So the six of them handle the harvest?"

"No, no. You're talking about nine to eleven tons of fruit, Jackie-O. We bring in help when the season peaks. *Señor's* the key to the harvest.

He keeps all the seasonals working and behaving. Without *Señor* out there I'd have to do it, and I don't exactly speak the language. They understand me just fine; don't get me wrong. I say jump, they jump. But I don't usually have to say anything at all because ol' *Señor* Ernesto de la Cruz is out there in the middle of it, morning, noon and night. He knows how to grow and he knows how to harvest and he knows I lean on him probably more than I should. *Señor* apprenticed under the Old Man, Victor Bruno, my late wife's late father. You've heard of him, I'm sure."

Jac cocked her head, as if on the precipice of memory.

"No? Really? Big beanpole of a man, white hair, mustache you could swing a tire from? Always in his overalls like he wasn't filthy rich?"

Jac looked at him without indicating. Conrad stared at his dual reflection, seeing only himself in her lenses, and could not tell whether the caricature of the Old Man had jarred loose some recollection in her mind. He assumed so. Everyone in the wine business, even peripherally, and anyone who *knew* anything about the wine business, had to know about the Old Man. He was legend. He had changed Conrad's life. He had taken him in for no good reason and treated him like a son. Everyone had a story to tell about the Old Man.

And yet Jac showed no sign of knowing or caring one way or the other.

Conrad surmised that it was her age. She was too young. Not too young for *everything.* She was just the *right* age for some things, of course. Just look at her. But she was too young to care much about the past. What counted as history for her generation was whatever had happened a week ago; six months to a year for the extraordinary ones. Jac here was smart, he could tell. But she was not fundamentally different than Iris. Or Celia. The part of life that was not happening this instant, or about to happen in the next instant, was essentially worthless. There was no value in the past for these kids. There was no legacy to honor. And since the truth in life always grew from the past – for history was nothing less than the soil packed around the root of all judgment – there was no truth that the newest generations even cared to claim. It was all but so much vapor. They evaluated everything and everyone in the moment, outside of any historical context. Abraham Lincoln and Al Capone could show up tomorrow with a handshake asking for a job and they would be on equal footing. History mattered not at all. Conrad's people hailed from the southern states where tradition was king and where a man was forever accountable for his transgressions and his father's transgressions and forever celebrated for his virtues and his father's virtues. But not here. Not out West. Not with these kids. Time was not the vine out here. Time was the great ocean, the great dilution. The moral ambivalence, Conrad found, was as maddening as it was liberating.

"Yeah, this whole operation used to be part of Victor Bruno's kingdom. Before he died, Victor had the Red Iron Vineyard over in the Carneros Valley, which was *huge* in its day, and the Bruno Acres up near Diamond Mountain, outside Santa Rosa, and then this one, Sol Ridge, which he passed to Clara. Sol Ridge was the smallest of the three. The big ones went to the Bruno sons. And Clara got the little one. Ironic 'cause Sol Ridge is the only one of the three that's left. The other two sold out oh, five, six years after the Old Man passed."

Jac nodded inscrutably.

"Anyway, *Señor's* been here at Sol Ridge from the beginning. And then one of his boys, Marco, and one of his nephews, Daniel, they each went out and got themselves enology degrees from Washington State. So they know the science. And now *Señor's* got it in his head that he's going to send little Celia to college, UC at Santa Cruz he says, so she can get a business degree. And just guess what business *that* might be."

Conrad knocked the back of his fingers against Jac's arm. His ring connected with the bone of her elbow. He didn't wait for her to guess.

"The *winery* business." Conrad pointed at her and nodded and winked. "He wants her to run Sol Ridge. You wait and see. Hasn't said anything directly, not yet, but one day he'll come to me, he'll sidle up to me one afternoon when he's showing me the berries and as I'm squatting in the dirt looking at all the fruit they've dropped, trying to judge the veraison and figure how far out the pick window is, and he'll take his big straw hat off like he's inspecting the inside of it and he'll say something casually into his hat like *Hefe, why don't you give little Celia a job when she graduates? Yes? She could help you sell the wine that I make. See?* That's how he'll say it, too. *Help you sell the wine that I make.*"

Conrad gave her a minute to ponder the significance of the phrasing before he continued.

"Secretly, *Señor* thinks all of this is his. He thinks he's the new Old Man. But the *real* Old Man was good about mapping out the future. This is a family business. Little Celia may be sweet as a dew drop but she's not exactly in the grand plan."

The weather, as Conrad called it, had thickened. Drops of rain appeared on the windshield. They streaked slowly down the glass, angling towards Jac in the breeze. She wished now she had brought the other pack. It contained more than just a toothbrush and makeup and her scant underthings for sleeping, the need for which might have been an excuse, if she wanted one, for not being able to spend the night. It also contained a hat and a heavy sweatshirt that would have been welcome protection from the damp.

Directly in front of them two dark labs bounded into view, each biting playfully at the other's shoulders as they ran towards the house and collapsed in a panting heap on a patch of grass off to the side of the front porch.

"But *Señor* is no Victor Bruno," Conrad continued. "Not by a long shot. He's good with the fruit. He knows those berries. And the soil. One of the best. But the business? *Señor* couldn't sell a bottle of water to a rich man in the desert." He jabbed his ring finger into his temple. "No head for commerce. He knows that, if he's honest with himself. And Celia's sweet as can be, but I don't make her as a businesswoman. She should be a singer. You should hear her sing at the Christmas pageant down at the St. Francis First Communion where *la familia de la Cruz* goes to worship. They invite me every year. And I show up every year and listen to Celia sing and hear all about Jesus turning water into wine."

Conrad snorted.

"See, I need grapes; Jesus," he said, pronouncing the name as *hey-soos*, "he only needs water. I call that unfair competition. Although

Jesus makes some piss-poor wine. I try it every year on my knees in that church. Let's see him turnout a decent Cab. Or a Pinot. Or a genuine Rhone Ranger Shiraz."

Conrad popped his eyes at Jac and smirked, holding back a laugh so that she might crack first. But to his disappointment, she sat there in her shades like a little stone bird, her beautiful rear end filling little more than half the leather bucket seat.

"I suppose I've never been much of a churchgoer," he said. "*Señor's* probably been trying to save my soul."

"Does it need saving?" Jac asked reflexively. Conrad laughed. The sound was sticky wet with phlegm. He cleared his throat.

"Oh, Lord. You a Jesus freak?"

"No."

"I mean, no big deal if you are. You just don't strike me as the type."

"No."

"My mother was a Jesus freak. She believed it all. Heaven. Hell. The Devil. Angels. The works. Got so she didn't make a lick of sense half the time. Every other day was like the day before the judgment day and she was makin' ready. 'Course, this was Georgia. Smack in the middle of the Bible belt. So she had a lot of company. Especially back then."

Jac nodded, pulling a knuckle in a slow arc down the dry side of the window. Like she was tracing the path of a comet across the sky. Conrad made a sound that was half laugh and half wheeze.

"My father had a rather direct way about him. He didn't take much guff from anyone, including my mother. And whenever she found herself on the business end of one of his tempers she'd tell daddy that Jesus was a-comin'." Conrad lathered on the accent. "Jesus was a-comin' to *shine his light.* Jesus was gonna *shine his light* to show the righteous the way home, and then, as for the all the rest, specifically including my daddy, Jesus was gonna *shine his light* to scour the world. And, boy, my daddy didn't put up with that kind of nonsense for long. No sir."

He shook his head, coughing.

"No siree. Poor woman. She just wasn't quite right in the head. Religion'll do that to you though, as far as I'm concerned. It'll pickle your brain. If she were sitting here today, she wouldn't like you one bit. She'd assume you were a bad person because that's just how she was. She was big into original sin. You were guilty first until you proved otherwise. She'd tell you to take off those shades of yours, Jackie, because you can't hide from the light of the Savior. If you've done wrong, the light will find you. You could argue with her all you want but she'd never come to reason. 'Course, then again, Momma predeceased. Went in her sleep a lot sooner than the doctors said. Then ten years later, Daddy accidentally caught the front end of a locomotive. So for all I know she was right. Could be that Jesus takes his time scouring. He's just out their waiting, biding his time. Shining his light."

Jac knew he was just trying to get a rise. She turned to him and shrugged, deadpanning, letting the idea of a stalking, homicidal Jesus hang there untouched like the bait that it was. Conrad laughed and swatted her shoulder with the back of his hand.

"Damn Jackie-O, if you don't know how to look right through a man. Let's get you a slicker."

———

The dogs were up and loping towards her as soon as she opened her door. One of them bellowed as they came, although their intentions were clearly friendly.

"They won't hurt you," Conrad said, opening his door. "Just push them away. Let 'em know who's boss and they'll mind."

Another bark and then a third dog, this one piebald and low to the ground, tearing around the side of the house to see what was new. They all clamored at Jac's feet for attention, taking turns to paw at her waist and popping up to her shoulders like she was the plank of a fence they were trying to clear. Jac cooed and tousled their hair.

"Gator!" Conrad roared, coming around the back of the truck. "Buddy! Get off of her!"

The dogs dropped and scattered as if hit with scalding water, each moving in different directions. They stopped in a rough semi-circle thirty feet out, craning their heads around defensively behind them, ears back, tails curled tightly between their legs.

"Show some manners around a lady!" He scolded.

"They're fine," said Jac. "Really. I like dogs." But Conrad was still at them, as if he were holding ground against wolves. He took a step forward and the dogs broke their positions, the labs running for the patch of lawn from whence they had come and the other, Gator, up the road to the bunkhouse.

"Go on!" he yelled. "You better run!"

"They really were fine," said Jac.

Conrad pulled her packs out of the truck and handed her one, winked, and strode off towards the house with the other over his shoulder, yelling for Iris. Buddy and Elmo watched warily as he passed then wriggled in the wet grass with a quiet, suppressed joy as Jac knelt to make amends.

In four or five minutes, Conrad was back outside with a forest green rain slicker and a maroon baseball cap that sported the Sol Ridge logo.

"The cap is yours to keep," he said, handing it to her. "A memento of your visit to Sol Ridge."

She put it on. Conrad moved around behind her and held open the slicker, beaming like they were about to head out to the prom. Buddy and Elmo stood uneasily and then resettled ten feet further away.

Jac stood, playing along, holding her arms behind her. She looked up as Conrad, taking his time, was sliding the sleeves up over her arms and shoulders reaching around her on each side to pull the front of the slicker closed over her breasts.

In the doorway a woman, Iris she presumed, was crossing her arms and looking down to avoid the spectacle.

"Iris, this is Jac," said Conrad from too close behind her. "Jackie, Iris."

Iris raised a languid hand, inclining her face eventually. She was an attractive girl with large, outrageously blue eyes and a prominent cheekbone allure that conjured a latter-day Alberto Vargas, although more of that was raw potential than anything now fully realized in the doorframe. She wore a drab, blackish smock and a pair of long sagging jeans piling up over pink bedroom slippers. Her hair, long and twisted into a thick rope behind her head, was an unnatural dark metallic black flirting with midnight blue undertones. And yet, for all of that, Jac could tell that here was a woman who had learned how not to be seen. Her stillness was an air-colored wall that she carried with her into the world like a portable blind.

"*Señor* up there?" Conrad asked.

Iris nodded.

"Is he ready?"

Iris nodded.

"Lemme guess; he's pissed and tired of waiting."

Iris was still.

"I figured. Impatient Mexican cuss. Though I guess I did dawdle a bit over breakfast with Jackie-O here. But I don't regret a single bite."

He winked at Jac and paused, holding himself in suspension for something – a blush, a smile, an apology – that never came. After a beat or two he scratched his little paunch.

"Jackie-O, I've got to go up to the high ridge and meet *Señor* to make some decisions. I'd take you with me but I won't be gone long enough for you to take your pictures and I can't leave you up there, so…"

"Don't let me get in your way," said Jac, waving him off. "There's plenty here to hold my interest."

"Iris will show you around, won't you Sugar?"

Iris nodded.

"We've got eighteen rows uphill and another sixteen rows downhill." He pointed simultaneously, like a scarecrow. "I can take you up to the plateau to see the bunkhouse and the juice box, and then up to the ridges later or tomorrow or whenever. You know how to ride?"

"A horse?"

Conrad gave a smile. "There's only a few things up here to be ridden, Jackie. We've got horses, an old bicycle, a tractor, and…" He didn't finish.

"If memory serves," she said.

"Good. We'll hit the upper ridges on horseback. You'll like it." Conrad turned for the truck and then stopped. Patting his pockets. "I leave my keys inside, Sugar?"

Iris shrugged.

"Damn." Conrad headed back towards the front door. As he approached, Iris cringed, closing her eyes and gripping the doorjamb, trying to squeeze herself out of existence. She pulled in sharply as he passed. They did not touch.

Conrad disappeared inside, leaving them alone with the dogs now lying head-to-head in the grass. The awkwardness between them was palpable, but pleasant in its own odd way, like air too saturated to hold any more water. Half a dozen openers occurred to Jac and Iris must have had her own list. They stared at each other instead. It was Iris who looked away first.

Conrad reappeared bouncing his keys in his hand. "I got an idea," he said. "How about Jackie-O here gets a picture of me and Iris and the dogs? Something we can put on the mantle. Whad'ya say, Sweetcheeks?"

Iris dropped her head and rolled away into darkness on the other side of the door as soundless as smoke. Conrad watched her go and laughed and shook his head and stepped off the porch. He stopped in front of Jac, standing close, chest-to-chest, under pretense of needing to speak softly. The dogs watched in apprehension.

"I'm just yanking her chain," he said. "Iris hates being photographed. Terrifies her for some silly reason. Poor kid. Like some old back-country wetback afraid of losing her soul to a flashbulb."

———

"You really don't have to do this," said Jac. She glanced over at Iris standing like a garden statue, silent in her blue serape. It had terracotta stripes and black piping along its edges. "I feel bad dragging you up here."

Halfway along the hike up to the Upper-Eighteen, as the striped field was called, the sun had punched a small hole through the weather.

God's single bright eye peered curiously down into his little pet-shop bag. It would not last, certainly. But it was enough to warm up the air and to hold off the rain. Shafts of light splashed extravagantly through the hanging drops.

"That's okay," said Iris at last, shrugging, arms crossed, trying to stay out of the shot. Buddy raced by, turning down one of the rows with Elmo hot on his heels.

"Now that I know the trail, I can easily get back to the house." Jac paused to find the fisheye in her pack. She uncapped it and screwed it onto the camera with a click. "And then you can just show me the way to the Lower-Sixteen."

"That's okay," she repeated. "Conrad doesn't want me to leave you alone."

Jac turned. "Oh?"

Iris nodded. Jac lowered the camera, waiting for more. Iris added, "Says he doesn't want you to get hurt."

"Here?" She opened her arms and looked around for wolves. "Doesn't seem especially dangerous to me."

She shrugged. Jac waited.

"The back way to the upper ridge can be real dangerous," said Iris defensively. "My father died up there."

Jac took a step closer. "Sorry to hear. How…"

"Fell. Rain weakened the slope. Trail just kind of sloughed off. My dad and Conrad just…" Her hands pretended to empty something small and precious down into the dirt. "There's a couple places up there where it gets steep. Nothing to grab on to."

"That's terrible."

Iris shrugged. "Long time ago."

"Guess I'll be careful."

Jac turned back to the falling land, and took several rapid fire shots of the valley, still boiling over with low-hanging clouds now blush with sun.

"There's nothing really to worry about," came Iris' voice, a bit grudging. "He's just like that."

"Like what?" Jac stayed focused on the valley, realizing that the key to Iris was to avoid aiming attention as if it were a lens.

"It's more about me than you," she said.

"I don't understand."

"He likes it when I spend time with... people like you."

"Like me. Photographers?"

"Women."

"Women?"

"Women that he's... you know."

Jac unscrewed the fisheye and placed it back in the pack. She extracted the macro and screwed it in. Her glasses were fogging in the humid air. The uphill hike had not helped. She was warm and wanted to shed the slicker. She settled for the Sol Ridge cap, dropping it on the ground at her feet.

"Conrad and I are not... he's not my boyfriend or anything. I just met him this morning. I'm just taking pictures."

"He's interested."

"No."

"I can tell."

"How?"

Silence smothered the question. Jac held the thickness of a vine between two fingers then weighed it on her palm. She bent to inspect a cluster of small hard berries. "Amazing what comes from these little guys," she said, deciding not to push. In the silence, she could hear Iris considering her next step.

"He asked me to make up Celia's room, the guest room," she said at last. "You're the only kind of guest he likes. He likes blondes."

Jac studied the berries from beneath and then from both sides, framing them in her head.

"Does it matter if I'm not in the least little bit interested in him?" she asked.

"No. It's always someone."

Jac lowered herself to one knee, moving the lens up so close to the grapes that they were almost touching glass. She pivoted so she could get the color of the sunlit fog in the background.

"Why do you think he likes you to be so… involved? In that part of his life, I mean. Being out here with me. "

A moment. And then, "I like your hair," said Iris.

"Really? This mop?" Jac stood and turned. "Thanks. I like yours too," she said, lying with a smile.

"No. You don't. It's not real." Iris pulled the dark braided rope out in front of her face so she could look at it. She picked at it with her fingers and wrinkled her nose disagreeably. "I let it set too long. Almost turned it blue."

Jac walked up the hill, letting the camera dangle from her neck. She stopped and reached out a hand, cradling the rope of Iris' hair as she had the vine.

"Not an easy thing to die this much hair," she said, squeezing gently. "It's healthy enough though. Beautiful." She was not looking at the hair. But she knew Iris could not see past the glasses.

Iris reached out, finding a thatch of blonde curls pasted in dried sweat to the side of Jac's neck. She entwined two fingers.

"I wish mine were this fine," said Iris. "Like angel hair."

———

Jac changed lenses, alternating zooms for a series of shots that captured the entire undulating length of a row of vines. She had unwittingly left the better of her two wide angles behind in the other pack. Not wanting to burden Iris, already a reluctant Sherpa, she had left the second pack inside front door of the house. Now she found herself wanting an intermediate breadth of view that she could not quite capture.

The photographer in her was muscling her way in, forgetting, taking over, worrying instinctively about things like color temperature and composition and exposure. As if any of that mattered.

She told Iris that she wanted to hike up and to the West to get an angle on the Upper-Eighteen with the house in the background and the valley below the house. Iris had turned and begun walking up the hill, brushing her fingers against each row of vines as she passed. Jac capped her lens, hitched up her pack and followed.

It was a longer and steeper climb than she anticipated. They stopped roughly every hundred yards so that Jac could turn and take a shot or two and assess the angle and ultimately conclude that they still needed more altitude to get the shot she had in mind. Buddy and Elmo raced ahead of them, nipping at each other and finding no end of distraction at sticks and burrows along the way, racing back to them whenever Jac stopped to take some measure of the vista, and then surging back up the hill and out of sight. Iris was quiet, as always, but less dutiful in her company. She did not question or balk. She swung her arms as she walked.

They stopped at a bare spot of ground marked by a prominent rock that jutted out of the ridge at a ninety-degree angle to the slope, providing a natural stone shelf. Both were panting. One of the dogs barked twice from somewhere up above.

Jac turned her back to the hill and cocked her head, looking sideways at the Upper-Eighteen, now well below them through a thin layer of white mist. The house – *the Barn* as Conrad had called it – was in the lower middle distance, off to the East. The swath of the valley, still spilling with pink foam, filled the background.

"This will do it," she said.

Iris nodded and walked over to the rock. She sat, bracing her palms against the stone and dangling her feet like she was sitting on an old chairlift. She closed her eyes to the filtered sun. Jac set down the pack and unclipped the tripod and began telescoping out the legs, extending two of them longer than the third, compensating for the slope.

"Do you like what you do?" Iris asked, her eyes still closed, like she was keeping the blue all to herself.

"What, photography? Yeah. I guess. It's a living."

"And you like taking pictures of vineyards?"

"Not particularly," said Jac still adjusting the tripod, not thinking to lie.

Iris opened her eyes, looked ponderously at Jac and closed them again.

"Then why are you doing this?" she asked.

"Oh, well, that's freelance photography for you. Got to follow the work." Jac screwed the camera onto the tripod, wanting to change the subject. "Conrad complains that you don't like having your picture taken."

Iris was still, as though Jac was talking to the stone shelf beneath her.

"That's a shame," said Jac, looking through the viewfinder. She needed the zoom and dug through her pack. Iris opened her eyes.

"Why?" Buddy and Elmo called to each other in the distance. "Why is it a shame?"

Jac stopped and looked up the hill for a moment. She returned to rummaging, pulling out different lenses and rejecting them.

"Because you're beautiful," she said. "Because that's how I see the world. It's the only way I know to save things. Protect them."

She found the lens and stood up, leaving the mouth of the open pack gaping. She fixed the lens to the camera and focused. She looked through the side pocket of the pack and pulled out her cable release, screwing it into the top of the camera.

"He's got nothing to complain about," Iris said. "He's got his pictures of me. He takes what he wants."

Jac pushed the plunger; once and then again, and again, trying to restart her heart, beating back the wave of cold dread in her veins. She forced herself to keep her back turned. To stay calm.

"Does he hit you often?" she asked.

"What …"

Jac listened for more. There was a long silence at her back. The breeze picked up, filling a vacuum.

"Not since we got the dogs. He can get frustrated. You can tell?"

Jac nodded. She repositioned the camera, taking away half of the house, and picking up more of the Upper-Eighteen.

"Ever thought of leaving?"

"You mean like since noon?"

"Why don't you?"

"I'm needed here."

"Christ, Iris. For what?" She had not meant to sound angry. "I'm sorry." She shook her head, cursing herself as the silence returned.

"How can you take pictures with those glasses on your face?" Iris finally asked, her voice petulant and punishing, betraying its own anger. Jac turned.

"It took some adjusting. But now I don't even know they're on."

"Why have them at all? Sun's not even out."

Jac turned back to the camera. Refocused. Pushed the plunger. She felt guilty for the anger.

"The sun *is* out. Even when we can't see it. It's everywhere. I can feel it." She squeezed again. "It hurts me."

Iris looked at her, intrigued and clearly unsatisfied.

"I have this condition. Hypersensitivity to light. Excruciating head-aches. The glasses are a small price to pay. Beats staying indoors." She forced a laugh. "It beats vampirism."

"You've had this your whole life?" No laughter, but the tone was softer now. Even concerned.

Jac nodded.

"I was born six weeks premature. The condition is rare, but it happens. I also have a nice little anemia problem. All for showing up to the party so early."

"Why... I mean what... why were you..."

Jac smiled, wanting to put her out of her misery.

"My mother died when she was pregnant. Tripped on the stairs on her way down to the basement. They were concrete. They had to cut me out."

Iris covered her mouth with her hand. Her eyes were stretched wide, like glacial lakes threatening to spill over.

"I know. It's gruesome. I'm sorry. It's an old, cold fact to me. I should remember that it's different for people who have to imagine it for the first time."

"That's so ... terrible," Iris nearly whispered. "Your poor father. Did he ever remarry?"

"Well, my folks were never married in the first place. But yes, he married a lovely woman some years later."

A cardinal alighted upon the crest of a branch. Jac quickly snapped up the entire tripod and repositioned the camera, trying to frame the house in the background. She squeezed off several shots.

"So you never knew your mother and I never knew my father." Iris was staring down at ground beneath her swinging boots. "That's an odd thing to have in common with someone."

Jac laughed softly, relocating the tripod. "Yeah. I suppose it is."

"My mother died of cancer a few years ago."

"Conrad said. I'm sorry."

"Thanks."

"That's a terrible time to lose a mother," Jac said. "You must miss her."

But Iris had fallen back into her silence. Jac left her alone, taking several dozen shots she didn't need. She wondered what in the hell she was doing. Way up here wasting daylight. She looked again at the Upper-Eighteen down below, not in relation to the house this time, but as a thing unto itself. A light-brown rectangle shaved into the foliage; the vines like eighteen parallel sutures stitched into the hill, binding deep wounds. She found another like it, much further down the hill on the far side of the road she and Conrad had traveled.

"I can see the Lower-Sixteen," she said more to herself than to Iris.

"You can take my picture," said Iris quietly, still looking at her boots. "If you want."

———

As they approached the house, conversation was regular and almost normal. Iris was explaining what she has to do to get Conrad's inventory and sales figures ready for the accountant. Jac followed along on the trail, the dogs between them, watching Iris from behind as she used her arms and hands to amplify her meaning. She bore little resemblance to the stiffly sullen woman Jac had followed up the same trail only an hour earlier. The sun was gone now. A breeze from the West was thick with new clouds, darker than their predecessors.

Conrad was sitting on the porch in a low wooden chair, petting Gator.

"I was just about to come looking for you," he called. Gator leapt up and met Buddy and Elmo in the closing distance. They all caught up on each other's scent. "But I wasn't sure whether you were up or down."

"Up," said Jac, when Iris did not respond. "I guess that's obvious now."

"Have you been down?"

"Not yet," she said. "Iris was just taking me."

"No need," said Conrad. "I'll take you." He stood up and stepped down off the porch as they reached the house. "Iris has got a lot of paperwork yet to finish from the looks of things."

Iris navigated around Conrad without a word or hesitation or so much as a parting acknowledgement to Jac and disappeared into the house. Conrad sized up Jac with an overly familiar stare.

"You do look *good* in that hat Jackie-O. I think maybe we should work you into our advertising. Whad'ya say?"

A whiff of chewing tobacco explained the slight distension of his lower lip. The smell mixed with his cologne into a sweetly disgusting tang.

"Sorry. I only work on one side of the camera."

The walk to the Lower-Sixteen was considerably easier than the walk up to the Upper-Eighteen. The first quarter-mile was down along the dirt road they had taken up to the house. As they walked, Conrad kicked every sizeable rock in his path. Every so often he spit a twisting, elongating tongue of coffee-colored chew juice into the low scrub.

Jac said little, letting him drawl on about the business of wine, alternating between the process of making it and the business of selling it, weaving in bits of his own personal experience. He was not born to this business, and he knew it. He was a latecomer without prior experience, unless decades of drinking wine counted as experience.

What he actually knew about growing grapes and selling the juice, he had learned for himself, on the job, doing whatever the Old Man would let him do and then doing the hell out of whatever that thing was until he got it right and the Old Man was pleased.

He spoke with an aspiring but lowbred arrogance that simultaneously celebrated his humble beginnings and bade them farewell. He had a keen appreciation for his place in the pecking order of California wine makers – *somma these boys have been at it so long and have such good real estate that they nearly piss pure Sauvignon Blanc. They could bottle their own urine and still make a fortune. My piss is still piss.* But, at the same time, he spoke as though he had been specially anointed to save a great and dying label.

"Victor Bruno was a great man," he said, spitting again. A glistening brown strand failed to cooperate and Conrad enlisted the back of his hand to relocate it to his pant leg.

"Taught me everything I know about this business. Everything. He was a better man than my own father and I'm not ashamed to say it. My daddy was great at being a mean son-of-a-bitch. He was great at being a husband to a crazy woman. And he was great at selling anything and everything Sears, Roebuck and Company cared to put out on the floor. But he was not a great man. Victor Bruno, on the other hand... *There* was a great man. More like my own father than my own father. And he chose me in this world just as surely as I chose him. See I don't believe we're born to family. I believe we end up choosing our family. Our real family. Even if we don't realize we're choosing."

"And you chose Clara," Jac said matter-of-factly, intending to complicate his simple narrative. "And little Iris."

Conrad paused and then covered it with another spit.

"I told you her name?"

Jac nodded. "And Iris."

Conrad nodded and kicked a rock. "Yeah. Okay, I chose Clara and Iris. But I also chose the Old Man. And he chose me. That's the point."

They walked another dozen yards and Conrad stopped and turned at the first and only place on the road from which the Upper-Eighteen was clearly, if only partially visible. Jac drew up short and turned as he pointed to the place that she and Iris had just been. He drew his laden ring-finger west, through the clouds, showing her the upper road that traversed from the field of vines across the slope to the plateau where the warehouse and the juice box and the stables and the tractor barn were, and then from that cluster of invisible buildings over to the bunk-house, also invisible, where *Señor* and the de la Cruz family lived. From the plateau, he drew his finger further west and up, tracing a road that skirted the slope at a steep incline and then eventually disappeared over the top of the ridge to an even higher, unseen field of vines.

"The Lower-Sixteen is our Cab Sauv. The Upper-Eighteen is our Chardonnay. And High Ridge is our Pinot. The view from up there is unbelievable," said Conrad. "Makes you feel like God."

The sun was long gone, leaving the wet air a bloodless white that leached all of the color from surrounding hillsides, as though all of the greens and browns and subtle plums were water-soluble, now burbling away along the valley floor, unseen beneath the cottony cloud stuffing, down toward a rusty aluminum drain somewhere in the basement of the world. The perspiration from the uphill hike and the chill in the strengthening breeze had left Jac cold. But she said nothing to betray her discomfort.

"I'd like to set up on the high ridge there for the sunrise," she said, her enthusiasm a credible counterfeit.

"Sunrise," repeated Conrad.

"How can you feel like the maker and destroyer of all things at any time other than sunrise? And I'll need time to set up."

"Well, I'm not coming into town at three o'clock in the morning to pick you up, that's for damn sure."

The next moment felt heavier, for both of them, than all of the others.

"Guess I'll be spending the night," she said, not looking at him. "If that's okay."

"Oh, that's more than okay," said Conrad.

"I left my things back in the car though. Think Iris will loan me a nightshirt or something?"

"That shouldn't be a problem, Jackie." Conrad patted her on the back. "We'll work it out."

Jac stared up dumbly at the hillside. It was Conrad who filled the silence.

"So Iris spoke of her mother, did she?"

Jac nodded.

"Seems you two sure got friendly in a hurry."

"She's nice. I like her. Quiet though."

"Yeah. She's quiet all right."

Jac pointed just below the ridgeline. "What's that?"

"What's what?"

"That road."

Conrad squinted. "Oh, that's the old horse trail. It's what we used before we built the haul road over the ridge. From that point down to the plateau, we built the haul road basically right on top of the old trail. But from that point up to the High Ridge, the haul road takes a longer route than the trail which is shorter and steeper."

"So that's not High Ridge?"

"No." Conrad spit, cleanly this time. "High Ridge is the next one back. Can't really see it from down here. This was all mostly horse work once upon a time, if you can believe that."

Conrad squinted again, shaking his head.

"Sunrise?" he asked.

"Sunrise," she responded flatly. "I can ask Iris to take me if you want to sleep in. You know. Get your rest."

It was the casual authority with which she had made the remark, as much as the remark itself, that snagged Conrad's phlegmy laugh and pulled it out of his throat like an ugly fish.

"You are a pistol, Jackie-O. You really are. I like that. But I'll be up and done with my first cup of coffee before you get outta bed and put those damn glasses on your face." He hunched, bowing his back to lower himself so that his nose was level with hers, his breath a hot cloud of decay, staring through the black lenses so that he could see the whites of her eyes inside their shadowed cave, pacing nervously. "You don't sleep in those things, do you?"

Jac turned and continued walking. Conrad followed, his phlegmy fish laugh flopping a couple more times in the dirt behind her.

A side road through an opening in the scrub led down another quarter-mile to the Lower-Sixteen, the rectangular patch of vines Jac had seen from above. Jac separated from Conrad, marching ahead of him down an aisle that bisected the field. On either side, decorous rows of vines were tied to stakes like injured soldiers propped up on crutches for a general's review.

She made a busy, overly occupied production of the photography. This way, that way. Uphill, downhill. Bending, squatting. Swapping lenses. Making notes. All of this said that she was too busy, too immersed, to talk. Conrad kept his distance, letting her work.

It was only when she was setting up the tripod and screwing in the macro for a close-up of a cluster of berries that he drew near again. His right hand found her left buttock and gave it a firm caress as she tried to focus. Jac forced herself to not react.

Focus, she told herself. *Focus*.

"So," she said, giving him nothing in her tone, "Cabernet Sauvignon?"

"Right," said Conrad, removing his hand and taking a step downhill as though her ass had been but a tree stump he had used for balance against the slope. Jac centered a cluster of berries and squeezed off several shots.

"They look kind of …"

"What," he said, spitting again.

"I don't know. Sparse. Not so healthy, I guess."

"It's early yet. Plus, I like to keep 'em stressed. Healthy vines spoil the wine."

Jac turned and looked at him, screwing up her face. "Huh?"

"Feel all the moisture in this air?"

"Yeah."

"A healthy vine leads to full berry clusters. Lots of fruit. Drier air can't circulate around the berries within each cluster. Then you've got a bunch-rot problem and you end up leaving most of your crop on the ground. Pinot does better with the full clusters, but not the Cab. These here have got to be small and loosely packed. When it comes to the Cab, I like stressed, struggling plants. They need to work for their existence."

"Sounds backwards to me."

"That's why you take pretty pictures and I grow grapes. Know what happens when these babies are starved for water?"

Jac shrugged.

"They decide that it's not gonna be an easy life. Long about late May they conclude that if it's dry now it's gonna be wicked dry come July. They start fighting to live. They send their roots down, looking for their own water, rather than laying up here near the surface to be baked in the summer sun. They stop putting all of their energy into the nonsense of growing up long and leafy and useless and they decide they need to put everything they've got into ripening those berries. More leaves mean more evaporation, which means less water to live on, so fuck the leaves. In fact, fuck the vines. It's all about the berries. I'm after good wine, not happy vines. They're here to make me happy, not the other way around. Keep 'em unhappy and they'll perform. Gotta be ruthless in this business Jackie-O. There's no room for sentimentality. Heavy on the stress. And if your vine is bearing fruit that'll just end up spoiling the wine, get out your knife, cut it off and leave it lay."

Jac pulled a water bottle out of her pack and doused the cluster of small, hard, dark grapes. The water caught the light so that they sparkled. She took another burst of photos.

"Isn't that cheating?" he asked.

"Nothing honest about photography, Conrad." She said, unscrewing the macro and digging around for the medium zoom. "It's all about framing the world you want, not capturing the world that is."

Conrad laughed. "Well, la-dee-da," he said under his breath.

She took a number of underwhelming shots of the valley, now much less photogenic, and then swiveled on the tripod to catch the Lower-Sixteen against the backdrop of the ridge. It was starting to rain again.

She pulled a beige rectangle of nylon out of the pocket of her pack and draped it over the camera and the zoom.

"Stand right there," she said to him. "This is a good shot."

Conrad struck a pose, hands on his hips looking off into the far distance. A man and his vineyard. A man who knew what he wanted in the world. She zoomed in until his eyes, a little milky and bloodshot and withered in the corners, filled the frame. A man who knew what he didn't want. She pushed the plunger.

"This isn't gonna let up," he said, holding out his hand to catch the drops. "We should go on up to the barn before it really opens up. You like steak? You're not a damn vegan are you?"

"Steak's fine."

"Good. I like a woman that goes for meat. And we'll open a bottle of Sol Ridge Pinot. What the hell, I'll invite *Señor*. You can meet him. Maybe he'll bring over little Celia."

"Sounds good to me," said Jac, fussing with the cable release.

"So tell me about your people, Jackie-O. Where do you call home?"

"San Luis Obispo."

"Your folks still there?"

"Mom's dead. Dad's remarried. Never see him. Which is fine. Pretty much just me and my camera."

"You ever married? Kids?"

"No. And no."

"Didn't think so." He paused. "Not with a caboose like that."

"What about you?"

"You mean kids? Just Iris." Then he spread his arms. "And all of these precious little berries. These are my children, Jackie-O. They're gonna' take care of me in my old age, when I can't traipse all over this hillside. Trick is to get Iris trained by then. That kid is not fond of learning."

Jac unscrewed and capped the zoom and put it back into the pack. Pregnant drops were now splatting against her slicker, exploding in small dull pops. She zipped up the pack and slung it over her shoulder, grabbing the tripod with her free hand.

"Seems smart enough to me," she said.

"She's plenty smart. It's not a question of ability."

"Maybe she's just not into making wine," she said, pushing back up the slope and using the tripod as a walking stick. "There's a whole wide world out there."

"That's not an option," said Conrad.

"Why not? I mean, if it's not her thing…"

"Because the Old Man had his plans for Sol Ridge just like he did for Red Iron and Bruno Acres. Could'a sold out a thousand times."

Conrad spit a rope of brown juice meant for the dirt that looped across one of the vines instead. He kept moving.

"But he didn't. This was always a family business for him. His other kids sold out almost as soon as they got their grubby little hands on those vineyards. Didn't give two hoots about their legacy and they were all too pleased to cut their own children off at the knees before they ever got the chance to step up and take what was theirs." He stopped. Turned. "You want me to haul that pack so you can handle the tripod thing and those sunglasses?"

"I'll manage."

"Suit yourself."

He turned his back again and pushed forward. They hiked back up toward the main road, Conrad leading by several strides. His words tumbled down behind him.

"Yeah, those boys were worthless if you ask me. Never got the wine gene I guess. Clara sure did though. She was born to this work. She loved it. That woman knew how to grow some grapes. She pled with her brothers not to sell. Offered to buy them out on installments. But they never could work it out. The boys wanted their money and the big labels were throwing it at them by the bucket load. Clara got offers too. Plenty. But she always refused. She wanted the business more than the money. She wanted to work the land. Everyday too. She was no slouch. 'Course, that was back before she got the cancer. Then she wasn't much good for anything except throwing up and crying and complaining. But she never stopped wanting all of this for Iris."

"Yeah, but if Iris doesn't want it…" Jac said to Conrad's back.

"What's that?"

"I said but if Iris doesn't want this…"

"Oh, she does. She just doesn't know it yet. She talks big. Sticks her lip out a lot. That's just the phase she's in. She's in her little bitchy phase. A bit slow into veraison."

"Excuse me?"

"Oh quit sounding so offended," he scolded. "You probably don't even know what the word means."

Conrad turned and looked at the inscrutable black mask, seeing only himself in the dark reflection. He sighed.

"When a grape berry starts to take on some color, when it stops growing and starts ripening, all of those acid levels start to fall off and the carbohydrates start converting into sugars. Okay? That's veraison. That's when you know what quality of grape you've got on the vine. Until then it's a hard, sour, bitter little thing. The berries that don't take on color and sweeten up on schedule get cut and left on the ground. What do you think you've been mashing into the dirt for the past half-hour?"

"I thought we were talking about Iris." Jac over-corrected, trying to keep the edge out of her voice. It came out as a laugh.

"Look, all I'm saying is that Iris'll grow out of her bitchy little snit and sweeten up and take to this life – her mother's life – just fine. She'll never leave Sol Ridge. Not as long as I have a say."

"And when you *don't* have a say?"

"That would mean I'm pushing daisies and then it's all hers any-way. The Old Man had his plans and I've got my plans. Immense plans, Jackie-O. If Iris hasn't ripened up by then…"

He let the sentence hang, spitting onto the trail. Jac stepped around.

"She said you and her father were best friends."

"Did she now? Well, that's true. Sandy was a good man. We hired up for the Old Man about the same time. I guess he had a season under his belt before I came on. He had more experience than I did, but then I worked harder than he did. He spent his extra time in the bunkhouse with Clara. I spent mine out here with the rest of the humps pickin' up the slack. Like rabbits, those two. Couldn't marry soon enough, if you take my meaning."

"Iris."

"Showed up eight and a half months later. Man. Been awhile since I thought of 'Ol Sandy. *Sandy, Sandy, he's no dandy, we're pickin' fruit while he's eatin' candy.*" He sang in a high, reedy voice that cracked and peeled at the edges of his tonal reach.

"We used to sing that loud enough for them to hear us all the way up there in the bunk house fuckin' themselves silly. *Sandy, Sandy he's no dandy...*"

Conrad laughed and spit as he reached the main road. He bent over and scraped the plug of tobacco from under his lip and flicked it into the weeds, spitting twice more and wiping his mouth with his hand. He turned and waited for Jac only half a dozen steps behind.

"His Christian name was Robert Sandoval, but everyone called him Sandy. And he *was* a good man. One of the best, if you ask me. Shirt off his own back kind of guy. 'Course, he was never the Old Man's favorite though."

"Why's that?"

"Oh. Don't know for sure. Didn't help that Sandy's mother was part Mexican. In fact, you'll get a kick outta this. This is kinda *small-world* funny; Sandy's mother was half-sister to *Señor's* father. Doesn't that just beat the band?" Conrad elbowed Jac in the shoulder and she bobbled towards the edge of the road.

"That makes Iris and Celia some kind of distant cousins. Don't get me wrong about the Old Man. He liked Sandy just fine as a worker. As a picker. He just didn't much cotton to the idea of Sandy as a son-in-law. Some of the crew thought Sandy was just angling for Clara's inheritance. I never thought that though. I knew he loved her. It was real alright."

"How did you and Clara get together?"

"Oh, we were always friendly, you know. We worked close. We lived close. It's one big family up here. That's just the nature of the job. But after Sandy... well he left a big hole and I guess we both just kind of fell into it together. Climbing out together meant gettin' married. I figured he'd want me to look after her and Iris. So I did."

"With Victor Bruno's blessing."

"Of course."

"Was that your first marriage?"

"Yep. First and last. Not doin' that again."

"Faithful to the end?"

Conrad laughed and cleared his throat.

"Faithful to the end. That's a good one. You are a pistol. Jackie, something tells me you know better. I won't bullshit a bullshitter. Married life isn't for everyone. I'm amazed it's for anyone. It's not for me, anyway. When I was a young buck I left Atlanta with my tail on fire and went to Pittsburg. Got a job on the railroad. Laying track at first. Then I worked in the yard. Then I worked in the office mailroom. Started wearin' a tie everyday. Cleaned up pretty good. And I started getting some attention. Women just started to come outta the woodwork. And these were not your run-of-the-mill city skanks, either. These were ladies. From good families. And not a one of them was interested in letting things follow a natural course. They were all angling for marriage. Right from the start. We'd start up and they'd all hold their tongues for awhile, but then they'd start pushing for something permanent. And that'd just ruin it for me. That'd be the end."

"And Clara was the one exception," said Jac, offering confirmation.

"Yep. Clara was the only one. Oh, there were a couple of close calls. One in Pittsburg, then the P&O transferred me out to Cleveland and I had a close call out there too. Jesus H. You'd think marriage was the gift of eternal life or something. She even gave me her daddy's ring. See that?"

Conrad held out his hand.

Jac laughed. "And you never gave it back?"

Conrad winked. "Gift's a gift, Jackie-O. She wanted me to keep it; just in case I changed my mind."

"You're terrible, Conrad. You are a *bad* boy."

Jac swatted him on the shoulder and he gave her a throaty pirate's laugh, ferris-wheeling his right hand backwards up into the weeping sky and bringing it around behind her to squeeze the flesh of her bottom. She squealed and squirmed away only to be caught by the shoulder and pulled back in. They walked in this way, shoulder to chest, in the rain, all the way back to the barn.

———

Dinner was served on a large, heavily lacquered slab of knotted oak. There were eight chairs, two at either end of the long rectangular table and three evenly spaced along each side. The chairs were all throne-like with high scrolled backs, wide, flat armrests, and broad seats. It was a table made for candle clusters and pewter goblets and decanters and ostentatious serving platters and bowls spilling fruit, although it actually had none of these things. A large chandelier made of elk horn dominated the airspace above the table. The lights blazed out from within the pointed bones which seemed to be burning in clean, white halogen flames, sparking off the plates and glasses and utensils in brilliant needles and broken shards of light, giving everything in the dining room a hardened, machine-made edge.

The dining room was actually not a room at all, but more of an island; a table perched on a huge woven carpet floating on a dark, hard-wood sea that lapped on the shores of a large kitchen at one end and upon the shores of a living area – driftwood in the shape of leather couches and a recliner chair – on the other end where an orange fire blazed and popped in its frame of river stone.

Conrad circled the table emptying the first bottle of Sol Ridge Pinot Noir and then started another, skipping over young Celia who rolled her beautiful brown eyes at the idea that she was not allowed to drink alcohol under Conrad's roof even though she drank wine regularly at her father's table up in the bunk house. But she did not object and Ernesto de la Cruz, seated next to her, did not intervene on her behalf. All of that had been tried before.

Iris, who might normally have occupied Celia's place, took advantage of the opportunity to sit directly opposite, next to Jac. Conrad's place was the same as always; at the head of the table, his back to the fire, the seats on either side of him empty, as if intentionally left vacant for those no longer present. The result was an invisible line across the end of the table; Conrad on one side, and everyone else on the other.

Iris was nervously atwitch, up and down from her seat, bringing things from the kitchen that she had forgotten. She placed a small bowl of mushroom gravy with a silver ladle, arching light into the air as she moved, next to Jac's plate. Jac smiled a thank you and continued cutting into her steak.

Ernesto de la Cruz held up his glass and watched as Conrad poured.

"Gracias, *Hefe*," he said softly with a slight bow. He was thick in the chest with wavy black hair just beginning to gray, and large, dark brown hands and wrists that emerged from the sleeves of a clean white peasant shirt. He buried his nose in the glass, sniffing deeply, sipped and nodded. Jac guessed that he was Conrad's age, maybe older, but the skin of his clean-shaven face held a dark, smooth luster that preserved his youth. She could see the boy still alive in the man, swimming in the eyes.

Ernesto waited until Conrad was out of the way and headed back into the kitchen with the empty bottle before answering Jac's question.

"Yes. This is true. I have two brothers who own a vineyard in Saltillo, this is in Coahuila." The words rolled effortlessly out of someplace deep and dark and protected from the world, coated in chocolate. "And I have also a cousin that works on a vineyard in Parras. This also is in Coahuila."

"My Uncle Javier makes wine, but my Uncle Eladio is the Birdman of Saltillo," said Celia with a glimmering smirk, her teeth holding the light. Her father elbowed her in the side pretending to be stern.

"This is not true," he said. "My brother has simply caught the attention of some birds – some parrots – that live near *Vides Felices*. That is the winery in Saltillo. He feeds them and they come to his window. He makes the wine just as much as Javier. They are good partners, my brothers."

"They peck at the window," said Celia, retaking the spotlight, "and if Uncle Eladio leaves it open they fly in and sit on the edge of the bed and squawk and bob their heads until he feeds them. Once Kiko got a broken wing and Eladio fixed it. They *love* Uncle Eladio."

376

"Your uncle sounds like a very good man," said Jac.

"He is," said Celia nodding and eating a fork-load of green beans. "I like your glasses," she added at half-volume with a knowing smile. Jac surmised that she had already asked Iris for an explanation, probably wondering whether Jac was blind or a movie star or both.

"Thank you," said Jac, volume off and mouthing the words.

Outside the front door came thumps and a whine.

"Can the dogs come in?" Jac asked Iris. Iris furrowed her brow shaking her head in a way that was as much a warning than answer. Jac looked across the table at Celia. She too was shaking her head.

Conrad, on his way back from the kitchen, detoured by the front door, whipping it open with a yank. If the dogs had had any hope that the opening door meant they might be coming in, it was short-lived. There were sounds of a panicked scramble from the porch.

"You've had yours," Conrad shouted after them. "Leave us be to have ours. Go on! *Git!*" He slammed the door and returned to the table.

"They're yours tonight Celia," he said without looking up, pulling in his chair. "I've had enough of those mutts for today."

Celia nodded, smiling to herself in a way that Jac took to mean such an arrangement was perfectly okay with her.

"So, you out here tellin' stories about Mexico?"

Ernesto nodded.

"Never met the brothers de la Cruz myself," said Conrad. "But I've sure sampled the wine."

"And?" asked Jac.

"They'd be well advised to take up training parrots. No offense, *Señor.*"

"*Hefe,*" said Ernesto de la Cruz under his breath, shaking his head.

"They over-macerate. And they baby those vines. Oh my god. Like they were growing little puppies down there. No discipline."

"No, *Hefe.* It is perhaps for a different palate."

"Different alright. Are you saying you prefer their way to our way? To *your* way, *Señor?*"

"No. *Hefe.* I am not saying this."

"Damn right you're not. You make the best god damned wine in the state of California. Am I right?" Conrad raised his glass. "Here's to *Señor* and to ambrosia done right."

Glasses rose above the table, too far away from each other for all to touch. Celia raised her water in a lackluster gesture, clinking the rim of her father's glass.

"*Cuenta con solamente agua?*" she asked.

"*Sí,*" he said winking. "It still counts. Gracias, Celia."

"*Hefe* says that you are taking pictures for a magazine," said Ernesto to Jac as the glasses returned to the table.

"Not a magazine, *Señor,*" said Conrad with a tinge of impatience. "A book. A *book.*" Ernesto remained focused on Jac, as though the noise from the end of the table was a squeal from a wet piece of wood in the fire.

"I'm just scouting for now," said Jac. "There are a lot beautiful vineyards out this way."

"Yes." Ernesto nodded, chewing his steak. "There are many. This is true."

"But none so personal as Sol Ridge," insisted Conrad. "In't that right Jackie-O?"

"It is breath-taking up here," said Jac, ignoring the question. "Iris took me up near the ridge today – not the high ridge," she corrected, raising her hand and then lowering it a foot, "this ridge right above the house here. And the fog had filled the valley below and the sun was streaking through. It was like heaven. I got some good shots, I think." She turned slightly sideways. "One or two in particular."

Iris blushed and fumbled through the basket of bread.

"Did you know Iris had blonde hair like yours before she colored it black like mine?" asked Celia, smirking again. It was Iris' turn to roll her eyes.

"Which way do you like it the best?" asked Jac.

"Blonde," said Conrad, emptying his glass and reaching for the bottle. "No question."

"I wasn't asking you," said Jac flatly. The table fell into a startled hush. Conrad paused in mid-reach. Celia's smile began to melt. "I'm interested in what Celia thinks."

Conrad poured his wine.

"Well," he said, "'scuse me for interrupting. Please, Celia, do tell us what you think about my stepdaughter's color from a box. We all do want to know."

Celia stared at her plate in silence, continuing to eat with a whipped shrug. Ernesto cupped his hand against the back of her head, her hair pillowing like a plume of fresh ink in seawater.

Jac drank, swallowed. She skewered another bit of steak.

"I'll bet she's beautiful either way," she said. "I've always thought it's important to try new things. It's a great wide world. We were all made for better lives. Don't you agree, Mr. de la Cruz?"

Ernesto chewed and nodded without looking towards the fire.

"Yes," he said. "This is true, Jac."

Conrad laughed as though to an off-color joke. Ernesto and Celia and Iris concentrated on their plates and the business of cutting their meat. Jac turned. Conrad planted both elbows on the table. He pointed at her with his knife.

"Beautiful either way," he said. "Well, that's pretty bold talk for a woman that never shows her eyes. Wouldn't you say Jackie-O?"

Jac smiled. Conrad smiled back, mimicking. Without turning her head, Jac removed her glasses, placing them on the table next to her plate. It was, Conrad realized, the first time he had seen her look at him. *Really* look at him. Look *into* him. Removing the glasses was like a black cloud scudding out from the path of the sun. He tried his best to keep his smile, muscles perceptibly quivering at the corners. But the smile had mostly faded by the time he was forced, more by the clarity of Jac's eyes than the intensity of her stare, to turn his head so that he regarded the food on his plate. He removed his elbows from the table and resumed cutting.

"You see, Jackie?" He said to his knife and fork, "No need to hide such pretty eyes anymore than Iris needs to hide her own hair. What would your momma say? God himself is in those eyes. In't that right *Señor?*"

"*Sí*," said Ernesto, smiling politely. "They are lovely eyes. Like the ocean."

"See there?" Conrad sawed his meat. "Like the ocean."

They all looked, but it was Celia who spoke.

"Wow. Is that a tattoo? That is so cool."

"No," said Jac. "It's a birthmark. I was born this way."

"Does it hurt?"

"No. It doesn't hurt."

"Is it like blood, or…"

"*Celia*," Ernesto's voice was hushed and stern. "*No sea grosero.*"

"No," said Jac, smiling at him in a way that she meant to hide the searing pain in her temples. "It's okay. Curiosity is never wrong. The smartest people ask the most questions." Then, to Celia she said, "Do you know what capillaries are?"

Celia nodded. Jac placed the tip of her finger on the sanguine stain that suggested a pooling of blood just beneath the skin in the hollow of her left eye.

"The capillaries in this part of my face are dilated. That's what causes the color. The color gets deeper as I get older. It's hereditary. I get it from my mother's side of the family."

As she spoke, Jac fingered her glasses on the table next to her plate. Her temples pulsed like the gills of a fish suddenly on the deck of a boat.

Iris stood, dropping her napkin, and walked to the dimmer switch on the kitchen wall, turning the knob so that the lights buried within the tangle of antlers faded down to something much closer to old starlight.

"What in the hell…?" Said Conrad, looking up.

"Does anyone mind?" asked Iris, retaking her seat. "Those lights were giving me a headache."

"*Oh, mi dios*," said Ernesto. "This is better. Gracias."

"Yes," said Celia, beaming at Jac with a secret enthusiasm. "*Much* better."

Conrad shook his head as if in a state of utter incomprehension. He stood and pushed his chair back and it seemed as though he was preparing to walk to the kitchen and turn the lights back up. Jac felt every muscle in Iris tighten; as if in the act of standing Conrad had somehow electrified Iris' chair.

But Conrad did not move towards Iris or the kitchen. Instead, he turned and walked over to the fireplace and pulled aside the wrought iron screen. He extracted two logs from a stone alcove beneath the hearth and tossed them in, replacing the screen.

"Conrad's taking me up to the high ridge tomorrow," Jac said. "So I can get some good shots of the sunrise."

"Oooo," said Ernesto. "*Hefe* have to get up early tomorrow, eh?" He laughed softly, his body bouncing in his chair. Celia snorted, exchanging glances with Iris. Ernesto straightened out his smile into something more earnest.

"*Hefe* is not so good early, Jac. I can take you up to the ridge."

"The hell you will," Conrad bellowed from across the room. "I'm up in the morning before any of your sorry asses. If girlie wants to see the god damned sunrise, then I'll be the one to show it to her."

"*Hefe...*"

"Don't *Hefe* me. You just better hope I don't come pull you outta bed just for the fun of it."

"I want to take the horses," said Jac. "Can we take the horses?"

"The horses?" Conrad looked at her, incredulity straining his once handsome features. "No. No, we *cannot* take the horses. Horses don't have headlights. We'll take the truck."

"I'd really like to have the horses in the shot, as the sun comes up."

"No way. It'll be early enough without having to mess with the horses." Conrad refilled his glass, emptying the bottle.

Jac turned her eyes away from Conrad to Ernesto. "Would you be willing to saddle up a couple of horses before dawn and take me up?"

"Hell no," said Conrad.

"I wasn't asking you," said Jac, keeping her eyes forward, speaking again to Ernesto as if Conrad were not in the room. "I can just see you, up on the horse with that big hat Conrad has told me about, silhouetted against he rising sun, dewy vines in the background."

Ernesto looked sideways at Conrad, then back to Jac. He pulled a piece of steak carefully off of his fork and nodded slowly.

"*Si.* I can do that for you, Jac. If this is what you wish."

"Oh, fuck *me,*" said Conrad, flaring his irritation. "You want horses, we'll ride the goddamned horses. This better be a great fuckin' book, Jackie-O."

"*Hefe,*" said Ernesto imploringly, gesturing toward his daughter.

"Oh Christ on a cupcake, *Señor.*" Conrad covered the distance from the fireplace back to the table in long, loud strides. "She's not a god-damned baby. She's a lot more grown up than you think she is. She knows what the word means. Don'tcha Sweetpea?"

Silence befell the table as the fire laughed from across the room in pops and whines. Iris looked carefully at Celia, who kept her head down, re-cutting her tiny pieces of steak. Conrad sat forcefully and resumed eating, not expecting an answer. His face was hard; features gouged into uneven stone. His anger was stubborn, occupying his eyes and patrolling the shape of his mouth, only slowly receding to allow a disingenuous expression of amusement, as though he was enjoying a good-natured banter with his guests by playing the irascible, salty old goat.

Jac raised her empty glass and turned to face the man no one else would.

"How about some more wine," she said. Only one half of her mouth rose to the occasion. The flames behind Conrad took to the new wood in the dim light and the blood seemed to slosh and quiver in the hollow of her eye.

Conrad smiled, the ropy tendons in his neck taking up their slack. He finished chewing his meat, set down his fork, and rose for the kitchen.

———

The borrowed nightgown stopped three inches above Jac's knees. It was made of a soft, thin midnight blue cotton and featured a glowing celestial theme with yellow suns, moons of white bone, cool blue stars, blood-orange comets and blooming spiral galaxies, all scattered from collar to hem like a wearable museum exhibit on the many disguises of light. She turned out the bathroom light and padded along the darkened hallway, back to the room she had been assigned, the polished wood floor cool to her bare feet.

"That was a mighty thorough cleaning," said Conrad as soon as she turned the corner. He was leaning up against the seam between the closed door and its frame, another full glass in his hand. "Get behind the ears?"

"Cleanliness is next to godliness," she intoned, expecting this encounter.

"Oh, I see. *Sister* Jackie is it?"

His words were thick and fuzzy at the edges. She had stopped counting at three empty bottles for the evening. A little less than two had been his alone. He took another drink, seeming to bite it out of the glass like a blood pudding.

"It's all the same to me I suppose," he slurred. "You're enough to make me go back to church." He wrinkled his nose and wiggled his ring finger at her. "Oh-Oh, Jackie-O."

"I think maybe it's time we go to bed," she said, slowing her approach.

The front of the nightshirt was soaking up the bath water from her hair, draping in a single strand over one shoulder. Jac combed her fingers through it absently as she reached the door and stopped to look up at him. He leaned down toward her. His breath was fetid and should have been visible. It should have had its own color. He did a thing with his mouth, stretching the already thin flesh of his lips into a bloodless gash, intending a smile.

"Why do you think I'm here?"

Jac answered quickly, starving the question of time to grow, like pinching the wick of a candle between wet fingers. This was her usual practice when men sought to hear her speak their own motivations. As though they were her ideas to be accepted.

"To wish me a good night sleep," she said. "To tell me that you will be up before I'm conscious and that you will be knocking at this door in roughly three and a half-hours to make sure we are up on the high ridge in time for the sunrise."

She watched the realities of that long-forgotten agenda play out in slow motion across his face. He blinked and swayed and leaned back against the door, lowering the glass to his waist.

"Three and a half... good God. Why the fuck do you have to see the sunrise? I don't understand why that is so all-fired god damned important to get up before... to get up so early and to see... to see..."

Jac's hands continued to comb through the wet hair. She nodded patiently, watching him clamber for purchase as his thoughts turned to mush beneath him and his anger began to rise.

"To see Jesus shine his little light?" she asked.

The words stopped his rising indignation in its tracks. His eyes locked onto her face like a hand grasping for something solid and strong rooted into the earth. She saw him thinking. Thinking. Thinking. Jac smiled. She reached out and patted his cheek, her fingers warm and wet.

"All the best coffee-table books have a good sunrise shot, Conrad. Come on. You know that. Silhouettes the topography. Brings out the romance. Gives Mother Earth her due."

"It'll be goddamned cold," he said, anger having congealed quickly into petulance, "and pitch black and... and shit-o-dear Jackie, we'd have to start headin' up there at four-thirty in the morning."

Conrad's bleary eyes lit up suddenly and he pushed himself forward from the wall.

"Tell you what," he whispered. "Let's take the truck. Then we could leave at six."

Jac appeared to consider the idea.

"Tell you what," she said. "I'll get *Señor* to take me up with the horses for the sunrise shots and then he can bring me back and you and I can go back up in the truck later in the morning. That way you can get some more sleep."

"Oh, god… *damnit*," he said, almost shouting, pulling up his shoulders. Jac forced herself not to flinch.

"No, no," she brushed his cheeks. "It's okay. I know how early that will be for you. I know how late it is. Let *Señor* take me. He's still awake. He must be. He only left… what… a half hour ago. I'll just call him. I'll ask him to come get me. I'll ask him to take me. He said he would take me. He's such a good man. He'll do whatever I need. I'm sure of it. You saw how he looked at me."

Conrad's eyes narrowed and she could feel his heart constricting itself into a small hard space, retreating like a mollusk into its shell. His red, wrinkled lids closed for several seconds. She felt him sensing her; feeling her presence in the reality of his choosing. He was young and she was in love. But not with him.

"*Señor* is a weak man," he said. "He is not a good man. He is a scheming man. A cheating man."

"No. Conrad. I saw how he looked at his daughter. I saw how he looked at Celia. He is full of love. He is goodness."

"You want him," he spat. "You want that no good Spic between your legs. That's what this is all about. Isn't it? You no good, sunglass-wearing, eyes-hiding whore."

"You're drunk, Conrad. Time for bed."

"He's always looking for that chance. Scheming wetback. Always looking to take what in't his. He'd take it all if he could. All of it."

"But *you* married Clara, not *Señor*," she said, assuring him, brushing his cheek. "*You* married the Old Man's daughter. Sandy died and then you stepped into Sandy's shoes, not *Señor*. God, *not Señor!* Come on now! All of this is *yours*, not his. Your house. Your land. Your vines. Your grapes. Your wine. It all belongs to you. And to Iris."

"Goddamned right."

"Why would I want *Señor*? I mean *really*? *Señor*? He has Celia, Conrad. That's all he cares about. She's his whole life. Where would I fit in with a man like that? Why would I want him when I can have you?"

Suspicion hung over his eyes. His face darkened like a gathering bruise.

"*Señor* don't know what he fucking thinks he knows," he said. "I'll tell you that, Missy. Little miss Jackie-Jac. This is all mine. All of it. I take what I want to take. I have who I want to have. Understand me?"

"Oh, I understand. You're the big boss man around here."

"That little glitter in his eye is mine. I fucking own it. I own him and I own her, whether he knows it or not. You fucking understand that?"

"I understand perfectly."

He stepped forward suddenly in a lurch-like stumble, throwing both arms around her. Wine sloshed over the back of her left shoulder. He pulled her in close, mashing against the plump dampness of her lips. The hand that was not holding a glass found the bare flesh of her flank beneath its borrowed cotton cover. Her skin smelled like soap. His heart thrilled in its chest of memory. He was young and love was still on the vine. Jac pushed against him gently.

"Whoa there, cowboy," she said with that mischievous half-smile. "Let me ask you a question."

Conrad took a short step backwards, drinking her in. He licked his upper lip and took another bite of wine.

"What."

"You mind terribly if I stayed an extra night?"

"Huh?"

"What if we got all of our business out of the way tomorrow and we spent an extra night exploring what's left? How would that be?"

He smiled, broad and toothy and his eyes shone in the dimness, gathering the light. He would surely have been something in his day, she thought. All smiles and southern charm wrapped around implacable desire. How easy it would have been to mistake willfulness for passion. To mistake it for love itself.

"Why Jackie-O," he said, "you're just full of surprises, aren't you?"

"Oh, I am *full* of surprises. My surprises will make your fucking head spin, boss. You like surprises?"

He breathed in deeply through his nose and finished his wine in a single swallow and exhaled.

"Not tonight then," he said as matter-of-factly as he could muster, falling back against he door, trusting that it was closed.

"We've an early morning, Daddy-O. Not tonight. Besides, you're drunk. I wouldn't want to take advantage."

Conrad laughed at this, then he stepped forward again, cupping her behind the neck. She resisted, pulling against muscle. Pulling against the thing she wanted. He kissed her on the forehead and withdrew.

"You be ready," he said. "I'm coming for you."

"I'll be ready."

———

Jac watched him disappear around the corner and then listened to his footsteps recede, irregular and alternately sliding and slapping against the floor. She opened the door, pausing suddenly in a veil of amber light. For as much as she had expected Conrad to be waiting for her, she had not expected this.

"Thank God," breathed Iris.

She sat at attention in the cushioned wicker chair at the foot at the bed, her hands curled tightly over the armrests, blood just beginning to return to the tips of her fingers. Her long hair – a genuine, blueless onyx in the low light – had been brushed out of its twisted vine into a kind of lustrous corvine plumage that disappeared behind her back. Her nightgown was blush and thin and covered her to the ankle like some diaphanous petal fallen from a trellis.

"I thought …"

Jac smiled. She stepped in and closed the door. "He's gone," she said. "It's late. Too late for what he has in mind."

"Do you want me to go?"

"No. I don't."

"I have insomnia sometimes. I thought if you were up..."

"Hey," she said self-evidently, "I really don't plan on sleeping myself."

"Why?"

Jac laughed at the predicament of her own making.

"Got to get up in less than four hours. Better off not sleeping at all than having to crawl up out of a dream."

She looked at Iris, soaking her in.

"I'm a night owl anyway. I sleep as much in the day as night."

Iris made a half gesture with a hand.

"Because of the ..."

Jac knew what she meant. She smiled and stepped around the pack she had leaned up against the nightstand and pulled back the covers. The bed was clean and white and cotton, the spread quilted and adorned with ruffles and eyelets. The headboard was large, made of roughly hewn Mexican pine, as was the dresser and mirror against the wall opposite the door, and the nightstands on either side of the bed. A frosted glass globe, like a smooth moon stuck to the ceiling, was dark. Light came, as if in a vapor, from a glazed pottery hurricane oil lamp burning dimly on the dresser.

"The night and I are old friends," she said. "Kind of a relief from the screaming days."

"Is that what it feels like? I mean really?"

"Sometimes," she said. "If I don't take the little white pills and wear the glasses. Let's just say I feel a lot better in the dark." Jac gave a soft laugh and shook her head at the familiar and the pathetic. "I guess that is a little vampiric, isn't it?"

Iris laughed in a sound that was small and hushed but tinged with a heightened attention; a child looking through a peephole.

"Thanks for the lamp, by the way," said Jac, nodding towards the dresser, "Nice touch. And for dimming those lights at dinner."

"I figured... I thought you might be more comfortable."

"You figured right. *Oh!* And thank you for *this.*"

Jac flared out the bottom of her nightshirt with her fingers, stretching the fabric taut. She looked to Iris like a dark Christmas tree, a perfect triangle of branches festooned with points of starlight and planets and comets, surrounding a slender trunk, white and naked and perfect, disappearing up the center. Jac opened her mouth in soundless delight. She curtsied.

Iris blushed, shifting in the creaking chair and picking at the hem of her own, much more feminine version of eveningwear.

"Kind of goofy, I know. I've had it forever. I went through an astronomy thing."

"No, no. It's great. I love astronomy."

"Really?"

"Come on. Cosmic gemology? A dark sky. Old, painless flecks of light? Absolutely."

"You can have it if you want."

"This? No. It's yours." Jac piled the pillows up against the headboard and slipped under the covers.

"Seriously. I never wear it."

"Really?"

"A memento of your visit," said Iris, mimicking Conrad, her bottomless blue eyes belying the sarcasm. "That and the baseball cap."

"Thanks. I promise never to wear them at the same time."

They laughed together at this, their eyes trying to hold the mirth like the air can hold the heat of the sun into dusk.

The silence came as an awkward force, pushing against them from all directions, even from below, as if the roots of the vines from the Lower Sixteen and the Upper Eighteen and the high ridge had all interlaced in the cooling soil beneath them. They listened to the hiss of the hurricane, burning light into existence.

"Can I ask you something?" Iris said after a minute.

Jac straightened herself, tucking the covers around her waist. "I think at this point, I'm obliged to answer just about any question you ask."

Iris unfurled her legs and stretched her feet out to push against the end of the bed, the flesh-pink pads of her toes peeking up over the bedcovers. The wicker chair creaked beneath her.

"What's it like being so…"

"So…" She waited. "What?"

"I don't know. *Free*, I guess."

"What makes you think I'm free? Free how?"

"You know. Going wherever you want. Traveling light. Taking pictures of things you like. Selling your pictures. Meeting people. Having… I mean doing… well, having whatever kind of relationship you want to have with them. Moving on. You're not chained to anything. You're not attached."

"We're all attached to something, Iris. Something that won't let go. Something we won't let go of."

"Really? I find that hard to believe."

"Believe me. I'm as attached as anybody. My life's not so romantic as you think."

"Could've fooled me," she gave a rueful smile.

"Grass is always greener on the other side of the fence," said Jac. "Well, the grapes always look juicier on the other vine, I guess I should say."

"Are you saying that you'd switch places? That you'd live here? With him?"

Jac shook her head, conceding.

"No. It *is* beautiful. But no."

Iris' forehead furrowed into a freshly plowed field.

"What do you see in him?" she asked. "I never understand that. Why do women…"

"I'm just here to take some pictures, Iris."

"I heard you." Her eyes were accusing and her tone sagged with distrust, waiting to be confirmed. "Through the door. I heard what you said about tomorrow night."

Jac sighed, looking into her lap.

"I say lots of things, Iris."

"So does that mean that you're not staying?"

"We'll see," said Jac, now trying to catch her eyes. "Can I ask *you* something?"

Iris looked back down at her hands then up again. Nodded.

"What keeps you here? I mean, is it the inheritance?"

Here eyes widened.

"Conrad told me," Jac said, reading her surprise. "Does that surprise you?"

"A little."

"Why?"

"Because he likes to act like Sol Ridge is his. Especially..."

She let the sentence drop. Jac picked it up.

"Especially when it comes to impressing women he's sleeping with."

Iris smiled a little and nodded. "Every woman he brings up here thinks he's Ernest Gallo. Not that his floozies are ever that smart." She looked up, stricken. "I didn't mean..."

Jac waived her off. "I've been called every name in the book."

"I wasn't..."

"Iris." Jac stiffened her gaze, holding Iris' attention. "It's okay."

The mortification dissipated. "Anyway," Iris said. "They should see the numbers. That's all I was saying. He's not Ernest Gallo. He's not even Victor Bruno."

"Okay. So he's trying his best to get laid. That's pretty normal, isn't it? Pathetic, yes. But normal for his gender. Particularly when there's a bunch of floozies like me to reward that kind of behavior."

She had intended levity, delivering the words with a mockingly accusing smirk. But Iris did not respond. The chair beneath her creaked as she pushed back gently from the bed. Jac restarted, erasing he tone.

"Or do you think he's in denial about this place?"

"Little of both," said Iris. "Legally he's just a trustee. 'Til I'm thirty. That's a fact he doesn't like much. He uses it to keep me close. Anytime I talk of leaving he reminds me of my sacred obligation. Other than that... forget it."

"Why is that so important?"

"What."

"To keep you close? To keep you here."

"I'm the grand-daughter of Victor Bruno," she said grandly, spreading her arms, mocking herself.

"The Old Man," Jac nodded.

"Right. The legacy. I'm the torch-bearer."

"And that's really such a big deal to him?"

"To Victor?"

"To Conrad."

"Well, he sure talks a good game."

"But it's all up to you. Isn't it? It's your decision."

Iris shrugged again.

"I guess."

Jac leaned forward in the bed, her elbows on her covered knees, her face in flickering light and shadow.

"Don't you think he's afraid that if you leave, if you go away, you'll either come back with some young buck of a husband and assert control, which I cannot imagine him liking one bit, or decide to sell the whole thing off to the highest bidder like your uncles?"

Iris looked, searching her from across the bed, but did not answer.

"Either way doesn't that spell disaster for King Conrad?"

Iris smirked at the sound of this. *King Conrad.* She nodded.

"So then isn't his best option to hold you close? Keep you under his thumb? Keep you under the spell of your obligation to the dead?"

Iris' smile faded. Invoking the dead so dismissively had gone too far.

"I'm sorry," said Jac. "It isn't my place. Let's just…"

She broke off, leaning sideways over the side of the bed to unzip her pack. She began extracting lenses, lining the black metal tubes in a decorous row on the other side of her shrouded legs.

"No. I know. I know. You're right." Iris came slowly back to life. "He says this is all for me. For mom. For Victor. But in his heart, I'm not really a part of this place. None of us are. It's all about him. You're right."

Jac paused the unpacking.

"What about in *your* heart? Iris. Is this something you even want?"

"It's something my mother wanted. For me, I mean. She wanted it for me."

"But ..."

"I used to imagine my father. I mean what he would have been like. I imagined him fighting with her. Even when she was so sick. I imagined hearing them through the walls. Yelling. Screaming. Saying the things to her I never said. I imagined him defending me. I imagined him coming to my room at night. When she was asleep."

Jac swallowed. "Why? What does he do? When he comes to your room? What do you imagine?"

Iris broke contact, turning towards the lamp.

"I imagine that he kisses me. On the forehead. He tells me to leave. He gives me some money. And he tells me that I don't need to be here for the end. That there is nothing I can do to save her. That it's not my fault. That I don't need to make her any promises. That she'll love me no matter what. That he'll love me no matter what. That I should just... go."

"Iris."

She looked back slowly. Passive. Beaten.

"I know this is personal. It's none of my business. Tell me to fuck off and I will. But..." she waited, giving her time, cradling a large black lens like the muzzle of a gun. Iris was still.

"How long have you been imagining these visits from your father? Visits from Sandy." Jac noticed a small jolt, a tiny pebble dropped into the blue of those eyes, when she spoke his name. "When your mom was asleep."

Iris looked away again. Not answering.

"Was it even before your mother got sick?"

Iris sighed.

"Was the first time a very long time ago, Iris?"

She nodded.

"And did imagining that it was your father help you get back to sleep?"

A long minute passed. The light paced and hissed in its cage of glass. The roots beneath them reached and groaned in longing.

"Why are you here, Jac? I mean..."

A thump, from somewhere deep in the house, traveled along the floor. Jac lifted an eyebrow.

"Conrad," explained Iris. "The door to his bathroom sticks. He's showing who's boss."

Jac nodded. She placed the telephoto in the row with the others and then fished around in the pack until she found the bottle of lens cleaner and a baggie of cleaning papers that were folded in half like a wad of small, clean white money. She inserted two fingers in behind the wad and pulled two home-rolled joints.

"Join me?" she said, holding them up. "Helps the pain a lot better than my little white pills."

Iris blushed a little. Shaking her head. Replacing one of the joints, Jac swung her legs out from beneath the sheets and padded around the end of the bed for the flame on the dresser. Iris pulled her legs into the chair so she could pass. Jac tipped open the glass and bent into the lamp. The paper glowed. A sweet cloud gathered around the glass moon.

On her way back, Jac stopped between the chair and the bed, looking down at Iris' face. Iris looked up in her innocent, sad perfection, inclining her cheeks, brilliant blue eyes flying open to take her in. Jac felt something snap and buckle deep in her chest, like a burning bridge under too much weight. She held out the joint.

"Sure?"

Iris smiled meekly, leaning forward over her folded legs and the flawless white flesh of her feet. She closed the rose of her lips around the end of the tiny roll, pressing them up against the pinch of Jac's fingers. Her hand lightly cupped the back of Jac's own, holding it in place. Iris inhaled with an obliging politeness, froze only briefly, and then leaned back in the chair releasing Jac's hand. They looked at each other until she exhaled.

"I know what it's like," Jac said, returning to her place in bed and setting the joint on a lens cap coaster. She pulled a lighter out of her pack and set it on the nightstand and then pinched the wad of tissue out of the baggie and wet it with several drops of solution. Uncapping the smallest lens, she rubbed the tissue in small circles over the glass.

"I used to imagine my mother all the time. Used to talk to her when I was in bed and the rest of the house was asleep. Like she was lying next to me. Face to face. I mean, you know, I never *actually* knew her. But it was like I knew her perfectly. In the womb of my own head. I knew her in darkness. Like I was still inside of her. As a child, I was always able to find her in the dark. Never in daylight. But, man ..." Jac shook her head. "Close the blinds and shut the door and I could just about imagine her into existence. I'd speak and she'd answer and off we'd go. And we would have these conversations."

"What kind of conversations?" asked Iris, newly entranced.

Jac laughed and took another hit, replacing the joint and the lighter on the nightstand. She blew towards the candle.

"Silly ones, mostly," she said. "Best lip gloss flavors. How I could convince my Aunt Alice to buy me a dog. She was kind of like a diary, I guess."

"Did she say things to you?"

"I imagined she did. Sure. Her favorite lip gloss was peach. Just like mine. What a coincidence."

They both laughed at this and the room seemed to brighten a little. Wisps of smoke carried the light around the room on soft shoulders.

"I complained a lot," said Jac. "Ghosts are good listeners."

Iris felt a sudden almost violent flutter in her chest. That word. *Ghosts.* She wanted to ask. She wanted to know. Did they have this, too, in common? Were the conversations real? Did Jac, too, have a specter whispering secrets in bed, when the house was dark and the valley outside was quiet, like a fallen green body waiting to be discovered? She wanted desperately to not feel crazy. She wanted to let it out. To tell Jac everything. To speak the words as she had heard them, night after night, year after year, in a whisper so soft and so cold as to be more likely a draught from the open window.

But there was, in that sudden flutter within Iris' chest, at least as much dread and fear as there was hope. She did not have the courage to risk such a confession in such a new friendship. Looking at Jac, she sensed a hardness. Something brutal. Or at least uncompromising.

Her eyes, now that she could see them, were sharp and discerning. Behind their blinds, those eyes had been narrow and busy. Evaluating. Measuring. Judging. The blood pattern that Celia had mistaken for a tattoo lent an other-worldly perception to Jac's gaze. Her loyalty, Iris surmised, was to the judgment of those eyes, not to people. Not to relationships. Not to good intentions. What would Jac think of her? If Jac knew what Iris believed, what would she think?

"What did you complain about?" Iris asked.

Jac shrugged and resumed cleaning. "Oh, I don't know. Everything. School. My Roy Orbison look made me a pretty easy target. I was not especially popular. And the headaches got in the way. I couldn't focus. I dropped back a grade. People thought I was either dumb or lazy or both. In high school the girls thought I was a slut and the guys thought I was desperate. I proved most of them right, I'm afraid."

"That's *terrible*," said Iris, her face aching.

"Yeah. Well, it toughened me up, that's for sure. That and Alice. A lot of people kind of conspired to toughen me up."

"Alice ..."

"My mother's older sister. Basically raised me until I turned fifteen. Then she kicked me out of the house."

"Why?"

"I was getting in the way of her love life." Jac glanced up for a second. "Basically."

She saw the confusion on Iris' face, laced with hesitation. Jac smiled.

"You're wondering if I actually poached my aunt's boyfriend."

Iris looked down at her fingers, which were busy worrying over a flaw in the fabric of her nightgown.

"Not exactly," said Jac. "Wayne was..." She rolled her eyes up to the dark frosted globe hanging from the ceiling. Remembering. "Let's just say he took a real shine to me from the beginning. Alice was as practical as she was unforgiving. When her sister died, she did what had to be done. She took me as her own kid. No husband. She just stepped up and became a single mother. Just like that."

Jac reached for the nightstand. She found the joint and lighter without looking.

"And those were prime man-grabbing years, too. Those were marrying years." She released an amber cloud and returned the lighter to the nightstand. "And Alice was not the looker my mother was. Mom got all of those genes. Would have been hard enough for Alice to get a man even without a weird lookin' kid in the picture. So when she finally found a guy that looked like he might just stick around longer than a couple of weeks, she was sure as hell going to keep him."

"And that was Wayne?"

Jac good another hit. Held the smoke. Released. She nodded and returned the joint to its makeshift coaster.

"That was Wayne. Good ol' shit-bird, whiskey-breath Wayne." She stared up into the dark glass moon as if she could see his face. "Alice did what she had to do. Believed what she had to believe. About Wayne. And me."

She capped the lens and picked up the next. She slipped another tissue out of the baggie.

"You're awfully forgiving," said Iris, hoping that maybe she had been wrong about Jac.

But Jac smiled, shaking her head. The expression on her broadening lips saddened her eyes, narrowing them to a kind of sweetly condolent wince, in a way that said there was so much Iris did not understand. About her. About forgiveness.

"No," she said. "And I'm cursed with a long memory."

"But where did you live?" Iris asked, horrified. "I mean … fifteen years old."

"Oh… there were a couple of friends." She broke off. Wetted the tissue. Started again, raising her eyebrows. "There were a couple of *guys*. They were willing if I was willing, if you catch my drift."

Iris returned to her worrying fingers.

"I toughed it out until I was halfway through my Junior year. Then I met this man who owned a photography studio. He was doing the senior class photos. He needed help. I dropped out." Jac shrugged her shoulders and held up the lens, pointing it at the lifeless glass moon like a telescope. "Here I am."

Iris looked up, shaking her head in a slow rolling disbelief.

"I guess I should feel lucky," she said.

"Maybe," said Jac.

"I mean, at least I had my mom. For awhile anyway. And a home. Where was your dad? Couldn't you have gone to him?"

Jac swatted at an imaginary fly.

"Why not?" Iris asked. "Was your dad all that bad of a guy?"

"Levi. I call him Levi. Every picture I have ever seen of him he's wearing those stupid jeans. It's the only name he deserves because it means nothing to me. I don't have a dad. I've never had a dad."

She seemed to Iris prepared to let the subject go and Iris was prepared not to push. Jac slowly twisted the rings on the zoom back and forth absently. The lens lengthened and shortened in a slow rhythm, breathing in the syrupy light from the hurricane.

"I'm no philosopher," she said. "Maybe we all start out perfect and living is just a process of … of exposure. Exposure inevitably brings corruption and spoilage. So maybe we should feel lucky if we're able to live in a way that allows us to control the rot. Careful avoidance. Not too much of this, or that. Not him. Not her. Not here. Not there. Limiting our exposure. Or maybe it's the opposite and we all start out like hard little sour berries and living is really a process of sweetening and taking on color. Maybe we should feel lucky if we get enough exposure in our lives to sweeten us up."

"Conrad's been lecturing you on veraison," said Iris in a laugh.

"The man knows his berries," said Jac, not looking up. She took another hit, holding it in her lungs. She released. "I'll give him that. He knows his berries."

She went back to twisting the lens. Iris watched her think, the stain around Jac's eye like a sideways question mark, wriggling in the growing haze.

"Or maybe it's all the same thing. The rotting and the sweetening. Maybe it's all just in the timing. Maybe Levi crossed my mother's path too early and maybe had it happened a hundred years later, by then he would have sweetened up and he would have been a loving husband and father. Or maybe he came along ten years too late, after the rot had already taken hold of him. Doesn't really matter, I guess. They met when they met."

Iris smiled, catching a memory like a sweet breeze.

"My mother used to tell me that we're all like tiny boats on our own little rivers. All the rivers are headed for the same sea, but they get there in different ways, by different routes. And we each get to pick the river. She believed there was no such thing as a bad boat, only bad rivers. Bad choices."

Jac nodded, thinking.

"Well, if that's true, then my mother should never have chosen to climb into Levi's little skiff. Because his was a river of darkness flowing no place good."

"So you didn't even try? I mean he was your dad. God, if *my* dad was alive… If I knew…"

"Yeah. Well. Levi had his own family. New wife. A baby girl to take care of. A good future in a solid job. He didn't want anything to do with me."

Iris leaned forward over her legs, indignant.

"He *told* you that?"

"Didn't have to. I looked him up. You know; followed him around. But I kept my distance."

"You've never actually met him?"

"I met him eventually."

"And?"

"Not exactly a heart-warming reunion," she said wryly. "Last thing he wants is another daughter."

"But that's so… that's so *cruel*," Iris said, almost pleading. "He can't just pick and choose his… his… He can't just decide…"

"Sure he can." Jac capped the lens and put it back on the bed, giving Iris her full attention. "He has. He has chosen. He has decided. From the very beginning. He chose my mother. He decided that he wasn't interested in marrying her. On the other hand he decided that he was *quite* interested in fucking her."

Iris blanched, almost imperceptibly, at the rawness of the phrase.

"He decided that he was quite interested in spending her money and accepting her gifts, including – as Alice liked to point out – things that have been in my family for generations. He chose to accept her optimism like it was some sort of bubble gum prize, stringing her along as he slept with half the town. He chose not to care about knocking her up. He decided he did not want a baby. That would be me, by the way."

Jac raised a hand toward the roiling ceiling and the enshrouded glass moon, identifying herself.

"Let's see, what else. Right," she counted on her fingers. "He chose to beat my mother for loving him; for wanting a family; for wanting to keep me. He decided that he *did* want to call the ambulance and even ride with her to the hospital, but he also decided that he would rather go to the bus station than hang around for the rest of my birthday or a bunch of pesky questions about my mother's broken orbital bone and bruises that were not exactly the shape of our basement steps. So, Levi *chose*. He *decided*. We all do. Just like your mother said. We all pick our rivers."

Iris was silent for most of a minute. Jac went to work on another lens.

"How do you know ... all of this? How..."

"Alice. She and my mother weren't really friends. But they *were* sisters. She was a nurse back then. She had a spare bedroom, compresses, painkillers. She said that even when they weren't getting along my mother came over when she had to. Which was a lot. Alice had a special hate for Levi."

"Because of how he treated your mother."

"No. Well, that was certainly part of it. But mostly I think it was because he was my mother's man and not hers. I'm pretty sure they had something going."

"You mean Levi and Alice?" Iris gasped. "No way."

Jac nodded.

"How…"

"I was a big snoop. What's a young vampire to do when everyone is asleep? I snooped. Alice had this photo of Levi that she kept in the back of a book." Jac shuddered visibly at the memory. "He had this look on his face. Cocky. Triumphant. Bottle in one hand, grill tongs in the other. No shirt. Hip jutted way out. Stupid boots. It was Alice's grill in the background. I could just tell. Why hide the picture in a book? I stole it from her."

Jac capped the lens and put it aside. She finished off the joint and crumpled the remains into a plastic film canister with a red lid. She dropped the lighter back into the open mouth of the pack. Iris waited, speechless. Jac combed her fingers through her damp hair in several contemplative strokes.

"I think Alice hated Levi for choosing wrong," she said at last. "For choosing the pretty one. For choosing her father's favorite. And then she hated him for leaving. And then I think she hated him for leaving it to her to raise me."

"Even though she knew …"

Jac nodded. "I didn't say it was rational. Or healthy. But what Levi did to my mother was the least of Alice's hate."

"Does she still hate him? I mean, like she did?"

"No. Nowadays, Alice doesn't hate anyone."

"Born again?"

"Overdose. Like I said; she was a nurse. She knew how to manage pain."

Silence came again, dark and thick, taxing the light. Jac extracted the camera from the pack and unscrewed the lens that was attached. She cleaned the glass of the lens as she had the others. She reattached it to the camera.

"Nice camera," said Iris, desperate for sound.

Jac looked at it in her hand, twisting it one way, then the other. Bits of chrome glinted in the firelight. She held it up to her eye, panning the room like she was scoping a rifle.

"Yeah. My trusty *Hemera Classic*. Best camera I've ever owned. She loves the light. I've got three digitals. Left all of them at home."

Jac lowered the camera and cocked her head, looking at Iris with fresh interest.

"You ever thought of modeling?"

Iris jolted. "Me?"

"Yeah. You."

"No. I... no."

Jac opened the back of the camera and pulled out the yellow canister of film and dropped it into the pack. She unzipped a side pocket and extracted a grey plastic tube. She popped the lid off with her thumb and let the new roll slide down into her lap.

"You'd be a great one," she said, lining up the sprocket holes on the lead. "You could make some really good money with that face. Those eyes. That body. I do a lot of portrait work. Magazines. Publicity stuff." She looked up. "I mean, don't get me wrong. Not forever. Modeling's not a good profession for long. But for a few years. Until you figure out what you want to do with yourself. While you're going to school or something. I can think of a dozen jobs off the top of my head."

They stared.

"I couldn't."

"You mean you won't."

"I mean..." Iris rubbed her face in her hands. Her eyes looked tired, the whites reddening with the smoke. "I mean I can't leave."

"The vineyard or him?"

"Both. Neither."

"Sol Ridge doesn't own you. *He* doesn't own you. No matter what has happened. Or how many times. You get to live your own life. Iris..." Jac waited until Iris was looking. "He's not going to settle for taking it out on the dogs. He's not going to sweeten with age."

Iris sighed, defeated. She picked at her nightgown as Jac watched, helpless. After a minute, she raised her face again and wiped her eyes with the back of her hand. She looked around slowly, as if taking in new surroundings. She sniffed.

"I used to like to sleep in this room," she said. "When I was a girl. It was kind of like camping to sleep in the guest room. It was where I came to kind of escape. My life. A little holiday. You know?"

Jac nodded.

"And I felt rich and privileged sometimes. To have two rooms that I could choose between whenever I wanted. Didn't even have to ask permission, as long as I made the bed and kept it clean. And then when my mom got sick, she kind of moved in here. Conrad kept the big room. She said she liked the interior room with no windows during the day because she could keep out the light. She liked it pitch black. And it was quieter. After she died it reverted back to a guestroom again. I've never come back to sleep in here. Now it's Celia's room."

"Celia?" Jac looked around for signs.

"Couple times a year this place can get pretty busy. *Señor* brings in his crew. The whole bunkhouse fills up for a few weeks at a time. Celia comes down here to stay. To live." Iris stared into the hissing flame. "Just the three of us."

Jac stared down at the heavy black camera in her hands, ashamed to have been so blind.

"It's about Celia. I should have…"

"I guess if I left, Celia could have my room. Then she'd have a choice just like I did. 'Course… it'd just be the two of them."

"Iris…"

But she wasn't listening.

"I'm going to bed, Jac. I'm tired. I'm not a night owl like you are. But will you do me a favor. In case you do leave tomorrow and I don't get to see you?"

Jac nodded. "Anything."

Iris unfolded from the chair and rose, eyes closed, as if seeing would make standing all the harder. She pulled the nightgown from each of her shoulders with a finger and let it fall to the floor at her ankles. Jac's heart all but stopped in its broken, burning cage.

The hurricane flame fluttered in an unfelt breeze. Each of them, rooted in their own private history of inexplicable experience, recognized the cool spinal sensation, like a goose flesh of the veins, and knew they were not alone.

Iris drew a slow breath and opened her incredible eyes.

"Will you take my picture?"

———

Jac knocked the side of her boot against Conrad's door. The house was quiet and dark. She listened and could hear him snoring inside. It was a wet and laden sound, a cheap tin shovel pushing through heavy slop.

She switched her pack to the other shoulder and knocked again. Sounds of conscious life sputtered and groaned. She heard a noise in the general shape of a question. She answered.

"It's me. Time to go, Conrad."

He grunted. She thought she heard despair.

"C'mon, let's go old man," she said. "Time's wasting. The light is coming soon." She waited. Hearing nothing, she said, "Tell you what. Never mind. Go back to sleep. I'll call *Señor*. He gave me his number in case this happened."

She clomped off down the hall. The door opened behind her and a weak, orangish light slopped out onto the wood floor, splashing up against the opposite wall. Jac turned.

Conrad stood naked and disheveled in the doorway. The skin of his torso and legs was hairless and a bluish pale, almost more aquatic than human, and it seemed to hang too loosely on his bones. He gripped the doorframe with both hands to stay upright. The thing he loved most about himself needed no such assistance, although it stood less than true and seemed to want to go back into the room.

"Keep your damned panties on," he mumbled, the act of speech requiring almost more effort and mental-muscular coordination than he could muster.

"Jesus Conrad." Jac made no effort to soften her disgust. "I'll be outside."

When he finally joined her on the porch he was moving slowly but fully dressed. Jac was sitting in the chair, legs stretched out on one of the packs. She looked up at him as he came through the door. He stopped next to her, looking out into the soggy gloom, bracing himself for the first step into a world without walls and tables and chair backs and other things that he could grip or lean on to guide his progress. He swayed slightly on his feet, balance negotiating with gravity.

"You're drunk," she said. "Still."

"I need coffee, that's all."

"You should have laid off earlier last night."

"Stuff it. Jackie-O." He managed a smile like he was adding another plate to the juggling act. "I'm as good as they come."

"Can you ride?"

"Shut up and get in the goddamned truck. Let's get this over with."

She stood and followed him as he stumbled forward. The air was cold and wet and close in the dark. Jac wished she had thought to bring a coat. She might have asked Conrad for a loaner. He was wearing sheepskin and denim. But she kept the discomfort to herself. It would have been wrong to ask him.

Jac winced as the motion lights caught them a few steps out onto the gravel driveway. The black *Erebus Charger* appeared in front of them suddenly, bathing in the floodlight. The rainwater gleamed along the hood as if the light had come from a bucket. Jac's breath was white, bleached and sterile in the light, boiling out in front of her.

They climbed in and Conrad fumbled with the keys so consistently that Jac volunteered to drive.

"God *damn* but you are a pain in the ass," he said, trying to be cutely irascible but missing by a mile.

Jac looked out her window, away from the floodlight pouring in through the windshield. She listened to the keys drop a third time. She had not slept. Not in two days. She could feel the pressure building behind her eyes. She saw Iris floating out beyond the window in the dark air, hovering over the sleeping valley, her skin like she was wearing the candlelight.

The key slipped into its metal glove. The engine roared to life and the truck lurched forward into the path of its own headlights, spraying gravel behind.

The wide road up to the plateau was rutted down the middle. Conrad seemed to be steering for the grooves, as if the truck were a train and finding the tracks would somehow ease the burden of driving. But the ruts appeared and disappeared and reappeared beneath them like invisible currents serpentining beneath a yawl. They swayed together, in perfect tandem, as if bound together in a dance to some silent music they both knew by heart. Neither spoke. It was a three minute ride that seemed to last an hour. They could feel the world beneath them rolling towards the sun.

When the truck reached the plateau, Conrad steered in a wide arc. The headlights swept the façade of a large, plain two-story building with a wide covered porch that she assumed was the bunkhouse. In the distant gloom were other buildings, too far for the headlights to reach.

"Bunkhouse, tractor barn, warehouse, juice box," Conrad said pointing, thumping his hand on the top of the steering wheel. "Fermentation. Bottling. Stables are out that way. You can see all of that when the sun is up."

"You said we could ride," said Jac.

"We are ridin' Jackie-O. In a *truck*."

"You said we could take the horses."

Her voice was as flat and as unemotional as she could keep it. But she still felt like a girl on the verge of a tantrum about a bicycle or a slumber party or an Easy-Bake Oven.

"You can see the goddamned horses later. I'm not going to saddle up in the dark."

"I want the horses in the shot."

He turned and looked at her, his face glowing red in the dashboard lights.

"We all want a lot of things, Jackie. We don't always get the things we want. Now I accepted that hard fact last night like a perfect gentleman. And you can accept it now. Understand?"

Jac looked back at him without acknowledging his words. Something in her silence must have been unnerving.

"I'll take you up on the horses at sunset. You can get a good picture with the sun going down rather than coming up. Sunsets are better around here anyway. You'll see." He reached out and cupped the back of her neck with his palm. "Then we'll ride back and have dinner, just the two of us. The Cabernet tonight. It'll be fine. You'll see. No need to wake the horses. Let 'em sleep."

Out in the darkness beyond Conrad's shoulder Jac saw movement, slow and large. She focused through the reflection of Conrad's head. She gave him a sideways smile and then opened the truck door and stepped out, pulling her packs behind.

"What... hey..." Conrad said, confused.

"*Buenos días*, Ernesto," Jac called out over the hood, closing the door.

"*Buenos días,* Jac," he said warmly.

"You brought friends."

"*Si.* I thought I would save you some time and trouble." He raised the reins he held in each hand by way of introduction. "Nellie. Diablo."

The horses seemed to look bashfully one way then the other, pushing soft clouds of steam into the air. Diablo shifted on his feet. Jac saw that Ernesto had hung large flashlights around each saddle horn.

Conrad opened his door and stepped out, plainly furious but at a loss for words.

"*Señor ...*"

"*Buenos días, Hefe.*"

"We don't need ..." he gestured towards the horses. The truck was dinging relentlessly behind him at the open door. He pushed it closed.

The black mare craned her head towards Jac, taking her scent. Jac set down her packs and brushed her neck gently, whispering as she did.

"Oooo, Nellie likes you," Ernesto laughed.

"I'll bet she likes everyone." Said Jac, breathing deeply, the smell of large animal like the earth itself.

"*Si.* She is a sweet horse. She is my Celia's favorite horse. But *Diablo* is not so gentle." He patted the nose of the pure white giant to his right. "Diablo is *Hefe's* horse. Temperamental. Skittish."

The stallion whinnied as if taking offense. Conrad, too, bristled.

"Best goddamned horse of the lot."

Ernesto winked at Jac, showing how easy it was to get a rise from both man and beast.

"Conrad doesn't want to ride," said Jac, still stroking Nellie. "You want to ride up with me to the high ridge?"

Ernesto shrugged.

"*Sí.* I will take you there if you would like."

"Will you bring your hat? I want to get a shot of you on Diablo there as the sun is coming over the ridge, vines in the foreground."

Ernesto nodded, handing her the reins. He turned in the direction of the bunkhouse, patting Diablo on the nose. Conrad opened the truck door and turned off the engine, leaving the keys inside. He slammed the door again angrily.

"No. Goddamnit," he said. "We don't need your stupid hat."

He snatched the reins out of her hands, not looking at her. Anger seemed to have restored some measure of equilibrium.

"You want to ride? Fine. We'll ride if it's all that goddamned important. In the dark. Let *Señor* go back to bed."

"Good," said Jac. "I'll ride Diablo."

"No!" said Conrad too sharply, turning on her. "You will *not* ride Diablo. *I* ride Diablo. Now climb up on that mare and let's be the fuck on our way."

He threw Nellie's reins at her and moved into position next to Diablo's saddle. His newfound equilibrium was only fleeting and mounting was a clumsy, grunt-filled affair, his boot repeatedly missing the stirrup.

Jac winked back at Ernesto, who did his best to suppress the humor in his eyes. He moved quickly between the truck and the horses to help Jac up. Before he could reach her she was already swinging her right leg over the saddle and leaning in to hug Nellie around the neck.

"You ride horses," said Ernesto, handing up one of the packs. Jac slipped her arms through the straps.

"I had an uncle Wayne when I was a kid," she said. "Aunt Alice's boyfriend. He managed a horse breeding business. He liked to take me riding a lot. Just the two of us."

Conrad looked suddenly back at her over his shoulder. His eyes narrowed to slits beneath a forehead wrinkled in confusion.

Ernesto handed up the second pack, supporting the weight as she secured the top strap around the saddle horn, removing the flashlight.

"I know some breeders," Ernesto said, lowering his arms to give the full weight of the pack to Nellie. "Was he here in California?"

"No, no," she said. "I grew up in Ohio. Cleveland area."

She nudged Nellie forward with a gentle heel, glancing back over her shoulder at Conrad as she passed. He was still staring at her, squinting at her in concentration, trying to think through his own haze. Trying to decide whether to believe his own ears.

Trying very hard to remember.

Behind him the night sky was dropping its veils.

"Come on, old man," she said. "Light's coming."

———

"In my room?"

Iris nodded. She sat in a chair on the bunkhouse porch, wrapped in a Mexican blanket with her feet up on the railing and cradling a cup of coffee. Celia sat on the railing itself, leaning up against the vertical post that held up one end of the porch roof. Buddy and Elmo slept on their sides in a fat yellow blade of sun slowly melting over the wooden planks.

Celia, having been dismissed back up to the bunkhouse after dinner, was full of questions about the evening, most of which concerned Jac. Iris had made the mistake of letting on that there had been some late night discussion that accounted for her yawning and generally somnolent demeanor.

"All night?"

Playing polite evasion with Celia, who could be ruthlessly insistent when she was of a mind, should have required more energy than Iris had to give in such a state of deprivation. But she had born the onslaught of questions with a patient humor. They kept her distracted from the gentle thrumming – a low voltage electric current – in every corner of her body. She could not explain the sensation, which had kept her awake long after returning to her room. She had expected to sink like a stone and to sleep until ten or eleven. But she had become strangely buoyant, her attention to everything around her unsinkable. She had lain in the dark, listening to the house breathe, listening to the vines dream outside in their beds of loam, listening to the darkened earth turn on its wheel toward the sun. She had lain in the dark, listening to Jac rouse Conrad, forcing herself to stay in bed.

At the first glow of morning Iris had dressed and made some coffee and then she had set out on the cool, wet road up to the bunkhouse, watching the sun silently explode over the high ridge in magnificent shards of day.

"Talking about what?" Celia insisted.

Iris sipped. Swallowed. Considered.

"Oh. Photography."

"What about photography?"

The valley beneath them, choked with white foam, blushed in the early morning sun. An osprey disappeared from view, banking and dropping down in the general direction of the Lower Sixteen.

"Oh. What the freelancing life is like."

"What's freelancing?"

"Oh…"

Buddy raised his head, listening. Then Elmo, one ear up. In an instant they were both on their feet, leaping off the porch. Gator, too, came barreling around the side of the bunkhouse from places unknown. The three of them converged near the middle of the plateau and headed off in a run to the far end, back around the juice box where the plateau narrowed into the road that wound its way up to the high ridge.

"They're back," said Iris.

Celia craned her neck to look and then spun her entire body around, swinging her legs over to the other side of the railing.

Nellie was sauntering. The reins were loose around her neck and her large black head bobbed in a slow steady rhythm. The pitch of her coat gleamed back the morning light.

Jac had one hand draped loosely over the saddle horn. The other rested on the butt of her camera, which she had slung sideways across her body on a strap so that the barrel of the long telephoto was hanging down near her hip. Her hair was loose about her shoulders. Her eyes hidden in their mask.

The dogs circled Nellie excitedly and then led her in toward the center of the plateau. There, Gator found sudden new interest in a smell that took him, nose scraping the dirt, back around the side of the bunkhouse. Elmo and Buddy left Nellie at a trot. They bounded back up onto the porch, retaking their former positions, where they all waited and watched the slow approach.

Celia was the first to move or speak. She waved and jumped down off the railing and walked out to intercept the horse.

"Morning, Jac," she said.

"Morning," said Jac as Nellie came to a stop.

"Did you get some good pictures?"

"Think so. We'll have to see." Jac stood up in the saddle and swung her leg over Nellie's enormous black rump. She stepped down trailing the tips of her fingers along the muscled hind leg as she descended. She nuzzled Nellie's neck and handed the reins to Celia.

"Great horse you have here, Celia," said Jac.

"Thanks," said Celia. "Dad calls us sisters. Where's Conrad?"

Jac unhitched her second pack and set it down in the dirt. She answered looking directly at Iris.

"He said he wanted to take the old high horse trail down. He said he wanted to walk the trail down to the junction. He told me to take the horses back on the road. I told him I'd get better pictures up there but he wouldn't listen. He won, of course. Nellie and I left Diablo waiting for him down at the trail junction so he can ride the rest of the way. He's one stubborn man. He seems to think the high trail is too dangerous for a girl. Mostly, I think I was just getting on his nerves."

Celia looked warily at Iris and then back at Jac.

"It *is* dangerous," she said. "They won't let *me* walk up the high trail."

"I'm sure you're right. I'm just disappointed. Could've gotten a good shot or two up there. The ridge was great, but the trail gets a better view off to the north." She patted Nellie's flank. "You need help with her?"

"Nah, I got her," Celia said. She clicked at Nellie in a way the horse clearly understood and the two of them moved slowly back across the plateau in the direction of the stables. Jac turned and watched them go, Celia's thick black hair in a long braid, moving in tandem with Nellie's black tail.

"Really a great kid," said Jac. When she turned again, Iris was looking at her with concern.

"What the hell happened to your shirt? Jac, you're bleeding."

With a forefinger, Jac found the long, red welt inside the frayed and dirty tear, flaying the fabric from shoulder to wrist. She looked at her finger and wiped it on her pants.

"Nah. Nasty scratch is all."

"*Scratch?* And your neck. What the hell happened?"

"Clumsy," she said, patting the tripod that bent oddly out of the top of her pack. "Got tangled in some scrub and tripped. Fell on my own tripod. Right on top of it. Bent it all to hell. It's junk now. I rolled maybe thirty feet down the slope before I stopped."

"Jac," the gasp seemed to come from her eyes. "That could have been serious. You could have…"

"Ahh," Jac said. "Ground cover was pretty soft. Could have been worse. Could've been a long flight of stairs."

Iris looked over Jac's shoulder in the direction she and Nellie had first appeared. The trail at the far end of the plateau was still empty and obscured in shadow. No sign of Conrad. Iris looked back at Jac.

"Want some coffee? Or breakfast?"

"No. Thanks." Jac kicked at the dirt. "I do have a couple of favors though."

"Sure."

Jac nodded in the direction of Conrad's truck, still sitting where he had left it. "Would you mind giving me a lift back to town? I don't think I want to wait around for Conrad."

They looked at each other over the railing, the landscape of Iris' face darkening beneath scudding clouds of emotion, from hope to confusion to disappointment to sadness to desperation to something darker still and more familiar. But she said nothing, leaving her thoughts to grope for solace in the old whispers that had gotten her this far; those icy aphorisms of the dead.

The brightest day makes for the darkest shadows.

The darkest night shows the faintest twinkle.

"He'll be mad," she said, stalling. "If his truck's not here."

"No he won't," said Jac.

Iris looked confused, ready to press her point. *Of course he would be angry.* But she just nodded, finished her last swallow of coffee and stood, leaving the blanket in the chair and her eyes focused on her boots.

"So." Her tone was hard, the old protective shell reforming with each word as she retreated back inside of herself like the sun slipping back into its granite slot in the mountains. "You said *a couple* of favors. What else?"

Jac pulled her glasses down the bridge of her nose so that their eyes might connect without any filter. She waited until the silence closed the distance between them, grabbing Iris before she disappeared into stone.

Iris finally gave in and looked.

———

Dear Celia:

I miss you so much. It feels like forever, doesn't it? I cannot believe you will be graduating soon! I am so proud of you, it makes my heart hurt just to think of it. You know I will be there in the very front row and Jac promises she will keep me from crying so I won't embarrass you. Especially when you are singing for all of those people! You can bet that you will have more pictures than you know what to do with!

I received a sweet letter from your father last week. Ernesto really is like a father to me. Thank you for sharing him. Now that all of the lawyers are gone and the paperwork and planning is done, it is kind of strange, being his partner. I think he feels the same way. But I cannot think of anyone with more love for Sol Ridge than him. I'll never forget what he said to me the night they finally found Conrad. It was late and the police had finally left. I asked him what we were going to do and he sat me down at the table and said, we are going to be kind to our fruit and grateful for the sun. Iris, he said, tomorrow is a new day. He's the right person for Sol Ridge. I know my mother would have approved. And when he is ready, he will hand it over to his family; certainly Marco and Daniel, but I know he hopes that you will take over the business after college. You should hear him talk when you are not around. He is so proud of you, Celia. You are already Queen of Sol Ridge. Maybe you will even have a couple of parrots just like your Uncle Eladio!

But listen, Celia, and this is important: that is not your future unless you really want it. As Jac says all the time, we don't have any claim on the future. We can only claim the present. That's the only thing we ever really have. It's the only thing we can own. The past that we know is gone and the future that we imagine may never be. They are like prisons that keep us locked away in other dimensions with only the ghosts to keep us company. Enjoy your life now. Every day. Go to college and learn. See as much of the world as you can. Surprise yourself. Do unexpected things. Make mistakes. Forgive yourself. If your path crosses Sol Ridge, and if that is what you want, then it is yours, Celia. Ripe for the picking. And if not, there are always other harvests.

I am doing well. Jac is teaching me a lot about taking photographs. I'm a slow learner, but she's patient. She has taken on a lot of new projects in the past year, so she's busy and I'm helping to manage the finances (which I am a lot better at than she is, so maybe it all evens out). She found a publisher for her winery photos, which she thinks will come out next summer. In the meantime, she has arranged four different modeling contracts for me. Can you even believe that? Me? Posing for photographers? The first one is for Vintage Pulp Publishers. They are reprinting a series of old 1940's detective novels by an author named McMannis. They want me to pose as the sultry blonde on the cover, holding a gun and smoking a cigarette and looking like mischief. Have you ever heard of anything so ridiculous? I will send you the first book as soon as it is published so that you can see the new me and laugh. I can't wait. I am having so much fun, Celia.

But I do miss you and I cannot wait to see you in all of your graduating glory. Give a big hug to your dad and Daniel and Marco and Nellie and Diablo and Oreo and Maggie Mae and Buddy and Elmo and Gator. I am enclosing a picture that Jac took of me on her first day at Sol Ridge. This is right below the granite notch, above the Upper-18. I have come to love this picture. Not because of me (how sad and terrible I look in my prison of fake black-blue hair!), but because of the light all around me, like thin golden veils. Jac says it was the moisture in the air that day, holding the sunlight. It takes a photograph to see it, Celia, but that light is all around us, everywhere, all the time. If we could see it with our naked eyes, as we walked around living our lives, I think it might be too much for our mortal senses to bear. Jac says it would keep us from doing all of the things we need to do to live. All of the things - the good things and the terrible things - that make us human. I think if we could see the light all the time we just might die of joy without ever living a single day.

Take care of yourself, Celia. See you soon.

All my love,

Iris

Chapter 9

PRECIPITATION LIKELY, CHANCE OF SUN ("THE MIGHT AND THE WILL")

Clement stared down at the pillar of wine. Four cases of pinot noir, one atop the other. He kicked the bottom of the pillar lightly with the toe of his boot. A man in a silver beard and a black baseball cap pushed open the door of the *Willing Spirits Emporium* with a six-pack in his hand and navigated his way around the pillar out into the mall heading in the general direction of *The Book Nook*.

Clement nodded congenially as the man passed, pulling one of the wine bottles out of its cardboard sleeve to read the label. The man in the hat nodded back warily, wondering perhaps whether the lanky man in the boots and the long, stoic face was planning to make off with a case of pinot noir once he turned his back. Clement watched him go, waited for him to turn back for a second look, then nodded again.

The man should have been less concerned about the wine and more concerned that Clement Merriwether might reach out and grab him by the wrist and take his six-pack of beer. Not to drink it – Clement had been clean and sober for five years and six months – but, rather, to confiscate it until the man was ready to leave the mall. Technically, alcohol was not permitted in the mall proper and all patrons of the *Willing Spirits Emporium* were welcome to enter the store through the mall entrance but were required to take their purchases out through the exterior door that opened out into the mall parking lot.

Clement had, in fact, thought of advising the man of the rule but had opted to let it go. He did not have the look of trouble and Clement knew trouble when he saw it. Experience had taught him that much. He'd keep an eye out as he walked the beat.

Wayne Kylie, the younger *K* of *K&K Distributors*, came back out of the liquor store for another load.

"Clem," said Wayne with a slap on the arm. "How you been, friend?"

"Been fine," said Clement.

"Looking for some wine? I figured you for a beer man."

"Am a beer man. *Was* one anyway. You figured right. This good stuff?"

"*Sol Ridge?* It's alright, I guess. I can't much tell one from t'other tell you the truth about it, Clem. It's gettin' popular so it must be good stuff to some people."

"Good way to lose some of it," said Clem, nodding at the pillar under his arm. "Leaving it this way out in the mall."

"Shoot, Clem. Not worried about thieves in here. Not your mall. Not with you makin' the rounds."

"Why not take it in through the front entrance?" *Like you're supposed to*, Clement wanted to add but didn't because he liked Wayne and Wayne's father, Joseph Kylie, and because Clement was just kind of like that, not saying everything he could. Leaving one in the chamber.

"Aww," said Wayne, jerking his thumb over his shoulder in the general direction of the outside world. "Some rascal parked his rig in the loading zone. This was just easier. Say, how's Quinn? Haven't seen him much since... well since he got back."

Clement smiled to himself a little deep inside where Wayne couldn't see. In hoping to change the uncomfortable subject of breaking the mall rules, Wayne had leapt headlong into the equally uncomfortable subject of young Quinn. *He should'a taken a second to think that one through*, Clement thought to himself but didn't say.

"Oh. 'Bout as good as can be expected."

Clement could see that Wayne now wanted desperately to change the subject back to the pillar of wine cases he had loaded in through the wrong door, but that he could not so quickly abandon his interest in Quinn's well-being.

"He's gotta job now. So that's good," said Clement.

"Job huh? That is good. Where's he workin'?"

Clement nodded his head in the same direction as the man in the baseball hat carrying the six-pack had gone, way past *The Book Nook*.

"Oh, down in F-Block at *The Shutter Shack*. Sellin' cameras."

"No kiddin?" Wayne was bad at concealing his surprise. "How'd he get that gig? You pulled some strings, didn't you Clem?"

"Nancy Havemeister needed some help. That's all. You should go see him. No one in there but him most the time."

"I will," Wayne lied. "I will. Soon as I get two minutes to rub together. The old man never lets up. But you tell Quinn I said hey. Glad he's back."

Clement gave the tower of wine another kick and gave Wayne a meaningful, over-the-rim-of-his glasses look – even though he was not wearing glasses – that meant *get the alcohol the hell out of the mall*. When he saw that Wayne got the message, he waved casually and was off.

"Tell Joe I said h'lo," he said.

He walked over to *The Book Nook* and stuck his head in looking for the man in the baseball hat. He was chatting up Calista May, who was behind the counter laughing in that way of hers, kind of a snorting sound from behind her hand that she used to keep people from seeing her teeth, which were probably worth hiding. The six-pack was on the counter.

"No alcohol in the mall, son," said Clement.

The man broke off from Calista and looked over at the door towards Clement.

"Huh?" he said. "They're not even open."

"No alcohol in the mall."

"I *purchased* them in the mall. Who are you, anyway?"

"Mall security. Not gonna tell you a third time. Glad you're feelin' better Calista."

Clement moved on.

He called it *walking the beat,* and it was what he liked most about the job. His office, the mall security center, was a tenebrous cave that glowed a sickly glaucous green from the three video surveillance monitors that jutted out from the wall above his desk. If ever he wanted to, Clement could sit in his chair and cover every square inch of the premises, as well as the east and south parking lots and the back loading bays. Every place but the restrooms and the interiors of each store, although most of the common area cameras had the capacity to capture and magnify most of the retail spaces.

But sitting in a squeaky chair in a dark, stale, windowless room looking at a tv screen was not Clement's idea of a good life. He liked to walk. He liked to see people and talk to them. He liked looking people in the eyes, which was the only way to tell what they're up to. Windows to the soul and all of that. And if security was the goal, well then there was nothing better than walking the beat. And Clement Merriwether was no stranger to walking the beat. Inside or outside. Not just seeing, but being seen.

Of course, if he were really serious about being seen as a way to deter mischief, then he would have worn his uniform. Without the uniform – unless you worked at the mall and knew who he was – then Clement may just as well have been another anonymous shopper, just another tag-along husband pretending to look at things in the windows but actually looking at the women half his age while the wife was busy maxing out the credit card in the *Cozy Kitchen* or the *Yarn Barn.*

No question; the uniform would have made the real difference. It was a starchy, blue and black get-up that Clement hated and had only ever worn three or four times in the eleven years he had had the job. He used to think that his police uniform had been unbearable. After that, he had complained to whoever would listen about his Department of Corrections uniform, almost envying the inmates for their loose, pajama-like attire and their slip-on shoes.

But as bad as those uniforms had been, the security uniform Clement had inherited from Henry Lancaster, the previous Security

Director, was worse. Almost like a polyester straightjacket that smelled like formaldehyde and burnt plastic and that chaffed the tender skin down his sides and under his arms and along his collarbone. It made all of his old uniforms seem like hotel bathrobes.

So *walking the beat* was mainly about security, but not enough so as to require that he endure the torture of the uniform. The real question was whether he would still choose to walk the beat if he had to wear the uniform, or whether he would, instead, choose to patrol the premises electronically from the confines of the security office. If the owner of the Summerfield Mall ever decided that his security director had to make his rounds in uniform, then he would probably not last much longer in the job.

Of course, that was a fairly ridiculous hypothetical since Diamond Pete lived in another state most of the year and was rarely around. Most of his contact with Diamond Pete (so named for the double studs in each ear) was by telephone or email. And whenever they had met face-to-face, Diamond Pete had never really seemed to care much about how Clement chose to dress himself as long as he did his job and kept the peace and didn't bother him about any employee overtime.

Clement passed from blue into yellow, crossing the imaginary divide between *Denim Denizens*, which according to the large maps encased in glass at each entrance, was the last store in *Zone C*, and *Gadgetopia*, which was the first store in *Zone D*. Although Clement thought of them as *blocks*, not zones. Walking a beat was something one did back and forth across a series of blocks, from *A Block* to *F Block* and back again. To Clement the term "zones" was really a child of science, not law enforcement, denoting ecological sameness or climatological continuity. It was really a weather term.

He knocked his knuckles on the entrance to *Gadgetopia*. Darryl Smoots looked up from the inverted helicopter cradled in his hands like an injured bird.

"Hey Clem," Darryl called out in his high breaking voice, attempting a wave only to drop a battery. Clement raised a hand and kept on moving.

When he finally reached F-Block, Clement made a slow beeline for the two men on tall yellow ladders. Diamond Pete, in all of his absentee landlord wisdom, had waited until the Tuesday before the annual *Summerfield Mall Swap-n-Shop* to finally upgrade the fire suppression system.

Fire suppression should not have been Clement's problem, except that Pete had called him and told him that since his people could not always be on site, he needed Clement to keep an eye on the progress. *Keep the pressure on*, is what he had said, referring not to the water pressure which would actually have to be turned off periodically, but to the pressure on the system installers who in Diamond Pete's estimation liked to drag the work out so as to pad the bill.

Cost concerns aside, the upgrade was a big job and the fire suppression technicians would need to stay focused in order to finish by Friday. Friday evening the *Swap-n-Shop* vendors would be setting up their kiosks in the halls and there would be no room at all for ladders. And by ten o'clock Saturday morning, and for the duration of the weekend, the entire Summerfield Mall would be so full of people that there would be no room for fire suppression technicians, with or without ladders. The system would need to be fully pressurized, back on line and ready to go.

Clement stood between the two ladders with his hands on his hips looking up at the two headless men. Everything above their armpits was inserted up through two dark square holes in the drop ceiling, as if they were reaching up into a thick bank of cloud.

Clement lowered his head, waiting. Looking through one of the ladders, he glanced over at *The Shutter Shack*. Quinn was behind the counter, looking blankly out into the mall.

It was a familiar, stuporous stare. The guards back in *The Alley* called it *the glaze*.

As in, *Rocky's got the glaze this morning.*

As in, *Digger be glazin' so he won't be no trouble.*

It was the way people looked when they were watching time itself, like the seconds and minutes and hours were walking around doing things out in the free world and all a man could do was watch them with a kind of forlorn envy.

Clement nodded and raised a hand. If there was any recognition in his son's face, any effort to return the greeting with a smile or a wink, Clement told himself that he was too far away to see it.

———

Quinn watched his father talking up to the men on the ladders, using the hands at the ends of his long arms to push his words up through the ceiling.

Like he was shouting up to God. Again.

As though that had ever done any good.

Quinn could count on Clement to check in on him at least two or three times a day. He tried not to be obvious about it. He rarely actually came into the store. But he always looked in. Always waved in that way of his.

I'm here. I'm watching. Don't disappoint.

Quinn did not know what kind of trouble his father thought was most likely. Or what kind of trouble he thought he might be able to prevent by walking past the store.

Not that it mattered. He knew his father had every reason to be suspicious and Quinn could not blame him for his worry or his vigilance.

It was enough at least to make him feel self-conscious about his idle, unproductive pose behind the counter and staring out at the shoppers trickling past the store. He stood up from his stool and busied himself unpacking the last shipment of filters, lenses and tripods and logging each new item of inventory into the computer just as Nancy Havemeister had instructed. Then he hole-punched the packing slip and put it in the corresponding wholesaler notebook in the back room above Nancy's desk. He threw the packing material in the trash and flattened out the box beneath his feet and put it in the recycle bin. When he was done with all of that, he unlocked the counter display cases where he made room for the new lenses. He put the filters on the front shelving and opened up the new tripods along the back wall near the camera bags.

All of that consumed roughly eight minutes.

Quinn sat back down on the stool and watched the people walking back and forth in front of the store. He watched them like a cat might watch fish from the bank of a stream.

No. Not a cat. A cat would have had some natural interest. A cat would at least have been entertained by the delicious potential of it all. So not at all like a cat with its scheming tail and quick attention. Much more like an old dog watching the fish. Or a horse.

One of the fish swam into the store swinging a bag of something from *Chocolate Dreams*. He had a star-shaped mole at the corner of his left eye. He circled the center display case, lingering over the new Olympus SLR's, and then swam back out. The mole had looked at Quinn but said nothing.

Quinn should have engaged the man. Should have actually spoken his greeting rather than simply nodding his head. Should have offered to take one of the cameras out of the case for him to hold and to imagine the substantiality of ownership.

But he hadn't the energy for that sort of engagement. And it would have been useless anyway. There would have been no sale to the man and the mole. They were in a chocolate frame of mind, not a camera frame of mind.

Still, Nancy would have wanted him to engage. To at least try. Maybe the next time the man and the mole were in the mall they would be in a camera frame of mind. Quinn might have had a chance to prime the pump. He should have engaged.

It was good of Nancy to give him the job. Good of her to take a chance on him. Cameras were expensive and easy to fence. Nancy knew that better than most. He may have been Clement Merriwether's son, but he was still a felon. And a thief, no less. She had really stuck her neck out.

Quinn did not know Nancy except through his father. That, and Nancy had been a good friend of his mother. In fact the first time he and Nancy Havemeister had spoken two words to each other was at the funeral. Back when his voice was just beginning to break and words did not come easy. Nancy's two words had been *I'm sorry*. Quinn's two words had been *thank you*.

Fifteen years later he had recycled those words when Nancy called the house a few days after his release, offering him the job for which he had never applied.

Thank you, he had said. *You're welcome*, Nancy had said.

And the next three months had passed one second at a time, all seven or eight odd million of them, cued up and shuffling forward in their quiet, standard issue laceless shoes like they were waiting their turn to drink out of the same rusty fountain.

But Quinn was used to time mocking him like that. He was in no position to complain.

Resigned, he stood up and walked out to the front window and turned on the video camera and uncapped the lens and then reached his finger up under the tripod mount and switched on the slewing servo. He unhooked the remote control and walked back around the counter and turned on the remote monitor. The mall outside *The Shutter Shack* windows glowed to life in full digital, high-definition color.

Quinn mashed a button with his thumb and the camera slew right. On the monitor, the mostly empty food court slid into view. The sprinkler techs were busy repositioning their ladders. He panned a little further to the right over to the *Hotdog Hut*. Donna Cole was busy cleaning out the bun warmer. He zoomed in until her long, lean face filled the monitor, her brown over-starched hair pillowing off the screen on either side. She had a smudge of mustard on her cheek.

Quinn zoomed back out. He spotted a woman in a white halter and a pinkish skirt carrying a bag from *Flouncy's*. He zoomed in again, tracking her out of the food court and into the hallway. For all of the feminine frivolity that she had just purchased and was carrying home with her, she wore a somber, scowling expression. Quinn imagined that maybe the pink tissue-wrapped enticement in the bag was a gift for someone she hated, her husband's suspiciously attentive secretary, and that the woman's only consolation was that she had deliberately purchased it, whatever it was, in a size that was a little too small.

He stopped slewing and let her walk out of the frame as she approached. He looked up as the woman passed by the windows. She looked in at him briefly and Quinn nodded a greeting, which she ignored.

It was an obnoxious way to pass the time. He knew this. His mother would have been ashamed. If it was true that the dead continued to monitor the living, then his mother *is* ashamed. Present tense. Full stop. Nothing conditional about it. She *is* ashamed to witness what she *is* witnessing. Although if the dead really did spend their afterlife time secretly monitoring the living, then Quinn felt something slightly hypocritical in the judgment.

Nevertheless, it was a slightly creepy and intrusive way to pass the time and Quinn did not need to imagine his mother's reaction in order to feel bad about it. *He* was ashamed. He tried to wait until as late in the day as possible before resorting to such life-saving distractions. But now, after three months, he found himself turning to the meager sustenance of recreational surveillance as early as 10:30 in the morning. He was as ashamed as the starving beggar who steals another man's bread.

Another woman stepped into the frame of the monitor, moving in a slow saunter. Quinn did a double take. He pushed the button and the camera kept pace.

He recognized her. It took him a second. He was not used to the casual clothes. Or the purse, like a black leather clam in a swing, hanging from her shoulder. And the background was certainly different. And she was in profile, which was probably the biggest difference. This time she was not actually looking *at* him.

Of course, she had *never* actually been looking at *him*, day after day, week after week, month after month. It had only felt that way. She had not actually had any idea that he was there watching her, just like she had no idea that he was watching her now.

But there was no doubt about it. It *was* her alright.

The weather girl.

426

The impulse of recognition, freighted as it was with the irrational loathing that he held for her, brought Quinn's thumb into contact with the record button. He pushed it. A red dot flashed three times on the monitor.

He zoomed in on her face, looking for that old self-satisfied sanctimony in her eyes. How many times had he wanted to smash those accusing eyes? To throw something heavy at those eyes? How many times had he tried to mute that piercing voice and its utterly irrelevant words?

The weather girl stopped and disappeared. Quinn had to zoom out and reverse the slew direction to find her again. She was bending over the glass display case in front of *Glitterati's* looking at bangles. The owner of the store – a man named Fred Kunch whose swayback posture and near obsession with oversized earth-toned cardigans made him about as *glittery* as a shitake mushroom – was in the back corner of the store trying to open a box of something for a disheveled red-headed woman. She was attached at the wrist to a bouncing, writhing child. The right side of her body jerked rhythmically earthward.

The weather girl languidly spun a countertop jewelry carousel with the tip of a finger. She opened a plexiglass panel, slipped a finger inside a gold metal watchband and lifted it off the peg. She looked at the watch face, holding it in both hands and frowned, as if she were looking at her own reflection in a mirror and not particularly liking what she saw.

Her purse slipped off her shoulder and down into the crook of her elbow. She dropped the watch into the open maw of the purse and then pulled the bag back up onto her shoulder. With the other hand, she closed the panel and resumed turning the jewelry carousel, fingering the baubles. Then, with that insufferably pleasant expression with which she so often lied to him, the weather girl turned her back to Quinn's disbelieving eyes and sauntered out of the frame.

———

The last place Quinn had worked was at the *Qwicky Pawn* on North Front Street near the lumberyard. Before that, he had been the Assistant

Produce Manager at the *Pay-n-Go Grocery Stop*, where he worked under the thumb of Edna Cornwallis, a woman almost twice his age and half his maturity. Edna had made it clear that she wanted a man, not an assistant, and she spent the better part of three years trying to show Quinn the difference. For not taking the lesson, Edna tended to punish him by imagining and then itemizing all of his shortcomings on the quarterly installments of his annual performance reviews. It was clear to Quinn that pay raises and promotions would only come at a price.

Not clear *eventually;* but clear almost instantly after his orientation. Almost before the dramatically demonstrative lesson in distinguishing between cucumbers and zucchini had reached its denouement.

And yet he had hung in there.

That he had endured the job for so long under those conditions without looking for some other job was as much a testament to Quinn's conflict aversion as to his antipathy to change if indeed there is any practical difference between those things.

For as consistently degrading as the job had been, Quinn had still managed to leave on something of a high note, telling Edna where she could stick her most recent disciplinary notice, dropping his green apron on the floor, and walking out on her in the middle of his shift. He had turned for one last look at her just in time to see the ball of iceberg lettuce Edna had thrown at the back of his head. He had caught it casually, with one hand, as if it were a softball in a park, and sent it hurtling back across the receiving bay and into the back of the truck, where it had connected squarely with Edna's stupefied face, detonating in cold, green shards of cellulose and sending her sprawling back into an open crate of tomatoes. It was, he would later admit to himself in a kind of reluctant pride, the single greatest triumph of his young life. It had taken him three years to do it, but *that* was how you put an end to a bad situation and got the last word.

The job at the *Qwicky Pawn* had only been to tide him over until he could find something better. Something that held a more promising opportunity for advancement. That, anyway, was how he explained the decision to himself. The truth was that Quinn was lost. Still lost. The truth was that for all of the satisfying decisiveness of the iceberg lettuce resignation, he had no idea what he was doing with his life and the *Qwicky Pawn*, like the *Pay-n-Go Grocery Stop* before it, was but a chunk of driftwood floating in an empty sea. He had seized upon it instantly, with all the desperation of a drowning man.

The gnawing truth of it was that his father had been right. Dropping out of high school was probably the worst thing he ever could have done. If nothing else, high school was constructive confinement. Even if he never actually learned anything, it would have spared him the hazards of personal freedom. At the very least it would have corralled him through a pre-structured life, moving him lock step into Summerfield Community College or some vocational training program and then into suitable employment, each year handing off securely to the next like a chain of fire fighters handing a limp, gasping body over burning obstructions and out the window and down the ladder to a place out onto an open lawn where it can breathe.

His father had done the most he was capable of doing, which was not, objectively speaking, very much. Anger had been the only emotion available to Clement in those days. Rage was his only tool and his only sustenance. It was rage that got him up in the mornings. Rage that made the funeral arrangements for Christy and that forgot to call *The Party Palace* to cancel the birthday clown. Rage that for months sat vigil at Carol's bedside, still in his uniform, every night, after every shift, fondling the black shard of Detroit iron the surgeons had extracted from her brain, until she finally gave up and slipped out of her coma. Rage that testified at the trial. Rage that got him drunk and that got him fired from the police force and that got him a job working ten-hour shifts guarding inmates locked up in *The Alley*. Rage that got him the reputation as the meanest screw in the joint.

And it had also been Clement's rage that had taken charge of young Quinn who, choking blind in the acrid smoke of his own life, was suddenly unwilling to sit at a desk and stare at a chalkboard and solve for X, day after day after day.

In the aftermath of it all, Quinn and Clement had become enemies of a sort. Each saw in the other the ruin of hope and they each banished from their lives what they could not comprehend. Clement's way was to fly into drunken tirades and to pretend to draw boundaries and issue edicts about what it meant to live under *his roof.* Quinn's way was to turn into stone and sink to murky, unreachable depths, where no teacher or guidance counselor or strip mall psychologist or father could find him.

So, yes, his father had certainly been right about dropping out of school. But, in Quinn's defense, his father had been right from a million light years away. The truth is simply unrecognizable at that distance.

The *Qwicky Pawn* on North Front Street was the original *Qwicky Pawn* that had, over the past thirty years, bloomed into a mini-empire of six *Qwicky Pawn* storefronts scattered throughout the county. The *Qwicky Pawn* king was Lonnie Mopes, a one-armed veteran generally known as *Mr. Itch* or *King Itch* or simply *Itch,* all nominally for the thing he could no longer scratch, but the moniker could just as easily have represented his professional devotion to impulse. The pawn business had been successful enough for Mr. Itch to retire from the nine-to-five grind and to help finance the ventures of his friends, such as *Blue Reels Video* and a strip club on Springfield Road called *Shocks & Struts.* Itch eventually purchased controlling interests in both businesses and devoted his time to counting his money, making spot inspections and sampling the goods.

Quinn's job at the North Front Street *Qwicky Pawn* was as part of a three-man crew that, in shifts of two, made sales, kept rigorous track of inventory, discounted sentimental value, and loaned money on the back of heartache. The store manager was Itch's cousin Mel, a mephitic fat man with a high voice, a quick temper and a deviated septum that kept his mouth dangling open on its hinge when he was not actually thinking about it. Which was almost always. The North Front Street *Qwicky Pawn* training program was for Mel to yell at you and hit you on the arm until you got it right. The health plan consisted of a promise to fire you if you ever called in sick.

Mel was not without a sense of humor. Particularly when he and Roddy P got going. Quinn never did know what the 'P' stood for, or even whether 'P' was Roddy's last initial or middle initial or just part of a nickname. All he knew was that Roddy P had been working at the *Qwicky*

Pawn even longer than Mel and that he was dumber than a bag of rocks. He wore a mustache that looked like something with a hundred legs had crawled up under the shade of his nose to get out of the sun and died there, sprawling out over the top of his upper lip. Roddy P liked to stroke the dead thing with his lower lip whenever he needed the concentration required of deep thought. He had thin brown hair and two plaid shirts to his name that he alternated every two or three days, one red on black and the other black on red.

Quinn and Roddy P worked adjoining shifts, but Roddy P always liked to hang around chewing the fat with Mel while Quinn tried to busy himself with whatever needed to be done.

"Hey, Roddy P," Mel would say with mocking concern from across the store, sitting down on his stool behind the counter like a glacial slab calving into a fiord, "You seen that Rolex we got yesterday?"

"Not since Junior had it I ain't," Roddy P would reply, referring to Quinn by their affectionate name for him. "You thinking Junior pocketed that watch, boss?"

"Pocketed? Junior steal from me? Better not. He dumb but not *that* dumb."

"King Itch gonna get that boy, Boss."

"Roddy P, I'm thinking Junior's got that Rolex puppy wrapped around his little dingly-dang."

"Bet he checks the time every two minutes or so, don'cha think, Boss?"

"Bet so, Roddy P. Bet he's th'only one give that little pecker of his the time a day."

They'd laugh across the store at each other, sometimes pulling the customers in on the joke if there were any around. If he were within striking distance, Mel would give Quinn a punch in the arm, ostensibly to show that it was all in good fun and to take away any basis for objection Quinn might otherwise have had.

But Quinn did not usually object. He took it. He put his head to his work or helped the next customer and let it pass, seizing upon the next comment from either of them that was about business or the weather or at least not intended to get a rise out of him. It was a paycheck. It was a place to go. Although Mel and Roddy P quickly put Edna at the *Pay-n-Go Grocery Stop* in a whole new light.

Not that he would have ever taken back the iceberg lettuce exit. But still.

Things at the *Qwicky Pawn* started to take on a serious edge when Roddy P learned that Quinn's father used to be a prison guard upstate. It had been Quinn's fault for not thinking. He knew Roddy P had done a stretch for assault and that he had friends cooped up in Granite Alley, or just *The Alley*, which is what they called the Summerfield County Prison up in Granite Pass. It was not that Quinn had any particular reason to think that Roddy P knew his father, but it clearly would have been prudent to let the connection go undiscovered.

One day Mel had come in uncharacteristically somber, explaining that his father had died of heart complications over the weekend. That disclosure had lead to a surprisingly sincere exchange of information about fathers and how they tend to turn into sons-a-bitches but how you love them anyway and when they finally go, man-o-Nelly how it hurts like a mutherfucker. Roddy P's old man had been killed in a knife fight and he surely had it coming but somehow it still wasn't right. And Junior? His old man was just like the other sons-a-bitches only he was still alive and kickin'. Where's he at now? What's he do?

And so out it came. Quinn could see Roddy P flinch at the revelation and then he went quiet as his lower lip stroked the dead thing beneath his nose and his tiny brain turned over the cards in a game of Concentration, trying to match the name Merriwether with a memory.

"You okay there, Roddy P?" Mel asked.

"Peaches, Boss," Roddy P mumbled. "I'm fuckin' peaches."

"*Peaches?* Who dat, Roddy P? Dat what you call Junior's momma?"

Mel and Roddy P had laughed uproariously at that, both of them trying to dissipate the stench of sincerity in the air. But even as his heart convulsed and collapsed at the reference to his mother, young Quinn could detect a harder edge to Roddy P's braying that had never been there before. He should have resigned right then.

But he did not resign. It took Roddy P's concerted campaign to drive him out, to pry his fingers one-by-one off the piece of driftwood that was the *Qwicky Pawn* before he resolved to once again confront the open empty sea.

The campaign started with simply an intensification of what had gone before. The ribbing was meaner and more personal. Quinn's mother was a favorite and recurring subject. And there was a reluctance to let the banter segue into anything else. On occasion even Mel had heard enough and seemed on the verge of taking Quinn's side.

"Now Roddy P let's give that mess a rest," said Mel. "Not like we can't say some nasty ass shit about you and yours."

Such remarks were always enough to temporarily stop the abuse but they only made the problem worse. Roddy P was back soon enough and worse than ever.

The game changed when a customer came in one day to claim a diamond ring. He was a good week past the deadline. *Qwicky Pawn* had the right to sell the ring and the man went away disappointed. All of that had happened in the hour before Quinn showed up for work. When Quinn walked in the door, he saw that Roddy P and Mel were all business. They wanted to know what he knew about the ring that the records showed was still in inventory and had never actually been sold but could not be found. They had looked everywhere. According to the sheet – Roddy P waved the clipboard in the air like a flag – Quinn had been the one to accept the pawn.

Quinn remembered the transaction. He remembered putting the ring in the safe. And that was all he remembered.

"You steal from King Itch he tear your fuckin' heart out with his one good hand," said Mel in all seriousness. "And I'll hold you down so he can do it."

Quinn had protested. Roddy P had then, after a measured silence between them, generously offered up Quinn's incompetence rather than venality as an explanation. Mel finally accepted that the ring had been miscatalogued and that it was probably tucked into an envelope corresponding to some other pawn. Hopefully it would turn up in the course of things as the pawns came due. Mel had called the managers of the other *Qwicky Pawn* stores and told them to keep an eye out for it since sometimes the stores redistributed the inventory.

The next thing to go missing was a twenty-two caliber, semi-automatic, Bernadelli P-90 pistol. The customer had not come to reclaim it and was not likely to. It had been sitting in the display case next to the Smith and Wesson Sigma that Mel always went on about and suddenly it was gone.

Roddy P brought it to Mel's attention in such a way as to suggest that Mel had taken it out to shoot squirrels as target practice, which Mel and Roddy P had been known to do from time to time with guns that came in that they wanted to try out. But Mel had not seen the Bernadelli. He stood up from his stool and huffed his way across the store to look in the display case and verify its absence just in case Roddy P was pulling his leg or had gone crazy.

Mel and Roddy P had both come down on Quinn like a couple of grand inquisitors. Mel thundered down the hallway into the back where they all hung up their coats. He went through all of Quinn's jacket pockets but found nothing. Almost as an afterthought he went through Roddy P's pockets, apologizing over Roddy P's protests at having been so quickly demoted from co-grand inquisitor to suspect, and explaining that no one was above the law. He found that Roddy P's pockets were also empty. The heat then turned right back onto Quinn. Mel pushed him up against the back wall as much with the stench of his body as his girth.

"Junior… I find out that you been fucking with me…"

There was no need to finish the sentence.

Quinn did not know how to account for the missing merchandise. It was possible that Roddy P was behind it, either because he was a thief or because he wanted to set Quinn up, but these were simply theoretical possibilities that carried no greater weight than other less dramatic explanations. Quinn resented, therefore, that Mel was unwilling to consider the possibility of Quinn's culpability as a similarly theoretical explanation. Instead, with Roddy's encouragement, Mel seemed to have made up his mind and had reached the stage of simply looking for confirmation. Quinn knew that it was time to go, before he was framed or fired.

And as he reached that conclusion one Thursday night in his tiny apartment looking out across a dirt road to a dilapidated grain elevator and an empty, tornado-ravaged silo that looked like a broken urn, eating his mac and cheese and drinking his beer and watching the evening news, Quinn found himself wishing that he actually *had* taken the ring and the gun. It seemed somehow poetically just that the wrongly accused inherit the spoils of the crime never committed, or, better yet, that the wrongful accuser be condemned to a lifetime of believing he was right all along and yet impotent to do anything about it.

The news couple – the mom and dad of current events – had blathered and gushed about a grand opening of some sort. The mayor would be there with his giant scissors. Something was long over due. Something would be a challenge. Something was a shame. Time was a shame. Waiting was a shame. But someone was optimistic.

Quinn had been looking out his window at the old defunct grain elevator, and beyond that at an old abandoned, snake-infested ramshackle garage in a corral with a rusty iron gate in front of it that used to be some kind of a bus barn however many years ago, and beyond that at the silo-dotted fields of wheat and corn and alfalfa that were collecting the ash of evening and losing their color.

At the limit of his vision was the horizon, lined with thick, dark clouds that were lit dramatically from below. And the world had seemed suddenly to him like a giant, earthen conveyor, inching everything solemnly but inexorably forward until, row by row, thing by thing, it all dropped off the end of the conveyor and down into the gaping maw of the sun's inferno, the molten heart of the grand crematorium.

The news couple had handed things over to the sports guy who then had handed things over to the weather girl who had greeted Quinn in her relentlessly chirpy way in front of a video of people rafting the Cleatchee River. She was bouncing her little remote control in her hand like it was a pair of dice.

Quinn actually knew the weather girl from Cleatchee High, before he had dropped out. He didn't really *know* her, know her. He knew who she was. Clarissa Day – all of her friends called her Clare – had been one of those kids who had everything she ever wanted and for whom life was one endless day at the fair. Money to burn. Smart. Adorable. So intimately involved in the lives of every single popular person in the school, and so central to every single after-school resume-padding program, and so devoted to cheerleading the football team and honing her forehand and arranging birthday celebrations for coaches and teachers, that there simply could not have been enough hours in the day for her to actually attend classes.

She had never been part of Quinn's high school world and she was not someone he ever thought about. Except that one day, many years after he had left high school for the last time, she had showed up in his living room talking about the weather.

Clare's father was not a prison guard. Her father owned a network affiliate. How nice for the weather girl.

And so that was who she became to him, night after night as the sun set fire to the distant wheat. The weather girl.

The video of the rafters had dissolved and the weather girl had started pointing at maps of Summit County and Deer County and Fulton County, changing the pictures with a squeeze of her thumb into her palm, and going on and on about how some unseasonably warm weather would be taking over in the next twenty-four hours and lasting through the weekend.

So go out and get it while you can, she had chirped. *Now's your chance! Now's your chance.*

Those words had unlocked an idea. Quinn bounced the idea gently in the center of his brain just like the weather girl liked to bounce that remote in the palm of her hand.

Now's your chance.

It was time to leave the *Qwicky Pawn* behind. Suddenly, there had been no doubt about it. Time to leave Mel and Roddy P behind. Yes.

But he needed to leave Mel and Roddy P behind in the right way. Not with a ball of iceberg lettuce. But still. In a way that they would remember. The next day was Friday and the weekend would be sunny and warm. So said the weather girl. Now was his chance. He needed to go out and get it while he could.

So said the weather girl.

Quinn thought for a while more as he finished is beer and his mac and cheese and then he stood up, grabbed the keys to his truck and drove out to the mall.

The next day had certainly *not* started out unseasonably sunny and warm. It was, in fact, more of the same bone-chilling slop that had prevailed over the past ten days with a stiff and frigid breeze from the north, scooping down from out of the pass. Quinn was at the *Qwicky Pawn* in time to meet Mel climbing down out of his minivan in the back parking lot. He was pleased to see the white plastic bag he had expected dangling from Mel's sausage-like fingers.

As was always the case on the last Friday of every month, Mel opened up the store, put the white bag in the juice box and asked Quinn to put the juice box by the back door for King Itch. And, as always, Quinn did as he was told.

The juice box was what they called the black iron box with a lid and a clasp and a combination lock that Mel used to pay his dues to King Itch. All of the *Qwicky Pawns* had a juice box and all of the managers paid his dues, which were collected by one of Itch's runners on the last Friday of every month.

The practice had started as a way for Itch to efficiently pick up the receipts and to make bank deposits every other day. Itch's runner needed only to open the back door, unlock the juice box, collect the deposits and be on his way. As a way of currying favor, managers started putting little notes and gifts to their employer in with the cash deposits. Often these gifts were simply interesting pawns that the store managers thought Itch might like. A diamond studded cigarette lighter. A pistol with bone inlays in the grip. A sterling silver pornographic belt buckle.

Eventually, after the South Town *Qwicky Pawn* was robbed, Itch required the managers of all stores to make the cash deposits at the end of every day so there was rarely any need for Itch to send a runner. But the fealty ritual continued anyway, albeit on a monthly basis. What had started as a gratuitous gesture of loyalty had become a kind of obligatory tax or, as Mel called it, *dues.*

Mel liked to pay his dues in alcohol, specifically, a bottle of Itch's favorite bourbon, which was *Lazy Sunday Kentucky Reserve.* Every month on that last Friday, Mel would bring in a new bottle of *Lazy Sunday* in a white plastic *Willing Spirits Emporium* bag and would put it in the juice box and then ask either Quinn or Roddy P to move the juice box out by the back door. Itch's runner came whenever he came. Usually no one knew he had been by, kind of like the tooth fairy, except that instead of leaving a quarter on the pillow, Itch's runner left the open padlock on top of the empty juice box.

On the Friday in question, Mel put the *Willing Spirits* bag with the bottle of *Lazy Sunday* into the juice box, locked it, gave it a kick, and told Quinn to move the box out to the back door. Quinn did as he was told.

Later in the morning, Roddy P dropped by to chew the fat with Mel. The sad truth was that Roddy P did not have much of anything else in his life except hanging around the *Qwicky Pawn* chewing the fat with Mel. Not that Quinn's life was brimming with distractions, but he would have rather hit himself in the head with a hammer than spend ten unnecessary minutes at the *Qwicky Pawn.* And while Quinn would ordinarily have started swinging the hammer after only two unnecessary minutes in the company of Roddy P, he had been very glad for Roddy's P's visit that morning.

Mel started laying into Roddy P about the football game the previous night and about how much money Roddy P owed Mel because of the points he had so unwisely given. Roddy P was in the mood to argue the issue and the two had gone at it, back and forth across the empty store.

Quinn had not wasted the opportunity. He had gone to the back of the store and closed the bathroom door like he was inside doing his business. He had quietly unlocked the juice box and extracted the *Willing Spirits Emporium* bag with the bottle of *Lazy Sunday*. He had slipped out the back door and tossed the bag under the front seat of his truck, simultaneously extracting an identical *Willing Spirits Emporium* bag in which was a sixty-four ounce bottle of *Flakes Away Canine Dandruff Shampoo* he had purchased at the *Noah's Arc Pet Store*. Quinn had then quietly opened the back door, slipped the replacement bag into the juice box, and locked it. He had then returned to the bathroom, flushed the toilet and washed his hands just for the sound of it, and entered the main room of the store in time to hear Roddy P tell his story about football referees he knew that took money to make bad calls. Mel called Roddy P a cheap bastard and a sore loser and said he wanted his money by the end of next week or he would dock Roddy P's pay.

Quinn's plan had been to finish out his shift and to then leave like he would any other day. They would not expect him back until Monday and when he didn't show on Monday they would wait to confront him on Tuesday. By then, Mel would have gotten an earful from Itch. Mel would instantly suspect Roddy P since *Flakes Away Canine Dandruff Shampoo* was exactly the brand that Roddy P always had to buy for his on-again-off-again girlfriend's dog-washing business and for which he had been mightily teased by Mel on the one occasion that Roddy P had been foolish enough to bring a bottle of it into the store.

Roddy P! You a mangy dog? You got you some worms? Hey Roddy P, show Junior here how you can lick yourself clean.

When Quinn did not show on Tuesday, Mel and Roddy P would put two and two together and Mel would be ready to fire him on Wednesday. They would call him a million times on Thursday and on Friday or Saturday they might come looking for him, depending on how upset they were. But by that time he would be in California visiting his old friend Gary Kilgore and learning about the San Luis Obispo job market. Quinn had not seen Gary in at least five years and it was surely a stretch to say they were friends. But Gary was a good egg and if Quinn showed up with no place else to go Gary would put him up and show him around and maybe hook him up with some work.

That, anyway, had been the plan.

But what Quinn had planned and what fate had planned were not remotely the same. About twenty minutes before the end of Quinn's shift, King Itch himself came shuffling in through the back of the store. The *Willing Spirits Emporium* bag hung over his shoulder and down his back from a crook in his finger that was so big it looked like something that belonged on the end of a crane. The weight of the bag pulled his only hand down over his shoulder and raised his only elbow so that it pointed up and forward and made it look like he only had half an arm, which is not a look any other one-armed man could really afford.

But King Itch *could* afford it. Half an arm was more than enough for Itch. He could accomplish more in the world with the point of an elbow than Quinn could accomplish with four more sets of arms and a couple of extra legs. He was as thick and broad as Mel was fat and as Roddy P was mean and stupid. His head was a cinderblock covered in stringy black hair – mashed inside a dirty *Shocks & Struts* baseball hat – that made the shampoo gag less of a joke. His face was Indian-tan and pockmarked like a leather moon. He wore a black leather vest over a red button-down shirt that was open to the sternum and only half tucked into his jeans.

Itch had stopped abruptly in the back of the showroom with a stomp of his boot. Quinn had seen him first and had said nothing because his heart was suddenly scrambling up into his throat, looking for high ground.

Mel and Roddy P looked up from one of the Japanese girlie magazines that Roddy P brought in every so often. He held himself out as something of a connoisseur of foreign pornography and liked to show off the latest acquisitions from his various erotic subscriptions. He stored them all in boxes stuffed in the crawlspace of his girlfriend's home. It was hysterical, Roddy P thought, that Mavis knew nothing of the glossy exotic ocean over which she walked.

"Itch!" said Mel, dropping the magazine.

"Hey, Itch," said Roddy P.

King Itch let his jaundiced, bloodshot eyes roam the room like a couple of prison dogs, from Mel and Roddy P to Quinn and back again.

"Girls," he said.

"What brings you out this way, Boss?" asked Mel.

"Makin' the pick ups my damn self on account of the goddamned weather," said Itch disgustedly, like it was something Mel should already have known. "Delray skidded his ass into the goddamned river this morning. He in County General with a fucked-up hip."

Roddy P, who had his issues with Itch's driver, found this turn of events amusing and let loose an improvident smirk. The prison dogs were suddenly all over him.

"Somethin' funny over there Roddy P? P for pencil-dick? P for pig-fucker. You laughing at my misfortune?"

"No Boss," said Roddy P, looking down at the magazine. "I'm sorry."

"You goddamned right you're sorry. My black caddy's upside down in the goddamned water and Delray's high on Percoset. Delray's a sorry fuck but he's the only one I trust to do the job. Now I got to drive my own ass doin' these runs. I ought shove this boot of mine right up your ass. Not a good day to test my sense of humor, Roddy P."

"It is a mess out there," said Mel. "Rain, hail, rain, hail. Roads must be something wicked, Itch."

"They wicked alright," said King Itch.

"Sleet, not hail," corrected Roddy P.

"Shut up Roddy P," Mel shot back. "Ain't no difference."

"One more temp'ture degree and she's gonna start snowing," said Roddy P, ignoring Mel and addressing King Itch clearly looking to redeem himself in the conversation. Itch looked at him in a way that made it clear redemption would not come so easily. Then he looked sharply over at Quinn whose senses flooded with quiet terror.

"You mighty quiet, Junior," said Itch.

Quinn tried his best to shrug nonchalantly.

"Nothing to say, I guess," he said. "Sorry about your car."

"I hear we got somethin' in common, you and me."

"We do?"

"I hear tell your daddy's upstate workin' *The Alley*. That true?"

"Not any more," said Quinn, shifting uncomfortably. "Used to."

Itch nodded.

"My granddaddy – name of Mopes – used to warden up at the old Summerfield County Penn. You know the old place? The Castle?"

"Yeah. I've seen it."

"Guess law'n order's in our blood then, ain't it?"

"Yeah." Quinn tried to give a little laugh at the craziness of coincidence. "I guess so."

"I gave my left arm for law'n order in Southeast Asia." Itch looked down at the place his arm should be. Then he looked back at Quinn. "You ever give up anything, Junior?"

"No sir," Quinn shook his head trying not to look at his two good hands.

"Didn't think so. Still too young. Waitin' for your bowl of cherries. But it don't mean nothin' without the sacrifice, boy. And we all got to sacrifice."

Quinn had simply nodded, not knowing what else to say. Itch pointed at him with his elbow and then slowly pivoted so that it pointed in the direction of the back room.

"How 'bout you step in the back for a minute and let me have a private word with my manager and assistant manager. Don't you go nowhere."

Quinn blinked and swallowed.

"Sure," he said. "Gotta use the can anyway."

The three of them watched in silence as Quinn walked past King Itch and disappeared into the back. He stepped into the bathroom and closed the door and stared at himself in the mirror. The terror on his pale face scared him almost as much as King Itch carrying a liquor bag full of doggie dandruff shampoo. His heart was shaking the bars of its cage like there was something horrible inside the cage with it.

Quinn had turned on the water in the sink, turned on the fan, slipped out of the bathroom, and closed the door behind him as quickly and as quietly as he could. He had then moved swiftly out the back door for the parking lot.

Outside, he leapt over the parking guardrail and landed on a patch of water that was just a little too cold to stay wet. His feet flew out from beneath him and he fell hard on his tailbone and knocked the side of his head on the pavement. He cussed and pulled himself to his feet, holding his head. It was raining and sleeting at the same time and he could see his breath.

"What the fuck are you doin'?" Roddy P was leaning out the back door.

"I gotta go," said Quinn moving quickly again for his truck.

"Go where?"

Quinn climbed in and closed the door and started the old raggedy engine that sputtered and coughed to life. He looked over at the door. Roddy P was nowhere to be seen. He put the truck into reverse and began to pull away just as Roddy P, Mel and King Itch were coming out of the door. All three were yelling and Roddy P was running for his own vehicle.

Quinn hit the gas and even though he tried his best not to look at them he could not help but see Itch's one massive hand wrapped around the bottle of shampoo. As he pulled away, King Itch hurled the bottle and it thudded hard against the back window of the cab, bounced off the toolbox, and rolled around in the bed of the truck like a small log.

He turned off of North Front Street and made a beeline down Cleatchee Junction, a long straight road without much traffic that allowed him to drive while looking in the rear view mirror. A quarter of a mile behind him Roddy P's sky blue van had turned onto the road and started closing the distance. Quinn had felt a surge of panic that pushed down on the accelerator without asking permission.

As he approached the intersection of Cleatchee Junction and River Road, Quinn had noticed two policemen directing traffic around a large knot of people gathered around the old River Road Inn, an eyesore of a hotel that had not seen a guest in fifteen years. The building was festooned with red and yellow crepe paper streamers that had grown heavy with rain and sleet, and that had spent the day pulling free of their attachments and bleeding color down the dirty white siding.

The umbrella-speckled crowd, which was too large to be contained to the sidewalk, had spilled out into Cleatchee Junction on the far side of River Road. Not that Quinn could hear it at the time, but as he had seen on the news later that night, they had all been listening to Mayor Bloom explain how pleased he was to see so many people turn out for the grand opening of the Summerfield Homeless Shelter.

"It speaks well of the community," the Mayor had read from a scrap of paper as an assistant held a bullhorn to his mouth and a wilting newspaper over his head, "that it cares so much for its least privileged citizens."

Quinn was simply traveling too fast to negotiate the ninety-degree turn onto River Road. He could have easily made the turn had the weather girl's assurances of unseasonably warm weather been anywhere close to accurate. A quarter of a mile up River Road and he could have slipped into the labyrinthine inner passages of the new Riverdale subdivision and then slipped out the other side as Roddy P got lost in the maze like a mouse trying to sniff out the cheese.

But the weather girl had been terribly, terribly wrong.

Quinn's front tires lost all purchase as he turned the wheel. The truck slid sideways into the parked and flashing patrol car, caving in the back door. Before he had known what was happening, the officers that had been directing traffic were pulling him out onto the road trying to ascertain whether he was injured and whether he was impaired. The answer to both questions was negative.

Some of the people attending the grand opening of the shelter were craning their necks backward to see what the commotion was about as the mayor talked about drugs and poverty and the hope for a better tomorrow. A blue van skidded to a stop on the opposite side of the road.

Roddy P approached as Quinn was touching his nose and standing on one leg.

"This man is a thief," he said in a loud voice, pointing his finger in Quinn's face. "He's just robbed the Qwicky Pawn up the road. I know because I work there. I was just chasin' him."

Quinn had yelled back that Roddy P was a lunatic and the officers were quick to separate them. One of the policemen took Roddy P back across River Road and questioned him. The rain grew harder and turned to a steady pelting of sleet. Quinn watched Roddy P pointing at him from across the street, talking a mile a minute like he did whenever he was upset that Mel did not see things his way. The officer took notes on a little pad as the mayor counted backwards from three. The crowd cheered and applauded.

When the police searched the truck, they found a white plastic *Willing Spirits Emporium* bag under the passenger seat. Inside the bag was a bottle of *Lazy Sunday Kentucky Reserve* and a bank bag with upwards of twenty-five thousand dollars in it. In the bed of the pick-up, they found a sixty-four ounce bottle of *Flakes Away Canine Dandruff Shampoo* and a beat-up hand-me-down toolbox his father had given him. Inside the toolbox they found a diamond ring and a twenty-two-caliber semi-automatic, Bernadelli P-90 pistol.

The officer hade carefully lifted the gun out of the toolbox with a ballpoint pen through the finger guard, the brim of his hat whitening with snow.

——

Quinn looked at the video one more time. Clarissa Day, Clare, pinching a watch from *Glitterati's* with Fred Kunch not fifty feet away. Even in slow motion, he still could scarcely believe it. He reversed the video to the place where he had zoomed in on her face.

The weather girl.

How he had come to hate that face. Its smug perfection. And the voice that was inseparable from the face. That bouncy, chipper, *everything's coming up roses and they're all for me,* chirping night after night after night.

Unseasonably warm through the weekend! So go out and get it while you can! Now's your chance!

She had simply lied to the viewing public. She had lied to *him*. There had been no chance in hell of unseasonably warm weather on that fateful Friday, and she had known it. She had lied. Who knows why she had done it. Probably so that she could be the bearer of good news, even if fraudulently. Like the weather was something she created and could get credit for. If it actually *had* been unseasonably warm, she would have expected gratitude. Like she was some kind of superhero.

Thank you Weathergirl! Thank you for the sun!

Well, there had *not* been any sun. There had been rain and sleet and snow. *Fucking snow!* Had there been sun, as promised, King Itch's driver would never have skidded off into the Cleatchee River and King Itch would never had made the pick-up himself. Had there been sun, had there been unseasonably warm weather, as promised, he would have made that turn onto River Road without any problem. He would have left Roddy P behind in the intestinal folds of the Riverdale subdivision and he would now be working in some California juice bar serving smoothies to women in roller skates and bikinis. He would have friends and a life and a tan because it was always warm and sunny in California. He had seen the pictures.

Instead, Quinn had been hauled off in handcuffs in front of Roddy P and a mob of Summerfield do-gooders and thrown in jail where he had spent the first night of what would become eighteen consecutive months of nights behind bars. And on almost every one of those nights, at six o'clock and again at ten o'clock, Quinn was forced to either hear the weather girl's voice or see the weather girl's face, chirping down at him from some concrete corner of a concrete room about how swell the weather was going to be, outside in the world where he could no longer go. And in that perfect, smug look of hers she knew that Quinn had been forcibly separated from the weather. She knew that he had to take her word about the weather. And all of that was okay with her because, *tsk, tsk*, he deserved to be locked up.

Twice a night, every night, from her perch. *Tsk, tsk.*

446

He was not delusional. Quinn knew that the weather girl had not actually orchestrated his incarceration. *That* had been the product of unbelievably bad timing and the collective ill will of Roddy P, Mel and King Itch. And, if he was to be fair, it was an ill will that he had largely inspired with a bottle of dandruff shampoo for dogs.

Quinn had been convinced that the bank bag stuffed with money was a payoff to Itch from some nefarious bit of business into which he had dipped one of his five fingers. But Quinn's lawyer, who was the best lawyer that Clement Merriwether could buy for his son on the little bit he made as a shopping mall security guard, could not be inspired to make the case that Quinn had unknowingly taken the ill-gotten gains of a criminal enterprise. Quinn's lawyer had eventually persuaded him that between the loaded bank bag and Roddy P's frame-up in the tool-box, there was nothing to do but cut a deal. So he did.

Fortunately, as a first offender, the judge seemed to think there was some chance that Quinn might come out of this a better man and a responsible citizen. The proposed deal was for five years, two suspended. The judge had worked on the prosecution to cut it to three years, one suspended. He had served eighteen months up in *The Alley*, where they all still remembered Clement Merriwether.

So he was not delusional. The weather girl had not been *actually* responsible for all of that. But she sure seemed to take the credit.

Tsk, tsk.

And now, here she was, in full high-definition color, the Weather Girl, slipping a cheap watch into her purse and walking off without a care in the world. *Tsk, tsk, Weather Girl.*

Quinn downloaded the video to a computer flash drive and put it in his pocket. His father dropped by later in the day and gave a knock on the side of the door of *The Shutter Shack*.

"Doing okay in here?"

"Doing good, dad," said Quinn from behind the counter.

Clement gave a nod and a wave and walked slowly on past the windows to check on the progress of the fire suppression system installers who had relocated to the other side of the food court. That was the only halfway good thing that had come out of the prosecution, Quinn thought. It had been an excuse for he and his father to put the past aside. Clem wanted to help and Quinn needed every bit of it. For the first time in a long time, Quinn felt like a son and Clem felt like a father and that one part of it had felt pretty good.

At the end of the day, Quinn went home to his little apartment, which was in the same building as his old apartment only one floor higher and a hundred feet further to the west. He would have preferred to live somewhere else, just because the continuity of it all was so depressing. But it was still the best deal in town and he still liked that it was quiet and out of the way. And he still liked looking out over the fields in the evening, with a beer in his hand and his feet propped up on the windowsill, measuring his distance from the light burning on the horizon.

He turned on the news promptly at six o'clock and ate a turkey TV dinner in his lap, impatiently suffering everything that preceded the weather. After mom and dad explained the news and little Johnny went on about the big game, the weather girl appeared, bouncing her remote control in her palm. She looked at Quinn with that familiar, knowing glint in her eyes, like she had figured him out a long time ago and nothing about him had changed one little bit.

She was optimistic about an early spring. It would be here before he knew it. She pointed to a radar map on the screen behind her and the sleeve of her blouse slipped part way down her arm.

The *Glitterati's* watch was right there on her wrist, plain as day.

Quinn turned off the television in disgust, his heart blackening in his chest before he was done eating the little bit of peach cobbler that the fine people at the Feast-O-Kings Food Company had put in the triangular aluminum depression next to his turkey. He stood up and threw the rest of his dinner in the trash and sat down at the kitchen table with a sheet of paper and a pen. He thought to himself for a minute, then he wrote: *Nice watch. Hope no one tells the police. Would sure be weird to see the weather girl on the news.*

He looked up the address of the television studio and prepared an envelope with a phony return address and stamped it and put the note inside without sealing it. He sat and looked out the window for awhile, strangely disappointed at having missed the sun devouring another bit of the world. He went to bed and fumed more than he slept.

The next morning at work, Quinn used Nancy's computer to print out a still shot of the weather girl's fingers holding the watch over her open purse. On the back of the photo he wrote: *fingers sticky with an 80% chance of incarceration. High pressure and unseasonably warm temperatures likely for the foreseeable future.*

Quinn dropped the photo into the envelope, sealed it, and handed it to Charlie Tidwell just as he was coming in to give him a bundle of envelopes and catalogues for Nancy.

"Morning."

"Morning, Chuck," said Quinn.

"This it?" asked Charlie, waving the envelope between his fingers.

"That's it."

"Okay then."

And off he went.

Quinn spent the rest of the morning processing the mail and helping a customer pick out accessories as a gift for a friend. She had only an inkling of an idea of the camera her friend owned and so it had taken a lot of time and a lot of questions and a couple of cell phone calls to her husband who needed to check with someone else and call her back. At every opportunity, Quinn let his attention leave the conversation and indulge itself, imagining the weather girl's face when she received the envelope; opened the envelope; read the note; saw the photo; read the note again; scrutinized the photo; turned the photo over; read the back of the photo.

Such reverie carried him up to just after one o'clock when Ed Phillips came by. Ed was a former *Shutter Shack* employee who had left to sell photocopy machines. Since Ed had the freedom to set his own schedule, he was able to help Nancy out in a pinch and for most of Quinn's employment this meant dropping by for a couple of hours in the afternoon so that Quinn could go get some lunch. He was a gangly, clean-cut, squarish fellow with an odd sense of humor and a devotion to vintage science fiction comic books that Quinn simply could not understand.

Quinn had an impulse to tell Ed about what he had seen the day before at the *Glitterati's* counter but concluded in a split second change of heart that Ed would not understand the irony or the reason it made him so angry. Quinn was not even sure that *he* entirely understood these things and he was not in the mood to explain to Ed Phillips everything he would need to explain in order for the story to make sense.

So Quinn let it go. He left the store to Ed and walked across the food court to wait in line at the *Hotdog Hut*. Donna Cole was like a whirling dervish behind the counter, filling cups with soda and dropping baskets of frozen onion rings into the fryer and pulling hot dogs out off the warmer and ringing everything up on the register like she had ten sets of hands.

"Hey Quinn," she said when it was his turn. "You want the usual?"

"You pretty much only serve one thing, Donna."

"Oh, your right," she said smiling and knocking her forehead with the heel of her hand. "Silly me. I'll just get you that raspberry iced tea and the cup of broccoli soup."

Donna Cole was one of those women who knew how to smile and take a demurely playful tone as she focused her free-floating anger to a point and drilled it in through your forehead.

"Okay, okay," he said. "The usual."

"Thought so. You have your punch card, Sweetie?"

Quinn pulled out his wallet and extracted the stack of coupons and punch cards for half the businesses in the mall and dealt them out into a pile on the counter like he was a croupier at a Vegas Baccarat table.

"You forget it today? Lose track of your punch card? No hurry. Take your time. We'll all wait for you."

He made it through the entire stack without finding his *Hotdog Hut* punch card and had to go through the stack all over again. He found the card, which had somehow adhered itself to the back of his *Movie Madness* punch card, just as Donna was putting his kielbasa and his cup of sauerkraut and his basket of onion rings and his large Coke on his tray. He paid and thanked her and walked out to the middle of the food court beneath the potted ficus to eat his lunch.

The tall, yellow ladders were now well down the main hall, set up like a giant "M" stretching between *Denim Denizens* and *Gadgetopia*. The technicians were leaning on their elbows over the tops of the ladders like a couple of mountain climbers testing their knots and setting their spikes.

"Excuse me?"

Quinn turned and looked up towards the sound of the voice. The weather girl handed him his wallet.

"I think you forgot this over at the *Hotdog Hut*," she said pointing behind her.

Quinn stood abruptly, jarring the tiny red table and upsetting his soda.

"Shit!" he said, dropping napkins over the spreading brown lake.

"You shouldn't cuss because it reflects poorly on your character."

The advice came from the young girl in the red glasses and coveralls holding the hand of the weather girl that was not holding his wallet.

"Sorry. Sorry," said Quinn, removing his food from the tray. "Damn."

"Damn is still a cuss word," said the girl.

"McKenzie," said the weather girl in a gently scolding tone.

Quinn turned to her and accepted his wallet.

"Thanks," he said, blushing. His heart rattled its cage. "It was really stupid of me…"

"Oh, goodness," she said in that familiar, chirpy voice and that broad sparkling smile. "Don't call it stupid. I do that sort of thing all the time. Last week I left my purse on the top of my car. Took McKenzie all the way out to the zoo before I realized it was missing. We pulled up next to a bus as we were turning into the parking lot and all of these people on the bus were pointing down at us. I couldn't tell what they were saying. I just waved back at them."

"I think zoos are sad," said McKenzie looking up at Quinn and scrunching her nose beneath her glasses. Her head was a mop of black curls. Quinn looked at her and cocked his head, seizing on any opportunity to look away from the weather girl.

"You do?"

"Yes because zoos are like prisons for all the animals but the animals didn't do anything wrong."

"But don't you think that zoos give the animals protection and food and shelter from the weather. And they get to watch all of the people going by."

"I wouldn't want to be cooped up in a tiny little cage watching people walk back and forth. That is very bad for self-esteem."

"It is? Do hippos even have self-esteem?"

"Everyone has self-esteem, silly bird," said McKenzie. "That's how we get up out of bed in the morning. 'Cause the esteem makes us. 'Cause the esteem is hot water in the air that floats you up."

"No, that's steam, Sweetie. That's different than esteem. Her father's a psychologist."

Quinn smiled, still looking down. He slipped his wallet into his back pocket. McKenzie ignored the correction.

"My daddy's birthday is coming and we're shopping and tomorrow I get to see *Hipporidiculous*." She pointed at a movie poster on the wall next to the *Hotdog Hut*. A large purple hippopotamus was hanging ten on a skateboard in front of a police car.

"Don't I know you?" he heard the weather girl ask. Quinn looked up at her. He feigned the sudden cloudburst of recognition.

"Hey... you're... you're the... you do the weather on..."

She smiled indulgently, waiting for it to pass.

"No. I mean, yes, that's me, but I think we went to high school together. Ridgeview? Wait, don't tell me." She closed her eyes and put her hand to her forehead. The stolen watch glittered at him from her wrist.

"Hey, mom?" McKenzie tugged at the arm.

"Wait a second, Honey. Clint. No. Quincy."

"Quinn," he said. "That's amazing. I'm terrible with faces and names. That was a long time ago."

"I think we sat together once at an assembly."

"No. Really?"

"Hey, mom?" McKenzie tugged.

"Yeah, yeah." Clare's face began to glow with memory. She reached out and touched him lightly on the chest with the tip of her finger. "In the gym. Top of the bleachers. You were wearing a blue t-shirt with like a… a Superman thing on it…"

"Superman represents our wish of invulnerability to disappointment. Hey mom?"

"…and you were… you had this pad of graph paper and you were making these paper airplanes and handing them out. And you just kept making them and you gave me one and then when Mr. Hanson finally came out to talk about… whatever… everyone threw the planes and there was like a dozen of these things whizzing out over the basketball court and everyone laughed. You don't remember that?"

It was one of those incarcerated memories. From the other side of the wall. He knew they were there, those times when he had been happy and normal. But he had stopped visiting. He had stopped longing for them. He had utterly forgotten them and they had forgotten him.

No. Not forgotten. Forsaken.

And now the weather girl had essentially busted one of those memories out, sailing it over the guard towers in a paper airplane.

"Yeah. That was me," he said, smiling at her and shaking his head with a kind of wonder. "God. I had forgotten all about that."

"Not me. I was the last person to throw and my plane hit him right in the face."

Quinn laughed as the memory circled. "That's right, that's right and then…"

"Oh my God. He looked right at me. I thought I was a goner."

"Wait, didn't I…"

"Yeah, you threw yourself in front of the bullet. You stood up and apologized and said you were trying to land it on top of his head not crash it into his cheek. Everyone cracked up. That was so funny. Even Mr. Hanson was laughing. He thought it was you. You saved me. I was so impressed."

"Well," Quinn felt himself blush a little, "the plane was my stupid idea in the first place."

"I'm Clare," she said, extending her hand. "Clare Day. But I guess you already knew that."

"Quinn Merriwether," he said. "But apparently *you* already knew *that.*"

They both laughed, shaking hands. Her face was not the same face as the one on the television. Everything of her personality was in that missing dimension. She smelled like sunlight. McKenzie reached up and grabbed his wrist and shook it back and forth.

"My name is McKenzie Day-Weaver but I suppose you already knew that. Did you also already know that I have to use the potty also known as the facilities?"

"Oh, Mac." Clare laughed and rolled her eyes and finally let go of his hand. "It was so great running into you Quinn. What a coincidence, huh?" She laughed.

"And you saved my wallet. Most people would have just kept it," he said without thinking.

"No. Most people are honest I think."

"Well, I really owe you one anyway," he said, again without thinking. McKenzie was pulling her mother backwards through the tables towards the restrooms.

"Maybe we'll bump into each other again and we can catch up. You out here often?"

Quinn jerked his thumb over his shoulder.

"Shutter Shack. Five days a week." He gave a casual wave. "Bye Little Mac who doesn't like zoos."

"Bye Superman who won't stop talking to my mom."

Quinn watched them disappear down the hallway to the restrooms and then sat back down and tried to salvage what he could of his lunch as he obsessed over the encounter.

Had she not actually been wearing the stolen watch, he could have convinced himself that he was dealing with twins; one a thieving and annoyingly incompetent meteorologist and one... *what*... one who was *not* those things. One who remembered him after all of these years; who had been glad to see him and who had fond memories of the person he used to be.

He thought about the envelope he had handed to Chuck Tidwell that morning and the note and the photo inside the envelope and he fleetingly considered running through the mall to see if he could find Chuck and ask him for the envelope back. But he knew it was far too late for that. Chuck was long gone and so was the envelope.

He could not help but doing what he had been doing all day long: imagining the weather girl's face when she received the envelope; opened the envelope; read the note; saw the photo; read the note again; scrutinized the photo; turned the photo over; read the back of the photo: *fingers sticky with an 80% chance of incarceration. High pressure and unseasonably warm temperatures likely for the foreseeable future.* Only this time, the face he imagined was not the weather girl's face, and her reactions did not make him feel like an avenger. This time it was Clare's face, and the reactions he imagined made him feel a little sick in the heart.

And that part he did not understand in the least.

Theft was theft was theft wasn't it? And being a cute and delightful thief did not mitigate the moral depravity of the act one little bit. If sending the note and photo to an incompetent meteorologist had been appropriate, why was it not just as appropriate to send the note and the photo to an attractive mall-crawling former classmate with a good memory? Quinn did not know the answer. Or, rather, he knew the answer he just did not know why he could not bring himself to *accept* the answer.

Could it have been that he liked her? Liked her because she was attractive and because she seemed to like him? Yes. That *was* possible. But the idea was so pathetic on so many levels – physiological, psychological, philosophical, moral – that he refused to entertain it. Was he that desperate to be liked? That he would instantly jettison his moral outrage for the sake of a brief touching of hands and a stupid little conversation? And if he was the kind of person for whom everything – even the fundamental questions of right and wrong, good and evil – turned on the issue of physical attraction, then what kind of person was he? And if everyone were like that, what kind of world would it be?

He slowly bucked himself back into believing he had done the right thing; the thing he could now not take back. He finished his food and then stood and carried his tray across the food court and carefully drained the lake of soda into the trash. He began walking but then stopped suddenly, forcing the man behind him to navigate around.

The thief had returned his wallet. Just what exactly did that mean?

He walked a little way down the hall, past the men on ladders, to the *Jumpin' Java* and bought a small coffee and a slice of pumpkin bread wrapped in cellophane. He walked around the mall for a few minutes – all the way to the *Airship Arcade* next to the movie theater – sipping his coffee and trying to distract his attention away from the memory of the feeling of Clare's hand in his own. It was an impossible task. He turned around and headed back to the *Shutter Shack.*

He had only been gone forty minutes, and the camera store was just about the last place he wanted to be, but he had to share the incredible weather girl coincidence with someone. He felt like if he kept it to himself another minute he might explode. Relief would not come any sooner or easier than Ed Phillips.

But then, halfway back to the store Quinn began to think more carefully about telling Ed that the weather girl had stolen a watch from *Glitterati's*. He knew that Ed Philips had an odd but lasting friendship with Fred Kunch. Ed's father, Gil, had served with Fred Kunch in Vietnam and had remained inseparable drinking companions and bowling partners until Gil's passing from lung cancer. Since then, Fred had withered from virtually all of his previous associations except his business, his sister, whom he purported to hate for her left-leaning political views, and Gil's son, little Eddie, now Ed, with whom he had bonded over a mutual interest in building replica models of World War II fighter aircraft. On any given weekend, whenever he was not selling jewelry, Fred could be found down at *The Hobby Horse* looking for new airplane kits, which he assembled in his basement, alone, listening to presidential biographies on tape. Every so often, Fred and Ed would bring their latest completed models to the mall to show each other and compare notes.

Quinn decided that maybe it was not a good idea to share the weather girl story with Ed after all. He would want to see the video. He

456

would want to show it to Fred Kunch. And Fred would go after her. Fred, whose only friend in the world might have been Ed Phillips, was famous for shooting his neighbor's dog for coming by his house and peeing on Fred's porch one too many times. There were also stories from the war and about his discharge from the service and about how he had treated his wife before she packed up their daughter and left him for good. Of course, the stories about Fred Kunch may or may not have been true. He was the kind of man about whom so little was actually known that the apocryphal was the only ready substitute.

Nevertheless, there was certainly no doubt about it in Quinn's mind. Fred *would* go after her for stealing.

And maybe she needed going after. Maybe she deserved it. That, after all, was why he had sent the note and the photo, wasn't it? Because she deserved it. She did.

But still.

When he walked into *The Shutter Shack*, Ed was behind the counter handing a customer a digital SLR. The customer was Clare Day.

"There he is, Mom," said McKenzie from beneath one of the display tripods. "Superman!"

Clare turned and gave him a small wave.

"Looking for a birthday present," she said. "McKenzie thought maybe a new camera."

"A good gift," said Quinn. "I've got this Ed."

Ed Phillips shrugged his narrow shoulders and went back to the stool by the register.

"Yes, but too expensive," said Clare. "Way too expensive. McKenzie doesn't think about the money."

"I think about money," McKenzie objected. "I think about money a lot. I'm thinking about it right now. And now. And now. And now."

"I thought we'd look anyway."

"And now. And now. And now."

"They're kind of pricey," said Quinn wincing.

"And now. And…"

"McKenzie."

"Money is not a substitute for love and attention, Mom. But you probably already knew that? Did you know that, Superman?"

"I did know that, yes," said Quinn.

He looked at Clare and they both laughed. She laughed with her eyes, he noticed. It was not something he had never noticed before. Not in watching her on a television suspended from the corner of a concrete room. And not in watching her on the little television sitting on the cloth-covered orange crate in the mostly bare apartment that was only slightly bigger than his cell in *The Alley*. He tried to remember whether he had *ever* seen her laugh on television. He was sure he had. They were always pretending to laugh at something, the television mom and dad and the sports brother and the weather sister, like they were sitting around the dinner table telling jokes as everyone else cupped their hands around their eyes and peered into the kitchen window at them.

So he was sure he had seen her laugh before. But he did not remember the eyes, their greenness, and how they seemed to pull the corners of her mouth up into laughter as if somehow instigating it.

He took her on a tour of the cameras and the less expensive photo accessories that might make for a good birthday gift. He was careful in handing her the cameras and the lenses and she was careful in receiving them, making sure that her hands – as if they were filled with helium – were right up beneath his when he released whatever he wanted her to hold.

"Mom." McKenzie was on the floor making a small fortress out of camera bags. "Can Superman come to the movie with us?"

Clare looked up at Quinn, handing back a telephoto. Then she looked over at her daughter.

"Mac, get off the floor. And put those back the way you found them. This is not a playroom."

"Can he?"

"I'm sure Superman has better things to do than to go see a two-hour cartoon."

"It's not a cartoon, Mom. Cartoons are on T.V. But *Hipporidiculous* is a whole movie."

"Just the same, I can't imagine that Superman would want to see *Hipporidiculous.*"

Clare laughed and shook her head, first at Quinn and then over at Ed Phillips, who was across the room by the register looking at Quinn with a dubious expression, which Quinn decided must have had something to do with everyone calling him Superman.

"Do you, Superman?" asked the girl pointing out into the hallway. "It's right down there and we're going tomorrow night 'cause mom has a five day vacation and daddy won't let me see movies and we have to go before I go back to his house. He says movies rot the brain but they don't really he just says that 'cause he likes books and newspapers. He says mom is spoiling me for the judge but I just like movies."

Clare sighed. Then she leaned in a little, so that their shoulders were almost touching, and spoke in a lower, not so chirpy voice.

"I'm going through a... thing."

"A thing?"

"A divorce."

"Ah."

"Ugly. You don't want to know."

"Okay."

"He has interim custody. I get her whenever he wants to take his girlfriend to the beach."

"Then I'd say camera equipment is too expensive. Maybe a t-shirt. Or a sock."

She gave a small, bitter laugh and touched his arm.

"I wish I had your sense of humor."

"Mom," said McKenzie in a voice that was tired and thirty years too old. "Janet's a fiancé. Not a girlfriend. And she's going to be a doctor someday. How many times do I have to tell you?"

Quinn and Clare both turned to look at McKenzie, across the store surrounded by camera bags. Had his face rotated even a little faster than hers, his chin might have brushed the high-arching bone of her cheek.

"I see Little Mac has big ears," said Quinn.

"I don't have big ears. Elephants have big ears. I have good hearing."

"Well, that's kind of what I…"

"And I have to have good hearing because everyone whispers. I call it ghost talking because it makes you feel invisible which is a tell-tell sign of adult-lessent depression and I don't want to get a depression because my nose will get all stuffy and I have my whole life ahead of me and I wont be adult-lessent for a long, long time. I'm just a kid trying to make it in a grown up world."

Quinn's mouth hung slightly open and he stared at the child in stupefaction. "Ouch," he said in a ghost-talking sort of way.

"We're sorry, Sweetie," said Clare. "You're right. No more whispers."

"So is he coming to *Hipporidiculous* or is Superman too afraid?"

———

The next day followed a sleepless night. Every time Quinn felt the world turning soft and slipping through the fingers of his attention he saw Clare's face and heard her voice and felt her breath on his cheek and the warmth of her hands under his, and all of that inevitably brought him fully awake again, re-inflating the world and amplifying all of its sounds.

Like the mechanic in the next room having another marathon session of grunts and moans with a woman Quinn had never seen but whose voice caused him to picture someone who refused to put down her cigarette and who flicked her ashes into a small glass that that swayed and bounced between the mechanic's shoulders.

Like the mutt a block away that wanted inside the empty house and the old windmill on the vacant lot where the gas station used to be, remembering the breeze in its fitful, rusted slumber. Like the dark air pushing through the wings of an owl and the moon in its harness of invisible creaking ropes, pulling the Earth on its axis towards another day.

The day passed in its slow stuporous sameness, only this time with an extra somnolence, like it was a rhino that had been darted and tranquilized and was looking for a patch of tall grasses in which to drop.

His conversations with the handful of customers that wandered into the store were excruciating, half-lidded exercises, as if each customer was a spotter who was there to grab the barbell of consciousness before it crushed his windpipe.

He finally began to perk up a little in the afternoon. Ed Phillips came by at one-thirty for an hour to read comic books behind the counter as Quinn slipped out for a hotdog and then a cup of coffee and a brisk walk to the North end of the mall and back. At three, Clement stopped by to apply the daily pressure to the men with ladders, who were high above a circle of orange cones arranged directly in front of *Glitterati's*. When he was done, he leaned in the doorway, knocking on the frame.

"Doing okay in here?"

"Doing good, Dad,"

"How 'bout dinner tonight? Couple of steaks. Game will be on."

"Oh. Thanks. But I've… I'm meeting someone tonight. For a movie."

Clement gave his slow nod with the pursed lips, which Quinn knew meant that his father didn't exactly believe him.

"Okay. Suit yourself. My steak will taste better than your movie."

"I'm sure it will. Next time."

Clement nodded and started to walk off and then leaned back into the doorway. He clunked the heel of his boot against the floor.

"What movie?" he asked.

"Death by Midnight," Quinn lied. He had no interest in suffering the look that surely would have followed his utterance of the word *Hipporidiculous*.

He walked the mall for the forty-five minutes after closing up *The Shutter Shack*. He stopped by *The Book Nook* and killed time picking up the latest best-sellers and pretending to read the back covers and then putting them back on the shelf and moving on. Unlike the earlier part of the day, he was now fully awake – too awake – like he had been pumped full of caffeine or was under the influence of a small electric current that darted around his brain, here and there and here again, like a bird looking for an open window.

He showed up at the theater twenty minutes early and sat in a chair in the middle of the atrium with his back to the ticket window and facing the three arteries of the mall, diverging off into the distance like rivers of fluorescent-lit tile. He was able to sit still for only six or seven minutes, after which he sprung up and walked over to the ticket window and purchased three tickets, two adults and one child. As he was returning to his chair, tickets in hand, he saw them.

"Superman!" shouted McKenzie. She was wearing jeans and a white shirt with purple suspenders. She scampered up and hugged him tightly around the waist.

"Hey Little Mac," he said, patting her on the head. "Hi Clare." He fanned two tickets in front of him.

"That was sweet of you," said Clare as she approached. "You didn't have to do that."

"Let's call it a finder's fee for the wallet."

Clare smiled in a way that was flat and perfunctory and that did not involve the eyes. She looked over her shoulder and then down at McKenzie and then up at Quinn, plucking the tickets from his fingers like a tissue from a box. Quinn noted her thin wrist, now bare of jewelry. Where a watch should have been were three thin parallel scars, the flesh between them like two frozen furrows in a winter field.

"Let's go on inside," she said and strode off towards the theater. McKenzie and Quinn looked at each other. McKenzie shrugged. She reached up and grabbed his wrist and pulled him forward.

They sat in the mostly empty theater eating popcorn and drinking sodas waiting for the lights to dim. McKenzie swung her feet and burbled with sound, nominating her favorite candy and colors and explaining the difference between the sexes.

"Boys have the edible complex and girls have the electrical complex."

"What does that mean, exactly?" asked Quinn.

"It means, exactly, that girls like their mommy but love their daddy and boys like their daddy but love their mommy."

"Oh. And why is that?"

"Because boys are afraid of losing their fellas and girls wish they had a fellas."

"A fellas?"

"That's a peepee, silly."

"Oh. Why do girls want a ... fellas?"

"So they can write dirty words in the snow."

"That doesn't make any sense."

"Yes it does too make sense. You just don't know."

"You're right. I don't know."

"Have you ever written words in the snow, Superman?"

"I guess."

"Is it fun?"

"I guess so."

"I would write in the snow if I could but I can't because I'm a girl and girls are held to a different moral standard that makes them shop and eat chocolate and redetect their rage."

"I like chocolate."

"No you don't. That's for girls. You get to write in the snow with your fellas so don't be greedy."

Clare sat quietly between them, nodding occasionally and tossing an unconvincing smile every now and then, always in pairs – one direction for McKenzie and then the other direction for Quinn – but otherwise like she was of another world entirely, one with its own worries and weather.

The lights finally faded. As the screen glowed to life and fat, wet, trumpeting sounds erupted from every direction, Quinn leaned over on his elbow and asked a question to which he, sickeningly, already knew the answer and, deeper still, the explanation behind the answer.

"Is everything okay?"

"No," she said, her voice quavering. "Everything's never okay."

———

After the movie they all walked down to the south end of the mall to the *Pizza Piazza!* and ate dinner. The idea came from McKenzie who declared that she was hipporidiculously hungry.

"Do hippos even eat pizza?" asked Quinn.

McKenzie, holding her mother's hand on the left and Quinn's hand on the right, stepped weightlessly over the tiles in the floor that she wanted to avoid.

"Hippos eat everything, Superman. Daddy thinks pizza is junk food. He says its tampamount to child abuse but he's being silly because my mom just buys me pizza, she doesn't hit me with pizza. Superman should not eat too much pizza or else he will not be able to fly and save any damsels in a dress. That's a woman who screams a lot because she's over-entitled."

Clare insisted she pay the bill and Quinn, based largely on the set of Clare's jaw and the edge in her tone, swallowed his guilt and his sense of how these things are normally done between men and women, and graciously accepted the offer.

After dinner, they stepped back out into the mall and Clare said it was time to get little girls headed for bed. McKenzie, spotting the pink polka-dotted *CreamNation* banner across the hall, insisted on ice cream because, she intoned with the perfect amount of broken-dream dejection, "daddy never buys me ice cream, even if Janet buys some, I don't get any because he says he's the responsible parent, but I don't think it's fair and one day when I have money of my own I will buy ice cream for every person that wants ice cream because ice cream is an alien right like suing for happiness."

After the ice cream had been purchased and consumed, Quinn and Clare took up a couple of chairs in the Grown-Up Zone that surrounded the *PlayLand Pit* in the South Atrium. McKenzie, eyes spinning with fresh sugar, waited in line for the plastic tube slide. Every so often she looked back and waved and they waved back at her.

"Too bad she's not cute," said Quinn.

Clare nodded but did not answer. Quinn pushed himself back in his chair, bracing his feet against a low, brightly cushioned bench. He had given up trying to draw Clare into conversation without McKenzie's help. He crossed his arms over his chest and looked out over the heavily padded pit full of shrieking, laughing children.

"I'm in some trouble," Clare said unexpectedly. He looked at her cautiously.

"What kind of trouble?"

"I took something."

"Took something?"

"Stole something."

"You mean like…"

"Yes."

"What did you steal?"

"A watch. From *Glitterati's*. Not two days ago."

"Mmm." Quinn nodded and looked away. McKenzie waved. They waved. "How come?"

She leaned back in her chair and was so quiet for so long that Quinn thought the conversation was over. But finally she looked at him.

"I honestly don't know. I've never stolen anything before. My entire life. Never. It was an impulse. A terrible impulse. You ever done something like that on… just on an impulse?"

"No." Quinn shook his head. "Stole a bottle of bourbon once, but that wasn't impulse. I planned that out pretty well. Threw a head of iceberg lettuce once. That was an impulse."

"What?"

He told her the story of getting the last word with Edna Cornwallis in the produce loading bay of the *Pay-n-Go Grocery Stop* and he was pleased that it made her laugh, with her eyes lifting the corners of her mouth, in just the way that he had spent an entire sleepless night remembering. When they had stopped laughing, Quinn looked at her.

"I guess even impulses come from somewhere," he said.

"Guess so."

"So where do you think yours came from?"

"I think …"

"What, Clare."

"I think it was the only thing I could control. Everything else in my life is beyond my power. My mother dies. My father dies. So suddenly I'm orphaned. My husband spends most of our marriage double-timing with his pretty young grad student. I walk in on them in my own bedroom. Then he divorces me and kicks me out of the house that is owned, I learn for the first time, by his brother's corporation. Then he convinces a judge that he should have full interim custody of McKenzie because I now live in a bad area of town."

"That's... that's outrageous."

"Well. There's a little more to it."

Quinn waited.

"He told the judge I'm... that I tried to..."

Clare looked away.

"Oh." Quinn winced. "Did you? Try, I mean."

"No. It was a bad reaction to a new prescription. I get these migraines. I'm also taking depression... I can't even believe I'm telling you all of this."

"Not like I'm going to tell anyone," said Quinn.

"I did take too many. By accident. The doctors overreacted. Peter made the most of it in court. God... if he ever got a hold of this..." she gestured in what Quinn assumed was meant to be the general direction of *Glitterati's*, "I'd lose her. I'm an idiot. What was I thinking?"

"You weren't thinking. That's why they call it an impulse."

She nodded, but unconvinced.

"You've got a good job," he said hopefully. "That should count for some kind of control."

"You mean the job where I try to predict the weather every night and pretend I have the atmospheric pressure under my thumb for the entire state? The job for the affiliate that has been going steadily under every year since my father died and that wants to pay me less than I've made in ten years? Would this be the job that barely covers the rent, let alone buy school clothes for my fourth grade daughter and that provides an opportunity for the news anchor and the sports reporter to take turns harassing me for a date? You mean *that* good job? And they'd fire me in a heartbeat, by the way. There's no loyalty there. One word about a stolen watch and I'm history. That'll help with custody."

Quinn looked down at his hands, the guilt rising in him like a polluted tide. Out in the *PlayLand Pit*, McKenzie had moved on to the *Trampoline Castle*.

"Sorry," she said, reaching over to touch his hand. "I don't mean to take it out on you. Nice date. Probably think I'm a psycho."

"Is that what this is?" he asked. She didn't answer.

"It's just... I don't own any part of my life. My life is like laying claim to the weather. It does whatever it wants no matter what I say or do. And I saw that stupid watch and... it was like proving that I was still alive."

"Maybe... maybe you can just decide that it was a really bad mistake and vow never to do it again."

"I can't."

"Give the watch away to charity."

"I can't."

"Why not?"

"Because the watch doesn't belong to charity. It's not mine to give to charity. It needs to go back to *Glitterati's*."

"Even if no one ever knows the difference?"

"Yes. Quinn. I'll know. I made a stupid mistake, but I'm not an immoral person. I'll know the difference. My father will know the difference, looking down on me and wondering what sort of person I've become."

He almost quipped that she might have thought about all of that before she had pinched the watch, but then, seeing the anguish on her face, thought better of it.

"And besides," she said, but then stopped. She swallowed and rubbed her face in her hands and pulled her hair back away from her head like she was trying to take off a wig and Quinn knew in the pit of his stomach what was coming. She let out a strong, stress-laden sigh. "Someone else knows about it, too."

"Who?"

"Now I'm being blackmailed. First time I ever break the law and I'm being blackmailed."

"Blackmailed? Are you sure? I mean… who is blackmailing you?"

"I don't know. But whoever it is got me on film."

"What does he want? Well, he or she?"

"I don't know. Probably a he, but I don't know. And I don't know what he wants. He'll want money. I'm on television so he thinks I've got money. That's my guess. He's threatening to go the police. And the station."

Quinn wanted to correct her. At best the threat was implied. She was reading too much certainty into his note. But he did not correct her, of course. What he really wanted was to tell her that there was no problem because *he* was the supposed blackmailer and he was not about to tell anybody about anything.

But he did not do that either. He had already gone too far. She would never forgive him. She would think he was cruelly toying with her. Stalking her even.

"What are you going to do?"

"I don't know. Give it back, I guess."

"What, just walk up to the counter and say I'm bringing this back? I stole this and decided that was the wrong thing to do?"

"Why? You think he would press charges?"

"Fred Kunch? In a heartbeat."

"You know him?"

"Yes. Fred's the guy you read about who waits for the neighborhood kids to kick a soccer ball into his yard and then stabs it with an ice pick. He shot a dog once. I don't think you should assume he is going to give you any points for returning stolen goods."

"I can't go to the police."

"No."

"I could just, like, leave it on the counter or something."

"Risky. Everyone knows your face."

"I could mail it to him."

"Yeah. I guess that's possible."

"I'd never really know for sure that he got it though."

"Look," said Quinn, turning to face her. "I know Fred well enough. Give me the watch. I'll tell him I found it on the floor outside his store after he closed. He'll take it and put it back on his little jewelry carousel and that will be that."

He saw her flinch a little when he mentioned the jewelry carousel. She had to be wondering how he knew that the watch had come from the jewelry carousel and not from the jewelry case. He cursed himself for being so sloppy.

"I mean it's a plausible story. I don't even have to say I know it's from his store. It could be from *Engagements* on the other side of the mall. I could just ask him if it looks familiar."

"What if the watch came from the case?" she asked with a hint of suspicion.

"Huh?"

"You said he'd put it back in the jewelry carousel. How do you know it didn't come from the case?"

"Did it come from the case? I just assume it came from one of the... you know, the little turny-things."

She didn't answer him and thought for a moment.

"Do you really think that would work?"

"Why wouldn't it?"

"I don't know. You would do that?"

"Why wouldn't I?"

"You've known me for less than a day. I've just confessed a senseless crime."

"I knew you in high school. Remember? I know that you throw a mean paper airplane. And you returned my wallet. So I know you're an honest person. Your daughter calls me Superman. How can I not help?"

"That wouldn't do anything about the blackmailer. He's still out there."

"Right. But aren't you better off having returned the watch than not? Clears your conscience. Rights the wrong. And, look, you may never hear from this guy again. I'm guessing he's had his fun. He's gone. If he were really interested in justice he'd have done the right thing and turned you in."

Clare looked away, flushing a little at the sentiment that turning her in would have been the right thing; the moral act for someone else.

"I'm sorry. I didn't mean…"

"No. No. You're right."

"He's probably some frustrated, immature little twerp. I bet he's the one with a rap sheet. I'll bet he's the one that's been to prison for theft. And I'll bet you twenty bucks that's the last you ever hear from him. I'll bet you a hundred."

"A hundred? You sound pretty sure of yourself."

"Okay. Fifty. I bet you fifty. If he wants more than fifty dollars out of you you're on your own. But I'll pay the first fifty."

"You're that confident."

"I've got a feeling, that's all."

Clare stared at the playing children for a minute. McKenzie, on all fours and being ricocheted around *Trampoline Castle* by a fat little boy who was hurling himself as forcefully as possible upon the cushion of air, looked up and found her mother as if by some telepathic prompting. She got in a quick wave before the next belly flop sent her flipping through the air.

Clare waved at the back of her daughter and then opened her purse and dug to the bottom. She held the purse sideways, her hands still inside, and looked at Quinn. He stuck his hand into the bag. Her hands clasped his on either side. She pressed the watch into his palm.

He kept his hand inside her purse, inside her hands. It felt dark and close and private. Her thumb caressed his.

"I'm grateful to you Quinn."

"Can I take you out again?" he asked. "Sometime?"

"Yes," she said. "Of course. But you don't have to do this. I'll see you anyway. I want to see you."

"It's the best way, Clare. Don't worry."

"When will you… give it to him?"

"This weekend. This place will be crazy with people."

"The *Swap-n-Shop*," she said.

"Right. Fred will be too busy to care."

"I'll watch. I can see from the food court."

"No. Don't come anywhere near. Just stay out of the Summerfield Mall. I'll take care of it this weekend and I'll call you Monday. Maybe the three of us can meet someplace else Monday night."

She squeezed his hand with gratitude.

When McKenzie joined them she was panting and disheveled and looking a little sick. She fell into Clare's lap holding her stomach.

"Well whose terrible idea was that?" she asked.

————

The Summerfield Mall annual *Swap-N-Shop* had quietly insinuated itself into a community tradition. Twenty years ago, at the request of the mayor, who was helping the city assembly respond to a complaint by various community councils, the mall had opened its parking lot to host a community swap meet. People from all corners of the county showed up with their folding card tables and their banners and their stacks of comic books, vintage novels, antique furniture, baby clothing, fresh baked zucchini bread, hand-made jewelry boxes, hand-tied fishing lures, hand-carved chess pieces, taxidermic bird collections, and all manner of objects with some perceivable or imagined value, to participate in a day-long frenzy of buying and trading that was a tribute to the roots of the modern social pathology of retail commercialism.

For five consecutive years the event attendance swelled until it filled the entire east parking area of the mall and the density of people looking to profit by unloading the contents of their garages onto their fellow citizens threatened to transform the Summerfield Swap Meet from a congenial gathering of townsfolk into a tragic news headline. The organizers of the event and Diamond Pete, the owner of the mall, divided the east parking area into two hundred and seventeen numbered lots and then devised a lottery to fairly determine who would be able to set up a table or a booth.

In the sixth and seventh years, the event came off beautifully and inspired similar shopping mall venues in Deer County and Fulton County. But in the eighth, ninth and tenth years, the event was marred by ill-timed spring rains that sent people scurrying for their vehicles with arm loads of their soggy comic books and crocheted woolens. Year nine lasted only three hours. Year ten was effectively cancelled and otherwise optimistic, good-natured people started making off-handed references to the Summerfield *Swamp* Meet.

But it was not all bad. In years eight, nine and ten – the soggy years – the Summerfield Mall experienced single-day revenue spikes that put to shame every other day in the history of the mall. Bigger than Labor Day. Bigger than the Friday after Thanksgiving. It was suddenly clear to Diamond Pete just how profitable the pent-up, frustrated energies of waterlogged swappers could be. The rains had come and washed in all of the money.

Year eleven, therefore, was the year that the retail beast fully devoured it's great grandparents, and the Summerfield Swap Meet became the Summerfield Mall *Swap-n-Shop*. Ever since, for one spring weekend a year, the mall divided up not only its east parking lot, but also every square inch of its interior common area, and invited all of Summerfield to come in out of the rain to keep its money dry.

Saturday morning saw more traffic in the *Shutter Shack* than Quinn had seen in the previous three months combined. Right on schedule, the rain was pouring outside in buckets, which meant that every last person interested in a *Swap-n-Shop* experience, including the vendors who had anticipated setting up their wares outside, were inside flirting with the fire code limits.

This was not unexpected. Nancy Havemeister had arranged her vacation to be back in time for the *Swap-n-Shop* weekend and had drafted Ed Phillips' to help out all day on both days. But, expected or not, it felt odd to Quinn to have both Nancy and Ed standing behind the counter with him, bumping into each other, talking over each other, reaching for the same merchandise. Not to mention the oddness of looking out into the store and seeing a dozen customers milling around and picking things up and asking to get into the display cases. It was like he had accidentally reported to work at *Gadgetopia*. Quinn could not imagine what the popular stores like *Gadgetopia* were like on the *Swap-n-Shop* weekend.

Beyond the showroom, out the store windows in the hallway, was a roaring river of people that boiled past and eddied around a series of identical tables. One featured elaborate dolls made from wheat and cornhusks; another, vintage vinyl records; and yet another, hand-painted mailboxes and flowerpots. They were like square boulders that stuck up out of the frothing humanity in a line that extended out of view in both directions.

Every so often Quinn found occasion to look out the window in the direction of *Glitterati's*, which was also packed with people. Fred Kunch looked to be helping three people at once and his vaguely simian nephew, whom Fred had no doubt hoodwinked into helping out for free, looked on the nearside of panic. Fred, dressed in an ochre shirt and a tan cardigan with reading glasses around his neck, wore the same dour expression that he wore every other day. The *Swap-n-Shop* throngs registered not in his expression so much as in the quickness of his glance. As he spoke in turn to his customers, his eyes darted left and right, flinging his suspicious scrutiny to every corner of his store, every display case, every countertop carousel, the register, and to the face of every new shopper to cross the threshold.

Quinn stuffed his hand into his pocket and felt the smooth glass face of the watch between his fingers. He wondered to himself just how and when he should approach Fred Kunch, a man he had never particularly liked and whom he had only really spoken to once, fairly recently one night as they were both closing up their respective stores at the same time. Fred had asked if he was Clem's kid and Quinn had said yes. Quinn had asked if Fred had ever seen a wetter spring and Fred had shrugged and said it was all the same to him and then walked off through the mall.

He had told Clare that he knew Fred well enough, and he still was not sure whether that was true or false. How well do you need to know someone to be able to return missing property? All he really knew was that in that moment, watching Clare watch little McKenzie ricochet around the *Trampoline Castle* like a kernel of popcorn, he had wanted to help. He had wanted to be the solution to Clare's problem. He would have said just about anything.

Clem stopped by late in the morning and rapped his knuckles on the doorframe. He was wearing his security uniform, which was too tight and too short in the legs. He was not moving with his usual ease.

"Everybody doing okay in here? Welcome back Nancy." He nodded over to Quinn.

"Hey Clem," said Nancy. "You're sure lookin' the part today."

"Diamond Pete gets nervous over all the swap-n-shoppers. My instructions are to see and be seen."

"Lot of people out there," she said.

"This year's a record for sure. It's cats and dogs outside again. Chased everyone in. Weather gal says tomorrow will be sunny. That'll help."

"Still a lot of people for one man," said Nancy.

"Oh, I'm an army of five today. Pete sprung for reinforcements."

"Well I just never felt so safe." Nancy shooed him off with the back of her hand and a smile. "Go be seen, Clem."

Quinn's father waived and disappeared back into the river.

Quinn, Nancy and Ed spelled each other for abbreviated, half-hour lunch breaks, each leaving the remaining two to handle the store. Quinn offered to take the last shift, resolving to devote the last part of his lunch to returning a watch to Fred Kunch and wanting to do that later in the afternoon when the crowds would be the worst and Fred would be feeling the fatigue setting in. Nancy, who was to take the first break, did not make it out of the store until well after one o'clock. Ed was not back from his lunch until after two. Quinn delayed until it was almost three.

There was a line of eleven people at the *Hotdog Hut* and Donna Cole had two helpers, one to take the orders and one to take the money as Donna handled everything else. From what he could observe, it was fairly clear that the Asian kid taking orders might have done better counting money and the orange-headed kid taking money might have been better at understanding orders and communicating them clearly to Donna. Most people left shaking their heads in irritation.

When it was Quinn's turn he ordered his usual kielbasa and cup of sauerkraut and a basket of onion rings and a large Coke and nodded hello to Donna who was sweating up a storm over the fryer. She nodded back distractedly, looking old for her years and like she wanted to cry. As he waited for his change he found himself feeling sorry for her. It was the second time in a long time he had felt sorry for someone else. He supposed that for the first time in a long time he felt strangely optimistic about his own life and that this had left some new room in his attention for the realization that not everybody in the world had it as good as he did. Not everybody made a decent wage working for a nice boss in a clean, up-scale store. Not everybody had a dad who was still alive and who wanted to share a steak and beer. Not everybody just happened to meet with new people or old classmates who trusted them and wanted to open up their lives and confess their sins. Not everybody was looking forward to Monday.

He wanted to say something to Donna as he was leaving. Something that she could hold on to that might help her get through the day. The orange-haired kid at the register counted the change into Quinn's hand and he stuffed it in his pocket.

"Hey, Donna," he said as he pulled away from the counter with his tray. She turned, her face twisted in something like grief. "Hang in there. The sun is supposed to be out tomorrow. Half of these people will be outside in the parking lot."

"What?" She could not hear him for all of the reverberating chaos. Her face said that she thought he might be the latest to complain about his order. Quinn raised his voice to just below a shout.

"I *said* the weather is about to change."

"What do I care about the weather, Quinn? Go eat your food." She waved him away with a pair of dripping tongs and turned back to the fryer. The Asian girl with the accent who was taking orders yelled out something incomprehensible.

"What?" shouted Donna. Quinn left to find a seat.

When he was done eating his lunch, Quinn navigated his way through the food court and out into the mall towards *Glitterati's*. Knots of people bent over *Swap-n-Shop* tables congested the flow of traffic and made forward progress difficult.

He reached the jewelry store and found it was full of people. Fred was all the way in the back corner opening up one of the wall cases for an older couple. An unshaven man in a blue cap was standing idly by waiting his turn. Fred's nephew was on the other side of the store, behind the register, ringing someone up. Two women were waiting in line for his attention. Quinn decided to peruse the tables outside the store as he waited for an opportunity to corner Fred.

On one of the tables were stacks of vintage comic books, pulp mystery novels and old movie posters from the 1940's and 1950's. Quinn flipped through each of the stacks, pulling out selections here and there as they appealed to him. He lingered over the Superman comics. One of them asked in bold yellow and red letters whether the Man of Steel could save Metropolis from Dr. Zeus, the evil genius who had invented a weather machine. On the cover, Superman was straining to catch hail boulders the size of small buildings as Lois Lane screamed in terror. She was wearing a yellow dress. Quinn kept it and moved on to the next stack. He picked up a book.

"Oh, now that there's a Jack McMannis mystery."

A tidy looking, white-haired man in his early seventies was standing across the table from him, arms crossed with a satisfied smile on his face. His nametag said: *Hello, I'm Marvin Hemmler.*

"You know your pulp, mister. That one's a beaut."

"Yeah?" Quinn turned the book over in his hands. On the front cover was a drawing of a busty blonde bombshell holding a large smoking revolver.

"Yessir. One of the first books I actually owned as a kid. Read that one a hundred times. Don't write like that any more. You like your crime?"

"Crime?"

"Mystery crime," said Marvin Hemmler.

Quinn nodded. "How much?"

"Ten bucks, full sentimental value, but you've got a nice face. You can have it for five and the Superman for another three-fifty."

"Deal," said Quinn. He dug out his wallet and gave Hemmler a twenty. Marvin put the comic and the book in a small paper bag and handed over the change, which Quinn stuffed into his front pocket. As he did, he felt the smooth face of the watch with the back of his fingers. He worried about it knocking around in there with all of the coins he was now carrying. He extracted the watch and dropped it in the bag with Superman and Jack McMannis. Quinn thanked him and moved on.

The next table seemed to be all about handmade pet wear. Collars, sweaters, booties, even hats were spilling out of several wicker baskets that were lined up on the table. Quinn began to turn away before the sellers – a man and a woman seated on the other side of the table – could launch into a sales pitch.

"What kind of pet do you have?" asked the woman before he could get away.

"I don't have a pet," said Quinn, turning back.

He looked down at the couple. She was heavy-set with a puggish nose and large cow eyes painted a revolting pastel blue. Her lips were puckered into the shape of a welt to cover yellowing, crooked teeth. Quinn did his best to avoid eye contact, and looked over at the man he presumed was unlucky enough to be her husband.

"Junior ain't got no pet," said Roddy P. "But I hear tell he played the bitch up there in *The Alley*."

He had grown a full beard and Quinn did not recognize him until he heard his voice. The stained plaid shirt – red on black – was the same. He tried not to react, but he knew it was too late. He could feel the blood running hot in his face.

"Roddy P," Quinn said, nodding.

"You like playing the bitch?"

"Nothing like that ever happened."

As he spoke he shifted his weight uncomfortably from one foot to the other. The bag in his hand knocked against his leg and he could feel the watch slide against the smooth cover of the Jack McMannis mystery.

The idea came to him in an instant, like it had already been planned long ago and as if now was simply the time to turn it loose into the world.

He would plant the stolen watch. He would let it slide out of the bag into Roddy P's little basket of dog collars. He would watch and wait until Roddy P found the watch and stuck it in his pocket. And then Quinn would go whisper into Fred Kunch's ear. Fred would get security involved. Security would hold Roddy P for the police. Then it would be Roddy P's turn to explain what he was doing in possession of stolen property.

Quinn thought about the long eighteen months that he had spent up in *The Alley*, feeling his insides devoured by anger at a God who would let something like that happen. The same God that had allowed a drunk to end his mother, and his sister, and that had then allowed that same drunk to walk away without so much as a scratch. The same God that had planted the seed of doubt in his father's brain about his only son. The seed that had grown into an expression that looked at Quinn every day now with eyes of concern and puzzlement over whether any of it was true and over what kind of person Quinn had become.

But God was making amends. For here, suddenly, on a day that Quinn just happened to have what he had in the bag he was holding, here was Roddy P, made to order and looking just dumb enough to steal a watch from a jewelry store and then spend the day sitting only fifty feet away. Quinn's heart thrilled at the poetry of it.

He eyed the basket of dog collars. Roddy P leaned over to the cow-eyed woman next to him and pointed at Quinn.

"Junior here's a thief, Mavis. Caught him red-handed. They put his ass a-*way*!"

The woman backhanded him along the side of his head and Roddy P recoiled like he'd been bitten in the face by a snake.

"Get outta my face, fool! And you leave this customer well enough alone 'fore I kick your sorry ass out into the parking lot. You on every last one of my nerves today."

Roddy P threw his shoulders back and tightened his lips like something bad was about to happen. But Mavis did not flinch and threw her own shoulders back.

"Oh yeah?" she said almost with a laugh. "Let's see what you got, Roddy P. You at the give-me-a-damn-reason stage, so you just come on and try me."

Roddy P almost instantly began to shrink like someone had opened up a valve in the middle of his back. He turned away, fuming.

"MmmHmm," said Mavis. She composed herself and readdressed Quinn with as close to a smile as she could muster.

"I apologize for my husband, sir. I hope you will not hold it against me."

Quinn looked at her and at Roddy P growing smaller and smaller next to her and something inside his heart snapped in two pieces. Inexplicably, he thought of Clare.

I'll know, she had said. *I'll know the difference.*

"I don't have a pet, ma'am, but I sure hope you do well today. I'd like to contribute twenty dollars for one of these beautiful collars."

He fished through the collars with a finger and pulled out a leather strip dotted with bits of faceted red glass meant to look like rubies. The name *Sunshine* had been stenciled across the middle in loopy cursive letters. He pulled the last twenty dollars out of his wallet and handed it over to Roddy P who stared up at him in ashen-faced humiliation.

"I'd like a receipt, please," he said.

Roddy P balked, leaning back in his chair and crossing his arms, looking at the money. Mavis snatched the bill from Quinn's fingers and slammed the flat of her hand down on the table so hard that Quinn could see Marvin Hemmler whip his head around over at the next table. Then she punched Roddy P square in the arm.

"I am *not* naming this baby after you," she said. "That's for damn sure. Roddy Jr. is out."

"A baby," said Quinn, glancing at Roddy P and then back to Mavis. "Congratulations."

"Thank you," said Mavis demurely.

Roddy P wrote out a receipt as Quinn and Mavis watched with a crushing patience. He ripped it savagely out of the little book and handed it to Quinn. Quinn handed him the collar.

"This is for you," he said. "Wear it in good health."

"You're lucky you're still walkin', Junior."

Quinn winked at Roddy P's wife.

"You don't deserve this woman, Roddy P. She's too good for you. How she puts up with you I'll never know."

Mavis beamed and gave Roddy P's beard a sharp tug. He yelped in pain. Quinn bent towards them a little.

"Maybe if you paid more attention to the mother of your child than all of those girly magazines you've got stuffed in her crawl space. Lotta money to be spending on personal entertainment with a little baby on the way. Don't you think?" He raised his eyebrows. "Roddy P?"

Quinn casually turned and walked across the hall into the jewelry store.

———

Glitterati's was no less busy than it had been. Quinn walked leisurely through the store, side stepping customers, looking at each of the display cases with an interest he did not actually have. Every so often he looked over his shoulder to make sure Roddy P was not up to something. He tried to make eye contact with Fred Kunch as he passed, but the proprietor was too involved in explaining the difference between a Mazarin cut and a Peruzzi cut. After a complete tour that included flipping through the class ring catalogues on the back counter, he slowly circled back around to the front of the store and leaned over the brightly lit glass display cases.

Strings of starlight glittered over rumpled black space. Quinn imagined what it must be like to actually purchase a diamond necklace and to fasten it around the neck of a woman, feeling the length of her body along his own. Eyes closed, holding her hair up. Eyes open. Eyes widen. Hair drops. Hand to the chest. *Oh! Quinn!*

He moved to the end of the display case to the jewelry carousel at which he had first seen Clare. He looked over his shoulder again for Roddy P and saw only a mass of people. He craned his neck until he could see the table of dog collars. Mavis was there, talking to two women with matching purses. Roddy P's chair was empty.

He scanned his surroundings as best he could and, seeing nothing, concluded either that Mavis and Roddy P had parted company for the day or that Roddy P had excused himself to the men's room or to the parking lot for a smoke break. He might have run home to clean out the crawlspace.

Still. Quinn did not trust him for a moment. Now that he had witnessed Roddy P's humiliation and spilled the beans on his stash of multi-cultural pornography, he found it just a little unnerving not to know where he was.

He spun the carousel with a finger. It was basically a clear box with four panels. Each panel had a clear door that locked at the bottom with a key. When turned to the locked position, the key pushed a small silver deadbolt through a hole in the plastic. At the bottom of one of the panels, the plastic had cracked, enlarging the hole for the deadbolt.

Quinn looked up to locate Fred Kunch. Fred was exactly where Quinn had seen him last, only now he was talking to his vaguely simian nephew who was doing a lot of nodding and pointing to a tall women in yellow who was drawing something in the air with her finger. Fred Kunch shook his head and as the vaguely simian nephew and his tall yellow customer dispersed, Fred turned to address a man in a blue tie.

Quinn returned his attention to the carousel, thinking that maybe the better plan would be to return the watch to the custody of the vaguely simian nephew instead of Fred Kunch. He touched the deadbolt rather idly with the tip of his finger. It slipped free of the hole. The panel door swung slightly open.

So that was how, he thought. *That* had been the birth of a bad impulse.

Inside the plexiglass panel, there were four rows of four felt-wrapped pegs. Each peg held a women's watch.

Every peg but one.

Quinn closed the door and straightened his posture and took another look around for Roddy P. He saw Fred Kunch's nephew loping his direction, swinging his freakishly long arms. Quinn drew a slow breath, preparing himself.

"I need to ask you to leave," said the nephew.

Quinn blanched and then sputtered in incomprehension.

"What? Me? Why?"

"Mr. Kunch has a strict no-felon policy."

"A what?"

"A no-felon policy."

"A no-felon policy?"

"That's right. A no-felon policy. He knows who you are."

"But I work right over there." Quinn half twisted and pointed in the general direction of *The Shutter Shack.*

"Like I said, he knows who you are. I'm sure he does not mean anything... well, I guess I can't say it's not personal, can I? I'm sorry. But you do need to leave now."

"So I couldn't even buy something if I wanted to?"

"No. I'm sorry. Please go."

"But... I was coming to see him."

"As you can see, just about everybody wants to see him. He doesn't want to see you."

Quinn thought for an instant about handing over the watch and explaining how he had found it on the floor behind a bench, *just right over there*, on this side of *Flouncy's*, and how he thought that it might have come from *Glitterati's* and how he thought Fred might be able to find the owner.

But now, in the face of such a sudden and personal distrust, the story felt all wrong. It felt more than wrong. It felt dangerous. Suddenly, he wanted nothing more than to be out of *Glitterati's*.

"Fine," he said coldly. "If you don't want my business, I'll take it down the mall to *Engagements*. And I'm telling my friends and acquaintances."

"Cellmates, you mean."

Quinn did not respond. He turned abruptly and threaded his way through the middle of a threesome discussing earrings, out of the store and into the torrents of the Summerfield Mall in the full throes of *Swap-n-Shop Saturday*.

He felt his blood boiling just beneath the skin. He had long grown accustomed to people thinking him a felon and a dishonest man. In fact, with the possible exception of his father and Nancy, both of whom were willing to give him the benefit of the doubt, he had long grown used to *everyone* thinking of him as a felon and a dishonest man. The truth was, he had given up caring, because trying to control what people thought of him was pointless. Like trying to predict the weather.

And then he had met Clare. Of all people, he had met Clare. And now the old, once accepted accusation by Fred Kunch, callously passed along by his vaguely simian nephew, seemed suddenly brand new and filled him with rage, as if he was still standing in the softly accumulating snow on the corner of *Cleatchee Junction* and *River Road* trying to explain the bank bag full of cash and the diamond ring and the Bernadelli P-90 as Roddy P looked on, watching his lie unfold its wings like a great tal-oned bird with a grip around his torso.

He had taken no more than ten steps out into the mall when he felt Roddy P's hands come down hard on each shoulder. Quinn did not think about it. Prison had taught him that much. He simply spun and swung.

His fist connected with the chin of a clean-shaven face that did not, he realized too late, belong to Roddy P but to a uniformed security guard. The guard was stunned but not as stunned as Quinn. The guard recovered quickly and took Quinn down to the tiled floor without any further resistance.

People parted. A hole opened. Suddenly they were no longer of the crowd. They were *other*. *He* was other. An outcropping of rock in the water. A drop of vinegar in a river of oil. People pointed. A second guard was on him in seconds.

Fred Kunch stepped out of the river and into the hole and picked up the bag that had gone skittering across the floor. With his cheek flat against the cool tile and a knee in his back, Quinn watched him slip his hand into the bag.

Quinn closed his eyes. He thought of Clare. He thought of slipping his own hand into Clare's purse. He could actually see her face in his mind. It was not like he was watching her on television. Not that face. It was the face she had shown him the night before, squeezing his hand in gratitude for telling her that he would take care of things. He would help her. Protect her. He was Superman.

The lights around him flickered and died and then came back to life in a burst, followed by a staccato sputtering from above. He felt a slight lessening of pressure in the small of his back as the guard twisted his head upwards.

Then it began to rain.

The people shrieked and ran for cover, confused and terrified at the implications. The crowd surged in one direction, then the other, knocking over *Swap-n-Shop* vendor tables. The other guard called for calm, but even Quinn could barely hear his voice. One of the vendors was trying to protect his vintage books from the sudden cloudburst. Another began yelling that people were looting his table.

Quinn felt like he was in a hole fifty feet deep. The wet chaos above him was a slow, muffled din, a storm beyond the horizon. He tried to think about what he would do. What he would say. There was an explanation after all.

He blinked the water out of his eyes. He could see his father's boots. Coming from a long ways off. Just his boots, through a forest of legs, running in his direction, pushing through pooling water. He felt the rough grout seam and the corner-point of tile pressing hard against his cheek.

He thought of the frozen furrows in the field and of the thin white lines across Clare's wrist where the watch used to be. He thought of little McKenzie.

He thought of King Itch pointing at him with the elbow of his one good arm. *It don't mean nothin' without the sacrifice, boy. And we all got to sacrifice.*

He thought of the rows of earth dropping off one-by-one into the maw of the flaming sun at the end of each day, as everything inched a little closer to the end.

In the middle of the fray, Fred Kunch stood motionless looking down at him, the stolen watch glittering in the falling water. The weather ran off his forehead in clear rivulets and his cardigan grew heavy and dark.

Fred did not pay much attention to weather. It was all the same to him.

Clement sat in his tiny, tenebrous office with the heels of his boots propped up on his desk. The space around him was much too small for his tall, lanky frame. He was like a bird in a shoebox, waiting for the lid to open.

He was working his way through a bag of breaded *Chicken Chunkadunks* and a cup of lemonade he had ordered down at *The Cluck Stops Here*, which was the Summerfield Mall's newest food court addition, slipping neatly into the space once filled by *The Hot Dog Hut.* His face flickered with electronic light from the three little holes in the shoebox, which were actually computer monitors fastened to the wall above his desk.

Two men were smoking out back, near the loading bays. Neither of the men was wearing any kind of uniform.

Three young teenagers who should have been in school were spending a lot of time in and out of the stores up in D-Block.

In C-Block, another youngster was standing on a skateboard.

In the food court an older man was leaning up against the wall of the hallway that led to the restrooms. He had been there for ten minutes.

Clement dunked a chunk of chicken into a small cup of honey-mustard and popped it into his mouth. He washed it back with the lemonade and decided that he missed the hotdogs. Although at least Donna Cole seemed a little happier in her new uniform and relieved to be working for an organization with a less austere, more employee-friendly business model.

The kid in C-Block with the skateboard was now actively riding the ramp that stretched between *CreamNation* and *Pizza Piazza!* He would need to put an end to that. The last thing Diamond Pete needed was another lawsuit.

There had been no fewer than six lawsuits filed over the damage caused to *Swap-n-Shop* vendors from the malfunction of the new fire suppression system. Two more lawsuits concerned injuries sustained by panicked patrons slipping on wet tile. The Summerfield Mall had been named in all eight cases and had filed one of its own lawsuits against the company that employed the men on the tall ladders. Although it was yet to be seen which, if any, of the cases would go to trial, the ratio of lawyers to mall patrons wandering around on any given day had grown steadily and the legal fees were proving to be significant.

Diamond Pete had not been a model of understanding. He had had a bad feeling about this year's *Swap-n-Shop*. He had told Clement to take special care to supervise those sprinkler installation technicians. He had told Clement to make sure he had sufficient manpower on hand to effectively contain any problem that might arise. And yet the sprinkler installers had cut corners and something terrible had gone wrong up in the ceiling clouds where the weather was made and Clement and his insufficiently numbered security force had been unable to contain the reaction below.

Diamond Pete had not outright fired Clement. He would wait until there was no more need for Clement to testify or to be of assistance in the storm of litigation. Then one quiet day Charlie Tidwell would drop a letter on his desk from one of Diamond Pete's lawyers. And that would be that.

"Hey Clem." Charlie Tidwell, speak of the Devil, came in with a bundle of mail wrapped in a rubber band and dropped it on the desk next to the lemonade and the cup of honey-mustard dipping sauce. Clement looked up and nodded.

"Hey Chuck. How you doin' today?"

"Oh, fair. Fair. Sun's coming out. That's good for a change."

"Yeah, that's good," said Clement. "High time."

"'Sposed to start getting hot by the end of the week."

"Good. Then we can start bitchin' about the sun for a change."

Charlie Tidwell laughed at this.

"Looking forward to it," he said. "We'll see ya' Clem."

"Yep."

It was not only the sprinkler fiasco and the raining of subpoenas that Diamond Pete would not be able to forgive. It was the fact that his head of security – the person whom every last store in the Summerfield Mall trusted for protection against theft and for whose services they all paid handsomely as part of their monthly leases – had pulled some strings to get a known felon, his son, but still, a known felon – hired to work at a high-end shop in the mall, and that said felon had, true to his thieving nature, robbed one of the mall jewelry stores. What the mall vendors did not already know, they read in the newspaper, and some of them, certainly Fred Kunch, had made their displeasure known. Diamond Pete would not forget. It was only a matter of time.

So Clement had started looking. At first, the available employment opportunities seemed so bleak that he thought he would have to either move to another state or change professions. The prospects of having to do either of those things, combined with the reincarceration of his son, had made him so depressed that he had taken his first drink in fourteen years and six months. That dark road felt the same as it ever had, like he had been walking it, stumbling it, laying in it, just the day before. The next day he had picked himself up off the dark road and had gone to a meeting and sat in the circle and said his name and said what he was, and then he had started all over again from the wretched beginning.

The day after that, after his first day sober, Clement had applied as Chief of Security for the Riverdale Homeowners Association. The RHA had recently built a clubhouse and a golf course and needed someone to spend a lot of time outside getting to know the home owners and acting as a visible deterrent to the river rats, which is what the RHA called the seedier element of Summerfield who lived on the other side of the Cleatchee River and who had targeted the subdivision with graffiti and petty crime from its first foundation. The position came with a budget, a golf cart, a uniform and an umbrella. The Treasurer of the Association was a good friend of Nancy Havemeister. He had survived an interview. They said they would call soon.

Clement tried not to count his chickens.

He ate another chunkadunk and watched the skateboarder talking with his friends outside of *Pizza Piazza!* He had longish hair and his baseball hat was on backwards. Clement could not help but think of Quinn, back in the days he now called, simply, *the aftermath*. Back in the days when he could no more connect with his son than he could connect with this skateboarding punk by yelling at the computer monitor. Like he lived in another dimension.

He had wanted to help Quinn. This time as he had last time. Last time he had nearly gone broke, but it had all been worth the feeling of re-establishing the familial bond. If there was one thing good to have come out of that nightmare it was that he and Quinn once again spoke as father and son. He did not know if he knew the whole truth about *The Qwicky Pawn* and that had never really mattered. He knew Quinn. And he had been in Quinn's corner, without question or hesitation. That was all that mattered. That had meant something to Quinn. It had demonstrated something vital. And that had started the thaw. A good thing from a bad situation.

So from the moment he had seen his son face down on the floor outside *Glitterati's*, in a pool of water with a knee in his back surrounded by pandemonium, his first and only instinct was to help him in every way he could. Upon hearing the allegations explained to him in a shout above the din of panic, as the deluge soaked him and people pushed past him in the hallway, Clement was already putting together a plan of action. A second mortgage. Or sell the house altogether. He would need to start looking for lawyers. One of the Swap-n-Shoppers had been yelling about looters. Clement was not listening. The only thing that mattered was Quinn, his son, who needed his help. It was too late for his wife and daughter. But his son needed help. That was something he could do. He could try anyway. That was all that mattered.

But his son had obviously had other plans. They had never even had a chance to talk. Summerfield police were on the scene within minutes. Quinn was taken into custody and had never been released. Clement had tried his best to work his influence behind the scenes, through old friends on the force. But it had been a lot of years. The friends were few and the influence was weak.

And everything had happened all too fast. Quinn, he learned, had declined any representation and had confessed within the first hour of interrogation.

The watch, it turned out, was almost as cheap as anything Fred Kunch sold. Four hundred dollars. For anyone else, a judge would have ordered restitution and community service and the misdemeanor would have floated away like a birch leaf on the Cleatchee. But for Quinn, possession of that spangly little timepiece was enough to violate the terms of his probation and almost before Clement knew what had happened, before he could mortgage the house or hire a lawyer, Quinn was on the bus heading back up to *The Alley* to finish out the last six months of his sentence.

He had had one phone call from Quinn the night before his transfer. The call had not been long enough for any explanation, but long enough for Quinn to say that he was sorry and to say that he was not a thief, that he had never stolen anything, but that he wanted to do what he was doing.

Six months was not a long time in the scheme of things. Except that not being able to see his son, the last beating heart of his family, made six months an eternity. Clement marked the time on a calendar he purchased at *The Book Nook* and pinned to the wall above his desk, beneath the holes in the shoebox. Quinn's release date was circled in red.

He knew better than to try to visit him. They had made that arrangement the last time. Too many people up in *The Alley* still knew Clement Merriwether. The fewer people that knew of his connection to Quinn the better. All he could do was wait.

Clement finished his chicken and wiped his hands and decided to head out to walk his first afternoon beat. He stood and finished his lemonade and eyed the monitor. The young skateboarder was trying to leap one of the benches. Clement flipped through the mail as he watched the kid hook a wheel on the bench and go sprawling.

It was the return address that caught his eye. He sat back down.

—

Dear Dad:

One down, five to go. Wanted to let you know I'm doing okay. You'd think after all of this time I would be better at writing letters. I'm not. It's like all of the thoughts get jammed up inside the pen. I know I'm not much better on the phone. Maybe if I was better at communicating I would not get myself into these messes.

I'm back in F Block. I almost thought they were going to put me in the same cell, but I'm up one floor and a little further west. My cellmate is from Fulton County. He's doing five years for burning down his own house. He's okay. Not real smart (he forgot one of the empty gasoline cans in the basement and two others in the back of his car), but he's okay. And big. No one is messing with us.

It is a lot different here than last time. The same, but different. Maybe it's because I'm only doing 6 months rather than 18. But that's not the only reason. I met someone before I was sent back up here to the Alley. An old friend from high school. You don't know her. Well, in a way, you kind of do know her. In fact, everyone in the Alley knows her. She's kind of here every single night. She talks

490

to everyone. But I'm really the one she's talking to. She uses phrases and gives me looks and gestures that only I can understand. I know it sounds crazy but that is all I can tell you. I will have to explain later because I don't know who might end up with this letter. Anyway, she keeps me sane and gives me hope about the future. She comes to visit me in person every week and sends me lots of mail. We are talking about moving in together when I get out. I am anxious to introduce you.

She has a daughter that calls me Superman as kind of a joke. I was wearing my old Superman t-shirt the first time I met her mom. Her daughter, who is all of nine years old, told me once that Superman represents our wish of invulnerability to disappointment. At first I thought that was a little crazy. And maybe it is. But I know how I feel every morning when I get out of bed and I know that today will be just like yesterday and the day before. And I'm not talking about waking up in the Alley. I know you know what I'm talking about. This is a feeling that won't let you out of your bed. It won't let you out of the bottle. It won't let you put on your clothes or smile or go to work or make a friend. I know you know that feeling.

But Superman is invulnerable to disappointment. He always shows up for the fight. It's not so much that he succeeds, it's that he always tries. He never gives up, even when he is up against chaos and forces he can't control. He'd show up to fight the weather if he had to. And that takes believing that today might turn out different than yesterday. Not that it will turn out different - no one can know that; only that it might turn out different. It takes an act of faith to get out of bed believing that today might be different than yesterday and believing a man can change a thing that might happen into a thing that will happen. Even when there is no hope, Superman always does something to change the day. He does something. Whatever there is to do, he does it. That's why we like him. That's what I think anyway.

Dad, I know I owe you an explanation. I do have one. But it is kind of complicated. Too complicated to cram through a phone line or through the end of this pen. It will just have to wait until I am out. If you think you have raised a thief I guess I can't really blame you since this is the second time I have been convicted, but that is so wrong. You and mom did not raise a thief. I am a good and honest person. The question for me has never been whether I broke the law, but why I am in prison.

There is a minister that comes by every so often. Charles something. We call him Chaplain Charlie. He says he knew you when you were working up here. I guess he was away for a couple of years in Panama and now he's back. He says hello. Anyway, Chaplain Charlie says that prison is not something around us that keep us in, but something inside us that keeps God out. He says that pushing God away shrinks our lives and that a man will never be free as long as he is running away from God. I know you are reading this and thinking that I've gone off to prison and will come out with a Bible in my hand preaching the good word and making an ass of myself every time you open a beer or say a bad word or look at Nancy Havemeister the way you do (yes, I noticed). Anyway, you can relax about all of that.

But I do think Chaplain Charlie is maybe on to something. Running away is like surrendering to something dark and hopeless. It's like giving up and the darkness then just walks up and plants a flag in your heart and claims you and some part of you dies and the rest of you lives like a slave. It's like locking yourself in a prison and allowing every day to be the same and taking some sick comfort in the disappointment of that sameness.

And I was thinking that I've been running away for a long time. Ever since the accident. I have been running away from Mom. And Christy. I have been running away from you. I think I have been afraid that I will not be able to bear it. I have been running away from every person and thing that life puts in front of me because I am afraid I will not survive the encounter. Chaplain Charlie's God has revealed my life as something that cannot be controlled or predicted and I have lived in fear that what I cannot control or predict will kill me; it will snuff me out, just like it did Mom and Christy.

And so I run. I fool myself into thinking that I am escaping to a better life but really I am just running into a smaller, darker place. It looks like escape. And freedom. But really it's the opposite.

I know it seems like I just gave up and that I did not put up any kind of a fight and that I just let Fred call me a thief so they could send me back up to the Alley. I knew that you would probably sell off just about everything you own to hire some lawyer and I couldn't see putting you into the poor house just so I could avoid six more months up here. I already have the felony on my record no matter what.

But that's almost beside the point. The thing is, even if we could afford a lawyer that could have won an acquittal, I didn't want an acquittal. Not because I am guilty (I am not), but because the price of that acquittal would have been too high. And because the confession, even though it was false, was something I could control. It was like proving to myself that I was still alive. It was the first time in a long time that I took a step toward something rather than away from something. It was the first time in a long time that I felt like tomorrow might hold something different than today and the day before. I know you will think that your son has gone crazy - and maybe I have - but I have not felt so good about myself and about my life in a long, long time. This morning I woke up knowing that I am the difference between the might and the will.

Don't get me wrong. I'm not saying I like the Alley. I don't. I hate it and I can't wait to get out of here. But I'm not running any more. And I do feel freer. And it makes me think that you could feel freer too. Because I think you have been running away from things just like I have. You're better than the Summerfield Mall, Dad. It's a great big world. There is room enough for everyone and everything. There is room enough for the past and the future and every kind of weather. And every day is different whether you know it or not.

So I'll tell you what Mom always told me when she came downstairs Saturday mornings and saw that I was cooped up in the den with the lights off, watching the same old sappy reruns: The weather today is beautiful. Don't waste it.

Love you. Quinn

Chapter 10

A BETTER PLACE
("THE CALLING")

He was a specimen, this judge. Henry O. Manumitt III. Like a young king, his father still cooling in the grave. Up there on his throne, casting down over the proceedings, stroking his coarse black beard, his right eyebrow cocked with interest, as if it were propped up on an elbow, stretching out from the king's brow to get a better view of the squabbling serfs.

The women on the jury, seven of them, would have gladly born the judge's children, had that been another part of the jury service requirements, along with not discussing the case with others, and keeping an open mind, and keeping their cell phones *off-all-the-way-off*, and submitting their parking reimbursement slips at the end of every day.

They smiled when he smiled. And when the furrows of concern deepened across the judge's forehead, they each offered their own furrows to help carry the weight. Were he to drop his pen and step down from his throne and climb into the jury box and take each of them, seriatim, moving from one to the other, pinning them against the burnished mahogany railing as the witnesses droned on about rights and expectations, contracts and contingencies, they would submit to his will without complaint.

The men in the box sat taciturn and emasculated in another man's house. In the palace of the king. None of them, Tyler guessed, would offer up any resistance to *le droit du Seigneur*, the rule of *Prima Nocta* transplanted into an American courtroom, in defense of their women. No indeed. A couple of the men had tried to assert themselves in *voir dire*, declining to answer questions about themselves. Declining to account for their beliefs and activities. The judge had looked down upon them with something short of a smile.

You can answer the question, Mr. Peterson.

You can answer the question, Mr. Collins.

You can. As if their objections had been but a public display of low self-esteem and doubts about their ability to form the words that might be arranged into the answer to a simple question.

Well, it seemed the judge was right after all. For they could. And they did.

Every so often the judge looked down at Tyler sitting at the table with Grace. This was usually whenever Grace stood to make an objection, swiveling the judge's attention from the witness, or from the debonair sanctimony of the plaintiffs' attorney, Mr. Glass. But not always. Tyler had caught several sly sideways appraisals by the judge, even as Grace sat quietly listening and doodling her three-dimensional boxes on her notepad, asking for no judicial attention whatsoever.

It was as if the Judge were trying to take Tyler's measure in small, unguarded moments, while everyone's attention was directed elsewhere. On each such occasion, Tyler had met the judge's gaze, directly and without apology, and the judge had slowly returned his attention back to the stilted, robotic repartee between witness and lawyer.

The looks from the bench might have been to remind Tyler who was king. That Tyler was in the courtroom at all meant he had already lost a battle with the judge and the justice system. The judge might have thrown the entire case out on a pre-trial motion. Or he might have at least discarded the claims against Tyler, leaving only the allegations against the studio to occupy the jury. But the judge had had other plans and the entire case had been allowed to lumber expensively and inconveniently forward, dragging him along behind, like a thrown rider caught in the stirrup.

After two years of argument and a small fortune in legal fees, today was Tyler's first day in the courtroom and the judge was obviously intrigued to see in the flesh the man about whom so much paper and argument had been devoted. He had tried mightily *not* to be in the courtroom and, truth be told, he was still not convinced that it was necessary. He had given his deposition. He had told his story. Said everything there was to say. So why did he need to sit and listen to every agonizing word in person? Why was *that* necessary? Yes, he owned the studio, but Kevin was the Director of Creative Development. This case was all about, and only about, creative development. Kevin had attended every hearing and every deposition. Kevin had made it his mission to account to the board at every twist and turn. When people at the studio had questions about the case, they did not ask Tyler. They asked Kevin.

In fact, Tyler was not sure that in the past two years Kevin had actually done any work at all that was not specifically related to tending to "the case" and feeding it money, like some pet monster that he had been allowed to adopt and keep chained up in the cellar, taking it for long daily excursions from the studio to the law offices of Meyers, Rudolph & Wagg, to the courthouse, and back again where the beast gobbled up bowls of profit and gnashed at its chains and bellowed for attention. At the request of the board, Kyle Wolzniak, Co-Director of Cinema and Television Projects, had temporarily assumed responsibility for all new development projects so that Kevin could stay focused on "the case."

Tyler had thought this an extreme reaction to what at that time was a new storm cloud on the horizon. He had counseled the board to adopt a business-as-usual-on-the-home-front approach to what would be a long court fight. But Tyler had abstained from the vote as previously agreed and he had bitten his tongue. "The case" was Kevin's baby. He would be the studio's point-person for the litigation. The lawyers at Meyers, Rudolph & Wagg had all but adopted him as an honorary associate, or a firm mascot, or whatever honor typically came with a million dollars in fees. They had given him his own office to facilitate document review and ready access to any one of four lawyers actively working the case.

So, in light of all of that, Tyler really saw no reason why it was not perfectly sufficient for *Kevin* to attend the trial in his stead. Kevin was his son, after all, and he knew all of the facts better than Tyler, even the parts about what Tyler should say and not say, remember and not remember, intended and did not intend. Kevin could tell the story to the jury, strategize around the clock with the lawyers and then report the status to the board of directors and to Tyler, its Chairman. Grace would be there, in the courtroom, looking up at the judge and over to the jury, to defend Tyler's interests as necessary. Why, then, did *he* need to be present?

They all had their answers, of course. Kevin had railed at him, face knotted in beet-red anger, that it was *Tyler's* company that had been sued and that Tyler *personally* had been sued, and that Tyler had been the one, stupidly without any witnesses or legal review, to negotiate the agreement that the plaintiffs now asserted never happened in the first place and so – here Kevin had pounded the dashboard of the car with his fist – *of course you have to attend the goddamned trial in person, dad!*

It was not an unusual tone for Kevin to take with his father. His passion for the case tended to get the better of him and poison his perspective, not unlike other things. After each day of Tyler's deposition, Kevin had laid into him for failing to remember the key points of his many and intensive prep sessions with Kevin and Grace and the suited savages of Meyers, Rudolph & Wagg.

It's like you weren't listening to a fucking thing we were telling you! I mean, do you even fucking care? About your own company! Your own reputation! Do you understand how much we have already invested in this fucking project? Do I need to show you the numbers again? Do you want to risk a jury telling you that you have no right make this series at all? That it belongs to that bitch Janice Lindstrom? Do you? You want <u>her</u> to own Winchester County? Because if so, dad, then let's just pull the plug right now and be done with it.

When she was present, Grace would always step in as the voice of reason, explaining how Tyler's deposition testimony had been fine and how overreacting was counterproductive. She and Kevin had exchanged some very sharp words, in fact, over Tyler's value to the overall effort.

The savages usually hung back during these exchanges, letting their client take the lead as they leafed through their notebooks and consulted their phones.

That Kevin hated Grace was no secret. He was not one for mincing words and Grace now had far too much control over a key witness in the case – indeed, *the* key witness – for Kevin to tolerate her with any equanimity. Initially, Kevin had liked the idea of investing in separate counsel for Tyler. Parroting the savages, he had told the board that it would give the studio a strategic numerical advantage at every encounter with the enemy. More objections. More motions. More time in front of the jury. But Kevin obviously had not factored in all of the consequences of buying Tyler his own lawyer.

And while the feelings were certainly mutual, Grace never gave Kevin the satisfaction of allowing it to become a personal contest between them. It was all about "the case." It was all business. Which made it all the worse for Kevin that he could not drag her down into the mire of his emotion.

But on this one point, even Kevin and Grace agreed: Tyler had to attend the trial in person. She agreed that not showing up was the equivalent of a forfeit.

And so here he was, arms crossed, tie pinching his neck, boxers riding up, listening to Mr. Glass ask Janice Lindstrom about her father John – Tyler had always called him Jack – and about what it was like growing up hearing stories of *Winchester County.*

"They were like real people to me," she said in a frail voice beyond her years. She was a prim, brittle woman with a saccharine smile and overly affected reactions to every question.

"Those characters are like aunts and uncles and cousins to me. And they were to my father too. His father, my grandfather, created those characters. He loved them like real people. My father used to improvise stories about them just for the fun of it. Sometimes he would start and I would pick up where he left off. He was proud of those stories and they were… well, I guess they were a kind of family bond. A connection to his father."

"Then why did he sell the *Winchester County* stories off to Warner Studios?"

"I was just a little girl at the time, but what I know is that Warner liked the stories. They wanted to make a television series. They thought it would be very successful and that people around the world would fall in love with the Winchesters. Those that had read the books would fall in love all over again. They were right. But my father didn't just... *sell them off.*"

Mr. Glass looked over to the jury, pretending to be confused. He clasped his hands behind his back and then looked back at Jack's daughter.

"How so, Ms. Lindstrom?"

"The contract with Warner was only for the development of a specific number of episodes based on the stories in these books." She placed her hand on top of the two black volumes in front of her. "Two hundred episodes. They only aired one hundred and thirteen episodes before the series was cancelled. My father was adamant about retaining all legal rights to the original material. Warner had nothing to sell to anyone."

"Not even to Milquest Production, a company in which, as you have already testified, your father owned a controlling interest?"

"No. Milquest Production never owned the rights. Warner had no rights to transfer to Milquest and my father never transferred any rights to Milquest when he became an owner of that company."

"But you heard counsel for the defendants state this morning in their opening statements that Mr. Tyler Freeman, then President of Shoofly Studios, personally negotiated the purchase of the ownership rights to the *Winchester County* stories, fair and square, I believe were the words..."

"Whatever Tyler Freeman and his studio think they purchased, the ownership rights to *Signs of Passing* or any of the *Winchester County* stories were never for sale. Not ten years ago and not now. That was never my father's intent." Janice's eyes went soupy and she pointed at Tyler, lecturing him from across the courtroom. "Those characters belong to the family trust and the trust does not consent to Mr. Freeman's *Winchester County* remake."

The judge looked again at Tyler, no doubt hoping for some reaction to the defiance in Janice Lindstrom's voice. Tyler did his best to look mildly amused in a disappointed way. He leaned over toward Grace, who tilted her head sideways to listen.

"Rhubarb, rhubarb, peas and carrots," he said softly, their joke for feigned conversation. He wanted to make her laugh. He wanted Grace to do what he could not do and show the jury just how ridiculous it was for Janice to believe the things she was saying. If Jack were alive he would never have allowed this sort of nonsense. Tyler wanted a smirk or a smile or a *come-on-now* headshake from Grace that would work as a down payment on the evidence to come.

But she was too professional for that sort of thing. It would have looked unseemly, laughing at Janice Lindstrom. She was sympathetic, even if, in their opinion, she had a weak case and little chance of success. Grace nodded her head once slowly and circled one of her three-dimensional box renderings on her tablet. She tapped the pad twice with her pen.

Tyler nodded as if in full agreement and leaned back against the back of his chair. At the adjacent table, Kevin and one of the suited savages were hunched intensely in conversation.

Mr. Glass asked a question about the business relationship between Janice and her father. Tyler took the opportunity to look up at the judge who, it turned out, was still looking down at Tyler. For an instant, their eyes met. He did not know what the judge was thinking. He only knew that the look left him feeling unsettled. It left him feeling... judged.

Tyler and Grace stuck together during the break, letting Kevin and the lawyers for Shoofly Studios pack into a small courthouse conference room to obsess over the morning testimony. Tyler and Grace went outside for a walk around the block in the warm spring air, fragrant with new blossoms.

"They're paying attention," said Grace when Tyler asked about the jury. "No one is asleep."

"Except me."

"Tyler," she tutted. "You want excitement?"

"No. I want freedom. Do I *really* have to do this every day for the next three weeks?"

"Yes. You really do."

"What if I fake an illness? I have an appointment with Doc Matthews this afternoon. He could give me a convenient disease. Lupus or something."

"When this afternoon?" she asked too seriously.

"After court, Grace. Relax. I'm not going to skip out on you."

"The abdominal thing still?"

"Gas. And depression," said Tyler. "He thinks I'm depressed."

"Are you depressed?"

"I'd feel better if I had fake lupus."

"You can't fake lupus, Tyler."

"Rickets then. Or the plague. That would get me out of court and it would keep Kevin's goons off my back."

"You're referring to the lawyers representing your own company."

"Savages," said Tyler. "All of you."

"You're a child, you know that?"

"Hardly. I'm an old man who has better things to do than sit in a courtroom listening to lies."

"You do realize you're the star witness."

"Kevin can ..."

"Kevin wasn't there, Tyler. You chose to meet with Jack alone, for years. You drafted the only piece of paper approximating a contract in this case. So you get to testify. Stop complaining."

Tyler sighed heavily "Yeah, yeah."

"Besides, what else better do you have to do?"

"Anything. Everything. I have a production studio to run."

Grace looked at him dubiously. They had known each other too long. She never let him get away with anything.

"What," he said indignantly. "I still do things."

"I thought you were tired of all that," said Grace.

"I am. But I still have responsibilities. Movies don't make themselves, you know."

She changed the subject with her tone. "We still need to work on your testimony."

"Let's have dinner after court," he said, stopping at the corner where they always turned around and retraced their steps. "My memory improves with wine."

"Thought you had a lupus appointment," said Grace.

"After that."

She gave him a smile and he tucked it away.

"Sure, Tyler. You're the boss."

———

The waiting room was ovular and blue with light yellow and tangerine accents that looked vaguely like exploded fruit on the textured curving walls. People in chairs hunched over in pairs or alone holding pens on strings tied to brown clipboards. Others communed with their phones. Still others stared vacantly forward in the direction of a burbling glass rectangle of fish. Skeleton Chinese pirates did sit-ups on the deck of a sunken junk.

Tyler knew the drill, which was to walk up the short hall connected to the oval waiting room like an air hose to a football and to wait for the only recently pubescent receptionist in her pretend-nurse garb to slide back the glass and check him in on her computer with a flourish of keyboard clicks and facial ticks and to confirm his insurance and to tell him to walk back down the air hose and sit inside the football and stare at the fish until they – the medical establishment, not the fish – called his name. He would be called.

So he did that.

And now here he stood, looking for an open seat. Some of his fellow detainees looked up momentarily, expecting to see a nurse, merrily embonpoint and colorfully clad in scrubs and wearing plastic clogs, carrying a familiar name on her lips, but then, disappointed to see that it was only Tyler, dropping their gaze back to their clipboards or phones or fish or pirates. He did not take it personally. As soon as he was seated, he would be giving the same disappointed look to the next poor bastard who wasn't a nurse in plastic clogs.

The waiting room was common to a suite of medical offices, so there was always a disparate collection of ailments and complaints that surrounded the fish. Every time Tyler came to see Dr. Matthews he tended to spend his time in the oval trying to imagine who had what medical problem. This was almost always an impossible task except on those occasions that a pregnant woman was there, fidgeting uncomfortably in her chair. And even then, pregnant women also needed to see the dentist, or they needed to bring their already born children to the pediatrician, or they developed inexplicable lumps, bumps and pains that sent them searching for answers unrelated to gestation. Pregnant women get skin cancer just like everybody else. So *guess-the-ailment* was mostly just a ridiculous way to pass the time. There was no way to tell what was wrong with people. What ailed them. What made them come to sit in the oval room.

Tyler panned the room for a place to sit, noting a chair next to a gangly, spaghetti-spined, teen-aged boy bent over a tablet device that flashed silently up into his face. On the other side of the chair was a low black table with a box of tissue and a stack of magazines. As much as he generally loathed video games, it was the only chair in the room that was not tightly flanked on *both* sides with people harboring secret ailments and so Tyler moved for the chair without any further hesitation. It was the best deal the room was going to offer.

Nothing about the boy acknowledged Tyler's presence, suddenly filling the empty space next to him. His face was passive. Eyes unblinking. He tipped the tablet sharply left and right, forward and back like he was trying to keep a bug from skittering out of a pan. Every now and then one of his legs twitched in a sympathetic urgency.

Tyler sat and leaned over to the table and flipped through the stack of magazines. Sports. Technology. Fashion. Gossip. All of them catered to interests not his own. Each of them, in its way, insulted and taunted him for his age. Generations looking back at him over perfect shoulders, laughing, not waiting for him to catch up. Not *wanting* him to catch up.

He was now, solidly, three life-phases behind.

He was obviously well past the phase when he could credibly claim a participative role in the dominant culture; which was more than just a little ironic, he thought, for a man who had built a small fortune in an industry that, more than any other, was *the* purveyor of dominant culture. Ironic, yes, but there it was. He had no personal claim to coolness. He was not James Dean. There was no pretending. That phase was simply gone.

Gone, too, was that phase of pretending to opt out of youthful preoccupations as beneath his dignity; looking with a counterfeit disdain at the American froth bubbling away around his ankles, deigning to be above it, to not want it, taking on arcane interests – collecting Tang Dynasty metalwork and ceramics – as if to prove some naturally contrarian nature.

And now, for many years, he was past even that elongated phase of focused, vicarious participation in all things young and insatiable, fueled by an increasingly unwholesome, vaguely prurient fascination as he looked through the wrong end of the telescope at a world spinning away from him.

What he would not give for those old unwholesome obsessions, he thought. He would settle for those.

But he no longer had the energy. Or the visceral comprehension.

He looked at the laughing, dripping, long-legged model sprawled over the surfboard on the top of the stack. She was not, in her proportions or the gleam in her eyes, unlike any of the nubile ingénues that regularly crossed his path looking to make a name for themselves in one of the movies or television events that Shoofly Studios launched out into the firmament every year. She might have been any one of them. And yet, as he looked at her, she was an alien being, the tips of her naked tentacles burrowing into the sand like earthworms into crystalline soil. Nothing of her touched him. Except perhaps the part of him that was still curious about things he did not understand. And even that part of him was increasingly too exhausted to care.

"Becky?" Everyone looked up at the nurse in the hallway. An unfortunately-shaped woman with an unknown ailment, presumably Becky, stood and shuffled off behind the receding plastic clogs.

Tyler leaned over to his other side and stole a look at the boy with the tablet, the only one in the oval room, other than the fish, who had not looked up.

It was a driving game he was playing. The vantage point was over the hood of a red Ferrari, navigating the winding roads across an idyllic, vaguely Europeanish countryside. Other cars darted in and out of view, often requiring sharp correction and acceleration. Not infrequently, in fact with suspicious regularity, these other cars ended up plowing through vegetable carts and split rail fences in clouds of dust and debris.

"Do you have to stay on the road?" Tyler asked.

"No," said the boy after an unnaturally long delay that left any answer at all in doubt. "You can go off road, but it will cost you points."

"What good are the points?"

He shrugged and shot past a yellow Astin Martin.

"They go on line," said the boy.

"What goes on line?"

"The points."

"To who?"

"Other people that play this game."

"Do you know them?"

"Who?"

"The other people. On line."

"No. They just play the same game. Everyone tries to get the most points."

"Then what?"

He shrugged again, this time without any follow up.

The red Ferrari crossed a finish line of flowers that had been tossed over the road leading into a small Italian-looking hamlet. Farmers and shopkeepers were waving their arms and shouting, presumably in celebration but the lack of detail in their faces left their emotion a matter of interpretation. They might have been rioting at all of the sudden automotive mayhem upsetting the chickens. It might be the beginning of the end for the clean windshield and the flawless red paint job.

The boy sat up in his chair, stretching out his spine. He held out the tablet.

"Wanna try?" he asked.

Tyler laughed a little like he was being given the opportunity to pole vault.

"It's easy," said the boy. "There's a super-simple level."

He handed Tyler the pad and gave him rudimentary instructions. Left, right, faster, slower. That was all there was to it, he promised. The boy reset the game and after a dramatic on-screen countdown, Tyler watched all the cars around him zip off in a cloud of bucolic Eurodust.

"You have to tip it forward," said the boy. "Give it some gas."

Tyler tipped the pad forward, leaning out into the room as he did. Scenery inched towards him on its digital conveyor belt, growing larger and disappearing off on either side of the screen in a simulacrum of forward movement, as though he were pushing a zipper painted to look like the hood of a Ferrari. He tipped and tipped until the countryside was suddenly a blur and he was quickly out of control.

Some of the oval room detainees looked up at him, perhaps misinterpreting his full body contortions, throwing himself over one side of the chair then the other, lurching forward and back, as if he were experiencing some form of seizure. Accidents abounded. Spinouts and ditch dives and splintered chicken coops. Twice the boy needed to reset the game.

But soon enough Tyler found a comfort zone and he was unzipping the Old Country, slowly, other cars passing him regularly, with relative ease. In the distance was the Mediterranean, shimmering an electric blue. Tyler tilted right, leaving the road. He broke through a split rail fence and headed out across a pasture. The cattle seemed indifferent. Like this sort of thing happened every day.

"What are you doing?"

"Going to the beach," said Tyler.

"You'll never get there."

"Why?"

"That's not the game. It's a driving game. The point is to stay on the road. And the road is back there." He pointed over toward the box of tissue and the stack of magazines. "You're losing points."

The pasture lands that lay between the front of the red hood and the glinting blue sea seemed to lengthen before him. It was like moving along a nightmarish rubber hallway that stretches and stretches out into the murky dream distance with a door at the end that moves farther away with every step, only in the driving game the hallway was a beautiful pasture and the door at the end was a glimmering blue ocean, and the murky dream distance was an exotic digital sunshine and everywhere there were cows, all of which Tyler was beginning to recognize as the same three cows over and over again.

"I'm losing points?"

"Yes. They're all passing you, dude."

The boy lifted the right side of the pad. The shimmering sea rolled away behind him and the broken fence and the road beyond loomed up over the hood as if he had never really been moving towards the sea at all. Cars on the road sped past. A French mime on a bicycle pedaled by and waved just to rub it in. The boy pushed down on the front of the pad, tilting it forward. The Ferrari rejoined the road in a spray of debris and sent the mime sprawling.

"That never gets old," the boy said, laughing.

There was suddenly a presence towering above them.

"Okay, kiddo," came the voice. "Let's beat it on home."

Tyler looked up as the boy was rising out of his chair, one hand extending down towards the pad. Tyler handed it up to him.

"Thanks for..." he started to say, but the man cut him off.

"Tyler? Tyler Freeman. I'll be damned."

He looked up at the man, focusing on his features. He was old, Tyler's age at least, but had a disconcertingly lively countenance; a broad smile and luminous eyes the color of the sea on the far side of the pasture he could never reach. It took a moment, but he got there.

"Warren Lemiski. My God if it isn't…"

Tyler stood and the two shook hands. The people around them looked up from their phones and clipboards and magazines, but only briefly.

"It's been…*Man-o-man*, Tyler, I bet it's been forty years."

"Oh at least, at least," said Tyler. "You were leaving your firm. Starting your own."

Pillsbury laughed and nodded.

"You still counting other people's money?"

"No. I'm mostly retired. Unlike you. I see you in the papers every now and then."

"Don't believe everything you read, Warren," said Tyler.

The boy next to him shifted his weight uncomfortably.

"This is my grandson, Stuart," said Pillsbury, tipping his head. "Stuart, this is one of my oldest …" he paused. "No. This *is* my oldest living friend, Tyler Freeman. We grew up together."

The boy grimaced awkwardly.

"Stuart was teaching me the finer points of auto racing," said Tyler with a wink.

"Well, he ought to know. He's got his permit now. He drives me everywhere. It's like having my own chauffer." Pillsbury elbowed Stuart in the shoulder. "Tyler here owns Shoofly Studios. He hobnobs with movie stars and probably knows a good chauffer when he sees one."

The boy's face brightened with what seemed genuine interest.

Tyler waved at the comment with the back of his hand like it was an offensive odor.

"It's not what it seems, believe me."

A different nurse, differently proportioned, wearing different scrubs and yet, somehow, the same plastic clogs, appeared in the hallway and called out Tyler's name.

"That's me," he said.

"Everything okay?" asked Pillsbury. "I mean…"

"Oh yeah. Check-up. You?"

Pillsbury pointed to his face.

"Lost a crown. You look good, old man," Pillsbury lied.

"So do you, Warren. You look good."

Tyler rejected words like *great* and *fantastic*. He did not want to sound insincere. But it was true. Pillsbury looked great. He looked fantastic.

"Let's get together for a drink. Tell stories."

Tyler agreed and fished a business card out of his wallet. Pillsbury pulled a pen out of his pocket and wrote a phone number on the business card and handed it back to him.

"I know how to find you," he said. "This is my number."

They shook hands and separated as the nurse was clogging across the oval to take more aggressive action.

"Thanks for the lesson, dude," he said unconvincingly to Stuart. "I'll try to stay on the road."

"That's where the points are." The boy smiled a little.

"And you try not to run anyone else over. You did that on purpose."

"Okay." Stuart's smile grew larger. "I guess a mime is a terrible thing to waste."

———

Tyler navigated elbows. Grace swirled her wine, watching his approach. Half a plate of cheese and spinach crostini sat accusingly in the center of the white cloth.

"You lupus people are always late," she said when he reached the table.

He sat without acknowledging the quip. He watched her face tighten around sudden concern. It was not like him to leave her hanging.

"Tyler." She leaned forward slowly, looking into his face. "What's wrong? Everything okay?"

He pulled in his chair and looked up at her. He had known her for too long to think he could hide from her. She had always seen through him, even back when Stephen was still alive and Tyler was to her, at best, simply her husband's employer. Even that long ago, Grace had had his number. She would certainly find out eventually. Everyone would. Hiding was pointless.

But he hid anyway. He did not know what else to do.

"Hmm? Oh, yes, yes," he said in irritation.

"You sure?"

"The drivers in this town. They all need to die. I'm lucky to be alive."

"Tyler, you've got more money than God and you're officially a senior citizen, why on earth do you not use a driver?"

"I've never used a driver. Never will either. That's Kevin's thing. I drive myself. Even if it kills me and everyone else on the road."

"What did the doctor say?"

He rolled his eyes.

"Yes?"

"He wants me to exercise more and cut out the booze. Speaking of which..." he looked over each shoulder at the rest of the dining room behind him with a hand half raised like he was preparing to hail a taxi. "What are you drinking?"

"Tyler."

"Hmm."

"You don't look so good."

"I'm goddamned hungry. I haven't eaten all day. That judge doesn't give us enough time to eat a decent lunch. Jury gets a full hour and we have to sit there listening to Richard Glass go on and on about this exhibit or that exhibit. Janice must pay him by the goddamned word."

Grace sat back and regarded him, measuring his tone.

"You're sure worked up," she said eventually.

"Bah."

"Are you concerned about the case? About testifying? You've testified before. It's..."

"I don't have the jitters, Grace. Relax. I'll say what everyone wants me to say."

"And what, exactly, does *that* mean?"

A server stopped by with menus. Tyler ordered wine and pretended to read through the specials. But there was no reading anything tonight. Meaningless black squiggles on the page. After a moment he looked up. Grace was still waiting.

"Well?"

"Nothing. It means nothing. It means…" He traded the thought for a crostini.

"It means Kevin is riding you like a rented mule," she said.

Tyler chewed.

"Look," she said. "He's your son, so tell me to butt out because it's none of my business, but I honestly don't know why you put up with that. Every dime to his name and every ounce of authority that he swings around this city like a club he owes to you. You gave him all of that."

"He does a good enough job," said Tyler, knowing that was not the point.

"I'm sure he does a fine job. That's not the point. Where is the respect? Where is the gratitude? And where… this lawsuit is not about Kevin. It's about you and the production company that you built from the ground up. If you wanted to fold up the tents and raise the white flag and hand Janice Lindstrom a check tomorrow so that you can move on with other business, then Kevin's role should be to defer to that decision and support it. His only words should be *yes, sir*."

Tyler laughed at the very idea. The absurdity of it actually lifted his mood a little. The white flag. Kevin's head would explode right off of his shoulders. He would want to pummel Tyler into the dirt. He would want to assemble an emergency meeting of the board. He would want to sweep all of the contents of Tyler's executive office suite into a great big box and kick it out into the hallway. But Kevin would not be able to do any of those things. Because Kevin's head will have already exploded off of his shoulders.

Grace was not as amused.

"Don't get distracted, Tyler. I'm not suggesting that you *actually* surrender. You're going to win this case. Easily, I predict. I'm just saying that Kevin needs to show some deference."

"He doesn't like me much."

"That's hard to fathom," she said, smiling with everything but the lips. She reached out and patted his forearm. "You're the most likeable person I know."

"Well, sure. You're a lawyer. Look at the company you keep."

She did not remove her hand. She squeezed gently.

He wanted to tell her. Suddenly. Urgently. The new fact, bound and gagged and hooded, held hostage on its knees in some soundless cavern of his brain, had suddenly, with the touch of her kindness, broken free and was making a run for the light. If anyone was to know, it should be Grace.

He patted her hand, smiling. He drew a small breath. But she spoke before he did. The new fact was recaptured.

"Mark went through a phase," she said. "When he was in college. He didn't want anything to do with us. We were footing the bill, of course. But that did not seem to matter. It was like he hated us. Blamed us for everything. And Stephen ... well, you can imagine how tolerant he was with that attitude. Stephen wanted to flat out disown him."

"Doesn't seem like Mark."

"Probably doesn't to you. He's always loved you. Alex too."

"Nonsense."

"It's true. You were very kind to them when Stephen died. They've never forgotten it. Neither have I. I'm just saying, before all of that, well... sometimes kids don't appreciate their parents like they should. Put it that way."

"But you knew it was just a phase," said Tyler. "And so you kept Stephen in check and you kept Mark in school and it all passed. You held it all together until it passed. You gave him a chance. And now he's a loving son with a family and a lot of well-designed New York buildings to his name. He grew out of it."

"Right." Grace nodded. "So I should have some credibility when I say that Kevin is not growing out of anything. He's what, forty-five? This is not a phase, Tyler. It's not going to pass. And in the meantime... well, it's just hard to watch."

He might have responded to the implication of his own emasculating infantilization at the hands of his over-bearing son. He might have defended himself. Grace knew more than anyone else, but she did not know everything. She was smart enough to deduce that Kevin had issues with sublimated anger. Hell, the *crostini* on the plate in front of him was smart enough to reach that conclusion, even without the cheese. But Grace could not know *why* Kevin was angry. He wondered whether, as a child, Grace had taken a back seat to her father's career as Kevin had. Somehow he doubted that Grace had essentially raised herself, or that she had watched one parent drink herself to death as the other, reveling in his own ascendance, pretended it wasn't happening.

So he might have provided her with some context for Kevin's anger and for his submission to it. But, frankly, it was all he could do to sit upright and pretend that he was having an actual conversation with his lawyer over dinner at *Le Goût*.

For he was doing no such thing.

He was still lying on the papered table in the doctor's office, staring uncomprehending up into the flaring nostrils of Dr. Matthews.

Breathe easy, he had kept telling him. *Breathe easy. In. Out. Listen to the sound of my voice.* And now that was all he heard and all he knew. Nothing else touched him and it took great effort to pretend otherwise.

The server came and took their orders and collected the empty appetizer plate and kicked the conversation in another direction. They spoke about the case, mostly. Grace, in that subtle way of hers, used their casual dialogue to add nuance and depth to the explanation of events that would soon be his testimony. When Tyler remarked that Jack Lindstrom had been trying for a solid year to convince him to buy into Milquest Production, Grace nodded as she skewered a radish.

"Negotiations are more than the words that surround a handshake," she said. "They can take a long time. You know that better than anyone."

"I do indeed."

"But the jury…"

"Right."

"Buying into a venture like Milquest was a complicated proposition. Jack wanted things out of the arrangement and you wanted things out of the arrangement. That takes time to work through. A lot of conversations. A lot of trips out to Jack's ranch. That's why they call it a negotiation. How long did it take you guys to negotiate the rights to *Gingerbread Canyon*?"

"Mmm. On and off for a year, I guess. Little less."

"Not a bad example. If it occurs to you on the stand."

"Difference is Jack *wanted* to sell *Gingerbread Canyon*. He didn't want to give up *Winchester County* and *Winchester County* was really the only reason I was entertaining the buy-in to Milquest in the first place. I liked Jack as a friend, and we played a lot of golf, but I was never wild about the idea of being in business with him. He was a better writer than businessman. Good writer. Not better than his old man, but good. No head for numbers though."

"But you *did* buy in," said Grace. "That was an affirmative decision you made. To do business with Jack Lindstrom."

"Not a controlling interest." Tyler pinched his fingers together. "A small interest."

"No, but you still decided to take the risk, however small."

"I was willing to buy in as long as I got *Winchester County* out of the deal."

"What I hear you saying, Tyler, is that you relied entirely on Jack's promise to convey the rights to *Winchester County* – ownership rights, not limited use rights – and that without that promise you never would have invested."

And so it went, through dinner and coffee; Tyler remembering the past out loud and Grace feeding it all back to him in a form that would help a lay jury recognize its legal significance.

Tyler knew the drill. It was not his first pre-testimony dinner with Grace. She had represented him in both divorces. When Shoofly had been sued over the profits from *Shadows on Saturn*, almost twenty years ago already, he and Grace and Stephen had put in some marathon sessions over dinner. She was working. It was dinner and the wine was good and the piano from the bar behind him filled the room, but Grace was working. He would receive a bill in the mail at the end of the month and this dinner would be on it.

And yet, he never spoke to Grace as his lawyer. Or, at least, it never really felt like it. It was as though her training and experience were merely incidental facts about her life, like his own stint in the Forest Service in lieu of college or his Tang Dynasty metalwork collection; something for texture but hardly central to the person.

Breathe easy, Tyler. In. Out. Listen to the sound of my voice.

When the coffee came, Grace drew a line in the sand.

"Enough of this. You're as ready as you will ever be. You'll do fine."

"When am I on?" he asked.

"Late tomorrow if we're lucky. If not, the day after. Since they're calling you in their case, we do not have a lot of control."

"Okay," he said. Resigned. Compliant. Like a child told to wash his hands before dinner.

"Tyler." She smiled in a way to show she was no longer a lawyer. "I'm off the clock."

"So?"

"So you want to tell me what in the hell happened at the doctor's office today, or do you want to keep pretending?"

He stared back at her for a moment, sipping his coffee as he wrestled with himself. Then he told her the story of meeting his old friend in the oval room and how strangely upset he was to learn that Pillsbury seemed so happy and fulfilled. He explained to her how ashamed he was to have secretly wished Pillsbury's tone had betrayed just a hint of envy or that his face had shown traces of regret and a legacy of ill-considered choices. The confession was humiliating. He wished he could take it back even as he was speaking the words.

But it was the only thing he could think of to talk about.

It was either that or his pancreas.

———

Sleep, fearing the very suggestion of death, avoided him like the plague. Tyler sat and paced and sat again. He had tried lying still in bed, eyes closed, hands folded over his chest. But he could not help seeing him-self from above. The bed was a stage supporting a one-man, one-act play about a man who lay dead, eyes closed, hands folded over in his chest. And Death was in the audience, ever the critic.

So at two o'clock he got up and never went back to bed.

Still in his pajamas and a robe, he sat downstairs in the living room staring up at his bookshelves and the ever-stirring ceiling fan and his original Martin Johnson Heade painting of a storm brewing on a watery horizon. Then he paced for awhile, hands clasped firmly behind his back to keep from grabbling little things, little keepsakes and doodads, Tang Dynasty metalwork, from the shelves and tables of his home and hurling them through windows. He took a seat at the dinner table and fidgeted with the tassels of the cloth mat beneath the centerpiece. And so on, until he had mulled his new reality from every room in the house. But no matter the room or the perspective, night pressed its oily black rags up against the windows, trying to suffocate him in dread.

As distracted and terrible as he had felt over dinner, when he returned home to his empty house – far too big for his needs, with its cool stone floors and its vaulted ceilings and all of its sycophantic echoes – he realized just how much he had been clinging to Grace's composed pres-ence to keep from dropping into abject panic. For as much has he had wanted to leave, upon saying goodnight through the window of her car, he was almost instantly desperate to be back inside *Le Goût* at the table, drinking coffee and pretending to be upset at other things.

For Tyler did not want to die. He was not ready. He was only sixty-eight.

The audaciousness of Dr. Matthews' words – *six to eight months* – filled him with rage. *Six to eight months*: Arbitrariness shellacked in cer-tainty and made into a paperweight that now sat atop his dwindling life with the weight of an anvil. If he had been sixty-nine years old, would the death sentence have been six to nine months? If he had been sev-enty, would Dr. Matthews have dropped the silliness of a time range altogether and predicted death in precisely seven months?

He tried to fight back with hopeful logic. He felt no different today than he had yesterday or the day before. He did not have *all* of the symptoms. A little liver pain. A loss of appetite. But no nausea. No jaundice. Stable weight. And depression? Who wasn't a little depressed? He'd been a little depressed for a hell of a lot longer than six to eight months. He couldn't even remember when it had started. It was the norm. Is that what depression meant now? A little disaffection was now a harbinger of swift and certain doom?

But these arguments were merely slick-thin soap bubbles against the searing hot pan of science. The blood tests. The ultrasound. The grave expression of the doctor, the man of science in the white coat who was adamant about making an immediate appointment for a CT scan. *Immediate. Immediate. Immediate.* If Tyler did not make an appointment, then Dr. Matthews promised him he would know about it and would hound him until he did. He would ring his phone off the hook. He would hunt him down if necessary. That was how urgently important it was. *Immediate.* Against all of Tyler's soap-bubble hope, the doctor man of science was that certain. And if all was as the tests indicated, if all was as Dr. Matthews, in his white robe and his stern expression, feared, then the gavel of science would strike the sounding block of fate and Tyler would be given a maximum of six to eight months within which to tidy up his affairs and deliver himself into the custody of Death.

At the dining room table, listening to the hum of the refrigerator from the kitchen and to the rows of ice, one by one, calving off into a frozen bucket of bodies, he wondered whom he should tell. A list of accountants and estate lawyers, the custodians of his assets on paper, scrolled through his mind. He would need to advise the Shoofly Studios Board of Directors, of course, and the various officers. He saw each of their faces reacting to the revelation. He heard each of their thoughts. Watched each of their silent contingencies rerouting themselves.

He had his thinning white hair cut once a month from a Korean man who liked to tell him knock-knock jokes that were difficult to understand through the accent. There were six to eight more of those sessions in store; no more than maybe twenty-four more knock-knock jokes.

He saw a dental hygienist every four months. Lydia. She smelled like citrus, bending over him, in up to her elbows, asking him questions he physically could not answer. She liked to talk about her son, deployed in some dangerous overseas hellhole. Lydia was no stranger to the sound of the scythe out in the dark, making its way. Only one more visit with her. Would he tell her? Would he go through the pretense of scheduling the next appointment?

And what about Maria, the woman who supported her three kids by cleaning houses, including his own? When did he tell her that he would have no further interest in a clean house?

What about his ex-wife? He and Rachael had not been on speaking terms or physically within a thousand miles of each other in ten years. Of his three ex-wives, she was the one who had survived the others. Didn't that status confer some rights of notice? Was it wrong to simply let her read an obituary? Were there applicable rules of etiquette?

And what of Kevin? How does a man tell his son such a thing?

Of course, all such questions were purely an exercise in hypothetical thinking; not hypothetical because pancreatic cancer was still only a possibility rather than a fact – in Tyler's mind, try as he might to resist it, the cancer was already calcifying as a hard, immutable reality, so dense in his consciousness that it was distorting everything in his spirit the way a black hole warps the fabric of space – but hypothetical because if he could not find the strength to share the fact with Grace Bell, then the idea that he would tell anyone else first, his son included, was a delusion.

At four o'clock he shuffled back upstairs to his bedroom and dressed himself in the dark. He might have turned on the light and looked for a new suit, shirt and tie. Instead, he dressed from the pile of clothes heaped into the chair in the corner and grabbed the tie from the doorknob that he had unnoosed from his neck only hours before. He slipped it over his head and cinched it up again. These were now his cancer clothes and it was not a new day.

He drove to the studio. He made small talk with the guard about the trial and about how one could get so much more work done in the early morning as the world slept.

"Bet with this case goin' on you've probably got to get a full day's work done in the morning just to keep up, don't you Mr. Freeman?"

Tyler smiled and stepped onto the waiting elevator. He went up to his office and closed the door and sat behind his desk in the dark and looked out the window at the lights of a city oblivious to the fact that he would be gone in eight months time. Maybe six months time. The lights would be there, burning for other eyes, and he would be gone.

He turned on his desk lamp and then stood, crossing the room to the bookshelves. Tyler extracted the second volume of Conrad Lindstrom's *Signs of Passing*, a collection of stories about people living in a fictional swath of the old American West called Winchester County. The book was so well read that the title had nearly washed away, the cursive letters like fading trails in the leather dust. The binding was half separated from the spine and the cover was starting to tatter.

He flipped through the book idly, spot reading here and there, reveling in the familiar. Loose pencil sketches separated the stories. He stopped at a drawing of a horse and rider, lasso in the air, black bull at the other end of the page, head down, one hoof up. Tyler studied it a moment and turned the page. The next story was *The Horns of a Dilemma*. He remembered it well and could not help but smile a little.

Sheriff Hank Winchester was out on a cattle drive with his oldest son, Luke, and a bunch of cattle hands. Luke had his own ranch and his own life and had moved out of Winchester County many years before up in the high country where winter came earlier and stayed later. Luke was a good man, even if rough around the edges and not everyone's favorite Winchester. He was stubborn to a fault and quick to fight, but all of that was wrapped tightly around a solid goodness that came with his last name.

Luke and Hank failed to see eye-to-eye on most things in the world, including how to bring a herd of cattle out of a box canyon during a thunderstorm. Luke would not have been along at all were it not for a request from his Aunt Kitty – Miss Kitty to most – who was concerned that his father was getting too old to be out on a drive without someone to look after him. Like any Winchester would have, estrangement or no estrangement, Luke stepped up for his family.

Hank Winchester, of course, resented his sister's concern and found no shortage of opportunities to show his son that he could still out-shoot, out-ride and out-rope every last one of them. At night, when most of the hands were lazing around the camp fire talking about the places they'd go and the women they'd court if they weren't hard-working ranch hands, either Luke or Hank would be off tending to the herd lowing discontentedly up into the night. It would always be one or the other. If Luke was at the fire then Hank was off patrolling the herd. If Hank was at the fire, then Luke was out walking around in the dark with a rifle slung over his shoulder, pulling from a flask of whiskey.

It was the presence of death that brought them together. It took Luke physically pulling his father off of the pointed end of a thousand-pound Texas Longhorn to get Hank to see his son in a different light. Hank, who had stupidly allowed himself to become cornered up against the canyon wall with his rifle still back with his horse, had shouted for help. When no one came and the bull began its charge, he began screaming for Luke.

And Luke did come. He came in a hard gallop through the sage-brush calling his father's name in terror of the inevitable, steering his horse with his knees and aiming his rifle. He shot the bull dead with one squeeze of the trigger, but not before it had skewered Hank cleanly through the rib cage and out the back.

Much of the story was about waiting for death. As one of the hands left as fast as a horse could carry him for Doc Chisolm's place just outside of town, the others set up camp right there in the canyon. Luke did his best to dress his father's grievous wound and held him tightly in his arms beneath a stack of saddle blankets as night came and the fire hissed and popped up into the dark, dry air.

"*I'm not gonna make this, son,*" breathed Hank.

"*Stop now. You're gonna make it fine. Don't you listen to that voice. You'll be laid up awhile, that's all. Tomorrow you're gonna hurt but you'll feel better. You will.*"

Lightning licked at the canyon rim like an electric snake. Blackie and the others whinnied and shuffled restlessly on their feet as the dry breeze carried the scent of the herd through the smoke.

"*Tomorrow,*" he rasped. "*Always tomorrow. What a curse that can be to hopeful people. You're a good man, Luke. You're my boy. I love all my family. Aunt Kitty. Ben. Papa John. God knows I do. But you're my boy…*"

"*Pa, now stop. Look here…*"

"*I want you to look out after them. I want you to protect them from the world. Do you hear me Luke?*"

"*I hear you, Pa. I do. Hang on now. Just hang on. Help is coming.*"

"*They're innocent. Like your mother was innocent, God rest her. There's good people in Winchester County, Luke. They need a firm, steady*

hand. *They need someone who's not afraid to
stand up and fight for them. You're not afraid,
are you Luke?"*

"I'm not afraid, Pa."

Of course, big strong Luke was sobbing by then, but the unchar-
acteristic emotion did not cut against his father's confidence in what
needed to happen next. Hank slipped his hand from beneath the
blankets, wincing in pain, but never crying out. He handed Luke his
Sheriff's star.

"No Pa. No, please..."

*"Your name is your badge, Luke. Wear it proudly.
Make me proud, son."*

"I will, Daddy. I will..."

———

Tyler awoke sharply to the sound of Kevin's briefcase dropping onto the
floor. He stood in the doorway to Tyler's office, mouth agape, arms outstretched. For a moment, Tyler imagined that he saw horrified incomprehension on his son's face. Perhaps a flash of fear in his eyes that Tyler had
been attacked in his chair last night by some stress-induced infarction.

"What the fuck, Tyler?" Kevin said angrily, never one for familial
endearments.

Tyler sat upright, blinking. The book slid from his lap onto the
floor. He bent down to retrieve it and hit his head on the edge of the
desk. He stretched his arm down to its full length, pulling down with his
forehead against he desk, finding the book with his fingers. He picked
it up and placed it near the lamp and sat back up. He had drooled in his

sleep. He wiped his face with the back of his hand. Still disoriented, he looked at Kevin and blinked.

"Have you been here all night? Have you been drinking? You realize we have to be in court in an hour? Were you just planning on sleeping through your own testimony?"

As the fog cleared, Tyler made a patting gesture with his hand.

"Calm down, Kevin. I just nodded off."

"Calm down? Really? What if I hadn't come by? You're lucky I forgot my brief case. I was planning on going straight to the courthouse."

Tyler stood and stretched. Sunlight poured in through the windows. "So let's go, already," he said.

"You look like hell. You're in the same clothes, you haven't shaved... Christ Tyler, have you no concept of a jury trial? What is *wrong* with you?"

What was wrong with him? The answer, for the first time since waking, exploded back into consciousness. He was a dead man. That's what was wrong with him. Six to eight months was what was wrong with him.

He looked up at his son in the doorway, radiating emotion. He imagined for his own benefit that Kevin would be terrified at the prospect of losing his father. Tyler made a couple swipes down the front of his suit coat with the palms of his hands and straightened his tie.

"You can drive," he said.

On the ride to the courthouse, Kevin railed about the case, venting his concern that Tyler might stupidly say the wrong things on the stand, convincing the jury to deny them the right to forge ahead with their remake production of *Winchester County*. Tyler looked out the window, watching the city blur past them. Every few miles he opened the window a crack to let the words out.

Kevin's cell phone trilled.

"I know. I'm one my way. Another thirty minutes with this traffic. He's with me. Yes. I found him passed out in his office. He looks like shit. I have no fucking idea. He's fine. How should I know? Sleeping. Yeah. I just hope Grace has done her job preparing him. No. Yes. We'll see. We'll see. Gotta go."

Kevin snapped his phone closed and dropped it into his shirt pocket as he accelerated around the side of an insufficiently motivated pick-up.

"That was Blake. He said the judge is waiting to bring in the jury. Nice, Tyler. Real fucking great."

"It will work out," said Tyler. "They'll wait."

"You don't get it, do you?"

Tyler looked over at the question. Kevin was looking at him, colored with anger. It always struck Tyler how little Kevin looked like Sarah. The hair maybe. And the hands. But not the face. His velvet gray eyes belonged to Tyler's mother. And the nose and cheekbones down through the lips and chin belonged to Tyler's father, Kevin's namesake. It was like old family photographs of his parents had melted together.

"I loved your mother, you know," Tyler said.

"What?"

"Her father, Grampa Joe, was a big drinker. It was in her genes all along, just waiting to assert itself. Once it caught her it never let go. It didn't make her a bad person. She was a wonderful person inside. She just couldn't free herself. And I couldn't be around her that way."

Kevin made a tortured, exasperated sound.

"Why are you... have you lost your *mind* or something?"

"She was innocent. You're innocent. I'm sorry for your childhood, Kevin. I am. I'm not so innocent. I know that. If I could do it differently, I would. All I can do is tell you that I'm sorry. And that I love you."

"Tyler... Christ. Can we just focus on the goddamned case? Can you just try to stay focused for one fucking minute?"

"I came from next to nothing. My mother took a powder when I was ten. My father raised me mostly with the back of his hand. That and leaving me alone in our dinky little apartment to be raised by the television. They weren't very good parents, but they did the best they could at the time. I'm convinced of that. Maybe I've just convinced myself because that's an easier truth to believe. Everyone has a life to live. My whole life has been devoted to a career that has culminated in Shoofly Studios. It's a good company and I'm proud of it. I'll admit that. But I would trade it all if I could go back and do things differently. Because

I knew better. Unlike my parents, I was conscious of what I was doing. I was better than that. I could have done better by you, son."

"Have *you* been drinking? You look …"

"But I can't go back. We look backwards but we live forwards." He looked back out the window at the fury of traffic. "Nope. Can't go back. I can only go forward. And when I stop going forward, I want you to go forward in my place. I want you to take care of Shoofly, Kevin. Those are good, dedicated people. I've handpicked every last one of them. They need those jobs and Shoofly needs them. You should keep them. Protect them."

"Protect them? From what? Wolves?"

"They need a firm, steady hand. They need someone who's not afraid to stand up and fight for them. You're not afraid, are you, Kevin?"

Kevin looked at him sternly.

"I'm afraid you've turned fucking senile over night. I'm afraid that you're going to testify like a crazy person and blow this case and that we'll have to flush a huge investment and pay damages on top of that. So yeah, Tyler, I'm afraid. I'm fucking terrified. If you're not going to help Shoofly, then get the fuck out of the way already."

"Your name is your badge, son. Wear it proudly. Make me proud."

———

Grace met them outside the courtroom. Kevin brushed past without saying hello and disappeared inside to join the suited savages.

"Tyler," she breathed. "You look…"

"I know. I know," he said opening the door to the courtroom. "I fell asleep and lost track of time. There's nothing to be done for it. Let's go."

His unshaven dishevelment registered immediately on the judge's face as well as on the faces of one or two of the women jurors. If Janice Lindstrom or Mr. Glass noticed, their expressions did not let on.

The plaintiffs finished up with Janice's testimony and called in quick succession two new witnesses: a close associate of Jack Lindstrom to testify to Jack's dying belief that the rights to *Signs of Passing* and the literary deed to all of Winchester County were still his, and an officer of Milquest Inc. to testify that the company had never considered the *Winchester County* stories, or anything else in *Signs of Passing*, among its intellectual property holdings.

Tyler listened without listening, his upright form an empty shell in a rumpled suit. His face slack and grizzled. Grace took notes. Grace stood and objected. The suited savages objected. The judge pronounced his rulings and instructed the jury as to what they could consider and could not consider; hear and not hear. The jury watched and fidgeted and scribbled their notes.

None of it touched him.

He thought of Hank Winchester dying in his son's arms in a desert canyon, a bloody hole through his body like a tunnel that had been bored through a mountain, without long left. Maybe six to eight minutes to live.

He thought about how much he wanted his last act to be one that would please is son. He wanted – suddenly, powerfully – to testify and to win this case and to hand Kevin the next big television series in the revival of the popular American Western. A franchise. A legacy. He would hand Kevin his sheriff's badge and then quietly fade away. Disappear. He'd go someplace tropical and spend the next six to eight months looking at the sea from a white sand island as the cancer ate him alive without radiation or chemotherapy to challenge its appetite. People would wonder, of course, but life would go on and then they would stop wondering. Grace would know. He would have to tell Grace. He would have to. But no one else.

And then he would be no more.

And when enough time had passed, Grace would be free to tell the others and they would understand how he had not wanted the fact of his illness to warp their lives. How he had not wanted his last six to eight months to be a time of guilt and tip-toeing and perfunctory tributes and jockeying for position. And how, as his last wish, he had wanted Kevin to be installed as the next Chief Executive Officer of Shoofly Studios.

The board would make it their decision, but they would do as he asked, one last time. They would need to wait for David Lewis' term to run its course. David was a good man and a hell of a CEO; better than Tyler had been in many respects. And Kevin would sure take some getting used to and would need to grow into the job. He would need to mend a lot of fences. A firm hand was a good thing, but it also needed to be steady and it needed to guide with wisdom and compassion and it needed to not choke the life out of the deck hands. It would be bumpy for a while. Maybe a long while. But that was just how it would have to be. He was as upset about the turn of events as anyone and they should all be grateful that they had more than eight months to be upset about it. They would all want to know if Tyler Freeman was really gone. Grace would tell them and they would all be stunned and some of them would cry and wonder and then life would move forward.

Tyler's cell phone chirped, bringing him sharply back into the present. The judge's eyes sliced down in his direction like a scythe through stalks of wheat. Every head in the jury box turned. The chirping continued, louder and louder with each trill, for a full twenty seconds as Tyler searched his pockets, Grace next to him looking on, Kevin fuming in humiliation at the next table, and finally silenced the phone.

"Our apologies, your honor," said Grace. "That will not happen again."

"See that it doesn't," said the judge. "Or the next time I will add another phone to my collection."

The jury laughed uncomfortably. The opening lecture about phones in the courtroom had been difficult to forget. The judge had presented a cardboard box and tilted it towards the courtroom, then full of candidate jurors, to show that it was full of cellular telephones rattling like a box of bones.

"It is your civic duty that calls you today, ladies and gentlemen, and only your civic duty," the Judge Manumitt had boomed, making a lasting first impression. "Not your spouse or your friend or your child or your boss. In this room the only call you can receive is from me and from God and neither of us need a telephone."

Tyler noted the caller as he turned off the phone.

Matthews, Benjamin, MD.

He should not have been surprised. Tyler had not made his CT scan appointment as promised. Now Doc Matthews was making good on his promise to hound him. The screen collapsed its light into black and Tyler slipped the phone back into his pocket. Mr. Glass uncrossed his arms. The judge nodded. The Milquest executive resumed his testimony.

After a vigorous cross-examination, the judge dismissed the jury for lunch. When they had left the courtroom, the judge inquired of Mr. Glass as to his intentions for the rest of the afternoon.

"Your Honor," he intoned, "it is the plaintiff's intent to call Tyler Freeman, which should take us through the end of the day and probably all the way through the next."

The judge nodded his approval and after making sure there were no other issues to take up, dismissed the parties until one-thirty. Even as the judge's black robe was whisking out the back door of the courtroom Kevin was standing before Tyler and Grace on the other side of the table. He leaned on his hands and spoke in a raspy whisper so as not to be overheard.

"Nice, Tyler," he said. "Maybe this afternoon you can play the fucking kazoo."

"It was an accident," said Grace, not looking up. "Let it go, Kevin."

"Don't tell me to let it go, Grace," he snapped, his eyes almost biting at her. "You don't represent me and you aren't my mother."

"Fine," she said dismissively. "Ready to go, Tyler? Let's go get some lunch."

"Negative," said Kevin. "We're all going to the conference room."

"He needs to eat," she said.

"No. He's up next for all the marbles. Nothing I've seen this morning has given me any confidence. I'll buy him an entire steak dinner if he gets this right. In the meantime, I've got a protein bar, because apparently I was the only one who thought ahead. He can have that. If you've done your job, Grace, this shouldn't take long. If I had thought to bring a razor and shaving crème I guess I'd shave him too."

Kevin jerked his head toward the other table where the Shoofly lawyers were huddled over a document like hyenas over a shank of zebra.

"They've got some new notes on where Glass is likely to go on his direct and you need to be up to speed Tyler. Grace, if you want to head off to lunch, we can handle it from here."

Grace stood, pulling her shoulders back.

"You need to show some respect, Kevin."

"And you need to know your place, Grace. This is a company matter and he's never needed separate counsel. That was an accommodation for strategic purposes only."

Tyler stood.

"Stop it, both of you. Kevin, I'll give you fifteen minutes, then my lawyer and I are going across the street to get a sandwich. Everybody needs to calm down and get along. Life's too short for this shit."

They all filed out of the courtroom and trooped down the hall to a small conference room where Tyler sat down in a hard, uncomfortable chair and allowed Kevin and the lawyers representing Shoofly Studios to bludgeon him with pointers and questions. After precisely fifteen minutes, Grace, who was standing behind him, laid her hand on his shoulder.

"Time for some lunch, Tyler. We need to keep your strength up."

Tyler stood. No one objected. The lawyers looked at each other and had then shrugged and nodded. He had answered their questions. He knew what he was doing. Even Kevin seemed satisfied.

They parted company and Grace led Tyler to the elevator and across the street to a small deli. They each ordered a sandwich and a drink and a bag of chips and sat down at a window table to eat and watch the passers-by and listen to the incessant jingle of the little brass bell over the door. They were halfway finished before either of them said a word.

"You like what you do, Grace?" Tyler asked. "Being a lawyer."

"Less and less," she said after a considered moment. "It's a kid's game. Like cops and robbers or cowboys and Indians. It only works if you can take it deadly seriously and at the same time not seriously at all. I'm not a kid any more. I find that I'm either taking it all too seriously or not seriously enough."

"Thinking of hanging it up?"

She shrugged and finished off her sandwich. Then she nodded.

"I think so."

"What will you do?"

"No idea. I don't laugh enough. Something that makes me laugh. What about you? It's a big world out there. When are you going to actually stop dragging yourself into that office?"

"Soon," he said.

"Right. You've only been saying that for a decade. I'll believe it when I see it. Soon when?"

"Soon."

———

When they had all reassembled back in the courtroom, the judge came in and went on record without calling in the jury.

"We have an issue," he said. "Juror Number Seven, Peter Philips, has advised Madam Clerk that he has just received news regarding his business requiring his immediate attention. Apparently, one of the shopping malls he owns has flooded. There are injuries and arrests and reports of general mayhem and he claims his personal involvement is critical."

The judge paused, scratching his thicket of beard and thinking to himself.

"Now, I can deny the request. The shopping mall in question is in another state and I am not convinced that the situation cannot be handled without him for the balance of the afternoon. There are only three hours left in the day. Having said that, I do not think you will have Mr. Philips' full attention and, if I deny the request, I am convinced we will have an angry juror on our hands. So," the judge leaned back in his chair and interlaced his fingers, "I am taking requests. Mr. Glass?"

"Your Honor," said Mr. Glass, standing. "If it is all the same to the court, since it is still the plaintiff's case, I would prefer to avoid the risk that my client is blamed for forcing Mr. Philips to stay. Our vote would be to adjourn and pick up with Mr. Freeman's testimony in the morning."

"Mr. Stebbing, what is the preference from Shoofly?"

The savage Stebbing stood, thrusting his bald, pointy head into the air like he was trying to pop a balloon.

"Move forward, judge. We're ready to go and think we should stay on track. Our concern is that Mr. Glass is taking tactical advantage of an unnecessary delay."

"Ms. Bell?"

Grace stood.

"You Honor, if it will help Mr. Philips tend to an emergency that we may not fully understand, I do not see any great harm in giving him the remains of the day to take care of his business. My client and I are fine with a recess until tomorrow morning."

A sound of strangled consternation came from Kevin's general direction. Neither Tyler nor Grace turned to look.

———

Grace dropped Tyler off at the studio to retrieve his car. She left him standing in the parking lot telling him that she was going back to her office to make use of the unexpected time that Peter Philips' shopping mall disaster had created. He watched her drive away. It felt like the blood was leaving his body. He felt hollow.

He had almost told her. At a long stoplight he had almost turned to her and blurted it out right there in the front seat of her car. But he hadn't and now he wished he had. It was getting too heavy to carry alone. He was as lonely now as he had ever been in his life.

He could have called Dr. Matthews, the only other person in the world aside from a couple of anonymous lab technicians, who knew why Tyler was now counting backwards. He could have gone to the hospital for the CT scan as he was supposed to do; throw himself upon the mercy of medical science and its white-robed brethren so that they could officially kick off the last phase of his life with grave expressions and batteries of confirmatory tests and orders – *immediate* orders – for radiation and chemicals and an early start on the embalming.

He knew he should. He was supposed to. But he couldn't. He did not want the ministrations of the white-robed brethren. Not now. Not ever. When his phone rang in Grace's car and he had seen that Dr. Matthews was again calling for him to account, to report, to begin the end, he had wanted to hurl the damn thing out the window on to the freeway. Instead, he had turned the phone off, vowing never to turn it on again.

Tyler walked the last few feet to his car, reached into his pocket and extracted the phone. He looked at it for a long minute and then broke his vow. He fished through his wallet for the card and then dialed the number.

"Warren?"

"Yes?"

"Tyler Freeman."

"Tyler! My old friend! *Man-o-man* what a good surprise!"

"I've got some unexpected time tonight. Want to have that drink?"

When they had finished coordinating, Tyler hung up and looked at his watch, wondering how he should spend the next few hours of his last six to eight months. He drove out of the studio lot believing that he did not know the answer to that question.

When Grace found him standing in her lobby she was in mid-stride, minding not to slosh a cup of hot tea. Stopping abruptly in surprise, she scalded her hand and spilled water on the floor. There was a minute or two of mopping up and running Grace's hand under cool water before she invited him back to her office. It was just the two of them. Tyler closed the door anyway.

"Can I get you some tea," she asked, sitting at the table by the window. Her desk beyond was clean, except for a bundle of pens, a tidy stack of files, a telephone, an antique lamp with a tasseled shade, and old photos of Stephen and the kids.

"No. Thanks," he said. "That stuff is dangerous."

Grace laughed her carefree laugh, like it was a kind of singing.

"True enough. I can ice it. That's safer."

"No."

"Okay. So then, to what do I owe this unexpected pleasure?"

"It's not a pleasure, Grace," he said sitting. He clasped her hand on the table. "I have something to tell you."

Her smile melted away horribly as he spoke, sticking grotesquely for a moment at a half-semblance of its former self and then continuing to dissolve as her face turned ashen. She kept her hand sequestered within his, using the other to wipe away the tears. When she spoke, it was part lament, part prayer, part curse.

"Oh, Tyler. Oh, Tyler. No, no. Oh God, Tyler."

She made a half-hearted effort to convince him to do everything that the white robes instructed. But Grace did not believe her own words. She had seen the radiation and chemicals go to work on Stephen. She had said many times that there was nothing she would not have traded to give him back his quality of life in those last months.

When that part of it had run its course, Tyler told her what he wanted her to do for him. She extricated her hand and got up and sat behind her clean desk, pushing aside the stack of files and took notes, still sniffling.

"I don't want anyone to know... until it's done."

"I understand," she whispered.

"For all they know, I'm on a long vacation after this goddamned trial. They'll be glad to have me out of their hair."

"I understand. Not a word." She hesitated. "Tyler, are you sure about Kevin? Can he run that business?"

"No. Not yet. But he'll learn. He's smart."

"Can he survive without you running interference? Will they have him? I mean he's not exactly... liked."

"They will honor my dying wish. They owe me that. And Kevin will do a whole lot better without the old man walking the halls looking over his shoulder. My very presence is like one big, never-ending second guess. And no one will give him a real chance to be his own man until I'm not around."

"It's just…"

"I know your thoughts about Kevin, Grace. But he's my son. I never gave him enough of myself when he was young. I learned that from my dad. Anyway, this is all I can give him now. The rest is up to him."

"And if he takes down what you've built?"

"He won't. He won't let me down. I would hope the board would intervene before that happens anyway."

"If it's your dying wish? Maybe not before it's too late."

"Grace…"

"Okay. I'm sorry. Whatever you want. Where will you go to…"

"To die?"

"Oh, Tyler. This can't be true."

A fresh surge of emotion threatened to break through. She fought it back.

"I don't know where I'll go," he said. "The middle of the ocean someplace."

"Are you sure? Would you be more comfortable here? At home I mean?"

"No. I wouldn't." He looked at his watch. Stood. Looked at her, destroyed behind her desk. "I'm sorry to tell you this. Here. Now. This way. But it's my first time dying. I don't know what I'm doing."

"You're leaving," she said. "Apparently."

"I'm meeting a friend."

She stood.

"You're okay for tomorrow? I can try for a continuance."

"I'll be there."

"I can drive you. I'll pick you up."

"No. I want to tell you something. The thing I came here to tell you in the first place. The hardest thing of all."

She began to cry and he stepped in to cup her cheeks with his hands, brushing her cheeks with his thumbs. He was on the hardwood; she was on the corner of the Persian. Their faces were level and close.

"Grace Bell, I love you. I love you more than I have ever loved any other woman in my life. And I always have. I loved you when Stephen, my good friend Stephen, was alive to be the perfect husband and father. Looking over the shoulders of my own wives, I envied him. I loved you then and I love you now. I have never told you this because I am a coward when it comes to my own feelings. And because there has always been another day. Tomorrow. Always a tomorrow. What a curse that can be to hopeful people. Well, not any more. I am running out of tomorrows. And I don't want to die a coward. I told my son this morning that I loved him and that I was sorry. He thought I was crazy. I am telling you the same thing and you, too, are free to think me crazy. But I do love you, Graciebell," he said, his own eyes welling. It had been Stephen's endearment, long out of use. "And I am so very, very sorry."

He leaned in, kissed her on her lips, and drank her into his senses.

"I'll see you tomorrow," he said, trying to smile. And then he left.

———

Pillsbury was waiting at a small table on the far side of the bar. Tyler stood in the doorway of *The Last Call Pub* and scanned the faces, not seeing him until Pillsbury stood up and waved his arms like a shipwreck survivor to a passing plane. There was music playing, but Tyler could not make it out over the human din of happy hour.

When he reached the table Pillsbury stepped around and gave him a hug and shook his hand with such enthusiasm that Tyler wondered whether he would ever let it go. They sat and Tyler flagged down a mannish-boy that looked too young to be slinging drinks and ordered a scotch on the rocks. Pillsbury was nursing something dark and foamy.

"Warren Lemiski," said Tyler with an appraising grin, "my old friend. How the hell have you been?"

"Oh, Tyler, I'm good," he said, beaming. "I'm real good. How about you?"

"Ask me after that drink gets here."

Pillsbury laughed like he had just heard the punch line of his favorite joke.

"*Man-o-man*, Tyler. It's good to see you."

They caught up with each other in fits and starts, summing up their lives in details and data and anecdotes that failed to do the job of summing up, something that was never really possible in the first place. How does one sum up a life without doing it a grave injustice in the process? Was there some averaging of events or some median of emotion or accomplishment or regret that could be rendered as some fair substitute for the whole? Were there representative moments or were there simply moments, each one an indivisible lifetime in itself?

Tyler watched as much as he listened. Pillsbury spoke with the same irrepressible enthusiasm sparking in the same clear blue eyes that Tyler had remembered after all of these years. His hairline was eroding up his scalp leaving a pattern that resembled the beginnings of flesh-colored peninsulas disappearing into soft, strawberry-blonde curls. He smiled and laughed easily in a way that seemed to open up his entire face. His teeth flashed the white bone of a young man. He was the picture of health and contentment.

Pillsbury's open, uncomplicated countenance, however, was rather at odds with his story. Warren, like Tyler, had been married twice. He had divorced his first wife, with whom he had a daughter and an unhappy marriage, in order to marry the second wife, whom he loved but who eventually died in a car accident on the evening of their fifteenth wedding anniversary. The only child of that second marriage, a boy named Jonathan, fell from a horse and broke his neck. He lived only for five more years, mostly paralyzed. Warren left his associate position at his corporate accounting and auditing firm to start his own business, hiring out his services to small mom and pop operations that needed someone who knew how to balance an income statement. The scaled-back practice gave him time to be with his son and, after that, to play violin with the symphony. He still misses Jonathan and he still plays the violin and he still has some of the old clients that he continues to help out, especially around tax time, less for the money than for his inability to tell them to find someone else.

But Warren explained that he was mostly retired from the business of *counting other people's money*, as Tyler had put it. Now he spent most of his time working for the daughter of his first marriage, Katie, a veterinarian with her own struggling animal clinic up on 54th and Val Vista. Warren did Katie's books and helped out with the patients whenever she was short-staffed. He knew the finer points of caring for dogs, cats, birds, lizards, snakes and rodents. On the weekends, he taught people, adults and children, how to play the violin. Katie has one son, Stuart, whom Tyler had already met.

"He seems like a nice kid," said Tyler, stirring his drink. "Knows his video games. Is that still what they call them? Video games?"

"I don't get those things," said Pillsbury. "Never have. He's a smart boy, though. He does well in school."

"Good genes."

"Yeah, all from his mother. How's... Keith?"

"Kevin. He's good. He works for me. Heads up our Creative Development Department."

"Takes after his old man," said Pillsbury, nodding with approval.

"I suppose. Spends most of his time these days working on that damn case."

"I read about that. How's it going?"

"No telling yet. Just getting started really. They say it'll take three weeks. The first *day* felt like three weeks."

"So, this is all about getting to do the remake?" Pillsbury asked.

Tyler nodded and sipped.

"And they say you don't have the rights and you say you do have the rights."

"Right. Correct."

"Think you'll win?"

"Hope so. Lot of money at stake. We charged ahead a long time ago. Janice Lindstrom kind of swooped in at the last minute and called me a thief."

"Oh, nonsense. You're no thief."

"Where were you when we were picking a jury?" quipped Tyler.

Pillsbury laughed again, like he was trying to catch rainwater in his mouth.

"*Man-o-man*, Tyler, I sure loved that show. Remember that? Every day watching that show? I mean, *every* day! Mom trying to get me to go outside and all I could do was keep my eyes glued to that little screen." His blue eyes suddenly widened, the memories coming too fast for him to process. "*Holy cow*, we ran away over that show! Remember that?"

Tyler nodded and smiled. Pillsbury laughed, rollicking in his chair. Tyler could not help but laugh back at him, now shaking his head in disbelief.

"I do remember," Tyler said. "Lasted what... eighteen hours? Hanging out in the woods behind the *Shop Stop* subsisting on rations of candy and gum."

"My mom was so mad. Said I was lucky my dad had shot himself."

Tyler winced, remembering that fact about his friend, but recovered quickly.

"Yes, I didn't walk for a solid week after that. I didn't watch television for two months."

The server dropped by a bowl of nuts and they each took a few and washed them down.

"What in the hell ever possessed us to do such a stupid thing?" Tyler asked, shaking his head and not really expecting an answer.

Warren's face began a slow collapse into a seriousness more befitting his age. He put the glass to his mouth and drank, dabbing at the foam on his lips with a napkin.

"Wasn't stupid," he said. "And I know exactly why."

Tyler waited. His eyes burned from exhaustion. He suddenly wanted to lie down. The noise around him was like a blanket he wanted to pull over his throbbing head.

"We got the call," said Pillsbury. "We were simply answering."

"The call. What call?"

"Boy," he said, rubbing his chin with his fingers. "How to explain something like this. It makes sense in my own head, but explaining it is kind of... weird."

"I'm no stranger to weird," said Tyler with a sip.

"Okay. Let's try it this way. Towards the end there, my son Jonathan knew he was not going to make it. We always tried to keep the talk positive, but the doctors were nothing but bad news. His organs were giving up on him. The only thing keeping him alive, other than a lot of medical machinery, was his sheer force of will. He was a strong-willed kid. He just kept hanging on. He defied all of the odds. Surprised everyone. The men in the white coats kept talking about months; weeks even. *Weeks.* He lived, technically I mean, he *existed*, for five years."

But they were right, thought Tyler, without saying it. *The white-coated bastards were right in the end.*

"I had him all set up at home for awhile there, which was really great. I kind of went crazy with bird feeders because he liked the birds. And the house abuts a greenbelt so every so often we got deer. But towards the end it just got too serious and we were spending most of our time at the hospital anyway, so..."

Pillsbury took a drink and gave a look around the bar, blinking, clearing his head.

"Sorry. Anyway. One day I was up visiting him, it was around the holidays, and these three girls, young girls, eleven, twelve maybe, came by to sing carols to patients. Part of a church group thing. And they came into his hospital room to sing. They sang Silent Night. In these beautiful, high whispered voices."

He made his fingertips dance in the air like falling snow.

"When they were done, they gave us a little curtsey and wished us a Merry Christmas and told Jonathan that they hoped he felt better, which was kind of silly because no one looking at Jonathan at that point could entertain any hope that he was ever going to get any better.

"And when they were gone and it was just the two of us, Jonathan told me that he was going to a better place. That's what he said. He didn't talk well then, but the words were clear. *Dad, I'm going to a better place.* And the next day he was gone."

Tyler watched his old friend, trying to understand but saying nothing.

"I think, Tyler… this will sound crazy. Or pious. I'm neither of those things."

"I'm listening."

"I think that those better places… kind of… call to us. I think we're wired to improve our lot in life. Not wealth. But happiness. You know? Contentment. Satisfaction. Peace. And I think we're capable of enduring great unhappiness and discontentment to get there. To get to that better place. But that's not enough. Not nearly enough. Because …" Pillsbury frowned, grappling for the words.

"Because we're afraid," said Tyler without really meaning to.

"Yes. Yes. Because we're afraid. We're afraid to let go of what we know. What we know about the world. About ourselves. We're terrified of disappointing the people we love by leaving them. Abandoning them to become someone different. We cling to the devil we know because we're afraid of doing the very thing we were made to do: which is to keep moving and changing. To improve our circumstances. To let go and move on. To get to the better place. And that tension lasts to our very last breath. Fear of death is just an extreme manifestation of the fear we have of any change. The more irrevocable the change, the greater the fear. And just as we are capable of enduring great unhappiness and hardship to get to the better place, we are just as capable of enduring great unhappiness and hardship to keep from letting go. To keep hanging on. We are always so …"

Warren abandoned the thought and shook his head instead, as if at something that could never be understood.

"Jonathan fought it to the very end. He was as terrified of dying as anyone else. He was afraid to abandon me. Afraid of what I would think of him for leaving me alone. It had been just the two of us for so long. But then I think Jonathan heard those girls come into the room and sing to him. And something in that sound punched through the veil and called to him. It was like a beacon that he recognized but could never identify. Something in that sound, something profound, made sense of his life. Something in that sound convinced him to just let go of everything he knew. And to go to a better place."

"Heaven," said Tyler matter-of-factly.

"No. Not Heaven. I don't know. Maybe Heaven. I'm not saying there is such a thing. It's not about religion. It's about ... *living*. Living means leaving. And arriving. We are always leaving and arriving. Leaving and arriving. Or at least we should be. In the same way a river is simultaneously leaving and arriving. The same way a movie is a river of still shots. The movie is not the still shot; it's one still shot handing off to another. And I think that same instinct to live even guides us *out* of life, across the line and into death. Because our instinct to live is simply the positive expression of the inevitability of change. Living is a process of change. Jonathan's last act of living was letting go."

"Dying, you mean."

"Yes. Dying. His last, life-affirming act was to die. He loved me. I know that. But clinging to me was holding him in stasis. It was killing him. He was alive, but there was no life left in him. In letting go of everything, including me, he lived again."

Another drink. Another glance around the room. Tyler waited.

"And when he was gone, I couldn't accept it. I knew it was coming, but when it finally came, I crawled into a bottle and deadened my senses to convince myself that time had stopped; that I could not live in the minutes and the hours and the days and the weeks and the months and the years after he ceased to exist. I wanted everything to freeze in place so that moving on from the last moment of his life was not possible. It did not matter how much pain and misery and anguish was in that bottle with me. I would endure it all. And that was the opposite of living. That was death-affirming and life-denying."

"So, what'd you do?" asked Tyler.

"I stayed mostly drunk for a year and a half. Went broke. Lost most of my friends. The world kept changing. I stood still, dying. Like those movies we used to watch on the gym wall at Dolly Madison. Tom Sawyer.

And the projector would stick on one frame and the bulb would melt ol' Tom Sawyer into goo right before our eyes."

Pillsbury took another long drink and wiped his lips on the napkin.

"And then one day I was walking across the lawn of the Center Street Plaza and I came across this young woman sitting in a folding chair under a cherry blossom, eyes closed, chin raised, practicing the cello. There was a lot going on around her, well, you know the Plaza, traffic on two sides, lots of people. But it was… God, how do I explain this… it was like she was in another world. Like I was watching someone in some other magical dimension. For that moment, however long it lasted for her, she had found that better place. I don't remember a thing about how she played. I only remember the look on her face. It was one of the most beautiful things I've ever seen. Not her face; her expression. Something in that expression called to me. I know that sounds ridiculous, Tyler. I know. But I glimpsed a better place too, maybe hers, maybe my own, maybe there's only one that we all keep aiming for and stumbling towards, like it's there in the background our entire lives looking for portals through which it can show itself. I don't know those answers. All I know is that that woman's face was like a portal to that other better place. I could see it. Through her I could see it. I could feel it. And it was like a call to me to keep living. It was like the better place was calling out to me.

"I sat down on the grass and I watched her practice. Utterly spellbound. Until she finally packed up her cello and folded up her chair and left." Pillsbury gave a small laugh. "I probably scared her. I was so riveted. I stayed there for another hour after that, lying on the grass looking up at the sky. And then, Tyler, I stood up and I let go of everything that was and everything that I knew. I let go of my son as he had let go of me. And I started living again. I left. I arrived. Like the river. Like the movie. I kept moving; kept trading one frame for the next and the next, each moment a little different than the last. I've been clean and sober and hooked on root beer ever since."

Warren laughed and raised his glass. Tyler obliged and they toasted to something he still did not fully understand. The server swooped by and switched out the bowl of nuts. They both waved off another round and he was gone.

"So what the hell does that have to do with us running away from home?" Tyler asked.

"We weren't running away from something so much as running toward something."

"A better place," said Tyler, nodding, remembering his father. Remembering his mother and Mr. Winston with Mr. Winston's family back East that became his mother's new family, and the sight of his mother's car turning the corner and never coming back. Remembering the small empty apartment smelling vaguely of greasy chicken scraps rotting in the trash, and the living room with the worn green couch and the ratty blue pillow and the window that would not open because the crank was lost. He remembered the dizzy feeling he got from watching that spinning wagon wheel on the television. And he remembered those horses, running full out. *Huckledy-buck.*

"Yes," said Pillsbury. "For me, that show – *Winchester County* – was like watching that woman at the Plaza play the cello. Or what Jonathan must have heard in the sound of those caroling girls. It's always calling to us, Tyler. *Live. Live. Live. Don't stop. Flow. Leave. Arrive. Leave. Arrive. Live. Let go. Float on the river of moments.* So… ten years old and we answered the call. We took off in search of something we felt and that we could touch with our imagination, but that we could not possibly understand. I still don't understand it. Not really. I just recognize it when I hear it beating in the background, or when I see it shining through a crack in the wall."

Pillsbury threw his head back and laughed.

"*Man-o-man*, Tyler. You must think I'm a loon."

"Not at all," said Tyler, finishing his drink, not knowing what to think, fearing that maybe his friend was a loon. A long while passed in which they said nothing and borrowed from the noise around them.

"Can I ask you something?"

"Yes," said Tyler. "Anything."

"You seem… Is everything okay? With your health, I mean? You're looking…"

He didn't finish. He didn't have to. Tyler mustered a smile. He nodded.

"I'm tired. That's all. Litigation is a young man's game, Warren. I'm losing sleep waiting around for them to call me to testify."

"So when do you think you will you get called?" Pillsbury asked, his eyes preternaturally blue, like the color of the distant sea in his grandson's video game.

"Tomorrow," Tyler said. "I get called tomorrow."

———

"Your honor, the plaintiff calls Tyler Freeman."

The judge nodded at Mr. Glass and then looked down rather severely at Tyler.

"Mr. Freeman, you may take the witness stand."

Grace patted him on the arm as he stood. He felt the extra meaning in her fingertips and the weight of her look. There was a stir in the room, a general holding of breath not unlike the collective, sharpened attention in the oval room around the fish tank when a nurse appeared at the entrance of the hallway with her clipboard and her plastic clogs.

He walked to the witness stand, a leather-padded chair pushed up into its little wooden enclosure, as if perched upon the prow of a small boat sticking out into the courtroom. The short walk across the room from one chair to the other seemed to have worn him out and he sat down heavily, the cushion hissing beneath him. The clerk took off her headset and stood and raised her hand. He swore to tell the truth, so help him.

"Mr. Freeman," declared Mr. Glass. His spectacles flashed fluorescent. "Good morning."

"Good morning," said Tyler, clearing his throat.

"You have been in the courtroom from the beginning of this trial, correct?"

"Yes."

"So you have heard the testimony of all of the plaintiff's witnesses."

"Yes."

"Including the testimony of the plaintiff, herself, Ms. Lindstrom."

Mr. Glass gestured. Tyler looked over at the table reserved for the plaintiff and her attorney. Janice Lindstrom, daughter of Jack, granddaughter of Conrad, met his gaze and looked away. She seemed oddly alone without Mr. Glass either asking her questions or sitting next to her.

"Yes," he said. "I heard her testimony."

"So then you heard the part of her testimony in which she said, under oath, just as you are now, that her father, Jack Lindstrom, never actually conveyed to you any ownership rights to that collection of stories about Winchester County."

"Yes. I heard that."

"And, just to be clear, Mr. Freeman, we are talking about the stories found in the two-volume book called *Signs of Passing* by Ms. Lindstrom's grandfather, Conrad Lindstrom."

Tyler's eyes skated, letting go of Mr. Glass. The jury hunched against the wall like commuters on a wide train with no windows. The transit authority supervisor fussed at something in her eye. The construction foreman, already uncomfortable, crossed his legs. The shopping mall owner, looking like he had put in a long night, picked at the diamond stud in his lobe.

"Mr. Freeman?"

Kevin sat at the Shoofly table in a tight suited, savage sandwich. The savage on his right was carving into his legal pad in sharp scribbles. The savage on his left, Mr. Stebbing, listened with an amused expression, twisting the ring on his finger like an over-the-top villain in one of Shoofly's Double-O-Seven send-ups. Between them, Kevin sat rigidly, jaw clenched, expression fixed, like a border guard, watching every word as it passed his father's mouth.

"I heard that testimony, yes."

"And are we to understand that you believe Ms. Lindstrom to be a liar?"

"Objection."

Grace and Stebbing are on their feet together, their voices blending in Tyler's ears. There is argument and the judge has to interrupt, his baritone stretching its legs for the first time that morning. Tyler hears none of it. He feels their words like waves slapping up against the prow of his little courtroom boat. He is so tired of being awake that he wants to push the chair back and curl up right there on the deck and go to sleep.

But there would be no sleep. He knew better. He was wise to this feeling by now. Exhaustion did not herald sleep. Not any more. Where once there might have been sleep, now there was only a widening ache. A thirst. The long, sleepless night had now begun to unfurl across its third day and he knew that this was but a taste of the next six to eight months to come. The ache would only grow. The thirst would only deepen.

The night, again, had been spent pacing in his robe from window to chair in his large, quiet home. His attention was like a scrap of bloody meat for a pack of savage dogs, pulling against one another. One dog was called *the trial.* Another called *death.* A third, *Grace,* and the cruelty of his declaration of love, and the ache that was blossoming in his dying heart now that he had spoken that truth. A fourth dog, *Pillsbury,* suddenly, after all of these years, Pillsbury and his dead son and his daughter the struggling veterinarian. A fifth, *Kevin,* his own son, and what would become of him on the other side of six to eight months. And there were others, hungry dogs with no name, yanking at the gristly scrap of attention, whose identities kept changing in the shadows. They all wanted his attention.

He had spent much of his time in the library, beneath a solitary lamp, attempting to read himself into unconsciousness. Words, those lullabies of letters, might have lulled him to sleep. They always had before. But no. Life was different now. No matter the book, the letters had all lost their adhesion, coming uncoupled from one another and shriveling into writhing worms of ash that rolled and crawled in agony across the page. Instead, his eyes read the empty, broken spaces behind the tortured ink. It was mostly the empty space behind the ink that kept him awake.

He decided that the words he needed were in a book he kept at his office, the only place he had experienced anything approaching sleep in the past two days.

So at four o'clock, Tyler went upstairs and pulled a clean suit and shirt and tie out of the closet and got dressed, thinking only afterwards that he should have showered and not thinking at all about needing a shave. He caught himself in the light of the hallway mirror, doorknob in his hand. He looked like hell warmed over in a nice suit. He didn't care.

The security guard at the studio had greeted him at the door, just as he had the morning before. He accused Tyler of becoming an early bird and Tyler kept walking and said there was nothing wrong with being an early bird and the guard had said something about worms and leaving some for the rest of the poor saps who liked to get up with the sun and laughed and laughed until the elevator door slid closed and amputated the sound and it fell away like something dead beneath him.

The office was dark and still and abandoned. This place he had built, from the ground up. It felt now like a husk of something dead. A place for homeless mollusks. For years now. For years it had felt this way to him. And yet he was only now identifying the feeling for what it was. He was a mollusk living in an abandoned shell. An imposter in another man's house. He had been, for years now, impersonating his former self as a dreamer and a maker of dreams from light and sound. The irony was not lost on him that from his youth he had shepherded the passion to build a dream factory and somewhere in the midst he had entirely lost the passion for dreaming. And now, even sleeping was lost to him. For ten years, maybe fifteen, he had been manufacturing a kind of simulacrum of dreaming. And now he was awake, a dying mollusk, in this still and abandoned place.

He had kept off the overhead lights and sat down behind his desk and pulled the brass chain on his desk lamp. Darkness fell over the top of the shade and onto the desk like a heavy rain. The desk beneath the light was empty except for a stack of transcripts. Kevin's red letters scrawled angrily on a yellow square of paper adhered to the top of the stack were difficult to ignore.

TYLER: READ!!

So he had tried to read his deposition. But even his own words were alien and would have nothing to do with him. The most he could do was turn the pages, every now and then stopping on one of Grace's objections and hearing her voice in the dark, and then moving on until he could take no more. He closed the cover and pushed the stack out of the light.

Signs of Passing, Volume Two, was still on the desk where he had left it the morning before. Tyler had opened it at random and began reading.

> "Never bet your life, your land or your love,
> son." Hank held up three fingers like a pitchfork
> and pushed his hand across the table so that
> the young blacksmith was sure to understand.
> "You lose any one of those bets and Death will
> surely mount his steed and come riding for you
> 'cause it means you don't value what the good
> Lord has seen fit to let you have."
>
> "Yessir, Sheriff," said Simms, chastened. The
> master blacksmith began pounding out a shoe,
> beating the red iron back into black. "I know'd
> it was a stupid thing to do. How was I to know
> he was holding a full house?"
>
> "That's the point, Billy. You never really know
> what the other man is holding. It's not worth
> the gamble, no matter how strong your hand."

Tyler knew the story, of course. It was *The Full House*, the story where Sheriff Winchester, in purchasing some grazing land that abutted the easternmost reaches of Winchester Ranch, stretching over into neighboring Granite County, had unknowingly traded on another man's poor judgment.

The seller was a Mr. Pickett, a mean drunk in need of money who had, in more sober times, won the forty-acre parcel fair and square in a game of poker. The loser of that fateful hand of cards was Billy Simms, a young widower who had taken up with a comely Sioux woman named Nakota, who Mr. Pickett usually referred to sneeringly as *Sue*, because that was just the kind of man Mr. Pickett was. Billy had inherited the land from his father after he died from tuberculosis, the disease that subsequently killed Billy's young wife, Frances, a teacher who was known throughout Granite County for her hats and her singing voice and her way with words on the subjects of drink and gambling.

Nakota had been one of Frances' do-good literacy projects. When Frances had fallen ill, Nakota came by the house daily to tend to her needs. After Frances died, Nakota lived up on the property in a little twelve by twelve shack Billy had built for her, about a hundred yards off from the main house where Billy laid his head at night. By day, Billy worked in Granite Creek as a blacksmith's apprentice. Nakota kept busy during the lit hours making Billy's clothing and tending to the garden and the animals and making sure he came home to a hot meal and a basin full of warm water for scrubbing the iron soot off of his face and hands. Fate's poker game meant that what small amount of money Billy had made from blacksmithing to squirrel away for a better life, was suddenly to be paid over to Mr. Pickett as rent for the land Billy once owned just as his father before him.

Once a month Mr. Pickett collected the rent from Billy in town, usually just as Billy was billowing the fire and putting on his apron and gloves. When he had collected from Billy, Mr. Pickett usually rode up the valley to the small house in the hills and collected a different kind of rent from Nakota.

A month after the sale, Hank and Kitty Winchester went out riding to survey the new boundaries of Winchester Ranch. Kitty had been moping over her younger brother Ben returning to San Francisco, and with Papa John and Evangeline Winchester off to a cattle auction in Santa Fe, Kitty had not been especially keen on staying back at the ranch as her brother Hank went out riding alone.

It just so happened that they rode up on the Simms farm at precisely the time that Mr. Pickett was there trying to collect his twisted version of rent for a parcel of land he had sold to the Winchesters a month earlier and no longer owned. From the look on Nakota's face and the tear of her dress, it had not taken Hank or Kitty any time at all to piece together what had been going on.

There was a scuffle of sorts, but Mr. Pickett, britches down around his ankles, was no match for Hank Winchester. Hank tied his hands with a length of rope from his saddlebag and threw the man up on his horse and rode him back into town, leaving Kitty to have a woman-to-woman talk with Nakota. After depositing Mr. Pickett in the Granite County Jail, Hank had paid a visit to the young blacksmith.

"'Spose I owe you rent now, don't I Sheriff?"
said Billy.

Hank looked at the young man and saw himself in those eyes and in the expression on his face, streaked with black iron grime, back when he was cuttin' up and giving Papa John a new gray hair for every day. Back then life was a card game you couldn't lose because every hand was better than the last and whenever you sat down the world just pushed everything to your side of the table. And then one day you lost a hand, like a wife dying, and the unfairness of it all was like a slap in the face and you realized for the first time that you might just be mortal and that maybe you always had been mortal, and that you had been surviving so far only on dumb luck and the indulgence of oth-ers and you don't like the sound of that one bit so you double down, betting everything just to feel the old you pumping through those veins. He remembered losing Papa John's favorite horse once in a poker game. He remembered the man with the inside strait shaking his head pitifully and telling him that a man never bets his horse and then agreed to take an I owe you for twice the money. Papa John had paid the debt and then taken it out of Hank's hide. With interest. An expensive lesson well learned.

"Nope. Don't owe me any rent," said Hank. "I knew your daddy. He was a good man, Billy. I know he'd want that land to stay in your name. He worked hard for it and you should keep it. So I'm going to give it back to you."

Billy Simms looked at Hank with extra attention, like he could not quite believe what he had just heard. Hank gave up a little smile at that.

"And I'll pay you to let me graze my herd if that's alright. You give me a credit 'til we're square. How's that sit?"

Hank fanned the hot air from his face with his hat as the master smith dropped the shoe in the bath. A ferocious hiss and a cloud of steam rose from the barrel and flattened up against the tin roof, forming gray droplets that hung in suspension. Billy Simms was too stunned to speak. All he could do was nod his head.

They sat awhile watching the master smith do his work. Hank put on his hat and started to stand up from the small table but then thought better of it and relaxed back down onto the bench and took his hat off again.

"Can I ask you a personal question, Billy? You don't have to answer."

"Anything, Sheriff."

"Nakota's been up there with you, what, three years?"

Billy's face flushed.

"Little over four I 'spose. She just does my cookin' and sewin' and tendin' and whatnot. It ain't nothin' like what people think."

"You love her?"

"No sir."

"You sure?"

"Yessir."

"How do you know you don't love her?"

"'Cause she's Indian. 'Cause I love Frances."

"Think you might consider makin' her an honest woman? A married woman, I mean?"

"Nakota? No sir. I married Frances. Once and for all."

Hank nodded, as if there was no arguing with that and he was going to let it go. He put his hat back on and stood, stretching his arms. He grabbed his rifle and tipped his hat to the master smith who nodded back, not saying that he could use his apprentice back and that he was glad the time for chewing the fat with the law from another county was done. Hank turned again to Billy Simms.

"Frances was a good woman. I know you loved her and she loved you. And I know you two had your dreams. But Frances is dead, Billy. God rest her soul, she's dead and gone. Long as you try to hold on to her, you're dead too. Or may as well be. Every minute's a blessing. We're all here and gone, just like those minutes and those blessings. Here and gone. Here and gone. Winking on and off like fireflies. You're takin' a big gamble that you're gonna be around tomorrow. That Nakota's gonna be around tomorrow. And what'd I tell you about gambling?"

Billy smiled a little and counted up to him on his fingers.

"Never gamble with your life, your land, your love."

Hank nodded.

"Time to let her go, son. Time to move on."

Tyler had awoken with a jolt, and a thin slick of drool on his chin. The sun, slicing off the tops of all the eastern buildings, was streaming in through the windows. The main lights in the office reception area were on and the circulatory hum of the office equipment blew along the corridors like an electric breeze. The book was in his lap, closed over his fingers.

There had been a surge of panic as he rose for the door, loaning him energy he would likely not have any ability to repay. He would be late. Kevin would be enraged. The judge would be angry. The suited savages would be in a hot froth. Much of his own board of directors would be in the courtroom to watch him testify. They were probably there already, waiting and looking at their watches. If the first of his last acts in this rapidly dimming life was to secure *Winchester County* for his son and for the company that was the organizational sum of his life's work, then he was off to a terrible start. He did not want to leave the world a disappointment.

He had made for the elevator in a hurry, not speaking to his employees, moving through the office faster than was safe for a man of his age.

"The witness can answer the question," said the judge.

"No," said Tyler. "I don't think Ms. Freeman is a liar. I think she does not understand."

"I see," said Mr. Glass, pursing is lips and looking over at the jury. "So it is your belief that my client's father, Jack Lindstrom, granted you, by operation of contract, the legal right to make a television series of the Winchester County stories in his father's book, *Signs of Passing*. Do I have that right?"

"Not quite. Jack granted me full ownership of the source material, which necessarily includes the right to make a television series."

"I see. And this contract right exists by virtue of what, Mr. Freeman?"

"By virtue of my many conversations with Jack Lindstrom before he died."

"I see. And what were the terms of this so called contractual understanding?"

The throbbing in his head, which on the drive over had felt like waves exploding against the face of a cliff, was now a continuous, unbroken, unrelenting sensation of pressure. Like everything inside him wanted out. He closed his eyes in an effort to push back against the building pressure. He supposed it must have looked like impatience with the question. Or irritation with Mr. Glass. How luxurious those petty emotions would have been.

"Jack had started his own production company," he said. "Milquest Inc. He wanted me to buy in. He needed the money and…"

"Mr. Freeman, I don't need a long narrative on what you perceive to be…"

Grace rose.

"Well, I object, your Honor," she said. "The witness is doing his best to answer the question and I think the context is entirely appropriate."

The judge was nodding before she finished.

"Sustained. Mr. Freeman, you may finish your answer."

Tyler's head was buzzing. He did the best to shake off the numbness stealing through his body. He wanted to sleep.

"Jack needed the money," he said. "In all modesty, he knew that if my name was associated with the business, Milquest would start bringing in big clients. I respected Jack as a writer. And we were good friends. To the end we were good friends. But I questioned his business acumen. I was not wild about the prospect of being an owner of Milquest."

Tyler paused, choosing his words. Mr. Glass opened his mouth to speak, but not quickly enough.

"So my involvement came at a price. The deal was that I would invest in Milquest, and lend my name to that business, in exchange for the rights to *Signs of Passing.* The negotiations occurred over a significant period of time."

"And by negotiations, you mean your conversations?"

"Yes."

"While playing golf."

"Sometimes."

"And at the baseball games."

"They were all part of an on-going conversation… negotiation. Yes."

"And you never reduced any of this on-going negotiation to writing, did you?"

"The negotiations were all oral. I trusted Jack. We put it in writing shortly after I bought in to Milquest."

"Really," said Glass with more than a hint of incredulity. "Did you put the whole deal in writing or just the parts you cared about?"

"The buy-in had already occurred by that point. The contract basically just dealt with the transfer of rights to the book."

"I see. Yes. How very convenient."

"Objection," said Stebbing.

"Withdrawn. Mr. Freeman," continued Mr. Glass speaking directly to the jury, "doesn't it seem odd to you that a man with his own production company would want to sell the rights of his father's famous work so that someone *else* could make a television series?"

"No."

"No?" Astonishment splashed from the word into the jury box.

"No, sir. Would you care to know why?"

Mr. Glass smiled.

"By all means, Mr. Freeman. Enlighten us."

The door to the courtroom opened in the periphery of Tyler's vision. Tyler looked up as Warren Lemiski and his grandson slipped into the back row, behind the assemblage of Shoofly directors and officers, and sat down. Pillsbury nodded at Tyler and grimaced a little as he sat amid the quiet of the room, as if apologizing for a disturbance. The boy looked as gangly and awkward as ever. He sat clutching his electronic tablet to his chest. Tyler looked back at Mr. Glass.

"Milquest Inc. is a production company now. But at the time, Milquest was a script writing company. Jack did not know the first thing, not he *first... thing*, about production. He was a writer. Like his father. He wanted me to make the thing – the series – and give him all of the script work. And then, if the show was a success, Jack was going to hit up his publisher to reissue the original book. He had a couple of his own books too that he was looking to publish. A successful series would help all of that."

"And he told you all of this, I suppose."

"No. But it was obvious."

"Obvious to who?"

"Obvious to me."

"I see," said Glass, strolling away from the jury nodding with his hands behind his back. "But you insist that Jack Lindstrom sold you the full ownership rights to the book?"

"Correct."

"Then it is not especially plausible to suggest that he would have any rights left with which to negotiate a reprinting of that book, is it sir?"

Tyler closed his eyes in a long blink, trying to heed Grace's advice to break up the cadence of the question and answer to avoid ceding any rhythm to the examiner.

But halfway through the long blink, he felt the brush of dream. A blue sea across a long, green pasture, dappled with cows. Calling to him to leave the road. The road one needed to travel in order to make all of the points. Calling to him to simply turn the wheel and head through the split rail fence for the sea. Calling him to sleep.

"Mr. Freeman?"

"Yes. Yes. I think Jack figured... I think he figured that I would jump right in and make the series. And that once the series was done and in the can, well, that I just wouldn't have any interest in the publishing side of things. The deal... the understanding... between us was for a full transfer of ownership rights. That's what I wanted and that's what it took to get me to buy into Milquest and Jack knew that. But I think Jack thought he would stick with *that* deal to get the series made and then..."

"And then what?" asked Mr. Glass, waiting to be outraged.

"And then he would assert that he had only granted me a limited right to use the book for purposes of the series. And that I would either agree with his memory of the arrangement or that I would not particularly care."

"So," said Mr. Glass with extra volume, "my client is a liar and her father was a conniving cheat, do I have that right?"

"Objection," chorused Grace and Stebbing.

"Overruled."

"I am not calling anyone a liar or a cheat. As I said, your client simply does not understand. And Jack was naïve, that's all. About my interest."

"And your interest was keen indeed, wasn't it sir?"

"Yes."

"You wanted every last page of that book and all of those characters, isn't that right?"

"I paid a lot of money. Yes."

"You wanted it all for yourself. Jack was interested in a collaboration while he was alive, but you wanted it all for yourself."

"It was to be a Shoofly project. Not a Shoofly-Milquest project."

"Isn't it true that you told Jack Lindstrom that you would invest in his company, that Shoofly would work with Milquest to produce the series, and that Shoofly needed the limited use rights to get that done? The right to *use*, Mr. Freeman. Not the right to *own*. That's what you told him."

"No."

"And then, after giving him only a quarter of the money you originally discussed, you gave Jack Lindstrom a piece of paper, the thing you call a contract, but that was comfortably vague about just what rights were being conveyed from him to you. Isn't that correct?"

"I'm not a lawyer."

"No. But you sure have access to lawyers, don't you?"

Mr. Glass made a grandly sweeping gesture at the three lawyers representing Tyler's corporate and personal interests.

"Yes."

"And yet, this," Mr. Glass stormed over to Madam Clerk's desk and picked up a piece of paper, "Plaintiff's Exhibit 12, was something you drafted."

"Yes. I drafted it."

"After his heart attack."

"Yes."

"And Jack Lindstrom signed it. Right?"

"Yes."

"It doesn't say the word ownership anywhere on this piece of paper, does it sir?"

"No. But we both understood that that was what it meant. That was what we had discussed."

"So Jack signed and then you just waited, didn't you? You stalled, for nearly ten years. You put the project on the shelf and waited for Jack to die so that you could misrepresent the deal – your *understanding* – to everybody else just like you are sitting here under oath and doing for this jury."

"Objection!" Grace was on her feet and Stebbing close behind. Jurors six and seven looked at each other and leaned in towards the front wall of the jury box.

"Overruled."

"No," said Tyler shaking his head.

"You knew about his heart attack. He confided in you about his health. You knew he was not a healthy man. He was fifteen years older than you. You were just counting the days, isn't that right?"

"Objection!"

"Overruled."

"No."

"You knew Jack would never just give up that world; those stories. You knew he'd never just walk away from *Winchester County*. Disinherit his own child, my client, of her family's literary legacy. You knew that, didn't you?"

"No."

"And so you waited until he died and then, suddenly," Mr. Glass thrust his finger in the air, "Suddenly! After all of those years of waiting. Suddenly, while his body was still cooling, you were ready to make a television series. Do I have that right, sir?"

"No."

"And so you forged on ahead, thinking that Milquest and Jack's daughter would never object since everyone knew that you and Jack had wanted to make a *Winchester County* remake. That's correct, right?"

"No."

"And after all, you had a contract, didn't you sir? A contract that you could conveniently interpret as granting you full ownership rights, not merely the right to use the source material while Jack was alive. Isn't that right?"

"Your Honor," said Grace standing. "Counsel is badgering the witness. It's uncalled for."

"Overruled," said the judge, looking up briefly from his notes.

"No," said Tyler. "That's not right."

"What does Shoofly have in mind anyway? Besides the television series, I mean? A motion picture franchise? A splashy reprinting of *Signs of Passing*? Action figures? Fast food tie-ins? Just how much money are you hoping to make off of my client's birthright?"

A sudden trilling seemed to come from everywhere within the quiet courtroom, like an invisible bird on the wing. The judge came to a sharp attention and sat bolt upright in his chair, panning the room. Jurors looked at each other. Several jurors and spectators fished through pockets and purses to make sure they were not the offender. There were four long chirps, each louder than the last, before Tyler realized that the invisible bird was in his own pocket.

"Hello?" he said into the phone.

"Mr. Freeman," said the judge sternly.

Jurors snorted and tittered into their fingers. Directors and officers shifted uncomfortably in their seats. Grace pressed her hand against her lips in what others would interpret as subdued mortification, but which Tyler could see was a kind of mirthful *Tyler-will-be-Tyler* bemusement.

"Yes. I've been busy. Listen, Ben, this is not a great time. I'm kind of in the middle of something."

"Mr. Freeman, I will ask you to terminate that call, and I mean immediately, or be held in contempt of court."

"Ben I've really... oh... I see. *The exact day?* Oh. Good grief. Who is it? I suppose it is confidential, but I'd say you owe me this, wouldn't you? Because I'm damned curious. Well that's just... Don't be so hard on yourself. It's not your fault."

The judge crossed his arms and leaned back in his chair.

"One thousand dollars, Mr. Freeman. Care to make it two?"

"Listen, Ben... Ben, yes. We'll talk later, okay? I'm surrounded by scowling lawyers. Don't worry yourself. I'm okay. Yes. I've just been very busy. Goodbye Doc."

Tyler tapped the face of his phone and looked up slowly in a kind of stupor. "My... my apologies, your honor. In my rush this morning, I guess ... I could have sworn it was turned off."

The judge reached his long arm down somewhere beneath his chair and retrieved his box of bones.

"Madam Clerk. Please take Mr. Freeman's cellular telephone and bring it to me."

The stout quiet woman with brassy hair stood and took off her headset and straightened her skirt with the flat of her hands. Tyler held the phone in his hand and waited. He glanced around the room, not seeing anything or anyone at first, hearing only the endless loop of Dr. Ben Matthews' words in his head. And then only two words. A name.

Taylor Friedman. Taylor Friedman. Taylor Friedman.

Faces resolved in the blur of his vision, like monuments clearing a fog, as Madam Clerk stepped out from behind her little wooden box.

He looked at Grace holding her expression of love and anguish and concern, all barely contained by her implacable professionalism. He wanted to stand up and walk across the courtroom and step around the table and kiss her full on the lips as he had in her office, not caring who watched or what they thought about it.

Then to Kevin, his beautiful son, inheritor of his hard-fought legacy, now a study in free-floating rage for being so powerless in his father's shadow; for being so insecure in a life not yet really his own. His arms were crossed tightly across his chest. His nostrils flared outward and his jaw-line pulsed like his heart was up and pacing the perimeter of his face. All Tyler could feel was sympathy and love for his only child, this boy of a man who looked for all the world like Tyler's mother and father and who needed his own life to live almost more than he needed oxygen. After all of the years that Tyler had been gone when Kevin needed him most, for the past ten years Tyler had been much too close when Kevin needed him to be gone.

And then Pillsbury, eyes wide as saucers. *Man-o-man, Tyler!* said the familiar blue exuberance of those eyes. He remembered, then, in that moment as he looked at his oldest friend, running away as a child. Stuffing the few things he could carry into a backpack, lying to his hung-over father and setting out into the world for what just might have been the best eighteen hours of his entire life. Setting out for a better place. Like he was entitled to be there. To find it. To get there. Like his whole life existed for that purpose. Getting there. He had been chosen. By whatever it was, he had been chosen. It had singled him out. It had called to him from, of all places, the television.

"You have to let go." Madam clerk pulled at the phone pinched in his fingers. "You have to let go, sir. Let go. Let... go."

She yanked the phone free and walked the few steps across to the judge and reached up and dropped the phone into the box of bones. The judge replaced the box as Madam Clerk resumed her seat.

"Mr. Glass, you may resume your examination," the judge said testily.

"Thank you, your Honor. Mr. Freeman, before you decided to... to *answer your call* in the middle of your testimony," he paused here to let his words gather weight so that they might drop into the jury box, "I asked you how much money you were hoping to make off of my client's birthright?"

Tyler did not answer at first. It seemed, suddenly, like many months since he had played the courtroom question-and-answer game. He looked at Mr. Glass as if whatever he was saying could not possibly apply to him. He did not realize he was smiling.

"Did I say something funny to you, Mr. Freeman?"

"No, no. I'm sorry. It was never about the money," he said. "It was always about... well, about *Winchester County*."

Mr. Glass shook his head and spread his arms.

"Sir, I don't even know what that means."

"Neither do I. Except that... except that chasing is so much better than owning. And wanting is better than having." He looked over at Pillsbury and then back at Mr. Glass. "And it is never too late to start over."

Collective incomprehension filled the room like an odor to which every face seemed to respond in unison. Mr. Glass looked back at his client, Janice Lindstrom, who was looking at Tyler with an undisguised consternation, and then up at the judge and then back to Tyler, seeking some confirmation, from anybody, that the witness was speaking nonsense.

"Your Honor," said Mr. Glass, "will the court please instruct the witness to answer the question asked?"

"The witness will be responsive to the question. Although I confess to now having forgotten the question. Please proceed, counsel."

"Mr. Freeman..."

"Look," said Tyler, feeling stronger, eyes clearing. "Jack was a good man. And maybe we really did just misunderstand each other. It was a long time ago."

There was something like a gasp from Kevin's general direction. Stebbing stood up.

"Your Honor, we would like to request a brief break so that everyone can stretch their legs and use the facilities. We've been going since..."

"Denied," said the judge, pointing at Stebbing and then at Mr. Glass. "Proceed."

"So," Mr. Glass said slowly, choosing his words, "you now think… that you… and Jack Lindstrom… may have miscommunicated – misunderstood each other, I think you said – about whether he was transferring a right to use the source material or all out ownership of the source material."

Tyler nodded.

"Yes, I think that's possible."

Kevin hissed something sharp into Stebbing's ear. Stebbing stood up and then, more tentatively, lowered himself back down into his chair.

"Would it be fair to say then, Mr. Freeman, that you are now uncertain as to whether there was ever a meeting of the minds between you and Jack Lindstrom in the first place?"

"Well, I think…"

"Objection!" shouted Stebbing. "He is asking the witness to testify to a legal conclusion."

Tyler looked at Grace, who read him as only she could. Something in her eyes understood that he had turned the wheel and left the road and that he was not coming back.

"Your Honor," Grace said calmly. "The witness should be permitted to answer. The question asks for my client's current understanding on a factual issue, not a legal conclusion."

Stebbing's mouth all but swung open on its hinge.

Mr. Glass stared back at her with equal parts dumbfounderment and suspicion, like a pilot who does not trust his own instrument panel.

"I agree, Your Honor," he said slowly, still looking at her.

"Overruled. The witness may answer."

"Your Honor," sputtered Stebbing, "if it is not a legal question then it certainly invades the province of the jury. He can't…"

"Overruled."

"Your Honor, we demand a recess. We…"

"Sit! Mr. Stebbing! The witness will answer!"

Grace nodded at Tyler and sat down, dropping her pen on her pad. She smiled, showing him her palms.

"Yes," said Tyler smiling back at her. "It is possible that Jack and I never really understood what the other expected out of the arrangement. It's possible I was expecting the impossible. I've been known to do that."

Judge Manumitt looked down thoughtfully, scratched the black thicket on his cheek, and nodded.

———

Dear Grace:

I am once again a man of letters. Having lost my phone in that unforgivably rude display of disobedience, I have yet to obtain a replacement. Believe me, I am in no hurry to do so. But it means that if I wish to have voice contact with the outside world - they call it 'off island' out here, or fuori-isola as my fellow islanders say it - I must leave my humble lodgings and walk half a mile or so along a cut stone path around the edge of a bluff that juts out over the Tyrrhenian Sea, to the general store where I buy my groceries. They have a telephone I can use - it was that phone from which I called you last Friday - but it is often in use by the fishermen and, as you know, the connection leaves something to be desired. I have a bicycle that will take me to the ferry and from there to far more modern environs.

So far though, I have had little interest in more modern environs. I have found more than enough here to keep me occupied. I am reading a great deal (what a lost joy I have found in reading again!) and I walk the local beaches everyday. I have long philosophical discussions with the sea, in which there is much give and take, point and counterpoint, like we could go on forever.

I am recently acquainted with a thriving community of chess players. I barely know enough of the language to get by. I'm lost most of the time. We drink coffee and talk about fishing and women. And sex, of course, which they all seem to think of as a spectacular type of fishing. They play chess and talk about the one that got away and sometimes I don't know whether they're talking about the women or the fish! And the movies. They love to talk about the movies. They all think Sergio Leone hung to moon. For a bunch of fishermen, many of them are impressive chess-players. But I hold my own. As you know, I'm a stickler for playing chess by the rules. I'm the only one in the group who seems to care about the rules. They all call me Sceriffo. That's my name around here now.

I received the estate documents you mailed. They are signed and enclosed. Everything seems to be in order, although I did make a couple of changes. You will see authorization for an immediate transfer of funds for the benefit of Taylor Friedman. I have written Dr. Matthews. Work through him to make the transfer. I would like it to be anonymous. I know you think this strange, Grace. It *is* strange. I admit that, particularly since the money is at the expense of several charities that could also use the help. But

I feel strangely connected to this person whom I have never met, whose gender I do not know, but who was born on the day I was born, under a ridiculously similar name, and whose life - or should I say whose impending death - was briefly confused with my own. I do not feel responsible, but I did spend three days walking in Taylor Friedman's shoes. My guess is that he, or she, has only another three to five months left. Money should not be the problem.

You will also see authorization for an immediate transfer to the Happy Tails to You Animal Clinic. This too needs to be anonymous. The owner is the daughter of a good friend and the business is on its last legs. I just don't care to argue with him about it. Besides, there is some self-interest involved. I have invited him to come stay with me for a few months. His daughter will need to hire an assistant. Again, money should not be the problem.

I understand, by the way, that Kevin has given notice and is going over to Warner's Creative Development Division. He was not happy with my parting recommendation to keep David Lewis in the CEO slot. I predict that Kevin will find his own way fairly quickly. That is my hope anyway. Whatever happens, it is now out of my hands. I believe the change is for the good.

Enough business. I am going out in search of the elusive red-rumped swallow and the barbary partridge this afternoon. I have taken to birding with a retired couple from Brussels. They have been at it for years. I have much to learn. I am lost and at their mercy.

I suppose that to live is to do foolish things. We play our bad hands and make bets we shouldn't. We play tomorrow like it's the high card in the deck. We gamble away the things we love and the life we have and we miss them when they are gone like we never had any choice in the matter. We cling to the illusion of living, and happiness, and success like some dear, dead relative in the open casket.

But faith in the act of living rests in letting go, Grace. In being lost. In aching for what you do not have and maybe never will. I ran away from home once as a child. Didn't last long. Most of a day. That's what my father called it: running away. That may have been what it looked like. But that's not what it felt like. That's not what it was.

I have let go, Grace. I have let go of everything and everyone. I have let go of my former self and I have found a better place. To be sure, this is a better place. A better life. Not the one I imagined, perhaps, but is the better life ever the one we have imagined? No. I have concluded that the better place, the better life, is never the one we imagine. And on this, the sea and I are in rare agreement.

That said, this place is not perfect. I still have reason to want. And, therefore, reason to live.

Perfect would mean that you have made your last objection, mailed your last invoice, closed up your practice, sold your house, packed your bags and that you are ready to let go of the fuori-isola world. Perfect would be a letter in the post that asked me to make some room for you on this incredible island of mine. Perfect would mean that we get to start again, together. That would be a place far better than even this better place. That would be perfect. Think of it. They have horses here. We could go out riding. Every day.

Run away with me, Graciebell. Let go of everything and run away. I am waiting. I will not stop waiting. I will live for that day, an old man with a young heart foolishly anticipating the impossible.

Until then, you have all of my love and now most of my money,

Sceriffo (Sheriff).

BRUEGEL, WILLIAMS, MATISSE AND ICARUS:
AN INTERPRETIVE NOTE TO *STILL LIFE*[2]

The myth of Icarus, as interpreted in the art of Pieter Bruegel and the poetry of William Carlos Williams, figures prominently in the symbolism woven into *Still Life* and the revolutionary art of Henri Matisse. From *Virgin and Whore: The Image of Women in the Poetry of William Carlos Williams*, Audrey Rodgers had this to say about the masterpiece traditionally attributed to Bruegel called "Landscape with the Fall of Icarus:"

Bruegel, "Landscape with the Fall of Icarus"

---

[2] A full color version of this note can be found at http://bit.ly/1IIYo6Z

"Landscape with the Fall of Icarus" touches upon the Greek myth of the tragedy of Icarus. As we know, according to Ovid and Appolodorus, Icarus, son of Daedalus, took flight from imprisonment wearing the fragile wings his father had fashioned for him. Heedless of his father's warning to keep a middle course over the sea and avoid closeness with the sun, the soaring boy exultantly flew too close to the burning sun, which melted his wings so that Icarus hurtled to the sea and death. The death of Icarus, the poet tells us "According to Brueghel," took place in spring when the year was emerging in all its pageantry. The irony of the death of Icarus, who has always been an emblem for the poet's upward flight that ends in tragedy, is that his death goes unnoticed in the spring – a mere splash in the sea [note the legs of Icarus, lower right]. The fear of all poets – that their passing will go "quite unnoticed" – is an old and pervasive theme. That Williams reiterates the theme is significant in the life of a poet who always felt the world had never fully recognized his accomplishments.

In his afterlife, Emily Foves has given her late husband wings. Emily has chosen to remember Robert as an idealized person that he never was. She has imagined in him a perfection, and even a fidelity, that is not only inaccurate, but that has kept her from living her own life. She has not grown. She has not lived. Her life is devoted to a careful stasis.

A paratrooper in the Army Air Corps, Robert was shot down during a night jump over the Rhone Valley, sending him spiraling into the Rhone River. Emily has always wondered whether it was the shot in the heart that killed him or whether he was still alive and drowned when he landed in the water. Marveling at the massive Carlyle seascapes in the local museum, Emily considers how easy it would be for a god to pluck a drowning man from the water, begging the question of why a god might choose not to do so. Not "God," but "a god." Her musing is both a nod to the polytheism and the Hellenistic context of the Icarus myth, and a foreshadowing of the revelation, then only moments away, when she learns that her beloved Robert is not all she had reimagined him to be. It is a revelation through which Emily experiences, emotionally anyway, Robert's fall from grace in her own eyes.

In *Still Life*, slightly different effect is given to the artistic (poetical and visual) interpretation of the Icarus myth, pulling focus away from the feet slipping into the sea and broadening it to encompass the surrounding pageantry of the living: even the tragedy of untimely death can be, and should be, dwarfed in the full bloom of young life. In her first dream, it is Henri Matisse's "Icarus" that dominates the dining room wall, a dark silhouette of a falling man, surrounded by stars that could as easily be exploding munitions and with a red mark on his chest that could as easily be a wound as a heart. In her second dream, Emily notes that Icarus is gone. Delia May laughs, saying to the old man that Emily "does not know her Bruegel" – Emily does not understand that this is her Spring and her beloved Robert should by now have gone the way of Icarus. Says the old man to Emily: *My dear, this is your spring. You are burning inside.* Seeing that Matisse's "Blue Nude," with all of its youthful sensuality, has replaced the falling Icarus, Emily's dream-self understands: *Icarus is gone.* And yet, *Everything was left. Everything.*

The old man in the dream is Henri Matisse, the artist who used variations on simple images and shocking colors to evolve impressionism. Matisse, the leader of a group of young, rebellious artists who ushered the age of modern art into early Twentieth Century Paris, was the central figure in the artistic movement known as "fauvism". The Fauves (or "Wild Beasts") were iconoclasts of the Parisian art scene using an insurrection of color and form to encourage an emotional resonance and the abandonment of emotional reserve too long associated with artistic appreciation. Admirers of Gauguin and van Gogh, the Fauves sought nothing less than to shock the artistic conscience. The Parisian art critics did not go along willingly, likening the style to "a pot of color flung in the face of the public." This "pot of color" appears on the table in Emily's second dream, albeit in the form of fruit that begins to liquefy and spill onto the table and the floor.

The wife of Henri Matisse was named Amelie. Here there is a phonetic parallelism at work in the name of the *Still Life* protagonist: "Amelie" becomes the Americanized "Emily." The character arc moves Emily from the actual wife of Robert Foves to the symbolic wife of Henri Matisse, where passion and color, rather than marital deference, rule her existence. She is simultaneously his wife and his daughter; he serves the role of Robert and the father figure whose legacy she is destined to inherit. Emily's last name, "Foves," is also intended as a phonetic slight of hand: Matisse was one of the Fauves, the Wild Beasts, who shocked artistic sensibilities with an unabashed use of color and form. Again, Emily evolves in this story from the literal to the symbolic, from Foves to Fauves. Clues to this progression are found in the fact that in the first dream, Emily is speaking English to Matisse's French, and in the second dream, she is speaking French to Matisse's English. In the first, she understands, but does not speak; in the second, she speaks and understands so well that Matisse may as well be speaking English, and he is.

The title of the story – *Still Life* – encapsulates its meaning, for this is a story about the suspension of movement; of growth; of change. It is a story about living only in the dry, dusty simulacrum of life. There are many examples of still lives in the story. The flowers on Emily's table. The carvings on Tom Douglas' mantle. The portraits by Artie Griggs, who renders his comrades in much the same way that Emily renders Robert in her own mind. Of course, Emily herself is a still life. Without any appreciation for the irony that she is describing herself, Emily asks Artie Griggs if he thinks a portrait is just another still life; a human still life. One is reminded of Emily's portrait of Robert, freezing him within the frame on her dresser, just as she has enforced a kind of stillness within the frame of her own existence. Emily has stopped living out of grief for a husband long dead in the Second World War. She has no spontaneously expressive existence. Once a promising artist, she spends her days faithful to a dead past. She takes anxiety pills to control an hysteria which we are to understand is only an urge to break free – to wake up – and continue living.

Emily has whitewashed the humanity from her husband's memory until he is perfect – until he is almost mythical. She has lifted him so high in her esteem that, like Icarus, he is bound to fall. And fall he does. When Emily encounters Artie Griggs, a painter and former soldier who attended basic training with Robert (Artie calls him "Bobby"), she learns that her husband was not who she had forced herself to remember. It is the continuation of an unraveling for Emily which began in the sudden and powerful presence of Delia May, and which ends in a resolve to move in with a friend in Florida and resume painting for a living. Before she leaves, Emily gives away one of her old paintings, a relic of her creative youth, to the milkman. The gift marks a rebirth, in every sense, including sexual, for Emily. She has transformed from a state of death to a state of fully empowered sensuality. From a vicarious existence through the memory of a dead husband to a burgeoning existence in her own right. That transformation is found in the painting that dominates the first dream (Matisse's *The Fall of Icarus*) to the painting the second dream (Matisse's *Blue Nude*). Emily's is a process of leaving behind the past and embracing the future; a process of reanimating all that has gone still.

There is also a sense here that the passion inherent in living is infectious; that it changes everything and everyone it touches. Thus, Delia May, with her confident sexuality and assertiveness, motivated by a new love for a crime writer she was initially hired to follow, nudges Emily back into motion, reintroducing her to the feeling of fresh longing. Tom Douglas, too, is changed forever, and we leave him restless with his station in life, wanting more from himself and the world than the still life of farm animals he has carved out of wood and arranged on his mantle. The flaming pomegranate, with its bright red juice and its spilling profusion of seeds, is an image of creative fertility and expressive vitality. This is the very fruit that, in the palm of Henri Matisse's dream likeness, bursts into flame. The story mixes blood and fire as the very essence of living.

Still Life also intends to present an under current of racial tension. The story is set in the late forties when African-Americans were still far from equal citizens. There is a veiled menace from the security guard in the first dream, as well as a furtive white guilt. Here is a black man wrapped in the white uniform of servitude. He also represents the interior beast-like quality that Matisse has befriended if not tamed and which Emily is afraid of in herself; for once it escapes, it will completely change her world. By the second dream, the black man is following Emily and then leading her by the hand, clearly her guide and ally.

In the end, it is a story of choices. There is a line in the first dream – " as she turned from *Mona Lisa* to consider *Whistler's Mother*" – that suggests the progression of Emily's arc through life if she does not choose to awaken from her living dream and resume the adventure of actually living: one from youthful beauty to an old withered spinster with no life but to sit in a chair and wait, perhaps for someone who will never return.

ABOUT THE AUTHOR

Owen Thomas, a life-long Alaskan with an abiding love of original fiction, is a product of the Anchorage School District and a graduate of Duke University and Duke Law School. While managing an employment litigation practice in Alaska, Owen has written three novels: *Lying Under Comets: A Love Story of Passion, Murder, Snacks and Graffiti*; *The Lion Trees*, winner of thirteen international book awards; and a novel of interconnected short fiction entitled *Signs of Passing*, winner of the Pacific Book Awards for Short Fiction. Owen maintains an active fiction and photography blog on his author website at www.owenthomasfiction.com.

www.ingramcontent.com/pod-product-compliance
Lightning Source LLC
Chambersburg PA
CBHW022232020726
47496CB00004B/871